The Hound in the Left-hand Corner

The Hound in the Left-hand Corner

A Novel

Giles Waterfield

WSP

WASHINGTON SQUARE PRESS
New York   London   Toronto   Sydney

Washington Square Press
1230 Avenue of the Americas
New York, NY 10020

Copyright © 2002 by Giles Waterfield

Originally published in Great Britain in 2002 by REVIEW, an imprint of Headline Book Publishing

Library of Congress Cataloging-in-Publication data is available.

ISBN: 0-7434-7553-4

First Washington Square Press trade paperback edition February 2004

10   9   8   7   6   5   4   3   2   1

WASHINGTON SQUARE PRESS and colophon are registered trademarks of Simon & Schuster, Inc.

Manufactured in the United States of America

Designed by Jaime Putorti

For information regarding special discounts for bulk purchases, please contact Simon & Schuster Special Sales at 1-800-456-6798 or business@simonandschuster.com.

FOR CARYL AND CORAL,
TWO TERRIFIC TRUSTEES

ACKNOWLEDGMENTS

I would like to thank a number of people for their help and advice in writing this novel, and particularly Charles Anyia, Rupert Christiansen, Jeff Fuller, John Hardy, Lucy Hughes-Hallett, Giles Ockendon, Sophie Plender, Paul Ryan, Luke Syson, and Martin Wyld; my agent, Felicity Rubinstein; the designers of this book, David Grogan and Peter Ward; at Headline, Hazel Orme, Ros Ellis, Mary Anne Harrington, Janice Brent, and my ineffable editor, Geraldine Cooke. For advice on various aspects of the book, Glynn Woodin and James Robins at Mustard Catering; Rob Van Helden, Robert Salter, and their colleagues at Rob Van Helden Floral Design; Jon Campbell and Sandra Patterson at the National Gallery, London; for her advice on evening clothes, Katherine Goodison; and on jewelry, Judy Rudoe.

THE CHARACTERS

Exhibitions Department
    Lucian Bankes (Head of Exhibitions)
    Louisa (PA to Head of Exhibitions)
    Diana Stanley (Deputy Head of Exhibitions)
    Hermia Bianchini (Exhibitions Assistant)
    Suzette (Exhibitions Assistant)
    Mirabel Thuillier (exhibition designer—freelance)

Conservation Department
    Friedrich von Schwitzenberg (Head of Conservation)

Education Department
    Melissa (Head of Education and Community Outreach)

Security Division
    John Winterbotham (Head of Security)
    Ian Burgess (Deputy Head of Security)
    Anna (warder)
    Bill (warder)
    Ralph (warder)
    Norman (warder)

Press and Public Relations Department
    Mary Anne Bowles (Head of Press and Public Relations)
    Julia (Special Events)
    Ben (Press Office Assistant)
    Luke (Press Office Assistant)

Guests at the Dinner
    HRH The Duke of Clarence
    Police Sergeant Ted Hoskins (Personal Protection Officer to Duke of Clarence)

The Characters

Tanya (lecturer, Queen Mary's College, London; Auberon Booth's girlfriend)

Lady Burslem

Sir William and Lady St. John

Mr. Kobayashi (Chairman of Japco; sponsor of exhibition in Japan)

Ronnie Smiles (picture restorer)

Valentine Green (journalist)

Denzil Marten (art dealer)

Lord Willins of Plympton (Chairman of Trustees, The Bloomsbury Museum)

Jonathan (Diana's boyfriend)

Ranald Stewart (Director, South London Museum)

Baroness Shawe and Mr. William Shawe

Gregory Noble (novelist)

Ms. Margaret Mills (Minister of State, Department of Cultural Affairs)

Mrs. Ferdinand Hill (lender to the exhibition)

George Evans (architect, Trusty Owen)

Imogen (Diana's hairdresser and friend)

Sergeant Major Jenkins, Corps of Commissionaires

Angel Cooks

"Mr. Rupert" Burnham (General Manager)

Leonore (Mr. Rupert's Personal Assistant)

Gustavus (Head Chef)

Fred (Head of Operations)

The Hound in the Left-hand Corner

The Museum, 3 a.m.

At 0300 hours the guard on patrol duty on the first floor is due to walk through Exhibition Suite One. In his central control room in the basement, with its cameras watching every public gallery, the staff corridors and meeting rooms and potential entry points (though not quite yet the offices), the exits, the delivery yard, the stores, the four streets around the building, John Winterbotham, Head of Security, can survey everything always. Now he turns to the camera covering Exhibition Suite One. He trusts his men, more or less, but Ralph, who is patrolling the ground floor at this moment, is a new boy. At 0300 hours precisely, the door to the first room opens and Ralph, small, neat, and dark, appears. He looks conscientious but nervous, as though an assailant might emerge from behind a showcase. He knows he's under surveillance. He looks around the whole room in the approved manner and presses the security button, which records his timekeeping. John Winterbotham is reasonably satisfied, though it's a pity none of his young recruits has his own military background.

On the morning of Midsummer's Day of 2001, BRIT is asleep. It was called the Museum of English History until last year, but with the millennium it was felt that a livelier name was needed and that "English" had exclusive connotations, so "BRIT" (subtitled "The Museum of British History") came in instead. At least, it seems asleep from outside: no passerby could sense the dim security lights glowing in all the rooms, or the sound of solitary steps along the marble and parquet floors. Anyone glancing at the

1

portico, with its ten enormous columns and monumental staircase, might think it the temple of an abandoned cult. Only a set of cords above the front door, waving in the night breeze, suggests it's ever inhabited.

Anyone who could enter the closed double bronze doors with their reliefs of Britannia and Saint George would reach a completely still entrance hall. It is a vast domed room, with screens of columns on four sides and a stone coat of arms above each screen. Opposite the entrance a gigantic staircase leads to the upper floor. Each corner of the room is occupied by a massive statue: Art, Industry, Learning, and Valour. During the day this is the busiest part of the building, constantly filling and emptying, babbling with a thousand tongues and a dozen languages, with inquiries for the lavatories and the cafeteria and Michelangelo's *David* and the Magna Carta, with hordes of near-rioting French schoolchildren and attentive Japanese. At night, empty and lit by pale security lights, its cavernous heights offer no welcome.

The room has perplexed generations of museum directors and designers. "So imperialistic," they said after the Second World War, "so huge, how can we persuade ordinary people it's a place for them?" "How *can* we make it look swinging?" they had cried in the sixties as they tried to disguise the dimensions under false white ceilings and walls. At the beginning of the new century, the management team agonizes over its authoritarianism and social élitism.

At the back of the building, Ralph walks slowly into the first exhibition room, apparently surprised at its transformation since the previous night. Though not quite finished, the exhibition, which is to open later that day, is almost in place. It's the museum's major event of the year, indeed its biggest exhibition ever, and has kept the place in turmoil for weeks. *Elegance*, it's called, *The Eighteenth Century Revisited. What a to-do*, thinks Winterbotham. The installation staff were working there until an hour ago under the supervision of Diana, highly professional woman that she is, and left in an unruly bunch, shouting and giggling as though they'd been drinking—though he kept a close eye on them and spotted no irregularities. *The big problem was the arrival of a huge painting by Gainsborough or somebody like that, it's all over the posters and stuff, came in at 10 P.M. in an unmarked van with a police escort, God, what a business, a Mr. Marten and a Mr. Smiles in attendance with their own crew of technicians, wouldn't let anyone from the museum near it, took it into the exhibition and hung it themselves. They seem to have had a bit of aggro with that German bloke, head of Conservation, who wanted to inspect it, wouldn't let him near the thing. He was furious, said it was his duty, but they wouldn't listen to him. Apparently it's worth an amazing amount of money, star of the show. Belongs to the Chairman of the Trustees, apparently it's the absolute prize of his collection; good man, Sir Lewis, knows how to handle authority, unlike some who are always asking your opinion when it's their job to lead. . . .*

Young Ralph seems tempted to linger. He must be spoken to. A good guard concentrates on the job at hand. That job's about security, not looking at objects. The only reason to look at any specimen on display is to check that it's in place and undamaged. After a pause or two, Ralph walks through the room at the correct speed and reaches the second exhibition room at 0302, the scheduled time. John glances at the camera covering the ground floor front. His man there is Norman, long-established, no problem, an ex-Welsh Guardsman like John himself.

Ralph is currently patrolling the Gallery of Early English

History: from the Stone Age to the Norman Conquest. It was the first gallery created when the museum was founded. A shaky government was persuaded that the museum would kindle patriotic fervor by celebrating England's political liberty, maritime endeavor, industry and science, literature and the arts, agriculture, trade, warfare. By the beginning of the twenty-first century it is one of the largest and most popular museums in the country, visited by over two million each year.

There's a great deal to see. Even the building, long derided as pompous, is now admired. On the South Bank of the river behind Lambeth Palace and Waterloo Station, it was paid for in 1902 by an ambitious purveyor of wine and spirits. He hoped the building might turn him an earl but, not being a gentleman, had to be satisfied with a viscountcy. Viscount Haringey wanted a proper building like the Natural History Museum, but up-to-date. He commissioned, from the architects Lanchester and Rickards, a palace in the quintessentially English Wrenaissance style. Built in red brick and Portland stone, its twenty-five-bay facade boasts a tower at each end, adorned with balconies at three levels, and unexpected finials on the hipped roof. The huge coat of arms of England over the main entrance has been a favorite target for paint-throwing political protesters ever since the museum opened.

The Gallery of Early English History is long. Having walked its eighty yards at a steadily increasing speed and glanced at some of its four thousand exhibits, visitors imagine they've seen the whole museum. They don't realize that beyond its marble doorcase, over three floors, stretch the Gallery of Medieval History, the Gallery of Early Modern History, the Tudor and Stuart galleries (sponsored by a firm of interior decorators), the Georgian and Regency galleries, two Victorian galleries, the Gallery of the Industrial Revolution (sponsored by a Japanese car production company), the Gallery of English Painting and Sculpture (supported by a major American trust), the London Gallery, the Gallery of Empire, the Gallery of World War (no sponsorship available here), the Gallery of Women's History, the Gallery of Technology and Science, the Discovery Room, and a number more, quite a number. The attendants are used to comforting visitors who, turning the corner and gaining their first view of the apparently eternal Gallery of Medieval History, turn pale, grip their bags convulsively, plead for escape. But there is none. "Museum fatigue can be a problem," admits the director.

At three in the morning nobody's suffering from museum fatigue. Only, perhaps, the security staff, who've been patrolling the building since midnight. In the Gallery of Early English History the slowly pacing Norman sees the yards of gallery stretching into a distant penumbra, interrupted only by the security lights glowing every few yards. The axe heads and sherds, the fragments of old shoes and fruit, the busts of Roman emperors, the illuminated manuscripts, slumber like rocks on the ocean bed.

When John arrived at the museum he had a great deal to do: a spot of tyranny was essential. Discipline had gone out of the window: the attendants would lounge around in gabbling groups ignoring the public, morale was rock bottom. One pair of attendants, a man and a woman and both married, were suspected of mistaking night duty for night pleasure. ("Too right those two like to be on the same floor," somebody said in the mess room, and everyone guffawed.) At night some of the men drifted completely out of control.

While they were supposed to check the offices of the senior staff, they were not meant to settle down on the furniture or peer at confidential memoranda. The curators hated having their space invaded by unseen strangers at night. It was realized that rules had to be tightened when someone scrawled "Old Jenkins likes shagging goats" in the trustees' lavatory (Sir Hubert Jenkins, authority and frequent lecturer on Agriculture in Early Medieval England, was director until three years ago). There's no more nonsense under John's rule. He keeps a tight grip on everything that goes on.

The control room is the heart of the institution. Unless the plant and the objects are safe, none of the activities the curators are so proud of (which personally he often finds a waste of time) could take place. Few of the staff know how intimately he surveys their activities, and might not like it, but the system is essential for good security. One day he hopes to be able to hear what is being said in all these public and staff spaces, to ensure that there are no breaches of confidence in conversation, but nonsense about civil liberties makes this difficult. He's mentioned once or twice to the Head of Admin irregularities of conduct he's noticed on the screen or on his walks around the building but the man's never seemed receptive.

When John left the army he doubted any civilian job (outside the police force) was worth doing and was skeptical about the museum. But when he realized that though the staff numbered only three hundred, there were over a million objects with a total value of £400 million for which he'd be responsible, his interest quickened. Now in his newly modernized control room, known to his staff as the Pentagon, he can survey his banks of cameras, the line of computers recording the action, the electronically guarded record files, the constant presence of a uniformed man, and feel that here at least, in this disordered muddle they call England's capital city, discipline and order rule.

He'll be going home shortly for some kip before returning for one of the busiest days in the museum's year. No family now that June's moved to Lichfield and the children have left home, so no need to spend time with them. His new girlfriend's pretty understanding about his irregular hours (though she was a bit too eager to be invited to the dinner that night, which of course was not possible, really went on about it). He looks at the day schedule for 24 June 2001, shaking his head.

0800	*Final exhibition installation begins—technical staff and exhibition staff arrive*
	Great Hall closed to public all day
1030	*Press view begins (NB beige press cards)*
1130	*Press conference in Lecture Theater*
1200	*Royalty Protection Group Security Advance Party arrives*
1230	*Trustees' meeting in Board Room*
1300	*Trustees' lunch in Board Room*
1430	*Rehearsal for Grand Pageant: actors arrive via Entrance for Groups*
1600	*Industrial Revolution, Early Georgian, Regency closed for caterers*
	Caterers arrive to set up Great Hall for dinner
1700	*Entrance Hall set up for drinks reception*
1815	*Guests arrive for reception—NB no glasses outside Entrance Hall*
1930	*Exhibition closes for guests*

	(RPG Security Advance Party check exhibition rooms)
1940	*HRH arrives at main entrance. Attends reception*
	(Personal Protection Officer RJH; Close Protection Officers POC and JF)
1945	*HRH leaves Entrance Hall for exhibition galleries—main elevator. Meets further group*
2002	*HRH arrives in exhibition*
2015	*Dinner guests commence move to Great Hall*
2030	*HRH leaves exhibition*
2040	*HRH arrives in Great Hall*
	Painting moved from exhibition gallery to Great Hall—to arrive after Duke is seated
2045	*Dinner served*
2215	*Speeches*
2230	*Performance of Grand Pageant*
2245	*Grand Pageant ends*
2300	*HRH departs (north entrance)*
2345	*Final guest departure scheduled*
0200	*Caterers depart*
	Museum closes

All OK, at least in principle. *The thing I'm most worried about is the Grand Pageant, which involves large numbers of extras, children from nearby schools (what are they doing there anyway, still up at eleven?), complicated lighting effects, and some tiresome actors and actresses. I won't be able to go home again until three the following morning, at the earliest. No problem about that. But I really must leave now—I should have left at midnight.*

Ian Burgess, his deputy, comes into the room and looks at him inquiringly as though wondering why he hasn't left.

Secretly, John's never happy leaving Ian to play boss at night and is sure he'll make a bad mistake one day, but he can't be on duty all the time. Ian just isn't tough enough, too soft with the staff—and the public, too, for that matter: you have to keep them in order, especially the types you get in south London. "Keep an eye on the new boy," John tells him, "and watch the screens for the exhibition galleries, especially the room where that new picture is hanging—belongs to the Chairman, absolutely vital no one goes near it." Then he leaves.

Ian rolls his eyes at the other guard in the control room (also nonmilitary, and his ally) and looks at the screens. Ralph has moved into the Gallery of Women's History, still on time. If he does look at one or two objects as he passes, and even stops for a moment, it does no harm, Ian considers. He and the boss disagree on that point, as on many. It's time for Ian to settle into the supervisor's office next door, although he'll be off himself at four; it never seems his territory when John's around. Ian's hoping for promotion to another institution soon, and will be glad to be number one, free to introduce a human working-with-the-public approach. It will be good never to have to see John again.

John passes through the entrance hall on his way to the staff entrance. He likes the hall at night, quiet, grand, powerful, its majesty undisturbed by crowds, the lights subdued, everything in order. *If only,* he sometimes thinks, *it could always be like this.* This evening, during the royal visit, the entrance hall and the Great Hall next door will look as they should look. Then indeed, with the highest in the land visiting the museum, the men in their black and white according to the code, the ladies richly dressed and jeweled, the movements of guests and staff prearranged, every action planned in detail and carried out by trained professionals—then this mighty building will be used as it should be. He's developed a proprietorial affection for the place; it appeals to something deep inside him. Lingering for a moment, he savors the sense of responsibility the great empty space gives him. He shivers a little at the thought of the day ahead. Could anything go wrong? No, of course not. He must get some rest.

GLOUCESTER STREET, PIMLICO, 7 A.M.

The alarm rings punctually at 7 A.M. It always rings at seven, winter or summer, weekday or Sunday, workday or funday. Occasionally Auberon wonders if waking at seven on a foggy Sunday morning is necessary, especially after a grueling night out. But the habit's strong and since he's talked about it more than once in profile interviews, he is strict with himself. He sometimes wonders if the idea of a form of monastic discipline subconsciously appeals to him. Tanya hates waking up early, of course, and can be cross, but then her crossness can lead to exciting physical contact just at the moment when his energy's at its peak, so that their limbs, more or less toned, surge under and over the luxuriant duvet. . . . Tanya's not there this morning, but in her own home a mile away preparatory to dashing out of bed and throwing on her clothes so as not to be late to deliver her 9 A.M. History of Western Philosophy lecture at Queen Mary's College (she's taught there for a while). She'll stay over this coming evening, probably, if they're not too exhausted. So nice they have the choice, the variety. . . . He's very fond of her, he thinks, though actually he's found her rather snappy lately: she keeps complaining that they always do what he wants to do, always see his friends not hers, always go to his type of difficult history seminar rather than her type of difficult philosophical forum, and attend pretentious house parties at weekends (lately she's completely refused to cooperate on that one, says it might be part of his job but it certainly isn't part of hers). Is he selfish? Hard to know—he finds it hard to assess himself, he often wonders what he's doing with his life. . . . And it's hard to know about Tanya, too. Maybe it's time for a . . . Ah, well, that can take its time, there's too much to think about now. . . .

Big day, he says to himself, caressing the sheets. *Big, big day*. He can spend ten minutes in bed, collecting himself, doing his stretching routine before the morning's regular workout. Well, almost regular anyway, it really is such hell doing those dreary exercises. Ten minutes in bed is much more pleasant: he can shape out the day, decide which events require concentration and which he can coast through. When he wakes up he always knows what's in his diary: usually six or eight engagements plus lunch (always) and dinner (almost always), and three or four private views or receptions from which it's nice to make a selection. He loves his glamorous life nowadays, so different from teaching or his quiet youth in Bradford . . . but should he be resisting this glamor, is it superficial and ultimately worthless?

Anyway, since he's chosen glamor of a sort, he may as well do it properly. These early-morning minutes allow him to choose clothes for the day and the evening. He always changes in the evening, never keeps on his suit. Often he has to change up, into a tux, or sometimes down—although his casual clothes are carefully chosen, too. Once an adventurous dandy, he's become less experimental recently, finding the people he deals with now are uncharmed by the crocodile-skin waistcoats and baggy scarlet silk trousers that made such an impact at High Table and provided his fusty colleagues with regular scandalized gossip. No more sartorial extravagances. On the other hand the chalkstripe suits he wore in the early nineties, with their red or yellow linings and waisted look, redolent he'd liked to think of old money subtly flavored with new vigor, now embarrass him. How could he have worn them? he sometimes asks himself, looking at the one or two he's kept (they were extremely expensive). They look so absurdly posh—what a frump he must have been. Now he has a New Look, a New Labor but at the same time Cool Academic Look. Dark suit, usually Italian, though there are one or two nice English suits around (he likes them understated, in very beautiful wool). Of course, he needs to dress just a little English for the job—a passing self-deprecating reference to his suit label to the right journalist shows he's in touch with contemporary design. One of those updated Savile Row-look suits, perhaps the dark gray, is probably right for today's business. White shirt—successful political figures always wear white shirts these days, but it's OK to sport good ones. A strongly colored tie—care's needed here, the tie should be striking but not obtrusive, though clearly expensive to the initiate. He cherishes his ties and owns around two hundred, which are arranged by color and fabric. ("It's the museum man in you," Tanya tells him.)

Odd, isn't it, how much time one has to devote to self-presentation these days in a museum? Not what I was brought up to expect. But this style business is essential if one's to make any impact on the media. . . . Do try not to think about the interview next week for the Bloomsbury Museum. I doubt I'll get the job— too young, too inexperienced, they'll say. And not all the Blooms- bury trustees (cultivated derelicts, some of them) will like my style of directing a museum, which is . . . well, what is it? Lively? Straightforward? Modern? Caring? Socially inclusive? God knows what it is, opportunistic and vacillating it often seems to me, trying to keep the waters from pouring in, maintaining some academic standards when the trend is to discard them as briskly as possible. But, then, I've had my successes and, of course, if Elegance *stuns the press (as it's already beginning to do), I'll go into the interview room with garlands of roses around my head and cannons firing in my wake. Tonight's so important—the opening and the dinner (the Bloomsbury Museum's trustees are mostly coming) matter in all sorts of ways. The other candidates for the job, according to the papers and gossip (I've tried not to lis- ten to it, but no success there), are a mixed bag, if gossip can be relied on. At least I'll be given a good reference by my chairman, who'll certainly not miss me.*

Yes, a lot depends on today.

He turns and stretches another way. He tries not to worry but hardly succeeds. *Do I truly want Bloomsbury or am I just impelled by feeling it's my duty to be ambitious? I think I want it, such a wonderful place, and after five years I could go on to a major job in the United States or a university chair, probably, if I keep up the publishing. . . .*

God, how pleased Dad would have been to see me in this job— from semidetached house in Bradford to national museum director- ship, and it would never have happened without all that support he and Mum gave me. I might have been running a local supermarket, and proud of it, too. Pity Mum is so vague now, but she's pleased when she grasps what I'm on about—loves the pictures of me in the papers: . . .

Four more minutes till he has to leave his crisp white bed, with its three linen-encased pillows to the left and three to the right. Linen sheet beneath, finest linen duvet above. Never did do the stretching exercises in bed, oh, well, he can make up for that at the weekend, probably, possibly, or whatever. He loves his bed, the source of such pleasure, and often in the evening after a day crammed with activity lies contemplating the soothing sheets, and the ivory paint and pale wood of a room in which every detail gives visual and tactile pleasure. It is a place of repose, of which there's too little in his life except when he's with Tanya and they're getting on well.

The room has a united color scheme, no strong accents, only whites, ivories, and creams, pale browns and beiges, and an occasional touch of pink and green. The vase of flowers, which always adorns the windowsill in front of the translucent blind, obliquely marks the seasons, reflecting nature in this cool elegance. No untidiness here: he dresses and undresses next door, in a little room where the clothes racks slide out of the cupboard at the touch of a switch, and where forty or fifty pairs of shoes lie in suppliant rows on a miniature conveyor belt designed by one of the museum's technicians. He smiles. Very silly, really, all this dandyishness . . .

Who'll get my job if I do move on? From odd dropped remarks, it might be none of them—the chairman may have in mind one of my staff. Don't know which. Diana, could it be, beautiful Diana, though she's hardly senior enough? Jane? Too close to retirement. Lucian? . . . It could well be Lucian. Lucian—that would explain why he's recently started appearing (he never used to) at functions whenever the chairman's there and is obviously establishing a humorous deferential relationship with that important individual. . . .

Not a nice thought, being succeeded by Lucian . . .

Usually this early-morning half hour is the time when he reads, not duty things like business reports on the museum and deconstructions of nationhood, but books he never speaks about to his colleagues or friends, and scarcely to Tanya. He's reading Pascal's *Pensées,* just at the moment. The world—which takes a great interest in him—thinks of him as a sunflower, its head turning constantly toward the sun. Auberon does indeed enjoy the media, just as they enjoy him, but people who think him superficial do him an injustice: the sunflower has no interior life. But he can't read this morning, too many teasing thoughts interrupt him. *Has the big Gainsborough arrived safely?* he wonders. And all this business of the loan of the Gainsborough to Japan, for example, that worries him, too. Can that idea be sound, should he be taking more of an interest in the whole idea, is it wise to let the chairman get on with it and not find out what's really going on? Lewis clearly doesn't want him to meddle, but all the same . . . God, Lewis is difficult. . . .

He thinks the exhibition will be OK—better than OK, pretty splendid—and intellectually coherent, and attractive to a wide public. They've had quite a lot of trouble with it, the chairman *would* insist on including lots of his own pictures, very hard it was to argue with him, especially when he said he wanted his Gainsborough to be the centerpiece. What really annoyed all of them was when they had to include a not very interesting picture belonging to that man Denzil Marten, the art dealer—Jane Vaughan said no art dealer's stock should be included in an exhibition, and certainly not when it was of doubtful quality, but Lewis began to look so furious when this objection was delicately mooted that they abandoned the subject. . . .

Downstairs he hears the splattering of mail through his letterbox, twenty or thirty envelopes usually. He's only recently stopped counting, more from pressure of time than any loss of curiosity. He has to admit to himself that he enjoys the public recognition asserted by a groaning mailbag. Ever-increasing numbers want him to attend private views and dinner parties and book launches and conferences, and make speeches and give lectures all over the country and indeed the world. His private address is not especially private, since he is a generous communicator and at parties dispenses his card widely to strangers, only realizing when they ring that he never wants to speak to them again. As the book jacket of his much-admired recent biography of the Earl of Strafford (his doctoral thesis) puts it, "Dr. Auberon Booth was educated at Cambridge and Harvard Universities and has taught at St. Peter's College, Oxford, and Princeton University. After a spell in the Department of Modern Antiquities at the Bloomsbury Museum, he became Director of the Museum of English History in 1997. He is thirty-five. Rooted academically in the study of English history, he regards himself as a citizen of the world. He has published many academic articles and a study of the cult of luxury at the Early Stuart Court."

It's definitely time to move. As his naked body rises from the bed he glances at his six-foot-two expanse of mildly bronzed flesh. It looks OK, but it should be better: his shoulders don't look firm enough. At least there's hardly any fat on him; his thighs are as firm as ever. Thirty-six is middle age by some definitions (though he prefers to think middle age begins at forty), but he's not really concerned about that. It's time to think about acquiring some gravitas—puckish youth can't be protracted. The full-length mirror at the end of his bed reveals his fine health and hair but also forces him to look at his face. He wishes he liked his face better: it always disappoints him. Regular features. Thick brown hair, shorter than it was: long hair's so unfashionable these days. Sensitive yet powerful mouth, that's the line. Strong chin. Tanya likes the chin. The problem is the eyes, which are brown (a dull color) and set too close together. When he was a child he overheard his mother say to his father, "He's good-looking, our boy, it's a pity his eyes are so close together." To which his father replied that excessive good looks never helped a man. Well, they probably didn't in Bradford in the 1970s, but they certainly do in modern London. Always the romantic, she was—typically, she chose his name, not at all the sort of name his dad liked, said it would give the boy a lot of trouble at school, and he was quite right, of course, though at King's it fitted in nicely.

Not good-looking enough, really. He wishes he were . . . Well, he wishes he were better at everything. He wishes success weren't such hard work, and often so disappointing once achieved. There are so many things he wishes. . . . "Stop being discontented, Auberon," he says to himself.

He pulls his exercise mat from under the bed and unrolls it. Tanya finds his exercise sessions infuriating. He runs a little on the spot. Then he stops. He finds the idea of all this morning training boring and unattractive. He's supposed (according to his brutal and highly expensive personal trainer) to do two sets of thirty push-ups and sixty stomach crunches and fifty repetitions with the dumbbells every morning. He really doesn't want to today. He decides that since this will be such a testing day he ought to give himself an easy start. He smiles a little at his own lack of resolution.

It's seven-thirty. Time to be getting on. He goes into his bathroom and closes the door.

HAY HILL, LONDON W1, 7 A.M.

Sir Lewis and Lady Burslem are asleep, and the world's quieter for it. Their flat on Hay Hill is large for a London flat, but it's not their home. Home is a rambling house in Suffolk, which they bought twenty years ago when they were first beginning to be seriously rich, and which they've handsomely remodeled and redecorated. Hay Hill is just a pied-à-terre, they like to say, a pied-à-terre with a dining room and drawing room, a library (for him) and a little study (for her). They still share a bedroom and a bed, after thirty-five years of marriage. He has a dressing room and they each have a bathroom, very distinct in character. They discussed the designs together with a specialist, who proposed for him an ebony and silver room, and for her a softly lit lilac and gold boudoir, which she loves to show her women friends after dinner. There is a spare room where nobody is encouraged to stay since staying with the Burslems happens at Herring Green.

The bedroom faces on to a light well, faced in white ceramic tiles. The interior decoration compensates for the lack of natural light. The walls are pale yellow, dragged a few years ago in a way their daughter (who works for a laddish magazine) tells them is completely out-of-date. "Terribly

Colefax and Fowler, Mum," she says, "we're all going mini-malist these days," but Lady Burslem likes it. The Regency–style curtains are so ample that closing them is a labor. They are made of glazed chintz ("Not really an 1830s material," said Mirabel Thuillier, the rather marvelous head of Historic Interiors who has done so much work for them and has become a friend, "but we'll allow it"), its faintly menacing pink roses crowding together on a gold and cream back-ground. The chintz gleams stiffly and nobody ever dares touch it.

In the *lit à la polonaise*, also by Historic Interiors, the own-ers of this comely apartment are lying. Sir Lewis is sleeping efficiently, on his side, an arm flung toward his wife. Above the sheets only a thick silver head can be seen. He wears dark blue silk pajamas with white piping round the collar. Even in sleep, it is clear that he is a man of determination, accustomed to command. The bulk under the sheets sug-gests a firm, compact body, rather less than six feet long. On his bedside table are an adjustable light for reading (he refuses to use Historic Interiors' clever obelisk lamp), steel-rimmed glasses, and a recent academic study of the career of Benito Mussolini. He reads at least a chapter every night: however late it may be, this is a man of intellectual curiosity and self-control, who has little time to waste on sleep.

Elizabeth Burslem does not read the books her husband likes. Before they were married she did a course at Lucie Clayton and worked as a secretary while going to parties every night, but it was a brief period of her life since they married very young. On her bedside table (plain Regency mahogany, like her husband's) lay *Vogue*, *Country Life*, and the most recent set of official instructions for magistrates. She wears a coffee-colored silk nightdress with lace around the neck, Italian and expensive-looking. She lies more or less on her back in sound sleep with only an occasional twitching, and snores faintly now and again. Lady Burslem's face is soft and pink when she is asleep; it is a face that has been expensively looked after for many years: although not always rich, she has always been aware of the importance of appearance. Her curling hair invites a stroking hand; her lips are parted in a little smile. She faces her husband, secure in her marriage, her wealth, her surroundings. She comes from a much better family than he does, as she sometimes reminds herself when he is trying her patience, but she cannot complain about the material and mental comforts he has brought her.

Each morning when he wakes Sir Lewis's eyes encounter a landscape painting on the wall opposite his bed. Just now it's his favorite possession, partly because it's his most recent acquisition. It suggests a yearning for the simplicity of Nature. He must be fond of the countryside, owning twelve and a half thousand acres of it in England and a further two thousand in Portugal. The picture shows a country river between pale green and gray banks lined with willows. A prominent gold label announces that the painting is by Renoir. The other pictures in the room are more modest: a little Degas pastel, a sketch by Toulouse-Lautrec, a Seago depiction of a boat on a breezy sea, a presentation drawing by John Ward (commissioned by one of his boards) showing Sir Lewis sitting at an official-looking table. The Renoir is the prize, but only the prize in this room: it does not compare so favorably with the much bigger, more important paintings in the drawing room.

Sir Lewis is a passionate collector. He's been buying art ever since, at twenty-four when he had very little money, he bought three works at Agnew's annual watercolor sale from the allowance his father gave him. Those watercolors are now consigned to a minor spare room in the country, but even the dubious Copley Fielding has been kept, out of sentiment. His houses bulge with paintings and he's recently acquired a villa in Portugal—primarily, his wife says, for pictures. At the private views he ceaselessly attends, gliding in his chauffeur-driven car to two or three chattering picture-rooms in an evening, he is one of the rare guests more interested in art than gossip or champagne. Every morning in the car, he spends a moment or two arranging the day's new invitation cards, by date and priority of interest, and talking to Denzil Marten, the art dealer in St. James's who has given him so much advice over the years. And just occasionally he likes to sell—especially if he can make a big. big profit. It gives him a thrill.

Eighteen months ago this sleeping knight was disappointed to be offered the chairmanship, not of the National Gallery (as he'd hoped) but of the Museum of English History (as it then was). He'd have liked to shape the art-acquisition policy of a great national collection. But he told himself that the museum was much admired, received £8 million grant-in-aid from government, had a large staff and a celebrated young director, and included a fine collection of English paintings and sculpture. He finds its affairs more interesting than he'd expected. It's disappointing not to be more closely involved in choosing exhibitions and acquisitions, and he finds the director headstrong and full of his own ideas. But at least *Elegance* was Sir Lewis's own proposal, and for once was enthusiastically received by Auberon. The exhibition's allowed him to contribute to the museum as he's eager to do, through creative ideas, sponsorship, loans from his collection. It's his exhibition, he likes to think, and will show the world that he's not only a man who takes but one who gives. And, of course, he has another major concept, which is very much his own. Today's the day not only to gain formal approval from the board of trustees but to announce his new scheme to the world. He's confident the world will be impressed.

Altogether, today will be a great day for the museum and its chairman, who will be revealed as a leader of London's artistic and academic life. He's never before shown anything from his collection in public, except as a discreet loan from "Private Collection." Now, triumphantly, he is lending eight works, each identified in the catalog as the property of "Sir Lewis Burslem CBE." He loves them all: the startlingly fresh Paul Sandby watercolors, the Samuel Scott view of the Thames, the Joseph Wright of Derby depiction of a forge, the portrait of a chambermaid by Ramsay. But one work will be a sensation: his spectacular Gainsborough of *Lady St. John as Puck,* the picture he acquired from the excellent Denzil Marten ten years ago and which hasn't been publicly exhibited since 1910. It's going to give so much pleasure when it travels to Japan after the exhibition here, and not just pleasure, either . . . marvelous how pictures can work for one. He's confident that the painting and the exhibition will impress not just the artistic classes but, much more important, the royal personage who's attending tonight's dinner. Sir Lewis would not at all object to becoming a peer. In fact, he has been working on the possibility quite hard.

Denzil Marten and Ronnie Smiles, the restorer who works on all his pictures, were very keen that the Gainsborough should not go to the museum until the last possible moment, which was last night— apparently Ronnie had some last-minute work to do on it in the studio, but nothing serious, he said. Longing to see it in situ, *should transform the exhibition . . .*

As the light filters through a crack in the curtains, his head shakes a little, his shoulders move, his forehead contracts, his eyes open. He's fully awake at once, as active and energetic in the morning as in the evening. It's a brilliant day, the sky suffused already with sunshine, a true Midsummer's Day. He surveys his Renoir and for once does not remind himself how much it cost. Today will be busy: he will hardly leave the museum; it will be a day crammed with achievement. Many people will want to congratulate him— and it will be such a pleasure for him, to offer congratulations where they are owed, to one person in particular. . . .

And there's his other project, announced today. "The Nowness of Now . . ." he murmurs proudly, and his chest expands.

Gently he presses his wife's shoulders, as he's done on so many mornings in the past thirty-five years, and murmurs, "Elizabeth." She opens her eyes and at once says, "Darling, it's the big day, isn't it?" as with her left hand she switches on the kettle for their early-morning tea.

Tradescant Road, South Lambeth, 7 a.m.

Jane Vaughan is at her desk. She is wearing a dark blue woolen dressing gown, once her father's, over her striped pajamas. The dressing gown has cording round the hem and might have belonged to an old-fashioned schoolboy. In the days of Hamish she wore silk in bed, but since he left for Vancouver she's reverted to the nightclothes of her youth.

Not getting dressed when she wakes up is part of her morning ritual: two early hours in her study before breakfast, dressing, and bicycling to BRIT (God, how she hates that idiotic name), where she's Chief Curator and Curator of Art. These two hours are disturbed by nothing: even the cat has to wait for breakfast. Every morning she slips out of her single bed and goes into the study, where her papers and books lay where she left them the night before. Her books remind her that she has a place in the world. They are trusty friends, even on days when waking is bleak.

This morning being this morning, she can't concentrate, as she usually does, on the book she's writing (this is her sixth). In spite of the delicious smiling morning outside, anxieties crowd upon her. What she can do (being perennially anxious about appearing ill-informed) is to study the catalog for *Elegance*, to arm herself fully against questions. It is an enormous catalog, so large it can hardly be held, so heavy it begs to be put down.

Never before has the museum enjoyed so splendid a publication, she reflects once again with raised eyebrows: none of her many exhibitions over twenty years at the museum attracted such opulence. Even her masterpiece, *The Court of George III,* which brought more visitors to the museum than any previous show, was accompanied by the mildest publication, every page communicating through its cheap paper and unimaginative design its ultra-economical production by Her Majesty's Stationery Office. The *Elegance* catalog, on the other hand, published by an international university press, has 624 pages, full-color illustrations, sixteen essays by international scholars, the thickest possible paper. At the front unrolls a symphonically modulated series of acknowledgments, the grades of gratitude indicated by size of typeface, elaboration of cartouche, degree of effusiveness. Page after page lists, in turn, the honorary committee for the exhibition (ninety-two names, none of whom have made the faintest contribution), the executive committee, the trustees, the catalog contributors, the lenders (headed by Her Majesty the Queen and arranged—the chairman insisted—by social precedence), the sponsors, the Magna Carta Circle (contributions of £1,000 a year plus), the Merrie England Circle (contributions of £500–£1,000, in smaller print), and museum staff (in smaller print still, meant to show how large the staff is, and to compensate for inadequate salaries). Every word has been read by the chairman. Nobody could accuse him of indolence. Naturally, he has never exercised censorship, though at one point he did suggest omitting the information that the wealth of a particular noble family, which has lent generously to the exhibition (and with whom he shoots), derived from slavery. Nobody opposed his suggestion. With his own pictures he has, as the man best acquainted with them, helped the curators to write their entries. He was particularly helpful over the Gainsborough, his prize, which normally hangs in a specially created gallery in his country house.

This enormous catalog is one of the few objects on Jane's immaculate desk. Civil Service tradition has taught her to keep a tidy desk, but she allows herself a few keepsakes. The pink marble egg was given to her by Hamish, many years ago, and though she's lost Hamish she has his egg. She bought the Roman glass jug more recently in Sicily, traveling with her friend Rosalind. The Elizabethan silver and ivory pomander is the most expensive ornament she's ever acquired: it reassures her of the moral benefits of occasional luxury. From her window she can survey the neat terraced houses of Tradescant Road, now increasingly expensive and done-up, not at all as they were when she moved in twenty-five years before.

She drinks her tea and rejoices that she does not have to leave her comfortable room for ninety minutes. Reading the catalog isn't too stimulating since she's read all the entries often and wrote many of them herself, but she enjoys the printed pages. This isn't just her exhibition: it was assembled by a committee of staff and outside experts. The curator in charge of administration was Helen Lawless, one of Jane's assistant curators, a young scholar who's recently emerged from an obstinately avant-garde university on the couth coast. Helen is anxious to make a mark and, with this exhibition, is likely to succeed. Jane finds her calculating and pushy, more interested in promotion (as though she were working in a business corporation) than in scholarship or the museum. Being a generous woman, she's tried to dismiss these thoughts, but recently overheard some of her young colleagues expressing themselves energetically on the subject.

Jane is proud that the museum can show such splendid objects, even though in places the exhibition—designed by an imperious interior decorator called Mirabel Thuillier, a friend and protégée of the chairman—looks like a Bond Street furniture dealer's. Rather tiresomely, Mirabel tried to exclude objects from the exhibition because they did not suit her designs, and to include other things (mostly from her stock as an art dealer) because she thought they would look pretty—but Jane (who can be formidable when necessary) squashed her. But over the decoration the chairman's taste, as interpreted by Mirabel, triumphed. The chairman's taste runs toward the gilded and in the exhibition gilding rules. She's not sure she likes the Gainsborough portrait, which Sir Lewis has persuaded the director (who, frankly, knows very little about pictures) to treat as the centerpiece of the display. In fact she's only seen it once, and then only for a few minutes in Sir Lewis's country house, before she was forced to go and have lunch. It's very impressive but there's something about it she finds unsatisfactory. Anyway, the thing's illustrated on the catalog cover, the posters, the leaflets, and the private-view invitations.

"We need good branding, Jane," young Ben in Press (why are all the men in the museum under thirty called Ben?) explained to her patiently. "We must use the same image on all the publicity material—and what better than this?"

"We don't want to be branded for life," she replied, but he never saw the point.

Why doesn't she like the picture? She looks at the full-page illustration of *Lady St. John as Puck* again, and at the four pages of enthusiastic exegesis written by Helen. The present catalog entry differs totally from the first version, in which Helen analyzed the painting as an expression of the social and intellectual subjugation of upper-class woman by a male-dominated social order, with the young woman obliged by a structure of power mechanisms to abandon her individual identity in androgynous role-play. Now, she extols its artistic merits as one of Gainsborough's finest achieve-ments, in a remarkable state of preservation (as the attached condition report establishes). Helen, although at first uneasy with the idea of direct contact with a man of wealth, was apparently converted by a succession of one-to-one dis-cussions with the chairman in his office. Champagne routed

Foucault, as her colleagues observed acerbically. Helen seems never to have glimpsed a work of art while at university and was obviously easily persuaded. But what is it about the painting that makes Jane uneasy?

The history seems straightforward. The provenance couldn't be more direct: "Commissioned by Sir Paul St. John, first baronet, 1772; by descent to Sir William St. John, sixth baronet; the Marten Gallery, 1989; Sir Lewis Burslem." A model provenance, only one real change of ownership in more than two centuries. The full-length portrait shows the twenty-four-year-old Lady St. John in 1775, shortly after Gainsborough's move from Bath to London. She is seen in a whimsical pose, one arm leaning against a tree, the other beckoning the spectator. The expression on her highly individual, rather pointed features is enticing yet ambiguous: while not exactly beautiful she is highly charged sexually. She wears a shimmering dark costume, half rustic bodice and skirt, half doublet, evidently the costume of Puck from *A Midsummer Night's Dream.* She stands in a forested landscape in the evening light. Around her head fly tiny fireflies—or are they fairies?—and in the distance, among the trees, flickers an almost indistinguishable group of figures possibly engaged in festive activities. Fairies serving Bottom, according to the catalog. In the bottom left-hand corner of the painting appears, for no very clear reason, a greyhound, rather an individual and English sort of a greyhound. It gazes lovingly at its mistress.

The thought of dogs makes Jane look out of the window to see if her neighbors are out walking their pets and, indeed, that crabby man from over the road is on his way home. She longs for a dog herself, sometimes, but it's hardly sensible to have a dog, which will spend the day shut up in her flat. In retirement, maybe . . . She tries not to feel anxious about the day ahead. Is anyone going to like the exhibition? Will they like the Gainsborough, on which so much emphasis is being placed? There are still questions about it. Despite its size and splendor, the picture wasn't exhibited at the Royal Academy (which the artist often found unsympathetic). But why was it apparently never shown elsewhere, at Gainsborough's showroom in Schomberg House or any of the other venues he favored? It is not mentioned in the artist's correspondence and none of his account books survive. On completion, the picture was presumably transferred from the artist's studio to Bytham Hall, the St. Johns' Suffolk house. It was never publicly exhibited until 1885, when the catalog of the Grosvenor Gallery exhibition of Thomas Gainsborough listed it as "No. 396, *Lady St. John impersonating Puck,* 91 x 58 (inches), St. John." It was fully (not to say fulsomely) described for the first time in *Thomas Gainsborough, The Artist and the Man,* published in 1898 by Mrs. Rupert Fountaine. Mrs. Fountaine, one of several writers on the artist at this period, apparently studied the painting closely. Her text remarks that "little is known about the sitter, who was aged twenty-four at the time of the portrait," but she includes a photograph taken by Messrs. Braun, the only early reproduction Jane has seen.

New information has come to light regarding Lady St. John. Her husband's family still live in Suffolk, although their old house was destroyed by fire in 1916 and many of their possessions burned. The present baronet inhabits a farmhouse nearby. Jane has not met Sir William St. John, but gathers from Helen (who disapproves of him) that he is an idle individual who devotes his time to traditional upper-class pursuits, such as selling off inherited possessions to save himself the trouble of working. The family archives are in the Henry Huntington Library in Pasadena and there Helen found out a little more. A discreetly worded letter from one St. John cousin to another written shortly after the picture was executed states that Lady St. John has retired from society and moved permanently to Suffolk. A more direct letter was sent by the lady's husband to his steward in the country. Among various instructions over improvements to the family house, it proclaims, in capital letters, "HER LADYSHIP WILL NEED NO CARRIAGE IN THE COUNTRY—SHE WILL NOT BE GOING ABOUT." Subsequently nothing was heard of her and she died in childbirth in 1778. There is a mention of her in one of Horace Walpole's letters: he remarks, "The young Lady St. John who lately made so fine an impression in the costume of Puck at the Duchess of Manchester's ball has it seems lost all taste for society and has removed to Suffolk to become a rustic vegetable—it is a pity, since such a fine woman will be quite wasted on country society. Why she has gone, nobody knows." Nobody knows even now, according to the catalog entry. The family letter hints that her conjugal behavior wasn't as dutiful as her much older husband, married for the first time, might have wished.

Jane is still not sure what worries her about the painting. She spends a good deal of time worrying, notably when she's thinking about retirement in two years. She is middling in height and size, not remarkable-looking but not forgotten by the observant. She wears her hair up and when she lets it down—at Christmas or parties—her luxuriant red tresses still amaze her friends. When she laughs her face is transformed from the faintly severe look of her official person into the air of gentle eagerness she must have worn all those years ago, bicycling to lectures at Cambridge. Nowadays she laughs less than she used to, but amusement still bursts forth.

Unlike her desk, her study is untidy. Bookshelves stretch from floor to ceiling, with more books stuffed in wherever there is space. Volumes are piled on the floor or coil across it, as it were organically. Her little Thomas Jones oil sketch of an Italian rooftop is the only picture still visible, now that the books have taken over like a paper fungus. It is her treasure, a present from her father, president of St. Magnus College, Oxford, when she took a congratulatory first in Modern History. The carpet is a rich Turkish rug; the walls, where they can be glimpsed behind the books, are painted in French gray. There is an armchair, but she never sits in it.

Though Jane (who has been working extremely hard in the past few weeks) is now rather hungry, her rules, which she observes strictly, knowing they avert gloom, forbid her to eat until eight thirty. But why are her thoughts wandering?

She gasps. She's realized something. She gasps a second time, and looks again at the reproduction of Lady St. John. Running to her bookshelves, she finds a large handsomely bound book with "Mrs. R. Fountaine—Thomas Gainsborough—G. Bell and Sons" on the spine, pulls it from the shelves with an eagerness it can't have aroused for years, and locates an illustration. She places the book beside the catalog illustration and stares at them both through her magnifying glass. She sees what she'd never noticed before. Her hands tremble.

"So what does this mean? What does this explain? Or what does it muddle?" she asks herself, staring out at the early-morning sunlight in Tradescant Road. It's going to be a hot day—how on earth will she be spending it?

Today Diana Stanley is wearing her hair short and layered, in a style she's recently adopted, with a long shiny fawn raincoat, which was fashionable last year but still does for early mornings, and high black leather boots, which she dons when she needs to grasp her head of department's attention. She likes to arrive at the museum early on the day of an opening, before anyone else, to make a final check on any exhibition that's about to open. As Deputy Head of Exhibitions, she runs the department, in her own opinion. She sometimes thinks that without her the museum would cease to function. Just under six feet tall and thirty-two years old, with a proud, regular face, straight ash-blond hair to her shoulders, blessedly attractive eyes, and legs that make men tremble, she sometimes adopts an air of haughtiness, her face raised toward the sky, her mouth slightly pursed, a faint tension in her lips. She doesn't want to appear haughty, being a woman of the left, convinced that wholesale change is essential for the development of European society. But she's not too austere in the present circumstances to compromise with the demands of the world, although sometimes she feels she compromises much too much. Although she disapproves of her family background, the expensive public school she left at fifteen, her parents' manor house in Lincolnshire, the connections her early life brought her, she still finds them useful. Nobody would suppose Diana was a victim of social exclusion.

She signs in at the staff entrance and smiles briefly at the security man. What *is* his name? She really ought to remember it. He has a stocky appeal she doesn't altogether discount, she likes the way his thighs fill his trousers, and there's an appealing coltishness to the face. . . . She always gives men's physique a quick assessment, even when she knows them well. At university, when the look was very direct, it became known as a "Diana burner." The staff entrance is heavily dingy—the dinginess is so unnecessary, she reflects, as she does every morning, but asserts the museum's character as a workplace. Its muddled brownness enhances her radiant, forceful figure as she strides toward Exhibition Suite One. She takes from her wallet the palm-top she uses everywhere (and which the Exhibitions Department identifies as her personal attribute). It is contained in an artist-designed aluminium and silver case commissioned for her in Zurich by a former Swiss admirer. Fortunately, it never reminds her of him.

On occasion at the museum, exhibitions are ready several days in advance. This happened in 1976, and again in 1994, when the display contained six objects, all from the museum's collection. That was the only time Diana experienced such punctuality. It's her ambition to make her department as efficient as her beautiful computer. But first, she must get rid of its head.

The museum's exhibition program has been created by Lucian Bankes over the past ten years. She frowns automatically as she thinks of him. Thinking about him is something she does not only at work but when she's away from the museum, maddeningly but irresistibly. The tall willowy body, the baby face, still handsome (people say, though she's certainly never seen its charm) at thirty-eight, the shock of blond hair (the color surely enhanced?), the silly first name, all these features of his obsess her, but in a wholly negative way. When she was on holiday last year in Greece, his face would intervene ludicrously between her and a temple front. Most annoying is his inefficiency, his failure to understand that never planning ahead and issuing last-minute contradictory instructions and bullying are intolerable. It is always she who has to soothe chaos, calm insulted lenders, comfort staff he's shouted at.

Maddeningly, it's his ability—oh, hell, the banner to the left of the exhibition entrance isn't quite straight—that's made the exhibition program so crucial to the museum. He is a historian by training, and his ideas for historical exhibitions have been consistently successful. *Royal Pets* and *Egypt and England* and *The Court of George III* brought crowds from all over the country. The museum's become famous for a style of display that is glamorous and entertaining and at the same time serious. In the past, exhibition titles had to include key words such as *Treasures, Royal,* or *Masterpieces,* but this expansive style has been supplanted by single keynote words. *Luxury* was a great success and so was *Garden,* while *Slum* attracted hundreds of thousands. *He has this flair,* she thinks, gripping her palmtop tightly, *even though he's essentially idle and bad-tempered and messed up things with his wife, who was an extremely nice woman, he has this maddening flair for clever ideas and publicity. . . . I'm sure I could be equally inventive if only I had the time. If I could maneuver him into making a fatal mistake . . . or show he'd been dishonest, or had knowingly exhibited a stolen work . . . or if I could subtly persuade him to mount an exhibition of staggering indecency . . . I could handle the results. . . . I could produce an authentic series of my own memos warning against Lucian's proposals. . . . I'd be the only person to appoint in his place, and I'd bring in a new style of exhibition, questioning, radical, socially aware, if necessarily subversive but at the same time*

*highly intellectual . . . blast this English intellectual complacency
and lack of adventure out of the water. . . .*

She hears a sharp footstep behind her. *Who's this with such
a purposeful step? Whoever it is seems to be catching me up, I don't
appreciate that. Should I be less worried about competition . . . ?
Turn, get the smile ready, may want to say hello. Ha! No need to
smile and certainly no motivation, it's Helen Lawless from Art.
Don't care for her one bit. Why don't I like her? Do I dislike too many
people? Is this a personality defect? No, on the staff it's only Lucian
and this one I can't take, this efficient, insinuating little number
(actually she's rather tall), hardly a year out of school, consciously
clever clothes, used to claim to be a woman of the left but no sign of
that now, always ingratiating herself with the director and the
trustees, particularly the chairman whose special friend she is . . .*

Seeing her turn, Helen tosses her a brisk "Hello."

Diana indicates Helen's existence with a nod. "You look
busy," she says, and indeed Helen does look busy, carrying
three meticulous files under one arm and a large parcel tied
up in pink ribbon under the other. Diana is struck by the
parcel. "Somebody's birthday?" she asks.

"No," says Helen coolly. "I don't do birthdays. It's files
and a leatherbound copy of the catalog for Mr. Kobayashi.
He's arriving today. They like nice parcels in Japan, you
know—you must have had an email from me about making
gifts to Japanese persons, I sent it to all senior staff."

This is a sensitive point, as Helen well knows. Mr.
Kobayashi is the chairman of the company taking *Elegance*
to Japan when it closes in London. For the organization of
this transfer, Diana, who would normally have been in
charge, has been replaced by Helen on the special instructions of Lucian (instructed by the director, who himself
seems to have received instructions from someone above

him). She resents such irregularity. Worse, Helen has been making visits to Japan (often with the chairman of the trustees and Lucian) and has returned with a lot of irritating chatter about Tokyo restaurants and design, dress, and literature. "Japan," she has taken to saying, "really is the coming country. . . . We must open ourselves fully to Japan. . . ." Some of her colleagues feel Japan would be the ideal place for her to find a new life, rather soon.

"How nice," says Diana. "I hope he likes the exhibition."

"He will, he'll love it. He already thinks it's going to be a wow in Japan. And he loves the catalog. Thinks it's one of the best he's ever seen."

"I'm so pleased," says Diana. It crosses her mind that she must have been rather like this herself when she joined the museum, ten years ago.

"We'll meet," says Helen, with a curt nod, as though she hopes this will not happen for quite a while, and turns off toward her office.

Diana surveys the exhibition galleries through narrowed eyes. *I've not seen them after all for five and a half hours,* she thinks wryly. She doesn't like *Elegance.* The concept's out-of-date, irrelevant, rich people's baubles. Who on earth's interested in the eighteenth century today—or, at any rate, this view of it? All those piles of gold and silver snuffboxes (in front of mirrors, simulated candles on either side), and a gold- and silver-laced court dress, and the swords with their extravagantly decorative handles, and the Canalettos and Reynoldses, and the views of Vauxhall Gardens—irrelevant, completely irrelevant. The only things she likes are the craftsmanship elements, the trade cards and workmen's tools in the re-created Georgian workshop (beautiful work by the museum's technicians), the lace-making and dressmaking, the displays of medical equipment and philosophical tomes. And she's proud of her own idea, the video recreation of the streets of London, the camera traveling through the wealthy squares, the City, the weaving quarters of Spitalfields, the slums—it's fabulous.

And she hates, she really hates *Lady St. John,* even though she hardly had time to look at it when it arrived so late last night. Huge self-congratulatory picture, shining in bright new varnish, lady simpering inanely in her theatrical tights as she prances in a glade. She doesn't like the implicit attitude, woman as eroticized semihuman fiction. "The movement of the body," its admirers say, "is so exciting, her outstretched hands are so vivid—what a work of imagination." Absurd—although it does look startling on the main axis of the third room, against a black background, surrounded by enamel and glass trees, under a subtly stronger light than anything else. Anyway, who were the St. Johns, no particular family, London trade one generation back, weren't they?

And she also dislikes the chairman's ridiculous idea of wheeling the picture into the Great Hall for the dinner.

There are still six object labels missing. There's endless wrangling about these labels. The final versions were only completed the day before following a furious meeting between Melissa in Education ("The labels must all be fully understandable by partially sighted ten-year-olds, it's in the museum's charter") and Helen Lawless ("How the hell do I develop a complex argument in fifty simple words?"). There are other problems. One or two objects have no light on them. The sight lines to the Beau Nash portrait need to be rectified. The miniature from St. Petersburg still hasn't arrived but is due at ten.

The display team has left one other mistake. The portraits of a husband and wife have been hung facing away from rather than toward each other, at different heights, and slightly crooked. This is deliberate. On his down-to-earth brass-tacks early-morning visit the chairman will be steered toward these paintings so that he can point out the error. This will stop him making trouble elsewhere and put him in a good mood for the day.

Otherwise everything's OK. It's been so marvelous working with my new exhibitions assistant, Hermia Bianchini. What a charming girl she is—can you call her a girl at twenty-five? She is girl-like, so slender, so graceful, with all the loveliest qualities of Italian girlhood. And then she's so enthusiastic, thoughtful, she always knows I'm overstretched and how to calm tiredness away. Close the palm notebook. Pull yourself together, draw in that beautiful stomach. The day ahead won't be fun. But at least my clothes are planned, well, sort of planned, but are they going to be OK and what about my hair and the jewels? Can I really carry them off, am I compromising my principles, should I really be wearing jewels?

She throws her mane of blond hair behind her head and sits for a moment on one of the Robert Adam chairs with her feet up on the matching fauteuil. *It's a relief to flout the regulations occasionally, when no one's looking, all those regulations, and the conservators fussing endlessly about the tiniest detail. Oh, God, will Jonathan enjoy himself? Will I enjoy Jonathan? Will he want me to go back to his flat afterward, or try to come back to mine? Quite a nice body, it's true, not a bad face either, though hardly interesting, but he's so bland, lacking in any real tenderness or understanding, superficial. It's so overrated, sex, once you get down to it. Do I need this kind of attachment, not much more than a fashion accessory? Nicer to spend the evening with somebody really understanding, noncompetitive, like . . .*

like . . . Hermia, for example. If only Hermia was . . . well, a man, really . . . though . . .

Diana completes her notes for the installation team, who will meet her in half an hour for a final briefing, and sets off to her office. This is located several hundred yards away, since the offices are scattered all over the building. She'll be the person the installation team meet, she thinks with irritated satisfaction—no chance of their seeing Lucian. He'll merely storm in later and order a few things to be shifted, though she may be able to dissuade him. She's found that if she can introduce into a discussion with Lucian the name of a foreign theorist or historian he's heard of but never read, he may retract. Today she has some spicy quotations from Habermas and Derrida in reserve.

What he hates is appearing intellectually deficient, his pigheaded ignorance exposed to the world. There was a glorious moment recently before the *Richard II* exhibition. Lucian insisted on moving the king's portrait from one end of the exhibition to the other. Diana said nothing, anticipating the return of the visiting curator, a choleric German-American scholar. She wasn't disappointed. Dr. Weiss shouted in a furious un-English way that made Diana tingle with pleasure. Although he tried mumbling about a joint decision, Lucian couldn't deny his responsibility. His mouth puckered as he explained that they (as he put it) had been assessing the visual effect—"This is not a textbook," he'd said. Dr. Weiss was not pacified. "Ah, if it is your decision, venerated Mr. Head of Exhibitions," he said, in horridly dulcet tones, "we must respect it. Your visual sense is infinitely more important than the findings of the Center for Medieval Studies at Princeton, which has just established the identity of this pair of royal portraits, executed in 1384. Husband and wife are here brought together for the first time since 1399. Now you have separated them! Of course, if Richard II looks charming in his new location, then forget historical problems. Please also remove my name from the catalog and all publicity. . . ." Diana often returns to this moment.

She rounds the corner of the Gallery of Empire. This has recently been reinstalled, no longer as a celebration of empire but as a denunciation of colonial oppression. The world maps covered in pink splodges, the uniforms and relics of Clive of India and Gordon of Khartoum, the portraits of colonial governors and letters from early inhabitants of Australia, the photographs of royal persons cutting ribbons and nonroyal persons tapping trees, went. In came a ten-foot-high and six-foot-broad sculpture (commissioned by the Projects Department) of a noble black man being buffeted by a nasty small white man in safari kit with a Union Jack on the seat of his shorts; photographs of people working in unpleasant conditions in convict colonies; whips and shackles, illustrating colonial oppression; graphs demonstrating Britain's exploitation of trade with the colonies. As Diana extracts from her briefcase her swipe card, she hears an intensifying sound, of squeaking shoes and rustling clothes and banging bags and finally a shriek of "Diana! Diana, darling! Save my life! My swipe card is in my office— do let me in or I'll be lost."

Diana smiles. These sounds emanate from Mary Anne Bowles, Head of Press and Public Relations. Her office is staffed almost entirely by beautiful youths with languishing eyes. As she says, with a director who needs a publicity department of his own, God bless him, one must have a nice boy or two around to keep one going. Diana once asked

Mary Anne whether she minded which schools the young men had attended. Mary Anne looked guilty and admitted she had gone through an Etonian phase but now doesn't really mind as long as they have nice manners and look alarmed when she's cross.

"Diana, you've saved my life," she says. "How can I have done anything so idiotic?"

"You do it about three times a week, it must come naturally," Diana replies.

"Why can't I be wonderfully efficient like you, darling?" cries Mary Anne, who was on the stage in her youth. "And what a day! Beastly press conference. Lots of people coming, thank God, though I wish they weren't so difficult about each having an individual tour, it's such a job finding the right person to take them around. Do you know that new man from the *Observer*, by the way, said he'd do a big piece?"

"Yes, I've met him." Diana has met everyone.

"What's he like?"

"Nice. Clever. Polite. Gay, I imagine."

"Oh, good. D'you think he likes hard or soft centers? Shall I try Luke on him? Or Ben? Or will he want to see Helen? Not everyone takes to her. Or Jane?—though she hates talking to anyone except the *Journal of Mid-eighteenth Century Studies*."

"Who's speaking at the press conference, by the way?" Diana asks.

"Auberon, then the chairman, so at least we don't need a sponsor slot." And, partly to herself, she remarks, "I suppose he may want to joke about being both sponsor and chairman—I'll have to caution him. You know, darling, I'm a little worried. Oh, Luke, there you are,' she says, to the shyly dazzling young man emerging from an office. "Who wants me from Radio Three? Oh, *Culture Vultures*—can't you deal with them? Oh, all right, I won't be a moment. Diana, one or two of the big critics who've already been seem to find the exhibition irritating. They don't like the title, they don't like it being eighteenth century, they don't like the poshness, above all they don't like Sir Lewis being the sponsor and a major lender as well as chairman. I've had one or two nasty questions from the *Guardian,* and even the others are a bit sceptical. I don't expect the *Guardian* to like it, they couldn't bring themselves to on principle, but if *The Times* and the *Telegraph* go the same way . . ."

"Any publicity . . ." says Diana.

"Of course, darling. But not 'this is a posh exhibition for posh people' publicity. And certainly not 'this is a self-promotion by the chairman of a public institution' publicity. I don't know—I just have a hunch. . . ."

As they reach the door of her office she says, "See you in a min, darling," before hurrying through a door labeled "Accounts Office." Though she and her team moved into these rooms six months before, the Works Department has not found time to relabel the doors.

THE ATTENDANTS' MESS ROOM, 8 A.M.

BRIT has just over a hundred attendants. Until recently they were recruited almost exclusively from the armed services. They wear outfits based on the police uniform, with dark blue trousers or skirts, and white shirts, black ties, and caps with shiny peaks. All but the most recent recruits have been trained to regard security as their prime duty. In the days when admission to the museum was free, tramps who wandered in looking for a warm corner were made highly unwelcome by these custodians of the public good. They would stand beside the intruders, follow them if they strayed, and gaze at them in oppressive disapproval, which soon sent them in search of a public library. The ranks that applied in the museum—warder, senior warder, assistant chief warder, chief warder, and head of Security—were rigidly observed, each rank enjoying its own mess room.

Auberon doesn't believe in hierarchy. On arriving at the museum he suggested to the Head of Security that the warders should call him by his first name. He was conscious of the effect of names on the relationships within an organization, and thought this would be friendlier, more appropriate for a modern museum than the old hierarchical system. This proposal met with such contempt (barely concealed) that he didn't pursue it. But he's still keen to change the system. "I'd like the warders," he said to John Winterbotham in early days, "to be known by a less institutional name, less reminiscent of a prison, something warm and welcoming. Maybe 'helpers' or 'visitor assistants.' What d'you think, John?" he would ask. John did not voice an opinion, but his expression was vocal enough. Ignoring him, "Don't you think," Auberon went on, "we should be in search of a caring environment, where the visitor assistants act as guides to our public? Let's have friendly staff who'll make 'guests' (isn't that a better name than 'public'?) really feel at home. We should drop the uniform, it's military, it's outdated— shouldn't our staff wear colored shirts, jeans even, or just their own clothes? What d'you think?"

"Very interesting, Director," John would reply.

John doesn't know that the management team has drawn up a restructuring plan. In five years the ex-services types will have been phased out in favor of "befrienders," people half their age, wearing postmodern red, white, and blue outfits and baseball caps quasi-ironically decorated with reversed-out images of the Union Jack, and keen to interact excitingly with "consumers." The befrienders will share roles with the rest of the museum staff, act as guides, assess objects brought in for opinion, welcome the public, do conservation cleaning. Auberon and the rest of the management team don't envisage cleaning the galleries themselves— unless a member of the press is present. Politically, it's perfect: out with authority, in with sharing. The curators have not been told about these plans yet; somehow, it seems easier to delay that moment. They may not be thrilled at the idea of acting as guards.

John's staff are less orderly than he realizes, and certainly than he'd like. He rarely enters the junior warders' mess room. It is an unattractive place, since an unadorned environment is thought suitable. The room is situated in the basement, and the dirty frosted-glass windows below the ceiling admit minimum light and maximum fumes. The neon strip-lights make the occupants look as though they're suffering from a hideous disease. The furniture is transitional. Until the female warders arrived it consisted of moldy armchairs with missing arms, strange stains on the fabric, and in one case only three legs, apparently on release from an institution for defective furniture. The women warders demanded change. Not easy. Providing new furniture for attendant staff, they were told by the perennially unhelpful officers in Admin, fell between budgets—not display, not office equipment, not health and safety. The senior warders resisted because they wanted the junior warders' room to be less comfortable than their own.

This is not a room to linger in. The most comfortable part is the corner for making tea and coffee. Here another drama's been enacted. Until a few years ago the noticeboard above the sink was adorned with invitations to take redundancy, health-and-safety warnings, startling girlie calendars, a yellowing photograph of a buxom lovely under the headline "Knock 'em flat, Nigella!" and in due season a picture of the England football team. These have been edged out, apart from the football team. Instead, postcards of the most appealing objects in the museum have fluttered onto the board. A recent shot of the director (known to the attendants as "Sunbeam") is always on view. (There's an almost constant supply in the press, since he is very fond of photo opportunities.) In today's photograph the director smiles expansively at a party of schoolchildren who have visited his office as part of the museum's accessibility campaign. A speech bubble ("You're simply revolting, tinies") has been added. The director will not mind: he has never entered this room.

At eight o'clock the day staff come on duty. Their first job is to clean the public rooms. Most of them hurry to leave coats and bags in their lockers. Only one lingers. He is about twenty-five, tall, slightly undernourished-looking, and fair. He looks tense but excited. He holds a carrier bag with a picture of a flower on the outside. Whenever someone comes into the room he looks up in expectation and blinks when it is not the person he is waiting for.

"Morning, Bill," they say to him. "You all right, Bill?" And one or two say, "Waiting for someone, are you, Bill?" He does not answer, only smiles perfunctorily. When he has looked up and been disappointed thirty or forty times, the door opens and a woman comes in. She is his age and has startling red hair and pale skin. When she sees him she raises her eyebrows a little and says, "Hello, Bill—you waiting for someone, then?"

He says, "Happy birthday, Anna. This is for you," and he holds out the bag.

She smiles but tucks the smile under control. "Thank you, Bill," she says.

He looks at her like a spaniel waiting to be patted, but she proceeds briskly toward the locker room. "Aren't you going to open it?" he says.

In spite of herself, his tone makes her stop. "All right," she says. "What is it?"

"Have a look," he tells her, rather squeakily.

She puts the bag on the table and opens it. Inside is a parcel, wrapped in thick crackling white paper with a green ribbon round it. *Green's my favorite color, and this dark green's my favorite shade. Does he know that, somehow? Did I ever tell him?* She unties the ribbon with some care while he offers her a pair of scissors, staring at her meanwhile. *I wish he wouldn't stare; is someone going to come in and find me doing this and jump to conclusions? What can it be? Beautiful paper, good taste—take the paper off carefully, it's pretty nice, too, what on earth . . . ? Artist's materials . . . a great box of them. Mmm—very high quality, not exactly what I need just now but . . . thoughtful, how sweet of him, he must be serious about me, can't imagine why, I must tell him more about what I actually do as an artist, God, what must they have cost? And he doesn't have any money to spare, giving so much to that awful old mother.*

She looks up and his air of anxious expectation is so touching that she puts her arms round his neck and gives him the warmest kiss she has ever given him during their extended complicated friendship. At this point Ros, Neil, and Charlie hurry into the room and stop short. Bill blushes deeply and makes to pull away, but she finishes the kiss properly as though the others were not there and then turns to them and says, in a friendly sort of way, "It's my birthday."

"Happy birthday," they chorus, and Charlie says, "Can we all give you a birthday kiss, then?" and she says, "Only if you give me a present first," and waves the box of artist's materials at them, and then they hurry to leave their things since they're all late, and bustle out of the room. Bill leaves last and before he goes, being a romantic soul and so violently in love he can hardly bear to spend a minute out of Anna's presence, does a little dance in the middle of the floor. "She liked them," he says to himself, "she really liked them. I was right, choosing those artist's materials. Oh," he allows himself to ruminate, "I'd do anything . . . Oh, how I love her, how I dote on her . . ."

AT THE MUSEUM, 9:15 A.M.

Fond of routines, Jane has another for beginning her day at the museum. Invariably, when she arrives in her office, she returns to the places where she likes them, the wastepaper basket and the tray of Biros, which the early-morning cleaners have invariably moved to the positions they favor. She opens the window. She waters the plants. She strikes off another day on the calendar and suffers a pang at the thought of how few remain to her at this beloved museum. She puts on the kettle. She sits at her desk. She opens her mail. She looks as rapidly as possible at the pile of internal memoranda from and about the forty curators who are responsible to her both in her own department and throughout the museum. They have a striking gift for complaining and indeed for being unhappy, which recently has often been justified since their role within the museum has been steadily undermined by the trustees. She puts on the floor (and sometimes straight into the wastepaper basket) the museum management team updates, which supply three inches or so of paper a day. She discards her emails.

This morning Jane does none of these things. Instead, she hurls her briefcase on to the floor, wrenches open a filing cabinet labeled ELEGANCE, and extracts a bulky file. It tells her almost nothing. On the loan form for *Lady St. John* the section headed "Conservation" notes only, "Conservation records held by owner. Painting checked on arrival at museum by Mr. R. Smiles, picture conservation adviser to owner. Apparently good condition."

Is it too early to ring Conservation? The head of the department is certainly an ally, if an unpredictable one. This is Friedrich von Schwitzenberg, formerly employed as a picture conservator in Munich and then at the National Gallery in London. Auberon persuaded him to leave the National Gallery a year or two before with the lure of a high salary and a handsome new studio. Jane finds him exciting and excitable, although she knows the National Gallery was not sorry when he left. He wears his gray hair protruding in many directions, and his clothes are unpredictable, ranging from a dapper 1950s Austrian look to something resembling an up-to-date tramp's outfit. (The latter is sported on formal occasions, to irritate the director and trustees.) He clearly enjoys spending the large sums allocated to him by the director, who wants the best conservation department in the country (a highly prestigious thing to have at the moment).

"Schwitzenberg!" he says, by way of greeting.

"Friedrich, it's Jane."

"Good morning, Jane. I hope it will be a good morning—one of the great days in the history of civilization, no?" He chuckles.

"I have a question for you, rather an urgent question. The Gainsborough—have you seen it yet?"

"The *Lady St. John*—I examined it last night, *ja,* but only very briefly."

"It's pronounced 'Sinjern,' Friedrich, you know that."

"Oh, so stupid, the English, with all these silly names. Anyway, however it is pronounced, I examined it."

"But thoroughly? Did you write a report on it?"

"But look, Jane, how could I, last night? Of course I would have wanted to, this interesting picture . . . but this man Mr. Ronnie Smiles hardly let me look at it, he just assured me everything of Sir Lewis's was in perfect condition and almost pushed me out of the way. He said he had written the condition report, no?" He paused. "Why do you ask?"

"What do you think of it?'

"Oh, it is a masterpiece. Of course it is a masterpiece. It belongs to Sir Lewis Burslem and it is the *Hauptwerk* of this exhibition. *Ergo,* it must be a masterpiece."

"But what do you think of it yourself? What is your frank impression?"

"Well, Jane, well . . ."

"No, not 'well, Jane, well.' This is important. What did you think of it?"

"What is so urgent? Why are you so agitated?"

"Please!" she says. "Please! What is your impression of the picture? I must know."

"Well, Jane, I have looked at many pictures by this artist and I have to say that even after this very rapid inspection I am a little puzzled with this one, I don't know why, *es ist ein bisschen* . . . There is something strange about the surface—I can't understand what. . . ."

"Did you look at it under ultraviolet or infrared?"

"No, I was not allowed to. Of course it would be interesting, that to do, since Gainsborough so often changed his compositions, did he not, moved arms, made again hairstyles? But little Mr. Ronnie was quite angry when I suggested I might examine it. Strict instructions of the owner, he said . . . all nonsense. . . . But one does not argue with the chairman's adviser, does one, even though he is a silly man who works entirely for the trade, polishing up nasty pictures so they look shiny and expensive? One does not argue with him because the chairman—God alone knows why—listens to everything he says."

"Suppose we did it now—looked at it under ultraviolet light, and under magnification? Could we do that?"

"My dear Jane, the exhibition opens in a few hours. The place is filled with people, the crew, the press will be here. And there is this strict prohibition—"

"I know all that," she says. "I wouldn't make the suggestion if I weren't really serious. There's something odd about this picture. Forget the owner's instructions, we need the truth. Friedrich, meet me in Exhibition Gallery C, with your ultraviolet lamp, in exactly ten minutes. I should be able to have the room cleared briefly. I want you to examine *Lady St. John* from top to toe, but rapidly. You can do it, can't you?"

"Jane, I have always admired you, you are so serious, but you're usually so English and reserved. I have never known you passionate like this. . . ."

"Ten minutes, OK? And speak to nobody about this. Nobody."

She ponders for a while. She needs help from somebody in the Exhibition Department. Somebody senior. The Exhibition Department—separate from her own curatorial division—is in charge of the exhibition space and Jane cannot do anything there without their permission. Who should she speak to? Lucian? She's not at all sure that Lucian would be helpful: from her observation he's become very friendly with Sir Lewis. One of the juniors? No, none has the authority she needs. It has to be Diana Stanley. She calls her.

"Diana—it's Jane."

Diana sounds faintly surprised. The two of them are not particularly friendly, though they've worked efficiently together on many occasions. "Yes?" she says. "We're rather busy—is it a quick call?"

"Diana, I need your help. It's an odd thing I'm asking, but it's important. There's a problem over the *Lady St. John*. I've asked Friedrich to make a close investigation of the painting on site in ten minutes. I need room C cleared of people, for around fifteen minutes. Can you please arrange it?"

"No, Jane, I can't, not possibly."

"You can—you must, really you must. This is not a favor, it's a necessity. I'll explain why when we meet. You must be there, too, yourself. Is that settled?"

"But, Jane, no, the place is full of people. . . ."

"I am asking you for this particular favor. It's in the interests of the museum, I promise you. We only have eight minutes now. Friedrich and I will be there, nobody else. See you then."

"I can't do it. You have to explain why."

Jane plays her trump card. "Potentially it's a source of great embarrassment to the museum. I want to make sure the person who's embarrassed is not you but Lucian." She despises herself for playing on Diana's well-known loathing for her head of department, but knows she has to.

"Lucian? How will he be embarrassed?"

"I'll explain. Nine o'clock, then, just for fifteen minutes?"

Diana, who is not used to being dictated to, says, to her own surprise, "Very well."

At nine o'clock Friedrich von Schwitzenberg enters the exhibition galleries, carrying his ultraviolet lamp in a long black case. The galleries are filled with people making final adjustments, like an orchestra tuning up. At the end of the second room the double door is guarded by a nervous-looking, tall young man.

"Good morning, Mr. Schwitzenberg," says the young man. "You're expected. Would you like to go in? I understand nobody else is to be allowed into this room." He gulps, since he knows this inspection is irregular. In Friedrich goes. He finds Jane, determined-looking and tense, and Diana, impatiently inquisitive.

"Look," says Jane, and she shows them a photocopy. "This is the reproduction of the painting from a book published in 1898. Do you see what I mean?"

"No," says Diana.

"Oh, but yes," says Friedrich after a moment. "The dog—its tail—the tail is different. I never saw that."

"The dog's tail is different?" asks Diana. "How's it different? Oh, I see . . . You mean—he's got his tail down in the old view, and up in the actual picture. How odd. But, really, is it worth all this fuss?"

"And the dog's eye," says Jane excitedly. "Do you see the dog's eye in the painting? Here in the photocopy it is quite normal—but in the painting, the stupid animal seems to be winking."

"Well, it's only a tiny wink. But it's true, there is a sort of a wink," says Friedrich.

"How much has it been restored, Friedrich? That's my question," asks Jane urgently.

"Please, please, will you examine it under your lamp? Can we have the lights out, Diana?"

"I don't think this will tell us much," complains Friedrich, "but if you are determined . . ."

Diana gives a rapid command on her mobile and the room becomes dark. Friedrich has extracted a long black tube from its case. He presses a switch and it emits a low mauve light. He puts the tube beside the painting, moving it slowly up and down the surface. It reveals nothing, only the smooth surface of the paint; there are no marks of any restoration.

"Nothing to be seen at all, someone must have applied UV-opaque varnish to the paint surface. This doesn't get us anywhere," remarks Friedrich.

"Suppose we look at it under your magnification head-loop?" asks Jane. "Diana, will you get them to put on the lights?"

As the lights come on again, Friedrich puts over his head

a metal band with a magnifying glass attached to it. They edge as close as they can to the painting and peer at it, trying to interpret what they're seeing. He peers at the picture and grunts before handing the band to Jane.

"No sign of anything," she says, in disappointment. "It seems to be in perfect condition."

"Or perfectly restored," remarks Friedrich crossly. "The only thing I find surprising when you look closely at this canvas is that the surface is so clean, so smooth, no signs of *pentimenti* here at all—surely Gainsborough was often changing his mind, no?"

"Quick, please be quick," says Diana, "we have so little time, we will have to reopen the galleries in only a few moments."

"It is a very smooth surface," Jane concurs, "but there's nothing to worry about on the evidence of this. I don't see where we are, any more than I did before. It just seems odd that the picture is so very perfect, doesn't it?"

Meanwhile Friedrich has been examining the canvas. "It's very thick, this canvas," he remarks, "as though . . . and very tense, like it has been relined more than once. . . . There's something about the canvas I don't like but what it is, I really do not know. . . ." But as he is speculating the door of the gallery is abruptly thrown open and an alien presence enters their little world.

"What's going on?" shouts a voice. "What the hell is going on?" A man moves violently toward them and then stops, glaring at them. It is John Winterbotham, Head of Security, in his best uniform, and looking as formidable as an ex-regimental sergeant major in the Welsh Guards can look. In spite of their maturity and seniority, Diana, Jane, and Friedrich are assailed by primitive emotions: fear of men, fear of the enemy, fear of authority, and guilt at being caught out like naughty children. . . . When he sees who is in the room, Winterbotham hesitates but stays furious.

"Mr. Schwitzenberg, Dr. Vaughan, Miss Stanley—for God's sake, what are you doing? It's against every rule in the book, extinguishing the lights in a gallery, closing the doors, ejecting the security staff—and when the room is filled with valuable loaned objects, it's unbelievable! We could lose our government indemnity. And tell me why you're looking at that picture—at that picture of all pictures. As you know I have the strictest instructions from Sir Lewis Burslem, no less, from Sir Lewis Burslem himself, that no one can inspect or touch the painting without an OK from him or Mr. Smiles."

"There was a worry about the condition of the painting, I felt I had to inspect it," says Friedrich lamely. The others shuffle around, horribly embarrassed.

"It was a necessary check," says Diana, but does not manage to sound convincing.

"Why did you have to turn out the lights and throw everybody out? Why didn't you alert Mr. Smiles? Thank God I was in the control room and could respond at once—with luck we won't have to put this in the day book, which means we won't have questions from the indemnity people but . . . The risk! You can explain yourselves to the director and for all I know to the chairman."

This is not an inviting prospect.

"In the meantime," continues Mr. Winterbotham, drawing himself up to attention, "I shall have to position a security guard on permanent supervisory duty next to the picture at any time when there are members of the public in the building—or members of staff who don't understand their responsibilities. That should stop any more . . . any more silliness. And now I must speak to the director."

As the three look at one another uneasily, Jane takes the lead. "If you're going to the director,' she says, "I'll come with you. It was my idea to examine the picture, not theirs."

"As you wish," John Winterbotham answers.

"I'll see you in a moment," Jane says to the others. They look at her dumbly and a little reproachfully—it was, after all, at her insistence that they found themselves in this situation. Diana in particular looks resentful—she dislikes being put into this awkward situation. And until now none of them had realized their actions in the building were so strictly monitored. The realization makes them shudder, rather.

AROUND LONDON, 9:30 A.M.

Lucian loves driving. It gives him, he realizes, a thrill that is almost as good as sex and much more reliable. If possible, he likes to drive fast, his little red convertible thrusting through the traffic before surging up to 80 mph. as he enters an empty road. He even loves doing it in London, especially now that cars in the city arouse such disapproval. It tickles him to drink heavily at dinner and remark to his hosts on leaving that he'll enjoy driving home fast: their reactions are so absurdly confused, their shock repressed by social rules in a way that makes him squirm with amusement. He keeps the hood down in almost any weather and never tires of sitting at the wheel on city streets sporting his goggles and his 1920s motoring hat. The outfit makes him remarkable to the gawking many, and easily recognizable to readers of Sunday magazines, since a goggles photograph is almost always selected for the articles about him in newspapers. He likes best a spread that appeared recently in one of the Sunday magazines and showed him in his neat Armani suit and his favorite green cravat, beside another of him wearing driving clothes. He doesn't care about the clothes, but he does like the attention. "Yin and yang," he will say agreeably to visitors, "sun and moon, male and female—rather good, isn't it?" And he waves his hand at the framed photograph on his office wall.

Even today he's not hurrying to work. He started the day as usual—long shower, two almond croissants with apricot jam, and four cups of coffee (the Japanese breakfasts he tried for a while after he began to visit Japan became rather depressing on winter mornings, and finding the right tofu was hell). He consumed all this (is he eating too much? he wonders—he thinks something like a paunch is developing, must keep an eye on this unwelcome addition) at the sitting-room window overlooking the communal gardens, before doing the news and arts pages and spending twenty minutes at the piano. His cleaning lady always arrives before he leaves. Since Fanny left him (what a stupid name, he always told her Fanny was a stupid name, period but dicey), he has relied on successive Portuguese ladies to look after his domestic affairs. Such a nuisance, having to look after the house—at least Fanny was effective that way. Big day, yes—everything under control, yes. His team has been trained (by him, of course), although they still need his guidance. Louisa, Diana, Suzette, each helps the machine run smoothly. "Teamwork, teamwork," he'll say, lying on the leather and steel chaise lounge in his office and gesturing toward the people scurrying about outside, "that's the secret of a good office." He's very impressed by their most recent recruit, Hermia, a delightful girl, half Italian, half English, educated at Milan University (which gives her an exotically cosmopolitan quality unlike all those worthy girls in the office from Nottingham University—at least he loves making jokes about Nottingham, though he has no idea of where they were actually educated). This Hermia seems to be acting both as his special assistant and, in some curious way he doesn't quite understand, Diana's.

Well, yes, Diana, of course, Diana. He frowns. *A fine woman, many good qualities, hardworking, sensible, conscientious. But, try as she may, she's not brilliant—something's missing. A good second-class brain, that's Diana. No vision, excitement, creativity, the qualities I can claim. Her political ideas, with which she used to keep boring us, were bog-standard New Labour—at least she seems to have calmed down on that one. Efficient to the point of obsessiveness. She believes the position of each object in an exhibition can be planned in advance—whereas I know works of art speak to one another and look different in a new setting beside an unfamiliar neighbor. Just like people in that way—you must seek out the best in them, the unexpected, no point trying to categorize them.*

Diana should be running a laboratory. She adores timetables and spreadsheets and budgets. Of course we have a good working relationship, I have to ensure that. She finds me inspiring, but I wish she were easier, less masculine in a way. And she has so many annoying habits—why must she make a point of being so polite to visitors to the office, whoever they are? There just isn't time to fit in everyone one meets. . . . At least she keeps things running smoothly when I'm away, and lately it's true I've been traveling an enormous amount. So tiring, going to Japan every two months—though the

Japanese visits have been very interesting lately. . . . And he smiles at the thought of his last Tokyo trip.

Lucian swings his car around Hyde Park Corner, pushing his way through a traffic light that has just turned red and waving toward the traffic advancing on him from Piccadilly. *Elegance should be a success. It's full of new display devices inspired by me. The video (again my idea), which takes the visitor through eighteenth-century London, has already been praised in the* London Sentinel, *and the design is brilliant, although I had to spend a lot of time guiding the designers. The Hampton enamel trees look especially glittering, although it was disappointing that the conservators wouldn't allow laser beams pointed at them.*

Forced to halt beside Victoria Station, he snorts and considers the morning's press conference. *They still haven't shown me the chairman's speech, my office is disgracefully inefficient sometimes. When will be the moment for my usual brief but essential remarks? And can I be sure the evening's speeches will mention the members of the department who are doing well, and leave out the lazy ones? And there are all those other things bothering me, though I don't understand why they're allowed to. Why aren't I sheltered from trivial problems? There's my overdraft, for example, so silly and difficult of the bank to refuse to extend it again.* . . . *They just must, it's no good them saying I must realize some assets.* . . . *So tiresome. Of course I'll have lots of money very soon—though paying off Fanny is a bit tricky. I can't leave the London flat, I simply can't, it's all my life in that place. Will Tuscany have to go? Monstrously unfair, particularly when I've made it so beautiful and the garden's just maturing—the framing of the view's sublime.*

More red lights in Vauxhall Bridge Road, it's like some sort of game. Auberon's flat is off to the right here. Do I have Auberon worked out? Not really, even now I don't understand him, I don't think he understands himself, he can't make out what he wants in life or at the museum. He's attractive in a way, at least that's how he presents himself, always looking for press attention. He likes to be thought progressive but is oddly inhibited, all sorts of old-fashioned ideas about academic standards. . . . It's hard to get him to understand that museums have changed completely nowadays. . . .

It's so unfair after all these years of work to have to retrench, and my salary's so meager, considering what I do. Well, at least I can earn a little from outside. The overdraft will have to wait till tomorrow, or the day after, and then the Cologne cash should come in, and my Hockneys will surely be shifted soon. . . . At least the present scheme looks set to work, think we can assume the picture will meet with approval from the buyer, and that'll help a lot. . . . Even better if Auberon gets the Bloomsbury Museum, and moves on—Sir Lewis hasn't exactly promised the position, but he's made noises . . . eighty thousand a year, and all those possibilities. . . . It'll be fun getting one or two people to move on elsewhere, and promoting others, like that little Hermia, who could become the director's special assistant, and even—delicious idea—transferring Diana to an access and outreach job in east London, without option . . . She'd certainly resign. . . .

The river is gray-green and sparkling as he drives across Vauxhall Bridge Road and turns left along the Embankment. *In the sunlight—it's going to be boiling today—the office blocks on the South Bank look like a row of Florentine palazzi. I like the South Bank, I think my revival of BRIT has transformed the area south of Waterloo, they're even starting to call it SOWAT. Used to be a dump, but it's a center of cultural life now, a rich slice of London, and the Underground station, too, now called "British History," that's a bit of a triumph, mosaics of great events from our history, selected to reflect landmarks in women's history, racial oppression, and class division. When I remember the moribund place I came to . . . and the moribund director I worked with. His only virtue was that he let me do as I pleased. . . .*

Into the car park just before ten. *Hardly any space left, lucky I have my own place. It's important to keep regular hours. This car park, of course, is the site of Nowness. What a great project, it'll transform the museum, allow endless exciting exhibitions, make the place more like an exhibitions hall and less of a site for display-ing old jam jars and tattered flags—God, how I hate the permanent displays, can't wait to dismantle them and sack the curators. At least some of them went last year, allowed us to hire some more essen-tial staff in Exhibitions and PR. . . . Pity Auberon is a historian, with old-style values. . . . Lewis has the right ideas, progress, moder-nity, newness—and Nowness is the best of them. Of course, a lot of the staff will complain when they hear what's intended. Most of them know nothing at the moment—I was lucky to have such a long talk with Lewis in Japan, very useful it was. I think I persuaded him of my full-fledged support, made him realize how useful I could be as a midwife for the great plan. . . .*

I think Auberon and I are the only staff members who call him Lewis. . . .

With his eager shuffle, legs slightly curved like a crab's, head and torso projecting forward, Lucian proceeds through the staff entrance. He extends his hand into the security booth for his keys without looking at the man on duty. They all know him here. This morning, though, there's a delay, which interrupts his train of thought. The man behind the desk says, "Excuse me, sir? What name is it?"

Turning indignantly, Lucian sees a mild-looking un-known. The name "Bankes" does not produce the usual immediate deference, and at least two minutes are wasted while his name is found on the list. "I'm a busy man, you know," he says, abstractedly rather than angrily, but he has to be concerned over inefficient bureaucracy.

To which the security man answers, also calmly, "My orders are to check everybody. I'm new here, sir, and I can't admit anyone without ID."

"Yes, yes," says Lucian, and moves on, impatiently clutching his keys.

The exhibition office is housed in rooms originally intended for the library. The first room contains the bulk of the exhibition staff, twelve of them: the catalog editors, the registrars, the exhibition assistants, the accounts officer. Some have worked for the museum for years and are used to him. Then there are several young enthusiasts who work long hours for little money in the hope of promotion one day. Lucian is amused that some of the nervous ones disappear when he's around (which is not so very often). They sit using the most advanced technology at mahogany desks inherited from the library and now in disrepair. The room is lit by hanging neon tubes, their fixings brutally inserted into the plaster garlands and roses of the neo–William and Mary ceiling. The walls are lined with dark walnut paneling, hardly visible behind the tottering bookshelves laden with bulging box files from which old faxes and papers seep, with brightly colored date planners charting exhibition plans for the coming five years, notice boards labeled URGENT with yellow stickers flapping in the breeze as though waving at passersby, press cuttings from recent exhibitions and assorted amusing photographs above the desk of Suzette, the fanatically hardworking editorial assistant, and the gleaming espresso machine, which is in almost continuous use. Each desk offers a little narrative about its occupant: the steely tidiness of Louisa's work surface, the elegant table occupied by

Hermia with its pile of crisp white paper, its sharpened pencils, and miniature glass vase containing a single rose, or the cascade of books, page proofs, travel mementos littering the desk of Suzette. Around this space, sometimes silently absorbed but usually frantic on the telephone ("The Vienna van is stuck at Dover" or "It's Manchester—they're being difficult about conservation again") or running about emitting brisk instructions to one another, circulates the flock of slender, black-clad workers. As Lucian enters the room they turn simultaneously toward him as though in warm loyalty—this is expected of them. He's late by anybody else's standards, but lateness does not apply to Lucian—as he likes to say, the moment he joins a meeting is the moment the meeting begins.

Lucian stands at the door, as though garnering recognition and applause. Then he says, "Everybody in my office in five minutes." The babble becomes more concentrated as his staff switch telephones on to voice mail, gather notebooks, subtly adjust themselves to be seen in public. Lucian advances across the room, finding time to smile at the delightful dark-eyed Hermia, who looks up at him—admiringly, he thinks—as he walks past her. Passing Diana's room, he sees her door is open (it usually is, indicating that she is constantly available to her colleagues). Diana is sitting firmly at her desk, as though she has been there for hours, wearing—but really he must not look at this—a pair of knee-high black leather boots of the most interesting sort. She is eating what seems to be a sandwich—a demotic activity to which she is prone (she eats a good deal, in his view). Diana's sandwiches are intended, he believes, to suggest that whereas he is thoroughly self-indulgent, she is so hardworking and down-to-earth that sandwiches are all she has the time or inclination for. This particular sandwich has clearly been planned to coincide with his arrival and indicate how long she's been in the office. Not catching her eye, he raises one hand in what is intended to be a neutral gesture but might conceivably, he realizes as he does it, look more like a Hitler salute. "Good morning, Lucian," she says, in a correct way that clearly is meant to suggest how constantly courteous she is in contrast to him. "There are sixteen messages on your desk." Sixteen messages, are there? How helpful of her, how very helpful, to imply once again that urgent business has been accumulating while he neglects it. He does not know she returned to her desk, rather less composed than usual, only a moment before he came in. The sandwich is to calm her nerves.

"Good morning, Lucian," says Louisa, his secretary. "I hope you enjoyed the skating last night." Lucian loves ice-skating and goes skating often. It keeps him trim, makes him feel the years have not affected him. She knows he likes her to chat first thing, so that soon he can show he is in charge and firing on all cylinders by turning the discussion decisively to business. This is what he does now. "Any messages?" he asks crisply, as though Diana has not spoken.

"Nothing very significant," says Louisa. "The *Daily Telegraph* wants a word with you, they'd like to photograph you in the exhibition. Auberon is anxious to talk to you about the press conference. The chairman is here and has some queries. In the broader picture there is a slight problem about the Australian exhibition, the sponsor for the Australian leg has fallen through and may be sued by Sydney. The figures for the Georgian Agriculture show have come in—the deficit is larger than expected but still under fifty thousand pounds if you look at it in the right spirit. Oh, and

Mr. Kobayashi rang from Claridges and would like you to call him as soon as possible. Nothing major."

"Hmm," says Lucian, who loves receiving calls and not answering them. He moves into his room. This used to be the librarian's office, and was originally designed to look like a seventeenth-century philosopher's cabinet. Lucian, a dedicated modernist, has painted the room white and hung a few Stefano della Bella etchings on the walls. This morning he closes the door immediately, and it stays shut for several minutes. When he presses the buzzer to tell Louisa to reopen it, he is discovered hunched at his desk, which is covered with small white sheets of paper, smirking with what seems to be satisfaction.

His staff advance into the room. Three of them squeeze on to a sofa intended for two, and two perch on each armchair. Hermia Bianchini, slender, graceful, poised as ever in her crisp linen dress, perches on the floor. Helen Lawless, who is cordially loathed by the whole Exhibitions Department, whose existence she scarcely recognizes since she considers herself as a curator to be a superior person to mere exhibition administrators, occupies the only comfortable chair other than Lucian's. She looks bored, as though this meeting were a tiresome and irrelevant duty. They all gaze expectantly at Lucian, who is yawning slightly and picking at some flaking skin on his chin. Is he in one of his good moods today, they wonder, or did he have a late night, making him liable to be short-tempered? He'll soon have to move into his public affability mode but may want to be horrid to them in compensation. Of course, if they can persuade him that *Elegance* is another stunner entirely due to his efforts, life may be OK. Much departmental energy is expended on Lucian's moods.

When everyone has almost stopped chattering in deference to the leader, Diana enters. She carries a chair from her own office, which she places close to the door as though contemplating flight. In one hand she holds her mobile phone, into which she is speaking softly, in the other her palmtop, ready for use. Her arrival soothes the gathering. Lucian again notices, though he tries not to, her long boots. They stop fidgeting.

"Had a marvelous time at the Hammersmith ice rink last night," says Lucian.

"How long did you spend on the ice?" asks Suzette. His staff couldn't be less interested in ice-skating, but they have learned which questions to ask. One self-promoter was once spotted studying an ice-skating magazine.

"About two hours," he says, and offers a satisfied grin around the room. One hand rests lightly on his stomach, indicating the improving effect this exercise has on his body.

"And did you meet anyone interesting?" they want to know.

Since the departure of Fanny two years ago roguish questions of this sort are well received by Lucian (and his staff, who love speculating about his personal life). He does not answer, since he is now ringing his hairdresser for an appointment and a little badinage. His staff wait patiently, half smiling in an accommodating way, while he banters with someone at the other end. Then he puts down the receiver, grips his desk and pushes forward his chin.

"All right," he says, "no time to waste, are we all set? Everything OK with the exhibition?"

"We need your input on a few problems," says Diana. It is her prerogative to speak first. "Perhaps on site? The technicians are keen to talk to you. They're a little anxious, a few things only you can sort out. . . ." Although she dislikes taking this deferential tone, she knows that the thought of being indispensable makes him feel secure. At busy moments this makes life more tolerable.

"OK, OK," he replies, "but I can't be everywhere all the time. Everything all right for the press conference? By the way, I don't have a copy of the chairman's speech. You must remember, Louisa, to give it to me as soon as it arrives. It's vital I'm informed fully on everything," and his voice moves toward an annoyed crescendo, "otherwise I can't do my job. Is that clear?"

There is a slight tremor in the office at his menacing tone, but Louisa has developed effective control techniques. "I'm so sorry, Lucian," she replies, with a concerned, guilty look. Frequent repetition of his name often soothes him, like an incantation to a peevish deity. "I thought I'd given it to you. My fault. I'll get you a copy now, Lucian." She gave him a copy four days ago and a revised one the previous day, but does not mention this.

Lucian enjoys these meetings. He loves to sit at his desk, which is broad and deep and piled with serious-looking papers. He seldom looks at these, but they give importance to the room. They are removed from time to time by Louisa and replaced with others. He likes to see his staff crammed in front of him, looking at him expectantly, laughing when he laughs, concerned when he is concerned, submissive when he is angry. Generally he is affable, because he is aware of how well he handles these meetings, but at certain key moments he knows how to be firm.

"We know that Mr. Kobayashi from Japco will be here today, and is arriving at the museum for the press conference. Has anyone met him—apart from you, of course, Helen?"

"No," they say. "Is he gorgeous?"

"Mr. Kobayashi is an extremely important person," Lucian replies gravely, "and it's crucial that he likes the exhibition. So please, everybody, extra effort there. Helen is his special escort for the day. . . ." There is some covert sniggering at this and he barks, "Please!" at which the sniggering subsides, more or less. Helen curls her lip.

"Helen, all the export papers are now in order, I imagine?' asks Lucian.

"Yes," she says, "and recorded on the confidential file."

"We know the file is confidential," remarks Diana, "though I don't understand why. But wouldn't it be helpful if a copy was available for myself and Jane? Presumably you'll want us to be involved in at least some of the arrangements?"

Helen yawns, very noticeably.

"Thank you, Diana," replies Lucian, "for offering. But as we have already discussed in earlier meetings, this exhibition transfer is being handled by Helen. I am sure she will consult you if necessary and use your services when required, but for the time being the chairman has insisted that anything to do with his property should remain confidential to the nominated staff."

"It seems a little unusual," comments Suzette, who has worked in the office for fifteen years and speaks with more freedom than most. "As though he had something to hide, almost."

Lucian frowns heavily. "Let's go to the gallery," he says. "Louisa, ring *The Times*—was it *The Times* that wanted me?— and then find out the chairman and the director's movements. Tell them I'm tied up for the next fifteen minutes but could talk to them after that. In fact, I must talk to them." (This is said emphatically. Lucian has a way of asserting things nobody wants to contradict.) "Fix something, would you? Oh, and we must get the conference right, a few problems might arise there. Is anyone coming from the chairman's personal office who we have to worry about? I'd like all of you to come to the exhibition, all of you. We can deal with anything else later. Ready, Diana, are we?" he adds, as though speaking to a deaf lady of advanced years. She merely raises her eyebrows.

Followed by his black-clad flock, with Diana striding slowly at the rear as though to indicate she hardly belongs to this procession, he leads the way out of the office. There is nothing more satisfying to Lucian than stalking through the museum with ten or twelve people in attendance.

THE DIRECTOR'S OFFICE, 10 A.M.

Auberon is sitting in his office and frowning. The cool detachment that he advocates for himself is not at all in evidence this morning.

Why did the chairman insist on a trustees' meeting on the day of an exhibition opening and a royal visit? The trustees are all here today, but that's hardly a reason for filling up the schedule in this absurd way. How can anyone think about policy today? I think the chairman's plotting, wants to introduce his new idea to the board just when everyone's too busy to think about it properly. If the trustees aren't concentrating they may nod through the first propos-

als and find at the next meeting that plans are far advanced and the government's been talked around and large sums have been committed to feasibility studies which it would be a shame to waste et cetera, et cetera.

And today we also have to entertain Mr. Kobayashi, who's taking the exhibition to Japan. He's inordinately rich and fairly genial, but not exactly entertaining. Great store's set by Mr. Kobayashi, however, and being nice to him is a major priority.

The Nowness of Now. Or the Newness of New, or whatever it's called. A dynamic "Now Center" to be built on the large empty car park next to the museum, designed in the most advanced materials by a famous British architect—apparently it doesn't matter who the architect is, as long as they're well known.

Wouldn't life be much easier if I weren't burdened with a chairman and a board who make the major policy decisions? They listen to my advice but don't necessarily follow it, not at all. The chairman has much more power than I'd like him to have. In any big museum the balance between the chairman and director is pretty delicate, but Sir Lewis overdoes it.

There'll be problems at Bloomsbury, of course, if I do get it. But at least I won't have to deal with such a self-seeking rascal—I really think that's the word—as Sir Lewis Burslem. His main aim in life is his own aggrandizement—oh, and getting a peerage. Whereas the Bloomsbury trustees are famously old-fashioned and amiable and, what's more, honorable.

Auberon stares gloomily out of his office window at the still empty street and the driveway up to the *porte cochère.* They're putting up the banners for *Elegance* at this moment, with a lot of shouting and contradictory instructions. Meanwhile the wooden scaffolds for the banks of flowers, which will be installed this evening, are being set out. This is a rare moment for reflection, stolen from the pile of business that threatens him every morning and which, in theory, is made worse by the time analyses that the Department of Cultural Affairs makes him fill in for each day. He has to give an account of how he has spent each fifteen minutes of his working day, whether on management, finance, staff, sponsorship, social inclusion, advice to regional museums, and all the rest of it (there's no box, of course, for research or study of the collections). When he started the job he took this duty seriously, but now he fills in the boxes fast and at random—or when he's feeling seriously frivolous he does it according to a code of his own, which is reworked every two weeks. No one ever notices that he's doing the same work on Monday the first as on Tuesday the sixteenth—he's confident that nobody at the department ever touches, let alone reads, the piles of paper this system produces. He's supposed to sign his staff's forms, but actually his secretary does this for him with a particularly convincing stamp.

He plays with the Japanese toy on his desk, a set of ivory beads suspended from a frame. It is one of the few non-British items in the room. This is an office which, as Auberon likes to put it, encapsulates the development of material culture in Britain from the early modern period to the present. Even in his predecessor's plain, antiaesthetic days, it was a fine room. The Edwardian architects, highly conscious of hierarchy, sited it in the middle of the first floor of the entrance front, next to the boardroom. When he arrived, Auberon contemplated moving to a more modest space. But soon, realizing that guests enjoyed it, and seduced by its noble proportions and the parade of anterooms (offices, really, but they feel like a suite of rooms in a Baroque palace) through which the visitor advances to the director's apartment, he decided to stay. He's filled it with objects from the museum's stores: portraits of famous Britons, eighteenth- and nineteenth-century furniture, a rich Turkish carpet, busts of poets and engineers. Among all this splendor hang two small engravings depicting early seventeenth-century London. These are his own, and at oppressive moments they remind him that he is also a writer and historian, and could return to that role. The three windows light one of the handsomest rooms in the city—the only museum director's office which is a favorite of *World of Interiors*. Nobody can accuse Auberon of lacking style.

But at this moment he is taking no pleasure in being stylish, or in the idea that all day he is going to have to kowtow to his chairman. Instead he worries about the Nowness of Now. Such a depressing concept, he reflects, his lip rising with an academic's disdain. Absurd name, too. Nowness will be a celebration of Britain today, "reflecting the volcanic dynamism inherent in the twenty-first century." This breathy tag sometimes runs through his head as he struggles with leaden directives from his paymasters in government. It comes from the Nowness of Now consultation document produced by a firm of media consultants at the chairman's personal expense—another example of his widely lauded generosity, of course. This document was presented to Auberon only a few days ago, apparently for his information. His modestly enthusiastic reaction obviously did not deceive the chairman, or bother him.

He knows just what will happen if the thing is built. The old museum will become a sideline, increasingly neglected, starved of funds and attention, while every available jot of money or energy will be pushed into keeping the new attraction running. Did he enter the museum world to create a pile of modish plastic or collect designer running shoes?

Nowness, main item for today's board meeting. Lewis must have a reason for pushing the project on. He hasn't explained what this reason is—can it be connected with Mr. Kobayashi? Is Lewis's idea for Japan really a good one? Perhaps it's better for me not to know more about it than I have to. It's really not my business.

Is it my fault that the chairman and I don't agree? I try to be fair-minded, but still I'm sure it's Sir Lewis who's the difficult one. I hate the way he meddles over exhibitions, purchases, appointments. I hate the way he keeps saying the museum's a business and should be run like one. However often I tell him the museum's essentially not a business because its primary purpose isn't to make money, he just goes on as though I hadn't spoken. Is the man stupid, or is this an intimidation technique?

He fills in his time-allocation forms for the next month and throws them into the out tray. Thwarting the chairman isn't listed as an option.

One stratagem, of course, is to deluge the man with papers, memoranda, reports of meetings, business plans there's no time to read, so that if he raises an awkward point, he can be silenced by a reference to a strategy document he hasn't looked at. But, of course, Burslem is pretty crafty and tough, can always strike back, use unexpected ploys, demand detailed difficult information—"immediately, now, I've no time to waste, the board has no time to waste in order to suit your convenience!"—or produce alarming new schemes. To date, Nowness is much the worst. Trouble is, he can block any initiatives that are important to the museum—though it's an awkward technique since he doesn't want to seem willful. Engagement with the man requires unceasing vigilance. Auberon sighs. He could, he thinks despondently, profitably devote a lot of his energy and time to his career development or his own intellectual life. Whenever is he going to write that book he's been planning for at least four years on the Anglican Church in early Stuart England?

So which of the trustees will be in favor of Nowness? John Percival, glossy retired politician and deputy chairman, supports the chairman from loyalty, although he's probably out of sympathy with many of Lewis's ideas. If Percival opposed the idea he could probably sink it, strong links with government, expected to enter the House of Lords. But Nowness will certainly appeal to some. Reynolds Brinkman, for example, chairman of Finance and General Purposes (a nasty little committee set up by Lewis and packed with his supporters), will certainly be in favor. Brinkman's favorite line to the museum is "Put your stock on view!" He loves saying that because successful retail outlets display 90 percent of their stock the museum should do so, too, or get rid of it. The idea of modernity and appealing to the market will excite him. Amanda Mann, Channel Four executive, is the trustees' link with the media: she's bound to like it. Aged thirty-eight, she's regarded by fellow board members as excitingly young and in touch. Though Auberon has the advantage over her on both counts, youth and popular culture are apparently felt to be her field. Auberon often sees her at parties, and for some reason feels he has to track the woman's movements: it sometimes makes conversation rather hard to concentrate on. If only she weren't so calculatingly spontaneous. Auberon had a lot of trouble with her when she wanted to rebrand the museum: she was the one who suggested calling it BRIT. . . .

And Alan Stewart—how will he vote? Professor of Modern British History at a large redbrick university, he's said to be anxious to move to Oxbridge or Ivy League. Very friendly, likes to ask about the progress of Auberon's writing—sadly there's never very much to tell him, must find more time. . . . He might well be in favor of expansion. Then there's the ghastly Mrs. Hobson, emeritus trustee who's long passed the sell-by date of seventy but stays on the board because the old bag's given so much cash and might give more. She's awful, so thoughtless, rude, self-indulgent . . . those are her pleasanter qualities. She's been a donor to many institutions and likes to make or destroy, preferably the latter: she once insisted that unless the director of a museum was fired she'd withhold a multi-million donation. Auberon has forced himself to remain on outwardly good terms with Mrs. H. even though she sometimes talks as though he weren't in the room, but he's become mildly obsessive about her. He keeps a photograph of her in a drawer at home and in moments of frustration thrusts the point of a pair of compasses into it, muttering a private imprecation. "So much aggression, darling, and such primitive fetishism," Tanya remarked to him, when she discovered the pockmarked photograph and the compasses beside it, "d'you think it's healthy?" Mrs. Hobson will almost certainly support Nowness, most especially if she thinks the staff are against. "Give them something to do," she likes to comment. "None of the staff here do anything at all."

Auberon takes a sheet of paper from the silver paper holder on his desk. It is thick creamy paper headed "From the desk of the director," one of his few official extravagances. He loves good paper and this is superior to anyone else's. On his sheet he writes *for* and *against*. Under *for*

he puts Burslem, Brinkman, Mann, Hobson, Stewart (?).
Under *against* he writes Percival (?) and hesitates.

They won't all be in favor, surely. Sir Robert Pound, for
example. Sir Robert is a former civil servant, impeccable in
manners, short on ideas, pinstriped in body and mind.
"Sound," they say about him, in Pall Mall clubs, "tremendously sound." They seem to mean that he has no wish to
improve anything except his own position but has risen
through punctuality, a frank smile widely deployed, an ability to keep to the rules and remember the prejudices of the
powerful, and stick to a stock of moderately liberal but
adaptable sentiments. He is famous for "not rocking the
boat." Sir Robert is cautious about money and may dislike
the idea of a new building going up with no revenue
assured. *Against?*

Olivia Doncaster—what will she feel? Nice to think about
Viscountess Doncaster. How can anyone be as charming, as
well mannered, thoughtful, intuitively intelligent, puckishly
humorous as this delicious aristocrat? Although she's so
much more than just an aristocrat. She's quite a new board
member, Auberon doesn't know her as well as he'd like to,
but they've already become friendly, almost intimate. . . .
Tanya is unenthusiastic about her, remarks in her best
Guardian manner on the outmoded tradition of appointing
people to official positions merely because they're titled,
though she's happy enough to accept dinner invitations as
Auberon's official partner to their house in Connaught
Square. Daughter of an ancient noble house, wife to the
heir of one of the oldest marquessates in the country, splendid Jacobean house in Yorkshire, and a collection of Italian
Renaissance paintings, every advantage life offers. . . . And
she's so *charming* and *beautiful,* and so intelligent, astonish-

ingly glamorous, not yet forty. Very keen on developing the party side of the museum, lots and lots of parties are the thing, she says, galvanize the place, make the museum *the* venue that people are *bursting* to come to for a good time . . . and then they'll be hooked and want to come back and give money and be part of the family and you've got them! Such good ideas, really, so sensible in the modern age, and already she's been madly helpful over the dinner and suggested all sorts of exciting people whom even Lady Burslem couldn't really turn down in favor of her boring friends from the City and the counties. . . . *Probably she'll be sympathetic to my views—I do hope so—and anyway her manners are so caressing, her hair so long and blond. Pity I've not really had a chance to explain to her what I think about Nowness. . . . God, I've got an erection, though only halfway, well, goodness. . . . I'll put 'Doncaster' in the* against *column.*

Trevor Christiansen—surely against. Trevor's an old-established artist, very fashionable in the 1960s when he was young and ran around with people in Notting Hill Gate and produced atmospheric paintings that explored the magical world of acid. His style has developed since then and his most recent work, obsessive studies of semiobscure interiors populated by shadowy figures, has restored him to favor at least with traditional critical opinion. His exhibition in St. John's Wood the year before called "Holocurst" in which he expressed his personal anguish about Nazi persecution (one of the finest pieces was a row of unbaked cakes on a baking tray, each labeled with the name of an actual Berlin Jew), showed his ability to wrestle with the toughest contemporary issues. Unlike most artists he enjoys public affairs, and is in great demand. Nowness of Now is likely to appal him.

Five to four in favor of Nowness, at best. It looks bad, especially since the tenth trustee, Sir John Blow, who's absent today, is an old business friend of Sir Lewis's and certain to be in favor. Six to four, then. But if they do approve the plans, Auberon can always set up working parties and financial reviews and emphasize the museum's difficulties and plant one or two subtly negative press articles—it might be possible to delay progress till Burslem loses interest. On the other hand, the man's determined and well connected and successful at ingratiating himself with government . . . and seems completely set on this project. . . . And the idea could so easily be presented as a way of opening up the collections to a broad audience, as museums are always being urged to do.

His eye falls on his print of Charles I's London and his thoughts are interrupted. "Do I really want to worry about all this stuff?" he asks himself. "Don't I want a more intellectual life, to explore ideas, not donors? Write books, not business plans?"

His buzzer sounds. No more time for reflection. It's his secretary, Emma. Emma is the model of a museum director's secretary: young, charming, humorous, interested in the arts and in people, patient. He is sorry Tanya doesn't share his enthusiasm for her. On the whole Tanya, it has to be said, is not generous about other women. Emma says, "The chairman's driver rang to say ten minutes. And Mr. Winterbotham has just arrived and needs to speak to you urgently, and he has Jane Vaughan with him. He says it's extremely important—something seems to have happened."

"Very well," says Auberon.

Enter John Winterbotham, red-faced, furious, with Jane, palely obstinate, behind him. "Unfortunately, Director," he says, "I have to report an infringement of security regulations by senior staff. . . ." He recounts what has happened.

Auberon, surprised, asks Jane for her version. She will only explain her actions in private. "Thank you, John," says Auberon. "You were quite right to inform me at once. But I think we'll keep this confidential for the moment, shall we? No word to anyone?"

Winterbotham looks put out. "Not even to the chairman?"

"If you don't mind, I'll discuss it with the chairman myself."

"Very well, sir," says Winterbotham, and leaves reluctantly with a sour look at Jane, remarking that the episode will be entered in the museum's confidential security dossier.

"I only have three minutes," says Auberon to Jane. "What on earth have you been up to?"

"I know it must all seem very odd. But I had to do it. The thing is—there's something strange about the big Gainsborough," she says. "We had to check the picture this morning, we just had to. After all, it only arrived last night after ten. Though actually we failed to check it properly."

"What do you think's strange about it? It looks very large and Gainsborough-like to me. A rich man's picture. Prefer the landscapes, myself."

"Its condition. Friedrich and I are both sure there's a problem, but unless we can examine the picture properly we can't identify what it is. We need to do it today, before the exhibition opens, to prevent possible embarrassment to the museum from a public exposure—"

"Public exposure of what? I wish you'd explain what you're suspicious of."

"I don't know what we're suspicious of. That's the problem."

"It's not very helpful, Jane. You know what the chairman's said—"

"I do indeed. And now Winterbotham's putting a permanent guard on the picture. Only you could authorize an inspection."

"Against the chairman's wishes? He'd be sure to find out. I don't think that's a very good idea."

The buzzer sounds again. "Sir Lewis's car has arrived in the car park,' says Emma, one of whose principal duties is to keep her director informed of his chairman's activities, including his rather mercurial business fortunes. "He's looking around the car park," she continues, "and talking to a man I don't know. They're consulting some papers, maybe architectural plans."

"What sort of man?" asks Auberon.

"A smooth-looking man," she tells him, "in a not very nice suit, carrying a couple of briefcases. Ah, they're on their way."

Auberon frowns again. *What now?* he wonders. It really is too tedious. He turns to his chief curator, who has adopted a denunciatory pose, her breast heaving slightly. "Thank you, Jane, we must end this talk," says Auberon. He thinks for a moment. "A problem with the Gainsborough, eh? Hmm." A wintry smile briefly agitates his mouth. "Have you spoken to anyone else?"

"Only Friedrich and Diana. I'll leave this photocopy with you—look at the dog when you have a moment."

The buzzer sounds again. "Sir Lewis is just on his way."

"Thank you, Jane," says Auberon. "But for the moment, hold off, would you? We have quite enough problems as it is."

In the second or two between Jane's departure and Sir Lewis's arrival, he tries to seize his whirring thoughts. *Problem with the Gainsborough? Bad for Sir Lewis—but bad for me, probably, too—terrible for the museum and the exhibition, if anything comes out—can Sir Lewis know the picture is questioned? Can I risk exposing the picture to cause Lewis embarrassment? No, I can't, too many potential complications, particularly for me—if only he didn't know about the museum publication I offered Tanya. . . . I never knew it was a breach but apparently . . . grounds for an investigation. . . . Hmmm, play this one carefully, Auberon.* He assumes his winning but determined Director's Smile, and opens the door to greet the chairman.

THE PREMISES OF ANGEL COOKS, 9:30 A.M.

Angel Cooks occupy nonangelic premises in Battersea. They've been established there for forty years, first under the leadership of old Mr. Burnham and now under his son, Mr. Rupert Burnham (known as Mr. Rupert by his staff and most of his clients, more from affection than deference). They cater for dinners, lunches, drinks parties for private and public clients, indeed clients of every sort (as long as they're rich), and are favored by the increasing number of people who like to give parties in museums. Mr. Rupert, who has run the business for over twenty years, is widely admired for his imperturbability, his blend of deference and firmness, his attention to detail, his imagination in creating alluring settings, his soldierly bearing, his raven hair, and chiseled features. He is, people agree, a paragon among caterers. Only occasionally is his smoothness ruffled. If guests are kept waiting for an hors d'oeuvre or a waiter fails to turn up, he'll shout furiously behind the scenes—though nobody front-of-house would know it.

This morning he is sitting in his office with his senior staff: Leonore, personal assistant, Gustavus, Head Chef, and Fred, Head of Operations and second in command. The office is utilitarian, its breeze-block walls painted cream, its floors linoleum, but among the filing cabinets lurk eighteenth-century English tables and Chinese export porcelain, and the walls are decorated with hand-painted prints of English gardens. These pieces, which belong to Mr. Rupert, are occasionally lent to his duller clients to liven up their offices. The staff are discussing tonight's dinner for BRIT. The menu is not one any of them would personally have chosen, since they know that dinner for four hundred prepared in a tiny museum space relies on compromises, however grand the host's ambitions and however deep his purse. Most of the food must be prepared in advance, particularly sauces; the main ingredients should be relatively straightforward; it helps if a course or two is cold. Mr. Rupert has had some difficulties with Sir Lewis, who has ignored his advice. This is the first time a member of the Royal Family (with the exception of a C-list princess) has visited the museum for almost thirty years, and Sir Lewis proposes to celebrate splendidly. A passionate royalist, he has looked forward to entertaining the Duke of Clarence for months. He wants this to be the best dinner of the year, the decade, and he thinks it will give the occasion additional prestige if as much of the cooking as possible is done on site. There was never any doubt for him that Angel Cooks would be the caterers; the question was what they would serve.

The menu's changed, Mr. Rupert reckons, something like sixty times. Sir Lewis's ideas had to be adapted to the tastes of HRH, who as a matter of protocol was sent three sample menus. HRH has pronounced likes and dislikes, which have been conveyed to the museum in an exquisitely courteous letter from his equerry. He likes shellfish (unlike many royal personages who avoid it), allowing lobster to be chosen for the first course. Beef hung on in there for some weeks (it's a favorite of Sir Lewis's), going through four transformations before disappearing in favor of chicken, which gave way to duck, though only briefly since duck soon lost its lead to beef, which finally streaked past the winning post in the form of an extremely complicated dish which for four hundred people poses a formidable challenge. The seasonal vegetables changed twelve times (everything's always seasonal somewhere, after all). Cheese came in, cheese went out, cheese came back, cheese was replaced by a savory, six savories were successively accepted and rejected, cheese returned ("But it must be English, Mr. Rupert"—"Yes, of course, Sir Lewis, we have a remarkable supplier. . . ."). Even the pudding went through numerous transformations, since Sir Lewis and his wife— who's acted as an advisory committee—disagree over puddings. A little extra course at the beginning of dinner flitted in and then was knocked on the head, port rose to the surface, port sank again in favor of dessert wine, the news that HRH liked port rescued it, there was much discussion over dessert wine, chocolates looked steady for a long while, but HRH does not care for chocolates so petits fours came off the benches. . . . From the relatively straightforward menu that Mr. Rupert optimistically proposed in March, almost nothing remains. All that has stayed unchanged are the potatoes and the vegetarian choice, which does not interest Sir Lewis.

"This is the final menu. We all know what it is in principle, but I want to familiarize you with the names of dishes Sir Lewis has chosen or rather invented. It's possibly the most ambitious dinner we've ever attempted," says Mr. Rupert to his team. "Ready? Vintage champagne on arrival—yes, after all he is going for vintage in spite of what I told him about how good the alternatives are. Supporting bar for those who can't manage without whisky, but keep it out of view. Canapés: the floured tortilla, the Japanese pancakes, the mini poppadums, the Parmesan shortbread, the mango and rosemary compote tartlets, the wild mushroom mousseline. Twelve canapés each."

"Generous," says Fred. "Very generous indeed."

"This is a generous occasion, Fred, you should know that by now. First course, Lobster House of Stuart."

"What on earth is that?" asks Fred.

"It's Gustavus's brilliant dish, Fred, with spinach laid between the portions of lobster and lobster pâté piped into the claws. By the way, when are the lobsters being delivered?"

"At six P.M. The Head of Security doesn't at all fancy two hundred live lobsters arriving at his precious museum. He's afraid they might escape and run all over the galleries like an invading army, snapping their claws at anyone who tried to stop them, a bit like *The Birds,* I suppose. Could you have a horror film called *The Lobsters?*"

"Thank you, Gustavus, can we stick to the point? Have you got enough staff to crack the claws and decorate the lobsters, and pipe in the lobster pâté?"

"I've got three extra boys, I think it'll be OK," says Gustavus. "Time is a bit tight, of course." For a moment he looks slightly sick.

"Good," says Mr. Rupert. "Main course, fillet of beef laid on a platter and layered with foie gras. Beef Plantagenet, we're calling it."

"Why Beef Plantagenet?" asks Fred. "What a silly name. Anyway, I thought this was an eighteenth-century dinner."

"It's our job to enter into the spirit of the evening and not make difficulties," replies Mr. Rupert. "As a tribute to His Royal Highness we're going for a royal theme, dynasties of England you know. Sir Lewis didn't like the idea of Beef Hanover, which I suggested, so it's Plantagenet. New potatoes with foie gras and red wine *jus*—baby carrots and sautéd spinach, *panaché* of beans with asparagus and baby turnips. No problems there, I think."

"Awful lot of vegetables," says Fred.

"Vegetables are the thing just now, as you know. The cheese course is called Queen Victoria's Cheese Platter. We don't know that she liked cheese, but it seemed a good way of bringing her in, and there are one or two things on it she might have eaten. With a June salad, a variety of leaves and baby beetroot to give color. And by the way, no vinegar, absolutely no vinegar in the dressing, please, Gustavus, you know it fights with the wine. All we need is just a touch of walnut oil, that extraordinary oil I brought back from Tuscany last year."

"I make a wonderful vinaigrette," says Gustavus sulkily (soon no one will push him around like this, he thinks, he'll be the one who decides everything and whose rages will make headlines). "People beg me for the recipe. To hell with the wine . . ."

"I must insist, Gustavus."

"Very well," says Gustavus, and does a shadow pout. His full pouts bring fear—and to some people, particularly certain sensitive young men and women, desire.

"And the pudding, no problems there, just a choice of berries and other fruit—Berries Tudor Rose. It should be good—apricots, dewberries, purple grapes, green figs, and mulberries. And Hanover Puddings, a.k.a. our individual chocolate sponges."

"It's an absurd menu, with all these stupid names," says Gustavus. "No one's going to have a clue what they're eating."

"Even less after they've tasted it," remarks Fred jovially.

"It's not the easiest dinner, but I expect we'll cope. And it is wonderfully expensive," says Mr. Rupert. "So that's the menu, and I'm happy to say it is *not* going to change." They all laugh. "His Lordship rang me up last night to propose adding celeriac purée to the vegetarian menu, which he thought he'd not given enough attention to. I said no, it could not be done."

"The whole thing's horribly problematic," announces Gustavus, running his hand carelessly through his sensual mane of brown curls. Gustavus is a recent recruit, a fine chef Mr. Rupert rescued from a country-house hotel in Wales. Every time Mr. Rupert looks at him he wonders how long he can keep him at Angel and off television. Not only is he handsome, but he's unashamedly gay in a "straight-acting, straight-looking" way (as the personal ads put it), an apparently irresistible combination to a large audience of men and women now that chefs have become symbols of sexuality. "Particularly synchronizing the starter and the main course—they're so fiddly. And, of course, the lobster's a nightmare."

"We can do it," says Mr. Rupert. "Just as long as the electricity doesn't fail . . ."

"I can't remember a more elaborate menu since I've worked here," comments Leonore. "It makes that Turkish dinner on a Thames barge when the barge started leaking look like a tea party."

Mr. Rupert's eyes glint. "It's a challenge, Leonore," he says. "We like challenges here."

"Yes, Mr. Rupert," says Fred. "But we don't like starters or main courses being late because they're too complicated, do we?"

"They won't be late," he answers. "They're never late and they particularly won't be late tonight." But they know their boss, and in his smooth manner detect unease. "Let's go through the program, shall we? Leonore?"

Time is not wasted at Angel Cooks. "Job sheets ready." says Leonore. "Staff arrival four P.M. Four hundred and three guests at the last count. Access via the staff entrance, all vehicles parked in staff car park. Security clearance via John Winterbotham at the museum, all staff to be cleared on arrival. They must arrive before five P.M. Personal protection officer to HRH is Ted Hoskins."

"We know him," says Fred. "Friendly but very precise."

She continues: "Security advance party will have checked the whole museum before we arrive, will recheck Great Hall seven P.M. Dinner in Great Hall. Cooking facilities in Gallery of Industrial Revolution, in front of the early steam engine. Reception in entrance hall. Serving tables between the statues of Art and Industry, they're all labeled underneath, supplementary tables in Tudor, next to the Dissolution of the Monasteries showcase as usual . . ."

"Will they have the place ready for us?" asks Gustavus.

"Last time they kept us waiting half an hour while they wrapped up a battleship in cellophane to protect it from the canapés. There was a madwoman there from the Conservation Department who screamed at us for hours. The guests started arriving while we were still unpacking. . . ."

"Everything will be ready," she answers. "Forty butlers in the entrance hall. Fred on duty in the entrance hall, with me. Rupert on duty in the Great Hall."

"I hope the canapés come out light," remarks Fred jocularly. "Usually Gustavus's canapés are so rich they don't want anything else. . . ."

"Our canapé chef knows exactly what he's doing. Each canapé will be a work of art," says Gustavus, who does not always enjoy Fred's teasing, especially on a big day. "You people in Operations wouldn't understand that."

"Now then, boys!" interrupts Leonore. "HRH arrives at seven thirty and meets a small group in the entrance hall before going to the exhibition. He's not attending the reception. No speeches at reception. Flowers by Perfect Plants, delivering six P.M. Sound engineers are Voicebox, we're giving them dinner, Fred?"

"Yes," he says. "Outmess for twelve."

"Equipment details," she continues. "Four ovens, three hot cupboards, four urns, three electric rings, six vats for lobsters, all to be set up in Industrial Revolution. Thirty-two tables for dinner, sixty-five waiting staff. Here's the room plan—the royal table is dead center, with the speaker's podium under the organ."

"What about the lighting?" asks Fred.

"Set up before we arrive, the Great Hall is closed to the public all day. It's Brightalite—they need a rehearsal with the tables in place. It's an elaborate scheme, meant to evoke the eighteenth century—pretend candelabra, ambient light on wall displays, simulated candles on the tables. We hope guests will sit down at eight forty-five. Speeches at ten-fifteen—chairman, HRH. Then the pageant, which is meant to last fifteen minutes."

"That may be optimistic," says Mr. Rupert, "but go on, Leonore."

"Guests can stay till midnight. We're meant to be out by two, but since it's the chairman's bash they can't do much about if it we aren't. Is that all clear?"

"All clear," says Mr. Rupert. "Gustavus, is everything all right at your end?"

"Apart from the nervous breakdown, yes," says Gustavus. "Have you ever had a chef drown himself in his own food?"

"By the way," says Mr. Rupert, ignoring him, "the new royal tablecloths arrived yesterday, with the rose, thistle, leek, and harp pattern on ivory damask. Here they are if you haven't seen them, chaps." They exclaim over one of the rich thick tablecloths woven in Lyon for the occasion. Mr. Rupert likes fine furnishings for his dinners. He has a store bursting with damask and velvet tablecloths in aubergine and ivory and lilac, floral-patterned cottons for summer and pure white for contemporary art events, eight varieties of dinner plates, mountains of wineglasses, sixty or so candelabra, approximately Georgian and Victorian and definitely modern Finnish silver, decanters by the dozen and ice buckets and wooden plinths and lengths of silk and velvet, all the apparatus used to make Mr. Rupert's dinners seductive. Tonight's decorations will, of course, be Georgian. Mr. Rupert will be lending an important service of Georgian silver from his own collection for the royal table, with replicas on the others. At this moment garlands of myrtle and rosemary adorned with violets and lavender, roses and pansies, and interwoven with silk ribbons, all in what Perfect Plants asserts is a perfectly Georgian manner, are being arranged around the walls. A choir is to sing airs from Handel, Arne, and Boyce from the musicians' gallery. The waiters and waitresses will be in costume. . . ."

"What about the costumes, Mr. Rupert?' asks Gustavus. "You haven't told us about the costumes." He evidently finds this amusing.

"Yes," says Mr. Rupert. "The costumes. They'll be ready for you at the museum. The waiting staff wear Vauxhall Gardens carnival costume. Senior male staff are dressed as eighteenth-century masters of ceremonies and female as ladies-in-waiting. I shall be coming as Beau Nash, of the Bath Assembly Rooms."

"I'm sure you'll look lovely," says Leonore.

"Thank you, Leonore. The attendants will be dressed as Georgian wenches and swains." He pauses. "I understand they're not altogether happy with the idea."

Gustavus guffaws. "I'm sure you'll all look great. I, on the other hand, will be dressed as a twenty-first-century chef. No need to try that outfit on."

"As a matter of fact, Gustavus," said Mr. Rupert, "that's not quite the case. The plan is that you should be presented to HRH after the dinner, so you're due to change into the costume of the great French chef Vatel. We've got the outfit—I do hope you'll like it."

Gustavus scowls, his handsome, good-humored face becoming darker and more aggressive than his colleagues are used to. "Is this a joke?" he asks.

"No, no joke," Mr. Rupert answers briskly, and snapping

out, "Kitchens," he leads them on a Grand Tour of the premises.

THE DIRECTOR'S OFFICE, 10 A.M.

Partial to Emma, the chairman always finds time to toss a smile at her. Being loyal to Auberon, she never smiles back too warmly. Today he allows himself a brief moment of full eye contact as he steams past her desk, waving his companion toward a chair. Then he turns back and says, "Oh, Emma, Mr. Kobayashi will be arriving shortly at the front desk. Go and get him, and bring him to wherever I am, OK? He must be made to feel extremely welcome."

"Yes, of course, Sir Lewis," she replies.

He has, she thinks, a faintly alarming walk, his head thrust out with his eyes fixed on the distance as though conquering it, his large strong torso also leaning forward, his legs in their well-cut trousers making long slow strides that cover the ground at speed. He affects a modern cut to his clothes, with narrow trousers, no vents to his jacket, his ties discreetly elegant and indiscreetly expensive. Even to the youthful Emma he is an impressive figure. If pushed, she reflects, someone could do worse than become Lady Burslem—though there's no sign of a vacancy just yet. Pretty tough she is, under that charm. As Lady Burslem one certainly wouldn't need to save for a pension.

Before Sir Lewis reaches the door of the director's office, Auberon emerges. He likes to keep the initiative when Sir Lewis arrives. This is partly because it gives the impression of being polite but also because if the chairman finds him at his desk, he always feels irrationally as though he's being caught pretending to work, like a naughty schoolboy. He likes to greet Sir Lewis at the door of his office, a courtesy that can be faintly threatening. Another reason, Auberon realized recently, is that, unlike anyone else, the chairman enters his office without knocking or being announced. He made it clear from the moment of his appointment that he was not bothered with such niceties. Auberon found this intrusive, a crude statement of the man's power. But it wasn't the only statement. At their first meeting Sir Lewis sat down without invitation at Auberon's desk, forcing him into another, less significant chair. Auberon now ensures that neither of them sits at the desk by moving his chair into the middle of the room before Burslem arrives. Even Sir Lewis, he thinks, would not shift the furniture around to assert his authority.

On this occasion, both assume the good-humored air with which they do business in public. Sir Lewis tries to maintain momentum by walking onward, as it were through Auberon, but Auberon is prepared and stands foursquare. "Good morning," they say to each other, before moving into the office, Auberon courteously indicating that as a guest Burslem should precede him.

"How is everything?" asks Sir Lewis. "How does the exhibition look?"

"Very good, I think," answers Auberon. "A few little adjustments still being made, under Diana's supervision. Shall we go and see?"

"I want to talk to you about the agenda for today's meeting," says the chairman. This habit of not responding to the director's remarks but continuing with his own train of thought is a recurring source of annoyance to Auberon. His only recourse is not to reply, in turn. This gives him a temporary edge, at least in his own mind, but he questions whether the man notices, and it rather impedes conversation. He sometimes wonders if Sir Lewis is aware of the symbolic discourse between them, which Auberon, as a historian of court politics, finds objectively fascinating if sometimes alarming.

Sir Lewis is resting his eyes on Auberon in a detached way that the younger man—even though he spends hours persuading himself not to be intimidated by his chairman—finds seriously unnerving. He tries not to look at Sir Lewis, who pauses before flashing his pure white teeth. "Now, the Nowness of Now—I think everyone will be supportive, don't you? I know you are, for what that's worth." This is accompanied by a jocular smile and a flash of the gleaming teeth.

"I'm sure people will want to consider the merits and demerits of the case," Auberon replies. "It's certainly very exciting. Of course, your term as chairman sadly only lasts another two years, Lewis—would you have time to carry the project through? Or would you seek another term?" His tone hints that the chairman might have to work hard to achieve that. He likes to stress the chairman's faintly ludicrous first name.

"I've brought some outline plans for the building, which Trusty Owen has just sketched out. You know them, don't you? They've done a lot of work for me, very reliable firm. As a favor, of course, there are no financial implications for the museum at present. They've done an elevation to show how a new building might hold the site, a plan." And he unrolls two or three large sheets of paper. "Of course, we'd want to hold a big architectural competition, involve architects from all over the world, exhibit the designs and so forth. . . ."

Auberon smiles gamely, fumbling at the sheets. "Very interesting," he says. *Am I going to be outmaneuvered on this one? What's Lewis been up to?* "They'll need a lot of thought, of course."

"Yes," replies Sir Lewis. "Of course they will. But the process will be much easier if everyone backs the idea in principle. I count on you to involve the staff. After all, you're the ones who'll be doing most of the hard work." His tone suggests that while their opinions are immaterial to him, the staff, and especially Auberon, will be working on little else for several years. "As for the trustees, I thought I'd introduce the idea this afternoon at the board meeting and gain their approval. An ultimate decision will depend, of course, on the business plan looking OK and on approval from government."

"Mmm," remarks Auberon, tested for a sensible response. "It is, of course, a revolutionary step. I wonder if it ought to be pushed through the board quite so fast. After all, it's hard for people to make up their mind rapidly on such a major issue. . . ."

"It's quite clear. Either you think this is a museum about the future, or you don't. Either you are in favor of progress, stimulus, forging ahead, the modern, or you aren't. That's all there is to say." This is a favorite phrase of his when he does not want to discuss an issue.

Auberon smiles politely and remarks, "There may be other issues to consider, of course."

"Undoubtedly there will be other issues," replies Sir Lewis. "We'll deal with them as they arise." He pauses. "I have your full backing, don't I?"

Difficult one, this. The director knows the chairman knows the director is not happy with the scheme, though how unhappy the director is the chairman probably does not realize. On the other hand, the director needs the general support of the chairman since without it he can't achieve much. Equally, the chairman knows that the director might, if hostile to the scheme, engineer its failure. He in turn needs the director's support. Within this delicate balance, the director, who has been learning recently how to impede the chairman's sillier ideas, must not appear negative. So he says, "I think it's a very interesting idea indeed—although, of course, I'd want to discuss some points with you."

"Good, good, and you like the elevations, don't you? Only preliminary thoughts, of course."

Auberon finds these computer-generated drawings, which ape the Edwardian building, immature and crude. "Full of ideas," he ventures. "Very interesting."

He wonders if the chairman believes him. It seems so— or at least he's willing to seem persuaded. "Good," says Sir Lewis. "Very good indeed. Shall we go and look at the exhibition? I haven't been in for two days, longing to see progress."

"I think you'll be pleased," answers Auberon, as they move toward the door, Auberon standing back to let his chairman go through first. As he watches the imposing figure walk through the outer office, again with a sidelong glance in Emma's direction, his mind wanders back to the Gainsborough—and the question, whatever it may be, that fascinates Jane.

In the outer office, a man is waiting for them. He wears, as Auberon immediately notices, an unfortunate suit. He eyes it with languid revulsion. Auberon's obsession with clothes is well known among his colleagues—those keen to be on good terms with him know that sartorial effort's essential.

"Mr. . . . Mr. . . . ," says the chairman.

"Evans," offers the unknown man. "George Evans."

"Oh, yes. This is Auberon Booth, the director of the museum. Important that you should get to know each other." Only the thinnest veneer of good humor conceals the contempt in this remark. Essentially, Sir Lewis considers that people who are not rich belong to a lower order of humanity. To him, Auberon reflects, what are we but two hirelings?

"Hello," says Auberon, offering what Tanya, who has studied his personality in some depth and gives him regular and often discouraging analyses of its development, calls his mark-eight smile. It is the least warm and friendly grin in the repertoire, barely more than an upward flicker of the lips and a thinning of the eyes.

"I'm very glad to meet you," says the man eagerly. "I hope you liked our outline ideas for Nowness. A wonderful plan—of course, we were only giving the very earliest indications of the way it might develop, on the computer, you know. . . ."

"Nothing worse than computer-generated architecture in my view, it's so meretricious. It stops architects from really thinking, irons out the creativity, don't you think?" says Auberon. He has not looked at the man, only observed his ill-fitting brown polyester jacket. He casts his eye in the direction of the man's cheek, not troubling about eye contact with somebody he never wants to see again.

Sir Lewis coughs. Auberon realizes he is not being espe-

cially polite. Icy superiority, Tanya tells him, comes naturally to him. Unless he watches out, he'll turn into a monster one day. Even Emma has made such remarks as "You
obviously didn't like that person, did you? You made it
clear."

He calls up the charm. "I'm sure there are lots of good
ideas there," he says, and wonders if this sounds better. "My
mind is rather on this exhibition and today's events, that's
all. I shall look forward to it." He does not specify what he
will look forward to.

"Come along with us, Mr. . . . . eh . . . ," says Sir Lewis. They
make their way toward the exhibition in silence. At the exhibition entrance, the press staff are arranging their wares on
two tables. Their banter drops deferentially as chairman and
director approach. On such days as this, the museum functions like an ancien régime court—particularly so today, the
apotheosis of Sir Lewis Burslem. As usual on press days,
Auberon can hardly recognize the junior press officers.
Generally dressed casually (allowable for junior staff, if it's
attractive casualness) they assume different personalities in
suits.

"You've seen the latest version of the press release, Lewis,
haven't you?" he asks the chairman. "*Lady St. John* is to the
fore, of course. We've had a lot of interest in her," and as he
says this Auberon feels a curious tingling. The chairman is
inspecting the choice of photographs (which includes everything he owns) and making encouraging noises to the staff.
He does it very competently, Auberon has to admit. From
the entrance to the exhibition Mary Anne emerges, carrying
a pile of papers and looking preternaturally calm. No longer
scatty, she has moved into the mood of heightened controlling awareness she adopts for major occasions. Meanwhile,

the chairman is advancing upon them. "The press pack looks very good, Mary Anne," he says. "Excellent. Who's coming to the press conference?"

"Oh, everyone," she says. "Not only the arts features people but a lot of the critics, who are coming back because you're here. If you have a moment, Chairman, there are one or two questions that might pop up, perhaps I should warn you . . ." Though the prospect of Sir Lewis's rage is agitating, she knows she just has to pretend not to be frightened. He generally responds well to a show of bright, unafraid competence.

Sir Lewis looks irritated at the thought of the press.

"I think I mentioned to you the other day that there's an aggressive young man called Valentine Green, a freelance journalist, writes for the *Telegraph* and *The Times,* one of those conservative radical types. As I briefed you, when I met him last week he asked at length about the selection of objects and your involvement. I tried to deal with it, but he may still want to raise one or two awkward points."

"Tiresome," says Sir Lewis. "Any other silly questions?"

"I've a feeling people may ask about the future direction of the museum, there've been a few rumors about the new building and plans to take the whole of the historical collection off view—d'you want to comment? And perhaps in the Press Office we could have some guidance . . . if you don't mind, Sir Lewis."

"You'll get some guidelines this morning," says Sir Lewis. "I will be speaking on that subject."

"What, the new building? Do you think that's wise?" asks Auberon, less coolly than usual. After all, the idea of a new building hasn't even been brought before the board. "Wouldn't announcing plans to the press be a bit premature?"

"I only intend," his chairman answers coldly, "to announce that plans will be considered by the trustees in the very near future."

"I think that will be great, a lot of fun," intervenes Mary Anne brightly. There is a silence. The chairman evidently does not care for the idea of "a lot of fun." "And if the building doesn't go ahead," she rushes on (*how aware is she,* Auberon wonders, *of the impact made by what she's saying?*), "at least we'll get masses of publicity."

This is not at all what Sir Lewis wishes to hear. Flushing slightly, he advances into the exhibition. Just inside the door is Helen Lawless. His manner changes. "Ah, Helen," he cries, with the warmth used by the great to their favorites to set off their coolness toward others. "Our brilliant curator! Is everything under control, Helen?"

"I think so, Chairman," she answers eagerly. Auberon and Mary Anne, an unwilling entourage, listen closely to the tone of this exchange. "I do hope you'll like everything. *Lady St. John* looks sensational with the new lighting."

"Let's go and look at her," he says. As they walk through the exhibition the chairman, again the pink of urbanity, doles out approval to left and right, to objects and staff, rather as the Sun King might have dispensed kind words to his courtiers on a festive day. He stops to watch the London video tour, nodding at the screen to include it in the circle of satisfaction and remind his listeners that this was his idea. He pauses briefly at each of his own pictures, remarking how different things one knows well look in a new context. This must be true, since he says it several times. Everyone in his entourage, which by now also includes Diana, Jane, and Lucian, nods each time as though at a revolutionary insight. Only Auberon maintains the bland half-smile he adopts in moments of tension. Mark-seven, Tanya would say. (Why does he keep thinking of Tanya? He's not at all interested in her, just now.)

Then Sir Lewis spots the error: the misplaced portraits. "But I don't like this!" he cries. "What have you done here?" They sigh with relief. And after some scornful remarks and expostulations and directions to the hastily summoned technical staff he sweeps on in high gratification, promising to return shortly to check that his instructions have been followed. Helen, who (alone) doesn't know about this ploy (the others don't trust her), is surprised that her colleagues seem fairly unconcerned. How would she feel, she wonders, if Sir Lewis caught her making such a glaring mistake? Mortified. Struck down. He's such a fascinating man. . . .

They arrive at *Lady St. John*. It has been artfully lit so that the whole area of the canvas is illuminated without light spilling on to the surroundings. In front of the painting, just for the opening, a wooden trough has been placed. It is painted with treillage and filled with sweet peas, lavender, and alchemilla, intended—according to Mirabel, who directed the flower theming—to evoke the freshness of the English countryside in June (in contrast to the atmosphere of an old bus station, which the theater usually evokes). It looks like a stage set, the climax of the exhibition.

They all stop to look at the painting. It is the chairman who speaks. "Out of this world," he says. "Out of this world."

As he speaks there is a bustle behind them. Emma appears wearing a look of detached efficiency and leading a large, powerfully built Japanese man in a raincoat. He is already fixing both Sir Lewis and the Gainsborough with an intent stare. "Mr. Kobayashi," cries Sir Lewis excitedly and loudly, and hurries forward to greet his guest. "How was your flight? How is your hotel? How do you like the museum?"

"This is the picture?" says Mr. Kobayashi.

"This is the picture. What do you think, Mr. Kobayashi? Wonderful, isn't it?"

"A very nice lady," says Mr. Kobayashi. "A very nice lady indeed. Yes, I like her very, very much."

GREAT HALL, MORNING

The Great Hall has had a splendid history. A large plaque under the minstrels' gallery and above the twenty-foot-high double doors, which lead to the entrance hall, announces that in this room on 24 June 1900 His Royal Highness the Prince of Wales in the presence of Her Royal Highness the Princess of Wales performed the museum's opening ceremony. They were attended by H. B. Truegood Esq., Mayor of Lambeth; The Right Honorable the Viscount Haringey DL KCB; Rupert Vaughan Lanchester Esq. and Edwin Rickards Esq. (architects); and M. D. Molson Esq. (Borough Surveyor). Following the ceremony, newspapers record, Their Royal Highnesses were pleased to favor the museum with their presence at a breakfast of remarkable length and splendor, attended by five hundred guests. The breakfast was provided by Lord Haringey, a fact that was discreetly referred to in the speech of thanks offered by the Prince. Following the banquet, a Pageant of English History was performed on the stage by local children. Given the scale of the repast it is hard to believe the guests benefited much from the reenactment of the Battle of Hastings by St. George's Church of England School, Blackfriars Road.

After that glorious opening day the Great Hall suffered a gradual decline. For most of the sceptical twentieth century it was viewed with as little favor as the entrance hall: bombastic and impractical, too large to be heated, too monumental for any but the most enormous objects. Numerous plans were made (but never carried out) to subdivide it. A Coronation exhibition was staged there in 1911 and again in 1953, but mostly it was seen as a white elephant. The hall was rescued from neglect by corporate entertaining. As museums realized in the 1980s that the best commercial use for places originally conceived of as temples of learning was as party venues, the Great Hall became an asset. "Marvelous, wow," potential clients would thrill. "What a space—and it can seat six hundred!" "Six hundred max," they would be told, "but it's more comfortable with five." And everybody would gasp cooperatively. "We're afraid," they were warned, "the catering facilities are almost nonexistent, so you'll have to introduce temporary facilities in the Gallery of the Industrial Revolution, next door." But ignoring this, "Wow," everyone would say again, "just look at it. It's so amazingly grand!"

The Great Hall lived again. After more meetings than seemed possible to the participants, and the employment of several contradictory experts on historic paint colors, a scheme of redecoration was decided on. In an expensive initiative, which had to be funded by axing the Research Department ("temporarily," the dispossessed scholars were told as they were turned out of their little Eden, but *temporary* proved an elastic term), the 1950s cocktail bar was removed, the walls were decorated in the historic shades of stone and cream, the doors were stripped to the original

Welcome to Northborough Free Library

Check out list for JANE S FREED:

1. **The hound in the left-hand corner : a novel**
   Author: Waterfield, Giles.
   Barcode: 30463000147896
   Item Type: Book : Book : book
   Due: 12/16/13

2. **Behind the scenes at the museum**
   Author: Atkinson, Kate.
   Barcode: A22501050417
   Item Type: Book : Book : book
   Due: 12/16/13

3. **Case histories : a novel**
   Author: Atkinson, Kate.
   Barcode: 30463000177067
   Item Type: Book : Book : book
   Due: 12/16/13

1. The hound in the left-hand
   corner : a novel
   Author: Waterfield, Giles.
   Barcode: 30463000147696
   Item Type: Book : Book :
   book
   Due: 12/30/13

2. Behind the scenes at the
   museum
   Author: Atkinson, Kate.
   Barcode: 30501950417
   Item Type: Book : Book :
   book
   Due: 12/23/13

3. Case histories : a novel
   Author: Atkinson, Kate
   Barcode: 30463000133007
   Item Type: book : Book :
   book
   Due: 12/10/13

...ORO 2013-11-25 17:33
...e helped by Circ

mahogany, the carpet was removed to reveal the oak boards, the heraldic achievements were repainted in their early colors, the bronze gasoliers were reinstated, a plywood cover was taken off to reveal the Foundation Day plaque, the two clocks, long silent, were set ticking and chiming once more. Most strikingly, the two monumental murals, very early works by Sir Frank Brangwyn which had been concealed behind wooden screens during the Second World War, were reexposed. Unfashionable though Brangwyn remains, his vigorous depictions of the youth of William Shakespeare and the defeat of the Spanish Armada (subjects chosen by Lord Haringey to epitomize English history) again make a powerful impact, and stimulate talk whenever social intercourse, steering through the difficult waters of corporate entertainment, hits the rocks.

The room is now in constant use. "Of course the location isn't absolutely central-central," Venue Promotions say to clients, "but it's awfully easy to access, close to Waterloo Station and Victoria Station and very handy from the City—and there's absolutely no problem about parking. Do try it." And try it they do, merchant banks and insurance companies and legal firms and official bodies, four or five nights a week. Venue rental, as it is known, has become one of the museum's most profitable activities. As the chairman says annually to the board whenever next year's business plan is presented with a note that government financing is once again to be reduced to promote efficiency, "Thank God for the Great Hall." He said it more than once when planning this dinner.

This morning the hall is as noisy as usual before a big event. The vanguard of Angel Cooks have deposited large packing cases and piles of tables and chairs behind a barricade in a corner. Mirabel's team are preparing their Georgian decorative scheme. On the stage at one end of the hall, where the Grand Pageant is to be performed, an ominous pile of props has accumulated under a tarpaulin with the occasional golden sword and trumpet peeping out. Melissa, Head of Education, who has devised the pageant, is hurrying to and fro on the stage without apparently achieving anything at all. The Head of Security is making himself disagreeable to the Head of Operations from Angel. Though hampered by the fact that this is an in-house event hosted by the chairman, he still needs to exercise control. He is assisted by the arrival of the Security advance party, in the form of two policemen and two police dogs, to check the building and particularly the rooms where His Royal Highness will be spending royal time. Their arrival allows John Winterbotham to clear the Great Hall, driving decorators and caterers into the entrance hall with curt commands. Mirabel is not pleased. She is blond and statuesque and of good family in Shropshire, accustomed to mix with the pink of society, and does not appreciate being ordered out of the room, as her increasingly strangled tones indicate. But out she goes, her pretty band of assistants rustling and shrugging in her wake.

Since the Great Hall's practically unfurnished, the security inspection does not take long. While the police officers guide their hounds round the inbuilt mahogany benches and the throne, and negotiate packages from Angel Cooks, John surveys the space closely. He notes, with surprise, that the security staff on duty are not the ones he'd expect. At one end of the room stands Anna—*OK, she does do the ground floor, and a very nice girl she is, too,* he thinks, *wouldn't mind doing a security check on her*—but on duty at the other end is young Bill. *What's he doing here? Goofy lad, one of the new intake, not really suitable, constantly mooning about and looking in the air—shouldn't he be on the first floor?* He approaches Bill, who is staring into the distance with an expression John can't understand—what's the matter with the lad? Nothing unusual to look at unless it's Anna and he's seen her often enough, hasn't he? Anyway, he's probably a poof. . . .

"What are you doing down here?" he demands of Bill.

Bill gulps. "I'm on duty, Mr. Winterbotham," he says. "Jim Baldwin's off sick, so I was transferred here. Mr. Burgess sent me down."

John looks put out. "I see. It's a bit irregular, having someone from another team working on a floor they're not attached to. You know the security procedures for the Great Hall, do you?"

"Oh, yes, sir," he says, "I mean, Mr. Winterbotham."

"You stay at this end of the room throughout your duty, you understand that, don't you?"

"Oh, yes," he says.

"Carry on," says John. There's something irregular going on here, he doesn't understand what. He must speak to Ian (who seems to be back early from his break, what's he trying to establish, then?). He leaves to deal with the police officers, who have now finished their check. As he moves away, the look of adoration, which has suffused Bill's face ever since by a blissful coincidence he was transferred to the room where *she* is on duty, returns.

The look is so strong that keen-sighted Anna can see it across the room. She smiles back just as Mirabel and her crew and the people from Angel flock back, followed by Melissa escorting what seems to be several hundred children for a rehearsal of the pageant. The more curious and observant among these many arrivals might witness the unusual sight of a uniformed security guard at each end of the monumental hall, smiling seraphically into the far distance.

PRESS VIEW AND PRESS CONFERENCE, 11:30 A.M.

Mary Anne and her boys adore a press conference. They like the tension, the unpredictability, the struggle to make trivial events appear important, the badinage, the excitement when a speaker enthuses his audience, the danger that somebody might offend an important journalist. They enjoy the beginning of press views when the doors open and early arrivals drift in, ladies in woolly hats from local papers and angular young men from art magazines with no discernible readership. These beginners are followed by a trickle of others—the man who claims to write for a (probably fictitious) journal in the West of England from which no article ever emerges but who comes to all the press views and drinks and eats for four, and the writer for a middle-market daily paper who's weak on opinions but hoovers up other people's, and the ex-museum director edged out of his job who finds journalism déclassé and sighs as he surveys the photographs on offer, always asking for something that's not there and pointing out errors of fact or typography. Mary Anne is more interested in the heavyweight critics from the nationals, although many of them prefer to make a personal visit before the press view. She likes the tweedy old-timers, people who have been working as art critics for twenty or thirty years (and can't stop, because the job never leads to anything else): they are generally good-natured and willing to see the best in any exhibition, and only write about one unkind review in four. She finds the younger art critics more professionally disagreeable, but when they arrive, anxious for confrontation, she almost always manages to soothe them. The new style of writer generally produces destructive criticism, since it sells papers, and writes about one kind review in eight. But Mary Anne is not dispirited by a bad notice: as she tells colleagues whose months or years of effort are dismissed in a few callous lines, "Don't worry, darling—they know nothing. Nobody remembers their actual comments except you—but people do remember the event is on."

Mary Anne likes to keep an overall view of press events. She circulates slowly around the galleries, ensuring the staff are playing their visitors correctly, neither neglecting the major figures nor being too attentive to the unimportant, and that the exhibition tours laid on by the staff are well attended. She measures the temperature of the event, observing who's making notes, whether the atmosphere's humming or chilly, whether attendance is good. No less than a hundred for a press view is obligatory for any success at all—they had two hundred and fifty for *The Age of Queen Elizabeth* and *The Court of George III*, whereas *Ceres Reborn— The History of Agricultural Implements in Britain*, in spite of its gallant title, only attracted the *Farmers' Weekly* and a couple of dreary craft magazines.

This exhibition's certainly arousing interest. The packs of journalists are dense, the discussions lively as they follow the tours given by Jane and Helen. They love the London video, the mixture of artifacts, the inclusion of objects belonging to people at every level of society. (This last was

Helen's idea. It was tricky to persuade the chairman to accept it till she convinced him that *Elegance* need not be a prerogative of wealth but could appeal to everyone.) The visitors are excited to see the "unknown" Gainsborough: "Superb," they say. "A hidden masterpiece—what a shame it isn't in a public collection—and who was she?"

Amid this enthusiasm there are only one or two dissenters. Notably Valentine Green.

Valentine Green is a freelance journalist, youngish, ugly, clever, and ruthless. He writes for more papers than he'd care to list, on a variety of topics associated with the arts. He is charming until he loses his patience and snaps. A true professional with a nose for anything suspicious, he loves hunting out a new story and sees himself as the scourge of the established order. For Valentine, there is a twist to the most straightforward story. He is a friend of Diana, but this does not make him write good-natured articles about the museum.

From the set look on his face, eyes thrusting forward and lips pursed, Mary Anne concludes he's not in a good mood. "Do you like the exhibition, Valentine?" she asks bravely.

"I find a lot of things about it very interesting," he replies, and closes his mouth tightly.

Into the throng of almost three hundred Sir Lewis Burslem advances. He wears an air of good humor, though it has an impermanent feel to it. Spotting his approach, Mary Anne, who thinks that an encounter between the two of them at this stage might be disastrous, maneuvers Valentine out of view behind a large showcase. Sir Lewis is accompanied by a little entourage: his wife, Auberon, his personal assistant from his own office, and Jeannie, the museum's only female press officer. They make a bustle as they advance, and the journalists, turning to look at them, hush and move slightly backward as though for royalty, perhaps intimidated by the air of conscious condescension that emanates from the Burslems. They advance toward the neighboring lecture theater, where the press conference is to be held. Behind the chairman's party swoop the young lady and the young gentlemen of the Press Office, firmly smiling as they propel the press into the theater.

There is a pause before the chairman and director, followed by Lucian, Jane, and Helen, mount the stage. From a distance comes the incongruous sound of trumpets and cheering followed by loud chanting. The chairman places himself in the center of the long velvet-covered table, Auberon to his right, the others at a tactful distance. Although the lecture theater is a hideous room in the Utility style of around 1948, the stage has been dressed up. Tall glass cylinder vases of arum lilies stand on Perspex plinths in a 1940s idiom to left and right of the table, and the stage is bathed in a softly flattering light, never seen here before. Behind the speakers' heads looms the image of Lady St. John's face, projected to three or four times life size. To some of those beneath her in the hall the image assumes a strangely ambiguous quality, as though her lips were moving, her eyes flickering.

Sir Lewis is less menacing elevated on a platform than he is close to—or so it seems to Mary Anne, observing events from the back of the theater. He's certainly no good at playing the house. His movements have stiffened, and his air of bonhomie seems perfunctory as he surreptitiously checks his text. No trepidation shows on the face of Auberon, who looks confidently at the auditorium, nodding at acquaintances. He's one of the most polished speakers she knows—

she loves listening to him. Auberon moves to the podium and it's curtain up. "Good morning, and I'm very glad to welcome you all to the museum," he begins. "Though the seventeenth century is my own favorite, I'm delighted the eighteenth arouses so much interest in you, as it now does in me. This is a very important day for the museum, the opening of our centenary exhibition. It might interest you to know that the six hundred and forty-two objects we've assembled make this exhibition almost twice as large as *The Court of George III,* our previous record. We're delighted to have with us today Mr. Kobayashi, chairman of the internationally recognized communications and property firm Japco which is showing our exhibition in Japan." (Heavy humming from the audience—they're obviously impressed by the idea of the exhibition going to Japan.) "Most important, of course, is the chairman of the trustees, Sir Lewis Burslem, who is of course my boss." This is said with a throwaway air as though the concept were faintly humorous, stimulating a ripple of amusement. "It's to Sir Lewis we owe the exhibition concept and its realization. Burslem Properties have generously acted as sponsors—extremely generous sponsors, since the costs have been huge. Sir Lewis will be speaking shortly and I won't anticipate what he's about to say—I'll get into trouble."

There is a further ripple at this point. Auberon can afford to flirt with his audience. He is much liked by the press, whom he rewards with pithy original insights when they ring him. Auberon thanks the staff and the expert committee and the committee of honor and the minor sponsors and the Department of Cultural Affairs (which was about to be renamed Access! when it was realized this might produce confusion), which has provided indemnity for the loans.

"But I shall not," he goes on, "try to outline our aim in mounting this exhibition—that's for Sir Lewis to do. We hope you'll help us make this event as widely appreciated as it deserves. . . ."

He does it so deftly, in Mary Anne's view. Really, he should have gone on the stage, he'd be a wonderful matinee idol, transferring to sexy character actor in a bit. Though the words aren't remarkable, the delivery, the smile, the air of distinguished youth and self-deprecation, are all so finely contrived. He's been speaking in public since he was at university, after all. He appears to do it so naturally. Only she—who's rehearsed him for so many public appearances—appreciates the hard work behind the charm.

But as for Sir Lewis, now making his way to the podium with hesitant arrogance, what about his public speaking? He's no orator, she knows well, and has received lessons in communication from nobody. Unlike Auberon, who addresses many of his remarks to the most distant corner of the lecture theater, Sir Lewis confides in the podium. He appears indifferent to his audience—though in reality, as she well knows, he's highly nervous about such events. "This great exhibition . . . the largest ever mounted by the museum . . . an entirely original approach, analyzing the art and industry of eighteenth-century England in the context of contemporary social, financial, political, industrial, intellectual, and medical conditions . . . we aim to contrast contemporary constructs of Augustan society with life as it was actually experienced. . . ." This bit was surely not written by him, more likely that insinuating little Helen. ". . . mirror to our society . . . we seek to analyze the development of an urban bourgeois culture in relation to traditional aristocratic hegemony," he stumbles rather over this word, "but we have not abandoned the consideration of visual imperatives. . . . The exhibition studies the aesthetic canon which to this day remains influential within the trope of Englishness. . . ."

This is not going down well. The journalists, deferential when he started, are rustling their papers. She finds herself resting her eyes pleasurably on Luke, particularly caressable today in his dark suit and gleaming green tie, which matches his eyes so well. . . .

Then the authentic voice of Sir Lewis reemerges. "This is not one of those occasions where the museum's representative forgets the sponsor's name. . . ." mild amusement ". . . I am delighted as chairman to be supporting this exhibition as sponsor . . . an unusual but I hope beneficial relationship . . . Burslem Properties if I may briefly blow my own trumpet . . ."

Auberon looks tense. But there's no alternative to smiling.

"Ours is the second largest property company in the country—including Scotland and Wales, which I'm happy to say don't offer much competition." This pleasantry evokes muffled protests in the audience, especially from a man who writes for the *Scotsman*. "We have developments currently under way in fourteen British cities as well as France, Germany, Japan, and the United States. We're proud to support this museum since in our humble way we regard ourselves as a part of British history."

This bit he certainly wrote himself. Then he embarks on a new line: "I want to take this opportunity to announce another initiative, which will shape the museum's future. At our trustees' meeting today we'll be discussing the possibility of a major new development here."

What on earth is this about? Entirely unscheduled, surely?

"We're investigating the possibility of a large extension. I can't tell you much except that it will offer a new display concept, based on advanced approaches to audience input and throughput." He looks at his notes. "It'll discard the traditional élitist statement of cultural capital in favor of an approach based on maximal social inclusion." *Somebody wrote this bit for him, too,* Mary Anne thinks, and her eyes swivel back to Helen. She's sitting upright looking cool, but the look of self-satisfaction on her face betrays her.

"It'll be a display by the public, about the public, for the public. It'll deal with life in Britain as it's lived by ordinary women and men, young and old, communicated through all sorts of media—personal possessions, videos of people's daily activities, Internet communication—with views of Britain as it is now shown nonstop within the museum. *Breaking Down the Walls,* that's what we call this program, and the whole extension will be called the Nowness of Now."

Mary Anne looks around the room. He's certainly caught them now—and her, too. Lots of press coverage . . . controversy . . . sounds a good idea. . . .

"One factor does encourage us. People love the idea—it excites them. We don't know precisely what it will cost, but we estimate twenty-four million pounds." Admiring gasps at the thought of so much money being needed. "I'm delighted to announce that a donor has already promised ten million pounds. Strictly anonymous, I'm afraid."

Excited at the thought of so much mysterious generosity, the audience applauds loudly. Glowing with the sensation he's created, Sir Lewis puffs out his cheeks and sits down. Mary Anne is so surprised she can hardly assess the scene but takes control of herself. Auberon is glaring into the distance, face pale, eyebrows raised and tense, hands gripping his chair. Beside him, Lucian looks nonchalant, Jane seems puzzled, little Helen smiles like a pussycat. Meanwhile her boys, standing together in a gaggle, are trying to attract her attention, Ben in particular. She ignores him reluctantly, he is really her favorite at the moment, those melting brown eyes are almost irresistible, if only her rules were not so strict, after all the Loved One would never get to know. . . . Instead she looks straight ahead. There's a peculiar silence until several members of the audience stand up or raise their hands. Auberon moves to the podium.

"Thank you very much, Lewis. Wonderful news—news to me, too!" he says. Controlled though he is, he can't avoid sounding annoyed: his rendering of "Lewis" evokes the French Revolution. "We'll be happy to take questions—though we must restrict our discussion to the exhibition. The exciting news you've just heard can't be elaborated on at this stage." Sir Lewis looks faintly disappointed and shrugs his shoulders but does not intervene.

The questions aren't too difficult. Mary Anne is often surprised at how docile arts journalists often are, apart from the little band of nasties. The well-upholstered ladies of a certain age who write in the glossy papers seldom have anything disagreeable to say. But she doesn't allow herself to relax—her eyes are on Valentine Green. He's stationed himself in the aisle, close to a wall light, which heightens the effect of his white face and aquiline nose. There's no doubt he'll speak. Yes, he's waving his hand.

"Valentine?" says Auberon. He seems to relish the idea of some awkwardness.

Valentine Green's delivery, a sneering innuendo shadowing every syllable, provides the perfect vehicle for his famous satirical shafts. He has a way of smiling into the far distance and not looking at the person he's addressing, which can be highly disconcerting. "It's very impressive to hear about these plans," he says languidly. "Congratulations." Sir Lewis twitches as though being mocked. "But I've two questions for Sir Lewis." The knight shifts in his seat. He detests direct questioning from the press unless they are wholly obsequious. "First, Sir Lewis, are you, personally or through Burslem Properties, producing this enormous sum?"

"That's entirely confidential," says Sir Lewis, "but I can state that though the board of Burslem Properties may consider a donation, they're not giving ten million."

"Thank you. We'll draw our own conclusions," says Valentine darkly. "My other question's about this exhibition. We note that the picture billed as the centerpiece of the show—visually and in all the publicity material—is the Gainsborough of *Lady St. John as Puck*. There she is behind you, after all, on a massive scale. I want to raise another issue, it's a rather delicate one but in these days of openness I'm sure you'll be glad to discuss it. As we all know, this picture belongs to you, Sir Lewis. Congratulations, again! A question emerges from all this. You're the chairman of this museum. Whatever the picture's merits, one might question whether an object belonging to a board member—the Burslem Gainsborough, as it were—should be given such prominence in their institution. It's as though a new product were being launched, like a new perfume or car. Isn't there's a conflict? And before you answer, I have a related question for the director. No, I insist, no, I insist! Auberon Booth, did you personally want to include *Lady St. John* in the exhibition? If you'd said you didn't want it, would you have been listened to? In short, is this exhibition, generously sponsored by Burslem Properties, acting as a huge shop window for one business and one businessman?" Auberon tries to intervene, but Valentine talks over him. "No, you must let me speak," he cries, his voice becoming more squeakily commanding by the minute. "Isn't it true that the intellectual integrity of this museum—a public institution, publicly funded—is being exploited for the benefit of the person at its head? What do you say to that?' Amid the rising buzz he lowers his voice and adds emolliently, "Only an inquiry, of course, only an inquiry—I expect I'm quite wrong."

Auberon replies, "Of course the museum is delighted to be showing this painting and the other seven works Sir Lewis is generously lending to this important exhibition. . . ." The members of staff on the stage try to look professional, detached, loyal, and enthusiastic all at the same time but succeed only, Mary Anne thinks, in looking confused.

"Yes, yes, yes," says Valentine, "of course you'd say that, wouldn't you? Of course in theory you're delighted. But let's have an answer, not this boardroom blandness."

Mary Anne tries not to enjoy these developments. How will Auberon handle this one? And Sir Lewis?

It's Auberon who answers. "The tone of your remarks, Valentine Green, is entirely unjustified. Sir Lewis is acting in his private capacity as a collector. The pictures belong to him personally, not to his company. . . ."

"Yes, but in that case," interrupts his terrierlike persecutor, "why aren't the pictures described as belonging to a private collector?"

Sir Lewis is about to speak—explosively, to judge from his bulging eyes and clenched fists—when Auberon forestalls him: "Why on earth should we disguise the paintings' ownership? Is there anything shameful about the owners of works of art sharing them with the public?"

"So you see no discrepancy between your chairman's official position and advertising these works in the exhibition? Yes, advertising—*Lady St. John,* an unknown work, will become one of the most famous Gainsboroughs in Britain. It's excellent publicity, isn't it, so that if Sir Lewis wants to sell on the picture one day he'll have no trouble? And command a much higher price than he paid."

This time Sir Lewis does intervene. "I have no intention of selling the Gainsborough, or any of my pictures," he expostulates. And then his face twitches and he stops abruptly.

Why's he stumbling? Mary Anne wonders.

Valentine is not deterred. Although the microphone has been wrested from his hand, he raises his voice with startling effectiveness. "Another thing—none of you has persuaded me that this picture has any valid connection with the exhibition. I've heard the party line, but it's just expensive wallpaper, isn't it, academic and visual decoration? Isn't this exhibition, and the accompanying nonsense, an exercise in vanity and self-promotion?"

This is going rather far, Mary Anne thinks.

It's Auberon again. "We can't respond to a question put like that. It's time to—"

But Valentine has more to say. There is an angry look to him: he stares at Sir Lewis Burslem as though he hates him.

Why? Mary Anne wonders. *Why should Valentine so dislike the man? As a symbol of wealth and power? It's not as though Sir Lewis were corrupt, is it? Is this some sort of personal crusade for Valentine?*

"I'd like to know," he says, "whether the museum had this exhibition forced on it. It's the chairman's idea, I understand, it contains the chairman's possessions, it's paid for by the chairman, it benefits the chairman. Chairman's bonanza. Shouldn't it be labeled 'This is an advertising space'?"

"This is a very serious exhibition with a distinguished academic committee," replies Auberon. Beside him Sir Lewis becomes redder and angrier, clenching his fists on the table and leaning heavily toward the audience. "Anyone who's studied the catalog and the selection of objects will see we're breaking new ground in integrating archival research and recent theoretical consideration of material culture. You should look at the evidence. And I think you've had your say—does anyone else have a question?"

Amid an eruption of chatter, Valentine, apparently satisfied, moves into the shadows. The next questions pose no difficulties. Seeing Sir Lewis reassume his air of a man fully in control of himself and others, Mary Anne reflects uneasily that though they can stop Valentine's talk they can't stop his writing. Since he writes persuasively, and his editors adore controversy, this may be a problem. At least he hasn't been asked to this evening's dinner—that would have been a nightmare.

Stage lights down, house lights up, principals move offstage, audience out. Mary Anne moves toward her colleagues, who are looking at her expectantly. She is not pleased. She'd thought she'd spiked this line of attack, and that her little lunch with Valentine the previous week had soothed him, but no . . . She assumes her brightest smile as she rejoins her team and says, "Went very well, don't you think?"

In the Special Events Office they're finalizing the seating for the dinner. Or, rather, Lady Burslem, chair of the dinner committee, is finalizing and the Head of Special Events is noting. The seating plan has been under discussion for the past three months and has become one of the most important features of the museum's life. As the guests responded, first, to the letter warning them that the event would take place and, second, to the ultra-thick heavily embossed invitation card, accompanied by a fleet of smaller cards outlining the program for the evening, the list has been revised over and over again.

"Imagine doing this before the days of the word-processor," Julia, Head of Special Events, remarks crossly from time to time (though not in front of Lady Burslem). Julia hates her job and would like another, possibly as project manager for the Workers' Revolutionary Party. She finds Lady Burslem efficient and amiable as long as she is never crossed and, in her posh way, rather amusing.

In the past few weeks the seating plan has emerged like an unruly quilt. Lady Burslem is famous for her skill in bringing together people who'd like to meet one another. Her husband delegates the seating arrangements to her, confident she'll loyally give him the cream of the guests. At one point, Auberon believed, his chairman was scheming to impose on him the dullest table possible within the bounds of decency—the most vulgar self-seeking members of the Magna Carta Circle, the ugliest titled lady with the largest overdraft, the most self-opinionated and verbose man of learning. Sir Lewis tried to relegate Auberon to the far corner, telling him some distinguished people must sit on the edges to show that all the tables had equal status—even though he plans to sit dead center under the speaker's podium. Auberon managed to squash that one but not to prevent one or two seriously boring people from sitting close to him. Sir Lewis and Lady Burslem are, of course, at the same table as His Royal Highness. The selection of the other occupants of that glorious board (twenty-four of them, instead of the usual twelve at other tables) has been discussed ad infinitum.

The meetings have been long and numerous, and Auberon has tried to avoid them. "It's ironic, isn't it," he remarks to Tanya, "that a museum director's principal duty these days is doing seating plans?" At each meeting they have reviewed the current guest list, decided whom to include from the B-list as refusals come in, perfected the royal table, tried not to group together the difficult or dull ("You can't put them all on the same table," Lady Burslem remarked. "They won't notice," Auberon replied. "They don't know we think their table mates are dull, they'll probably get on extremely well"). They have assessed the potential for future financial donations from people they don't know well, moved touchy creatures to better positions, patched up fragmented tables, counted and recounted and yet again counted the numbers. "It's not the food and drink that make a party," Lady Burslem likes to remark, "it's the host and guests." Wearily, Auberon assents.

One of the issues that has been discussed at length has been the naming of the tables. They worked on the principle that table numbers would be inappropriate since they imply an order—whereas names create a benign nonhierarchical atmosphere. They settled on the names of thirty great British persons of the eighteenth century, including appropriate women and scientists and representatives of most political leanings, and came up with a curious and varied list, from George III (the royal table) and Queen Charlotte to Pitt and Fox, Gainsborough and Reynolds, Johnson and Delaney, Burney and Goldsmith, Handel and Arne, Vanbrugh and Adam, Herschel and Hume. Thomas Paine was rejected as too radical and with unfortunate digestive connotations. In the end they decided they had done a good representative job.

This morning Lady Burslem, apparently insatiable in her appetite for organizing things, is sitting in the Special Events Office. This is their last opportunity to revise. The final lists have to be printed at one o'clock.

"Any more withdrawals this morning?" asks Lady Burslem.

"A few people are ill," says Julia.

"So inconsiderate," replies Her Ladyship. "Anyone important?"

"The Duchess of Wiltshire . . ."

"Oh, she's practically dead anyway, no loss, but that table—Chatham, isn't it?—becomes rather difficult." By this time either of them could win a quiz on the evening's table plan. "Julia, do we have a duchess substitute? We thought she'd do for that dreary businessman who might join the Magna Carta Circle. Has anyone else dropped out?"

"Mr. and Mrs. T. Sergeant, who are on Hunter. Their daughter's ill."

"Can't remember who they are. . . . Oh, corporate patrons, are they? Who else?"

"Vivian Blow is not coming, the artist, didn't give a reason, just said that she'd decided she had no time for bourgeois festivities."

"So tiresome, why couldn't the silly girl have thought of that before? . . . Not really a girl, just dresses like one, must be fifty if she's a day. . . . But what a nuisance, she's on Hervey, that table's very short of girls."

A not too aggressive baroness is found to replace the duchess and a member of staff is put in her place; the Sergeants disappear, bringing that table down to ten; the artist . . .

"Is that it?" says Her Ladyship. "No late additions? You've put Mr. Kobayashi next to me, haven't you? Very important. On my left, with HRH on my right."

"Yes, yes," says Julia. "I suppose I couldn't know a little more about Mr. Kobayashi, just in case I have to introduce him to anyone?"

Lady Burslem looks thoughtful. "Mr. Kobayashi is Lewis's opposite number in Japan, chairman of one of the leading property companies. He has been very kind over taking on this exhibition and promoting it in Japan, so that we—that is to say the museum—should make a lot of money out of the event. He's very fond of English painting, and even collects it, I believe, not something many Japanese people do. Is that enough? So, I think we have everybody. Oh, and are all the staff on dinner standby alerted?"

"Yes," says Julia, suddenly resentful again. She is one of the standbys herself, condemned to parade all dressed up before dinner in case she has to fill a vacant place instead of being consigned to the outmess table.

"Thank God it's done," says Lady Burslem. "I hope never to have to organize a dinner for four hundred again. The things I put up with for my husband! You must feel the same, Julia. Shall we print out the final list?"

The telephone rings. Julia answers. "Oh, I see," she says. "Well, I'm so sorry. . . . Of course we understand. No, no trouble at all. I do hope you have a good holiday. And do come and see the exhibition. . . ."

"Who is it?" asks Lady Burslem.

"Bad, I'm afraid. It's Lord and Lady Pomeroy. They're flying to South Africa tomorrow and can't risk a late evening."

"Maddening," says Lady Burslem. "It's always the grand ones who are most cavalier. And they're on the royal table, too. . . . Well, we'll have to start again. Who do we promote?"

DENZIL MARTEN GALLERIES, ST. JAMES'S, LATE MORNING

Yes, Mr. Marten can see Jane that morning. Via his secretary (apparently he could not find the energy to speak to her himself, though Jane was sure he was in the same room), he intimated that a few moments could be spared. Could she touch on the reason for their meeting? . . . Ah, it was about the Gainsborough. What was the problem? . . . It seems rather late in the day. . . . Well, if she could only tell him in confidence . . . Eleven thirty should be fine, he was surprised she wasn't too busy—it must be urgent. . . .

Before she leaves, Jane twitches her clothes and in spite of herself examines herself rapidly in the vanity mirror concealed in her desk. Though she does not care for Denzil Marten, she knows what sharp eyes he has and does not want to feel uneasy under scrutiny.

I can't make out if he's anxious or apprehensive or neither. He must know that the picture's been substantially restored (if that is indeed the case); he probably commissioned the restoration. What am I going to say to him? I need to find out what he knows about the picture's condition . . . about its state when it came into his possession . . . about the restoration. I suppose I'm showing my hand by talking to him, but otherwise I won't make any progress. . . .

I'll take a taxi to the gallery. It's against my principles, but I've so little time and I don't want to arrive at the luxurious premises of Denzil Marten, art dealer, Bury Street, St. James's, in a post-Tube flurry. It would be nice to step lightly from a purring cab looking crisp, worldly, soigné. I used to be like that, when I was living with Hamish. . . .

On the way she considers her destination, physical and human. Denzil Marten is one of the best-known art dealers in London. He does not belong to the almost-extinct category of condescending old-established firms occupying opulent Bond Street premises, nor sell contemporary art from the pure white premises of Cork Street or Shoreditch. His is a different style. For the past thirty years he has inhabited an externally discreet establishment in Bury Street, St. James's. In the window one painting, usually a flower piece but occasionally the portrait of somebody rich, announces his trade, but only the initiated would brave the glass door in its neo-Baroque frame and the lofty young woman making lunch appointments behind a Boulle *bureau plat*. Inside, the atmosphere exudes calm luxury. The Dutch genre paintings and classical landscapes glowing on the dark brown velvet walls beneath discreetly bright lights seduce the trustees of large American museums and the wealthy collectors who buy from Denzil Marten. Nothing indicates overtly that the pictures are for sale or that the place is in any way connected with financial processes.

Generously, he has lent a picture from his stock to *Elegance*. It is a depiction of a serving wench by Henry Robert Morland. Privately, Jane does not think it is a work of any great quality, and she even doubts the attribution. But Mr. Marten was very pressing in his suggestions that the picture would contribute to the exhibition's social themes as well as its artistic qualities, and a note from the chairman of the trustees to the director in favor of the loan ensured its inclusion. Well, it looks OK, in Jane's view, but no more than that.

Although not brought up as an English country gentleman, Mr. Marten has adopted the style of one. In London he wears pinstripe suits with a stripe slightly too broad for comfort, and a scarlet or orange silk lining. He belongs to a club in St. James's Street where he has lunch most days, since it makes him feel he's arrived at the heart of the English upper classes. He's said to have an old rectory in Devonshire, with some acres, where he can indulge his passion for the country clothes he demonstratively sports on Friday mornings in London. He is rumored to be enormously rich and his passion for the aristocracy amounts almost to a disease. The body within this apparatus is not notably appealing and the face is on the bulbous side, but he has a well-groomed mustache and a mass of smooth black hair, which glistens in the sun.

Jane knows him well, having bought one or two paintings from him for the museum. She feels calm as she negotiates the glass door and says good morning to the lissom Annabel decorating the desk.

From the main gallery a little staircase leads down to the viewing room and then to Mr. Marten's office. The office walls are covered in red silk and brilliantly shiny cabinet pictures, which, Jane knows, are likely to be less good than they appear. The proprietor sits behind his desk. He waves at her and points to a chair, but indicates he is in the middle of an exceptionally important conversation that cannot be interrupted. Clearly it concerns sums of money, referred to in a code, which makes them sound mysteriously enormous. From time to time he slips into Italian or French or German, often, mysteriously, in the same sentence. It is an impressive performance, but Jane has heard it before and is short of time. After five minutes she looks at her watch.

"I have someone here," says Mr. Marten instantly into the telephone. "*Ciao, caro.* My dear Jane . . . what a pleasure to see you. Have you seen my little Terborch, very fine, don't you think? Private collection, not been out of the house for two hundred years, wish I could tell you where it came from . . . not your sort of thing, of course . . ." He is fond of secrecy and peppers his conversation with sly references to persons of unimaginable wealth and importance. "How can I help you with this matter of yours? It must be very pressing—on the day of your big opening, when you're so busy . . ."

"I need to ask you one question," Jane says.

"Please," he replies, simultaneously scrutinizing a message pad on his desk as though unwilling to waste one second. "Just one moment." He presses his intercom. "Annabel, could you call Lord Woking's office, and say I can't make Brooks's until one fifteen? Oh, and ring Mr. S. at the London house and check they'll be coming here at three—and they are bringing an additional car for the bodyguards and does it need a *Parkplatz?* Thank you, darling. Yes, Jane?"

Jane tries not to be irritated. "I'll only be five minutes," she says. "Then I'll leave you in peace."

"But I've all the time in the world for you," he replies unconvincingly.

"Thank you," she says. "The Gainsborough that belongs to Sir Lewis Burslem—you sold it to him, didn't you?"

"Yes, you know that, it's in the exhibition catalog," he answers. Does he stiffen slightly?

"I need to ask you about it."

"Ask whatever you like. I'm an open book. Within limits, of course. By the way, would you like some coffee, a little drinkie?" And before she has time to answer, he presses on, "Naturally you understand I can't tell you anything that remains in confidence between myself and my clients."

"Of course. You bought the picture directly from Sir William St. John."

"Yes. That's all in the provenance, too."

"What condition was it in when you bought it?"

"Oh, surprisingly good, really. It needed a little attention, of course—it had been hanging in a cold country house for a long time."

"I haven't been able to examine the picture in detail," she says, "and it looks splendid, of course, but I am a little concerned about its conservation history. I just want to be briefed in case we have any questions from the press—you know how hot they are on overrestoration, even though they understand nothing about it. So—do you have condition reports for the picture while it was in your possession and may I see them?"

Mr. Marten no longer looks so friendly. "I don't see," he replies coldly, "why the past condition of the picture is in any way your concern. I'm not prepared to release any documentation. You must know that Sir Lewis has given strict instructions—on our advice, to be honest—that the condition of all the paintings in his collection is a private matter and that they're not to be analyzed by any borrowers. People are so ready to make negative judgments. It seems to me you're abusing his generosity."

Jane sits very upright and stares at the exceptionally glossy painting of two nymphs disporting themselves in a strangely blue glade, which hangs above his head. Then she speaks rather slowly and deliberately: "You know perfectly well that by showing the picture—any picture—in our exhibition we are giving it our stamp of approval, academic validity, if you like." As she says this, she remembers the questionable Morland he has lent to the exhibition, but she cannot retract at this stage. "In a sense the picture becomes our responsibility when we give it wall space, and even more so when we engineer so much publicity. It becomes the intellectual property of the community, of all of us, not the personal possession of the legal owner." Marten sneers, and shrugs his shoulders. "What a strong presence he has," Jane remarks to herself. Can it be the remains of his aftershave, or one of those scents that are meant to arouse desire, or sweat, or . . . ? "So—I must be prepared, in case . . ."

"In case what?"

"In case its condition, or its quality, is questioned."

"Absurd," and he waves his arm dismissively, "all this ethical hocus-pocus. It doesn't convince me for a moment. The picture belongs to the legal owner."

It's odd, she thinks, how he's not allowing himself any eye contact with her. Not a good sign. "That's how it may seem to you. But you'd be happy to show anything you have for sale here in a museum, wouldn't you—to lend it to an exhibition, for example? You recognize the seal of approval it gives."

"I don't have time for arguments of this sort," he says. "And if you're thinking of the picture I've lent to *Elegance,* I lent it because I wanted to help the museum."

"That's as it may be. But museums have their own values, and those are what I want to protect."

"Museums are the graveyard of art. I shall tell Sir Lewis his instructions have been disobeyed. I'd seriously advise you, Jane, not to cross him in this matter." He fixes her with a hostile glare. "Of course the painting was restored after I'd bought it, but no more than many of the pictures in public galleries. It was a highly competent restorer who did the work."

"Who was that?" she asks.

"I'm not at liberty to tell you. But what I can tell you is that you'd be unwise to spread stories in search of a sensation, if that's what you plan to do. Foolish and damaging, that's what it would be. Sir Lewis owns a very fine painting, bought directly from the original family. He's very happy with it, the details of the restoration are incidental. And now, Miss Vaughan, I know you have a great deal to do. . . ."

"I won't keep you," she says. "You've been more helpful than you realize." This remark startles him. He fingers the huge glass and gold paperweight on his desk. "You're coming tonight, I think, to see your picture and all the rest—and thank you so much for your generous loan," she concludes insincerely. He nods frostily. "We'll meet then."

He does not reply. They do not shake hands. Jane departs.

Back in her office, she looks up Ronald Smiles in the telephone directory. She's known him, too, for years (small place, the art world), since they were both students at the Courtauld Institute of Art, but she seldom speaks to him now. "Ronald Smiles, Picture Restoration Studio" is how he is described, with an address in Fulham. *He's probably at home recovering from a hangover,* she thinks to herself, but she'll try the studio.

"Hello," says a voice. It sounds like him. Perhaps his studio is also his home.

"May I speak to Ronald Smiles?" she inquires.

"I'll see if he's in," says the voice. "Who shall I say is calling?"

"Jane Vaughan." There is a muffled sound at the other end. "I know that's you, Ronnie," she goes on. "I want a word."

"Oh, yes, it is me," he says. "The phone was handed to me by my assistant. What do you want a word about, Jane? It's been absolutely ages. You must have retired by now, darling—are you looking for consultancy work? Don't know if I can help you, really, things aren't good at the moment. . . ."

"I want to talk to you about the Gainsborough of Lady St. John," she says. "The most prominent picture in our show."

"Oh, yes," he says. "It's rather good, isn't it? Beautiful brushwork, don't you think? The artist at his most refined."

There is a curious tone to his voice, which is loaded with ambiguity at any time. She must not let him realize that she's trying to find out what has happened to the painting, if it can be avoided. They don't want Sir Lewis to think they might be unhappy about his precious picture. She must be discreet. Being discreet is not easy with Ronnie, whose snakelike mind can usually extract information from anyone he talks to.

"Yes," she says. "It's quite remarkable. But I was looking at it yesterday with Friedrich. . . ."

"Who is Friedrich?" Ronnie asks. He knows quite well who Friedrich is. "One of your colleagues?"

"Friedrich von Schwitzenberg, our Head of Conservation."

"Your Head of Conservation? Really? I've never heard of him. What is his field?"

"Ronnie, don't waste my time." He makes vague remonstratory noises down the line. "I wanted to ask if you were involved in its conservation, so that we can give the proper credits if we're asked. The picture's arousing so much interest, you see."

"Oh, yes," he says, "I'm so pleased. I did it over ten years ago—that is to say, I worked on a few problems when it came on the market, and cleaned it, of course, remarkable how well it came up after all those years in a dim country house." And then, more sharply, "You know you're not allowed to examine it in the museum, don't you? Sir Lewis is strict about that, on my advice I may say. I'm the only person allowed to handle his pictures, we don't want a lot of so-called museum experts crawling over everything. . . ."

Ronnie worked briefly at Leicester Museums and Art Galleries in his young days and left hurriedly. He does not like museums at all, and happily is never asked to work for them.

"No," she says, "we were just looking at it, in the exhibition. I suppose that's allowed. We were wondering if any areas had had to be repainted."

There is a pause.

"Not really," he says, "not what you would call repainted.

I did have to do some work on the edges, the landscape background was a little damaged. . . ."

"And the dog?"

There is another pause and a noise like a stifled giggle. "Oh, yes, the doggie," he says, "he's nice, the doggie, isn't he? Well . . ."

"I noticed only this morning that whereas the dog in an old photograph of 1898 has his tail pointing down, in the actual painting his tail is in the air. It seemed a little odd."

"Well," he says, as though considering, "well . . . I did have to do a bit of work there. I realized from the X-ray there was a *pentimento*. It looked as though originally Gainsborough showed the tail in the air. I could see exactly how it had been. And then he, or someone else, shifted the tail downward, it must have been considered more decorous or something. So I went back to that earlier version, I thought it brightened the picture up, more cheerful, better for the composition."

"So you removed later paint layers? Don't you think they might have been Gainsborough's?"

"Maybe, yes, but an afterthought, not his original idea. Anyway, I took a snap of the painting. I suppose it was a little irregular, but these ethical questions are awfully difficult, aren't they?"

"Indeed they are," responds Jane, "though I've never thought they interested you much." But this is not the moment to antagonize Ronnie, irritating though he is. "I mean, you're always so original," she continues emolliently. "What about the rest of the painting—did you have to do a lot of work on that?"

"Oh, no. Absolutely not. I cleaned it, of course, but it was in beautiful condition, really. Don't you think it looks good?"

"Yes, yes," she says hastily. "Unforgettable. Shall we see you at the dinner tonight?"

"Yes, I'm coming," he replies. "Looking forward to it. A great day for Sir Lewis, isn't it?"

"A great day indeed," she affirms, putting down the receiver. And what on earth, she asks herself, does this highly unusual conversation mean?

GREAT HALL, 12:10 P.M.

There's been a burst of activity in the Great Hall. Garlands and wreaths in the style of Vauxhall Gardens, decorated with gold and scarlet ribbons, have been nailed to the walls by Mirabel's crisp assistants. In the center of the hall, two marbled plinths have been prepared for allegorical figures, which have not yet arrived. One of these, people have been told, is to be the goddess of True Love, designed by Mirabel from an original idea by Rysbrack. The other figure will be False Love, a beautiful young woman holding a mask, with the legs of a scaly beast protruding from her skirt. On the balcony the technicians from Brightalite are arranging spotlights, while the sound engineers, keen young men in yellow shirts whose mobile telephones have apparently become integrated into their anatomies, are setting up their equipment.

Amid the slow crescendo of preparation, a figure in white and blue stands at each end of the room, following instructions that warders are not to move around the hall but to stay fixed and keep their eyes on everything. At one moment Bill ventured on a tour of inspection, which took him ten feet from Anna. As he moved toward her, he continued to survey the preparations, till he was so close that a glance at her could not be avoided. The sight of her, looking half in his direction and half, nonchalantly, into the air, made him stop, open his eyes wide, and twitch his mouth into a tentative half-smile. It seemed tentative, because his heart was filled with conflicting excitements and he was afraid that if he looked at her too long he would lose control. When she saw him coming nearer she tried to look neutral. She was still wondering if she liked him enough to let him think something serious might happen between them, since she is a highly moral person who believes one should only embark on an intimate relationship when truly committed to the other person. Her relationships have been few. She still isn't sure about Bill: she was telling herself he's a kind and nice man, and she'd like to put her arms round him, but wonders if they'd have anything to talk about. He's so keen, it's almost off-putting. . . . As he approached, much closer than he was supposed to, surely, she intended to give him a cool, appraising look. But when she saw his peering eyes and his funny, shy smile she was so touched and amused that she gurgled with laughter, and waved at him in a nonofficial sort of way. He did not know what this meant and thought she might be teasing and his smile waned so sadly that, unself-conscious for once, she put her fingers to her lips and blew him a kiss. His mouth fell open and he stopped walking, gazing at her speechlessly—until a crash from the far end of the hall forced him to investigate. As he stands again at his post he thinks she is beaming in his direction, though he is not sure of this. Is it a contemptuous smile, perhaps? She is so much better educated than he, how can she be interested in him except as a friend? Maybe that's all he can hope for, like a medieval knight, though he does not want a life of chastity, enduring hopeless love for his lady. . . . At one o'clock Ian finds them still standing dutifully at their posts, half a mile it seems away from each other.

"Everything going all right?" he says to Bill. "I nearly forgot about you two. Any problems?"

No, no problems, really.

"Oh, well," he says, "I suggest you both go and have something to eat. I'm sorry everything's so irregular today."

And yes, he wants them to have a break at the same time, and he will stay in the hall and keep an eye on things, and no, they're not to come back a minute before two, and since it's Anna's birthday (*how on earth does he know that?* she wonders) why doesn't he take her out somewhere nice? They'll be on duty together all afternoon, and if they want to confer (*why does Ian use that word so emphatically?* Bill wonders) from time to time, no harm done.

Bill is puzzled. What can Ian mean? His thoughts are always so apparent that Ian smiles. Bill is not particularly thrilled by this. Why do people always smile when they see him?

"Oh, go on, Bill, it's no secret, the whole museum knows."

What is no secret?

"Go on, off you go."

But he still hasn't said what isn't a secret and Bill doesn't like to ask and suppose she doesn't want lunch? She might want to go shopping, or have a rest, or go to the chemist. . . .

But he asks her all the same and, yes, she would like to

have lunch with him. If only she wouldn't laugh so much—he really can't understand what she means by it . . . but, oh, God, the happiness of it, how can one stand being so happy?

THE BOARDROOM, 12:25 P.M.

The boardroom is one of the museum's most sumptuous apartments. Located over the entrance hall and almost as large, it is lit by a massive Palladian window. This window overlooks a road, which the founder intended as a monumental avenue leading to the river. Only a few houses were constructed and nowadays the processional route dwindles into a traffic-filtering system and a bus station. On the paneled walls of the boardroom hang portraits of the queen and the duke, the museum's founder resplendent in the robes of the Bath, and successive chairmen. At the huge mahogany table (rescued by Auberon from the basement) innumerable committees have debated; candidates for senior jobs have trembled before panels of dignitaries seated kilometers away across the polished board, wealthy applicants for the privilege of making donations to the museum have eyed one another surreptitiously and wondered if it is a bonus to be invited to lunch here in the company of their peers. In rare moments of nonactivity, Auberon likes to sit here on his own, enjoying the room's noble proportions, and considering the many things that worry and console him. Above all, he wonders if he is happy here, if he is wasting his talents, whether he should not be back at Oxford and setting some prints on the sands of time by writing real books as he knows he could do. . . . He would miss the glitter and the power, but doesn't he realize how insubstantial they are? Is the great world really so great after all?

Today the table's set for a minimal lunch, which would gladden the civil servants who oversee the museum's finances. All these guests will get are sandwiches laid over dispirited lettuce leaves on brittle metallic trays, which bend dangerously when lifted, and own-brand mineral water from one of the dimmer supermarkets.

At twelve twenty-five precisely the room is silent. Sir Lewis Burslem is lounging, as though indifferent to any observers, in the ornate mahogany and leather armchair designed for the chairman. In front of him lie papers which he is studying carelessly, one arm drooping languidly beside his chair. Auberon, resembling a smoldering volcano rather than a man of the world, is rising from his seat on the chairman's right, perhaps to move toward the principal door, which is opening. Among the muted tones of the half-shadowed rooms, Emma, wearing white linen, crisp and startlingly light, provides a higher accent as she enters the boardroom through a side door. She carries a pile of papers, apparently architect's drawings. Outside, the warm morning has been growing hotter, and at this moment the sun fills the room with the heady radiance of flaming (but frustrated) June.

Through the door walk three of the trustees, then another, then two more. It is well known that Sir Lewis requires exact punctuality for the meetings he's chairing, with only a moment or two for amiable preliminaries. As they come in, the men all in dark suits, except Trevor in his artistically licensed green corduroy outfit, and the women equally but more competitively somber, they exude assurance. Auberon greets them at the door, sharing a cheerful remark between two or three to save time, while the chairman casts off his threatening mood in a burst of controlling good humor. "Good to see you," he cries. "Starvation rations, I'm afraid, but they'll leave space for this evening."

Auberon and Sir Lewis have been discussing the Nowness of Now. Auberon raised the question of running costs for the new building. Sir Lewis had not thought about this matter but regards it as irrelevant. He does not appreciate the director's apparent determination to diminish his day of achievement. Typical of the modern age, when people won't acknowledge success but insist on quibbling.

"Lunch," announces Sir Lewis, "and shall we get started?" As the trustees munch their official sandwiches unenthusiastically, he begins. He hopes they like the exhibition. Yes, they evidently do, judging by their approving hums. He thanks them for their support. The staff are to be congratulated, he continues, especially Helen Lawless, the special curator, who has given so much time and expertise. "And Jane Vaughan," interjects Auberon, who is less keen on Helen. "And, of course, Jane Vaughan," Sir Lewis echoes, with what passes for warmth, "and the exhibition team and not least the director."

"Hear, hear," the trustees say.

"And let's not forget the sponsorship team for finding a sponsor, not so easy these days."

They all laugh.

"Tonight," continues Sir Lewis, "will be a great event. I don't need to remind the trustees of the need to arrive punctually and act as joint hosts. There's a guest list ready for you all—four hundred and three, at the last count. We expect you to recognize them all!"

They go through the program: the reception, the distribution of catalogs (all the guests are to have one, but trustees must ensure nobody gets two), the presentations to HRH ("What a shame *she* can't come," they say), the seating plan. "This is being finalized as we speak by the chair of the dinner committee," remarks Sir Auberon. More appreciative chuckles.

What I most dislike about these meetings, thinks Auberon, *is their pretence of good humor. What's the point of this pantomime of cordiality, this deference, when actually the board's almost always split? And it's so galling that the views of board members— who know nothing about museums—are always rated more highly than the staff's. If only the sensible members would say more. Like Olivia Doncaster, for example. She's so sensitive.* At the thought and still more the sight of her—*Surely I can allow myself another glance, I haven't looked in her direction for . . . well, for minutes*—he relaxes and nibbles meditatively at an egg sandwich, his teeth delicately extricating the cress that escapes from the bread like a tendril of hair. . . . *She's always so special, and today, she's delectable. So soft, her arms, a brush of golden down disappearing into the sleeves of her dress, the sleeves are short but not short enough . . . her peachy skin, her faintly vulnerable shoulders, her smooth neck, begging to be caressed . . .*

Talk has stopped and the chairman is looking at him. They all are. Clearly he's expected to say something, and he tears himself away from studying the bones of her neck. She blushes faintly—has she noticed his contemplation of her? Has anyone else? He is confused by her look and by having no idea of what's being discussed.

"I need notice of that question, Chairman," he says randomly, but with what he hopes sounds like witty insouciance.

They all laugh, even the chairman, who does not press him. *Obviously this is an OK response—that was a narrow one. I must concentrate. I'm tired, I suppose, after all the recent pressures, but however tired one is, losing one's grip at board meetings is madness. Now they're talking about the press and I must listen, but who cares? What I realize is that I no longer care about Tanya, not even a little. Why should I realize this now, at this moment? Tanya's so aggressive, so practical, so angular and strident, so intellectual, always going on about moral values and our obligations, and pointing out my faults, which may be good for me but isn't at all nice . . . unlike . . . Dear God, I can't be in love with Olivia, I hardly know her, this is fantasy . . . but, then, it isn't just lust on my part, it's her character I really like, it's pure feeling on my part, it's her gentleness, her kindness, her natural elegance. . . . Oh, God, what are they talking about now? Museum security? To hell with that . . . We've had such delicious talks in her conservatory, stretching in huge deck chairs in the soft green twilight that inches through the massed plants, talking about business and sometimes other things. She's so attentive, sympathetic, thoughtful—yet perceptive. . . . Of course, if we . . . if she left Tony Doncaster she'd never become a marchioness, and would she mind that? And if she remarried she'd have no title at all. . . . Isn't this a bit premature on my part? I mean, I've no idea if she even notices me. . . . Of course some titled divorcées hang on to their handle whoever they hitch up with. . . . I must concentrate, but I've heard this stuff a hundred times. . . . Maybe she's Lady Olivia in her own right. . . . Isn't it time I got married? Really, it's not so cool in your late thirties to be single, people think there must be some reason, they think you're gay, not that I'd mind, but it's just not true. . . . God, this meeting is boring and it's so hot in here. I wish I were in a green meadow under an apple tree with her. . . . It lends cachet to a man, they say, to have a titled wife, absurd shibboleth but persistent. . . . Would she be interested in some-*

body like me from such modest origins, would she like me if she knew me intimately, what on earth am I aspiring to? . . . Am I quite mad?

"Do you have anything to add, Director?" asks the chairman. He has nothing to add. *Except that one of the trustees is the most enchanting woman I've ever met and I want to live with her on a desert island and make passionate love the livelong day (with a simple flat in Paris for occasional weekends, and possibly a studio in Venice. . . .)* "No, I think that's all very clear," he says briskly.

"Shall we have a break from formal business," concludes the chairman, "and resume at two for the real meat of the meeting?"

THE MUSEUM CAFÉ, 1 P.M.

The museum café is huge and noisy, filled with eager ladies from the Home Counties dressed up for a day in London. It is easily located by the smell of food, which permeates the surrounding galleries. For many years it was apparently designed to evoke a wartime British restaurant, but when Auberon became director, the interior was about to be reinstalled as a French bistro. He persuaded the board that BRIT should be serving English food in an English setting, and energetic boardroom disputes between the country-pub party and the let's-pretend-we're-in-one-of-those-exciting-places-off-Piccadilly school finished with a victory for tradition. There are more important battles to be fought than this one, Auberon (who was of the Piccadilly tendency) felt. In any case the country-pub fit-out might well be interpreted as an ironic postmodernist look, at least by sophisticated visitors. The staff detest it, but one of the minor rules of a museum is that the staff always hate the café.

Today there are very few members of staff behind the sign saying PRIVATE. When Diana, fraught after this tiring morning, arrives with her tray, she recognizes only Terence, the curator of Agricultural History. As usual, he looks mournful, eating soup as though it were the final nourishment of his life. His department, which flourished under the previous director, has dwindled under urban-minded Auberon, who is bored by plowshares. Confronted by empty tables, Diana has to join him. She interprets a twitch of his mouth as a greeting. "How are you?" she says cheerfully.

"Mmm," he replies noncommittally. At least this is better than his previous style of greeting, which was "I can't remember which department you're in."

"Things all right in the department?" she perseveres.

"Oh, fine," he says. "Absolutely fine. It's marvelous having a post frozen every time someone leaves. We're down to two and a half, compared to nine four years ago. Before the Great Panjandrum arrived."

Diana thinks it better not to respond directly. After all, her own department has more than doubled in the past four years.

"Ah, well," she says. "But at least you have your wonderful collections intact. And you haven't been abolished, like the Instruments of Warfare Department." This is not very constructive but she must say something. *There's Hermia at the traditional English puddings counter. Oh, Lord, oh, Lord. Why should I be so affected by seeing Hermia? It was only yesterday I noticed how special she is—of course I've always liked her, but in the six months she's been here I've never been so struck by her, not in the way I am now. . . . In any case, what's Hermia doing here? Is she alone? Is she buying something absolutely delicious and special to take away, or eating her lunch in the café? Hermia is so exceptional—perhaps we could at last get the chance to talk a little now, away from the office. It would be so . . . so . . . reviving. It's hard to have this dreary curator sitting at the table—surely he's almost finished the stodgy shepherd's pie with carrots and peas he's boringly chosen? But no, he's still talking.*

"Who cares about collections nowadays?" he is saying. "There's nothing glamorous about collections, it's all exhibitions and P bloody R, begging your pardon, ma'am. Who cares anymore here about history or academic achievement? We might as well give up bothering with stupid old objects and turn the museum into a permanent funfair. *ELEGANCE*—I ask you!"

Diana keeps her positive good-humored look in repair and says in a warm but noncommittal way, "Well . . . mmm." *Hermia's now looking around the café, as people do, to see if there's anyone to avoid. Or perhaps someone she wants to join—who would that be? Who, now? Will she even come over to the staff section?* Diana tries to look encouragingly toward Hermia, while maintaining an air of patient concern toward old Terence.

"It's cuts, cuts, cuts all the time," he is droning. "Our dedicated acquisition budget has gone completely, even the trust funds for departmental purchases have been absorbed into the general budget. There's hardly any travel money, no vote even for volunteers' petrol, everything's moldering away—and meanwhile that bloody Bankes is traveling the world first-class in search of another pretentious exhibition."

I love conversations about Lucian's enormities, but I must defend my department. And then—oh, heaven—Hermia is coming in our direction. Say nothing, Diana, just look calm. Smile at her, noncommittally if you can. She's smiling back—warmly, I think. Suppressing irrational joy, she points out to Terence that temporary exhibitions bring in crowds of people, often make a profit, and are essential for the museum's financial survival. As she chats she is clearing a space on the table, eagerly but, she hopes, unobtrusively. And Hermia does sit down at their table.

Oh, how I love you! How I dote on you! What am I saying? I'd so enjoy these few moments with you, if only Terence would go away. But he stays, even though there's nothing left on his plate. What will he do now? Is he going to start talking about employment grades in a fantastically dreary way, or how curators are now on a lower salary scale than other departments? He does not know Hermia and she's forced to introduce them. Though not moved to speak, Terence watches Hermia minutely as she lays out her salad, glass of water, and knife and fork on the table. She creates a zone of elegance around her on the pseudo-cottagey table. *But why does Terence stare at her? Can this torpid old thing—in his dusty tweed jacket with leather patches on the elbows and his expression of permanent irritability—be conscious of the ash-blond hair, the high arched eyebrows and the pale olive skin of this young woman, who radiates grace among banality?*

"Have you seen the exhibition yet?" Hermia asks him pleasantly. *There's absolutely no need for her to be pleasant to this old has-been, but how do I tell her that?*

No, he hasn't seen it, not since he installed the agricultural implements—but he tells her this regretfully, not aggressively as he would tell Diana.

"Oh, but you must," she cries. "After all, the section you have lent to is of such an interest, it is so central to the narrative—the creation of a folklore around the pastoral ideal and agriculture in the eighteenth century. . . ."

He seems to have melted completely, gazing spaniel-like at her as she eats her West Country Farmer's Salad. This is almost unendurable—Hermia will be leaving in a moment and I've hardly spoken to her. Seething, she notices that Lucian—*Oh, God, not him, that really is the limit*—has come into the café and is surveying its occupants. Seeing the group at her table, he frowns, shooting, she is sure, a look of irritated dislike in her direction. Hermia follows her look and waves at the new arrival. "Ah," she says, "I told Lucian I'd be here, he said he might come along, too, to talk about progress on the exhibition."

"I thought he never came here," says Diana. "I thought it was beneath him."

"I don't think he comes very often, in fact I had to give him directions," replies Hermia mildly, "but I suppose he's so busy today . . ."

"The department is busy. That doesn't mean he is." She must not sound disloyal. It must make her seem so unattractive.

"Don't you think Lucian is the busiest of us all? He just has a different way of working. . . ." Hermia remarks, innocently as it were. But his arrival brings one advantage. Terence, muttering something bucolic and still gazing at Hermia (if one can be bothered to listen, he seems to be saying he'll pop into the exhibition later though he can't be doing with private views), collects his utensils and hurries away as though terrified of having to share a table with the Head of Exhibitions.

This individual advances upon them, showing no sign of having noticed the agricultural depression. He holds a large tray, decorated with a painting of a picturesque cottage and peasants after George Morland. The tray bears one large espresso *(they'll be serving traditional farmhouse espressos shortly, too ludicrous, this place)*. Lucian grips this tray like an offensive weapon, staring forward as though avoiding superfluous eye contact. As he approaches them, his eyes fix on Hermia. Diana recognizes this look of Lucian's: she has seen it when he has been in pursuit of an elusive exhibit, ruthless, single-minded, mesmerized by the object he's pursuing and determined to possess it. The intensity of his emotion makes him strangely compelling. Now, though, it's not a work of art he wants. . . .

Amid the genteel bustle Hermia remains calm. *She doesn't seem excited by Lucian's arrival. She might well be flattered by his interest, of course—repulsive as he is, he's a magnate of the museum world. But her smooth, untroubled face tells one nothing.*

"Hello, Hermia," says Lucian anxiously, almost nervously, not at all in his usual confidently abrasive manner. *Ah, he's at that stage. Not sure how to deal with this situation. I want to say, "Go away, you revolting man, how can you imagine for a moment that this delicious girl"—my God, what am I feeling?—"could be interested in your bloated power-hungry body or your unpleasant personality? It's impossible, even for a moment."* As these thoughts run through her mind she offers Lucian, out of politeness, a nod. He responds with a vicious leer, a caricature of courtesy. During this mute exchange, confronted by a man, Diana realizes that her feelings for Hermia are wholly new to her. *No man's ever aroused such intensity in me. . . . I must be what I now realize I am and not what I thought I was. . . .*

In the agitation of this internal strife she leans forward and knocks over her glass. It does not break, merely strikes the table gently and spills its contents over the polished wood. This must be a good omen, or at least not a bad one. All three, two of them at least struggling with pressing thoughts, watch fatalistically as the water slides over the table, absorbing crumbs and fragments of lettuce and carrot before dribbling onto the floor. Then she and Lucian look up and at each other. Each instantly understands the other's state of mind. He seems astonished, as though seeing her for the first time. Meanwhile Hermia, faintly flushed perhaps but otherwise composed, looks conscientiously at her watch as she finishes her salad. Can she be aware, this pure young woman, of the desires surging in their hearts? *Ah, well*, thinks Diana, *the course of true love never did run smooth.* . . .

"I'm so sorry," she says.

There is a pause.

"Worse things can happen," says Lucian. "At least the glass didn't break. That's bad luck, breaking glass, you know, old superstition. . . ."

"Bad luck for whom?" Diana asks.

"For you, I suppose. Perhaps for all of us," he says, and for a moment he and Diana study one another, each newly curious about a person they have long known and generally disliked, whom now they see afresh. For the first time in years, she later reflects, she does not feel viscerally hostile toward him, and he seems intrigued by her, not just by her boots. . . .

"There's a strange sensation, like excitement, in the museum today. Is it Midsummer's Day madness?" remarks Hermia, for whom the silence at their table, amid the surrounding clatter, must have become uncomfortable. "Have you noticed it?" As one, they turn to look at her. Each marvels at her grace, the fascinating Anglo-Italian coolness of her warmth, her sophistication, and yet her naturalness. For a moment neither speaks, and then they turn to look at one another and both in unison say yes, and smile. It is unclear whether they are smiling at her or one another or the atmosphere within the museum or the oddity of the human condition.

"How strange you all look, as though you're obsessed by each other," interrupts a well-bred voice. It is Jane. She speaks humorously, but as they turn toward her she realizes she may have spoken the truth. She continues, "May I join you?" but she sounds unconfident that they want her to penetrate their little circle.

"Yes, of course, do," they answer. Lucian remarks, neutrally, that Diana has poured water all over the table and that Jane must take care.

As she sits down, Jane realizes that though she is bursting to ask Diana for more help over the Gainsborough there's little she can say in this company. After a moment Hermia declares she must leave and goes, in spite of their voluble protests. Lucian and Diana both become quiet as soon as she departs, both stare at the table, and frown, and look melancholy. Jane examines them, and does not at all understand their behavior.

"What is it about this girl that makes them so keen for her to stay?" Jane asks herself, in the midst of this silence. Is it her looks, her gentle manners, her sympathetic shyness, her willingness to listen? Is it the mysterious glancing sexuality, which even Jane thinks she can detect in her? She braces herself for questions from Lucian about why she was inspecting the Gainsborough so closely this morning, but no such questions come. Obviously he does not know about it—or perhaps he has a secret reason for not asking . . . or perhaps Auberon never told him—and why should that be?

ANGEL COOKS, 1:45 P.M.

Angel Cooks is not disorganized today. Of course, Angel Cooks is never disorganized. But compared to the usual strict control, the atmosphere is a trifle tense. Mr. Rupert's features betray the flicker of a frown as he restrains himself from breaking one of his cardinal rules, which is to keep out of the kitchen in moments of tension. Instead he is issuing a string of orders to his secretary and tapping angrily at his computer, listing and relisting the evening's order of events. He is not anxious, of course, no, not at all anxious, only concerned about dinner being delayed by the guests not sitting down, or His Royal Highness arriving late, or the lobsters not being acquiescent, all problems that would make the menu even harder to deliver. . . . Much as he admires the Royal Family, he's doubly anxious when they attend one of his events, the potential problems are so much greater. And there's always the possibility of a security alert and everyone being evacuated from the building just as the dinner is reaching its culmination. . . .

Guided by an instinct he can't ignore, he hurries down the passage into the kitchen. Gustavus is not to be seen. In the canapé kitchen, the five thousand canapés for the evening (thank goodness they refused to do that cocktail party for the Lord Mayor tonight) are being assembled as though on a conveyor belt before being placed in the cool room. Six people are working on the vegetables: the *panachés* are beginning to take shape though the turnips are slow today, the new potatoes have been cleaned and are ready to be packed, the *jus* to be poured over them stands in twenty glass containers. The salad is ready to go. Four jeroboams of walnut oil are being packed into cases. As for the beef—well, where is the beef? It should surely be well advanced by now but there's no sign of it at all.

"Where's Gustavus?" asks Mr. Rupert, of one of the sous-chefs.

"Oh, he just popped out," she says, blushing slightly. "He's been here all morning, he was getting a little tired. It was the beef and foie gras that was worrying him—he didn't seem completely happy about the recipe. . . ."

"Not happy about the recipe?" exclaims Mr. Rupert, his voice rising steadily as he speaks. "What right does he have not to be happy, or happy for that matter? It's irrelevant, whether he's happy or not. We've done it at the National Gallery, we've done it at Chatsworth. He's not happy?"

"I meant," she replies, her hands shaking slightly, "that he didn't think he was doing it terribly well, he thought his interpretation was wrong. Oh, Mr. Rupert, he's trying so hard."

"Where is he? I don't think he's popped out," says Mr. Rupert. "I know where he'll be." And striding toward the back of the huge white kitchen he raises his voice: "Gustavus! Gustavus!"

Gustavus is in his office. He has taken off his chef's hat and is sitting in front of his desk, his head in his hands. Beside him are an empty wineglass and a plate on which lies a slice of beef, looking as though it's been violently assaulted. He does not turn when Mr. Rupert comes in.

Mr. Rupert inspects the back of Gustavus's head before speaking. The situation is not wholly unfamiliar to him, though he has never had any trouble with Gustavus. He speaks gently. "Gustavus," he says. "Gustavus. Are you all right?"

Gustavus turns. His face is crumpled and his eyes are red. "The beef's no good," he says. "I tried it and it's just no good. It's too heavy. I know it's one of your specialities, but I can't get it right, it's too rich. I have your recipe, but I tried a little experiment, I thought it would be exciting, I shouldn't have done. The way I've done it, it's hopeless."

Mr. Rupert cuts a sliver off the beef.

"Don't eat that," says Gustavus, in a miserable voice. "It's disgusting, and cold, too. And I did so want to do you credit on this great occasion, and His Royalness, and everyone in the world here and all I do is produce this shit."

"I can assess beef at any temperature, and I know good beef from bad beef better than anyone in the country," replies his boss, sliding the meat with its succulent coating of foie gras into his mouth. Gustavus looks at him pleadingly. Mr. Rupert raises his head toward the ceiling, bites, chews, pushes the meat round his mouth, and considers. Then he looks Gustavus in the eye. "It's excellent," he says. "Better than I've ever made it. What have you added, though?"

Gustavus opens eyes and mouth wide in amazement and gratitude. "It's a tiny hint of mustard glaze," he says, "mustard from Morocco, with a little tarragon and lime in it. Do you really like it? Aren't you just pretending, to make me happy?"

"I really like it. You are very talented. This will be perfect," says Mr. Rupert. "Now, I have some orders for you. I want you to give your instructions to your chefs for the next hour and then I want you out of here till three. A run around Battersea Park, d'you understand? Definitely not a trip to the pub—you're not to drink any more until the end of the dinner. The more you drink, the less capable you are. And no pickups either, just a nice run in the fresh air. And no other substances, either. OK, is that clear?"

Gustavus shudders. "I just wanted to feel more confident—at least I don't hide it if I drink. That's a good sign, isn't it?"

"That's quite a good sign. Back at three. Run in the park, OK?"

"Yes, Mr. Rupert," says Gustavus, gasping a little. "You're so kind. And you really like the beef?"

"Yes, Gustavus. The beef will be unforgettable."

JANE'S OFFICE, 2:15 P.M.

There is a message for Jane, back in her office. Sir William St. John would like to speak to her.

Why has he rung her? Has Marten spoken to him? Is he going to tell lies about the state of the painting when it left his possession? Does he imagine he has some sort of a reputation to defend? Will he be as arrogant as most people of his sort (a member of the intellectual aristocracy, Jane despises the territorial variety)? Will this be a *mauvais quart d'heure?*

As it turns out, Sir William is extremely amiable. "Sorry

not to have been in touch sooner," he says. "Had to go out with my wife, she insisted on collecting some jewelry from the bank for tonight's bash, awful bore, normally wouldn't let it out of the vaults, but I can't stop her having her way, ha- ha. She wants to look as glam as possible, after all she is the modern Lady St. John you know, doesn't want to be upstaged by the historic one—not sure she's going to dress up as Puck, though. The picture looks glorious on the poster, I must say . . . hmm . . . Actually I think Delia will look OK in her glad rags, much younger than me, you know, and quite a looker, too, but I can't help teasing her. Anyway, how can I help you—I think we've met, haven't we?"

No, Jane doesn't think they've ever met. She just wants to ask him a question about the Gainsborough. Of course, he'd be happy to tell her anything he can.

What was the condition of the painting when it left his possession? Sir William does not speak for a moment, but laughs. "Oh, not so bad, really, it needed a clean, of course, wonderful what restorers can do, isn't it? Yes, it had been damaged a bit, there was a fire at the big house long ago. When was the fire? Oh, during the First World War, they never really got to grips with the house again after that, Father sold it in the twenties, just for the building materials—yes, we lost a few things but nearly everything was rescued. The problem with the Gainsborough was, it was so big they had trouble getting it out. It was kept upstairs, yes, upstairs, Father told me, in a cupboard or something, seems odd now, doesn't it? Actually," he says, "if you won't think me awfully inquisitive, why d'you need to know all this?" When she reassures him that she's only interested in historical accuracy, he remain loquacious but becomes more cautious. Yes, during the nineteenth century the picture was hardly ever shown—it had a bad reputation, was meant to be unlucky according to family tradition, broke up marriages, had a strange effect on people who spent too much time near it, made them lose control of themselves and fall in love with all sorts of unsuitable people. That was the story anyway, lot of bunkum, really. What did it derive from, this story? she asks. But he does not answer. Instead he says, "I know where we met, we were at Cambridge together, weren't we?"—and as she digests this unfamiliar idea he goes on, "We acted in *Love's Labour's Lost* together at Girton. You were the Princess, I was Dumaine, one of the lords, as I recall—do you remember? I knew I knew the name and when I heard your voice on the telephone you sounded just as you used to—you wouldn't recognize me now, awfully fat and ugly, but I was OK-looking then, I believe, and you were certainly much more than OK-looking. . . . Wasn't your old man a bigwig somewhere?"

Jane is so startled by this development and by the half-lost recollection of a hot summer at Cambridge, and of the beautiful young man who played Dumaine and held her hand whenever possible during rehearsals, that she can hardly speak. But finally, "Yes," she says, "I do remember—but you weren't called William St. John then."

He laughs. "No, I didn't think it was cool to have a name like that, liked to be known as Bill John. Used to madden my father, that was the point. I turned back into William St. John when he died."

"I seem to remember calling you Billsy."

"Billsy to my friends—that's me, was me, anyway. Not much Billsy about me nowadays. Anyway, Delia can't stand the name. Well, we'll meet tonight, can't wait."

"Oh, I'm nothing to look at now," she says, "nothing at all. Plain and dull. Just an old curator."

"Don't believe you," he answers. "There'll be lots to catch up on, won't there? But in the meantime, this picture. Well, Janey—wasn't that what we called you?"

"Yes," she says. "In the past."

"Janey—just to wrap up the story, now that the catalog's printed, and you can't publish what I say. . . ." there's a teasing note to his voice. "The Gainsborough was never shown in the house during the nineteenth century, for the reasons I've given you. And also because that particular Lady St. John was thought to be a terrible bad lot and there were stories about her in the family, which no one else was allowed to know. Supposedly she had a great affair with a man in the Life Guards only a few months after she was married, then ditched him because she got bored with him. He killed himself, it was hushed up, but the husband got wind of it, he was older than she was, worried about his beautiful wife, worried about whether his little son was really his son, and his heir, you see what I mean. . . . It would have been pretty disastrous, you know, would make all of us into bastards, no right to the title or anything. There's no way of proving it now, of course, but it may well have been true. . . . He forced her to leave London and move to Suffolk, where he kept her more or less a prisoner. She died a year or two later, in childbirth, and only the little boy survived her."

"You've never told anyone all this, have you?" she says. "There's nothing about it in any of the files."

Sir William sounded reflective. "Well, it's a miserable story, it may be exaggerated, I don't know. But you can see why they wanted to keep it quiet. Even now there's still a bit of family property, you know, a few pictures and an acre or two, we don't want our rights questioned, do we? lots of cousins around . . . I'm not at all sure they wouldn't sue, the other branch of the family, greedy lot they are. I'm only telling you because you're a scholar and an old friend, too, I know I can count on you not to tell anyone. The story was always passed down in the family as a secret, father to son, mother to daughter."

"And the picture? What did her husband feel about the picture?"

"Her husband didn't like it, not surprising, really. The story is he told the artist to paint the dog in, because he said he'd married a bitch. And he hated the fact she was painted as Puck, thought it was terribly déclassé." There is a silence at the other end of the line and Jane wonders whether to prompt him. But he resumes. "After her death he put the picture in some out-of-the-way corner, it upset him. When he remarried, the last thing his new wife wanted was a huge portrait of her glamorous predecessor staring at her every morning over the Rice Krispies. It came out again in the son's time and began to acquire this peculiar reputation. It was meant to affect people's emotions if they looked at it. Silly story, of course, but it's true that the son and heir did marry his cook at a young age, she was a very good wife and bore him fourteen healthy children. But marrying the cook wasn't at all what the family had in mind."

"So when the portrait reemerged recently," asks Jane cautiously, "how did it look? Was it much damaged?"

He does not answer at once. "Well, as I say," he responds, a slightly different note in his voice, "it was not in prime condition. But perfectly all right, just a little . . . eh . . . Funnily enough, the greyhound in the left-hand corner was particularly fresh, I always liked that bit. Well, if that's enough for the moment . . . I've got a few things I should be getting on with. . . ."

"Of course," says Jane, "me, too. I look forward to seeing you tonight."

There is a pause. "D'you think we'll recognize each other?" he asks ruminatively.

"Oh, I think so," she says. "Look out for the hair, it's not really changed so much, though the rest of me has, unfortunately."

"Your hair, your beautiful red hair. I remember that. And all you girls wore white, didn't you? It suited you particularly well. What are you wearing tonight?"

"Green actually," she says. "I suppose I should be wearing black, to suit my advanced age."

"I'm wearing black," he says, and then "Good-bye," rather gently.

THE BOARDROOM, 2 P.M.

The heads at the boardroom table are not all gray. Though grizzled, the one at the top of the table is compact, clipped, and forceful. Two or three are pepper-and-salt and one is hairless, but there's a fine variety of coiffures on parade—a fashionably cut blond male head and a ditto female, one or two short-back-and-sides in tones of black and French gray, a mane of rich curly brown hair arranged with loose elegance on a female support, and even a blue head supporting a diamond net. This is not a fusty board: the chairman has assembled exuberant youth (relatively speaking) as well as wisdom and gravity. A yard or two from the main proceedings, a short-cropped red head, bent over a laptop set on a little attendant table, hardly looks up.

Nearly all the heads are turned toward the head at the top of the table. It is producing sounds to which the others respond, angling sideways or bending downward as though thinking deeply. The talking head sometimes looks forward but more often to left and right, driving its gaze up and down one row of attentive listeners, then down and up the other.

A great many words flow from the chairing mouth. "We're thinking out of the box, looking at a new museum concept, a museum about people, not objects . . . intensely of today . . . radical reevaluation of our society . . . robust . . . new . . . robust media-inclusive material reflecting life of every person. An architectural competition attracting world attention . . . world-class building by internationally known architect . . . make us a totally innovative destination venue . . . a place not for the élite but for all . . . social inclusion's the name of the game . . . showcasing material culture, popular music, sport, shopping . . . globalization . . . multiracialism . . . humor . . . color . . . consultants . . ."

At least, thinks Emma, taking the minutes at her little table, *he's reading from a text so there must be a copy somewhere. Sounds quite fun, actually, but Auberon will hate it.*

The blond head to the talker's right is the only one not turned toward the speaker. It surveys the table, while the right hand attached to it takes notes. Only occasionally do its eyes fix on the speaker.

After quite some time the talking mouth closes. The other heads look at one another to see how the rest will react, and shake themselves and bob up and down, and the hands attached to them even clap, discreetly but supportively. Then the talking head announces that a gift of £10 million has been offered toward the project, on condition only that the board is satisfied with the final result. More clapping, followed by a pause and coughs and paper shuffling.

So far so good. Never taken minutes before, I'm already exhausted. What do I do when they all talk at the same time?

"Well?" says the chairman. "What do you all think? No progress possible at all, of course, without the board's full approval. Shall we go around the table? John?"

This is John Percival, deputy chairman of the board. Unlike the others, he already knows about the proposals.

How do I write down the names? "Percival" or "John" or "JP"? How do I record what they say? Wish I could do shorthand like Mum—must concentrate—hard to catch what some of them are saying. . . .

Self-assured, patrician, John Percival compliments the chairman on his foresight, energy, ability to raise enormous sums of money apparently without effort. . . . He wonders about the impact of the new building on the existing museum, which is already almost more than they can manage. . . . Running costs are a problem. . . . In the past year or two they've had to lose so many curators, close the Research Department. . . . Shouldn't they commission a feasibility study before making further commitments?

". . . *JP expressed his general approval of the scheme and admiration for energy and enterp. of Ch.*" That should do it. . . . "*approved of the idea in princ. but we have to look at overall implics.*"

The chairman draws these comments firmly into his grasp. These are important considerations, he agrees, but housekeeping mustn't halt exciting initiatives. . . . Museums must adapt to a new audience and new technology. . . . Nowness should offer a reflection of modern Britain's financial and business achievement . . . infinitely extended access, making heritage part of now. . . .

How much of this do I have to put down? Some of it's just hot air. . . . I can give him a draft and a sexy smile, that should do the trick.

Doris Hobson, to John Percival's right, is enthusiastic, her blue-rinsed curls darting, bowing, and jerking as she speaks. "A wonderful idea . . . we must show the best of contemporary design and prove how dull and old-fashioned other museums are. Much of our museum is out-of-date and could be closed without loss, and look at the opportunities for corporate lettings this new building will give us, and it will create close links with exciting aspects of the modern world—and the staff here don't have enough to do" (this is said with a jerk of the head toward the director). *I certainly won't minute that. How dare she, the old harridan? The sooner she dies the better, but let's get some more cash out of her first.* She'll see if her trust can find some money—she has an idea there might be some funds uncommitted over the next three years, would that be helpful? *DH said a further contrib. might be available. . . . Isn't that the right sort of note? The polish comes later, thank goodness some of these people are so verbose you don't have to write down everything . . . and OH NO, now they're all talking about minuting, will I have to say something? . . . PANIC . . .*

"May we minute that?" says the chairman, with a conniving laugh.

"Certainly," says Mrs. Hobson, "but please keep the amount open. A substantial sum, you might say at least three million pounds. . . . Do you understand that, young woman?"

That must be me—the old cow. . . .

Appreciative gasps erupt around the table and the chairman beams expansively. Even Auberon beams, in Pavlovian reflex. "Yes, Emma, will you minute that with great care?" says the chairman jovially. "Maybe in capitals." Everybody laughs.

"A contrib. of at least three mill. would be made available from her trust. . . ." Big deal—it's easy to be generous if you're rich . . . and it allows you to be courted all the time and be horrible to people who work for you. . . . Auberon hates her, quite right. . . .

The master head bobs almost uncontrollably at this announcement and if possible harder yet when Amanda Mann (who actually has to dash, in a few moments, to a frightfully crucial meeting at Channel Four, so sorry, but simply must say something before going) intervenes: "What I find terribly exciting," Emma thinks she's saying, "is the opportunity to mix media. There's no need to stick to the conventional museum. Here's a chance to combine film, photography, video art, the most sophisticated contemporary communication with the stuff that goes on in an old-style museum. We can use Nowness to analyze and celebrate—yes, I mean it, celebrate," and her glowing contralto glows even more richly, "things from the home, things people can relate to from their everyday experience, bring them into the stuffy museum context—put a VCR beside a vestment, a Ryvita next to a Rembrandt! This is one of the most thrilling moments of my life. Well done, Chairman!" she concludes, the warm emphatic contralto that has energized so many executives at Channel Four meetings resounding like an organ.

What an idiot . . . hate her makeup, pretending to be so funky when she's not that young. . . . "AM said this was the most thrilling moment of her life" . . . *???* . . . *What kind of a life d'you have, darling?*

The temperature in the board room is rising, both physically (the room, lofty as it is, is absorbing the growing heat of the day) and mentally. The heads are leaning inward eagerly, eyes flashing to and fro as they assess others' reactions, mouths opening and closing as each seeks to make a dynamic contribution.

As Amanda gathers her papers into her black and silver attaché case and prepares to leave, it's Sir Robert Pound's turn. He, too, is swept into the current: Auberon's projections, he realizes, were quite wrong. Bold scheme, says Sir Robert, will cost a lot of money, but we can't reject such an idea and the amount of money already raised is astonishing. . . . Can we afford to turn down such a possibility?

And Lady Doncaster likes the idea, too, so up-to-date, and can it involve the young?, so important to get them interested in museums and the countryside and traditional things; sometimes they seem to have no knowledge of their roots, it's so sad when our heritage is so rich *(What's she on about? Doesn't she realize this thing is about Nowness not stately homes? She's really not so bright, though Auberon seems to think so, ho hum)* as well as our future. . . . "I wish," Lady D. goes on, "I wish I could contribute seriously financially as so many of you have promised to do"—*Typical of the aristocracy, they all say they've no money however rich they may be, just mean, that's what they are*—"but perhaps I can do something about organizing a ball or a fund-raising dinner. . . ." *"Lady D. offered to organize a ball or a FR dinner"* . . . *Please not, please not, balls are the pits, I'll end up doing most of it and there's so much work and so little profit at the end of it. . . .*

There's vigorous assent at the end of the table. "Yes,

young people are crucially important," says the chairman. "They have a vital role in all of this," and the heads nod again like porcelain Chinamen's. *Clearly there's full agreement about this fascinating insight of Lady D.'s—though actually no one's likely to say young people are irrelevant.*

Reynolds Brinkman, captain of finance, a man with such a reputation for fierceness that those who meet him are captivated to find him relatively polite, welcomes the proposal, too. Links with industry and the City could be immensely fulfilling. . . . He could get six men around a table for lunch to discuss this scheme and by coffee time the museum would be richer by six million pounds . . . ongoing support, too, almost guaranteed. . . .

Brinkman UK should be able to make a contribution, and is there any chance of one of the rooms being named for us? Not on the same scale as some of the figures mentioned, but would something around five hundred grand be any use? Are you accepting small donations, ha-ha? . . . Nowness will create a shop window for the UK, sorry, I mean Britain or do I mean England? . . . It's a pity we can't rebrand again—a Museum of Europe would be fabulous, branches all over Europe, Brussels, Berlin, Paris . . . HQ, of course, here in London . . . business opportunities, trade openings would be incredible, with this place as the center of an international empire. . . . We should really be pushing the envelope on this one. . . . *Even more money—this is extraordinary. Do I have to minute that stuff about Britain not really being relevant? Actually RB is quite sexy, though Viv in his office says he can be really foul . . . What is this, am I fixated on older men? Auberon's looking tense, obviously not enjoying this orgy of generosity. Will any of them say no?*

Trevor Christiansen, Auberon's old friend Trevor, even

Trevor is carried away. *This is vibrant, exciting talk,* he thinks, *just what is needed.* . . . He asks about contemporary artists and whether they will be represented in Nowness. It will be a showcase for the best of contemporary British art, he hopes. *(Why do they all talk about "will" instead of "would"?)* Of course, he's assured, contemporary artists will be well represented, there are wonderful opportunities here for patronage, lots of exciting site-specific commissions are envisaged illustrating British art at its best but reflecting contemporary British life and culture and particularly the lives of ordinary people. . . . Trevor purrs.

"Alan?" says the chairman cautiously. "What do you feel?" He can't rely on Professor Stewart. He is a large man, both physically and intellectually impressive, and when he speaks he has a way—which can be annoying to those who don't agree with him—of filling the space. In the ensuing pause the heads calm themselves, no longer glancing to left and right but concentrating on the professor's polished and pleasant dome, the curly brown hair that clusters around it still vigorously youthful.

"I've listened to this discussion," he says, "with the greatest interest, and I congratulate the chairman on his bold proposals. But I do have a few reservations, if I may?"

"But of course," says the chairman.

Unlike anyone else in the room, Professor Stewart allows himself a moment's consideration before he speaks. His voice is mellifluous and measured, authoritative but humane. He is not, the others instinctively feel, a man who is easily intimidated. "This is what I'm worried about," he says. "Practical problems about this new extension have already been voiced, notably how we pay for the running costs of this new building once it's up. As we all know, the government in its wisdom reduces its grant-in-aid every year, whatever we do. Like John, I'd remind fellow trustees that recently this has led to serious cuts in staffing and conservation and care of the collection—which we tend to forget on a day like this, when everything's so positive and cheerful."

The heads are now looking not at him but at the table or the ceiling or even out of the window. Only Auberon revives like a flower plunged into water (though he tries to disguise this). The professor goes on: "I think this museum is doing wonderful things. But I don't subscribe to the view that curators are redundant or that scholarship has no place here. They represent what is really important, and they're at risk here now, as they have been for years. They are the people who understand what we possess, they hold the keys to all the objects we look after." Mrs. Hobson sneers at this, and Lady Doncaster looks politely surprised. "In my view it would be completely unacceptable to cut expenditure on the main museum to run this extension. We don't want all icing and no cake, do we?" *How does that go in? "AS stated that the museum should not be all icing and no cake. . . ." God, it's hot in here, I wish they'd stop.*

"Many thanks, Alan, these are crucial issues," says the chairman equably, "and ones I've given a lot of thought to, as we all have. I see Nowness as self-supporting, with an admission charge. Contributions to the endowment fund are built into all donations. . . . There are major possibilities for fund-raising events. . . . Hopefully it will make a profit, which will support the loss-making main museum. . . ."

Stewart listens impassively. "Well, I don't want to be a bore," he says, "or to go against the general mood, but I think I must put my point of view. When I sit around this table and other similar tables, and listen to talk about cultural institutions, and how they need to be renewed and the importance of visitor figures and marketing policies and accessibility and new buildings, I sometimes wonder if we're forgetting their ultimate purpose."

"I don't think that's true, Alan—through you, Chairman," says Reynolds Brinkman. "We know very well what museums are about."

"What *are* they about, then?" asks the professor, turning inquiringly toward his colleague.

Brinkman looks firm for a moment, and then uncertain. "As far as I'm concerned the point of a museum is . . . is . . . to be a welcoming, well-run, efficient center of activity where the public feel at home and can have a really good day out. . . ."

The tension's rising, no doubt about it. How about "There was some general discussion over the role of museums"?

Professor Stewart surveys his colleague with narrowed eyes. "Well, yes. With respect, your definition of a museum's more appropriate for a shopping mall. Men like Tradescant or Denon or Eastlake or Bode, the men who created the great museums, would have been astonished. I know the world's changed, but I still see no fundamental reason to abandon their ideals. What I've heard so far about the Nowness of Now doesn't convince me it would add anything substantial to what the outstanding museum in our care already offers. I don't want to be aggressive, but is this idea truly what we're about? Can't other organizations do it better?"

Brinkman does not relish these remarks. "There's no point in being rude. . . ." he begins, but Stewart overrides him. "I'm sorry to be a bore, Chairman, but give me one more minute. The original purpose of a museum is to collect, preserve, display, and interpret objects. Those are still the essential purposes—the other activities that have emerged recently are just subsidiary. Scholarship is what's crucial in a museum, knowledge, conserving and understanding the past and studying the present—not just presenting it in a jazzed-up form without comment. I'm sorry to be so dogmatic, but we do tend to forget these objectives. The only thing that makes museums special is their collections. If we forget it, our museums will turn into theme parks, probably not very good ones. They're the guardians of our past. We need our past, and if we're going to understand the past we need to work at it." He laughs. "I'm sorry," he says, "I'm used to lecturing to large groups of dozing undergraduates. But I hope you see what I mean."

Oh-oh-oh, how do I minute this?

The sun beats more hotly than ever through the boardroom windows. The heads waver uncertainly, unsure whether they should respond to this speech (which most of them have found hectoring) or seek guidance from the leading head. One gray pate, overcome by the hot afternoon, nods at its chest before jerking unhappily upward. The leading head seems briefly nonplussed. But it has met more aggressive opposition in boardrooms, and at rallies.

"We all agree with you," it asserts. "Of course, our core purpose here is looking after our collections. But we can't sit about and hope for the best. The days of dusty old museums filled with arrowheads are past. We must animate our museums—they must contribute to today's debates." Most of the heads nod and emit a consenting hum. "As I see it, the Nowness of Now will be full of contemporary objects—not just works of art but advertisements, cosmetics, cars, cleaning equipment, bicycles, commercial products, film, photography. It's just that they won't be historic objects, they'll be about today, for today. Must a museum only be about the past? Don't we all spend too much time looking backward?"

Professor Stewart stares into the distance. "You've put your point of view, Chairman, and I've put mine," he says. "On a practical level, I do think we need to know more about how the Nowness of Now is going to work. It's one thing to build an extension, another to keep it going. I'd like to know, too, what the staff feel. They'll have to do the work, after all."

No problems about that bit. . . .

The chairman looks briefly uneasy. "Of course it's important that the staff should be involved. They're completely behind these proposals."

"Perhaps I could say a word," says Auberon tentatively. The chairman turns toward Auberon, who avoids his eye, but instead fixes on Sir Lewis's large, white, sharp teeth.

"I should make one point clear. It would not be accurate to say the staff are happy." He pauses in an unconsciously dramatic way, and blushes. The faces show faint surprise. This is not the cool Auberon they're used to. "They're not happy with this idea because most of them don't know anything about it. It's never been explained to them and they've played no part in developing it. This should be understood by members of this board."

Quite so, but this is bold and even bald. I'll have to get Auberon to write this bit out.

The chairman assumes a new look, this time of patience, as if he is dealing with an able but somewhat unruly child.

"I might have consulted further," he says, "but I wanted to clear the idea at the highest level before taking it to the workers, as it were. I really couldn't clear the proposal with the staff before speaking to the board. What I'm looking for now is the board's approval for a feasibility study. All costs will be met from the promised donation, that's been sanctioned. Leaving aside what the director thinks just for the moment, do I have the board's approval in principle?"

Clever. Puts Auberon in his place, makes him look like a fusspot. And once they've committed themselves to spending money, nobody's going to want to waste that money, even though it's only a fraction of what'll be spent in the end.

The heads look around and nod at one another and at the chairman. All except Professor Stewart.

"How do we express reservations?" he asks. "Are we voting formally?"

"I prefer to avoid votes," says the chairman, "but if you want one . . . I suppose I hoped approval would be unanimous," he ruminates, as though suggesting disloyalty. "Those in favor?"

Six hands are raised.

"Those against?"

Up goes Stewart's hand.

"And I'm an abstainer, for what it's worth—but I'd like my abstention recorded," says Percival.

"We're all abstainers until we know more," replies the chairman smoothly. "Thank you all for a most interesting discussion, and thank you all for your support, in all sorts of ways. At the next meeting we'll report further—won't we, Director?"

The meeting is at an end.

"The meeting concluded at 3:48 P.M. All present congrat. the chairman on the proposal he had put forward. Working group set up . . ." Oh, Auberon, poor Auberon . . . he looks so upset . . . none of that sparkle. . . .

The Exhibitions Office is empty, its usual inhabitants whirring around the exhibition. Two ceiling fans hum above the unoccupied desks, setting the piles of paper rustling. In the swelling heat, more indolently powerful by the minute, the potted plants droop as though wanting refuge in their roots. The windows are scarcely ever opened here because of the traffic noise, but when the blinds are left open, as they have been today, the afternoon sun assaults the room.

Into the stuffy emptiness steps a figure in a soft cream cotton dress. She moves to the windows, opens a little casement, and pulls down the blinds. The room is calmed at once as Hermia, cool amid the heat, walks to her desk and sits down. She shifts one or two papers that lie in front of her but hardly pretends to work. It's too hot today. She looks reflectively into the distance. No expression appears on her face.

This lassitude is not unusual in Hermia, when she's alone. She blooms in the company of other people, changes according to their characters, reflects unconsciously what they want her to reflect. It's very easy to fall in love with her, not only because of her looks but because she can so readily be transformed by lovers into the person they're looking for. When her office reaches its high points of frenzy (several times a day, on the whole) she becomes as animated as the rest of them, but alone she finds it pleasanter to remain quiet—and contemplative, no doubt, though no one knows what she contemplates.

Her thoughts are interrupted by a red-faced, impatient

noise. It is Lucian, desperate for a telephone call. For Lucian telephone calls are like the call of nature for other men. He tears across the room to his office, but as he passes her desk he notices her, stops, and gasps. "Oh, Hermia," he says, and blushes.

She smiles, just a little, and raises her eyebrows. "Can I do anything to help?" she asks. "I have some work for Diana. But Diana is not here."

"Oh, yes, I have something that needs to be done urgently," he says. "If you could . . . if you could . . . if you could help me with my speech for this evening."

The telephone stops ringing and he jumps nervously. The door opens again, admitting Diana. She walks into the room slowly, looking at the two of them, and advances toward Hermia's desk. She stops. There is a silence. This is broken by the telephone ringing again. Lucian jerks as though to answer it but, pulled by some force he cannot analyze and which surprises him by its strength, he stays where he is. The two standing figures both gaze at the young seated woman. She looks questioningly from one to the other but does not speak.

"Hermia," says Diana, "you were going to help me with those faulty labels—but perhaps you have other things to do for Lucian. . . ."

"No, no," says Lucian politely, and then, "or, rather, yes, I have got things that need doing. Can you help me?"

"Of course," says Hermia. "You are the head of the department, so if you need me you must take the precedence."

"Take the precedence?" Lucian repeats the words as though this foreign-sounding phrase conveyed no meaning to him.

"In matters of work, you must take the precedence," she says.

"What does this remark mean?" Diana and Lucian ask themselves. "What is she thinking? Is this peculiar triangle apparent only to two of the people involved? She seems so innocent, so unaware. . . ."

Diana cannot endure this situation. She is sure Hermia means more to her than she does to Lucian—oh, to hell with what Lucian is feeling, anyway. Recklessly, she asks a question that has to be answered, one way or another.

"Lucian is clearly senior in every respect," she says, "but if you had the choice, which of us would you sooner help?"

Hermia looks perplexed, but not Lucian, staring as he is at her lips, her firm, curving lips.

"What do you mean? How can I answer that?" she asks, and laughs. "Working here is not a matter for gratifying one-self."

They still regard her silently. *Is she right?* Lucian wonders. *Can working in a museum—or anywhere—ever truly offer plea-sure or self-fulfillment? Has he been deceiving himself all these years?*

"But it is true," she continues, "that Diana did ask me to help her with the labels some time ago, and that does seem to be quite urgent. So unless Lucian has something very important, perhaps he will forgive me. . . ."

How charmingly, they both think, *how modestly, with what thoughtful deference, she makes this inquiry.* How can Lucian insist on anything in such company? They look at one another instinctively, as though sympathizing with the other's admiration for this perfect girl.

"No," he says, "nothing so essential, or that it . . . that . . ."

What he intends to say is never known. The telephone

rings and this time Lucian answers it in his own office. After a moment he closes the door.

Diana continues to stare at her young colleague. *What does her answer mean? Can it be a statement of love? Can I hope?* "I . . . I . . ." she says, and chokes.

Hermia smiles. *Warmly,* Diana thinks. "So, shall I help you with the labels?" she asks. *Oh, yes, you certainly can, sweetness. Oh, how vulnerable I feel—I, Diana, sophisticated, good-looking, fashionable, clever, politically committed—I could be a teenage girl, I feel so unsure of myself. . . .*

GALLERY OF MODERN TECHNOLOGY, 4 P.M. ONWARD

Bill and Anna are on duty in the Gallery of Modern Technology. It is situated at the top of the main staircase, overlooking the stairwell. The wall opposite the stairs is interrupted by two large official-looking doors, one leading to the boardroom and the other to the director's suite. It is a thoroughfare for the public and staff, who hardly notice the highly improved displays (sponsored by an IT firm which, by coincidence, has been invited to provide at least half the exhibits).

For the warders, excluded from the museum's official business and kept rigidly in their place, this is a favorite duty point. It lets one glimpse goings-on at the top, if only by guesswork. Who's in favor, who's out, who's rising or waning can be assessed from the way people walk, their expressions, the weight of the files they carry. Some passersby forget they're being overheard, and speak much too freely—forgetting that their words will be scrutinized by the junior attendants' staff room minutes later.

The room is little visited today by the public. A few people enter, gaze without enthusiasm at the instructive diagrams and flashing screens, and inquire where the toilets are. On this bright afternoon the museum looks dispirited, its exhibits tired and uninviting. Even the traffic on the Trafalgar Road and the tinkle of the ice-cream van are more appealing than anything indoors.

Internal staff activity, on the other hand, offers lots of distractions today, enough to interest even Bill and Anna, who are now on duty there and who, after all, have many other things to think about. They had a successful lunch, they both think, their first ever. She talked to him about her art—another first—and explained why she works on making models of human torsos out of newspaper and mud sprayed with paint even though she actually prefers painting recognizable landscapes. He reacted more intelligently than she expected—indeed, he appeared to know quite a lot about contemporary art. She realized that she'd expected him to be ignorant on the subject, she'd seen him as a museum attendant with very limited interests, while she was an artist who made a living working in a museum. Class prejudice, in fact. She shuddered at herself. Now they approach the afternoon expectantly, unsure where it will lead them but confident they'll like it. The heat makes them languidly amorous.

But they're not left long to enjoy this mood. Almost as soon as they are on duty, the door of the boardroom opens and out come the board members. At the sight of these remote, august figures, powerful, mysterious in their actions and faintly absurd, Bill stands unconsciously at attention, the unruly curl at the back of his head standing up in sym-

pathy. Anna adopts a pose intended to express simultaneously politeness, efficiency, artistic integrity, and the rebel-
liousness aroused in her by authority. In any case, none of
the trustees notices them. The little group at the front talk
excitedly in a hum of approval: "Marvelous," they say, and "It
must be Lewis who's giving the money, mustn't it?" and
"Shhh," and "We must move the place forward, no good just
sitting on what we have." They make for the stairs. They are
followed by two men who look less filled with enthusiasm.
One is Mr. Percival, Bill and Anna recognize: he looks up as
he passes them and nods. "I'm very concerned," the other
one is saying, and "Will it bring the whole place down? The
figures look so very bad, and the department's being so
impossible. . . ."

After a while the door to the director's office opens, and
the director and chairman emerge. They seem tense and
glare at one another, as they stop in what they think is a solitary space. Instinctively, Bill and Anna have hidden behind a
showcase.

"There's no evidence for what you say," says the chairman, "or, at any rate, your account's greatly exaggerated.
The picture wasn't in perfect shape when it was put on the
market, but fundamentally it was in fine condition. Without
any doubt, it's a key Gainsborough. I have certificates, three
in fact, from important scholars, to prove it. I think you're
trying to embarrass me."

"I'm not trying to embarrass you," replies the director.
"I'm just warning you that doubts have been expressed
about its condition and questions may be asked."

"In which case," Sir Lewis goes on, in a hectoring tone, "I
expect you to defend the picture absolutely. Any doubts cast
on it publicly would be calamitous—not for me, I'm just its

owner, but for the museum. You'd look the biggest fool, Auberon. It was you who sanctioned the publicity material."

"Under pressure from you."

"You had the chance to say no, you said nothing. I'm not responsible for your lack of courage, am I? Remember what I say. And don't forget, any negative publicity will look bad for all of us. It certainly won't help you. D'you have a date for your interview at the Bloomsbury Museum, by the way?'

"Yes," says Auberon fretfully. "A week today."

"The Bloomsbury board will be here in force tonight, won't they? Better make sure your collar's clean." He sounds sneeringly dismissive.

You can see, Bill and Anna think, *why people are said not to like him.*

And on they walk.

Bill and Anna emerge a little flushed from their hiding place as Auberon returns to his office. As he approaches his door, a voice calls him. It is that airy-fairy expensively dressed trustee, Lady Doncaster, who keeps featuring in photo magazines you see in the dentist's waiting room. She hurries along the gallery toward him, eagerly expectant. "Auberon!" she calls. "Auberon!" His frowning face lightens. He turns and strides toward her and they meet in the very center of the room, between Bill and Anna who are standing by the walls. As the director and the lady meet, they clasp hands and gaze into each other's eyes. Then they realize they're being watched. For a loaded moment, the emotions linking the two couples crackle in the stuffy room among the unconsulted computers. Auberon and Olivia, bound up in one another, become aware for the first time of the two motionless figures to either side of them. Then Auberon says, "Shall we speak in my office?" They disappear through the great mysterious door (through which neither Bill nor Anna has ever gone), as though these other lovers did not exist.

Bill and Anna gape at one another. There's so much to talk about, but they can hardly say anything when they're supposed to be patrolling the gallery (and then they'll be under observation from the security cameras). How strange it is, Anna reflects, to stand so close to someone you think you're falling in love with, yet not speak to him. And he thinks, *If I'm going to be worthy of her* (in fact he first thinks, *If I'm to be a worthy husband,* and dismisses this term as absurdly optimistic), *if I am going to be a worthy partner, I'll have to give up this futile job where all I do is stand and stare, and never get anywhere. . . .*

They're not alone for long. An anxiously eager lady from Education who is organizing a session called Finding Yourself in Yesterday appears with her class, which consists of one small and faintly tearful child. He is her sole pupil and she is not letting go of him. More bustle at the end of the room, and a string of people comes in: *Mr. Bankes from Exhibitions, and that bossy Diana, the man from Early Modern, isn't it?, the sweetly smiling lady from Education who likes everything done exactly as she wants it and nearly always gets it, and a couple of curators we hardly know, and Mary Anne from Press, oh, and Miss Vaughan from Art . . .* They march toward the director's office, preoccupied and determined. As they reach the door, it opens and Lady Doncaster emerges, slightly flurried and hot-looking. She smiles at them distractedly and hurries down the corridor, tweaking at her skirt.

"Isn't she called Lady Bonkaster?" Anna offers, and they giggle.

Silence resumes. Only for a moment. A group of neatly

suited ladies wanders through, bright-eyed, drinking in the knowledge imparted by their voluntary guide—though Bill, who's read the labels several times, knows that almost everything she says is inaccurate. Then the torpor resumes, and in the afternoon quietness, broken only by the noise of traffic, they are too hot and sleepy to talk to one another. They do not have to wait long for the next development. The director's door opens again and this time the staff tumble out, chattering like little birds.

"You can't think it's a good idea, Lucian," says Jane, in resonant tones. "You simply can't. It's so crude. The Nowness of Now—it's embarrassing!"

Lucian looks away from her. "Not to me, it isn't," he says. "It's contemporary, it's exciting—we have to embrace the here and now."

"Oh, come on, Lucian," she urges. "You can't believe in this stuff. Where's the Lucian I know, the man who made the museum's exhibitions the best in Britain?"

"We could have a series of themed events," suggests a woman, Bill and Anna think she's the Head of Press, "like a Dutch picture exhibition, *The Downess of Dou.*"

They seem to be amused by this.

"Or an agricultural exhibition, *The Cowness of Cow.*"

"Or one on etiquette, *The Bowness of Bow.*"

"Or a prisoners-of-war installation, *The Powness of POW.*"

"And how about a pussycat happening—*The Meowness of Meow?*"

Lucian alone does not smile. Following his sternly forward-looking figure, they giggle their way down the corridor and disappear from view, meeting on the way John Winterbotham. He glares at Anna and Bill as he passes toward the director's door. They return his look in what they hope is a keen but deferential way, and peer around the gallery as though it might contain something for them to be watching out for. They hope the next passerby will offer them yet more entertainment. And as Mr. Winterbotham disappears through the director's door, Bill mouths something to Anna, who laughs, and they clasp hands, and together they do a silent waltz along the sunny parquet.

GALLERY OF INDUSTRIAL REVOLUTION
AND GREAT HALL, 4 P.M.

The Gallery of the Industrial Revolution is one of the "unimproved" galleries, as Auberon puts it. Laid out in the late 1940s, it contains a replica of the original spinning jenny, paintings of Manchester in the early nineteenth century, cases of complex machinery, and in the center a steam engine. But displays about Britain's past industrial prowess are no longer acceptable to most senior curators, who think it hopelessly old-fashioned to present any picture of Britain's success as an industrial nation or its technological advances, and consider that the portrayal of social otherness in early industrial Britain is of much greater importance. Unfortunately, reinstalling the gallery, and removing the huge pieces of machinery that crowd it, is financially impossible. To save the public from inappropriate messages, which might be interpreted as nationalistic self-congratulation, the room is frequently closed, particularly since it is now used to prepare events next door in the Great Hall. On such occasions, and particularly when the dinner is large and magnificent, the room is closed for days and many of the exhibits are wrapped in thick plastic, filling the room with white-sheeted, indecipherable forms. These have excited a number of conceptual artists interested in the decline of industrialism, and have, indeed, sometimes been mistaken for works of art in themselves.

This daunting space has been invaded by a group of formidably efficient people led by Fred, Angel's Head of Operations. They carry an arsenal of heavy metal objects, curiously appropriate to the room in their way. "Urns over there, under the picture with the smoke," says Fred, "and the ovens next to them, yes, it's four ovens today, which means we can't do the usual, just put them below the case with all those shiny things in it, would you? No, Nick, you idiot, not so close—hold on, it's my mobile—oh, hello, darling, hold on a moment, would you, I'll ring you back—yes, immediately—yes, Mr. Rupert, everything's cool—hot cupboards under that model thing, the factory or whatever it is—yes, close to the power points, obviously—do we have the spare generator ready?—hello, Jim, have you checked the power again? No, there should be no problem in a big place like this—what? They haven't rewired this side of the room?—I think it'll be all right—cool, then, cool—two more electric rings, yes, there should be room for them under the steam engine." The metal objects are disposed around the room and the delivery team goes. Fred's mobile rings again. "Hello, oh, Sam, yes, hello," he says, "not a great moment, actually—look, darling, we're just setting up, absolutely crucial time, just got into the venue—I know we said we could go out properly on Saturday, but I have to do this event, I just have to, I'd be letting Mr. Rupert down—he has to be away—no, it's not always me who ends up doing all the work,

Mr. Rupert works all the time, he's amazing, it's just—No, it's not silly calling him Mr. Rupert, it's just what we call him—No, I am not a toady—Yes, I know your sister's going to be in London, I know, dearest, but look, petal, maybe I can join you after the dinner, it should be over by eleven, we could go out clubbing or something—Yes, I know I fell asleep in the club last time, but I'll take it easy before we go, I mean the night before—OK, if I have to work I'll get up late—look, Sam, I love you, yes, I do, but I have a job—oh, fuck fuck fuck . . ." and as he utters these words the team comes back saying, "Where were you, then, Fred, we missed you?" and Fred says, "Canapé table in Regency, yes, Regency, that one through there, yes, two tables, and the dessert table in that room over there, Early Georgian, yes, we can use as much space as we like, it's the Chairman's do, two dessert tables, yes, and the lobster unit," at which they all giggle, "the lobster unit, keep it clean, Nick, on its own in Late Georgian . . . Main preparation table here in Industrial—no, Jim, this is Industrial, that's Early Georgian, look, it's got a steam engine, Industrial, get it? Can we have the tablecloths ready?—" and as the rooms take on their new guise as a temporary kitchen his mobile rings again and he answers it desperately, "Samantha, hello, darling, great to hear you, yes, we're still very busy," with a clenched smile. "No, our relationship is not on the rocks, but I really can't talk about our relationship now, I've got a huge reception starting in two hours—No, receptions don't matter more to me than relationships—Of course I love you, look, we're going to the Cayman Islands, aren't we, next month? Well, of course that's got everything to do with our relationship, we'll laze about and love each other and—No, I will not stuff my face with food all the time," and then he loses his temper and shouts down the phone, "Oh, get stuffed yourself, it's better than being a fucking anorexic," and turns shaking but still competent to his team, who have returned with more metal objects and are looking at him quizzically, and says, "I'm a bit worried about the electricity, we don't usually have this amount of machinery, it's having so much on the go, can we get Harry to come and do a check for us?" And as Harry is summoned Fred nods to the team and says, "OK, we'll set up the reception next, please, all the stuff into Early Georgian for the moment ready to move into the entrance hall at five o'clock. After that, tables for Great Hall, please." And they disappear. The mobile phone rings and he switches it off, then switches it on thinking this may be work rather than wife, changes his mind and turns it off.

"Check the Great Hall," he says to himself, and moves into it. What he sees does not delight him. Instead of the empty space he'd expected, ready for forty round tables and four hundred chairs, he finds the hall filled with tiny children. Some are dancing in a ring around a peculiar pole in the corner covered with ribbons and flowers while dozens more are lying on the floor cutting colored paper into small pieces.

"What the hell . . . ?" he asks himself, and of one of the children, "Is anyone in charge here?" She points out a tall lady with a seraphic expression and a bleached linen smock, who is smiling gently and making cooing noises to the children around her as she moves around the room. "Can you tell me . . . ?" he begins to ask her.

"My name is Melissa," she says. "I'm the Head of Education and Community Outreach. Can I help you?"

And when he tells her that he has to set up for a large dinner that evening, she says, with untroubled calmness, "I know about the dinner, to which I am coming, and I'm sure if you have everything organized it will all be fine. In the meantime my team of young helpers are working together on the pageant. That's the maypole over there."

"Is that thing staying there all evening?" groans Fred. "Nobody said anything to me about it. It's just where we need to put two of our serving tables."

"Yes, it's staying, it's the maypole for the prepageant dancing," she replies calmly. *(Does she ever stop being calm?"* Fred wonders. *It's extremely irritating.)*

"You see," says Fred, "the maypole is right between several of the tables and I'm afraid the dancing tots will collide with the guests, which may not be very popular particularly if the tots get trampled on. . . ."

"Oh . . ." she says, less serenely, and blushes and Fred sees she isn't as bad as he'd thought and gives her one of his twinkles, which makes her blush.

"We do have to set up, you know," he says. "Any chance . . ."

"Yes, really it's time they went home anyway and the coaches will be waiting—but we do have a pageant rehearsal on the stage later. Will that get in the way?"

And in a few moments, as though in the dramatic finale of a grand opera, the paper-cutting children are removed, the doors are thrown open, and forty round tabletops are rolled through, followed by trolleys bearing hundreds of little gold chairs, six-foot-tall flower arrangements in rococo vases appear through a distant door, the Head of Security bustles in with his clipboard and informs Fred he shouldn't have started work without authorization, and is told in return that he's failed to give Fred any warning about the maypole, so they reach a not very cordial truce which includes the maypole being moved into a corner. A sound engineer repeatedly intones, "One two three four, one two three four," from the stage, the lighting engineers experiment with an extended range of effects. Through all this activity, order is maintained, narrowly. Only the children rehearsing on the stage, endlessly singing a ditty to the effect that "Elizabeth's our Queen, Elizabeth's our Queen, Yours is One, Ours is Two, Elizabeth's our Queen," makes Fred grind his teeth, as does the certainty that his mobile, switched off though it is, is trying to get him. . . . At least, he reflects, this event is more of a strain for Gustavus than it is for him. *How is Gustavus?* he wonders. He hasn't seen him for a while. But when he goes back to Industrial Revolution he finds Gustavus, subdued but in control, conferring with his team of twelve chefs.

"Oh, Fred," he says thankfully. "Fred, collecting the lobsters is Operations, isn't it? What time are they being delivered?"

"Six on the dot," says Fred, "by the staff entrance. I'm taking charge of them personally. I'll deliver them to Industrial Revolution, shall I?"

"Yup. I'm not sure exactly where we're setting up—at least the beef is done, sort of, apart from the garnish. I'm still not quite happy with it. . . . The lobster, that's what makes me anxious. . . . I just hope the spinach is ready in time for all this layering we're doing."

Fred smiles at him reassuringly. "Of course it will be OK," he says, in a warm, encouraging way. "Angel's dinners are always OK, and a lot more than OK."

"There's always a first time. . . ." replies Gustavus lugubriously, and his chef's conference continues.

Bill and Anna have not been bored at all this afternoon. Although there have been few visitors to look at or talk to, the movement into and out of the director's office has been most interesting. After his staff had left, the director emerged from his office with John Winterbotham, both carrying clipboards. They were discussing the details of the royal arrival this evening, particularly the security arrangements. "Can we do this walk-through pretty quickly?" said the director. "I have to get home and change."

"No problem," said Winterbotham.

Once again Bill and Anna looked brisk and assumed efficiently self-deprecatory smiles as the pair passed.

A moment or two later, a new group arrived up the stairs. It was the Chairman of the Trustees, and that rude Lucian man again, and a large Japanese man, and that tall nasty girl, Helen, who everyone knows is having it off with Sir Lewis. Helen was carrying a bottle, for some reason, looked like champagne. As they passed, Sir Lewis talked about an export license—"all sorted out, Lucian, no worries there, the minister was completely understanding, special exemption against Waverley, the chairman of the Export License Reviewing Committee raised a bit of trouble but a few cases of Château Something, his favorite, dealt with that one. . . . He said if we could prove the picture had been shown abroad in the recent past . . ." They disappeared into the office. A few moments later Emma, the director's personal assistant, came out, looking seriously annoyed. She carried her briefcase as though going home but did not seem happy about it. "Bloody rude," she said to herself, as she hurried past them, not even saying good night as she normally would.

Anna and Bill thought it unwise to talk to each other, as they would normally do. Not only were there the cameras, but the door might open again and the chairman emerge. Though Sir Lewis never bothers to acknowledge the staff's existence, he's very observant when any detail is not exactly right. They merely moved a little closer to the great door, just to keep an eye on things, as it were. But of course they could hear nothing, since behind that door was the secretaries' office, and then the personal assistant's office, and only after that the director's office where the meeting—whatever it might be—must have been taking place.

A little while later the door opened and the group came out again. They were laughing, and seemed triumphant. Bill and Anna had anticipated this moment, and were almost concealed once again, this time behind particularly large interactive displays. "I am so pleased," said the big Japanese man. "It is a wonderful arrangement. You get what you need—I get what I need: a lot of Gainsborough! It's a good exchange, I think!" Then they all shook hands. "Keep that document safe, Mr. Bankes—it's valuable!" They all laughed heartily.

Somebody must have looked inquiringly at Lucian, since a moment or two later he said, "In the control room, with Winterbotham, it'll be as safe as a document could be anywhere." Then they all went.

When they have all gone, Bill and Anna emerge from their retreat and look at each other. What on earth does this mean? Should they tell anyone? "It's not our job to interfere," she says, "we're only the slaves around here."

"Something very odd is happening, that's clear," says he.

"Yes, but what can we do about it?" she wants to know.

"We can tell someone who'll know whether to take it up," he insists.

"But it's not our job," she repeats, "and all we've done is overhear a conversation we weren't meant to overhear, just because we're under-persons and they don't think we're worth bothering about."

"I don't care about that," he says, "I know something's wrong, and they ought to know."

"They?" she asks. "What sort of they?" She is impressed by his determination.

"Here's Ian, we'll tell him," he says, with relief, as the deputy head of Security comes around the corner.

"How are you two doing?" he asks genially. "Had a nice afternoon?"

"We've had a very interesting afternoon," says Bill, "and we think we ought to tell you about it."

CONTROL ROOM, 5 P.M.

John Winterbotham sits in his control room and growls at the screens. The day's been chaotic and makes him wish he only had to supervise the daily routine without these special events. *Staff all over the place all day, two of them behaving in the oddest way, staring at one another all the time like maniacs and even dancing in the galleries at one point, senior staff shouting at each other, director in a rage, and then three of them turning off the lights and trying to examine that painting . . . and when I take them off to the director nothing happens. After all, the instructions from the chairman were very strict and that Mr. Smiles keeps going on about it, too, and Sir Lewis has shown how strong his feelings are financially (very useful it's been, too) as well as threatening major trouble if anything goes wrong—funny, actually, you wouldn't think a bit of old canvas was worth so much worry. . . . Very friendly Sir Lewis was, when he left a short time ago, but it seemed best not to mention the incident in the exhibition gallery this morning since the man has a temper. . . . And this evening there'll be hundreds of strangers in the building and the catering staff are full of actors and dancers and unreliable people of one sort or another and there's the delivery of lobsters, which I don't like at all. . . . It's my job to keep the place in order and what does anyone do to help? All they do is make trouble and resent me when I try to sort it out.*

There's Diana leaving from the staff entrance, funny one that but at least she's organized . . . and that young girl from Art, well, I could tell a story or two about her and someone who shouldn't be mentioned—why on earth they had to do it in History of Women's Freedom after a private view . . . Don't they know I can see everything that goes on in the galleries, even in the dark? . . . Girls going home no doubt to put on their frocks . . . Odd, those two don't seem to be speaking to each other . . . Lucian going off as well, he seems to be OK, at least Sir Lewis thinks he's a good thing—though I've hardly had the courtesy of a good morning from him in seven years until this evening when he arrives in my office with an envelope, says it's high security, would I put it in the museum safe, wonder what that's about . . . attendants leaving for the evening, some of them back in an hour, have to allow the buggers out for a bit—pity I don't get a break myself, not that I'd want it really. . . .

He looks at the entrance-hall screen. Final visitors are out promptly, as usual. He loves the organized way the museum empties every evening: first warning 1645 hours, second

1655, final one at 1659, but by then the building's always clear. Hardly any public in today, weather too sunny and hot, it's been stifling, and there's no big exhibition open, but they expect crowds and crowds when *Elegance* opens the day after tomorrow, he may have to take on temporary staff. At least the Lodge will help him find reliable types again.

The temporary exhibition galleries are empty, as per instructions. Only one attendant in there, standing beside *Lady St. John*. No one, but no one, to go in until six-fifteen.

As for the Great Hall, they've finished fussing around on the stage making all that din with the kids, damn nuisance in my view. The tables are laid. The flower arrangements, some huge, some small for the tables, have been delivered. God knows how much they must have cost but probably it's all necessary, like regimental dinners—at least in the army everything's done in the same way each year and you don't have to worry too much about temperamental women the way you do here. . . . I wonder what's going on in Industrial Revolution, I sometimes almost prefer not to know, but it seems to be in good order, that man Rupert has it all under control, good man at that, amazing the way they can start with a table with hundreds of empty plates on it and within an hour every plate is all set up with its fancy starter in place, twelve different items sometimes on each plate. . . . There seems to be a bit of agitation in there just now, but Mr. Rupert is dealing with it. . . . Ah, well, only eight more hours . . . and I have to be all over the museum during that time, making sure every detail is in order, no good just staying watching the screens, they don't tell you everything . . . at least I'll get some dinner, looking forward to that. . . .

He'll be on duty here for another hour or so, then let Ian take over for a while when the Royal Guest is due to arrive.

It's good to be able to keep an eye on things. . . .

In two hundred or so houses and offices, people are embarking on strenuous preparations for dinner at BRIT: in official residences, in mahogany and chrome offices in the City, where slipping into evening dress is a regular activity, in handsome flats overlooking Eaton Square and Regent's Park, in the discreetly expensive hotels masquerading as private houses round Sloane Square in which BRIT puts its foreign guests, in gentlemen's clubs in St. James's Street, where members find it handy to change in the loo, in Fulham and Wapping, Dulwich and Hampstead, men are squeezing themselves into tailcoats rented for the occasion and protesting vigorously ("Cheaper to take you out to dinner, darling, somewhere really nice, than go through all this palaver"), and women are willing the children to shut up and worrying about their hair and whether somebody else will be wearing the same dress. Instructions have been strict: guests must be at the museum by seven-fifteen, before a Certain Person arrives. The prospect of venturing across the Thames (even if only four hundred yards) is so alarming to many of them that dozens of emergency plans have been made. Diaries have been wiped clean, fleets of cabs commandeered, baby-sitters bribed heavily to stay from six till one, jewels removed from bank vaults by the treasuryful. An invitation from Sir Lewis Burslem is not to be ignored.

This is, after all, one of the most heavily publicized social events of the year. The exhibition has been generously previewed in the *Sunday Times* and elsewhere; interviews with the director and others have appeared as extended features that morning, along with the usual shots of technicians pretending to put finishing touches to exhibits that were actually in place days before; the Duke of Clarence is one of the most popular members of the Royal Family, and known to be a good speaker; the guest list is said to be glittering, if traditional; and gastronomically the dinner (already gossiped about by the diary of a well-known evening newspaper, which succeeded in being wrong about every single detail except the name of the chef, who was profiled under the headline "The Great Gustavus" as the culinary star of the coming decade) will clearly be memorable.

Police Sergeant Ted Hoskins MVO (he's proud of his membership of the Royal Victorian Order) of Metropolitan Police Royalty Protection, who is driving in from Surrey, has reached Wandsworth. He concentrates on the road conditions: traffic flow pretty fair, density fair to middling, weather excellent (he can hardly remember a more beautiful evening, it would have been nice to stay at home and play cricket with the boys). Has to be at the boss's place by 1830 hours, ready for departure for venue at 1930. This evening should be pretty straightforward, at least it's all in one place, no public access other than the strictly controlled lists of guests, museum and catering staff. The latter can be a problem since caterers tend to draft in dubious extras at the last moment, but this outfit won't do that. Ted Hoskins is a fine figure of a man, all blond six feet two of him, and the old-established tailors behind Burlington House who make the evening dress and the morning dress, the dinner jackets (winter and summer varieties), the pinstripe suits, the tweed jackets and the sporting outfits he needs for official duties, contemplate the results of their tailoring with satisfaction. A devoted but not uncritical royalist, he is proud to be considered a friend by the Duke and Duchess (whom he's known for a decade and sees on more than half the days in a year). At public engagements he manages, like his colleagues, to be both invisible and highly present, never noticeable until trouble arises. To his wife and his friends he claims to feel detached about the celebrities, the parties, the visits to places all over Britain and the world—"All in the day's work," he tends to say—but in fact they still fascinate him. Only occasionally does he want to offer his own point of view as an individual rather than a reassuring shadow. But he expresses forceful views at home.

Ted, used to wearing black and even white tie two or three nights a week, has had much less trouble organizing himself than some of the other participants. Lucian is in wild disorder, can't find his collar studs, finds it hard to tie his tie (Fanny always did it), has lost a crucial part of the white waistcoat's internal mechanism, has a taxi waiting outside, will have to set out half-dressed and create his armor en route. He is excited and apprehensive about the evening. It's crucial to his future, he thinks, as he pushes his face into the little boxes on his bedroom table and casts their contents on the floor and wrenches open drawers in search of his gold cuff links (he really can't wear the flashing Mickey Mouse ones tonight). *Thank God everything looks promising, this afternoon's meeting with Mr. Kobayashi went well—at last the paper's signed and safe in the museum, export license sorted out, things moving on nicely. As for one's own career, let's just hope the evening is a huge success and dazzles those old fools at the Bloomsbury Museum into thinking Auberon is the brightest star in the museum constellation so that we get rid of him. The competition for Bloomsbury—one gathers—is pretty dim.* He smiles as he thinks of Sir Lewis wringing his hands at a recent private view and remarking unctuously to Lord Willins of Plympton (Chairman of the Trustees at Bloomsbury) how much he'd miss young Auberon but "gosh—he's able!" *And Hermia—how delightful she was this afternoon, and she'll be at my table this evening. But I mustn't be too attentive to Hermia, I must be seen being extra-nice to Helen. Helen—hmm—need to take a lot of trouble over her. If everything goes according to plan, how am I going to promote her? My job, Head of Exhibitions? Is she up to it yet? Better to think about Hermia—what a dream she is, I thinks she likes me, too, I thinks maybe she likes me very much—Is there any chance . . . tonight . . . a bit soon? Funny about Diana, she really does seem to have made the leap . . . actually I find her in the role of a dominating dyke rather exciting, can imagine her in enormous thigh-length boots, I've always liked her in boots, only thing I do like about her really, must be something about her Germanness. . . . Must concentrate. . . . Who invented these fucking collar studs? Impossible to squeeze them through these stiff white holes.* And he dashes out of the door.

Naturally, Diana is much more organized. Her hairdresser and friend, Imogen, has come round to check her hair and arrange the silver comb with a spray of egrets which she's bought for the occasion (rather cheaply, she was pleased to find). Diana has decided not to wear black—she hates grand parties that look like funeral wakes, men in black and white, women in black and black. She doesn't approve of spending large sums of money on clothes, and felt it was loyal to her principles to choose her dress in a secondhand design boutique—although even there the price she had to pay was a shock to her principles, and her purse. She has to admit she's pleased with the dress she found, gray and silver layered organdy, over cream silk, shimmering almost to the ground. From the low neck, her creamy shoulders and arms (she never tans) emerge like the necks of two swans.

All day her thoughts were darting back to her outfit. Everything looked OK when she did a dress rehearsal for her very critical friends Susanna and Dolly, but how will it be this evening, at the real thing? And is she even going to have time to enjoy herself, or will Jane keep her running around the museum in search of clues? Just before she steps out of her bedroom into her sitting room to try the effect on Imogen, she seizes a silver organza wrap (given to her years ago by some man or other), which for some reason she pulled out of a drawer days ago and dropped onto her bedroom chair. She's been vowing not to wear it, but now, intoxicated by the moment, she throws it around her shoulders. She doesn't look at herself before she goes out of the room, she's too full of nerves—does she look too commanding, or too tall, or as though she's trying too hard or . . . ? Imogen says nothing for a moment and Diana peers at her nervously at which Imogen says, "Darling, you look *astounding!*" So Diana turns to inspect herself in the mirror, and in the soft light of the sitting room, more flattering than the one in her bedroom, realizes that, yes, well, she does look quite striking. . . . "You look like a princess, a Scandinavian princess!"

"Do I look like an ice queen?" asks Diana nervously.

"No," says Imogen, "you look like your namesake, the goddess."

"Not over the top?" says Diana.

"Totally, darling, but it's magnificent. And we haven't done the diamonds yet!"

"D'you think I need to wear diamonds, with all this silk and stuff, couldn't I just wear . . . ?" asks Diana.

"You absolutely must," cries Imogen. "If you're ever in doubt about diamonds, say yes."

"But it's not correct, according to my principles, to wear so much jewelry," cries Diana. "I mean a diamond and pearl sunburst necklace, and diamond and pearl earrings— they're not very comradely, are they?"

"Oh, darling," says Imogen, "don't take life so hard."

"Do I take life so hard?" asks Diana in surprise.

Just as Diana is coming to terms with wearing jewelry and whether she takes life hard, the telephone rings. "Shall I leave it?" she asks Imogen.

"It might be important," says Imogen. "It might be Jonathan."

"Oh, to hell with Jonathan," says Diana, but she picks up the receiver. It's Jane. *Oh, no, not Jane,,* says Diana to herself, *at this moment I do not want to have to think about Jane and her mad schemes, really I do not want to be involved in this peculiar Gainsborough business at all, it's too much for me just now, I want to think about myself and her . . . her . . . Hermia.* "I'm so sorry to bother you," says Jane, "are you struggling with your jewels? I have to tell you something. There's some strange sinister scheme afoot here, I don't really understand the details, but Ian Burgess, the security man, rang me and told me that two of the attendants overheard the chairman talking about some secret arrangement over the Gainsborough, it wasn't quite clear what. Some crucial document has been put in the Security control room, Ian's going to try to get hold of it for me. . . . Yes, I know it sounds bizarre but museums are bizarre places. . . . Diana, I know this is asking a lot of you"— *It certainly is,* thinks Diana—"but I want you to ring your friend Valentine Green and insist he comes to the dinner, he has to drop everything, he must be there, he's exactly the sort of troublemaker we need. I can't ring him, I don't know him, but you and he are great friends, aren't you?"

"Yes," says Diana rather grudgingly, "I suppose so. What do I tell him?"

"Tell him everything you know but not quite everything so that he's intrigued and needs to know more—yes?"

"All right," she says, "I'll try." All she really wants to think about at this moment is her clothes.

"And there's another thing—I want you to arrange for us to inspect the picture. . . . The Gainsborough, of course, Diana, which picture d'you think? As soon as HRH is out of the exhibition and before it comes into the Great Hall . . . No, it's a loan, it comes under you and Lucian, not me, I can't do anything about it. . . . Diana, I know I'm being impossible, but it's very important. And what is emerging is that Lucian . . ." She pauses.

"Lucian?" asks Diana, rather more interested.

"That Lucian is deeply implicated in all these plans. My feeling is that if and when the whole story comes out, Lucian will be a goner as far as this museum is concerned. His position will be untenable, and not just untenable here." She pauses again.

Diana hesitates, too. *Lucian? His career destroyed? Forced maybe to leave the country? Of course he's a remarkable man . . . I owe a lot to him . . . one should not be vindictive . . . but then it's only the truth we're trying to reveal, he's obviously behaved badly. . . . Just imagine, Lucian out of the museum, oh, bliss, and probably out of Hermia's life, too. . . .*

"I'll do whatever you ask, Jane." She feels horrible as she says it, and she also feels triumphant.

"Wonderful," says Jane, and rings off.

God, she's so bossy, this Jane, Diana tells herself. *And I always thought of her as a bit of a mouse. Still, I can't let her down.* "I have to make a call," she says, "persuade someone to come to this stupid dinner at short notice."

"You look as though you could persuade anyone in the world," says Imogen.

Lady Burslem is wearing diamonds, too. Her husband found them for her at Tiffany's a few years before, when he was ending a longish affair and as usual in these circumstances felt guilty toward his wife. (She has a great many jewels.) On that occasion he gave her a tiara, a necklace, a brooch, pendant earrings, and a diamond and ruby bracelet. Privately she feels that all this jewelry en masse is rather overpowering, and she knows wearing a tiara for this sort of occasion isn't right, but since Lewis is so keen on it and (she suspects) insisted on white tie for the event so that she could wear the blessed thing, she has invested herself in the full array. Her outfit has been made for the occasion by her dressmaker in the country, a reliable woman whom she's persuaded Lewis to approve of (though he'd much prefer her to buy a famous label). It's a black velvet dress over which, since she no longer trusts her arms, she's wearing a soft, loose *devoré* jacket in very dark blue—she thinks the contrast with the black is rather successful. Reluctantly she agreed to buy a new pair of black velvet shoes for the evening (she has several pairs already, but Lewis insisted that they had to be new). She thinks her favorite place in Mayfair have done a beautiful job with her hair—though it was disconcerting when she went there this afternoon to meet two friends who'll also be at the dinner having their hair done in the neighboring seats in exactly the same style. She thinks she looks OK and she does hope Lewis will approve—he can be so outspoken if he doesn't like something. As she meets her husband, who's assumed his tails with ruthless speed, they smile at each other warmly.

"My God, those jewels," he says. "I certainly did you proud with that lot!"

"And do you like the dress?" she asks.

He looks at it and does a thumbs-up. "Fabulous," he says.

"Best of British!" she says. "Such an important day for you, darling."

"Speaking of which," he replies, "one never has time for a drink at those dos. Shall we have a quickie before we go?"

"Why not? We've got ten minutes," she says. "I'm sure Mrs. Sterling will have it all ready." And indeed Mrs. Sterling has laid out a tray in the pantry with two glasses and a linen napkin, and in the fridge are two half-bottles of champagne.

Auberon is not drinking champagne but glass after glass of water. He is perspiring with anxiety. There's a leaden feeling in his stomach. He cannot understand precisely what's going on in the museum, whether Jane is exaggerating over *Lady St. John*, what on earth they were all doing in his office this afternoon when he was elsewhere, whether Sir Lewis supports his candidacy for Bloomsbury or not, what the critics will say about *Elegance*, whether he likes elegance himself, whether his clever friends will sneer (one caustic piece in an influential weekly can set swathes of less courageous people mocking). He feels quite sick at the thought of the Nowness of Now, and having to smile and look enthusiastic when plans are announced, especially after this afternoon's board meeting. There are so many complications . . . oh, and can he put the cost of hiring the tails on expenses? Tanya reacted badly—he might have been a bit abrupt, suddenly he can hardly bear to speak to her—when he said they'd meet at the museum because he hadn't time to collect her.

"How low-key d'you want me to be this evening, sweetest?" she'd said aggressively.

"As low-key as comes naturally," he'd replied.

What's crucial is to keep the show going, make sure the guests enjoy themselves (especially the guests from the Bloomsbury Museum), and see the exhibition gets good reviews soonest. I will not have the staff manufacturing difficulties. . . . They must remember this event is a public performance . . . like a court masque, with comparable financial, social, and political implications. Then there's their own pageant. . . . Oh, Lord, the pageant . . .

He glances at himself in the mirror. He looks awful, eyes almost glued together and bloodshot, tired, slightly red in the face, bags under the eyes, faint air of dementia—he should have given himself time for some meditation. No doubt when the party starts he'll revive. He always does.

In the taxi to the museum he peers at the evening paper. Nothing much in it. The private lives of assorted manufactured celebrities have taken surprising turns—one has to be aware, at least, of this brand of futile popular culture. He turns to the City Dweller's Log Book on page seven and his whole body jerks. The lead story is about the directorship of the Bloomsbury Museum. Prospective candidates are listed . . .

Oh, NO, we're just arriving at BRIT. . . . What's the fare? Surely not so much . . . Why bother with this kind of article? It's always inaccurate. . . . Can't read it now but I must, won't be able to concentrate on the party if I don't. . . . Did I give the driver too much? The flowers outside look fabulous. . . . What does this article say? "Professor Alan Stewart . . . highly admired, a very strong can-

didate . . ." *Alan Stewart—my trustee? Is he applying, for God's sake? How do they know? He'd certainly be a strong candidate, much too strong. . . .*

Auberon pretends not to notice the Head of Security approaching with his usual officious air as he hovers behind a column scanning this idiotic article. . . .

"Liz Birley, Keeper of Urban History at Bloomsbury . . . well respected, a lively, feisty woman . . ." Rubbish, she's got no chance at all, sheer tokenism, but then maybe she has connections I don't know about. . . . Aren't I in here? Ah—"Auberon Booth, the clever and high-profile Director of the Museum of English History (now oddly rebranded as "BRIT"), is admired for his highly developed social skills and his unrelenting pursuit of a stylishness or 'elegance' (the awful title of his new exhibition at the museum), which some think he never quite achieves"—Ooh, nasty, who wrote this? Could it be that horrid little journalist I told to wait the other day because I had no time? "He is considered aloof and superior, slightly surprising from a graduate of Bradford Grammar School and Southampton University. He has not made much impact during his brief period at the museum. . . ." Intolerable, what makes them say that? ". . . he is thought to be too young for the Bloomsbury Museum job and could wait till next time around, especially if he achieves more at BRIT. . . ." Will anyone read this stuff, will anyone serious be influenced by it? No, surely not. A heavy scowl at John Winterbotham, who retreats. *"A dark-horse candidate is Ranald Stewart, Director of the South London Museum. . . ." Aha, little Ranald, goblinlike, humorous, heart-of-gold, look-at-me-caring-for-the-socially-excluded little Ranald, what do they have to say about him? "He has attracted attention for his lively and innovative approach to accessibility. . . ." Exactly, he must be good at something. "His flamboyant manner conceals highly developed managerial and fund-raising skills." Huh, why so nice about*

little Ranald, twit of twits, never stops boasting about his working-class background? But on it goes . . . "The trustees may want to show their interest in the regions by appointing a non-London figure in the form of the only nonmetropolitan-based shortlisted applicant, Susan Higgins, Director of Manchester and Region Art Galleries and Museums. A plain-speaking former opera singer famous for her sense of fun"—*Where does all this drivel come from? She's as lively as a wet Sunday in Oldham*—"she has done a superb job, experts feel, in solving the problems of the area's numerous underfunded museums. . . . If appointed, she would be the Bloomsbury Museum's first woman director and her appointment would show the way the trustees want to steer the museum. . . ."

He drops the paper behind the pillar, realizes this is not helpful, picks it up again and greets John Winterbotham, who is lurking at a discreet distance (and no doubt has read the article, too). "Just a few points I wanted to clear with you, Director," says John.

Auberon sighs. "I don't have long, you know."

Upstairs in the museum, Jane is making her toilette. As the curators' corridor outside her office fills with noisy steps and slamming doors and loud good nights, she opens her cupboard and extracts a plastic dry-cleaning bag. Inside is a green satin evening dress bought at Christian Dior by her mother in a moment of uncharacteristic abandon in the 1950s. It was stunning when new and still looks pretty good. She thinks it will be OK this evening—and it fits pretty well, she knows from experience, and doesn't look too young for her, even now. She hopes it won't look eccentric with the jewelry she's chosen, an amber and silver necklace she bought as a girl traveling in Syria, and silver hoop earrings from a trip to India. Hardly a self-conscious woman, she knows that in a museum—nowadays more a party venue than a house of learning—people in her position are obliged to be reasonably well dressed, if subtly less elegant than the genuinely rich. It takes her ninety seconds to arrange her hair in the mirror inside her cupboard door, and around three minutes to put on the dress. She smiles to think how long some of the other guests will be spending on dressing, and her thoughts drift back a long way to how pleasant it used to be, in those days of sweet intimacy, to chat to the man one was going out with as one changed one's clothes. She smiles again, more sadly. Is it the loss of such intimacy that makes her so aggressive over things like the Gainsborough? No, she thinks that sort of tiresome integrity was born in her, though sometimes she worries about her own fierceness.

But Jane has things to attend to, and wants this dressing business finished. And once she's changed her clothes her personality should alter just a little, too.

She can't resist one look at herself full-length and hurries along the corridor to the ladies'. *Green always suited me, at Cambridge I had a beautiful floaty dress I'd wear to May balls—perhaps at one's advanced age one should bow to the years and just wear black. . . .* She passes one of the attendants: his eyes widen as he presses himself against the wall. In the ladies' she turns off all but one light, and stands in front of the mirror. *Faint moment of dread. Must do something about my hair. But the dress? It looks OK, I really do think it looks OK.*

There are more important things to worry about this evening than clothes. Such as meeting Ian from Security in Early Georgian, which we chose because if the meeting's observed in the control room and arouses suspicion I can say that as chief curator I wanted to check the catering arrangements from a curatorial point of view. I'm sure my movements are being monitored, maybe my telephone's being tapped.

Early Georgian is surprisingly quiet and orderly. On an enormous trestle table four hundred plates are laid out, each with a minimal garnish—these must be the plates awaiting lobsters. Beside the table stands another table, covered in sealed boxes, some marked "Spinach," others "Lobster Pâté," and rows of huge metal vats, filled with water and plugged into sockets on the wall. Her precious Rysbracks have disappeared under wooden boxes, the Haymans are swathed in thick plastic sheeting, the ship models encased in protective wooden cases so heavy they are hardly removed even on the rare days when the room is open to visitors. There is Ian, looking amiable and anxious. They pretend to look around the room and gesticulate now and again at the cooking equipment, just in case they are being watched. "It's my turn to take over in the control room," says Ian. "The boss is busy with the royal arrival. I think the papers we want are in the control-room safe, I'll get Bill or Anna to come over and collect them, make a copy, we'll sort it out somehow." Eight-fifteen is clearly the crucial moment for their plan, after the crowds have left the exhibition and while the Duke's making his way toward the Great Hall. Ian knows who'll be in the control room at eight-fifteen—no problem there, it's one of his own men, Ralph, he won't say anything to John. He'll make sure that Bill and Anna are on duty in the exhibition room beside the Gainsborough . . . they already know a bit about what's going on, they're the ones who overheard the conversation about the document. . . . They don't like Winterbotham, won't report anything to him. Jane should have six minutes clear, but not a second more, the inspection absolutely must be done in that time. . . .

As they conclude their plans, they hear flustered bustle from the direction of the staff entrance. A procession enters the room. At its head walks John Winterbotham, looking stern. Behind him, wheeled by Angel's junior chefs and manual team, trundle four large metal containers, each labeled FRAGILE—DO NOT TOUCH. On either side of the containers walks a file of attendants, most of them grinning. It is an impressive, if mystifying, sight.

"What on earth . . . ?"

"It's the lobsters," replies Ian, "arriving for dinner. Your dinner, not theirs."

"The lobsters?" breathes Jane.

And indeed it is the lobsters, and already the water in the waiting vats is being warmed, and sixteen chefs and souschefs under the leadership of a devilishly handsome young man with a flushed face are waiting to embark on lobster preparation. Four people to a vat, it seems. Jane and Ian abandon their discussion to watch the containers being opened and the live black lobsters, clenching and flailing, being pulled out and thrown into the now boiling water. Recalling herself, Jane remarks, "It's awfully improper, I'm sure lobster preparation is not allowed here. . . ." to which Ian replies, "Chairman's orders, you know, HRH and all that, loves lobsters . . ."

As they confer, a tall urbane man, evidently in charge, appears and bows slightly. "Is everything OK?" he asks. "I'm Rupert Burnham, the managing director of Angel Cooks. I think it's Miss Vaughan, isn't it? We had the pleasure of meeting on the occasion of the Chaucer private view. Ian, how are you? Is everything all right from your point of view?

The lobsters are a bit demanding, but lobsters always are, we can cope. . . . They're going to be stuffed with spinach, you see, and lobster pâté, I think it'll be delicious."

"It looks very organized," says Jane. "If it weren't you and your team doing it I should be rather nervous," and so she is, but not as nervous as she is about her other activities.

"Can I offer you a glass of champagne?" asks Mr. Rupert agreeably. "Then I'll leave you to the lobsters."

ENTRANCE HALL, 6:15 P.M.

The preparations are perfect. When Sir Lewis and his lady emerge from the Jaguar and give a gracious wave toward the well-mannered group of spectators being held back strenuously by a line of policemen, they can allow themselves to glow with satisfaction. The enormous blue and gold banner proclaiming *"Elegance"* (no subtitles, it was decided, no dates, just the one word) has been hoisted above the main entrance. Even though it's a golden evening and extremely warm, blue and yellow gas flames are shooting from the Edwardian gasoliers on either side of the main steps.

On each step, left and right, bewigged footmen in eighteenth-century livery hold flaming torches. A red carpet of huge width and depth runs from the pavement under the *porte-cochère* up to the front door, which is flanked by a bevy of Georgian country wenches. There were wench-recruitment difficulties among the staff since some buxom potentials refused to oblige on principle while less promising ones pressed their services, but now the ranks of wenches look very fine in their white dimity dresses sprinkled with flowers and their pink sashes and their poke bonnets, poised to bestow programs and beams on the arriving guests. The appearance of the chairman stimulates an electric shock through the senior staff waiting at the door. Auberon, again in his courtierlike mode, emerges from the museum precisely as the Burslems step out of the car.

"Good evening, Auberon," says Sir Lewis. They cooperate well on an occasion like this, when both are being watched by many eyes.

"Good evening, Auberon," says Lady Burslem. "It all looks marvelous, doesn't it?"

"It certainly does, thanks to Mirabel," says Auberon diplomatically. Praise for Mirabel always pleases. At the moment he needs to please the chairman.

Sweeping up the steps, the Burslems nod graciously at the wenches, who curtsy in ragged deference. *The curtsies aren't quite right yet,* notes Auberon, *oh, well, it's a bit late now.*

"Those curtsies are a bit rustic," remarks Lady Burslem, and laughs. "Shall I give them a lesson? My mother taught me. Look, girls, this is how you curtsy." And to her husband's embarrassment she demonstrates, until he pulls impatiently at her hand.

As they walk into the entrance hall, the Burslems stop short and she puts out a hand to clutch his arm. The windows have been blacked out for the evening and the room is transformed. It's not only the vast array of delphiniums, peonies, larkspur, all white (the flowers for the evening are rumored to have cost more than £100,000) twisted around ten wicker columns, or the lighting from dozens of tiny electronic candles twinkling on gilt candelabra supported by carved Moorish pages, not only the practically naked full-sized statues of classical deities on plinths or the army of footmen extending silver and glass trays with the whispered inquiry, "Vintage champagne, madam?", not only the costumed chamber orchestra on the balcony playing Handel's *Water Music* with amplified enthusiasm or the scented clouds of vapor pumped by half-naked children from little silver bellows. It is the gloriously harmonized combination of all these elements, brought together this evening like the instruments in an orchestra, which makes the museum feel like the antechamber to Paradise. The Burslems exchange a tiny nod, and Sir Lewis almost beams.

"Very good," says Sir Lewis. "Immaculate."

"Marvelous," says Lady Burslem. "It's all perfect. What time did you close the museum today, Auberon?"

"Five o'clock, as usual," he replies, trying not to sound smug. "Teamwork, you know." Meanwhile he's wondering if his warning to Jane and Diana will be listened to. He caught the two of them whispering to each other just before the Burslems arrived and penned them in a corner behind the largest candelabrum. "What are you plotting?" he asked them.

"Oh, nothing," they replied.

He didn't believe them. They were to say and do nothing about the Gainsborough, he told them—no doubts were to be cast on the picture's condition. Diana lowered her eyes. Jane looked inscrutable. This was not helpful. He went further. Any improper conduct would lead to dismissal, he told them. At this their heads jerked upward and they fixed him with what he saw as nervous but resolute defiance, Jane in particular. Something's certainly up.

Meanwhile Sir Lewis is greeting the staff, who are grouped in readiness (and order of precedence) for his encouraging words. They have certainly tried their best with their clothes, he notes with satisfaction, and for museum curators on pathetic salaries they really look quite creditable. That woman Diana, for example, is stunning tonight, in silver and gray. Helen's all in black, very nice little number that dress, just to the knee, showing her arms and lots of the rest of her, He probably paid for it, he thinks, with a slight stiffening of the groin, and her toes look very sexy painted red in those little sandals, wonder what the shoes cost, they can't have been cheap either, well, no doubt they were paid for by him, too. In fact he seems to have paid for everything on her except her body . . . and in a sense, well . . . what a naughty girl she is . . . worth every penny he's spent on her, though. He winks slightly at Lucian, smiting him on the arm with a muttered word of congratulations, kisses the hand of Diana (good-looking she certainly is, but there's something a bit chilly about the woman, can't say what), shakes the hand of Jane, but then realizes he'll have to kiss her if he's not going to look too conspicuous kissing the next one in line, who is Helen. So he embraces Jane, who looks startled and faintly resentful, and then with much more enthusiasm takes Helen, who's wearing a minxish look, into his arms. She wriggles seductively at his touch, a movement observed by everyone except Lady Burslem who's looking in the opposite direction.

An enormous man dressed as an eighteenth-century night watchman advances, asserting himself by occupying a great deal of space.

"Sir Lewis, this is Sergeant Major Jenkins of the Corps of Commissionaires, who will be announcing the guests," says Auberon.

"Ah, Mr. Jenkins, a very good evening to you," remarks Sir Lewis genially. He is good at shows of geniality. *Pretty shallow shows,* thinks Auberon sourly.

"Good evening, sir," says Mr. Jenkins. "I just had one question for you and your lady, sir, if I might."

"Yes?" asks Sir Lewis.

"Where would you be proposing to stand, sir, to receive your guests? I would suggest just here, so that those in the line can be indoors. And do you wish the guests to be announced by their full names and titles in every case, or may I abbreviate as and when, sir? It does save time."

A rustic wench hurries up to them, rosy and squeaky. "The first guest is arriving, Sir Lewis!" she cries, looking as though she's about to faint at the excitement.

"Time to get into position," says Sir Lewis. "Come along, Elizabeth, come along, Auberon," and into position they go. "Who can it be?"

"Baroness Shawe and Mr. William Shawe," booms Commissionaire Jenkins as a commanding female with a modest husband in tow approaches the hosts for the usual rapid exchange of civilities. *God, what a dreary beginning,* thinks Auberon, *the bossiest sort of right-wing life peeress, always wanting to improve the nation's morals and knowing best.* She passes on, husband behind her, and there's a pause.

"I always wonder on these occasions," says Lady Burslem, "if anyone at all is going to turn up. Maybe this will be the evening when nobody does."

D'you think we could make a go of it on the basis just of Baroness Shawe? wonders Auberon.

"It might be a bit sticky," she replies.

"Think of all the food she'd have to eat, though I dare say she'd make a good job of it."

"Where are all the trustees?" grumbles Sir Lewis. "I told them to be here in good time."

As he speaks, they arrive. "Sir Robert and Lady Pound!" announces the commissionaire. Auberon is not thrilled to see them either. *Lady Pound is one of those constantly thrilled, insincere upper-class types, and Sir Robert is looking more of an old bore than ever, continuously stroking the medal around his neck as a bride might stroke her bouquet.* "Viscount and Viscountess Doncaster!" *Better. Olivia's wearing a tight-fitting scarlet dress, Versace, I should think, her arms are tanned and beautiful, her face smiling and soft, her lips like kissing cherries, her hair particularly soft and flowing, a choker there's hardly time to admire is sparkling around her neck. . . . Have to say hello to her beastly husband, why must he slap me on the shoulder?* They move on. "Mrs. Hobson!" *and here's the old cat, nose pursed, in something much too young for her, looking around venomously to see how the room compares to the Moorish tent she organized for her own seventieth birthday, and hardly bothering to greet me.* "Mr. Kobayashi, Mr. Shimuzu, Mr. Tanaka." *Our Japanese friend with his two henchmen, to whom the chairman's again being unctuously polite. Ah, there are Lady Pound and Lady Doncaster, like social commandos primed for the task, swooping on the Japanese guests and smothering them with kindnesses.* "The Bishop of London, Mr. and Mrs. William Beckley-Smith, Miss Amanda Mann and Mr. James Mantling . . ." "So glad you could come, so glad you could come, so glad you could come, isn't the hall looking good, all done in seventy-five minutes, yes, it was Mirabel, isn't she clever?" prattles Auberon. *Is there an alternative to "So glad you could come"? Lucian and Mr. Kobayashi, over there, conferring together—what's going on?* "Professor Hilary and Professor Gabriel Ironside." *Ah, the Ironsides, my role models, so successful, so serious, he took her name when they married, such an effective move. Brilliant, the way they combine academic weight with big popular reputations, their recent books (particularly his* Crunching the Apple: Culturing Consumption in Augustan England, *which has been hardly less admired than her outstandingly original* Identifying Identities: Signifiers for a Post-Industrial Age) *are constantly in the learned journals and on television. . . .* "Amanda, darling," Hilary cries, and the Bishop turns sharply toward him *(Why on earth? Can "Amanda" be his nocturnal name?)* as they embrace effusively. "James, how nice to see you," he asserts, though he can't stand Amanda's husband. "D'you know the Bishop of London?" *It's amusing to introduce people who've not one thing in common. Wish those cameras would stop or perhaps it's glamorous, is it? And who's this with Trevor Christiansen, this woman like a mobile duvet?* "Trevor!" he says, less warmly than usual.

Trevor has been pretty annoying about Nowness and has the presumption to say, "Marvelous about Nowness, Auberon."

"Marvelous to see you," intones Auberon, and then "I did enjoy the latest, many congratulations" to Gregory Noble. *Noble's a peculiarly successful novelist—I've never managed to read more than a few pages of any of his books but have to pretend, he can sometimes be flattered into making passable donations to the museum, wasn't it five thousand last time? God, why are English-women so badly dressed, even for a big occasion like this—the men look terrific in their tails and decorations, but honestly, the women, how do they do it? The inexact cut, the lack of color sense, the grazing bosom, the careless shoes . . . This one looks OK and somehow familiar—oh, Lord, it's Tanya, heavily made-up and hard-looking tonight. Screws up her face when I kiss her cheek. Red around the eyes, not good. Has she been crying—oh, no, surely not? For heaven's sake* . . . "Sir William and Lady St. John." *Further flutter. More flashing of teeth and jewels. Sir William's tall, red-faced, broad-shouldered, she has a blond boiled, posh look.*

"Marvelous you could come," says Auberon. "Actually we're longing to have a photograph of you beside the other Lady St. John, is that really OK, and you, too, Sir William?" and as he speaks the mildly blushing Lady St. John is swept off to be photographed.

"Professor and Mrs. Alan Stewart." The Professor and Sir Lewis exude antipathy as they exchange cordial handshakes. Obviously unaware of the *London Sentinel* article, Stewart greets Auberon warmly and says, "God, what a meeting that was this afternoon, I felt for you." Decent of him. "Very difficult situation . . . well, at least you may not be forced to do battle. . . ." and he gives Auberon one of his rare but charming smiles.

His lawyer wife merely jerks her head toward the festivities. "The Sacrifice of Athena to Mammon, I suppose," she remarks.

The guests are pouring in. "Sir Richard and Lady Frazier," proclaims Jenkins proudly, "Sir Thomas and Lady Frazier." *The Frazier brothers, in their sixties, owners of the family business, unfailingly generous patrons of the arts. The country's studded with mementos of their generosity. "Where would we be without them?" people often ask. Much jollity as they greet Sir Lewis. Not that they like each other, but members of the wealth club must appear to be on good terms.*

Behind them treads Lord Willins of Plympton, life peer, Chairman of the Bloomsbury Trustees for quite a while. Large bushy mustache, thrusts it into people's faces, staring eyes, quite alarming. "Ah, Noël," says Sir Lewis. *No doubt Lewis envies him his title and the Bloomsbury Museum, definitely a notch above BRIT.*

Their director always gets a knighthood; the director here's lucky to get a CB. "Nice of you to find your way here," says Sir Lewis.

"Enormous contribution you've made, Lewis," remarks Lord Willins, in an only faintly patronizing way, "splendid event, looking forward to it hugely . . ." He embraces Lady Burslem.

"You know Auberon, don't you?" she asks.

"Of course," replies Lord Willins, and nods at Auberon with a half-smile. "Looking forward to seeing what you've been up to in the exhibition, was looking at your displays the other day actually. . . ." *Is he teasing? Stomach churning, I really do want that Bloomsbury job, don't I? They say Lord Willins is decisive, brisk with his charm, controlling, shrewd in detecting talent (or its lack).*

Each time Auberon glances to his left he gives a little gasp. Over half of the guests have arrived and the entrance hall has become a place of celebration, the noise convivial yet not too loud, the festive music still audible, the flash of cameras enlivening, the candle-type light showing soft and haggard cheeks to advantage, the liveried footmen (apparently selected for their looks and fine calves, and much handsomer than most of the male guests) moving dextrously from group to group. Thank goodness he's been able to invite some of his own friends, so not everyone's a frowsty friend of the chairman. Tim and Vanessa (performance artists who fit in anywhere) look particularly decorative this evening, Tim in his wittily deconstructed tailcoat, one tail red, the other white with a slash down the back, Vanessa delicious in full male evening dress, the dark trousers hugging the thighs that once Auberon knew so well. . . .

"Mr. and Mrs. Denzil Marten . . ." *Why does he have to be here, little creep? Nobody really wanted that picture of his.*

"So glad you could come," Auberon remarks, looking beyond them at the next guest. . . .

"Mr. Valentine Green." No friendly greeting from the chairman, who looks appalled to see him. And what on earth is Valentine doing here? His name certainly wasn't on the guest list. "Nice of you to make it," Auberon says coolly (but he hopes not too rudely, this is an influential man in his way). Valentine smirks at him. Auberon looks quizzically at his black shirt and white bow tie outfit, remarking, "Reversing out? That's rather clever."

"Mr. and Mrs. Ranald Stewart," enunciates Jenkins rotundly, though not with the rotundity he applies to a title. There's a certain flatness now in his announcement of any mere Mr. and Mrs. though only those who've heard him delivering several hundred names at the top of his voice (almost always accurately) would be aware of it. What he loves is introducing a titled person: when a duke or duchess appears he becomes almost ecstatic, as though announcing the arrival of a divine being.

Hmm—Ranald. A rival. Pity he had to be asked. Ranald will be aware of the impression he's making and, no doubt, will find himself talking to Lord Willins. He's a snappy dresser in a flip way and is wearing an enormous silver bow tie, which rotates—he's demonstrating it to Lady Burslem. This stuff is considered amusing by the great, like having a court jester. Ranald's managed to make his little museum, which has nothing in it, into one of the most visited places in London. He's created this personal cult, it's hard not to be irritated. His choice of his favorite socks and tie of the month fascinates the press, there's even a special display case to show the rubbish in the museum hall. He's still cooing at Lady B., won't he move on?

*Well, no doubt he'll want this job if I move on to Bloomsbury—
BRIT's a big step up from South London. . . .*

Ranald and Auberon greet one another as though presenting swords before a duel.

"Nice to see you," says Auberon coolly.

"Lovely to see you. You must have been so busy," replies
Ranald, "what with the exhibition, and I hear you have an
extension planned—oh, it was on the news, didn't you hear
it? Too busy reading the papers, I suppose—and then
there's next week, of course."

"Next week?" inquires Auberon, as though surprised.
"What d'you mean?"

"Little museum job, isn't there?" says Ranald archly.
"Tiny interview. Darling, you know Auberon, don't you?
He's just about to be appointed Director of the Bloomsbury
Museum."

"What makes you think I'm applying?" asks Auberon,
with a pretence of calm though he knows other guests are
pressing to speak to him.

"Little bird."

"Aren't you applying, Ranald?"

"Me? Oh, no, it's all nonsense that stuff in the *London
Sentinel.* I'm not grand enough, am I? I just scrabble around
in my little museum dealing with my local public. . . ." *All this
is said archly, suggests he can't be telling the truth. Oh, God, that
draining stomach again. Now, social inclusion, crucial issue these
days, we haven't really grappled with that yet at the museum. It's an
omission, especially given the views of the person who's arriving
now. And, of course, Ranald's wife's a teacher and he'll know all the
current education jargon for the interviews . . . haven't had time to
do any proper preparation on that, will they ask me about it in the
interview? Oh, shit . . .*

"Ms. Margaret Mills, Minister of State at the Department of Cultural Affairs," announces Mr. Jenkins, and the hosts stand up straighter and smile harder, knowing that this plain woman in an unidentifiable but faintly ethnic costume will shortly be deciding their financial fate for next year. She moves rapidly past the Burslems and stops at Auberon. "We expect a lot from your exhibition. I gather it's very innovative," she says to him. "Is there any chance of a little pretour from one of the experts?"

"Certainly, we've arranged it," he replies, and there indeed is Jane, looking competent but slightly flustered.

The names go crashing on, countesses and MPs and business people and chairs of trusts and historians and the rich and the great and the good and media people and the merely fashionable and dozens of owners of objects shown in the exhibition, and all the people who—how wearisome it all is, he finds sometimes—keep the whole commercial and public relations and glitter operation rolling along. But he goes on smiling and chuckling and exclaiming and kissing and repeating his mantra. Finally there's a slackening in the arrivals, and an extended pause, only briefly interrupted, and a longer break, and Lewis says, "Well, I think that's about it, don't you? We can go and wander in the crowd." The arrival of Friedrich von Schwitzenberg wearing a dinner jacket seriously too small for him and green with age encourages the Burslems to wander. The noise level is rising. The party is a success.

For Angel Cooks, everything is going well, too, front of house at least. The dinner-waiting staff have been cleared by Security and have piled up their crash helmets and handbags in Early Georgian and slipped discreetly into their

Georgian footman's or maid's costumes behind the show-cases. The tables are all laid, the knives and forks and the five glasses are gleaming in ordered lines, the name cards are in place (though a certain noble lord has left his wife behind, pressing the reluctant Julia into guest duty). In the entrance hall, the forty butlers are pouring rivers of cham-pagne (mutteringly identifying the vintage, as instructed) and dispensing the fascinating canapés arranged on replica Royal Worcester and Chelsea serving dishes, each with a lit-tle porcelain Chinese person in the center playfully pointing to the food.

Mr. Rupert is ready. He's allocated all the staff to their tables (the girls to hand the plates, the boys to serve the main dish, the girls to follow with sauces and vegetables). He's delivered his talk explaining the name and nature of each course, the wines, the timing, the directions for visi-tors. He's quelled the resting actress who claimed she'd been promised the chance to serve HRH with her own hands. Salt and pepper are being poured into eight hun-dred tiny silver pots, two for each guest. The places of vege-tarian guests have been identified. Now the waiters and waitresses are sitting on the guests' chairs, gossiping mildly and admiring one another's variations on blue liveries and white dresses, hoping Mr. Rupert will not reappear to propel them into activity.

Returning to Industrial Revolution from the Great Hall, Mr. Rupert senses more than ever that everything's not quite right. He does not know that Gustavus has just seen a name on the guest list that means nothing to anybody else (and certainly not to Mr. Rupert, who on no account must be allowed to guess): the director of a leading television com-pany is coming to the dinner. This is the man Gustavus has been talking to about a television series, his own series, his very first—he's due to see him again tomorrow. From time to time he sips his glass of water. Although there are sixteen people working on stuffing the lobsters, this turns out to be even less easy than they expected. Four hundred lobsters are needed (although, of course, there are some veggies among the guests) and fewer than half have been finished and stuffing these obstreperous creatures is taking the chefs away from everything else. The beef is almost ready but not quite since a few touches have to be made at the last moment, not least heating the stuff. At least the vegetarian *compote frappée de légumes italiens* is done, and the salad dressing is pretty reliable. It would not be quite true to say that Mr. Rupert is nervous . . . but he's had better evenings . . . if only HRH were not coming . . . and to calm his spirits he throws himself into stuffing lobsters, too.

Stripped of their champagne (which they relinquish protestingly at the exhibition entrance), the guests involve themselves in *Elegance*. The completed effect is triumphant. Sir Lewis and his party parade complacently around the rooms. "How clever you are," the guests say to Sir Lewis, "what a marvelous show, it will be such a success." Some of the guests move past the material about the working classes with raised eyebrows, but the silks and the swords, the portraits and the country-house views, the busts of kings and poets, the virtual London, have them cooing and glowing. Since so many of them try at home to pretend the eighteenth century is going strong, it's not surprising they are thrilled.

The owners of objects stand obliquely close to their possessions, enchanted if people say, "Darling, I know who that one belongs to!" pointing to something labeled: PRIVATE COLLECTION.

To this the owner replies, "Well, we have to say Private Collection, you know, the insurers insist, absurd, isn't it?" or "I never thought there was anything to it, but the curators seemed to like it," or "Henry was awfully against lending it, such a hole on the drawing-room wall, but I persuaded him—isn't it gorgeous?" *Gorgeous* seems to be the word for the evening.

Surveying the scene but wondering what is going on behind it, Diana wanders through the exhibition. Her sleeve is pulled—or not exactly pulled but touched, urgently. She turns to see one of the women attendants whom she recognizes vaguely—pretty girl, startling pale face, odd how she's never really looked at her before. The girl says to her, "Miss Stanley, there's an envelope for you, top secret. Ian Burgess asked me to give it to you, but please would you not let anyone except yourself and Miss Vaughan look at it?"

Diana stares at her and abruptly realizes what this means. Where on earth is she to put this envelope? She has no handbag, being at home as it were . . . but as she struggles with this problem she is accosted by the Hon. Mrs. Ferdinand Hill. This lady is one of the more difficult lenders, who has had to be asked to lunch or dinner and stroked at least once for each of the loans she eventually agreed to make and endlessly fussed over loan conditions and government indemnity. "Where is the exhibition, then?" says Mrs. Hill loudly, oblivious of the large notices pointing to it and the hordes of people moving in its direction.

"I'll show you," says Diana. "You'll see how splendid your objects look."

And out they go toward the exhibition room, meeting

Jane on the way. She has a harassed air and rolls her eyes at Diana. "Can I have a word?" she asks. "I mean, when you're ready."

"Do, do," says Mrs. Hill, unexpectedly affable after a glass or two of champagne, "catch me up, will you, Miss um . . . eh . . . and show me where my little things are—oh, there's Rodney, how nice to see him, what fun this party is, all one's favorite people," and she yells, with surprising vigor, "Rodney!"

Heading toward Jane, Diana encounters Jonathan, and reminds herself that he's supposed to be her partner. He is looking smooth and slightly disconsolate.

"Hello, darling," he says. "Wow—you look fantastic, what an outfit! And those diamonds—they're just brilliant."

"Thank you," she answers, making herself accept a kiss. "I'm afraid I'm rather on duty. Will you be OK? Lots of people from the City here—you'll know masses of them."

"Aren't you going to speak to me, then?"

"Yes, later, at dinner. Enjoy the exhibition. See you!" and she hurries away, suppressing a hint of guilt.

Jane is nearby, and anxious. "I think I'm being watched. And followed. Don't you think you are, too?"

"No," says Diana, "I don't." She looks at Jane in concern. *Is the pressure affecting her?* "But I have something to tell you. . . ."

As they speak, John Winterbotham passes them. He does not greet them, as he normally would. He merely turns his gaze toward them for a moment, impassively, and walks on. When he reaches the entrance to the exhibition room, he stops and turns back toward them. He is speaking into his mobile.

"You see, look at that," says Jane. "Someone wants me to

know I'm under surveillance. I suppose I'm being watched from that control room, too—but with all these people the control room probably can't follow me. I find it horrible. . . . Anyway, we don't want them to think you're involved in all this, go away, don't talk to me."

"But I must tell you about this document. . . ."

Helen passes them. She looks determined, as though on a mission. She conveys subtly that she's noticed them but doesn't need to acknowledge their existence.

"Dear little thing," says Jane.

"You should have seen her ogling the chairman," remarks Diana, with distaste.

"I suppose it's true. . . ."

"Oh, I think undoubtedly. What are you doing now?"

"I'm progressing," says Jane. "Eight-fifteen. It's all set up. But I don't know what we're going to do if we find real problems with the Gainsborough."

"Quite," says Diana. "Auberon was very severe."

"He can be as severe as he likes. Do you think Auberon is part of this conspiracy?"

"Conspiracy?"

"Obviously there's a conspiracy," says Jane, "but personally I doubt he's part of it. If we can get hold of that document . . . or will you, in the ladies' or something?"

She looks so anxious that Diana can't help smiling. *I do admire her, she's so passionate, so determined, so unlike me in her resolution and courage, her assurance of what's right, and as for me, I don't even know that I believe in anything, even my political convictions, they're pretty lightweight, aren't they?, all conveniently set aside on an occasion like this—but at least I seem to be doing the right thing by helping Jane over this peculiar business. And now Jane's off again and talking to one of the guests.*

"Oh, good evening, Professor Ironside," she is saying. "Are you on your way to the exhibition? I do hope you'll think our interpretation of the role of the canals in the industrial economy of late eighteenth-century England is reasonably lucid, within the confines, of course, of the imposed discourse . . ."

Back in the "kitchen," there's been more tension. "No more lobster pâté in the lobsters, they'll do fine without, we'll just have to make sure the top tables get the full works," Mr. Rupert has decreed.

"What?" says Gustavus. "We've only got about a hundred more to do."

"No time even for twenty," says Mr. Rupert, "you'll be lucky to get the spinach into them."

"Who's the chef round here?" cries Gustavus angrily. "Me or you?"

"You," answers Mr. Rupert, still calm, "but ultimately I'm the boss. Do as I say. Six of you finish spinaching the lobsters, the rest on the beef."

"But what will they say," wails Gustavus, "all the people who don't get any pâté in their lobster? They'll be furious."

"They'll be fine," he is told. "If we give them enough to drink, they won't even notice."

Gustavus obeys scowlingly. "Put the proper lobsters on to that table," he orders, "and keep them well away from the unstuffed ones. And carry on with just the spinach." As he moves into the other room to deal with the beef he wonders how life will be if he does become a television chef. Can't go on working for a caterer, unless they triple his salary. He'll need a better showcase than this kind of event, but he'll miss

Mr. Rupert and the sense of excitement . . . and he'll miss some of the chefs, too. . . .

Fred is showing some strain. His mobile rings at intervals and he hustles into a corner of the room from which he emerges looking flushed, and swearing. "All the ovens functioning?" says Gustavus.

"No problem," replies Fred. There is a strange humming sound, a click, a flickering of the lights, and darkness.

"Christ," says Gustavus. "Power failure." And he starts to laugh, softly and then less softly and then so unsoftly that his cackles sound around the room, which is suddenly hugely threatening in the dim emergency lights.

"Steady!" says Fred. "Get Mr. Rupert, will you?" he says, to an underling. "And ring Security. Gus, it'll be all right, old man. A power failure's par for the course, power for the course if you know what I— We'll get it fixed in a jiffy."

"It's a hot night," says Gustavus, "why worry? Let's serve the beef cold. . . . After all, His Royal Bloody Highness is due any moment, isn't he?" He laughs again in a stagey way, which makes the chefs look at one another anxiously.

There's been much agitation about the royal arrival. Sir Lewis wanted His Royal Highness to be received at the main entrance by a bevy of petal-throwing wenches and a row of trumpeters. The duke's detective felt this might lead to complications, and suggested the royal guest should enter by the staff entrance. Sir Lewis was distressed by this proposal, which would have had him greeting the Duke among unmovable sandbags and fuse boxes. They compromised: HRH is to arrive quietly at the front entrance at 1940 hours, and will then move along a prepared route through the crowd to the Gallery of Early English History, which will lead him circuitously and secretly to the exhibition by 1953 hours. On his way he will shake some waiting hands and in the exhibition meet the curatorial team, plus three visiting scholars, plus the managing director of Burslem Properties, plus Mr. Kobayashi, plus the entire board of trustees. The tour of the exhibition will conclude at 2025 hours when HRH proceeds to the Great Hall for dinner, where he is due at 2030 hours. By that time the entire cast of guests will be ready for the royal entrance, to be announced by a fanfare of trumpets from the minstrels' gallery. This program has been discussed and rehearsed for days and weeks and months. All the relevant staff have walked through the program several times, with Sir Lewis, more red-faced than usual, directing the proceedings and Auberon languidly surveying progress from as great a distance as possible.

On her way to the entrance hall Diana sees Hermia directing people to their positions for the royal welcome. A blush rises rapidly from her neck, suffusing her fair face. And OH BLISS, *Hermia is abandoning her duties and moving in my direction and, yes—yes—coming to talk to me.* Seized with irresistible irrational happiness at the chance of speaking to the girl she's not seen for at least thirty minutes, happiness intensified by Hermia's eagerness and Diana's awareness of her own glamor this evening and by the rushed intimacy they're enjoying in the midst of so many indifferent people, Diana is transfixed. . . . She takes Hermia by the shoulder and gently turns her face toward her, searching her with her eyes—although what exactly she's asking, she doesn't know. An impulse propels her to turn and just behind them she meets the thunderous face of Lucian. Following Diana's gaze, Hermia also turns towards him. She, too, starts and blushes. The three stand immobile in an unhappy triangle until the crowds push them apart.

Back in Industrial Revolution, the lobster preparation is as complete as it ever will be. Two-thirds of the lobsters are approximately perfect, though many look rough around the claws where they have been pulled apart in a frenzy of stuffing. Garnish in the form of parsley and lettuce leaves from the emergency supplies disguises the worst gashes. Some lobsters have spinach only, some have lobster pâté only, a few strays have neither, but Gustavus has found some ersatz caviar, which has been dotted gaily if indiscriminately around the plates. The effect is strange and not altogether appetizing. "Harlequin Lobster," he says. Nobody laughs. Mr. Rupert's face has lost all color at the amateurishness of all this, amateurishness such as Angel Cooks has never witnessed except on the evening when the catering tent collapsed half an hour before a dinner. His jaw is set rigidly. "For God's sake, make sure the top table and the director's table get the proper lobsters," he says. "It's my fault, I should have known this menu was too ambitious for four hundred. . . ."

They are working on the Beef Plantagenet, which with luck will be heated in time since the electricity supply is reconnected and the ovens (bar one, which refuses absolutely to oblige) are again functioning. The beef is being carved by harassed chefs, sweat trickling under their white hats on to the food. The foie gras is the finest of its type, rich, thick, smoothly packed with goosey entrails, but is has been overchilled and has to be cut with heated knives. The thinnest slices of foie gras are inserted precisely between the slices of beef. "I'm sure the beef will be OK," says Mr. Rupert to Gustavus, "though there's a lot of work to do. But it's quite straightforward." *If only it were,* he thinks; nothing could be less straightforward. As for the puddings—well, that preparation has not even started, nor has the savory, but after all it's only seven thirty and the guests won't be eating their pudding until ten . . . two and a half hours away, ages, really. . . .

Mr. Rupert thinks Gustavus is OK, but he's not quite convinced: at least he looks self-controlled as he darts around the room, commanding, cajoling, encouraging, sometimes shouting (but not too often). From time to time he's still sipping his glass of water. "At least," he remarks to Mr. Rupert as he runs past, "the tables won't collapse."

"That's one thing that's never ever happened," says Mr. Rupert, in a chuckling sort of way. Being superstitious he tries to touch wood, but finds only Formica.

The entrance hall is full, burstingly, magnificently, richly and sonorously, chatteringly and glitteringly full. Many of the people there see members of the Royal Family repeatedly, some dine or sleep with them, but tonight even the most blasé are caught up in the mood of anticipation. At the front door, where John Winterbotham now stands guard, a little reception party is formed by Sir Lewis and his wife, the Mayor of Lambeth and her husband, and Auberon. Behind them the people being presented are ranged in two lines, while the Head of Special Events, wearing an expression of fierce resentment over her deconstructed and safety-pinned black Lurex evening dress and her gold Wellington boots, is marshaling them backward and forward, slightly to the left and then again a bit to the right, so that they are in the ideal spot. She is making them move around slightly more, perhaps, than she needs to.

For Ted Hoskins, accustomed to such events evening after evening, the prime concern is attention to every detail, to every face that comes close, to the possibility of unforeseen interruption. It's not only the surprise attack he needs to beware, it's the approach by an erratic enthusiast with an unsolicited present or autograph request. Keeping undesirable members of the public away from the royal person is a key element of his job. The ideal event in his view is the one where nobody's present except one uncontroversial foreign head of state and plenty of detectives.

At least this job should be under control, and I've got good close-protection officers in Pete and John. There's not much of a chain gang here for the Principal to deal with, only the Mayor of Lambeth and husband. A bit of flesh to be pressed, we all know the form. No possibility of industrial disputes here—always one of the worst worries—the place is well run. Given how much territory we have to cover and the numbers in the building, I'll have to work hard on eyeballing the Principal, but we know each other so well we can almost always tell what the other's thinking. Not so simple with the Duchess, she has her own little ways, but that's another story. . . . Dinner—wonder who I'll be next to this evening. They're not always so easy, my fellow guests. Some of them like the thought of meeting a genuine detective and want every detail about what it's like working for the royal person, others resent being next to a copper. It's going to be difficult to keep a Purple Corridor in the Great Hall, such a lot of people and not enough space, but we've worked out a reasonable escape route from the staff entrance if all goes horribly bent.

They walk up the outside stairs. *Not a bad crowd, all well behind barriers. Reception party at the top of the stairs. Mayor*

*clearly nervous but heaving with excitement, funny how these Old
Labor types love a royal, it's the New Labor ones who are dodgy.
Sir Lewis and Lady B., know them well. Auberon Booth, not seen
him before. Indoors now. Bit of a rumpus in here, lot of noise, as
usual all goes quiet when we come in. The lighting's a bit strange,
odd on Midsummer Night to have all these candles, they obviously want to make a major splash. John Winterbotham being presented. Give him a wink. Twenty-eight hands to be shaken in the
hall, all the trustees plus others. We'll try to get the Principal
through in four minutes, trouble is he's so good-natured he enjoys
meeting people and spends a lot of time on them. Can't push him
too much. Eight hands shaken, two minutes up, definitely won't
make it on time.*

    *Bit of whispering going on now, but they're mostly engrossed.
Passage between the guests has opened up nicely. All the trustees
chatting hard, the Principal knows a lot of them, makes it harder
to move him onward when he wants to gossip but there's a lot of
ground to cover before we get to the exhibition and HRH wants a
proper look at it, says he enjoys the eighteenth century, lots of things
lent from the Royal Collection. Over halfway down the line now. Is
that woman with the big nose going to try to speak to him? Quick
glance at the equerry whispering in the Principal's ear. Goodness,
the smell in here is overpowering, what are they playing at? Quite a
lively crowd, not all oldies at all, some peculiar dresses, it's odd people don't think they should dress formally for a royal occasion, but
then some of these girls do look pretty gorgeous even if they're showing all that flesh—no complaints about that, mind you. I've often
wondered what would happen if I talked to one or two of these girls
in the way I'd like to. . . . Enough of that, concentrate, Ted . . .*

    *The boss is pretty nearly at the end of the line. We must make sure
we get him out of the room double quick for the next stage. . . . Yes,
he's finished pressing the flesh. Sir Lewis is doing his business, "Sir,*

would you like to . . . ?" and they're away, off down the human corridor, Winterbotham at the head, and out of the door. Two minutes over time, but that's within the allowance. . . .

They've laid out an alternative route to the exhibition, avoiding the crowds, which takes us through all sorts of odd corners. It's very quiet here, strange, low lights, almost like being in a forest with all these odd things looming out at you. God, what dreary places museums are, full of old bits and pieces like exhibits in a law court, though at least there's not much crime around here. Into the main exhibition place, where everything seems in order. Another line of people. Sir Lewis does the honors. Big Japanese man at the front of the queue, Sir Lewis seems keen HRH should talk to him, almost prevents him moving on to the next character, oldish woman, nice face, long red hair. Through the exhibition pretty fast. Stop finally in front of a big picture of a fairyish sort of figure dancing around in a wood, is it a bird or what, or some kind of a poof? They all exclaim with excitement, which is obviously the thing to do—can't see much in old pictures myself. The Principal's asked his opinion by the big Japanese man who seems to have joined the party (rules about not starting a conversation with the Royals have gone completely these days). HRH says, in a jokey sort of way, "Well, is it genuine?" This goes down like a ton of bricks, so then he says, "What a remarkable picture, Reynolds, is it?" When someone whispers to him he says, "Gainsborough, Gainsborough, of course, do you know the great works at Windsor Castle, Mr. Kobayashi?" Mr. Kobayashi seems to like this and says no and HRH says, "Well, we must arrange something, a special tour with the Surveyor of the Queen's Pictures, I know you'd enjoy seeing them." Mr. Kobayashi smiles and rubs his hands and Sir Lewis grins like a Cheshire cat and they all seem happy. We get a talk about this picture, quite a long one, from a little girl in black who seems to be very important here for some reason. Finish the exhibition. Dead on schedule, now. Off to dinner, arrival scheduled for 2030 hours. Everyone's moving correctly into the Great Hall. Trumpeters bursting to do their fanfare.

Meanwhile, back in the exhibition galleries, *Lady St. John*'s been lowered by the handling team on to a wooden trolley. Bill and Anna are in charge of the picture as it's wheeled into a dark side gallery. Friedrich von Schwitzenberg, carrying his infrared lamp, emerges with Jane from the shadows. "How much time do we have?" they ask Bill and Anna.

"Five minutes, sir," Bill replies, grinning nervously. It's all their jobs are worth to be discovered involved in this caper, important though it clearly is.

Friedrich passes the lamp slowly over the surface of the painting. "Very odd, Jane," he says. "I can't see anything. It appears to have no underpainting or restoration at all. Could it be—do you think it could be a completely intact canvas, in perfect condition?" He taps it. "If only I could take it out of its frame . . ."

"No, I'm afraid not, sir," says Bill, looking anxious but conscientious. "We have to take it into the Great Hall in less than two minutes, sir."

"But feel, Jane," says Friedrich, ignoring him, "the canvas layer, it's so thick. When has it been relined?" He scans the picture again and asks that the lights should be put on again. "I wish I could see the edges. And what's this? Jane, what is this? Is it a signature?"

"The picture was never signed, as far as we know," she answers.

"But look at this. It's an initial, tiny, look through my lenses, in the hair on the tail of the dog. *R*, isn't it, and an *S*? Who on earth could that be?"

"That could be, that almost certainly is, Ronnie Smiles," she says.

As they gaze at one another, mystified by this discovery, the head of the picture-handling team and Bill edge deferentially toward them. Friedrich inspires some apprehension among the staff.

"If you don't mind, Jane, Mr. von Schwitzenberg . . ." they say.

"No, no, wait . . ." says he.

"Of course we must go," says she. "And we must move quickly into the Great Hall ourselves, Friedrich, or people will notice we're not there. And we shouldn't go in together."

Friedrich has become very agitated. "What's going on?" he cries, as they hurry down the dimly lit Gallery of Medieval History ("Yes, yes, but do come along, Friedrich," she urges.) "What is the history of this picture?"

He storms his way through the Gallery of Early English History toward the entrance hall. It is strangely quiet, and the blinds over all the windows allow only the dimmest light to penetrate even on this warm, glowing evening. The entrance hall is now almost silent, no guests left there, only a few wenches and swains collecting glasses, removing furniture, picking up nefarious cigarette stubs. From the Great Hall comes a roar of chatter.

"We're awfully late," says Jane. "You go in first, I'll follow."

But in vain. At the entrance to the Great Hall stands John Winterbotham. As he sees them, creeping in like errant children, he nods heavily. "Been busy?" he asks.

"Oh, just some essential details in the exhibition, you know."

"Ah," he says. And he gives, as though humorously, a discomforting smile. "I hope they really were essential. In any case, your movements will have been recorded on camera. It's double security tonight, as you must know."

Jane's spine tingles disagreeably as she gropes her way toward her place on Sheridan, embarrassed that the Great Hall is filled with expensively dressed people milling about and refusing to sit down, that the lights are low, that she has to weave her way through the crowds without looking confused or anxious although she's so obviously late. As she advances with what she hopes is not too much of a scuttle, she turns back to look at Winterbotham. He is following her once again with his eyes, and speaking into his walkie-talkie.

The Great Hall always looks impressive for these dinners, much better lit and more seductive than the galleries that surround it, but this evening it is outstanding. The royal coat of arms above the stage, the garlands on the walls, the tightly structured pyramids of white roses interwoven with mixed foliage on the tables, are bathed in soft, gently flickering light. Each table is lit by an almost completely convincing chandelier with flowers intertwined in the branches, the pools of light creating sociable islands within the surrounding dusk. In the center of the room the life-size statues of True Love and False Love have finally been installed. The two female figures are more beautiful than one would believe possible, extraordinarily lifelike, naked but for a wisp of material around their loins. The colored lights playing over their bodies give them, for a moment, softly blue heads, mauve breasts, scarlet thighs, golden legs until the colors change again. Each table is a little work of art adorned with a portrait (commissioned for the occasion) of the celebrity it is named after, framed in gold and poised at the summit of the floral pyramid. The linen tablecloths and napkins assert their starchy perfection through the mass of silver, the crystal decanters, the little round glass vase of white roses at each place, the stiff hand-illuminated menus. And the royal table is a sight that even the royalest or serenest of highnesses might admire. The table has been set with a Sèvres dinner service made for Louis XV and presented by him to the ancestor of the present noble owner during his embassy in Paris. This descendant has alarmed the staff of his rural priory by agreeing to lend twenty-four complete settings for the dinner. It's good of him, one might suppose, to lend so generously to Sir Lewis, whom he's never met. The rosy pyramids on this table (George III, it's called, in spite of some doubts about the associations) are twice as high as the pyramids on other tables, their peaks disappearing into the darkness. As Auberon notes with some asperity, there's no doubt which is the top table. The tablecloth on George III has been ruched into bows adorned with silk roses, which alternate neatly with the gilt tapestry-covered chairs from the museum's stores. The guest of honor has been given the gilt chair on which a royal duke sat at the coronation of George III, surmounted by a red velvet canopy. The display cases in Late Georgian and Regency have been emptied to provide the most sumptuous table decorations, dominated by the two Paul de Lamerie épergnes, which have been laden with pale green grapes exquisitely arranged by Mirabel Thuillier. It's a table not to be forgotten, and it won't be forgotten—already it's been photographed for two historic-interiors magazines. Competition to sit at this table has been keen, and several also-rans consigned to neighboring tables such as Handel or Gainsborough (where Auberon is) are stealing disconsolate looks at the luxury so close but so remote. The lucky persons admitted to Paradise are preening themselves, chattering with assumed ease about the table's adornments, and effusively introducing themselves to one another as they await the royal arrival.

It is perhaps fortunate that the happy guests cannot see what is happening in Industrial Revolution. Although the lobsters have now all been plated, in the process the correctly stuffed ones have become confused with the semi-decorated lobsters and the not-at-all-decorated lobsters. Mr. Rupert's attempt to sort them out has not been successful. Gustavus is running from beef preparation to lobsters and pleading with the waiter looking after Chatham, where his prospective television producer is sitting, to check that every plate is a perfect one. The waiting staff, all unwilling to give their tables incomplete servings and risk complaints, are surreptitiously replacing B- or C- with A- lobsters on their trays and shaking them about as they do so, while Fred (still persecuted by his mobile) guards the royal crustaceans. As for the beef—well, the beef is ready for the ovens although some of the cuts look as though they've recently been involved in a rugby match.

"He's arriving," the word goes around Industrial Revolution. The trays are finally put in order under Mr. Rupert's stern eye, accompanied by noisy complaints and covert kicking of shins by staff whose A-lobsters have been stolen. "Consistency! For God's sake, keep your tables consistent!" cries Mr. Rupert, though he knows consistency has vanished. "As long as every plate on each table is the same no one will notice, they're too plastered to care." The forty waiters are lined up, so that when Mr. Rupert shouts, "In!" they will enter the hall in a long procession. As they wait, the ones at the front can see the guests standing to greet the royal party, the duke unmistakably tall at their head. The fanfare of trumpets blares through the hall.

The royal party sits down. The royal table sits down. The other tables sit down gradually, like ripples receding on a beach. There is another fanfare of trumpets, and the orchestra strikes up with *The Arrival of the Queen of Sheba*, immediately inaudible in the chatter, which rises like a cresting wave, then abruptly halts as, to a further burst of trumpets, *Lady St. John* is wheeled into the room. The spotlight on the picture follows it along the hall but flickers slightly so that the figure of Puck seems to be moving. Auberon has particularly dreaded this moment—the whole business is so dreadfully unprofessional and theatrical, he's sure colleagues in other institutions will mock, though it does have a certain dramatic effectiveness. In front of the humming expectant hordes, the huge object is lifted on to hooks by the handling crew (dressed in rustic Georgian outfits like Stubbs's peasants) and raised on ropes operated by invisible hands. *Lady St. John* judders a little as she approaches the right height, is lowered again (out of the corner of his eye he notices his chairman staring forward with a fixed grimace), rises once more and is finally steadied—upon which a new floodlight bathes the picture in soft warmth and the trumpets sound yet again. The guests burst into applause. Sir Lewis's grimace broadens into a complacent grin.

No complacency for me, thinks Auberon. *Been to lots of din-*

ners here but never has so much depended on the evening, for me or the museum. I wish I knew nothing about Sir Lewis's plans, not even their outline: what's proposed for Lady St. John *worries me, it's not illegal but the idea of the picture being lent to a Japanese museum for a long period immediately after it's been shown here makes us seem faintly disreputable. What the hell is this bread? Tomato, tarragon, and garlic—for God's sake! Anyway, nowadays can we realistically associate museums or even universities with moral standards or the search for truth? Aren't they commercial operations now? Are moral standards relevant any longer, now that old absolute values have been abandoned? Museums are just extensions of the marketplace, dependent on commercial or political pressures. Why bother with serious issues, when all the public want is interactive videos and period prurience? God, this bread is disgusting, who wants to bite into a chunk of fresh garlic? All I am is an impresario, using scholarship and intellectual integrity like animals in a circus.*

Olivia's at the next table, I can see her if I turn my neck just a little. She looks delicious, the slit up the side of her dress just revealing a hint of that fabulous leg. . . . If I look at her just briefly, now she's turning away from that odious newspaper magnate and opening her bag, she might see me. She's taking out her lipstick . . . she's caught my eye . . . she's smiling faintly and looks a bit embarrassed to be seen attending to her makeup . . . she's blushing. Those few moments in my office this afternoon, such pleasure, such abandon, such closeness, intimacy . . . her suggestion that I should go around next week when the husband's away . . . Shall I? Do I dare? It's potential headline stuff, could ruin my career, then again it could make it. . . . Odd, dinner's taking a long time to arrive, longer than we expect from Angel Cooks.

He has a second sip of white wine, is surprised to see his glass almost empty, he must make sure he doesn't drink too much, though it's wonderfully soothing. But as he begins to let himself feel anxious about the dinner, Mr. Rupert's celebrated grand entrance is again enacted. Led by Mr. Rupert himself, wearing some extraordinary eighteenth-century concoction with a three-cornered hat, the waiters troop in again in their two perfect files.

Auberon turns to his neighbor on his left and amiably opens conversational proceedings. She is one of his favorites among the museum's patrons, a wealthy lady of singular sweetness of disposition, who finds consolation for her widowhood in dispensing large sums of money to her favorite charities and prefers paying for the essential things that other rich people dislike supporting. Such people make the odious business of fund-raising supportable for Auberon.

"You seem anxious," she says.

"I am anxious this evening," he replies. "Of course, it's my job to be anxious—but I'm sorry if it's obvious."

"Probably only to me," she answers. "What are you anxious about? Everything's going swimmingly. You must be delighted."

"I am, of course," he says, and she laughs.

"Exciting about the Nowness of Now," she goes on.

"Mmm," grunts Auberon.

She laughs again. "Are you wanting a modest contribution from me for that one?"

Auberon is not able to reply quite at once.

She looks at him seriously. "Do you think it will happen?" she says. "Of course, you may not be here to deal with it. Do you really want the Bloomsbury?"

So obviously everybody's talking about my application, it's taken for granted. Do I really want the job? Will it mean more of this arti-

ficial hospitality, trading culture for cash, night after night? No doubt at all, it will. . . .

The lobsters arrive. Auberon looks routinely at his plate and again more searchingly. There is a hush as others peer at the menu to see what they're supposed to be eating. Most of the lobsters have a windswept look, as though they had been walking along a beach in a storm, and some have gathered a strangle sprinkling of black dots. "Caviar?" says Auberon's neighbor doubtfully. "With lobster? Gilding the lily, isn't it?" Auberon, realizing he is frowning, pushes up the corners of his mouth and looks at the top table in case of trouble. But Sir Lewis looks contented—the top-table lobsters must be OK.

"Perhaps it's an eighteenth-century way of serving lobster," remarks Auberon lightly. But as he wonders once again how one's supposed to tackle the thing—they never had lobster when he was a child—there's an interruption. From the farther reaches of the hall emerges the tall, white-clad figure of a wild-looking chef, moving at speed. In his hand he holds a plate, his other hand curved protectively around it. Advancing like a flurried Doom from a morality play, he clearly has a target. Auberon knows he should not be staring across the room but feels it's his duty to know what's going on. The target turns out to be a tall residual Bohemian, recognizable as the director of a television production company. The chef seizes this man's plate from under his fork and thrusts the plate he's been holding into its place. The producer stares furiously at the chef, who gives a sickly smile and disappears.

There is further movement from behind the top table. Mr. Rupert, who has been overseeing the service of His Royal Highness, is off.

*   *   *

"Well," says Sir William St. John to Jane, "who'd have thought we'd meet again like this? D'you still see many people from those days?" When she'd stumbled to her table in a flush of embarrassment, she'd known him at once, with the alarmed pleasure felt by those who re-encounter people they knew twenty or thirty years before. She could still see why she'd liked him all those years ago. He looked at her consideringly and gave her a kiss. "I remember you very well, better than you might suppose," he said, and looked at her quite tenderly. *Could she ever have been Lady St. John?* she'd wondered, *and how would it have been?*

"Some," says Jane, "mostly from my college. A frightening number have become senior civil servants, or headmistresses. Tremendously worthy. I went to a Gaudy the other day, it was fun but sad, too. . . ."

"Why was it sad? Just *tempus fugit?*"

Jane does not answer. Instead she says, "What do you feel, seeing *Lady St. John* set up in triumph?"

"Good, this lobster, isn't it?" he replies. "Though mine looks quite different from yours. I seem to have green stuff in mine, spinach, I suppose."

"I've got pink stuff—can it be lobster pâté? I think that's what they intended to put in it."

"Regional variations, I suppose. What do I feel about seeing *Lady St. John* here? Not narked, no, not really. We had our time of grandeur as a family. It's no good looking back."

"I mean—has the picture changed a lot since you last saw it, whenever that might have been?"

He does not answer directly. "To be honest, I was a bit surprised when I saw her again in the exhibition. Hadn't seen the picture, actually, since it was sold to that chap

Denzil Marten, d'you know him? Never quite sure about him. Anyway, it certainly looks different now from how it was at home, not that we ever looked at it, we just kept it in the attic."

"Oh, yes," says Jane eagerly, "in what way different?"

He hesitates before answering. "Shinier, I suppose, and brighter, and just . . . different. Still, Marten was so persuasive . . ."

"I hope you got a reasonable price," remarks Jane innocently.

He smiles. "If you're anxious to know . . ."

"Oh, no, not particularly, I just wondered."

"Since you're such an old friend, I'll tell you . . . but not tonight. It was a useful bit of money, but Marten assured me they'd have to spend a huge amount to make it look OK. I mean, it did look a bit odd, after the fire and all that. I suppose I shouldn't be telling you all this, in fact I had a call from Marten telling me to stay quiet, hadn't realized it was so important. . . ." He looks at his lobster and grunts a little. "Well, to tell you the truth it does make me rather angry to see this performance here tonight, wheeling the picture in for goodness' sake, as though the thing were a sacred icon when it's only my naughty old ancestress who's been through the wars, cleaned up to look expensive."

"It was in poor condition, was it?" ruminates Jane. "You might be interested to know it's now insured by Sir Lewis for ten million pounds." She hopes this will provoke him into indiscretions.

"What?" says Sir William, dropping a little lobster on his shirtfront. "Ten million? Ten million pounds, not dollars? I've been done." His handsome ruddy face clouds over.

"Something's been done, anyway," says Jane.

He broods for a while. "I hope Burslem enjoys it," he says, not very convincingly. "I suppose he's been done, too, in a way. Never liked Marten, shouldn't have trusted him. I'll tell you something, Janie. I mean Jane. Oh, well, to hell with it, Janie. I think this may interest you. The fact is, when I say the picture was not in very good condition . . ." He stops as they hear a muffled sound from offstage, followed by the noise of clattering and shouting. A door closes and the sound is blotted out. Then Sir William is claimed by his neighbor and Jane has to wait.

She looks about her. *In this huge room, amid this theatrical spectacle, four hundred mouths are opening and shutting; eight hundred eyes assessing their surroundings, their table companions, the dresses, the decorations, the lighting, the statues, the hosts, the royal duke, the Gainsborough, the food; four hundred minds seeking amusement, influence, gossip, mention in a newspaper. Are they all enjoying themselves, or deceiving themselves? Lady Burslem, for example, smiling and talking so easily to HRH up at the top table— is she aware of her husband's penchant for dear Helen, now seated (and just why is she at a better table than I am, after all she's considerably my junior at the museum?) next to Mr. Kobayashi to whom she's dutifully cooing? Is Tanya aware that Auberon's fascinated by someone not younger but more glamorous than she is, richer, more smiling, thrillingly unobtainable (I suppose)? What's Alan Stewart thinking about this event, and the possibility of becoming a museum director? And Auberon, who's confused by what's going on in the museum now and doesn't know which side he's on or, indeed, which side is which—what's he experiencing? Does Sir Lewis, surveying the scene from up there, find his moment of triumph as satisfying as he'd hoped? Or is he subject like so many of us—why not be moralistic?—to unease and disappointment over success? And all these other people, concealing so many hopes and ambitions and anxi-*

*eties, so many blossoming and wilting affections beneath their silk
fronts, what are they deriving from this exercise, from all the words
exchanged this evening between these chatterers? God, how many
words will be spoken in this room this evening, at least two million
and most of them garbage or banalities. If only we spoke less and
thought more. . . .* Professor Hilary Ironside beside her claims
her attention with an oblique reference to his most recent
publication and she promptly replies with a flattering allusion, making it clear she has read it.

At other tables they are talking about publications, too. At
Walpole, "What is the next novel about?" Diana asks her
neighbor. He is a successful novelist she has not met
before.

"It's about global warming," he answers. "Ordinary people, humble but serious working people, and how our
planet is being destroyed."

She cannot think of a sensible reply to this. There is a
silence. Then she rallies. "That sounds good," she says wanly.

"As you may or may not know," he says, "my last book was
about the destruction of a family by pedophilia, a father
molesting his daughters and his son, set in a deprived community in the north of England. It was intensely painful to
write."

"It's been very well received, hasn't it?" says Diana, who
has not read the book but has seen a précis prepared by Special Events.

"It's doing well," he says. "I'm afraid it just shows what a
cancer this child abuse thing is. . . . Terrible, terrible . . .
We've sold over forty thousand copies to date, film rights
under negotiation. . . ."

"Your novels are always searing, aren't they?" asks Diana.

He looks huffy. "I hope they're strong but not formulaic."

"No, no," she says. "I mean you always deal with the most difficult problems in a fearless way."

This remark goes down better. "Novels today have to be fearless, don't they?" he ruminates. "And they need to be about ordinary working people, not élitist, privileged people. After the global thing, I'm doing a black saga set in inner-city Manchester. Should be a winner."

"A winner?"

"I mean, it will confront some of the most acute problems of our day, for a broad but thoughtful audience. Look at Dickens—face the problems, get the readers. If you want to change society, it's no good writing endlessly about neurotic women in middle-class suburbs."

Diana has decided she dislikes him quite strongly. "I never read novels," she tells him, "and I'm afraid I've never read any of yours."

"Oh, that's all right," he replies, looking deeply offended. There is a pause. And then, to her amazement, he looks at her body intensely from her chin downward and asks, "Have you got a boyfriend?"

Denzil Marten, sitting next to Helen, is having an easier time. Turning toward the Gainsborough, he remarks, "She looks good, doesn't she?"

"She looks wonderful," says Helen. "Lewis—Sir Lewis—is a great judge of art. It's remarkable, isn't it, in a man who has so many concerns, and has to worry all the time about huge sums of money, that he can give so much attention to pictures?"

"Remarkable," says Denzil. "What do you think of the Gainsborough yourself?"

"It's superb, one of the finest of his later—period portraits," she says.

He looks at her sharply. "Oh, good, I'm glad you like it. You must come into the gallery one day and have a look at my stuff," he says.

"Sir Lewis tells me you have beautiful things," she answers politely. "He speaks very highly of you, says he can always trust your advice. I'd love to come in."

"Come and have a spot of lunch. We do quite a nice little lunch at the gallery." He looks at her sideways, charmed by her long sleek body and the heavy black eyelashes adorning her pale face under the shining black hair coiled on her head. *She's like a fox,* he thinks, *there's something feral about her, under all that clever poise.* He'd like to put his hand on her knee and work it slowly upwards. . . .

There seems to be a lot going on in this room, Ted Hoskins considers, *more than I'd expect of this sort of dinner. And speaking of the dinner, that lobster was a bit rough—mine looked as though it had been struck by a blunt instrument. It still hasn't been cleared, but at least they've poured the red wine—pity I can never touch a drop at these events—let's hope the beef is coming soon, we're slipping behind schedule. Odd, that chef appearing from the kitchen, what on earth was that about? And why is John Winterbotham running around, taking messages to someone, looks like that man Bankes we met in the exhibition, and why's Bankes standing up and leaving the hall? Don't like this kind of unexpected activity. The Principal, though, is having a good time . . . chatting away to Her Ladyship . . . Must keep on talking to my neighbor, wife of the chairman of a large company, about her travel plans and what the Principal did when he went to Canada recently and her children's school and my own children. . . . What on earth's happened to that beef? We've been waiting ten minutes now. One thing the Principal does get cross about is being kept waiting, and the schedule's pretty tight, we must be home by twelve-fifteen, we may have to cut the pageant—no great disaster, though the kids will be disappointed—and I have to drive home, but of course that's the least important thing. . . . Lovely girl three places down on my left, wish I could give her a lift home. . . .*

Lucian is sitting next to a woman who's unimportant except that her husband's one of the richest men in England. On her other side is the secretary of a large grant-making trust, whom he's keen to charm. He has to talk across the uninteresting lady (while pretending to include her in the conversation, which annoyingly she wants to participate in) to the man in his sights, while trying to suppress his anxiety over the progress of the interesting little plan he's involved in. On Lucian's other side is Baroness Shawe, who's negligible politically just now but might wield influence if the government changes. He needs to give her adequate attention and laugh moderately at her quips while not seeming too friendly (facing him on the next table is a government minister who could have a major impact on his own future). This evening he finds Lady S. not too bad, in fact—there's a certain vigor to her dark features that is almost appealing, and he's never minded a faint mustache on a woman. On her other side sits a business friend of the chairman, who also needs attention, and could be touched for money. All this requires concentration and more's needed for his struggle with his lobster. (What on earth is Angel Cooks up to? His looks as though it's just arrived economy class from Tokyo.) In the midst of all this he's surprised to find John Winterbotham leaning over his chair. John wants a word, urgently. When Lucian returns to the table five minutes later and Baroness Shawe asks in a jolly way if anything is wrong, he has to reply, "Nothing that can't be sorted out, I hope. A little security problem." But he looks furious.

Meanwhile Sir William has just finished his story to Jane. "My God!" says Jane, and stares at him in horror. "How disgraceful—everything except the dog—how ironic!" She feels almost inclined to laugh, though when she catches the eye of Lucian resting on her from two tables away she does not feel amused at all.

Ronnie Smiles and Mirabel Thuillier are on Hume ("Who was Hume, anyway?" says Ronnie. "Oh, really? Wish I could have had someone a bit more rococo—like Madame de Pompadour"). They have finished discussing the decorations and Mirabel has successfully revealed no trade secrets at all. They have enjoyed a satisfying (though loyal) gossip about Sir Lewis and Lady Burslem, with only the most discreet giggled references to his love life. "Did you see the nice young lady's sitting on the royal table?" Ronnie burbles. "A bit brazen, isn't it? But then Elizabeth's so good about it, I don't really think she minds, do you?"

"She'd have an awful life if she did," chuckles Mirabel, "but you know the funny thing is how well the two of them get on, they're really happy, you should see them choosing curtains together. . . ."

"How are things going on the royal table?" asks Ronnie. "I can't really see from here."

Mirabel, trying to suppress her rage that she's not sitting there (when she's worked so hard and given them a substantial trade reduction), peers toward it. "HRH was talking to Elizabeth," she says. "Now he's moved on to the woman on his other side. . . . Lewis—well, Lewis is not looking very relaxed, poor man, I suppose it's because he has to make a speech. But he seems to be having a nice time with Lady St. John, who looks good—I suppose it must be the candle-light."

"Very odd, this lobster, isn't it?" says Ronnie. "It tastes all right but my claw seems to be filled mostly with spinach."

"Mine's mostly lobster pâté, no spinach at all," says Mirabel. "I wonder why they don't take the plates away, time's going by. Perhaps that's why Lewis looks unrelaxed."

In the Gallery of the Industrial Revolution, people are unrelaxed, too. The power supply for the ovens has failed, apparently irreversibly. The beef is as ready as beef could be, the foie gras perfectly layered between the slices of meat. The vegetables are done, the sauces prepared. But they are all stone cold. Fred has hurled his mobile phone into the corner of the room where it has hit one of the wrapped-up museum objects with a disturbing thud, and is shouting, "Fuck! Fuck! Fuck!" Gustavus is not to be seen. There is an uneasy silence.

The chefs and the waiting staff cluster around Mr. Rupert. *This is a moment for decision,* he thinks. It is possibly the worst moment of his life: he's lost control. "Well, the show must go on," he says, in a cheerful manner. "We must serve the food cold. Say nothing to anybody, no apologies, no explanations. From now on, a cold entrée is what was always planned, cool food for a hot evening."

Fred stops saying, "Fuck," and instead asks, "What do we say to Sir Lewis?"

"Nothing," says Mr. Rupert. "Leave that to me. If the

rest of the evening goes well, he won't really mind and he'll mind even less when I cut fifty percent off the bill. OK, everybody? Lobster away. Claret's poured. Then it's Beef Plantagenet frappé. And where the hell is Gustavus?"

The waiters are in line. The doors open. "We haven't told the trumpeters we're ready," cries Fred, one of whose many jobs it is to coordinate the music with the dinner. He is distracted just now by his wife's extremely clear-cut pronouncement that unless he is back home within an hour she is leaving with the children and going to her mother's, probably forever. With their silver dishes held with one hand above their heads, the forty waiters advance into the Great Hall, announced a minute later by an only slightly ragged fanfare of trumpets. Mr. Rupert, trying not to look conspicuous but hampered by wearing an enormous ribboned wig and a silver court dress coat, remains close to the service door, not anxious to be behind Sir Lewis when the plates of cold beef arrive. It's not long before he's summoned to the high table by a po-faced footman. As he walks he looks ahead to gauge the mood of the great man. It seems curiously subdued. The flashing eyes and whirling hands of the chairman's worst moments are not in evidence.

Instead he's confronted by a slightly menacing jocularity, possibly considered more suitable in mixed society.

"Ah, Mr. Rupert!" says Sir Lewis, turning in his chair and speaking with sinister softness. "Anything wrong in the kitchen? Some of the lobsters looked as though they'd been hit by a hurricane."

"Yes, Sir Lewis." Better not to offer an explanation.

"And the beef is cold."

Make something up? Tell him this was a period touch? Admit the truth? Blame someone else?

"The power failed. I'm very sorry. There was nothing we could do."

"No emergency generator?"

"The emergency generator failed, too. Everything failed." Judicious pause. "You might speak to the museum staff about it."

A nasty one for Sir Lewis, though he isn't prepared to acknowledge the fact. He maintains his savage smile, but he's silenced for a moment.

"The beef's disgusting, cold. We shall have to review our long-standing relationship, Mr. Rupert."

Mr. Rupert cannot bring himself to be courtly. "With great pleasure, Sir Lewis," he says.

Lady St. John, sitting beside Sir Lewis, shows signs of wanting to listen to the conversation. Sir Lewis flicks his hand imperiously to dismiss Mr. Rupert and turns to her urbanely, remarking that cold food is so appropriate for a warm evening. Mr. Rupert leaves, telling himself that nothing will persuade him to work for this horrible old party again. He feels, all the same, that he has to explain himself to Auberon.

Auberon is clearly not enjoying his beef. "This meat is not one of your great successes, Mr. Rupert," he says. But seeing—to his amazement—tears welling into the eyes of the great caterer, he goes on, "Not your fault. Idiotic menu for this number of people, anyway. And the canapés were delicious."

"Thank you, I appreciate that," says Mr. Rupert.

As he speaks, a waitress runs up to him. "Mr. Rupert," she says, "there's been a disaster. I mean, there's a little problem.

I mean, we need you—we need you urgently. Gustavus . . . Gustavus . . ." But she is unable to say what is so serious about Gustavus.

"What about Gustavus?" asks Mr. Rupert. He reminds himself that in the army much worse things could happen. "What about Gustavus?"

"He's . . . he's rather tired."

"We're all rather tired," says Mr. Rupert. "What's special about his tiredness?"

"Well," she says, "he's fallen into the raspberry coulis. The coulis in the big vat. He doesn't seem to be able to get out. In fact, he seems to have passed out."

"Will you excuse me?" Mr. Rupert asks Auberon.

The dinner remains buoyant, more or less, sustained by the rivers of alcohol. Not many people mind particularly that the beef is cold, since the menu does not suggest it should be hot. The claret chosen by Sir Lewis is of such spectacular quality and poured with such generosity that merriment spreads uncontrollably. *Are we just drunk?* Auberon wonders. *Is the sociability we think we're enjoying artificial?* He does not like the way this conviviality is presided over—ironically, as he sees it—by the portrait of Lady St. John. In the golden spotlight, her teasing smile seems to quiver, her eyes to interrogate him, the wooded hinterland behind her is more mysterious than ever. Looking at her, he sees in her features—for the first time—the pure beauty of Olivia Doncaster.

His attention is torn away from the portrait by new activity. John Winterbotham has reappeared. He is moving purposefully toward someone—who? Jane? He is speaking to her, holding the back of her chair as though to help her. She

does not seem eager to move. He looks insistent, even bullying. She is standing up, she is leaving . . . What on earth? He
hides a lump of foie gras under his knife and fork and asks
his neighbours to excuse him. As he stands up, Lucian
appears at his elbow.

"We had to ask Jane, as chief curator, to come and look at
something in the exhibition, Auberon," he says. "Small matter of conservation, slight damage to an object, reported by
my staff. Just thought it should be attended to immediately."

"Shouldn't I come?" asks Auberon.

"Oh, no, no need at all," says Lucian. "Just a little problem with a manuscript, nothing serious. It's all under
control."

The entrée is not under control. Piles of beef and foie gras,
of discarded vegetables, congeal on the plates of the four
hundred guests. Over the stiff white tablecloths red stains
and little heaps of salt appear. People are leaning back, tilt-
ing their chairs and talking to friends at neighboring tables,
fingering the flowers in the huge table decorations, resting
their hands not just on the backs of chairs but on the backs
of their neighbors. More than one hand, it seems, has wandered into a nearby lap. More than one cigar has been illic-
itly lit. More than one bread roll has been tossed, and tossed
back. There is a sense of bubbling anarchy.

Ted Hoskins isn't happy. *This is getting out of hand, the
party's loosening up too much. And we're way behind schedule.* He
catches the eye of the Principal, who raises his eyebrows and
rotates his left wrist as though to indicate the time. Ted nods
and shrugs. But at last something's happening: Sir Lewis is
walking toward the microphone.

*   *   *

Sir Lewis hates the annual general meetings at Burslem Properties unless no questions are asked; only if the audience is silent can he begin to savor his powerful position at the center of the platform. He equally abominates having to attend the Friends' AGM at the museum, when all sorts of fuzzy history enthusiasts not wearing suits ask unexpected questions. Even today, at the apogee of his triumph, at an event which (he is confident) should help him toward the title he's deserved for many years, he'd much sooner not be making a speech. But a speech must be made—first by him as chairman, then by the Royal Guest, then again by him as sponsor of the exhibition, and finally by the director. His speeches have been rewritten and rehearsed many times, and contain a number of jokes and one startling announcement.

The first speech goes well. He proclaims the success of the museum and the exhibition, thanks the lenders, thanks the patrons, thanks the sponsors (loud applause, here), thanks the designer, "the incomparable Mirabel Thuillier." He says a few words about the importance of exhibitions to the museum, how they are its lifeblood. He announces—to even louder applause—that that very afternoon the board of trustees has agreed to commission a feasibility study on a new project, the Nowness of Now, and—to tumultuous applause—that £14 million has been raised already. Then (more confident in the face of so much clapping) he lowers his voice, and with more expressions of gratification than it seems possible to crowd into a minute, welcomes the Royal Guest.

The Royal Guest is an accomplished speaker, and his private secretary an accomplished speechwriter. His lead joke is genuinely funny and the laughter hesitates for a second, as though surprised at the idea of being spontaneous. Many more thanks, many more congratulations, many more references to the excellence of the museum and the dinner (only one or two slightly hollow laughs at this). The guests burst into cheers.

There is a further fanfare of trumpets. In the distance the waiters reemerge like a row of clockwork dolls, carrying above their heads large silver platters laden with cheese. From his seat on the platform Auberon can see a tall figure dash toward them, waving its arms. The front waiters stop, the waiters behind don't. The liveries sway and push and curse, metal clatters on the parquet floor, and hundreds of kilos of Queen Victoria's Cheese Platter hit the floor. The waiters retreat higgledy-piggledy through the service door, leaving the trampled cheese behind them.

Sir Lewis stands up again. He is so happy to be supporting this exhibition, which he'd have wanted to sponsor even if he hadn't been Chairman of the Trustees. It's given him a wonderful opportunity to help the museum . . . and such a chance for his company . . . the largest property company in the UK, extensive interests in Australia, New Zealand, et cetera, bringing architecture and building together . . . Burslem Properties, "dedicated to people, dedicated to quality . . . We look forward," he concludes, "to another wonderful millennium for Britain." Bow, smile, wave of the hand, second bow, he sits down at the back of the stage. Thunderous reception from the audience.

It's the director's turn. A lot of speeches tonight, think the guests, as they slip out for a discreet visit after all that wine. Auberon thanks his staff and his chairman. He gives a brief account of the exhibition's themes and academic purposes. He does not mention *Lady St. John*—she's written into his speech, but he's sick of her. He also sits down to loud clapping. From the corner of his eye he can see Lord Willins of Plympton, clapping hard. Bloomsbury looks a step closer.

The applause dies down and the speakers return to their seats. It's time for the community pageant, the moment nobody in the audience has been looking forward to. Announced by yet another fanfare of trumpets, several tiny children dressed as flowers run on to the stage and burst into a pretty song. But for only a moment, since a voice, a much louder voice than all of theirs put together, interrupts them.

"Shut up!" the voice shouts at the children. Aggrieved, or possibly not understanding him, they sing rather louder. "Shut up, you little bastards." This person is evidently not fond of children. The audience hisses at his brutality. The children hesitate, several burst into tears, and the singing peters out. The pageant has not started well. The tiresomely insistent voice goes on. "Sir Lewis, tell us about the Gainsborough. Hasn't the picture been dramatically restored? Isn't most of it done by restorers? Isn't all this fuss sheer hype?"

Sir Lewis waves his hands distractedly in the air. "What?" he says. "Be quiet! No questions, please!"

"Answer me," shouts the voice. The guests stir and crane and chatter and try to spot the speaker. It's a man, but who? Youngish, in a black shirt, intense, anxious-looking, determined—who the hell is this?

"Isn't it true," he says, "that you're sending the picture to Japan, and making lots of money out of the deal for yourself? This whole event's a promotion exercise for your property. Can you deny that?"

*   *   *

Ted Hoskins is looking in the direction of the Principal, who just for the moment is pretending to be happy with this development. *This is not going well, not one bit. He'll be wanting to leave soon, we'll have to get out of the place as discreetly as we can.*

"Shush, shut up," cry some of the guests, but not many, since this interruption is compensating splendidly for the deficiencies of the dinner as well as halting the pageant.

Tense moment for Auberon. He loves to see Sir Lewis embarrassed and floundering. He's fairly confident of being able to deal with Valentine Green better than his chairman can, even though he's not quite sure what Valentine is suggesting. But the general atmosphere is not promising.

The children on stage try once again to burst into their song and dance routine ("We have a mania, For dear old Britannia"). Auberon pushes them gently but firmly offstage. They look fiercely resentful and one or two utter some very unflowerlike words as they go.

"D'you want to speak?" he asks Sir Lewis.

"No," says Sir Lewis. "Get rid of the man."

Auberon takes hold of the microphone and says, in a jolly way, "I'm sorry, everybody, this is not a press conference, it's a dinner. Some journalists never know when to stop!" There is some uncertain laughter, which halts when John Winterbotham and one of his men take Valentine by the arms.

"Go on, Auberon," he shouts, as they drag him off, "you tell them, you tell them about the Gainsborough. . . . Let me go, this is a free country, let me go, you pigs. . . ." but a guard places a hand over his mouth and he is led out of the room.

"Thank God," says Sir Lewis. "Intolerable . . ."

"Don't thank God yet," says Auberon, as the voices in the

Great Hall rise in a raucous crescendo. To a further fanfare of trumpets, strong, confident, and extremely loud, the line of waiters, their liveries slightly crumpled now and some of their wigs missing or at a strange jaunty angle, reemerge with their platters above their heads, heaped this time with fruit. They are greeted by thin applause and a few jeers. "Shall we go back to our seats?" Auberon asks his chairman, noticing uneasily that at the royal table movement is going on. A large solid-looking man has mounted the dais and is whispering into the ear of the Royal Guest. The Royal Guest has stood up and now advances to shake the hands of the chairman (who looks like a disappointed child) and the director (who doesn't). The large man and His Royal Highness vanish. They are followed a moment later by the minister, who does not shake any hands. *Oh, God, there goes our grant-in-aid increase,* thinks Auberon furiously.

Jane has disappeared and Valentine has been taken away, Diana realizes. *Goodness knows what they've done with them. I may be the next to be spirited away. And some of the most important people are leaving. I have to do something, say something—it has to be done now, in public, at the dinner, we can't rely on action tomorrow, which might be suppressed, just as we might be. . . .*

Auberon is completely confused by these developments. *Have I been deceived by the chairman?* he asks himself. *Is this stuff of Valentine's justified?* But his thoughts are interrupted by another loud proclamatory voice. *It's like a meeting of the Seventh Day Adventists, this dinner,* he thinks. *Who now?* A clear female voice . . .

"When it gets to Japan, the Gainsborough is being sold by Sir Lewis," the voice says. "Sir Lewis has made an arrangement with Mr. Kobayashi, to sell him the Gainsborough for twelve million pounds."

Sensation.

Sir Lewis seizes the microphone. "This is rubbish," he says. "I have no intention . . . I mean, nothing has been decided—anyway, the picture belongs to me. . . ."

Auberon realizes who the speaker is. Diana—competent, calm Diana. Why on earth? And where does she get this strange information from? Can this stuff conceivably be true?

"And what is more . . ." she is saying, when Lucian jumps out of his chair and seizes her from behind by the arms, in an intimate yet threatening gesture.

"Enough!" he shouts. "Enough!"

Around them the guests are being plied with seasonal berries by the waiters, by now determined to deliver their wares. Many of the guests are standing and whispering incredulously to one another.

"Let me go, Lucian!" Diana cries. "There's more to say. This is where the money for the Nowness of Now is coming from, not from anyone's generosity. And Lucian Bankes is involved, for a huge fee. Let me go, Lucian!" she shrieks, as he grips her neck. He releases her, he stares around him at the gaping faces. He scuttles to an emergency exit and disappears.

Sir Lewis's blood is now as up as blood can be. He shouts into the microphone, causing acute pain to the ears of the people nearest the loudspeakers. "Yes, yes, yes, it's true," he bellows. "Yes, I am selling the picture, and I'm proud of it. It's my picture. I've a right to sell it. I'm not selling it for myself, but for this museum. Yes, for the museum. From this sale I'm making a donation of ten million pounds for the Nowness of Now. I wanted it to be a secret, but since I'm being treated like a criminal, I want my generosity to be properly acknowledged, not vilified by an ignorant reporter."

Auberon takes the microphone and tries to think of something dynamic to say. He fails. What should they all do? Sit down? Pretend nothing has happened? Eat their pudding and propose toasts?

"Let's get off the platform," says Sir Lewis to Auberon. "This is all new to you, Auberon; I should have told you, but there are one or two complications, export licenses and so on, I would have preferred to keep it quiet. Anyway, it's all out now. . . ." There is a triumphant yet faintly manic look in his eye. Auberon, mystified, stays quiet.

But as they make for the steps, they're again prevented. Through the door from the entrance hall bursts an Amazon, long red hair flowing behind her, green velvet dress torn at the arm. Behind her run two men in security uniforms. As they enter the Great Hall they stop, embarrassed by the hundreds of eyes on them.

"Get away!" Jane shouts. "Get away, leave me alone. I've something to show you. All of you, all of you here. . . ." and she advances like a warrior of ancient times toward the platform. So rapidly yet majestically does she move, with such disheveled assurance, that nobody dares stop her. The chatter hushes: the only sound comes from the last plates of dessert being smashed on to the disordered tables by the furious waiters.

Jane mounts the stage. "I am Jane Vaughan,' she cries, in a thrilling tone. Mrs. Siddons would have admired her. "Jane Vaughan, chief curator of this museum. I have something to tell you all. It's about the Gainsborough. This picture we've all been admiring, this masterpiece, it's hardly a Gainsborough at all. It's the pretence of a Gainsborough!"

Sir Lewis is back on the platform. "It is not a pretense," he says, in a strange panic-stricken voice. "It's a great masterpiece. It's a top masterpiece by one of the greatest British artists, Sir Thomas Gainsborough."

"Maybe it once was," she says, "but not any more. Friedrich!" she calls.

Friedrich von Schwitzenberg is on the platform beside her. "We have good evidence," he says, "that this picture has been so much restored that it is hardly the work of Gainsborough."

"No!" cries Sir Lewis. "Don't damage my beautiful Gainsborough. No, no, no!"

"I won't damage it," says Friedrich, "at least, not the original picture. Look!" He stands on a chair. And with a scalpel he cuts, vigorously, the top and sides of the painting. The piece of canvas on which the image is supported rolls slowly forward. There is a groan from the audience, such as you might hear at a public execution. Auberon finds himself giving a feral gasp, high and warbling. He tries to restrain himself, and notices he is not succeeding.

"Look!" cries Jane. "There's the Gainsborough underneath, the real Gainsborough."

Under the fine intact canvas which supports the glossy portrait of Lady St. John, is now exposed another canvas. It is black, mottled, with great ridges and cracks—hardly a picture at all. Only in the bottom left-hand corner can an image be recognized: it is a dog, a noncommunicative greyhound, with its tail slightly drooping.

"Different, isn't it?" cries Jane mockingly. "That's the picture that was going to be sold to Japan for twelve million.

That's all that's left of the Gainsborough, after fire damage. It's hardly worth twelve pounds."

There is a strangled scream from the top table. The scream is in Japanese and few people can understand it precisely, but it is generally clear that Mr. Kobayashi is very upset indeed. Then there is no more sound from Mr. Kobayashi.

Into the appalled silence Jane looses a few more words. "They stuck a new canvas on to the old one and painted the picture again," she announces, to the world in general. "This isn't Gainsborough 1780, it's Ronnie Smiles 1990." She laughs cruelly. "What price Ronnie Smiles now?"

She stands triumphant as Sir Lewis, staggering toward her, clutches his side, utters the words, "My Gainsborough . . . my Gainsborough . . ." and falls heavily onto the floor.

At this moment the two statues of False Love and True Love, who have been extremely well trained by their agency and have remained immobile for the past three hours, decide they have endured enough. They step down gracefully from their pedestals and leave the room.

THE BOARDROOM, 2 A.M.

Only a moment ago Angel Cooks was still in action clearing the Great Hall and the Gallery of the Industrial Revolution under the weary but still decisive command of Mr. Rupert. Fred, having disappeared for an hour or so ("I'm sorry, I had to go, it was Samantha, major crisis. . . . No, I was able to sort things out, she's fine. . . ."), returned and seemed calmly detached as he assessed the damage to the new tablecloths. Gustavus, recumbent in the coulis for three hours, awoke dripping with scarlet juice but with a beaming face. "Was I asleep for a minute? It was all that vodka," he proclaimed joyously. "If it's really good quality it knocks you out but you feel fine when you wake up. So, where are we at, how's the dessert doing? Oh . . . oh, God . . ." as he recalled the events of the evening. A moment or two later, changed into his Vatel outfit, he reverted to cheerfulness, as though relieved of a burden. He was remarking to Fred, "Ah, well, no television programs for little Gustavus just yet," when a call came through on Fred's ever-busy mobile, inviting him to participate in a program on chefs' disasters the following day. He said, "No," and then, a second later, "Yes." As Fred and Gustavus were leaving the room, Fred caught Gustavus's eye. Gustavus rolled both eyes in return. Fred giggled, Gustavus giggled louder, and the two of them burst into an orgy of uproarious laughter. "The beef," they cried, "and the foie fucking gras," and "You should have seen yourself lying in the coulis," and Fred was vividly describing the waiters' repeated attempts to serve the pudding ("without any coulis, but it didn't matter a toss because everybody was shouting and nobody wanted the fucking stuff") when they were quenched by Mr. Rupert. "Come along, boys, it's been a long night," he said. "I just hope it's not the last night Angel Cooks are ever employed." Now, after the last slamming door, the last laugh, the last flurry of lipstick-stained napkins retrieved from dark corners, the Great Hall is swept and quiet.

*   *   *

The human detritus was more difficult to manage. It took quite a while to remove Sir Lewis. Diana was able to dispatch her Jonathan with a few curt words ("Too much to worry about, can't come back with you now"—"Wouldn't it cheer you up to come home?"—"No, it wouldn't, I don't need cheering up thank you, and I have professional responsibilities, too, you know," though as she snapped out the words she regretted being so disagreeable). It needed much longer to clear most of the guests, who milled around discussing the evening's mysterious events and fingering the torn remnants of the Gainsborough. Only when the lights were turned on at full strength did the sign of their raddled friends persuade them to move on. On the way out they were bemused to be offered party favors, neat little bags containing scent and catalogs and postcards of *Lady St. John* and information about Burslem Properties, even though the exhibition posters showing the now discredited face were already being taken down.

Despatching the guests was complicated by the suspension of John Winterbotham. At this delicate moment, he was thought to be too closely involved in the plot to continue his duties. He was told to stay in the control room under the supervision of his own staff—the ultimate insult, as far as he was concerned—before being sent home. Ian, who took his place, disliked this obligation and was even sorry for him. They had a little conversation in the control room a while ago. "I thought I was doing the right thing," said John. "Sir Lewis is the boss here, after all. I was doing what he wanted, wasn't I? They told me Jane Vaughan and the rest of them were trying to create mischief, so I kept an eye on them." Ian shrugged and offered him a cigarette, a wholly forbidden action in the museum. "I mean," John went on, "how was I to know Sir Lewis was planning to sell a picture to Japan, and even if he was . . . well . . ." He took the cigarette. "I mean, when you're trying to do your best for the place you work for . . ."

It was Lucian's movements that particularly interested Diana, now acting Head of Exhibitions. She was to begin her duties at six in the morning. Had she got rid of him at last? What's more, he was no longer a rival for Hermia, who in any case can't have liked him much. . . . She noticed that Helen, who was surely implicated in Sir Lewis's plans, hadn't dashed out of the room like Lucian, but made an elegant withdrawal with all the other guests. Perhaps she wasn't seriously implicated, in spite of appearances? Or was she just being very cool about it all?

As soon as the guests began to shift, the trustees and senior staff convened in the boardroom. "Like the last meeting of the provisional government in the Winter Palace, isn't it?" remarked Alan Stewart, as they fell into chairs or leaned wearily against the paneling, "though let's hope not equally disastrous." John Percival, as acting chairman, called them to order. The exhibition would proceed as planned, he announced, obviously minus *Lady St. John*. All the posters and publicity material showing her image would have to be withdrawn and destroyed, and replaced with another image immediately. A press release would be issued the following morning. "The show must go on," they all said sagely.

"I offer my resignation," Auberon announced vigorously. "I think I should leave."

"Your offer is not accepted," said Percival. "But we'll want to consider what's happened very closely. Clearly, serious mistakes have been made. Of course there'll be many questions to be asked—particularly why nobody spotted that there was a problem with the picture much earlier. I think I speak for everybody in saying you have our confidence." And they all nodded, all except Mrs. Hobson, who treated Auberon to one of her hatred looks.

The telephone rang and Mary Anne answered it. A moment later—"It's the *Daily Telegraph*. They want a story at once—every paper in the country is trying to reach us. Will you speak to them, Mr. Percival?" And half to herself, she breathed ecstatically, "The attendances are going to be sensational."

"Very well," Percival answered. "Auberon, you and I must issue a joint statement."

"And there's a television crew on the way, should we let them in? I hardly ever get television for anything positive," Mary Anne muttered, "but let's make the most of it."

"Someone told me," said Auberon, "that Ronnie Smiles is the press's new rogue hero, and has given six interviews already. He's billed as the new Tom Keating."

"Little creep," said Jane.

"Ah, Jane," remarked Percival, "outspoken as ever. We owe you a special thank-you."

"And Diana, too," she said stoutly.

"And Diana, too. Many congratulations. We won't forget what you've both done. Very incorrect procedurally, of course, but then there was some pretty incorrect behavior going on here, wasn't there? We have some tricky days ahead of us, ladies and gentlemen, but I'm sure BRIT will survive."

The telephone rang again, and Auberon answered it. He

spoke for a little while. As he put the receiver down, he said, "That was a surprise call. It was Lucian Bankes."

"Lucian Bankes!" they exclaimed. "Where is he?"

"He's at the front desk. He said he was on his way to Dover when he realized how foolish he'd been. He said he'd disgraced the museum he loved. He wants to apologize, and face the consequences of his behavior."

They gaped at him.

"And he's on his way up to the boardroom, if that's OK by you."

"Shall we drink a toast?" suggested Trevor Christiansen.

"To the Nowness of Now?" asked somebody.

"To the Thenness of Then," someone replied.

AROUND LONDON, 3 A.M.

Bill and Anna are asleep, together. They were brought even closer by their joint adventure, notably their information to Ian, which had such unexpected consequences, and their release of Jane and the others from the Medieval Manuscripts store in which they had been locked. When they finally went off duty at 2 A.M., it seemed natural for Bill to ask if Anna would like to be escorted home, and natural for Anna to agree, and natural for Anna to ask Bill in for a nightcap, and even more natural for them to subside onto Anna's futon almost as soon as they were inside. It will surprise them when they wake in the morning to find that they fell asleep immediately in each other's arms, and are almost fully dressed.

*   *   *

Diana is at home, her hair rather on end, too tired to take off the dress that has earned her so much admiration. She is excited to be appointed acting Head of Exhibitions. She is exhilarated that Jane has triumphed, and even more so that Lucian has vanished. But as for Hermia—well, she does not know about Hermia. When the state of the painting was exposed, Diana felt a strange uncertainty. Was she really in love with Hermia, and was Hermia in the least bit attracted by her? As she stood motionless among the confusion of the Great Hall, she found Hermia beside her. She said, since it seemed the only thing she could say, "Do you have a lover?"

Hermia replied, "That's a very old-fashioned saying. Yes, of course I have a boyfriend, but he is in Milano, why do you ask?"

Suppressing her flooding disappointment, Diana asked, "Do you still want to be my friend?"

Hermia answered delphically, "You are a wonderful person, Diana. I admire you so much." What was one to make of that?

Now back in her little flat, she contemplates her diamonds and pearls with disgust. *Better paste than these glittering rocks, paste that at least doesn't pretend to have value. Do I understand myself any better than I did before today? Will I go back to Jonathan and his like, to unenthusiastic affairs with uninteresting men? Or have I really changed? Am I—yes, am I—liberated?*

The telephone rings. Who can this be? "Diana," says the voice, "it is Hermia. I cannot sleep. I had to ring you up. . . ."

Jane, meanwhile, sits in her study, still in her torn green velvet, unable to contemplate bed. This—ah, this—is indeed a moment when a lover is needed. But, then, so many moments are. She looks at her books with a cold eye. She looks at the catalog of *Elegance,* still open where she left it this morning—what on earth will they do with the sixty thousand copies they printed with such pride, all worthless and laughable now? She thinks about the way she behaved today. Was she courageous? Foolhardy? Is this what her grandfather, the general, would have done? And what about the chairman—or ex-chairman, probably? He can't have known that the picture was a fraud—she's almost sorry for him. She feels overcome by a sense of anticlimax and gloom. In three hours she'll have to go back to the museum, to repair some of the damage, but now she can't bring herself to go to bed.

The telephone rings. Auberon. "Jane," he says, "I'm sorry to ring you at this nocturnal hour, have I woken you up?"

"No," says Jane, "I can't sleep at all."

"Nor me," says Auberon. "But I wanted you to know how pleased the trustees are with you. Much more than they are with me, actually, which isn't surprising."

"But you haven't done anything wrong," she says.

"I haven't done anything right, either. After you'd left, Percival said I was to ask if you'd consider accepting the position of Deputy Director, for a period of five years."

"What do you mean?" she cries. "I'm due to retire, you know that."

"Not if you take that job, you aren't," he answers. "No reply needed for a while. Just thought I'd let you know."

When he has put down the receiver, she thinks, *Deputy Director? Five years! The little house in Oxford delayed for three and a half more years! This calls for brandy. I certainly won't accept this offer.* She has some brandy. *Well, maybe I will.* She drinks a little more. *On the other hand, do I want to work for those trustees? Do I really care about the place, after all this? Is there any point in working oneself stupid for a bunch of self-seeking ignoramuses?* And she drinks just the tiniest drop extra, and goes to bed undecided.

No telephone calls and no brandy in the Burslems' flat. Lady Burslem has returned only minutes before from the hospital. Lewis's heart attack was a mild one, and he will be home in a day or two. Of course she will be there to look after him. She sits at her dressing table for a long time, brushing her hair, and looks at herself pitilessly in the glass. Then she tears her tiara from her head and hurls it violently at her husband's Renoir. Both suffer damage—the Renoir, on balance, rather more.

Auberon, in his elegant bedroom, still in his evening clothes, still too stimulated to sleep, lets his mind range over the day. Does he want to stay at the museum, after all this? Doesn't he look like a public idiot? Will anyone respect him? Is it worth his while going to the interview at Bloomsbury? Will anyone take him seriously?

He throws off his tailcoat and does not pick it up from the floor. *Not like me to do that,* he notes. And does he really love Olivia, isn't that a fantasy? Tanya was so kind and supportive this evening, so gentle when she found him. How had she guessed where he was, having a little cry in his office? Has he been wrong about Tanya? Has he been deceiving himself over Olivia, just as he's been deceived over so many other things? Isn't he a fool, gullible, easily distracted, unserious? Hasn't he been seduced by glamor, and forgotten the questions that absorbed him when he was young? When this business has sorted itself out, shouldn't he take a good serious look at himself? He lifts *The Imitation of Christ* from his table and stares at the spine without opening it.

He thinks he should leave the place. He's made a total fool of himself. He'll resign the day after tomorrow, when everything's calmer, and this time he won't allow his resignation to be declined.

The telephone rings. Who on earth, at this hour? There've been enough calls for today, surely.

"It's Valentine Green," says the voice. "I've been released from the cleaners' cupboard where your staff decided to put me, and I'm writing a story about this evening's events. It's due in shortly, but I wanted to invite you to comment." He sounds more vituperative even than usual, but Auberon does not care.

"Sorry about the confinement, not my doing, I assure you," says Auberon. "I hope you weren't too uncomfortable."

Valentine snorts furiously. Perhaps Auberon doesn't sound sufficiently concerned. "Do you have any comments on this evening's events? It might be to your advantage. The story isn't very favorable to the museum, as you might expect, or indeed to you."

"No," says Auberon. "No comments tonight. It's just been a midsummer folly, hasn't it?" And as he puts down the receiver he falls asleep on his sofa.

Back at the museum, there's no activity at all. Ian, sitting in the control room and hardly able to stay awake, looks in turn at all the cameras—which now, he reflects, belong to him. Young Ralph is walking through the exhibition galleries. Norman is progressing through the Gallery of Early English History. The Great Hall is empty. The entrance hall is empty. The streets outside are empty, too. If anyone were passing the museum, they would never guess that anything ever happened behind the closed bronze doors.

than a whisper. "You trying to give me another heart attack? Oi, Dom, glad you're here. You heard that, then?"

"Somebody fell in the pool. They haven't climbed out. Mac, keep behind me and don't come outside until I say so." Dom was leading us down the hall, out into the courtyard, Mac trotting obediently behind her. I tucked in behind him. If Dom wanted to lead the charge, I was damned if I was going to argue.

We hadn't got completely out of doors before Dom changed her stance. I've seen her do it before—when something even looks like posing a threat to Mac, she basically becomes a killing machine with an *on* switch—but it doesn't get any less impressive over time.

"Stay here." She'd contracted somehow, but expanded as well: whatever she'd done with her muscles, she was tighter and more compact, but also a lot more menacing. Looking at her, you knew this was someone who could fuck you up without taking the time to blink. "Both of you, until I tell you it's okay. I don't want anyone getting in my way. Clear?"

"Of course." Mac usually manages to sound slightly amused when he's dealing with his bodyguard in full protect mode, but not tonight. He was tense as an overwound guitar sting. "Go."

Memory—what sticks with you and why, the pictures you retain in your head when things a lot more immediately important or personal fade out—is really peculiar, you know? There's probably a thousand small things I've forgotten in my life, things I'd like to remember, but the mental image of Domitra moving across the open courtyard, keeping low to the ground and looking from side to side as she went, is right there in my brain, and has been since it happened. If I close my eyes and bring it up in my head, I can actually hear the nightingale.

The moon was up, just starting to come down, a half-moon that looked a lot brighter than we get in Europe or America. It washed everything out except Dom, moving across the courtyard in the moonlight like Bree's Siamese, Farrowen, when she's stalking a ray of moonlight, looking to be made of liquid silver herself. I found myself crossing my fingers, holding my breath, wishing to myself the way a kid might hold his breath and wish for something: *please let her be disappointed, let there not be anything for her to find, let it all just be moonlight and no more than that...*

There were nine full pools in that courtyard, and she looked at every one of them. She went for the far side of the courtyard first, keeping close to the base of the outer seraglio walls, the side away from our suites. Mac muttered something under his breath, very quiet; I couldn't make out what he'd said, but it sounded anxious. We were both watching Dom, moving from the paths between the outer pools to the inner ones, through the centre and back out, ending up at the pools closest to our windows.

At the far end of that cluster of three pools, she stopped. That's the clearest memory of that whole bit of weirdness, Dom stopping, her shoulders tensed up the way Bree's do, her head locked sideways. She was looking into the third pool.

Mac took a step forward. That brought it home to me, just how rattled he was, because she'd told him to stay where he was and when Dom tells him that, he does it. That's what he pays her for. No point paying a bodyguard to protect you if you're not going to do what she tells you to do, you know?

"Wait." I put a hand out, keeping my voice low. "Mac, wait. She's found something. Look, she's heading back."

Another memory with total clarity, Dom heading back to us. She wasn't running, but somehow, in some way, she covered the distance in what seemed a few quick breaths.

"Problem." She was breathing through her nose, like a racehorse. "Big problem, yo. Someone in the third pool, face down. There's blood in the water. A *lot* of blood."

We stared at her like a pair of waxworks. Mac seemed to be holding his breath, and as for me, I couldn't seem to get my throat to work. She hadn't sounded dramatic, but the picture she'd brought up in my head was really vivid, and really unpleasant. Someone in the pool, face down, blood. Right.

"Domitra?" Mac had his voice back, and he'd forgotten about keeping it lowered. "Why in hell are we standing about? So we can wait for whoever it is to drown—Johnny, what are you –"

"Shit!" The path alongside the suite wing was suddenly bathed in a different kind of light. "That's our room—Bree's woken up. I'm off."

I turned back into the corridor, a few seconds too late. There were doors opening, people talking, movement. Luke was out, calling back in to Karen to stay put. Cyn and Stu Corrigan were both heading towards me. I could hear voices as everyone else woke up to it. And here came Bree, her hair tousled and her eyes wide, in her yoga clothes, and with bare feet.

"John...?"

"Dom's found someone in one of the pools. I haven't looked, but it sounds bad. No, Bree, damn it! Stay here, will you please? I'm going to see if I can help. Just wait, all right?"

The corridor was full now: Tony and Katia, the Wilsons, Ian. Karen had got enough clothes on to pass for decent, and come out. There was something very primitive about it, as if everyone was clustered together for some kind of tribal protection against who knew what, monsters or something.

"Where in hell is Patrick?" Katia sounded sharp, scared. "Isn't this a security thing?"

"Patrick's not quartered in the seraglio, remember?" Ian had gone just outside the doors to the courtyard. "He's got a first briefing with two hundred hired security professionals tomorrow morning at eight. He needs to be with the security details. Fuck! What are they doing down there? Hang about, people, I'll be back."

Bree reached out suddenly, and got hold of my hand. Her own

was cold, much too cold. I let go and got one arm round her, pulling her close up against me, the pair of us stepping out into the courtyard, watching the group at the edge of the pool: Mac, Domitra and Ian.

They were arguing about something, Mac and Dom waving towards the pool and gesturing, Ian shaking his head *no*. Whatever it was, Ian apparently won. He stood up and pulled out his cell. Words, bits of information and conversation, floated across to us.

"Patrick...? Look, mate, we've got an emergency...dead...in the pool...no, not drowned...throat cut...a fucking mess...get Bengt out here you too, yes I said Bengt....just get here now... royal family... five minutes, good..."

I didn't realise I'd let go of Bree, much less that I'd moved, until I was halfway down the path. *Royal family.*

Shit, shit, *shit*. If those broken sentences had meant what it sounded like they'd meant, there wasn't going to be a fan in the world big enough to cope with what was going to hit it.

Ian saw me coming. He met me halfway up the path, getting his body in front of me, like an American footballer. He shook his head at me.

"JP, look, you want to go back up and wait, please? There's nothing you can do and it's pretty grim down there." He sounded gruff. "No need to give yourself bad dreams over it, and we don't want Bree heading down this way either. No, trust me, nothing in hell to be done but deal with it. He's dead, all right." His shoulders sagged, suddenly. "God, what a fucking mess. I don't know what's going to happen now, about the gig."

"He?" The royal family, he'd said. He'd demanded Bengt. Oh Christ. If this was Ali in the pool with his throat cut, the gig was going to be the least of our worries—getting out of Manaar alive would be more like it. "It's not one of the twins?"

"The twins? No." He craned his neck, peering around me.

There was cars coming towards the seraglio, moving hard and fast, screeching into the drive, doors slamming, Patrick and Bengt and God only knew who else. The nightingales were still making noise out there in the dark, trilling like mad things, lacing the cold night air with birdsong. "It's Nordine. Sorry, JP, but I don't think Bree's driving that Bugatti in the morning."

Over the past few years, I've seen more late nights that involved dealing with coppers on the hunt, and dead bodies lying about, than I want to think about. But the hours of Boxing Day morning, what happened after Ali's people had come and fished what was left of our personal equerry out of the water outside our bedroom window, was new to me. It was completely outside my experience.

It was clear, straight off, that the people in charge were Patrick and Bengt. I was too freaked and too rattled at the time to give any real thought as to why that seemed so weird, but it would have been obvious if I'd been thinking straight: what were two heads of security, both foreigners, doing in charge of investigating how a dead bloke, one who'd worked personally for the Emir, had fetched up in a pool in Medin-Manaar? Ali had plenty of local rozzers, but Patrick and Bengt were definitely running the show.

I'd got hold of Bree again. The pair of us clustered near the suite wing corridor entrance with the rest of the Blacklight contingent, waiting for someone to tell us what needed to happen next. Just then, I was concentrating on being ready to get between Bree and the body they were fishing out of the pool. The shortest route from the pools to the ambulance that had just come screaming into the courtyard was straight past where we were standing. If Bree showed any signs of not doing what she was told when they carried that shrouded stretcher towards us, if she even looked like giving me any argument when I pulled her back indoors and away, I was prepared to get heavy about it. Ian had called it grim, and he'd mentioned nightmares. That was enough for me—I wasn't having my wife exposed to it.

"Patrick, for heaven's sake, what's going on?" That's another visual that's stayed in my head: Barb Wilson with her hair in a mess, her in fleecy pink pyjamas and a pair of shiny black stilettos. Turned out they were the nearest shoes she'd had to hand, since she hadn't unpacked her suitcase yet. "What do you need us to do?"

"I don't know any more about what's going on yet than you do, Barb. As soon as I get details, I'll report them, believe me. For now, it's just the bare fact: Nordine Benhamou's dead. As for what you need to do, I'd say nothing yet, except stay back and out of the way."

Patrick was watching Bengt, who'd left the ambulance people at the other end and come up to us. That bony Scandinavian face was locked down hard, but I could see his Adam's apple working as he kept swallowing. I wondered if he was actually trying not to have himself a sick-up. "Bengt, I'd like to get our people back to their rooms. It's a pity we don't have a space in the suite wing large enough to fit everyone, but if everyone's back where they belong, we know where to find everyone."

Bengt managed a nod; he really did look as if whatever he'd seen in the pool had left his supper wanting to come straight back up again. He kept staring off towards the city, then jerking his back towards us again. "Yes." The Adam's apple went all the way, held, went down again. "All right."

"Sounds good to me." Dom was in front of Mac. You'd think that, surrounded by everyone else and with what passed for Manaari security two feet away, she'd have relaxed a little and eased up being quite so protective of Mac, but no. "You guys want me up first? Since I found the dude?"

"I don't know yet, Dom. I don't think it really matters." Patrick was doing the same thing Bengt was: staring off towards the city, then remembering we were watching him, and jerking his attention back to us. Really bizarre, you know? I couldn't sort out what they were on the lookout for. It wasn't as if someone was going to show up with some way of getting Nordine's blood back inside, and bringing him back to life again. "Look, if I can please get everyone to go back to your rooms? That will make our job a lot easier…"

His voice tailed off. A car had pulled into the courtyard, a big bullet-proof job, the Manaari flag fluttering behind it. I suddenly got what Bengt and Patrick had been watching for.

For all that the Emir of Manaar had his own personal security chief, he'd seemed to me to be quite casual about his personal safety. He strolled about the place with only a single detail covering him; once or twice, visiting the studio, he'd actually come out with no security at all, just a driver. He really hadn't seemed worried about someone having a go at him, at least not since we'd got here.

Yeah, well, things had changed, and damned fast, too. Ali's usual deal was to wait for his driver to open the door and stand there like a stuffed waxworks dummy while Ali did his cock of the walk, it's-good-to-be-king thing. Tonight, the driver opened the limo door and four pairs of black boots, worn by four commando types, hit the pavement in a big hurry. The commando types were carrying what looked like serious firepower, and the firepower, whatever the damned things were, were pointed straight at the rest of us.

I looked up, and made a mistake: I locked eyes with the nearest commando. Next thing I knew, he'd moved, not just himself but the gun, as well; he'd gone from pointing it towards us to pointing it at us, and the muzzle of the fucking thing was aimed straight at my midsection. Next to me, Bree sucked in her breath.

"That's not necessary." Patrick had somehow got himself between me and the gun. "Everyone is right here, present and accounted for. Lower that, please. Your Excellency…?"

"Lower it. You insult my guests with your nonsense." Ali was out of the car, and I was getting my first look at just how opaque that cold smooth face could be. There was nothing there I could read, nothing at all. Behind him, the commando lowered the gun, and my stomach settled back into its proper place; it had been trying to crawl behind my spine. "Bengt. What is happening here? I will hear all of it, and at once."

Bengt told him. That's how we got the details of just what Dom had found in the third pool, and the more we heard, the paler Bree got. Bengt wasn't out for the shock value, but the thing was, he was taking his boss seriously, and Ali had said he wanted all of it.

I'm not going into what Bengt was telling Ali. It was bad enough hearing it the first time. Short version was that someone had done a very nice job severing our equerry's throat nearly from ear to ear. Even without anyone having time to take more than a fast look, one thing was obvious: whoever had nailed him hadn't been messing about. There was blood spattered for a few feet along the edge of the pool, and the water was full of it. In the meantime, I had hold of Bree's hand and I was keeping an eye on what they were doing down by the pool, lifting something weirdly limp and bloodless-looking out of the water, onto a gurney, pulling a sheet over it, strapping it down, turning the gurney round…

"Ali." I'd got his attention, and everyone else's with it. "Look, I'm not having my wife made to stand about watching the parade, all right? If that's a problem, sorry mate, but we'll have to argue it later. Bree, no, don't even think about arguing with me." I leaned up and kissed her. "I'll be along in a minute, I swear. You don't want to see this, and I don't want you having nightmares. Off you go."

She opened her mouth and shut it again. I had my back to the rest of the crowd, and one eyebrow up. I mouthed it at her: *Please*.

She turned, and went. Down the corridor, I heard the door open and shut quietly behind her. The rest of us stayed where we were, watching the blokes in the dark blue jackets wheeling the gurney along the path, directly at us.

No one was saying anything, not a word. As they got up close, Ali stepped out in front of them, and they stopped.

"Show me." He sounded completely alien, about as old school as I'd ever heard anyone sound. I was suddenly reminded, full stop, that this was another culture, another set of rules, another world. "He was my servant. I will see the wrong I must redress. Show me."

There was no hesitation, none at all. One of them held the gurney in place, and the other pulled away the sheet, down and off Nordine's face, halfway down his chest.

There was a moment of absolute quiet. Then there was noise, plenty of it, Barb Wilson saying something I couldn't make out, and Luke muttering under his breath behind me—*bloody hell oh bloody hell no don't Karen don't look*—and people shuffling and moving about, Tony whispering to Katia to shut her eyes for fuck's sake, and Domitra peering round me, focusing on Nordine's face, saying something about how much blood he'd lost to be that blue.

I'm not going into detail, but I was damned glad I'd got Bree to head back inside. I was going to have enough bad dreams over this one to do for both of us. Then he was decently covered again, and Ali had waved the gurney off towards the ambulance, and away to wherever they were taking the body.

"Okay." Even Patrick was rattled, and that's saying quite a lot. He doesn't rattle easily, and almost never visibly. It's not as if he hasn't see his full quota of dead bodies, either—Christ, he's a retired homicide copper. "Your Excellency, may I ask, how would you like me to proceed? My first responsibility is to our people, but I understand that this changes things. What do you want me to do? If this is over to Bengt, I'll be happy to –"

"No." Ali had been looking away, but he turned toward us. For the first time, with the ambulance headlights on full and brightening up the courtyard, I got a look at what was happening to his face, in his eyes. "You will find out, both of you. Your duty is to your people. This is understood. But before you leave here, you will find out. That is what you owe me."

Flat as a stone in one of those deserts in the north, that voice was, and just as cold. No argument was possible, not that I could see, and from the total silence around us, I got that I wasn't the only one thinking that way. Ali had turned, looking off down the trail towards the pool, taking a step in that direction. I suddenly thought *right, is he wondering how to drain the bloody water out of it?* The commandos still had their hands on their guns. My skin was moving on my bones, and it wasn't from the chill of the night air.

"What about the show?" Ian had got his voice back. "Is that still on? Look, I'm sorry, I know this is a loss and I don't want to sound crass, but we need to know, and fast. It's not a small question—there's a lot of gear and money and time invested in this at both ends. We still playing New Year's Eve?"

Ali turned back, and locked eyes with Ian. Neither of them seemed to be blinking, and no one else was making a sound, except the damned nightingales.

"The show will proceed as scheduled." His voice was dead calm. "To cancel now would serve no purpose. Continue as you have been—request what is required, and it will be provided. To tell a quarter million guests to stay away is too foolish an idea to consider, and the negative publicity would be impossible to control. My staff will handle all media contact. You will say nothing to the press, no word, without clearance from my people. It is understood."

It wasn't a question, and we all knew it. If I'd thought it was quiet before, I hadn't known the half of it. You could practically have heard hair growing, it was that silent.

"Sounds good to me." Ian's voice had gone almost as flat as Ali's. "I don't fancy dealing with the media on this one anyway, believe me. I'll send all the vultures along to your people, with pleasure. Excuse me, I need to ring Carla in LA. She's coming out the day after tomorrow and she needs to know what's what. We don't want any cock-ups."

He turned away, reaching for his phone. That seemed to break some of the tension, somehow; I could hear people letting their breath out, feet shuffling. Everyone had been standing about like storefront mannequins. Ali was still staring down the path, and I wondered for a moment if he was planning to trot along and have a look at the blood, the way he'd demanded a look at Nordine, but no. He jerked his head towards Patrick and Bengt.

"Do what you must. Bengt, the Guard are at your disposal—use them at need, and at will. I will meet with our publicity liaison and make certain this is kept as quiet as possible. There will be penalties for any media crossing what lines we choose to set: expulsion for foreign nationals, more severe for any of our own people foolhardy enough to disobey. Goodnight."

He turned on his heel. A moment later, the courtyard had emptied out of any trace of the Emir and his entourage.

"Wow." Domitra was watching the limo's taillights disappear. "The dude doesn't mess around. Patrick, you want to ask us questions tonight? Because if not, I'm going back to bed. I was all the way out when that murder shit went down. No? Cool. See you in the morning."

105

Chapter Seven

I know I've said it before, that everything to do with that gig in Manaar was a new experience. Weirdly enough, someone getting murdered basically under our windows wasn't new, but the follow-on was: having our sound designer drag us out of doors to make noise at two thousand portable toilets was a first.

Not only that, they'd called us out early. I got that Ronan was twitchy about the sound, but the thing is, Ian should have known better. There was no reason at all for Ian to ring everyone up at a quarter of ten in the morning and tell us that cars were coming to bring us out to the stage in half an hour, look sharp and be ready out in the courtyard and no backtalk from you lot, either. And that was nuts, because no one knows better than Ian that we don't do early mornings, on or off the road. Bree'd been seriously cross over it; neither of us had slept well, and I had a few ominous little twinges of myokimia letting me know I'd underslept.

I'd soothed Bree down as best I could, got a mouthful of breakfast and my meds, grabbed Little Queenie and stomped out into the courtyard to wait for the cars. I was just awake enough to think that something was off here because Ian had gone straight out of character, and just groggy enough to shrug it off and decide I was being paranoid.

When the limos hit Amina, we saw that the first two towers were in and powered up, and a lot of the trenching they were going to need for the wiring was already dug; there were blokes laying in cables. It turned out Ian wasn't even actually there. He'd left this up to Ronan.

It was right round that point that my feeling that something was going on stopped being foggy and got more immediate. Ronan's about as incisive as it gets, and just about as anal. When he gets a soundcheck going, he's got an invisible clipboard in his head and he's ticking items off as they get done the entire time. That morning, he didn't seem to know what he wanted us to do.

The longer we were out there, the more I woke up. The more I woke up, the more convinced I got that I wasn't being paranoid. Something was very weird about all this.

I wasn't the only one worrying over it, either. Standing onstage, noodling bits of the set list, the rest of the band was as edgy as I was, being pissy about things that wouldn't have normally caught their attention, and just generally being cranky.

"Bloody hell." Luke had come over to hang out next to my stool. The day was shaping up to be a scorcher, even with the breeze coming in off the sea. I'd promised Bree I'd take it easy and not let myself forget to take rest breaks; that promise was damned near the only thing that had stopped her ringing Ian back and telling him *sorry mate, fuck off, not happening.* "I don't know about you, JP, but I'm ready to call it and head back to the hotel. What in hell did Ian and Ronan think they were doing, dragging us out for this rubbish? And where is Ian, anyway? If he's dragged us all out for this and gone back to sleep, I swear I'll sack him."

"Right with you, Luke. Bree wasn't happy about it, either." I shifted on the stool. "Christ, it's warm out here. I'll tell you what, mate, I'm this close to packing it in and getting a lift back to the seraglio."

"Fuck it, let's call it a consensus." Stu had headed over, with Cal at his heels. "This is rubbish. We're not needed out here. Any of the techs could have handled this—we're not playing, we're just making noise to check levels."

"I'm not even doing that. They haven't got the vocal rig set up yet." Mac was looking about as pissy as I've ever seen him. He's a solid pro, Mac is. He works his arse off, he doesn't whinge and piss and moan about having to get the work done, but just then, he looked fed up. "I can't see a single reason we're out here. If I had a nasty suspicious nature, I'd be wondering if there was some reason they wanted us away from the seraglio this morning—oh, bloody hell!"

"Right." I was up on my feet. The bulb had lit up in my head, nice and bright, and apparently, it had lit up for all of us at the same moment. "I want a car. Where the fuck is Ronan? And where's Jas?"

"Here, JP." My guitar tech, Jas, had been dozing in a folding chair on one side of the stage. He uncoiled and headed over. "Last I saw, Ronan was out at the far remotes—I think he's checking levels. Is there a problem?"

"No idea, but we're going to find out, and properly quick, too." Mac jerked his head. "Get Ronan up here, will you, and it had best be in the next five minutes, or else there's going to be—ah, here we go, lovely. The man in the kilt has joined the discussion. Ronan, a word with you, and then we want cars. And let me clue you in, right upfront, that dodging the question won't end well. What in hell is going on? Why were we all dragged out here?"

Ronan Greene's been with Blacklight for decades. This was the first time I'd ever seen him looking uncomfortable, or out of his depth. He's like most obsessive expert types: if something doesn't fit, he'll just shrug and pretend it isn't there. Not that day, though.

"I don't know." He swallowed, hard. "No, Mac, don't flip your shit at me. It's the truth, I don't know. Patrick and Ian told me to get you out here, and to make sure you stayed out here for a couple of hours."

He took a breath, and waited. Luke found his voice first.

"Patrick and Ian? What the fuck?"

"I told you, I don't know." At least he was showing enough sense to not twist about it. "I haven't got the first clue why. And if you think I'm any happier than you are about it, you're off your head. We've got a couple of dozen remote towers going up, plus eight 40-foot generator trucks and I have to…"

He stopped. We were all staring at him, even Jas.

"Hang on a moment." Cal sounded pretty normal, but both hands were balled up hard and tight. "Ian and Patrick had you drag us out here, and you didn't bother asking why?"

Right about then, I found myself wondering if maybe I hadn't actually woken up yet. This was so far beyond anything believable, it didn't seem real. Maybe it wasn't. Maybe I was still curled up back in our suite, Bree next to me. As ideas went, that wasn't any weirder than our manager and chief of security conspiring with our sound designer to get us off the premises for a few hours. And it certainly wasn't any weirder than the possibility of our bassist knocking Ronan off the edge of the stage with a roundhouse punch, which is what Cal looked about ready to do.

"Of course I asked." Ronan was keeping a wary eye on those balled fists. "Tried to, anyway. Ian said they needed the hotel clear for a few hours, orders from Bengt Ekberg, just shut up and do it and don't ask questions. He's the boss, Cal. Since that guy got slashed last night, I wasn't about to push the issue. Ian told us this morning that Patrick and Bengt are handling it. He told us not to ask any questions, just cooperate with them." He shrugged. "I cooperated. Ian, Patrick and Bengt all said, do it. I did it."

"Yeah, well, we're undoing it." Luke's mouth was a thin line. "Cars, Ronan. Right now. We're done here."

We had to wait about ten minutes for the two limos, and it felt more like ten years. I've been with this band, played with this collection of people, for over half my life. We'd gone through ups, downs, and everything in between. Christ, I'd nearly fucking died on them twice. But the tension on that empty stage, that day in Manaar, was like nothing I'd ever come across with these blokes. You'd have needed Bree's best chef's knife to cut that silence, and trust me, it would have dulled the blade.

"All right." Mac waited until both drivers were out on the grass, and he wasn't wasting words, either. "Back to the Queen's Palace, fast as you can. And there'd best not be any bullshit later about taking the scenic route, or claiming you didn't get what I just said. Where in hell is my bodyguard? Domitra!"

"Here." She'd been here all along, staying out of the way, keeping an eye on things. She sounded nice and terse herself—she picks up on Mac's moods, the way Bree picks up on mine. "Ready when you are."

The first thing we saw, when the limos rolled to a stop just inside the main gates, was a small tanker truck.

It hadn't been there when we'd left, but there it was at the far end of the pools, perched between the farthest two, on the widest bit of the paving. It looked as if the driver had got lucky; either that or he was really skilful, because the tires were right at the edges of the path. One inch either way and he'd have had the thing in the water.

There were two huge hoses, out and working. One of them was pumping the bloodied water out of the pool where Nordine's body had been dumped. It took me a moment to realise that the second hose was also pumping, but not from the same pool.

"They had to hocus us away for this?" Luke was out, squinting across the courtyard into the sun. "What the fuck, we're supposed to believe that Ian and Patrick were so worried about upsetting our delicate sensibilities with the sight of trucks pumping water that they tricked us the hell out of here on five hours sleep? Bollocks to that."

"Yeah, that's bullshit." Stu was staring at the tanker. "If they tricked us out of doors, where in hell are the women? Why are they cleaning out the second pool over? Was there another body no one bothered mentioning?"

"You sort it out, Stu, you let me know, all right?" I was heading for the suites. My heart was giving the tickybox a major workout, and the fact that I couldn't get air into my lungs properly wasn't helping things. The corridors were dead silent. *Where in hell are the women?* "Bree? Bree!"

Fumbling with the key, pushing the door open. My heart was trying its best to act like a bullet train, making the wrong sort of commotion under my ribs.

Of course she wasn't there. Nice empty suite, bed made, tray set aside to be put outside later for the staff to remove. Everything was normal, except that we'd been tricked away, apparently so that the women could be taken elsewhere, all of them but Domitra. And the whole bloody thing had been done by people we not only pay, but by people we trust.

I went back out into the corridor. There was a shot I was wrong, that Bree was out but Karen or Barb were where they'd been when we left, but as shots go, that one was as long as odds get. The Queen's Palace wasn't easily walkable to anything; if you wanted to get round the place, you rang for a car and a driver.

111

And if Bree'd rung for a car and driver just to go out somewhere on her own, then yanking us off to the venue on a pretext made no sense at all.

There were voices, coming from everywhere: Cal calling for Barb with some serious urgency in his voice, Tony swearing like a navvy, Stu sounding like blue murder. I pulled the suite door shut behind me. My palms were wet. Right. If anything had happened to Bree, there was going to be a second murder done, and maybe a third.

"Karen's gone. Suite's empty, both rooms." Luke was back out in the hall, and one look at his face made it clear that I wasn't the only one wondering if Ian and Patrick might not be on the next plane out of here, both of them looking for jobs, or else being wheeled out on gurneys. Cal's mouth was clamped into a thin tight line, and Stu was a dark mottled red, clearly about to lose it. "If anything's happened to my wife, someone's going to bleed."

"Get in line." Tony was breathing through his nose. "I'm going to kick some ass from here to Istanbul. Where the fuck is Katia? What kind of Arabian Nights bullshit is this!"

"Let's find out, shall we?"

We all jerked round to stare at Mac. He had his phone up to one ear and he sounded calm, but of course he hadn't got a missing wife to worry about.

"Fair warning, mates, I'm about to get really high-handed— Ian? Oh good, I was hoping you'd pick up. Let's make this short and sweet, shall we? We're all back at the Queen's Palace, and everyone's rather cross because their families have gone walkabout. Sorry, ducks, but Ronan played copper's nark. He split on you. I don't know what's going on here, but you're about to come back and explain yourself, aren't you? Oh, and you'd best bring Patrick along with you."

He stopped. We could hear Ian's voice, crackling away. Had he been able to see Mac's face, he probably would have just shut his gob and not argued.

112

"Ten minutes or less, Ian." Mac's voice had changed—there was steel in there, now. "Because if it goes to eleven, we're not playing New Year's Eve. Yes, that's what I said. You get back here now or the show's history. And you may be, as well. Cheers."

Right after Mac hung up on Ian, he'd offered up a fiver on how long it was going to take either or both of them to get there, with that ultimatum ringing in Ian's ears. Mac's own bet was that we'd get Ian in seven minutes, without Patrick.

If I hadn't been so frazzled by the whole mess, by the empty suite behind the door with our name on it, by all those open doors with no one behind them, I might have wondered why I was more pissed off than I was worried. Everything was wrong about that whole morning, and by all rights, the top of my head should have been blowing off. It wasn't. There was a part of me that knew, all the way down where you know things, that Bree was fine. I couldn't have told you why, though, not then.

No one took Mac up on the bet, either, and that was a pity, because it would have been a quick five quid in pocket. He'd actually got it wrong. It took Ian nine minutes, and Patrick actually got there first, on his own.

We'd headed out into the courtyard to wait, full band, a solid united front. The tanker truck was gone; it must have finished doing its thing while we were inside, flipping out and ringing Ian. I'd slipped off down the path for a quick butcher's at the pools; both of them were empty.

Going by Ali's taste in wheels, I'd expected Patrick to show up in some shouty little red thing that made a lot of noise and went like a scalded rat. Considering the Bugatti, that would have made some sense. Turned out the car Patrick had been given for his personal use was just a newer, meatier-looking version of Tony's old Range Rover, back in San Francisco.

It takes quite a lot to ruffle our pet detective, but he pulled into the courtyard so hard and fast, the tires squealed and smoked. He must have taken one look out the windscreen at the six of us, at least half of us looking like murder and any one of us able to give him the sack, and known he was for it.

But he climbed out and headed straight for us, no hanging back. If he was worried, either about me or Luke or Tony beating him to death with his borrowed truck or about losing his posh job, it wasn't showing.

"Sorry if I'm late, but the car had just been requisitioned about two minutes before you called. They had to bring it from the auto pool." He glanced down towards the pools. "I passed the tanker truck on the way in. Empty?"

"No, you're not late. But about those pools, you're asking the wrong question, Patrick." Mac had got his attention, and ours as well. "You ought to be asking whether or not we're pissed off enough to give you a week's notice and show you the door. First things first, and we'll save the rest for when Ian gets here. Where are the women?"

"Having lunch with the Emir."

There'd been no hesitation, none at all, but no surprise at the question, either. So yeah, he'd known it was coming, and he knew why we were narked. He was looking at all of us, going face to face. Somehow, though, I got the feeling he was really looking straight at me, maybe because he was doing the 'one eyebrow up' thing. We could have been alone out there; he might as well have said "Bree's having lunch with the Emir" and been done with it. And, right then, I suddenly got why I hadn't seriously considered that anything bad might have happened to Bree.

Patrick wouldn't let that go down, and I knew it. I may not like that he fancies my wife, and I may not like the bloke very much on a one on one basis either, but I trust him to take care of Bree. Nothing bad was going to happen to my wife, not while Patrick Ormand was about.

114

"Lunch with the Emir?" Luke was keeping his voice steady, but his jaw looked like a bit someone had chipped off Mount Rushmore for a souvenir. "Is that why you and Ian felt you had to lie to us, and get Ronan to keep us away for the morning? One more try, Patrick. We're not dim, we're not puppets for you to jerk about on strings, and we're not going to be talked down to by someone we employ. We clear?" His voice went up, sharp and hard and loud. *"Where the hell is my wife!"*

"Having lunch." Patrick was locked up with Luke, stare to stare. He seemed to be pulling out every old cop trick he knew; the eyebrow up, the steady stare, the answering only the bits of questions he wanted us to know. It was all very familiar, and it brought back the bad old days, when we'd been obliged to answer him, instead of the other way round. None of us were saying anything—this was Luke's to handle. "I wasn't talking down to you, Luke. The Emir phoned Bree personally, shortly after you left for Amina Plaza. He'd remembered that she was supposed to be driving the Veyron this morning, with Nordine. He offered to let her drive it anyway, with him accompanying her in the passenger seat. She declined the offer, and he apparently decided that, in that case, everyone was having lunch with him. So he sent cars. They were just starting dessert when your call came in to Ian. He said something about taking everyone and personally showing them the shopping district in downtown Medin-Manaar. Apparently, it runs from an old-school souk to an Armani boutique."

I opened my mouth, and shut it again. The words were there, and ready—*oh for fuck's sake, mate, try it on the dog, all right?*—but Patrick cut me off. We could all hear a car, heading for the seraglio, full throttle from the sound of it. Patrick jerked his head over one shoulder, towards the sound of the engine.

"And that's all I can tell you. But it sounds as if Ian's here. Maybe he can tell you more, if you aren't satisfied with my answer. And I do understand that you probably aren't."

115

Patrick might have been pulling out everything in his copper's arsenal. Ian had nothing to pull. He got out of the car, looking about as harassed and miserable as I'd ever seen him look.

Out of nowhere, I got hit with a memory: sitting on a hotel bed at the Four Seasons Brickell Key in Miami, not quite one in the morning after a show. Bree'd come up missing, and Ian and Carla had come up to help me find where she'd gone. They'd sat there, the pair of them, side by side, using their cell phones, ringing airlines, trying to find her for me...

"What were you thinking?"

It was there in my voice, that feeling of trust betrayed. There's nothing worse, you know? There's nothing that can cut you into pieces as small as that can do you. I hadn't planned on saying anything, I've always left the Blacklight band business up to the band's two founders, but there it was, and everyone shut up and let me go, and the words kept coming.

"Christ, Ian, have you gone round the fucking twist? We trust you, mate. We've always trusted you. You've never let us down, never. I'm not speaking for anyone else, but here's the thing: if we can't trust you, where are we, then?"

"I had no choice." He had control of his voice, but it wasn't going to last. Stressed as we've seen him get, I'd never seen him quite like this. "None. I got called in this morning and given orders, no arguments, this is how it works, period. I've officially had my access to anything to do with Nordine getting killed revoked. You want to tell me what else I could do under the circs?"

I don't know what I'd expected him to say, but whatever I'd been expecting, it wasn't that. I stood there gawking at him. The rest of the band was doing the same.

"Everything goes through Bengt, full stop." Christ, yeah, our tour manager wasn't happy. "I wasn't what you'd call in an ideal position to argue, not unless I fancied telling him to fuck off and tell you lot I'd decided we were blowing off the gig. Besides, he

116

had a double handful of his own rozzers backing him up. Like I said, not ideal."

He looked me straight in the eye, and took a breath. "And I tell you what, JP, I don't much fancy being accused of being a backstabber. I've worked my arse off, keeping shit together for this band for twenty years. I haven't got that coming, not from any of you lot. I deserve better."

"JP knows that." Luke was looking thoughtful. "We all do. Never mind that. He told you hands off? What the hell is he up to?"

"'He' being my old school chum, I gather." Mac was tight-lipped. "Remind me again why I suggested we come within a hundred light years of Ali al-Wahid and his high-handed bull-shit? Oh, right, he's funding two charities that matter to us. So let me see if I've got this, Ian: we went to bed with Ali's an-nouncement that Patrick and Bengt were jointly in charge ring-ing in our ears. Now you're telling us that sometime between then and this morning, our pet pasha did a one-eighty, put Bengt in complete control of the investigation, and locked you out?"

Ian nodded. He wasn't talking, not then, and I wondered if he felt he could trust his voice. Mac turned back to Patrick.

"So, where does that leave you? You're our head of security. The contract's nice and clear about that: all matters concerning band security are up to you, and of course Dom. I don't really think I want to let Ali or anyone else fuck with that—in fact, I know I don't. I'll walk away from the gig before I agree to that. Where are you in the New World Order?"

Patrick snorted, a sour, angry little noise, very unlike him. This was definitely shaping up to be a day of unknown quantities. "I handle anything that concerns Blacklight security. But that's all I'm officially allowed to handle. And before anyone asks, no, of course I don't like it. But I have to respect it. We walked into a situation where existing security was already in place. It's damned good security, too, very efficient. Bengt's a solid pro. You don't run security for three winter Olympiads unless you're at the top of your game. Besides, that's also written into the contract, that everything to do with Manaari security issues is Bengt's to call. But this is the main reason I wanted to wait for Ian. It wasn't my place to tell you about al-Wahid's little backflip, it was his. I wasn't there. I got my orders from Ian and I'm following them, unless and until someone tells me otherwise. So was Ronan."

We were all quiet, letting that sink in. I'd moved back into the shade of the corridor. My legs were beginning to shake. Brilliant, just fucking perfect. The entire time I'd been stuck out onstage at Amina, I'd remembered my promises to Bree: that I wouldn't stand about exacerbating the ataxia, that I wouldn't forget to take rest breaks to keep the MS under control. And of course, we'd got back here, and I'd been standing in place the better part of half an hour.

"JP, dude, you look shaky as hell." Domitra had noticed. She wasn't offering any help, that's not her job and not her thing, but she spoke up. "You want to park somewhere?"

"Yeah, I do." I had to talk over my shoulder—I was already heading down the corridor, key in hand. "Sorry. You want me in on the rest of this, it's happening where I can sit."

Back in our suite, I hit the fancy fridge and managed to find liquid for everyone. I'd barely got myself settled with my legs up when Mac spoke up. He'd obviously been thinking.

"Is anyone else getting the delicate aroma of fish off this situation? Because I am. JP's equerry got his throat cut in the pool—and I must say, the fact that we were all snoring gently just the other side of the wall when that happened makes me very glad that these walls are nice and thick, because the idea of some nutter roaming about with a machete or a scimitar or something isn't the stuff pleasant dreams are made of."

"Not in the pool." I'd actually found Patrick a beer in the

fridge, God only knew how it had got there. He'd got the top off in a hurry, and was taking little chugs. "At the edge of the pool."

"We sure about that?" Ian sounded as if he might be getting some of his balance back, now that no one was questioning his trustworthiness and threatening him with the sack. "How sure?"

"Completely. There was blood spatter along a broad expanse of both the paving and the edge of the pool. He either fell in or was pushed or lost his balance and fell in, and he died in the pool." Patrick got another mouthful of beer down. "He bled out in the water, but he wasn't killed in the water. I got a good look last night, remember?"

The picture was much too vivid. Mac shook himself suddenly, the kind of movement one of our cats would do if he or she happened to fall into the tub and wanted to get all that water off in a hurry.

"Oh bloody hell. Right, okay. Wherever he was killed, Ali told Patrick that he and Bengt were both in charge, absolute authority. We all heard that? I wasn't having some sort of nightingale-induced hallucination?"

"That's what he said." Luke was watching Mac, eyes narrowed. "What's your point? Go on, will you?"

"My pleasure." Mac wasn't smiling. "My point is that something must have happened this morning. Whatever it was, it got Ali to basically forbid anyone except his own people to even look at what happened to Nordine last night. And more than that, it's clear that he wanted the women out of the Queen's Palace as well. Fuck, he wanted it so badly, he bullied our own tour manager and our own sound designer into jerking us about and lying to us." His mouth thinned out suddenly. "And believe me, he and I are going to have a conversation about that at some point down the road. Count on it."

"It worked, too." Stu was a dangerous colour. "Used our own

119

people to fuck with us. That bleeding little shit!"

"He's all of that." Mac was up and pacing, nice and taut. If he brought this level of intensity to the stage at Amina in a few days, he was going to melt the remote towers and all the portable toilets, as well. "But that's not my point. We're missing something here. Whatever went down, it went down here. *Right* here. This was where he wanted everyone cleared out of for a few hours, enough to invite everyone to lunch—no, right, sod that, invite's the wrong word, isn't it? And whatever it was, we must have slept right through it."

My legs were throbbing, a dull nasty jangle of stabbing pain. I rubbed them, feeling them wincing away from even the touch of my hands against the skin and muscle. My brain was kicking into high gear, always a bad sign where the MS is concerned.

"That tanker." *Shit.* This was going to be a bad one, a major bitch of a relapse. I could feel it, roaring down the track straight at me; my jaw was numbing up. Hopefully it would be gone by tomorrow, assuming we were staying in Manaar long enough to play. "When we got back here today. Two hoses, two pools. Why did Ali need to get the water out of the second pool? Only one dead bloke. Just Nordine."

They were all staring at me. I managed to get to my feet. I'm not proud about the disease, I don't try to hide it, but that doesn't mean I want to flash the results at my mates.

"Sorry." I sounded like a stroke victim, and I was hot and cold, pain coming in waves. Yeah, this was going to suck. "Not feeling well. Need to lie down. Can someone go find Bree? I need my wife."

Chapter Eight

"JP, can you back off the reverb? No, not that much, it's just that I'm getting some wash. Right, that's got it—Ronan? What have we got…?"

It was a nice clear early evening in Amina Plaza. The sun was just beginning to ease off into something that didn't actually leave my eyes watering. We had three days left to work out the few remaining kinks from two years of not playing together, until we hit the stage for the biggest show we'd ever played, and God knows, there had been distractions for miles.

Still, it was business as usual, at least as far as the rehearsals went: Ronan tweaking things, Luke picking up ghost echoes from Little Queenie, Cal worrying about whether there was enough bass in the mix, Stu rolling his eyes, Tony being diffident about the entire thing because he was just a guest and not a full member.

"Okay, set list, where are we? Yeah, cool, does anyone think we need to work on 'Liplock'? No? Good, okay, so what's next, 'Long Day in the Hot Sun', Stu, you ready…?"

Onstage, rehearsing, we could forget about anything that wasn't actually connected to the gig. Offstage, things weren't quite so normal.

For one thing, I couldn't get used to those lines of toilets and tanker trucks, stretching down both sides of the park. Yeah, I know—that sounds nuts, letting myself get distracted by portable khazis. But there was something off-putting about them, and something scary as well: a mass of people is just a crowd, but a crowd needing all those toilets was something else again.

The small army of security people Patrick was deploying during the onstage rehearsals was another issue, at least for me. He'd told us he wanted to get them used to hitting their assignments while there was actual noise, making sure their headsets worked properly. There was no way to simulate what the crowd was going to do in terms of ambient noise, but at least we could rattle their headphones with music cranked up good and hot. And yeah, he had a point, and that was clear thinking and proper planning on his part, but it was still a reminder of just how big this gig was. I didn't really need the reminder. None of us did.

"Mac, hang on, I'm going to need you to run through that harp break again. No, not yet, hang on a minute. We're not picking it up on two of the channels—no, still not getting it. Can someone check those damned wires, no, damn it, behind me, second trench…"

I resettled the guitar on my shoulder, and shifted my weight from foot to foot. I thought about parking myself on the stool until everyone got their shit together; hopefully, the stage was high enough up and far enough back to keep Bree from noticing how shaky my balance was. That last MS hit I'd taken had been a corker, but it had been mostly gone by nightfall. That's one thing about the bad ones, they move quickly. Not much of a consolation prize, not considering the rest of the shit the disease dumps on you, but at least it's consistent.

That was another difference, something completely new. I generally make a point of not dragging my old lady to tech rehearsals. After all, rehearsals are long and boring even if you're actually involved in what's going on. If you're not doing anything for hours on end but watching your old man getting progressively more cranky and irritable, you're probably not having a good time.

But the women were all out there, sitting on the grass or—in Karen's and Bree's cases—on the folding chairs Luke and I had demanded the road crew find them. The rest of the women had waved away the offer of back support, and opted for the grass. Cyn Corrigan, who's very fair-skinned, had found a parasol somewhere; I could see both Barb and Katia, stretched out on the grass with their hands under their heads. They looked to be asleep.

"Hang on—what? No, I said we need to do some fine tuning on that piano. We're losing too much of the high end in the mix...what? No, not the bleedin' Strat, the Strat sounds fine. The piano, mate, I said the *piano!*"

Like I said, rehearsals are a stone bore, especially when they're tech-heavy. None of us want to subject our wives to that. Normally we don't have to, and under any other circs, we wouldn't.

But these circs weren't normal, and we all knew it. It had taken me knowing Bree was safe, back from whatever had got Ali to manipulate the band wives into vacating the seraglio, before I could relax enough into that short sharp MS-induced high-gear brain pyrotechnics thing the disease provokes in me, to sort out why things felt so bizarre. But I got it, finally.

The bottom line was, we'd got spoiled. We'd got used to having a retired homicide copper between us and the rest of the world. Patrick Ormand might not be my favourite human being out there, but he's very good at what he does, and what he does best is ferret out information, and sort out the best way to use it. And right now, he couldn't. He'd been hamstrung, not only by the situation, but by the bloke who happened to own the country we were working in.

Ali had told Patrick and Ian to back off, no guest list privileges, the whole thing was Bengt's turf, thanks very much and we'll keep you posted if we fancy it. And while Ali might not have actually said anything upfront about trespassers being shot on sight, Patrick isn't any kind of dim. He had to know that that was just what Ali had meant, whether the threat was stated or not. Besides, one section of the contract that Ian had signed with our approval said, nice and clear, that we agreed to respect the authority of the Emir while we were on Manaari soil.

So Patrick was stuck. Unless Bengt felt like keeping us in the loop about what had happened and what was being done to sort it out, we were locked out. And so far, Bengt hadn't told us a damned thing. Not a comfortable feeling, for any of us.

I don't want to be a diva over it, but the way I saw it, Bree and I had reasons to feel more involved than the others. Nordine had been our personal equerry, our driver, assigned to make our time in Manaar easier, and he'd done just that. He'd shown up within minutes of any call, from bringing me bandages the day I'd bunged up my knees to Bree ringing him to ask where she could get a shoe repaired in Medin-Manaar. Under different circs, he would have made a fantastic concierge at a five-star hotel somewhere.

And yeah, I know, that was his gig. I get that Ali would have probably had him beheaded or thrown into a pool full of electric eels or something if Nordine had slacked off or been cheeky or done anything to piss us off, but in my head, that was irrelevant. The point was, he'd done it all, without a blink or a question or a word of complaint. He'd sat with Bree in that pricey chunk of automobile, side by side, sharing information, answering questions.

Christ, I'd trusted him with my wife's safety. We'd called him by his first name. And he died right under our bedroom window. I wanted to know who, and I wanted to know why.

"Ronan, is that better? Good, because I want to have another go at 'Hammer It Home'. I'm still not getting my voice round it properly. You chaps up for that? Brilliant, let's do it. Luke, do you want to do the full lead-in again? 'Aftertouch' all the way through? Okay, right. Ready? Fuck, I've gone dry, going to need some spring water—oh, thanks..."

"JP?" It was Jas, holding one of my lightweight chambered guitars. "You want the Paul for this? Here you go."

I handed Little Queenie over, and watched Jas get her safely in her stand. Of course the Paul was perfectly tuned and ready to go. No surprise there; Jas has been my guitar tech for a good long time now, and he really knows his stuff. More than that, he knows the way I want things done, and he makes that happen. Now that I thought about it, Nordine and Jas had a few things in common.

My effects array was on the floor in front of me, ready and hot. On the black stage we'd used for Book of Days, the effects had been set into the floor itself, and I'd had to learn which lights in the surface activated which stomp box. Since we were using a standard Tait end stage, rather than the invisible set we'd done for Book of Days, everything was right there and visible. While I was checking settings, Luke got his PRS Blue Waterfall off standby, and ready to go.

"Aftertouch" is entirely Luke's piece. It's a gorgeous instrumental, shimmery and light at first, but it's full of twists and surprises; the deeper you get into playing it, the denser it gets, and the more layers start showing. It runs between four and five minutes, depending on whether we're doing any jamming on it, and as it moves, it takes on weight, getting darker and deeper.

125

By the time we hit the final thirty seconds, the music's so ominous that the audience is probably jerking their heads round to make sure there's no demons jumping out at them from behind the towers. And then, right at the point where even playing it starts feeling too heavy to deal with, it takes one short sharp musical breath and becomes an entirely different song, because Mac steps up and opens his mouth, and suddenly bob's your uncle, here we go, we're off and away, and it's Blacklight's third-best-selling single ever.

"Every time the big man tries to nail you, every time the jackboot finds your door..."

We settled into it, and for a few minutes, I was able to push the imaginary picture of Ali cutting us off from what was happening all the way to the back of my head. Just as well, because that meant I could push the other picture away as well, the one that wasn't imaginary: what was left of Nordine, on that gurney.

"Every time your self-respect has failed you, when you think you can't take it anymore..."

Mac was working the vocal, playing with it, testing inhales and punches. If you'd happened to be out on the grass listening—and there were quite a lot of people out there, what with Patrick's security people, our staff, workmen, riggers, Ronan's crew—you'd likely have thought Mac sounded perfect.

The band knew better, though. We'd played that song for well over two hundred shows on the Book of Days tour, and we knew to a breath where Mac still thought the vocal needed tuning up. That was quite heartening, in its own way, because it meant we were finally coming together. The instincts were still there.

"You don't have to take it, you don't have to buy it, you can make that nail your own, just hammer it home, I tell you hammer it home!"

Mac let the instruments spiral off into quiet. "Ronan? Anything that wants adjusting, best tell me now. And can I get a consensus from everyone? Because that sounded quite close to where I want it. Tony, you haven't lost one fucking note off the piano on that, have you, mate? Absolutely brilliant, people, cheers. Anyone up for a break? Because I want a sit-down and something very, very cold to drink."

I handed the Paul over to Jas, and wandered offstage. Bree'd been sitting in her chair, probably dozing under the floppy sun hat she was wearing. She saw me coming, and hoisted herself upright.

"Wow, that was a really good version of 'Hammer It Home'. Mac's sounding better and better. Are we done for the night? What do you want to do about dinner? Cyn was telling me about this French restaurant she and Stu went to last night in town, down near the port." She lifted the hat off, got a good look at me, and her voice sharpened up. "John? You're shaky, hang on, here, sit —"

"No, it's cool, Bree. I'm fine." *Shit.* Last thing I wanted was having her shoulders hunching up, she'd been through enough recently, but there's no sneaking anything past her, you know? She was right, I was shaky; there were some trembles in both legs, just bad enough to be noticeable. "I just stood a bit too long, that's all. Not to worry, this isn't a relapse. Just the usual bullshit. But yeah, sitting down's probably good. And I need my meds— where's your purse, love?"

We had a nice little break, hanging out on the grass with the rest of the band family, watching the moon beginning to edge itself up on the horizon. There were people camping already, all the way at the back of the Plaza—we'd seen them the last two days as we'd driven in. They were mostly trying to stay out from underfoot. They were probably afraid they'd get turfed out of the park, and maybe the country, if they were too obvious about pitching tents and settling in. And yeah, we knew we were getting the wide-eyed stares, but again, they stayed out of our way and out of our faces.

I stretched out on the grass next to Bree, and closed my eyes. A nice lazy break was just what I needed. There was a warm breeze blowing, just doing its thing. It tasted of the sea.

"I tell you what, I think we've got the world's best fans." Mac sounded mellow and relaxed, himself. Next to him, Domitra was sitting with her ankles crossed. "Or the best-behaved, anyway. There's got to be at least a couple of thousand people back at the entrance to the plaza, and they've stayed damned near invisible. Civilised."

Stu snorted. "Fuck yeah, of course they're behaving. We've got two hundred people who look like they ought to be trotting round behind some head of state. Have you taken a butcher's at that lot? Whoever came up with that ought to have got the sack straightaway. Do these people think they're blending in with the crowd? Inconspicuous? Christ, they're wearing black suits and Ray-Bans. For all we know, they've got something with a full clip in it tucked under their arms or in their socks, or something."

"Well," Cyn pointed out, "you're assuming they want to blend. If I were doing their job, I'd want everyone within eyeshot to know what I was up to. Preventing trouble is a lot less trouble than coping with it while it's actually happening. Isn't it? Come on, Dom, some backup here, please?"

Dom shrugged. "Less trouble, sure. Less fun though."

"I'm fine with the security types. It's the Manaari police worry me." Cal was chewing on a blade of grass. "I'm not about to piss that lot off. The ones I've seen look like they get off on killing people. They wouldn't have to put a lot of welly into it, either, not with what they're carrying in the way of firepower. What are those damned thing? Uzis, or something? Scary as hell. Oh good, here's Ronan. I'm damned if I fancy going back up for more work tonight. I want my supper."

Ronan wove his way towards us through a small crowd of Patrick's security people. Stu'd nailed it, spot on: they were all wearing the sort of suits that made them look like Secret Service, or maybe extras from a James Bond movie.

"Sounding good, you lot." From Ronan, that was a high compliment; it was clear he'd meant the music, not just the tech, and he's not one to notice whether we're cooking musically or not. He lowered himself into Karen Hedley's empty chair and jerked his head past us, looking down the length of the plaza, away from the stage. "Four more towers up, two more to get done. That'll happen by end of business tomorrow. I wish Patrick would keep his hired bruisers off my patch, though, and nobody bother telling me they need to be here, all right? I already know. That doesn't mean I've got to cheer them on or send them flowers. They're in my way."

Mac opened his eyes and propped himself up on one elbow. He'd sprawled out in the grass, eyes closed and ankles crossed, almost touching hips with Katia. Since Katia makes no secret of the fact that she thinks Malcolm Sharpe is hotter than a blast furnace in Lucifer's kitchen, I suspected she was enjoying the moment. Tony didn't seem bothered, and neither did Domitra; she was sitting just at his other hip, watching the security people. I had no clue what they were doing, they looked to me as if they were just wandering, but apparently, there was more to it than that. Whatever it was, Dom seemed to have a handle on it, or at least recognised what they were up to.

"Ronan, dude, they're not in your way." She bent forward, stretching out like a rubber band. I swear, if I tried some of the moves she and Bree and Mac do with that yoga stuff they're all into, I'd probably snap like a rubber band, not bend like one. "There's, what, maybe two hundred of them total, and the plaza holds three hundred thousand people. You're just pissed off because you have to pay attention to them."

"Wrong. I'm pissed off because they're breathing my air. And they're in my bloody way." Ronan was still staring. "Okay, people,

I think we're done for the day. I'll want you back here tomorrow, but probably not until mid-afternoon. We should have the rest of the line arrays up by then, and we can set some marks and get some of the fine tuning done. Patrick! A word with you, please? Look, I can't have these people wandering about. I've got towers going up, and there's fans being allowed to sleep at the back of the plaza…"

"Right, that's us done for the day." I really had needed the rest break; my legs had stopped trembling. "I'm with Cal, I want some food, and then maybe a good long kip and a nice warm bath. We'll be back at work tomorrow."

The French place in the city centre turned out to be just as good as Cyn had said it was. Even Bree made happy noises, and she's fussy about French food.

We had a very nice dinner, relaxing over it, taking our time. Work was done for the day, and the cars were waiting outside to take us back to the seraglio whenever we were ready. Ian hadn't come out with us; he was trying to catch up on stuff long-distance, things that had got pushed to the back burner by the gig. Having the entire band in one place for a casual meal, with all the wives but without the braintrust turning food into something that's more about business, that's a rarity, you know?

They gave us a private dining room, away from the rest of the customers. That was necessary, because, as I've already mentioned, Medin-Manaar was already filling up and beginning to spill over with Blacklight fans, and apparently not all of them were checking their sleeping bags back at Amina Plaza. We got some double-takes and not very well-muffled gasps between the front door opening to let us into the restaurant and the door to the private room closing behind us. Heading out after dinner, we had to run the gamut again, with an entirely new set of fans.

Still, they were quite well-behaved, all things considered. I did catch a couple of looks at Mac by a table of wall to wall women in what looked to be their forties, but nothing went down beyond the inevitable *oh my god it's Malcolm Sharpe!* whispers. They stayed in their seats, probably because they'd got a good look at Dom. It's not just outraged boyfriends with fake paternity suits he pays her to handle.

Back at the seraglio, we brushed our teeth, I took my night meds, and we curled up under the silk coverlets. Sex definitely wasn't happening that night; at my age, digesting that much dinner takes all my energy, and Bree, with her diabetes, is in the same boat.

"John—those people at the restaurant."

"What about them, love?" She'd snuggled up next to me, her hair fanning out across the pillows. She'd cut it quite short for awhile, getting ready to have to go deal with her cookbook being published, but the publisher had decided to bring it out in the spring instead of for Christmas, and now her hair was coming back in long again. I wouldn't have said so to her—she worries far too much about how I'm going to react to how she looks—but it made me really happy, her letting it grow longer again. All that hair swinging round her when she moves, that's always been something that can get all the blood deserting the north of me for the south. My first sight of her, still sixteen years old, she'd leaned forward and all that auburn hair had leaned right along with her, nearly to her waist. I've never forgotten that. She says full long doesn't work on her at her age, that it's better on girls than women or something, but I'll take as much as I can get.

"I was just thinking about the hotels here." She sounded not quite drowsy, but getting there. "I just can't figure out how this can possibly work. I mean, there's supposed to be a quarter of a million people at this show, right? But there can't possibly be enough hotel rooms for that many people here, can there? I mean, Medin-Manaar's only got about that many people actually living here, at the most. So where are all those fans going to sleep? Out in the plaza? Because I know there were a lot of them already hanging out right by the entrance when we drove in today, but I thought that wasn't allowed. There are signs everywhere, in about eight languages, pretty much warning that vagrants will be fed to bears or flogged outside the local Starbucks, or something."

"Yeah, I know, but they've suspended that rule, just for this gig." There was a light breeze coming in through the window—bloody hell, I'd forgot to close it again, and tonight the temperature was really dropping. "It was in one of Carla's emails, after she'd come out here that first time. Ali didn't want to, but you know Carla. She's barely old enough to remember Woodstock, but she knows what happens when you've got a shitload of people and nowhere to put them. She had the numbers, and that was that: not enough room for everyone, you've got to put them somewhere, end of story. She put it in as part of the rider. Ian told us he thought Ali was fighting the idea mostly because he didn't want a quarter million people having a piss all over his nice green park, but with the portable toilets in place, he finally gave in. And don't ask me what they're doing for showers, because I've no clue. There's drinking water being provided, but I've got the feeling most of the crowd's going to smell a bit ripe come New Year's Day."

"Except the ones who actually scored hotel rooms. I'm pretty sure there's no such thing as a room without a private bath in this town." She yawned, warm breath tickling up against my shoulder. "I bet Carla will know. She gets here tomorrow night, doesn't she? If I remember, I'll ask her about it then. Damn, it's getting chilly in here. Is the wind blowing straight in at us, or something?"

"Yeah, it is." I swung myself out of bed, feeling the cold air coming in through those high skinny casements, hitting bare skin. She was right about the wind direction. "Hang on, I'll get the things closed and—"

With one foot on the floor and the other not quite there, I stopped. Behind me, Bree was sitting up. I put a hand up to hush her, but it wasn't needed; she'd already heard what I'd heard.

Voices, outside the window. They were being kept lowered, all the way down; if the wind had been moving in any other direction than straight through the window, we'd have heard nothing at all. Somehow, even as close to inaudible as those voices were being held, I got a feeling of urgency, panic, something like that.

Shit.

Something had gone very tight at the base of my spine: the instinct for self-preservation, announcing itself. The last time we'd heard night noises under that window, Nordine had been slashed to death a few feet away, just the other side of our bedroom wall.

"Chairs." Bree had her mouth up to my ear; she breathed the word, rather than said it. "Under the window. I'm going to see."

She was out of bed, still nude, shivering and hurrying, keeping quiet. I was right behind her, reaching for a robe, throwing one over to her. She stopped just long enough to knot the belt round her waist, and headed for the window. There was a small ornamental chest in the way, not tall enough to be useful. If we wanted to put chairs there, the chest needed moving first.

I got my hands at one end, and she took the other, and I nearly dropped it. It was damned lucky I didn't, because we were both barefoot, and it would have broken a few toes; the bloody thing weighed as much as one of my Marshalls. It brought back years of pictures in my head, Bree helping me move amps and guitar cases from local gigs, or from room to room, or even just when I wanted to reorganise things in my basement studio back home in San Francisco.

We got two of the chairs out of the dining room and up against the bedroom wall. I had a bad moment, wondering if the caned seats would hold either of our weight. I got a hand on the caning and pushed as hard as I could against it.

It held just fine. That was just as well, because Bree wasn't bothering about being careful, or testing for strength first, or whatever. She just got one hand on the chair back and one up on the casement, and hoisted herself up.

I held my breath, but nothing happened: no crash, no foot through the caning, no broken ankle, nothing. She reached out her free hand and slowly, carefully, adjusted the ornate grille so that we could see out without being seen ourselves.

Right. If it was holding her, it would hold me: I'm not mad enough to ask her what she weighs, but she's a good stone heavier than I am, and maybe more. I took a breath, and climbed onto the chair next to her.

Moving the chest out of the way had taken about a minute, and as it turned out, that cost us any shot at a decent look. By the time I'd got up on tiptoe and craned my neck to see who'd been whispering, they were heading away from us. They'd already gone down the length of the pavement, all the way beyond the second pool and out past the first one. I saw their backs, no more than that: just three people, covered head to heels in the same dark loose clothes. I had a better view than Bree, but it still wasn't much of one.

"Who is that?" Bree's voice was low, but it was audible. There was no way they could have heard us: they were too far away, and the wind was blowing in the wrong direction. "John? Could you tell? I can't really see anything."

"Sorry, love, but no, I couldn't. I can't see which direction they went, either—which road they took, I mean." I pushed the grille slats shut, cutting off the cold air. "These casements are too deep to see off to the right or left properly. Let's get back to bed, yeah? I'm too old to be climbing about on caned chairs in the middle of the night. Besides, I'm freezing my bollocks off. No, don't bother about the chairs, all right? We can get them in the morning."

Back in bed, we curled up close, not talking. I'd wrapped myself round my wife, and it was a good long while before either of us slept; my nerves were jangling and twitchy, and Bree was as rigid as an old tree trunk in my arms.

When she finally did relax enough to drop off, I lay awake in the dark, listening to her breathing even out, light and smooth. She made a small noise and snuggled in. No nightmares there, and thank God for it. I wasn't so sure I wasn't going to have a few of my own.

I'd told her the truth, about not knowing who'd been standing about having a tense conversation under our windows. I had no idea who they were: I couldn't even guess. They were just three shapes, all completely covered with black robes.

Whoever had been wearing them, the robes were probably the long black deals we Westerners always associate with Arabs. Djellabahs, or burnooses, or whatever they're called, big loose things with a lot of movement in them. I'd caught the movement of the cloth, billowing out behind them as they moved away, two smaller shapes and a taller one between them, hurrying to—where? I hadn't got the first clue.

That one in the middle hadn't just seemed taller. Even in the look I'd managed, that one had just seemed bigger, somehow. I'd have bet even money that the shape in the middle had been a man.

Chapter Nine

That marital mind-reading thing Bree and I do sometimes, it's really peculiar, as if just letting our eyes meet can get across what's going on in both our heads. We've had it going on for years, but it can still surprise me.

On 29 December in Manaar, with two days left before the big party, it kicked into overdrive. Not only that, it did it first thing in the morning, and that was a surprise. All I'm generally good for first thing in the morning is mainlining coffee and seeing what hurts, and how badly.

That morning, I woke up early. The suite was still mostly dark, shadows in all the corners—I could see across the bedroom, but only after my eyes got used to it. That meant the sun was still down a goodish way. I did my usual morning thing: flexing, testing, being careful not to disturb Bree while I tried to sort out what the MS was likely to dish out, and where it was planning to dish it. Nothing seemed too noisy that morning except my bladder, and that was just business as usual, first thing in the morning. Good. Any time I begin a day with minimal pain, I can cope.

I rolled over and got my eyes unglued all the way. The first thing I focussed on was that pair of caned chairs, still sitting side by side under the window casement, where we'd dragged them last night.

I lay there, ignoring the demands my bladder was making and the faint jabs and tingles in both feet. I was still staring at the chairs, but I wasn't really seeing them. Something was moving at the back of my mind, edging its way towards the front, wanting me to look at it. Right. We'd been standing on those chairs, me craning my neck round the casement, trying for a good look…

People, three of them, hurrying away. It hadn't been anyone from the Blacklight contingent, I'd have put a fiver on that; it's hard to mistake a back and a walk, when it's someone you know well. Whoever that lot was, they weren't ours. But what in hell was it, that wanted me to look at it…?

No car, Johnny. Wherever those three were off to last night, it was close by. No sound of a motor, none at all.

At just about the same moment that thought popped into my head, a warm hand landed on my shoulder, and rested there. Damn, I'd woken Bree—I hadn't meant to.

But this wasn't her soft light *are you awake, are you okay* touch. There was something imperative about the pressure of her hand against my skin. I turned over and found myself staring into a face about as wide awake as she ever gets that time of day.

"John—last night." The hand against my bare skin was nice and warm. That's always a relief; most mornings, her hands are chilly because she's got crap circulation, and the diabetes doesn't help. Her voice was low, and clear, as if she were trying to keep it pitched down quiet enough for just us to hear. Silly, really, because the seraglio walls were nice thick stone. Unless you'd planted yourself right under someone's window, and they happened to have the casement slightly open because they'd forgotten to close it against the chilly night air, no one was likely to hear what you were saying. "They were on foot, weren't they? They were walking. I mean, walking to get to—where? Somewhere. John…?"

"Yeah, I was just thinking the same thing. No car, was there? Just feet."

I got out of bed carefully; if the MS was going to oblige by not taking me out for the day, I was damned if I wanted to trigger anything. Bree's hair was tousled, and she'd sat up. "Means whoever it was, they've got to be right in the neighbourhood, doesn't it? And it was the same story the night Nordine got slashed, yeah? They were running, not driving. I don't remember hearing an engine, either time. Do you, love?"

She was already swinging herself out of bed, reaching for the clothes she'd pulled off last night. That was a sure sign we were on the same frequency: it takes a lot, a crisis or a brainwave or something along those lines, to keep her from her morning shower. And that was peculiar, all things considered, because really, there wasn't any urgency, not beyond us both having just realised the same thing at the same time, and both of us wanting to know what in hell was going on.

"No." She got one leg into a pair of knickers. "But what the hell, John? Aren't we supposed to be the only people in the Queen's Palace? Blacklight, I mean? No one said anything about other people staying in any of the other buildings, or at least, no one said anything to me. The other buildings are closed off— they're supposed to be empty. I haven't really gone and explored or anything, but the one right across from us is deserted. There are padlocks on the doors. I'm pretty sure the Emir actually said we had it all to ourselves, when we first checked in."

"Yeah, he did." I was thinking back, remembering. She was right, Ali had been pretty damned clear that we were all alone in the Queen's Palace. If I was remembering properly, he'd made rather a formal song and dance about how much he respected our privacy, about us not being bothered. "But now I think of it, that's three times we heard people under our window. That first time, we thought it might be Tony and Katia. Remember?"

She paused with the zipper of her jeans at half-mast. "You don't think it was them?"

"No way of knowing, is there? I'm just saying it's possible that first lot was also whoever our little night visitors were the other two times. Or at least, it's possible that one of them was, anyway."

She blinked at me. "Nordine was one of them," I told her. "And he's dead. So obviously it wasn't him last night. Look, hang on a minute, all right? I need a piss and if I don't get my morning meds, I won't be good for much."

I'd known it was still early, but I hadn't realised quite how far from full morning we actually were. We slipped out of our suite, and down the corridor towards the courtyard, with almost no light to speak of coming through the high grilles. There was no sound either, not from the courtyard or from behind any of the suite doors.

By the time we got out of doors, I realised we were tiptoeing. And while I wasn't sure about Bree, I was actually holding my breath.

"Wow." Bree had both arms wrapped round herself. Her voice was barely above a murmur, and she was shivering. "This place really is all about cold nights and warm days, isn't it?"

She was right. I'd noticed it before, that temperature differential, the way an eighty-degree day would suddenly drop into the mid-forties. Outside our own quiet breathing, the only thing I could hear were birds calling, perched somewhere at the back of the trees behind the seraglio walls. They sounded plaintive, somehow, as if they were in mourning for something, lamenting. I wondered what they were. Larks, or doves maybe...

"Wow, listen to those doves. It's like they're singing dirges, or something." Bree slipped her hand into mine. "Which way were those people going, last night? Were you able to tell at all?"

I closed my eyes, thinking back, trying to remember. It was amazing, how fast and how clear the picture was there in my head: Three black shapes moving away from me, the way one of the smaller ones had looked hunched over somehow, the way the fabric had flapped at the hems...

"John?"

"Got it." We'd reached the end of our own white path, the first intersection between the pools farthest from the Queen's Palace. Now that we'd cleared our own quarters, I wasn't bothering about keeping my voice down. "They turned right, hard right."

"Are you sure?"

"Yeah, I am. They must have done, because whatever the tall one in the middle was wearing flapped hard left just before I lost them."

"Okay." She still had my hand, and she wasn't showing any sign of wanting to let go of it. She wasn't moving, either. "Now what do we do?"

I'd started forward, but that stopped me where I was. It was spot-on, that question. Here I was, about to go roaring off, and I hadn't got the first clue what we were doing, never mind what we were actually looking for.

So I raised an eyebrow at Bree—*come on, love, help me out here*—and damned if the old marital mind-reading thing didn't kick in again.

"Maybe we should go see if there's anyone down that way." Her voice had dropped again, quiet enough so that no one was going to hear her but me. "Maybe we should go see if Ali was wrong about us being alone out here."

140

"Wrong, or full of shit," I agreed. "Come on, love. Let's go for a reccy, yeah?"

I know this sounds nuts, but neither Bree nor I had explored the compound beyond our own corner of it. That probably makes us both out to be as self-absorbed as all get-out, but to be fair about it, I was there to work, and when I work, the job gets all of me. We were on a really compressed schedule, with a massive show coming up; that meant the band had been largely split between Ali's state of the art rehearsal studio and Amina Plaza.

Still, I was surprised about Bree not wandering about. She's got more curiosity than I've got at the best of times, and a lot more awareness of her surroundings, as well. It made me wonder whether she was even more uncomfortable with being here than I'd thought.

We got out beyond the three sets of bubbling pools, and stood at the head of the crossroads, looking to see what might actually be visible off to the right. I'd already worked out some of the geography in my head: the right-hand road led west, and so far as I knew, there was nothing out there but desert, dunes and lizards, and the stretch of blacktop that Nordine had said Ali had deemed unsuitable and unsafe for Bree's drive in the Veyron—too curvy or twisty or something to work with the car's speed. So unless someone had got some tents set up or something, there was no reason for anyone to have –

"Whoa." Bree'd stopped in place, craning her neck, pointing with her free hand. "Have those been here the whole time? Or am I having a mirage moment, or something?"

I jerked my head back into the moment, and followed her pointing finger.

There was a small jumble of buildings over there, just beyond where the road curved out west to meet the desert: I couldn't quite tell how many, not at that distance. But there were at least four of them, low squat things made of the local sandstone, topped with what looked to be tin roofs. From where we were standing, compared to the minarets and curving arches at our end of the compound, they looked ugly and graceless. The sun was coming up, touching them with colour, but even the distance and the dawn light couldn't make them look anything other than dismal.

The sun was moving up faster in the sky now, full sunrise. Even though we were both looking west, the sand was reflecting enough of the day's first brightness to make anyone with normal eyesight wish for sunglasses.

Bree was squinting. "Holy shit, is that a *slum?* In Manaar? That's a pretty far cry from his grandmother's antique blue tiles and silk lounging cushions. John, are my eyes playing tricks, or does that little gulag over there actually have corrugated tin roofs?"

"Looks like it." There was something disturbing about her using that word, *gulag*. She was right: small as it was, all it needed to make it look a proper POW camp was barbed wire round the perimeter. Something about it made me think of old photos of Viet Nam in the sixties, those miserable little Quonset huts all over the landscape. "I'm just trying to wrap my head round the fact that I never even noticed it was here. Christ, I'm dim, some days."

She squeezed my hand. "If you are, then so am I. I didn't notice it before either—when I came out with Nordine, we went straight. And I'm not surprised you didn't see it. If you're heading into the city to get to Amina, it's in the opposite direction, and I bet it's invisible half the time, with the sun hitting it—it would be too bright to focus on. But I never even glanced this way. I was giving the equipment in the Veyron all my attention. Let's go check it out."

I'm not a particularly heroic type, but I don't actually spook easily, either. You need imagination before stuff can get to you that way, and the truth is, I just haven't got much imagination. Creativity's a different thing; I've got my share and more of that. But that whole 'distant early warning' thing that people like my old lady have, I'm missing out on that. She's got imagination. She thinks there really may be ghosts out there. She's sensitive that way, and I'm not.

But I'll tell you what: that morning, heading for that dull-looking huddle of sandstone shanties, something was tingling up and down the full length of my nervous system. No idea what it was, not then and not now, either; if it had been straight-up caution, that would have made sense. After all, we didn't know who or what was down this way. Besides, I'd seen what was left of Nordine.

This wasn't caution, though. It was something much deeper, something that felt a lot more primitive, somehow. Last time I'd got that kind of tingle down what was left of my nerve endings after all these years of the MS, I'd been walking into a federal prison. This felt a lot like that: *look sharp, Johnny, there's bad craziness out here waiting to jump out and nail you.*

From the crossroads to the first of the buildings took just about fifteen minutes of walking, and neither of us said a word the entire time. Bree had stopped shivering; the sun was climbing now, and the day was warming up. There was no one else out there on any of the roads, not a car, not a human being, not even any of the local camels. It was so empty and quiet out there, we might have been the only people alive in Manaar. And that was in spite of the number of people who'd already piled in for the party...

Down along the blacktop, hugging the edges, until the buildings came into full view. They really were dismal little holes, nothing more than square sandstone boxes with crap corrugated tin roofs. There weren't even any proper windows, just slits in the stone, not big enough to let anything bigger than a fly or one of the small desert lizards in or out. I couldn't make up my mind whether they looked more like old slave quarters or small individual prisons. The only thing that made it clear we weren't looking at some kind of prison colony outpost was how flimsy the doors looked.

"Man, this place is creepy." Bree has a good strong grip, and she was using it; my own hand was going numb under the pressure. She had her voice pitched all the way back down to low again. "It's like someone moved Viet Nam to the desert instead of the jungle. Or maybe some old nineteenth century plantation, those shacks where they kept the slaves. What was that look for? Did I say something wrong?"

"Read my mind, that's all. Bree, love, can I have my hand back, please?" I shook it and got the blood flowing again. "Okay. So, now what? I'm not really up for knocking up one of the residents and asking them if they've been flapping round the posh end of the seraglio in the middle of the night, you know?"

"Me either." She turned to stare at the huts. "But you know what? We walked all this way to check this out, and someone from down here was probably trespassing on our space, and, well, I want to know, John. Don't you?"

"Bree, what, no, wait –"

No joy. She'd already turned and moved, going fast and quiet, straight ahead. Before I could get my wits together and get the heart to stop slamming long enough to scuttle after her, she'd reached the first building, slipped up against it, and was peering in through one of the slits, calm as you please.

Brilliant, just brilliant. We were visitors on someone else's turf, probably trespassing. I had a sudden parade of nightmare visions: the Manaari police leaping out from behind the other buildings and slitting our throats the way someone had done to Nordine, or some hulking yobbo in a black burnoose kicking the door open from the inside and leaping out of doors brandishing a scimitar, or…

144

"Huh." She was back at my side. For a moment, I thought about throttling her for scaring me that badly, but she was back unharmed, no damage done, and I let my breath out. My hands were slick with sweat. "There's no one in there. That one's empty. I mean, totally empty—there's a bed and a table and a toilet and small chest and nothing else at all. There's not even any linens on the bed. Just like a prison cell."

I lifted an eyebrow at her. "You planning on having a look at the rest of this lot? Because if you're going back over there, so am I, and no argument either, Bree."

"I was hoping you'd say that." She smiled at me, but it was gone in a moment, and I realised that her shoulders were hunched up tight. "I think we should, John. Don't you? Do you want to check out the second one, while I go do the third? Okay, bad idea, don't glare at me like that. We'll stay together."

We'd gone on tiptoe out of our own quarters, and here we were, back on our toes again. I doubt, now, that anyone in any of those buildings could have heard us walking; there were no paved white walkways, not here, just the fine grainy sand of the Manaari desert. But we tiptoed anyway.

Peering in through the slit window in the second of the four shacks, it took a moment for my eyes to adjust to the dimness in there; if the slits weren't letting people in or out, they weren't letting any proper light in, either. This one had linens on the bed, and a coverlet spread over the mattress, but nothing else. There were no towels in the room, and no tissue on the holder for the toilet tissue roll next to the loo. Nothing at all to be seen in there.

That thing about there being no paper, that sealed it for me: this was just another empty room. You can live without blankets and pillows, but not without toilet tissue. I shook my head at Bree—*no one here either*—and we moved on, to the third shack.

This time, Bree got to the window first. She slouched a little under the low roof, getting her eye up against the outer wall, lining it up with the slit...

"Bree?"

I didn't think I said it out loud, but maybe I did. I was watching her from a few feet away, hearing her breath suddenly shorten up, watching her profile, watching all the colour drain out of her skin, leaving her face the colour of old parchment. The eye I could see looked about the size of one of our salad plates, back in San Francisco, stretched wide.

"Bree, what –"

She stepped back from the window. One hand went to her mouth, but she was a fraction of a second too late. A moment later she was down on both knees, losing the remnants of last night's supper.

I got to the window slit. My heart was making some serious noise, clattering behind my ribs. From down near my feet, I thought I heard her say something—*no oh god John don't look*—but I was there, and already looking.

When I was a kid—damned I remember when or where, or even why—I read a description of the room Jack the Ripper had used for his only indoor killing. I remember a phrase used in there, about what the rozzers found, about there being blood on the walls and ceiling. Whatever I'd been reading, a phrase had stuck in my head over the years, the way phrases do: *blood frenzy*. Looking into that third hut, that phrase came straight back to me. I don't know if there was blood on the ceiling—it was too dark in the corners to tell—but the rest of that description fit, much too well.

There were no linens on the bed in here, either. There had been, but they'd been stripped free and tossed in a hideous little pile on the floor. Even as dark as that room was, I could see that they were streaked and smeared with blood. I couldn't be sure, not in the bad light, but something about it, the colour or how dark those stains were, felt as if the blood had had time to dry awhile.

Recent or not, there was a lot of it. The bare mattress looked to be nearly soaked through. There were spatters on the wall next to the bed, as well. Through that thin slit, I got a waft of stale air, and felt my stomach tighten up, making me have to think consciously about not retching: the air was laced with a genuinely ugly smell.

Bree was still on her knees, down in the sand. She was staring up at me, not saying anything. Her chest was heaving. I stepped back and got both hands out to help her up.

"Right." I was speaking normally—I wasn't worrying about whether anyone could hear me or not, just then. For one thing, all the puking would have let on to anyone hanging about that we were there, and that we'd had a look inside. And for another, I was too rattled to think straight. "Let's get the hell out of here. I want a good hot wash and some coffee. And after that, we need to decide what to do."

That walk back took a lot less time than getting there had done. I don't remember much about it, not beyond the fact that I kept glancing behind us, wondering if whoever had left all that blood on the bed and the linens and the walls had got any bright notions in their head, about following us back. I remember that I had hold of Bree's hand, that I wasn't letting go. And yeah, we hurried.

We didn't meet a soul. Except for the sound of car engines in the distance, the road back was as empty as the walk out had been. We'd just made it back through the peacock-gilded gates and into the corridor when the door to Tony's suite opened, and both the Mancusos came out.

"Hey, guys, you're out early –"

He stopped, staring at us. Even in the dim light, we must have looked like hell. Katia took a good look at Bree's face, and one hand went up to her mouth. Both of Tony's eyebrows were up near his hairline.

"JP? What's going on? You two look like you just saw a dead

147

body or something." He changed colour. "Oh fuck no, man, not that. Tell me it's not that."

"Not a body." Bree let go of my hand, finally, and pushed her hair off her face. She'd gone sweaty, whether with the heat or the fear or just a delayed reaction to our morning so far, I didn't know. "Just the blood."

"Blood?" Katia looked to be having trouble getting words out properly. "Bree, what are you talking about? What –"

"Blood. Just what Bree said." Down the hall, other doors were opening; we'd attracted some attention. Stu was heading towards us, and Mac, with Dom right behind him. Out of nowhere, I got hit with a thought: *I wonder if the rest of the band is as tired as I am of mornings in Arabia.* "A lot of blood. I think someone else got themselves killed. I also think maybe we need to sit down with everyone. And then we're going to want Patrick."

"Every good story starts: Once upon a time...You listen to the rhythms, you scramble for the perfect rhyme..."

It was Blacklight's last full rehearsal before the show, and the only one we were getting under the full night sky. Tomorrow night, the thirtieth of December, wasn't going to be an option for rehearsals, or anything else; that was going to be dedicated entirely to letting the crowds in and getting all that sorted out and managed. There was no way we could possibly rehearse. If anything still needed nailing down, it was going to have to happen tonight.

What with the stage being a pre-packaged rental, there was nothing fancy or even particularly complicated going on, but Nial and Ronan were both edgy anyway. Even though the number of people in the Plaza was nowhere near what tomorrow night was going to look like, we still had an audience. Medin-Manaar had been steadily filling up with Blacklight fans; the crowds had begun spilling over into the Plaza, and there was quite a good-sized crowd already camping out on the grass farthest from the stage, near the park entrance. The headcount near the back, just the early arrivals who'd been let in already, was a big enough audience to make most stadium bands happy.

So yeah, thirty thousand people or so had pitched their tents and sleeping rolls and bits of blanket on the grass. They were being kept well out of the way, though; Ronan had thrown a serious tantrum and completely flipped his shit over the fans getting in the crew's way.

Ian had handled it. He'd told Ronan not to get his Utilikilt in a twist, and had got some of Patrick and Bengt's security troops to shepherd everyone away from the work area. I wasn't sure what the blokes in charge were using to keep the front of house clear—there was nothing obvious in the way of security muscle. Whatever it was, though, it was working. We'd been rehearsing the best part of two hours and I hadn't seen anyone near the stage except the people who were supposed to be there: grips, lighting crew, techs. Our lot.

Tonight, with all the towers up and all the wiring trenches in place and covered over, the rig was about as ready as it was going to get. The PA was getting its final tune-up. We were slamming through tweaks to the set list, getting the standards out of the way early on so that we could concentrate on a couple of songs that wanted a last minute rubbing up. That meant the early arrivals were getting a one-shot chance at something none of our fans had really ever had access to before: a good look at Blacklight in "work out the kinks" mode. We don't generally sell tickets to band rehearsals, you know?

"*So just what rhymes with 'cry'? And just what rhymes with 'why'? I'll tell you if you tell me why you never kissed me goodbye...*"

"Damn, Mac really works this one, doesn't he?" Tony had wandered over from the piano, and he was watching me watching Mac. "Heavy duty."

"Yeah, he really does." Mac was leaning into it, pushing his body against the vocal as if the song were something solid he wanted the contact with. Just then, it was Mac, Luke and Stu working out the intricacies in the tune; Tony and I had stepped back, and Cal had his Alembic bass ready to roll, if needed. "That's the cool thing about Mac, you know? Doesn't matter whether he wrote a song or not. He just brings it, every time."

"I noticed." Tony was watching Mac himself, now. He had a very odd look on his face. "Believe me, I noticed. But with this one, he really seems to want to nail the sucker. It's like he's going after a whole different thing when he sings it. I remember noticing that, back during Book of Days. I know we only did this one a handful of times, but it really seems to matter to him. That's pretty weird. Because isn't this the one Luke wrote about Solange's mom? I mean, about her dying?"

"Yeah, well, Mac probably wants to do it perfectly, for Luke's sake. Hell, Mac knew Viv as long as Luke did—they all met right round the same time, you know?"

Now I thought about it, Tony was right. Luke had been writing the music to most of Mac's lyrics for well over thirty years now, but he hadn't written lyrics much himself until Book of Days, and he hadn't written a word about what had happened to Viv until this particular song, at least not that I'd ever heard. "You Never Kissed Me Goodbye" was a stunner, straight from the heart, and very bittersweet.

It's actually rather tricky to play, just because there's so much feeling behind it. The song really did seem to hit some peculiar buttons for Luke's best mate. Tony was right about that: something found its way into Mac's vocal for this one that wasn't really there for anything else. For some reason, that line of thought was making me uncomfortable.

"*I see your ghost round every corner, trapped forever in the looking glass, I thought we were free but how can that happen when I can't tell the present from the past?*"

150

"Man, he's fucking nailing it. But like I said, he just brings it for this one, every damned time." Tony dropped his voice. "JP, you get a chance to talk to Patrick or Ian yet? About what happened this morning, I mean?"

Mac had his eyes closed, and both hands behind his back. It was almost as if he needed them wrapped round something, but with the mic system completely wireless, there was nothing for him to hold. It's not often Malcolm Sharpe doesn't know what to do with his hands.

"JP? Hello?"

"Sorry—I got distracted, there. No, I haven't, not yet. Neither of them were around this morning, and we haven't had much in the way of time to hunt them down. Bree said she'd look out for them, though."

Christ, that full-on band conversation that morning—yeah, well. Short, sharp and tense as hell, and that was even though we'd got the entire band crammed into our suite. That was a return to tradition, something I'd noticed during Book of Days a few years back: when Blacklight's on tour and Bree's along with me, the entire band family gravitates towards our digs, even if we've got the smallest suite in the place.

That morning, Bree'd got everyone some good strong coffee and some of the local pastries, filled with chopped nuts and soaked in honey; she can't eat them herself, not with her diabetes, but they'd gone down well as comfort food. We'd let everyone wait a few minutes while we got ourselves calmed down enough to not flip our shit. After that, with everyone wrapping their tonsils round their coffee, we'd dished.

The conversation, about what to do, had lasted all of two minutes, maybe less. The choices were pretty limited: tell Ian, tell Patrick, or tell both. The fact that we discussed it at all, that we'd asked for input on what to do, just shows you how rattled we were. When you came down to it, the band could do sod-all

151

about any of it. About the only thing they could do was tell us to tell Patrick and Ian, and of course, that was exactly what they'd done. The consensus on that one—all hands voting, one for all and all for one—had been a no-brainer.

But neither was answering their phones. I'd left short sharp voicemails for both of them—*um, chaps, went for a stroll this morning, found something I think you need to hear about, you want to check in, please?*—but no one had got back to me, at least not by the time we'd left for rehearsal. It was really frustrating, and I found I was even less happy than usual about leaving Bree behind while I went off to rehearsal.

"*I'd give the world if you could come back and kiss me goodbye, oh baby...*"

Luke took a lead break, all sharp edges and minor progressions, up and down the scale. The PRS sounded like someone's throat trying to cope with swallowing tears. It worked with the song, almost too well; that was something I'd thought from the first rehearsals, more than three years ago now. Something about the melody said pain, or maybe the memory of pain.

Right now, though, Luke's lead was nowhere near as sharp-edged or pain-soaked as Mac's vocal. If he could bring this to the stage tomorrow night, he'd have a quarter million people sniffling and reaching for their hankies. Christ, it was even having an effect on me, and it's not like I'm not up on everything Mac puts out there.

"*I need to learn to let you fly, let our story just soar on high, but I can't let go because you never kissed me goodbye, come back to me, baby, you never kissed me goodbye...*"

"Brilliant." Stu did a little flourish on the snare, and got up. "That sounds about perfect. I don't know about you lot, but I want a break and a nice leg-stretch and something cold to drink. How are we for time? Oi, Ian, there you are. We have room in the schedule for a stretch and a cold beer?"

"More than enough. You're running about a quarter hour ahead. And yeah, before you ask, the sound out in the house is good. Nice and crisp."

Ian had come out on stage, with Carla right behind him. It occurred to me that, right, this was one reason Ian hadn't been answering his phone—Carla'd only just got in and there was probably a fuckload of detail to be sorted out. "All right, lads, break time. JP, got a moment? I want a word with you."

"Yeah, I was just about to hunt you up. Carla, glad you made it in time for the gig. You all right?"

She was just coming off the better part of thirty-six hours on planes, and she had to have been jetlagged half off her nut, but it wasn't showing; she looked just the same as always. Patrick's got that same thing going on, and it makes me want to bash him sometimes; for some reason, though, it doesn't worry me with Carla.

"I'm fine, just a little sleep-dep." She yawned suddenly, a proper jaw cracker, sucking down air as if there wasn't enough in the world. "Wow, sorry about that. I'm having my floors refinished and I underestimated how strong the smell would be. Not nearly enough sleep last week. Can we go backstage for a few minutes? Hey guys—this is sounding really great. Excuse us, okay? I'll get JP back to you in a couple, I promise."

She led the way between the amps, offstage and down to where the road cases and the rest of the gear was stashed. Ian was right at her heels, with me trotting after them. I wasn't sure why I was so convinced, but I was: they knew all about what Bree and I had found that morning.

That particular mystery got cleared up as soon as we below. Patrick was waiting for us, and Bree was with him.

"Hey, JP. Sounding good up there." Nice conventional opener, and the only problem was, it was rubbish. There was nothing conventional about Patrick's voice, or the way his eyes had gone all over dirty ice. He'd gone into predator mode, and he wasn't wasting any time trying to hide it, either. "Bree told me what you guys found this morning. Have you got a couple of minutes, so we can talk about it?"

"Hell yeah. I was hoping you'd get back to me." I headed over to my wife, and got an arm round her waist; she was looking worried, for some reason. Or maybe it wasn't worry. Whatever was going on, she was as tense as hell. "You all right, love? Glad Bree got hold of you, Patrick. I left you a voicemail this morning, but I didn't want to leave any details, not under the circs. And we've been nose to the grindstone all day."

"I know. That's why I called Bree. You guys were in full rehearsal mode and Ian told me nothing short of blue murder was acceptable for interrupting the band." He paused for a moment, choosing his words. "And while it's possible that murder is just what may have happened, we've got no way of finding out, at least not that I can see."

"Why do you keep saying that?"

My wife sounded furious. I got it suddenly, the tension, the look on her face. She wasn't worrying I'd be sniffy about her having given Ian and Patrick the gen without me there; she was worried that someone had got killed, and that whoever had done it might walk.

She went on in a rush. "That horrible little room was absolutely streaked with blood. Someone or something died in there. How can you say you can't find out? That's insane, Patrick. Just go look in the window. That's what we did. You'll see."

"I did look." Flat as a rock, that answer was, and it was pretty obvious that this was the first Bree'd heard of it. "I was on my way over there in the Range Rover even before I got off the phone with you. There's nothing there, Bree."

"What!" I was gawking at him. "Sorry, mate, but that's bullshit, all right? Unless you think me and Bree are both off our heads, or fucking hallucinating, or just straight up lying to you —"

154

"None of the above." He was watching me, nice and steady, and cold as January. Frost on the sidewalk in winter, those eyes were, just ready for someone to slip on, fall, hurt themselves. "I'm reporting, JP. I'm not arguing. I'm just telling you what I did, and what I found as the result of what I did. I checked the slit windows on all those huts, just to make sure I wasn't getting the wrong one. I checked every window, every hut, from every angle. There's nothing there, not in any of them. Those huts are nice and clean."

We both stood there, staring. His voice had gone careful. "One of them was much too clean, in fact, especially when I compared it with the other three. In the third hut from the road, there was no mattress at all."

"Yeah, I'd guessed that one already, ta." For some reason, my own edginess was ratcheting up to match Bree's, and it was taking my temper with it. I sounded about as pissed off and grim as I felt. "That's the one we were talking about, the one with all the blood. Nothing there? Someone already got in there and tidied up, did they?"

"So it would seem." Patrick was still being careful, and I was damned if I could see why. There was no one within earshot of us in any direction. "The question, absent any overt physical evidence, is what everyone feels the next step should be. Because I've got nothing to show any of the Manaari authorities, not a single piece of evidence beyond your statement, and Bree's. And I'm afraid that isn't enough. There's nothing in that room that would support –"

"My word not good enough for you?"

Patrick went quiet. I was staring straight into his face now, and Bree was white-faced, either with rage or with shock, I couldn't tell which. I was a bit too close for comfort to telling Patrick what I thought about an employee of the band telling one of the members that he couldn't be arsed believing what he was told.

155

Ian and Carla were still not saying a word, just watching and listening. "Bree's word not good enough? Because if that's the way it is, mate, I'm taking the rest of the evening off. If you're not up for believing me or Bree, we'll go straight to the bloody Emir and let him tell us he doesn't believe us. That do you?"

Something flickered in his face. "It would, if I were disbelieving your word. But as it happens, I'm not. I don't doubt for a moment that you and Bree saw exactly what you say you did. That's not the problem, JP. You're not thinking this through. Suppose I go find Bengt and tell him all of this. Don't any of you understand what the problem is, here?"

"We can't tell who to trust." Carla let her breath out and finally put her tuppence in. "That's it, isn't it, Patrick? Whoever cleaned that room up and got rid of the evidence, it could easily be someone high up in the royal family or in the Manaari security forces, or who knows who else. And if we stroll in and tell them what we saw – "

"Fuck!" Ian sounded harassed almost beyond what even he could deal with, and he can deal with quite a lot. "I'll tell you what, people, I don't have time for this. We don't have time for this. We've got the gig the day after tomorrow, and not thirty seconds worth of wiggle room anywhere between now and then. The way I see it, Patrick's right. We can't do a damned thing about any of this, not if they already know what's going on and decided to handle whatever it is themselves. And they must have, because otherwise who the fuck got in there and got rid of the evidence?"

Patrick was watching me, one eyebrow up. I wasn't saying anything. Neither was Bree. There was nothing to say. They were right.

Yeah, I could do what I'd threatened Patrick with. I could stalk into the palace with Bree at my side. We could demand Ali front and centre on the carpet right now, no backchat from the Emir's personal thugs, thank you very much and be quick about it. We might even get him; he had very nice manners, and a respect for guests under his roof that was almost as obsessive as Bree's.

And if we told him just what we'd seen and demanded he do something about it—then what? All we had was a wild story and nothing at all in the way of backup. Besides, if Ian and Carla were right, there was a good chance Ali knew all about whatever was going down anyway. Fuck, I was sure of it. No flies on the Emir, you know? I'd be willing to bet that damned near nothing went on in Manaar he didn't have an eye on, or a finger in.

Next to me, Bree's shoulders suddenly relaxed, and I let my own breath out. Whatever had gone down, whoever had been involved, however it tied in to what had happened to Nordine, we were stuck. Whoever had done whatever it was, they were going to get away with it. There was nothing to be done about it, nothing at all.

"I'm sorry, JP." Patrick had seen it, seen us reason it out. "If anything changes, I'll be on it. But right now, there's nothing to do."

"He's right, JP. You know he is." Ian sounded gruff, but there was sympathy at the back of his voice. He knows me very well, does our band manager, and he knew just how frustrated I had to be. "Look at it this way, though. Two days from now, it'll be a whole new year and we'll be on a plane home. And after that, whatever is going on around here can go right ahead and happen. It's not going to be our problem."

Chapter Ten

If you want to know who came up with the idea of tracking down Bengt Ekberg whether he fancied being tracked down or not, I couldn't tell you. I remember it being Bree's notion, she remembers it being either my idea or Ian's, and Ian says he remembers fuck-all about anything beyond the actual confrontation with Patrick backstage before I headed back out for another hour's worth of final fiddling and song tweaking and tech run-through. All I can tell you is, the whole time we were smoothing out those last few rough spots, I was getting more and more pissed off about the whole mess. And the more I thought about it, the more pissed off I got.

(Cal, what happened to that tasty off-timing thing you were doing after the second chorus? No, I mean that thundery rumble trill thing, the one that comes right before the bridge, I'm not hearing it. Luke,

sorry, that Strat's out of tune. JP, can I have an A…?)

I hit the harmonic on the A string, and Luke tuned his axe. Conversation, people talking, tech and tweak and all the stuff that gets done. And unless someone was calling my name, I wasn't hearing any of it. My head was elsewhere.

Right off the bat, from that first phone call from Ali to Mac, this gig had been a piss-poor idea. Nobody had wanted to do it, no matter what they'd said. And what's more, we'd all known it. We'd all known that any dealings with the al-Wahid family were going to mean trouble.

Bree hadn't wanted to come. Katia hadn't wanted to come. No one had wanted to do this gig. So what in sweet hell had all of us, any of us, been thinking? The money?

Yeah, twenty four million quid was a lot of dosh. Truth is, we had enough to cover that ourselves, if we really needed to. The Book of Days tour had been the most profitable tour in industry history, and not just in Blacklight's history, either: in anyone's touring history. A few years after the CD's original release, we were still getting royalty cheques that left me blinking, and left Bree looking for charities to send some of the money to, because it was more than anyone would ever need and having that much coming in after the fact sent her "all wealth is greed and all greed is evil and up against the wall, motherfucker!" needles redlining.

(What? No, we're going to need to do something about Mac's harp right there—it's getting washed out. Yes, I know it'll sound different when the venue's full. I'm not dim, mate.)

Why had we agreed to do this? It wasn't as if we hadn't known the al-Wahid connection was septic. We'd lost staffers and family because of it. We didn't need his twenty four million quid, we didn't need his horny little brats, and we didn't need his moneyed privileged bullshit.

We didn't need to play his opening party, either. Christ, we could have been back in San Francisco, hanging with the cats, spending New Year's Eve with the Fog City Geezers playing the 707 Club. So what in hell were we doing here –

"JP?"

I jerked my head back into the moment. Luke was watching me, the Strat at the ready. He knows me quite well, does Luke, better than most people out there, and besides, he's one of the shrewdest people I've ever met. I'd have bet my last royalty cheque that he knew just what I was thinking. "Check in, mate," he told me. "Keep in touch. You've got a guitar solo right there, last I looked."

"Sorry." I settled the Paul against me, ready to roll. They were all watching me, just waiting. "Here we go. Luke, you want to give me the last eight bars...?"

Why had we agreed to do this damned show? Right, of course, there'd been another reason. It hadn't been just the money for my recovery centre, or Luke's diabetes research foundation. There was also Mac's idea, wanting to put a few gigs on for our fans, free festival dates, a thank-you thing. He'd liked the idea of bending Ali over a barrel for double what we'd been offered initially, and getting Ali to end up footing the bill for the festival dates. I remembered just how dark Mac's grin had been when he suggested that; he's not usually malicious, or vengeful, or any of that.

Now that I was actively thinking about, I found myself wondering if Mac himself had even really wanted to play this gig. Hell, maybe the idea that Ali would agree to what was being demanded hadn't occurred to him; maybe he'd thought Ali would balk at the kind of numbers Ian had thrown at him. Christ, had that meeting really been only a month ago? It felt about twenty years had gone by.

But Ali hadn't balked. He hadn't even blinked. He'd just agreed to everything we demanded, and signed the bank transfers like some sort of indecently wealthy performing seal. What the fuck? We were back at the original mystery: why had the Emir of Manaar been so determined to have us play this party? For a lot less dosh, he could have had damned near anyone else in the world. Hell, for what he'd been willing to pay us for this gig, he could have booked the Pope to come out and do magic tricks, maybe pull a rabbit out of one of his hats. Apparently, though, only Blacklight would do. Why?

"Fuck me, Johnny, that was blistering!" Mac's voice cut through the noise in my head. "That little solo would have taken all the paint of the walls, if we were happened to be playing somewhere with walls. Seriously, what got into you? And can you do that again when we play it for real?"

I came back to the here and now with a thump. The rest of the band had stopped playing completely; they were all too busy gawking at me.

"Sorry again." There was a nasty little jolt of electricity up and down my right leg, deep under the skin, where the damaged nerve endings are. The pain wasn't doing my temper any good, not with me already feeling pissy and ready for a brangle. "I've got no idea what I was playing, none at all. The fingers were here, the head was elsewhere. Aren't we recording all this, though? I'll give it a listen tomorrow and see what's up. Look, what else have we got on? Because I've gone achy round the edges, so whatever's left to do, can we just get it done now, please?"

Another twenty minutes, polishing things, fine-tuning, getting it down and getting it done. My fingers knew the drill and just got on with it, and thank God for that, because no matter how much I tried to concentrate, I couldn't manage it. Pulling my mind off Ali's motives just wasn't happening, any more than shrugging off the idea of someone getting away with what looked to have been a really ugly bloodletting was.

"Time to call it a night, I'd say."

Ian had been watching from the side of the stage just behind Tony's piano bench. He doesn't need to waste his energy checking how we sound from out in the house. That's Ronan's thing, and he's very territorial over it. But Ian's not above reminding Ronan—or anyone else he thinks needs the reality check—that he's the manager, and that he's not having us get too tired out. "Brilliant job, mates, let's call this one and put it to bed. Cars are round back. There's a couple of restaurants offered to stay open if we fancied a late supper."

Bree was waiting backstage. It was late, and yeah, I was hungry; fact is, with her diabetes and my everything else, we can't afford to be missing meals. Used to be she'd be fussing over me, nagging me into making damned sure I got enough food to keep the MS hanging back. These days, since she got the diabetes diagnosis a few years back, we nag each other.

That night, though, it didn't go down that way. I hit the bottom of the stairs, we took a good hard look at each other, and well, yeah, there you go. Any ideas about plumping back in the limo, heading for one of the city's chichi eateries, and having a nice plate of goodies before bed went straight out the window. She was pale, and pinched; all that outrage, the same stuff that had been building up in me since that face to face with Patrick at the break, was reflected right there in her face. There are times when that marital mind-reading thing can be a proper nuisance, but there it was: neither of us was going to be able to enjoy anything at all until we'd done something, taken some kind of action, handled it as much as we could. And we both knew it.

"Ian." I jerked my head, and he was right there. Bree was at my shoulder. The rest of the band was already piling into the cars; I saw Carla, one leg already half inside the last limo, stop and turn to watch us. "If I wanted a shot at finding Bengt, where would I look? And don't even think about trying to talk me out of it. Where?"

"No clue, JP." He wasn't stonewalling me—he meant it. "You're asking the wrong bloke. I scratched Bengt off my list of people I needed to keep up with after al-Wahid ordered me off. You want Patrick for this one. Hang on, let me get him over here, or at least get him on the phone. I saw him about three minutes ago."

He'd already got his cell out, but it wasn't needed. I caught Carla, one arm waving in a *come over here* gesture and then pointing at us, and there was Patrick, coming up behind Ian. He must have been near enough to have seen us, and truth is, I'd have put a few bob on him knowing what we were talking about, as well. He knows me and Bree very well, does Patrick.

"Patrick?"

Bree had hold of my hand, and she'd caught Patrick's eyes with her own. Patrick likes to say he hasn't got a thing for my wife—he's been saying it so long, there are times I think he's actually convinced himself it's true—but that's rubbish. When Bree speaks, Patrick jumps, and I don't give a toss whether he's willing to admit it or not. Most times it drives me round the fucking twist, but there's no denying it can come in useful, and this was one of those times. Saves arguments, yeah? "We want to find Bengt," she told him. "Where should we look first?"

He opened his mouth, caught my eye, and shut it again. From the look on his face, I sussed he was probably just trying to sort out a good answer to Bree's question, but she can't read him as well as I usually can, and she misread him being quiet. "Please, Patrick? We don't want to get you involved in a turf war thing. We don't want to get you into any kind of trouble at all, but I'm not going to be able to sleep unless I do something, and I know John won't. We won't tell him you told us, I promise."

"I'm not worrying about that, Bree." There it was, that gentle note he gets in his voice at any evidence of Bree's warm-heartedness. It's one of the few things he doesn't seem able to control, or maybe he just can't be arsed to try. He was avoiding my eye, though; too busy smiling and being gentle at my wife. "I was just trying to think of the likeliest place to start. What time is it? We can check the production office first..."

So, yeah, we missed the post-rehearsal supper. The limos pulled off without us, and we trotted along after Patrick as he headed around the side of the stage and off towards the little trailer where I'd first asked Bengt about whether the Tahini Twins were being kept off our patch, as promised.

No joy, not on the first try; the trailer was dark and locked. Bree made a frustrated little noise under her breath, and I got one arm round her waist. Patrick shot us both a look, and got his cell out.

"Let's see if I can get him on the phone." He smiled at Bree. "I know you guys must be starving—Bengt? Oh, good, I was hoping you were around. Listen, have you got about five minutes? I've got JP and Bree Kinkaid with me, and we need to talk to you about something. Where are you? Oh, at the Palace—do you want us to come there?"

He actually ended up coming to us. Looking back, I think that was probably a mistake; we gave him enough time to put a good mask over whatever he knew or didn't know. Or maybe the mistake was Patrick letting on that me and Bree were along for the ride. Either way, he showed up in his Range Rover about ten minutes later, and he hadn't even got all the way out of the truck before I knew it was going to be useless.

Forewarned, forearmed, all that rubbish. It was right there, in the nice careful blank look on his face. That look was so unrevealing, it might as well have been armour.

"Oh, *damn it.*"

Bree, muttering, hadn't managed to keep it low enough for Patrick not to hear. He shot her a look, and then one at me. Yeah, he'd seen what we'd seen. Waste of time. We weren't going to get told a damned thing Bengt didn't choose to tell, unless

Patrick had some way, some sort of cop-speak thing, of getting what we wanted to know.

"Good evening, Patrick." He smiled at us, and that smile set the tone: this wasn't the cheerful Southern California thing we'd got before, it was the formal European front, the same one he'd used on me when I'd asked whether the al-Wahid twins were really being kept out of our way. "And Mr. and Mrs. Kinkaid, a pleasure. Is there some way in which I may assist you?"

Patrick may have had some cop tricks up his sleeve, some way of getting Bengt to turn loose of the gen we wanted. I'll never know, though, because Bree'd apparently made up her mind that playing protocol games was going to get us fuck-all in the way of information. She just went straight for it.

"Yes." She was looking straight at Bengt, holding him with her eyes, making sure he kept his attention on her. She's lived with a European long enough to totally get where American and European manners are different. "We had a very odd experience last night, and then this morning…"

She told him, no whitewash, no frills, just the simple facts: people under our window last night where no one had any business being, no sound of an engine, obviously on foot, reasoning it out, and then what had gone down this morning. She kept her voice as even and uninflected as possible; she'd already sussed that giving him or anyone involved with the al-Wahid family any excuse at all for not taking her seriously would bury our chances at the start. Being written off as an emotional bird would have done it, and she knew it.

So she stayed calm. It got a bit dodgy near the end; talking about what she'd seen through the window slit, she had a bead of sweat along her hairline that had nothing to do with the weather. She got to the end of it, no interruptions from anyone, and waited.

"Ah." Bengt sounded completely neutral. "I'm familiar with those huts, of course. They were put up many years before my association with the royal family. If I remember correctly, they were mostly used for storage while the motorway was being completed, with the occasional emergency housing provided for a worker. But if you looked through the windows, you will have seen that they are very sparse in terms of accommodations. No one lives in them, these days."

"Maybe not." I was keeping my own voice level. There'd been just a shade of emphasis in that *if you looked through the windows*. "But someone was using that third hut for something, and whatever it was, mate, it left a lot of blood."

Bengt opened his mouth, but Patrick got in first. "I'm not primarily concerned with whatever happened in that hut. But the terms of our contract state very clearly that the Queen's Palace is Blacklight's, for the band's exclusive use, for the duration of our stay in Manaar. Then there's the specific rider, forbidding the al-Wahid daughters from interacting in any way with the band family. We already know Nordine was on the premises when he had no business there. JP himself encountered the two girls skinny-dipping in the mineral pools, right outside the palace. Both clauses have been breached, Bengt. I've already discussed this with Carla Fanucci and Ian Hendry. If band management chose to enforce it, we could turn around and go home right now."

Bengt and Patrick had locked up, eye to eye, and no one was saying a word. I was remembering, a bit too clearly, just how tricky it was hiding things from Patrick, back when he was a cop. I've always thought he'd make a brilliant poker player. There's no reading that face, not if he decides to keep it shuttered. But Bengt was matching him. Pair of stone faces, there...

"Yes." Bengt broke the silence, finally. "That is true. It would be unfortunate, however, and would cause a great deal of trouble to all concerned. It would also do some harm to Blacklight's reputation for reliability, if such things matter to your organisation. I would also remind you that the Emir has absolute say on

166

whether or not a plane leaves Manaari airspace. I do understand your position, of course. But whatever happened has already happened. What would you have me do?"

"We want to know what happened in that hut."

I jerked my head round to stare at Bree, and got a shock. Between outrage and frustration, she was about ten seconds away from dotting Bengt Ekberg a good one, straight across the chops. My wife doesn't play poker; she hasn't got the face for it.

"That's very natural." If he'd read it, he wasn't showing. "The huts, of course, are well beyond the grounds of the Queen's Palace. But I understand your desire to know. Patrick will understand, I think, when I say that I have nothing in the way of spare time until after the show. But I will look into it then, and keep you informed."

I got hold of Bree's hand held on hard. She was breathing through her nostrils.

Bengt looked at his watch. "And now, if you will excuse me, I have much work to do. Good night to you."

"Ladies and gentlemen, His Excellency the Emir and the Royal Family offer you warmest welcome to Medin-Manaar..."

"You ready for this?"

Tony had come up behind me, and he sounded shaken. That wasn't much of a surprise; yeah, we'd done crowds of over a hundred thousand on the last tour, but there's a difference between that and the decibel levels that come out of a quarter million people, you know? Just then, you could barely hear anything over the crowd noise. You couldn't really see where Amina Plaza ended, either. Something about all those bodies out there made the horizon look different, and of course it was getting dark. Good job we'd gone for all those audio towers and all that extra gear...

"Yeah, I'm fine." I had Little Queenie strapped on and ready to go. "Not a problem."

"We know that you have come to Manaar from the far corners of the world, and we have an extraordinary show for you…"

Of course that was bollocks. Truth is, I was nervous as hell, stomach fluttering, nerve endings jangling, the lot. I always get edgy on opening nights, even if the opening night is a one-off. I was damned if I was letting Tony in on that, though. He'd been through enough shit this past year. There'd been so much going on around us, it would have been too easy to forget that he was barely ten days out of a gruelling rehab, trying to get his life and his marriage back together.

I wasn't forgetting. No way I could, you know? I've been through that particular horror show myself. If dishing out a double handful of little white lies was going to make any part of it easier for Tony to handle, I was prepared to keep dishing until I ran completely out of the damned things.

"…to ring in a new era of entertainment and luxury in Manaar, and to ring in the new year…"

"Ready for this, Johnny? Tony, don't look so freaked out, mate. It's just a gig." Mac had breezed up next to me, running in place, loosening up, doing all the usual stuff he's been doing for forty years just before the spotlight finds him. If he's ever been nervous about a show, I've never once seen him show it. "Honestly, though, I still haven't quite wrapped my head round not having the ramp and the side stages out there. Not quite Book of Days, is it?"

"Bigger crowd, smaller stage." Luke was right behind Tony, and the Bunker Brothers right at his shoulder. "Jesus, listen to that audience. Everyone ready? What's the noise level out there, do you think? Hey, Bree."

I turned, just my head, and smiled. Bree was behind me, literally pressed up against me, one hand ready for her traditional way of wishing me a good show: snaking between my thighs and grabbing. She knows, and I know, that there's nothing like sending the band onstage all primed for sex to get that out to the audience, as well.

I don't know what she'd been thinking since the encounter with Bengt, where he'd basically told us to fuck off and keep our noses out of their business. Whatever she was worrying about or imagining or anything else, she'd put it away and was apparently planning on keeping it put away until we got back to London, or maybe all the way back to San Francisco. She hadn't brought it up, hadn't said a word about it, nothing at all, since that backstage meeting. If Ian hadn't dragged the band off for a long last-minute full run-through in Ali's fancy studio, I might have spent more time worrying about what was going on in her head. As it was, I had no attention to spare for anything that wasn't the show. Probably just as well, yeah?

"...*one of the greatest bands in history, legends of rock and roll, in a once in a lifetime show...*"

"Dude, you've been talking for a year. Just shut the fuck up and let the band onstage, yo." Domitra was looking cross and concentrated, and she was muttering. The women were all dressed to the nines, but she'd gone the other way; normally she'd be in stretchy stuff and her Docs, but tonight, she'd apparently decided that being even scarier than usual was the way to go. She looked like a ninja from one of those Japanese black and white movies. Everything she had on was black.

"*Ladies and gentlemen...*"

The stage lighting shifted and flickered, a pool of gold and indigo, the logo that's identified the band for coming up on forty years, and of course the audience noise levels went up a few notches. Bree got one hand between my thighs and did her usual 'sending hubby off to the office' deal. She had her lips against my ear. "Do a good gig, baby."

"*...BLACKLIGHT!*"

That whole thing, about being a bag of nerves on opening

nights—I always forget that, as soon as we hit the stage and the lights find us and we hit those first chords together as a band, as a unit, the nerves get out of the bag and just let me do my thing. The Amina Plaza show was no exception.

We'd actually opted to do something unusual for us: we'd included a few numbers we don't do live, as a general rule. It could have been risky, that; it was Mac's idea, and he'd suggested we all brace for an argument when we let Ian know. But Ian was fine with it. He'd told us, usual gruff Ian style, that he was the tour manager and not the musical director, the set list was Mac and Luke's worry and not his, get on with it, play whatever worked for us.

So we opened the Manaar gig with a thing called "Locked Me Out Again", a B-side off our first mega-selling album, *Pick Up The Slack*. There was a good chance half the audience wouldn't know it, and yeah, you generally want to open a show this size with a standard or a hit. I wondered what was going on in Mac's head, but I hadn't asked him. I don't question him about this stuff often, or Luke either. Some part of me is still the new kid, still just being allowed to sit in, you know?

So, first chords—it's a sharp jumpy off-rhythm run on Luke's Strat. Cal and I played a call and response, Stu hit the kick drum, crashing low end of the piano from Tony, like distant thunder. Then Mac hit the spotlight.

"...*Same old movie, same old thing, here we go again, same reactions every time, been doing this since I don't know when...*"

I was holding my breath. I probably wasn't alone, either. Mac never shows nerves, but yeah, it was risky.

The crowd went nuts.

I glanced out over this endless tidal wave of faces and moving shoulders and hands in the air, a quarter million bodies swaying like rows of ripe corn in some field out there in the American heartlands. If there was anyone among the first few thousand people who didn't know the words, I couldn't see them. They all knew every word of a B-side that we've played live maybe three times ever, and which gets basically no airplay. They were all singing.

"...*Same old story, same old song, it never seems to change, I make noise and you get weepy, I put myself right out of range...*"

The portable toilets were shaking. Now that's what I call being on it, yeah? Even the crappers were dancing. I realised I was grinning, something I hadn't really been doing much of since we'd got back to Manaar. I wasn't the only one, either. The whole band was grinning along with me. I could see Tony's face over the long shining expanse of piano lid; the rider had specified a Mason & Hamlin grand, and Ronan had kitted it up with an assortment of internal mics. Tony's face—crikey, he was shining almost as much as the damned piano.

"...*So I'm out on the porch and the sun is sinking, my key don't work, don't know what you were thinking...*"

Bree was dancing off in the wings, my side of the stage. I had a fantastic view of her moving, and the rust-coloured dress she'd got for the show was moving right along with her. It had been too long since I'd had her there offstage, visible during a Blacklight show; the Book of Days set had been a revolutionary bare stage, 360 degrees open to the audience. That meant there were no wings for her or anyone else to dance in. This—my old lady shaking it, getting down and rocking out, just lost in the music, right there where I could see her and draw on that energy—was fucking brilliant. It was old-school Blacklight.

Right, Johnny, and there's you answer. That's what was going on in Mac's head.

That's why he'd wanted to open with a thirty year old B-side. All the tech, all the gear, Ronan had got us all totally twenty-first century, Brave New World stuff. And musically, Mac done a one-eighty. He'd taken us back to the band we'd been when we first crested, back in the late seventies: amps, light show, the lot. It wasn't retro, any more than Book of Days had been. It was just another take on what we'd done with that last tour: Blacklight then, Blacklight now, here we are, rock on with us. The contrast was brilliant. It was like listening to an eight-track in that Bugatti Veyron Bree wasn't going to get to drive after all.

"...*Banging on the sliding door but it's double-paned, I might as well leave—you locked me out again!*"

So yeah, the opening night nerves were gone by the time Luke hit a scorching little solo three minutes twenty into that first tune. Some nights are good right out the gate. Some nights, especially when my body's playing Judas on me, I've got to go deep into the physical reserves and pull up stuff so that I can give the fans what they're there for.

But once in a while, we get the show where just a few bars in, everything comes together and you know, straight off: this one's historic. It's legend, magic, not something we can repeat. This is one for the ages. They aren't always the big gigs, either; some of the ones that get talked about longest are smaller shows. It's something to do with the energy, what happens when energy becomes alchemy: crowd anticipation and band and venue and maybe just the smell in the air come together and become one thing, and bob's your uncle: lead into gold.

I'm glad, now, that the crowd had something amazing to take away with them. They came a long way for that. They deserved it, the loyal buggers.

We finished the first set with "Liplock". It was a nice safe way to bring down the house, and it probably led to more than a handful of babies for some of that audience, nine months down the road; you give Malcolm Sharpe a song about oral sex, there's going to be rather a lot of belly-bumping by the time the night's over. Down the side stairs and straight into the tent that had been put up for the band's use, towelling off for a twenty-minute break, sucking down mineral water, hydrating.

"Damn, JP, that sounded fantastic!" Carla had glass of something bubbly in one hand. Right behind her, Bree was balancing two plates of food. "Way to rock the Kasbah, guys."

"Thanks." I'd headed for a chair straight off; my legs had gone shaky, whether from the adrenalin or the MS being pissy, I couldn't have said. My stomach was rumbling, as well—playing music is like good sex, the way it uses energy and burns off the calories. "Bree, is one of those for me? Great, because I'm hungry. We sound as good as I think we do tonight?"

"Better." She'd pulled over a chair and settled in next to me herself. I took a quick look at her plate—good, she'd gone for sensible food. Some show nights, she's so damned busy making sure I've got the right nosh, she just grabs whatever for herself. "John, you know something? I never realised until tonight just how much I missed dancing where you could see me. It feels like the good old days. And wow, I haven't heard some of those songs in years—actually, I don't think I've ever heard you do 'Locked Me Out Again' live, ever. Whose idea was that, the oldies stuff, I mean? Because it was totally kickass and I'm loving it."

"Bree, angel, how sweet of you to say so. My idea, mostly, with some input from Luke. But of course the entire band had to approve it." Mac was bouncing from foot to foot, shaking both legs and arms. "God, this lactic acid can just sod right along now. I feel as if I've just ridden three stages of the Tour de France. Ian, what have we got? Ten minutes…?"

We opened the second set with "Hammer It Home", Mac's pissy political monster of an anthem, and that pretty much locked up the way the rest of the gig was going to go. He always does this one edgy, but tonight he brought this weird sort of trembling concentration to it.

"…Every time the Big Man tries to nail you, every time the jack boots find your door, when you think your self-respect has failed you, think you can't take it anymore…"

I've got a really nasty guitar solo mid-song, and it came out dirtier and rougher than usual. Not a bad thing, that's what the vibe was that night, but as I was playing it, a thought popped into my head, maybe because I suspected Mac was envisioning Ali when he sang about the Big Man: I hadn't seen Ali anywhere, not before the show, not in the band's private tent, nothing. What the fuck, the bloke had coughed up twenty four million quid for the pleasure of having us come out here and play this gig, and he couldn't be arsed to actually watch it? It didn't make sense.

"...Hit it hard, hit it fast, make them work if they want your ass, you don't have to take it, you don't have to play it, just make that nail your own, I tell you hammer it home..."

I shot a look into the wings, both sides of the stage. Not there. Maybe he had a royal box somewhere, but even if he did, something was still off.

"...I tell you, hammer it home...!"

I had it now. Whatever I didn't like about the bloke—and that was damned near everything—he did have a huge respect for hospitality. Yeah, we'd been paid a metric fuckload of dosh to play this show, but we, the whole Blacklight family, were guests under his roof. And he hadn't come out to wish us good luck, hadn't sent someone, nothing.

I pulled my mind off it. I had to, basically, because two hundred and fifty thousand people were demanding our attention and that's where the attention had to go. So Ali, and why he hadn't come out, why he'd blown us off, that had to wait. The next hour and twenty minutes were all about the gig.

We closed the show with "Remember Me". That was hard, making that choice. It was one I'd written, words and music, a love song to our world, to the music we make, a way of saying thanks and a way of calling us all out on our bullshit. It was also a love song to my wife.

Unfortunately, it was what had been playing on the overheads at Wembley Stadium the night I'd gone into V-fib and flatlined. For Bree, that song is always going be about me on the floor, watching what she thought was me dying. She hadn't even been let touch me because her mum was busy using paddles to restart my heart, and she didn't need her daughter electrocuted in the process. The song is Bree's personal soundtrack to her worst nightmare.

But "Remember Me" is also one of the best-selling singles in music history, and our fans expect it. And the gig wasn't about Bree, it was about them. So, when Mac and Luke put it down as the closer, they did check with me first. Nice of them, you know? They didn't have to do that. But they were all at Wembley, and they all knew just how Bree reacts to it. I'd told them yeah, she'll be warned that it's coming, but I'm with you, this is about the fans, and she'll have to cope.

Halfway through the song, the entire stage and Amina Plaza and all those towers seeming to shake with how much music and feeling and magic and everything else was happening out there, I looked for Bree. This was the first time we'd played the song, the first time she'd seen me onstage with Blacklight, since I'd almost died at Wembley. I needed to know she was actually dealing with it, that she was okay. There was fuck-all I could do about it if she wasn't, but still, I needed to know.

She wasn't dancing. She was standing very still and watching me. Not the band—just me, I could tell by the way her head moved slightly whenever I did, following me movements. She was far enough back in the shadows to where I couldn't see her face. But she was there, offstage, still visible.

Arms around each other, bowing. Fireworks shooting off behind the stage; they were actually out past the city, being set off from boats out in the Medin-Manaar harbour. Offstage to towel off, letting the chanting and screaming and flickering cell phone display lights build up to insanity pitch. Back out onstage for a three-song encore, instead of the usual one tune. Lights up, announcement over the PA, and the largest gig Blacklight had ever played was in the bag, and done.

"Right." Ian was waiting for us in the tent. "Brilliant show, guys. That's quite a lot of happy people going to be going on about this one for good long time. I've got the cars just outside— there's a late supper waiting for everyone in the corporate suite, back at the Royal residence, if anyone fancies it. You lot ready? JP, what?"

"Just wondering about something." The show was over, and my brain was back in gear, looking at what I'd put aside for the past couple of hours. "Am I the only one thinks it's pretty damned rude that Ali never bothered to show? Or was he there, and I just didn't see him?"

If anyone had told me it was possible for silence to be that absolute just the other side of the wall from a quarter million people, I'd have thought they were bonkers. Maybe it was the look I got off everyone's face.

"Shit." Mac had gone very still, and Domitra, next to him, was reacting. "Good eyes, Johnny. No, I haven't seen him at all today. And if someone wants to reassure me that there's nothing ominous about that, I'll be delighted to hear it. I just won't believe it. Ali's got a very strong sense of what the host owes the guest, and if rudeness isn't a beheading offence in Manaar, it's bloody close. Ian? Suggestions? Because I've got a very bad feeling about this."

"Fuck!" Ian had gone even stiffer than Mac had. "No clue, Mac, and no, I haven't seen him today either. I was so busy concentrating on the gig, the Emir never came into my head. Look, let's get back to our digs. We can have the full confab once we're safe out of here."

"Safe?" Katia was staring at Ian. "You mean, you think we might not be safe?"

176

"I don't know, do I?" Ian turned and headed for the tent flap. We were right behind him; getting out seemed like a good idea, suddenly. "I just know I'd rather not be in a tent in the park if there's bad news no one's shared yet. Let's go –"

He stopped. There was noise, just outside the tent flap. Not voices—a different sort of sound entirely. A clicking, oily, a bit metallic somehow.

"Mac." Domitra was in front of him. She looked like a coil, ready to let go. "Behind me. *Now.*"

I didn't see Mac move, so maybe he didn't. Maybe Dom did the moving. But she was there, blocking him off. There were people in the entry to the tent, and they were heading in fast.

Uniforms. Ali's guard. They were all carrying guns, and the guns weren't in holsters. They were pointed at us.

I wasn't thinking, or anything else. It's a funny thing about moments like that—you don't think, you just do. I'd got one hand out and hard on Bree's arm, and I'd yanked her behind me before I'd even realised I moved. No one else seemed to be moving, not even the muscles of their mouths, because no one was saying anything yet. I had a mad thought: *might need a new ticky-box if we get out of this alive, Johnny, the old one's working so hard it's going to blow…*

"Excuse me. Let me through, please."

It was Patrick's voice, coming from the back of that swarm of armed guards. They let him through, but they weren't lowering the guns.

"Patrick?" I don't know that I'd ever heard Mac sound completely unnerved before. "What in hell's going on?"

"There's been another death." Dirty-ice eyes, cold cop looks, the smell of blood, of something wounded: everything I dislike most about Patrick Ormand. I'd never been so glad to see any of it. "And we've got one hell of a mess. It's a member of the Royal Family."

177

Chapter Eleven

I've been in a few crises in my day. I don't know about you, but I always think I'm right there in the moment, nice and calm, keeping it together, voice of reason. Then it's over with and I realise I was freaking out, losing it, flipping my shit. After that, the only way to suss out what really happened and how I really reacted is to ask someone else who was there.

I've been in the middle of a firefight in Cannes, in a club fire in Marin County, and saddled with a few too many dead bodies. I thought I was calm for all of that. But that New Year's Day in Manaar, I did a complete one-eighty: I remember myself being too freaked to put words together to make a sentence. Not my usual way of remembering how I handle the bad moments.

"The royal family? Someone's been killed?"

Ian had somehow got himself in front of the rest of the band, but the armed thugs didn't seem to give a toss about who was standing where. There probably wasn't any reason for them to worry; I don't know much about guns, but I was pretty sure that what they had pointed at us were the kind of things that could spray a hail of bullets before anyone could duck—automatic, or semi-automatic, or whatever. "Patrick, for God's sake, talk to us. The Emir? Has something happened to him?"

Patrick had his back to that collection of muzzles. I didn't know if that was some sort of show of courage or defiance or something, or whether he honestly didn't believe they'd open fire and shoot him in the back; either way, it occurred to me that our pet detective really has got glacial runoff in his veins. My own chest was thumping away like a bad drum machine track on some piece of eighties synth-pop rubbish.

"So far as I know, the Emir is unharmed. I don't have any of the actual details yet. All I have is the bare fact." He took a deep breath and looked around at us, frozen there in place like the Blacklight exhibit straight out of Madame Tussauds. "Princess Paksima has been killed."

There was noise behind me, murmurings, voices. Bree was still leaning up against me; I felt her let her breath out, realised that the reason my chest was throbbing was because I was hanging on to my own breath for dear life, and exhaled. The rush of air to both lungs made me giddy.

"I'm very sorry to hear that. I'm sure we all are. But I'm not really clear what it has to do with us."

We all jerked our heads. Carla had come up to stand at Ian's right shoulder, and she nodded her head towards the guard. She wasn't gesturing with a hand, not at that point, and I got why straight off: she wasn't pointing, or doing anything else that might get any fingers tightened on any triggers.

"Why are these people pointing guns at us? The band's been onstage for hours. They were in full view of a quarter of a million

179

people. Besides, most of us didn't know the princess—in fact, it was specified in the band rider that the al-Wahid girls would stay away from anything to do with the band while we were in Manaar. The Emir and I both insisted on that. It's pretty obvious that no one here interacted with the princesses in any way, at least not willingly. So I really don't see the point of this."

She sounded just the same as she always does: nice and calm, and completely competent. Not only that, she looked to have sorted out who was in charge of that lot, because she was talking to one particular bloke, forcing him to make eye contact with her.

She waved one arm, finally, a nice easy gesture. You'd have thought she was confronting someone blocking her driveway back in LA, or something. The gun in his hand wavered, lowering just a bit, just enough.

Carla had both eyebrows up, completely in control of the situation. She wasn't looking at Patrick, so I don't know whether she caught the tiny nod he gave her. I saw Ian reach for her hand suddenly, and hang onto it.

Funny thing, but with just that one gun not aimed at us any longer, the whole vibe in the room shifted and changed. For starters, Patrick suddenly found his voice again. He must have also realised what he'd been presenting his back to all this time, because he turned round, not too quickly. Most of the guns were still pointing our way.

"I've got a call in to Bengt Ekberg." He'd picked the guard in charge, as well, and he was talking straight at him. "I'm as puzzled as you are, Carla. I have no idea why the Emir or anyone else would send armed guards out here, or what their orders are. After all, you said it yourself: Blacklight's been onstage all evening. I'm guessing we'll have to wait for Bengt before we find out anything solid."

We were all quiet. Bree wasn't behind me any longer; she'd slipped out and come to stand right beside me. I'd been concentrating so hard on what was going on with Carla and the guards, I hadn't even noticed. Domitra was still planted in front of Mac, and she still looked dangerous as hell. So far as I could tell, she hadn't moved an inch the whole time.

And of course, Sod's Law being what it is, both my legs picked right then to get shaky. That was probably inevitable: the gig, the adrenalin, standing in place for too long. The MS is an opportunistic bitch of a disease. If there's any opening for it to ratchet up and give me grief, that's what it does.

"Excuse me."

Shit. Bree'd noticed. I know that tone. When my wife's voice gets that controlled and even, she's not taking no for an answer. Of course she'd felt the tremors start up in my legs.

"Patrick, can we get John a chair, please? He needs to sit."

Patrick opened his mouth and shut it again. He looked about as close to being confounded as I've ever seen him. Bree's tone got even sharper. "*Now*, please, Patrick."

The guard in charge went stiff around the shoulders. The gun came up, not all the way, just an inch or two, just enough.

Bree rounded on him. She fixed him with a stare worthy of that bird in the Greek stories, the one who turned you to stone if you met her eye—Medusa, is it? She looked like one of the Fates or something, assuming the Fates ever got tarted up in designer gear and high heels. For one really bad moment, I thought she was going call him *little man*. If she'd done that, he'd probably have opened fire. It didn't help that, in that particular pair of shoes, she was taller than he was.

"Is this your idea of Manaari manners?" She snapped it out at him. "Do you think the Emir would approve of you treating his guests this way? I have trouble believing he would be so discourteous, or send you to be so discourteous. My husband is ill. He needs to sit. Unless you're planning on shooting someone, lower that gun, please."

For a good long moment, the whole situation just hung there. I couldn't hear a damned thing behind me—for all I knew, the rest of the band, the crew, everyone else, had keeled over from shock, or slipped out the back of the tent, or been beamed up into some kind of alien ship or something. That device in my chest never had to do a harder few moments' work than it did just then.

He dropped the muzzle. This time it went all the way down, until it was resting on the floor. Behind him, the rest of the guard followed suit.

Someone, one of the crew I think, brought me a chair, and I sat down. My legs were shaking like the bloody San Andreas Fault about to let go, or maybe like all those portable toilets a few hours ago had done. I wouldn't have put tuppence on it being from the MS, either. The back of my shirt was plastered to my skin, soaked through with sweat.

With me safe in a chair, Bree went and got one for herself, and settled down next to me. I reached out and got hold of her hand, and kissed it. We've got some amazing women around us, and thank God for it.

I don't know how long we waited, but it felt like hours, or maybe years. I remember Luke getting Karen into a chair and bringing her a plate of food—when you've got Type One diabetes, the bad kind, you can't pretend you don't need to eat. I remember my guitar tech, Jas, bringing over a couple of bottles of cold Volvic water, handing one to me and one to Bree. That's my usual tipple, and of course Carla had made sure it was in the rider that all the band's areas be stocked with it. I remember Cal wondering out loud how many people were still in the park outside, how many were still camping out there.

And at the back of my head, I kept hearing something Bengt had said, during that useless confrontation we'd demanded with him. Patrick had pointed out that the contract had been breached just by the twins being in the seraglio in the first place, that under the terms of the contract we could turn right round and go home.

And Bengt had said something about Ali having the last word on who got to fly out of Manaari airspace. I was wondering just how I'd been dim enough to miss that being a threat.

Because, yeah, it was a threat. It might have been no more than Bengt pulling a higher face card than Patrick's in the dainty little game of power poker that conversation had been, reminding us that we were on Ali's home turf and that gave Ali complete control, but any way I looked at it, that had been pretty damned ominous. He'd slipped it in there like the business end of a knife, and I hadn't sussed it.

I was so deep into thinking about that, I nearly missed the stir from outside. Then all the guards were standing with their backs straight and their eyes carefully not fixed on anyone or anything in particular and all the guns pointed straight at the roof of the tent.

Ali al-Wahid walked through the flap, and into the band's tent. And if I'd thought it was quiet behind me before, I hadn't known what quiet was.

For a bloke we didn't know well and didn't much want to, we'd seen him in quite a few different moods, you know? We'd seen him resentful when Mac and Luke called him out on his shit, back in San Francisco. We'd seen him calculating, nearly every time he'd had found himself around Bree since we'd first got here. We'd seen him doing his imperious privileged thing pretty much twenty four-seven, and of course, we'd seen him looking scary and relentless, the night Nordine had bought it. I hadn't really given him and his moods a lot of time; he just wasn't someone I thought much about if I wasn't given a good reason to.

That night, though, he just looked wrong. Different, stripped down, as if someone had peeled off flesh, taken everything inside out and then stuffed it back in again, but forgot to put all of it back. There was something indecent about it, I'm not sure why—it made me uncomfortable for a moment, as if I was looking at something through someone else's curtains. I don't do the voyeurism thing.

Next to me, Bree made a small noise at the back of her throat, but she swallowed it. Whatever it was that wanted out, sympathy or shock or whatever else it might have been, that wasn't the moment to be showing anything at all.

He came in, not looking around him at all, not looking at any of us. He looked as if he was seeing something maybe far away, something no one else could possibly see but him; no way to tell whether what he was looking at was brilliant or terrible, or maybe both.

The guards on either side held very still. A couple of them were visibly sweating, and that had me wondering until I realised the poor sods didn't know whether to risk moving to one side to let their boss through without interference, or whether moving and catching his attention was riskier than having him bump into one of them. They probably weren't sure which option was likelier to get them flogged, or maybe beheaded.

"Outside."

I had no clue who he was turfing off the premises, but whoever it was, his voice sounded different, as well. He'd never had much of an accent, not beyond that sort of moneyed-ponce modulated thing people get when they go to posh schools. Mac's got a touch of that in his speaking voice, as well.

I wouldn't have known that was Ali talking if I hadn't been staring straight at him. All the expression, all the body, had run out of his spine and face. It seemed his voice had taken a hit, as well. It was thin as wire. All the personality was gone out of it.

He hadn't sounded like this, or looked like this, when he'd stared down at Nordine's bloodless corpse, and told Bengt and Patrick to find out who'd killed his servant. This was a whole new level.

184

Since no one from our contingent was moving, it was just as well that Ali's personal guard got that he was talking to them. The bloke in charge, the one Carla and Bree had locked up with, shouldered his gun, and the rest of them followed suit. A moment later, they were on the other side of the tent flap. You could practically hear the sighs of relief, but that might have been in my head. We'd all gone quiet again.

The problem was, no one seemed to know what to say. The bloke had the power to keep us from going home, he had that troop of armed thugs waiting outside and a small army stashed somewhere else, and I was pretty sure that if he told them to slowly break all our arms and legs, they'd queue up and ask him whose fingers to start on first. But he was also a father, and he'd just lost one of his kids. None of the usual conventional rubbish was likely to work. Even Bree, who's got a nurturing streak you could park a tour bus on, didn't look to be able to summon up the necessaries...

"We're very sorry for your loss."

Bree and I both turned, and so did everyone else. Karen Hedley's got a wonderful speaking voice, good enough to give your ears a massage, very mellow and soothing. She was also the last person on earth to have any warm feelings for either of the al-Wahid twins, dead or alive, not after the damage they'd done to her own daughter; she dotes on Suzanne. But she wasn't putting it on—Karen's not capable of that. She meant what she'd just said. Maybe it was just being a parent herself, being able to feel what Ali must be going through.

"Thank you." Nothing was moving in that face, not a feeling or a muscle or anything else. "I regret my guards' behaviour. I gave them no instructions. They will be required to explain themselves, but this is not the moment."

"Your Excellency, is there any way in which we can help?" Patrick didn't sound as gentle as Karen had, but the official cop voice probably did a lot more to get things moving than the conventional regrets Karen had offered up, however genuine they'd been. "I'm happy to offer any assistance I can give Bengt while we're still in Manaar, if that's appropriate."

Oh, bloody hell. Yeah, he'd slipped that one in nicely: *happy to help, experienced copper, you letting the band out of here and if so, when?*

"If Bengt needs assistance, he will tell you." Ali looked around, starting with Bree, moving to me, just looking. I got the impression he was making sure that he made eye contact with every person in that damned tent. "I have no reason to believe that any of you are involved, but I cannot know. And no one will leave Manaar until I can put a name and a face to the person who executed my daughter."

There were probably fifty people in that tent just then: the band, the family, the crew. If you asked me whether any one of us happened to be breathing just then, I'd probably say no, we weren't. There was something about that word, *executed*, something about the way he said it, that didn't leave much room for breathing, or anything else.

"As the head of the house of al-Wahid, I thank you for your performance tonight. I regret that my daughter's death made my attendance an impossibility." He had his hands in his pockets, and he was back to looking at something we couldn't see and probably didn't want to. "You are all tired. Go back to the Queen's Palace. If Bengt has questions, or desires your assistance in any way, he will tell you in the morning."

"John?"

It was probably not too far off daylight, New Year's morning, and Bree sounded wide awake. She was keeping her voice quiet, but she wasn't worrying about whether she might wake me; she knew damned well I hadn't slept more than a couple of minutes at a time. Neither had she. I doubt either of us had got within twenty miles of actual REM sleep that night.

"What, love?"

"Do you suppose those guards are still outside?"

I rolled over, and faced her. Sunrise was definitely coming up shortly; the light in the room was a chilly blue, but it was morning blue, not midnight blue, and there were birds calling outside. I could see her face, and the blue light wasn't nearly as dark as the blue circles under her eyes. She looked exhausted, completely wiped out.

"John...?"

"I don't know, Bree. Just guessing, but I'd say yeah, seems likely. Not really sure what they're up to, or why they're out there in the first place, though. It's not as if anyone's going anywhere." I got a hand out from under the cover and touched her cheek. "At least we won't have any midnight visitors under our windows, not if the Forty Thieves or whatever Ali's gang calls themselves are still patrolling the place. Why?"

"I just – " She stopped, and took a breath. She had her voice under complete control, but it was a visible effort. She was putting her whole body into holding it even. "Shit. John, are we prisoners?"

Even with her not letting her voice go up at all, keeping it straight up, that question should have sounded like melodrama. It says a lot about the situation that it didn't. It sounded terrifying and logical.

That was the result of hearing those boots out there all night. They weren't loud, but they were there, rhythmic, not stopping. We'd heard them echoing across the seraglio, back and forth between those damned pools, ever since we'd got back. The brief periods when we hadn't heard them had been even worse; both of us had strained, waiting for them to start up again.

There'd been no band meeting last night, no putting our heads together, no trying to sort out what the hell was going on and what we were going to do about it. That was a definite boot to the arse of my personal comfort zone. We'd had thirty years of dealing with anything that came up as a group, a unit, a pooling of brains and opinions and ideas. Last night, that hadn't happened.

So yeah, I couldn't answer my wife, and my comfort zone had gone walkabout. Not having that meeting was also a pointer as to how big this was, how much potential it had to fuck up our world: The cars had brought us back from the tent, motorcycle escort to cut through the crowds outside the venue, thousands of happy fans cheering when the limos went by. It was just like the post-show after any big outdoor stadium gig, yeah? Everything had been normal, right up until the limos got us through those peacock-gaudy arches and we'd seen Ali's guard, full uniform, and those damned guns.

Nothing was normal that night, not after Ali had used that word, *executed*. And Ian, who's so nuts for meetings that given half a chance he'd probably call a band meeting to discuss whether we were having enough band meetings or not, hadn't even bothered suggesting a huddle. He'd waved us off to our suites and told us to try for some kip, maybe things would shake out in the morning and he'd do his best to get some gen on what the hell had actually happened. He hadn't hung about waiting for anyone to answer him, either, just climbed back into the limo where Carla was waiting. They might have been going off for a management-level confab on their own, but if that was what was on, they weren't including us. Not exactly reassuring.

"John...?"

It would have been nice to be able to chuck her under the chin, grin, tell her to stop being silly, don't talk rubbish of course we're not prisoners. I couldn't. I didn't know, not for certain, and I was damned if I wanted to offer up soothing nonsense that might turn out to be a flat-out lie. It wouldn't do any good; she wouldn't buy it anyway.

"I don't know, Bree. Not sure if not being allowed to leave on schedule fits the definition or not, but –"

I stopped because she'd begun to shake. I pulled her up close, just holding on. Moments like this, only Bree will do me for comfort, and yeah, she feels the same way. The best I could offer just then was comfort, skin to skin, heart to heart.

"It's okay, baby." I was talking into her hair. "If we are stuck here, it won't be for long. There's a consulate right downtown— we passed it on the way to the restaurant. If there's any smell of us being detained here indefinitely, Carla will be down there handling it, even if she's got to get the bloke in charge out of bed. It's not as if we're what you'd call low profile. Besides, I didn't get any feeling off Ali that he was targeting us for anything, you know? So there's that."

She was quiet, but she wasn't relaxing. I kept both arms wrapped round her good and close, just holding on. I'm not sure what you call it, when that whole primal need thing kicks in and we just sort of slip back to wanting to do what our ancestors did, huddling together round the fires because something big and toothy is out there prowling in the bushes and wanting to eat us. Atavistic, or something like that? Whatever it is, that's where we both seemed to be just then.

Even if the reality of what was going on outside our bedroom walls hadn't been keeping me awake, the MS would have done the trick. There were little stabs and tingles everywhere. Both legs were twitching from heel to groin, to the point where the normal night dose of antispasmodics was barely making a dent; the twitches were becoming straight-up spasms and jerks. There were ominous little movements under the skin on the back of my left hand, as well, a sort of weird fizzing sensation. That was new to me. It was also painful as hell.

I could hide those from Bree, but I couldn't hide the small continuous case of the shakes. And Bree wasn't saying or doing anything that showed she'd even noticed. It takes something huge to get her attention so locked up that she hasn't got enough to spare for what's going on with me.

"I hate this place."

All of a sudden, her voice wasn't under control anymore. She sounded pretty damned close to the edge.

"Glad to hear it," I told her, and brushed my lips against her forehead. "I was worried you might want a little summer bungalow in the desert, or something. Seriously, Bree, once we're out of here, I'm not planning on coming within a hundred miles of this place again. He can have his tents and his peacocks and his mineral pools and the rest of it. I'm out."

She was quiet, and so was I, just holding on. We were both straining our ears, listening for that rhythmic footfall from outside in the seraglio, Ali's boys doing their thing between the pools. And either they'd got a lot quieter, or else they'd stopped.

My head kept trying to come up with a picture, any picture, of what might be happening back at the palace. Was Bengt there, burning the midnight oil, talking to people, coping, dealing? Had Ali slept, or was he awake, maybe staring at that distant thing he'd seemed fixed on, back in the band's tent? Was he pacing, walking the floor? I couldn't seem to bring up any kind of picture in my head; there was a just a blank, somehow.

"You know what?" Bree was muffled, her face up against me. Her voice seemed quieter than it had been; maybe she was getting sleepy, finally. I hoped so. "I'm worried about..."

Her voice trailed off, and I moved back a bit. "Sorry, love? I didn't quite catch –"

"The other twin." The sun was almost up, now, and for some reason, I found myself remembering sunrise, the two of us not sleeping, going out at first light, finding that blood-spattered hut at the edge of the desert. Christ, was that really just a couple of days ago? It felt like half a lifetime had gone by. "Azra. They were almost like one girl, somehow. Weren't they? Identical twins come from the same egg. She must be—I don't know. Destroyed. Ripped in half. She's lost the other half of the egg she came from. It's like someone smashed the other side of her mirror."

"Yeah, I know what you mean." She was right, of course she was, but I hadn't actually stopped to think about it until she'd brought it up. The way she'd put it was almost too vivid. "And them being almost like one girl, that's spot on. You couldn't tell one from the other, not unless you knew who was wearing which colour headscarf."

"Her sister's been killed. Her twin." Her voice was under control again, very quiet. "That's got to be so hard, John. Like losing, I don't know, half the person you were—hello?"

I'd heard it as well: a tap on our door, quiet, rhythmic. For some reason, we'd both gone stiff. Silly, really. It wasn't as if we were in any danger from anyone...

"JP? You awake?"

I let my breath out so fast, I got dizzy. Bree was already up, knotting a robe around her waist, heading for the door; I was rubbing my hands, shaking my legs a bit, trying to get the pins and needles out and get the MS to back off. I had a strong feeling that today, of any day, I couldn't afford to let myself fetch up incapacitated and helpless.

Luke was still in pyjamas, and he didn't look as if he'd slept much either. Neither did Stu or Cal, who were right behind him. Mac, just letting himself out of his own room with Domitra already on guard in the corridor, had pulled jeans and a tee-shirt on, but he was looking tousled and rubbing his arms. Tony was out in the hall, with Katia already waiting for him. I saw her glance over at Mac; if she thought he looked any less lickable in what he had on, she wasn't showing it, or maybe she was too

191

busy shivering. That corridor was always chilly, what with the small high windows not letting the sunlight in, but that morning, it was bloody cold.

Bree held the door open, letting everyone in, peering out into the corridor to make sure no one else was coming along. I'd pulled on my own robe and swung myself out of bed. The floor felt as if small pins were sticking up out of it, straight into the soles of my feet. I could feel the nerves trying to squirm away from the source of pain, but of course, there was no place to go: the pain was entirely internal. You can't squirm away from your own body, even if there's days you wish you could.

"Can everyone hold on a few minutes, please?" Bree was keeping her voice down, but she wasn't whispering. Apparently, she was only worried about waking the rest of the band wives. She didn't seem to give a fuck whether the guard out of doors could hear her or not, assuming they were still there. "Are we expecting anyone else? No? Okay. Then could I get everyone to sit down while I put a kettle on? John needs his meds before we do anything. It's been a bad night. Stu, you do tea, not coffee, right? Dom, is tea okay? I don't think I have any of that drinking chocolate you like…"

So she'd noticed the MS was flaring, after all. For some reason, that made me feel better about things, more normal somehow. I caught her eye, blew her a kiss, and headed off for our posh khazi. I heard Tony say something about wanting a shave and a shower himself, as I was closing the door behind me.

I not only got my meds while my wife was sorting out who wanted what to drink, I actually managed a fast shower. I learned a good long time ago that when the brain gets into wide-awake mode but the body's reeling under the MS, a strong short hosing down can be just what the doctor ordered, and the hotter the better. I've run that one past my neuro, and the quack agrees: a good hot shower can't hurt. And one thing I could say for the

Queen's Palace: what with the hot mineral pools running underground, I couldn't whinge about not having enough hot water for a good wash. Besides, I'd snuck a fast look at the clock on my way into the bathroom, and it was twenty minutes of six. The rest of the band probably needed a few minutes of wake-up time, themselves. There was no need to rush.

By the time I'd got myself dried off enough so that the silk robe wouldn't glue itself to the wet patches, Bree'd got a second pot of coffee going, and the suite smelled brilliant. We'd also been joined by Karen Hedley. Bree was fussing over her, and one look at Karen was enough to make it clear why. She looked as if she hadn't slept at all, and you really can't do that, not with what she's got wrong with her. Even with Bree's less aggressive and serious form of it, sleep deprivation can mess with the levels and balances.

"All right." Bree'd saved me the rocking chair—it was more like a rocking throne, really—and I settled into it. "Bree, is there a cup for me, love? Great, thanks. So I'm guessing I wasn't the only one who thought we should have had a band meeting last night?"

"There probably was one." Mac likes his coffee loaded with sugar and cream, which means he can chug it while the rest of us are still waiting for ours to cool down. "In fact, I'd lay good money on it. What a pity the band wasn't invited to be there for it. Do you know, I'm rather cross about this."

Domitra snorted, and he gave his bodyguard a look. He wasn't joking about the mood he was in. "Well, honestly, Dom, can you or anyone else imagine that the braintrust wasn't up all night, figuring out what to do?"

"Of course they were." Stu got a mouthful of hot tea and swished it round like mouthwash. "Ian and Carla and probably Patrick, as well. I don't know whether I'm pissed off or glad we weren't invited."

"Don't you? I know exactly which one I am." Mac set his cup down, and Bree refilled it halfway. He didn't seem to notice. "I have to say, I'm not thrilled with this secrecy rubbish. In fact, I think I'm going to have a few words to say to our management on the subject. And yes, that includes Carla."

"I couldn't agree more. They do seem to be forgetting who pays them, don't they? It's not exactly a habit I want to encourage." Luke's voice was at normal volume, but had both of Karen's hands between his own, and he was rubbing hard. It reminded me of all these years I'd been rubbing Bree's in just that way, trying to warm them, get the blood circulating properly. "Hopefully it'll stop once we're the hell out of this bloody emirate and back home. It seems to only happen here. Bree? Is that someone at the door? No, you have your coffee, I'll get it—ah. Good morning, ladies. Sorry, did we wake you...?"

That was the only full-on band meeting I can remember where all the wives were there, and none of the management. Unusual, to say the least. Of course, we don't generally hold them at six in the morning in our pyjamas, either. But as I say, nothing about that night was normal.

Still, we did get a lot sorted out. It was interesting, because all the wives had opinions and they were all putting them out there, making damned sure they got heard. The one thing everyone agreed on was that, if we didn't have a definitive time by lunchtime for our plane getting the fuck out of Medin-Manaar Airport, management was going to be very busy.

"And I don't care how much it costs, either." Barb Wilson sounded pretty much the way I imagined her great-grandmother must have sounded during a suffragette march, back when Queen Victoria was still alive. Just the right tone to scare the hell out of generations of schoolboys, yeah? It would have been even more impressive if she hadn't been wearing paisley silk slippers that turned up at the toes, like something out of a 1920s movie about Arabia. "I'm not spending one minute longer than I have to in this place unless someone gives me a real reason to do it. If the Emir thinks he can keep us here indefinitely, he's got another think coming."

She stopped, because it was pretty obvious Karen wanted to say something. She'd opened her mouth and closed it a good four times while Barb was talking.

"Come along," Luke told her, and he was smiling. "No need to be shy, love. Put your tuppence in. What's on your mind?"

She'd gone bright pink. Odd, that, because she and Bree have almost identical colouring, but Bree goes white and Karen turns red. It might have something to do with the freckles—Karen's got masses of them, and Bree's got none—but whatever the reason, it's bizarre seeing them side by side.

"I do, actually. I just can't see why you don't call them and tell them to get over here. They work for you. They're supposed to be protecting the band's interests, aren't they? And really, they're quite good at that. But why should Ian be the only one who gets to call meetings? Can't you do it?"

"She's right." Bree was nodding, nice and fierce, her own hair bouncing against her shoulders. "You know she is. I get that they've probably been up all night, but tough shit. Shouldn't they be in on whatever we decide? I think Karen nailed it. Anyway, if we're going to bitch at them for not including us, we shouldn't be hypocrites and not include them."

"Bree, angel, how right you are. And yes, you've both nailed it." Mac had his phone out, and was punching in a number. "Besides, we've had one instance too many this trip of being separated as a family. I've personally had more than enough of—Ian? Good morning, mate. Mac here. Sorry if I woke you, but take comfort from the fact that you're in good company—I'm afraid none of us slept very well. We're just having a band meeting and we think you need to come play. No, we're in Johnny and Bree's suite. Yes, I know it's six in the morning. A pity we didn't do this last night—if we had, everyone might be getting their beauty sleep. See you in a few, and mind you bring Carla and Patrick with you."

Chapter Twelve

It turned out the guards outside actually had packed up their tents—or rather, their high-powered guns and whatever the hell else they'd had with them—and gone off to scare the shit out of someone else. We found that out when Patrick, beating Ian and Carla to the punch by about five minutes, stuck his head in through our suite door. It was a pity that was about the only good news he brought along with him.

Bree'd left the suite door propped open, letting everyone know to not interrupt the conversation inside by tapping on panels and waiting to be let in. I wasn't admitting it to Bree or anyone else, but I was edgy over that; between the guards charging into Blacklight's tent and having them stomping about outside our windows, I'd have felt a lot safer with any sort of barrier between me and the Forty Thieves. And yeah, I don't need to be told how much protection that flimsy little door would actually have been against a hail of bullets. I still would rather have had it shut.

We'd actually been quiet for a couple of minutes after Mac rang Ian, so we heard the Range Rover Patrick had been using since we got to Manaar pull up outside. Listening to his footsteps, I wondered why they sounded so loud—he's a soft-footed bloke, is Patrick, probably thanks to all those years he spent as a cop. Then I got it: they were the only footsteps out there. The Forty Thieves had gone off and left us alone. So everyone was watching the door when he came down the corridor and poked his head into our suite.

"Good morning." If he was worried at having a dozen pairs of eyes fixed on him, it wasn't showing. On the other hand, it might have been the first time I've ever seen the bugger actually human enough to look the worse for wear. His eyes were looking nearly as puffy as mine get, and he needed a shave. "I'm sorry to see everyone up so early. Did anyone manage to get any sleep last night? Bree, that coffee smells wonderful. Would it be possible to snag a cup...?"

"Not much in the way of sleep, no." Luke was watching him load his cup with cream and sugar. "Personally, I find it tricky trying to sleep when you don't know if you're under some richer than fuck potentate's house arrest, or not."

"Not to mention having the potentate's personal goon squad marching back and forth under your windows all night." Bree was cradling her cup, letting it get cool enough to drink from. "Patrick, are they still out there?"

"Ali's house guard?" He'd gone very still, suddenly. "They were in the seraglio courtyard last night? They weren't there when I pulled up. Not a sign. How long were they here?"

"Bree just told you, mate." I was watching him. There was something happening there—finding out about the guards being here had flipped a switch somewhere, or maybe clued him in to something. I've been around the bloke too often to miss that when it happens; everything tightens up, tautens, focuses. It's as scary as hell, even when you know why it's happening. When you haven't got the first clue, it's even scarier. "All night long. They were here when the cars brought us back from the Plaza, and they were still out there when Mac rang Ian. If they've gone, they've only just gone."

"Interesting."

He sounded nice and detached, noncommittal, whatever. And it was complete bullshit. Something in his head had opened, and let some light in from somewhere. I could tell.

"Interesting is one word for it." Bree had her eyes aimed at him as well. "But what I want to know is, why were they out there at all? I mean, why here? They had to know we weren't going anywhere, Patrick. We can't. So why were they guarding us? What did they think we were going to do, flap our wings and fly away home like a bunch of ladybugs, or something?"

She glanced at me, less than a blink's worth, and I got a shock, because it was there for me to see, even if no one else in that room could. She'd sussed it, figured it out. She already knew what the answer had to be.

Right then, the light went off in my own head, and I wasn't alone. You could practically here the bulbs popping, all round the room.

"Shit! They weren't guarding us, were they?" Tony was up on his feet. "They were doing something else altogether—or guarding something else altogether. What the fuck! This place is starting to piss me off. Anyone have any ideas?"

"You asking, dude?" Dom seemed to have gone as restless as Tony had, because she was on her feet, shaking her legs, limbering up, loosening muscles. "Because I think maybe it's got something to do with those damned pools. Remember when they got us all split out and shit, drag the band out for practice and everyone else gets lunch with the Emir and no arguments, and we came back and found those tanker trucks emptying out two of those things? No? Patrick, you think it's something else?"

"Oh, you could be right, Dom." His eyes were dirty slits. "It does leave me wondering about something related to that, though. Why come here at all?"

Bree was nodding, and Mac seemed to have caught up, as well. The rest of us just waited.

"JP and Bree heard and saw people having some kind of rendezvous under their windows." Christ, yeah, our pet rozzer had gone into full homicide detective mode: his teeth were showing and you could see the gears meshing. "Nordine died under their windows. Something happened with the pool adjacent to the one Nordine died in, and no, don't ask me what because I don't know either. And last night, Ali seems to have sent the house guard over here before you ever got back from the show. But why here at all? What was Nordine doing here, or anyone else? There are mineral pools all over the compound. Why come to the only occupied area, and risk being seen?"

Back during the Book of Days tour, the morning our long-time security chief had been killed and I'd suggested Patrick Ormand as a replacement, I'd been functioning on not enough sleep and a bitch of an exacerbation. I remember Mac making a comment at the time, something about how, if this was how my head worked under circs like those, Bree needed to wake me every couple of hours during a crisis. He'd been joking, but I must have been in pretty much that same place New Year's morning in Manaar, because I heard my own voice coming nice and clear, and my own voice was the last thing I was expecting to hear.

"You sure about that, mate?"

Patrick turned to face me. "Sure about what, JP?"

"How do you know they came from somewhere else? Whoever they were, I mean? Because maybe they were right here all the time. Maybe they did their thing right here because it was the closest place to do it, whatever it was."

"Oh for fuck's sake!" Mac slapped his coffee cup down on the nearest flat surface. "Johnny, that's brilliant, and do you know, if you mean what I think you mean and you happen to be right, then I'm really going to want a few words with the bloody Emir, bereaved papa or not."

"I'm not following this." Cyn Corrigan, sitting on the edge of our bed in a pair of pale yellow pyjamas, sounded fuddled. She hadn't quite got all the lash goop off after the show last night, and she had a few streaks up high on her cheeks. "What do you mean, here all the time? How could anyone have been, and us not know?"

"Fuck! Are we idiots?" Stu looked ready to put the boot in with something, he was that narked. "We've never actually explored the rest of this place, is how. I can't speak for the rest of you, but I've never gone past Cal's suite at the end of the corridor. Anyone else? Yeah, that's what I thought. I never even tried that fancy painted door at the end of the hall, to see if there was anything on the other side of it. They told us we had the place to ourselves, I just believed it. JP's just sussed that we were probably wrong."

"Nits." Cal had his fists clenched. "Bloody hell, we're a bunch of nits!"

Stu snorted, a pissy angry little noise. He's got that Irish temper, has Stu. "That's one word for it. Cor stone the bloody crows, I feel a proper divvy right now. I don't know about you lot, but I'm off to have a butcher's and see for myself."

"Yes, let's." Mac held a hand up, and turned to face Patrick. "But before we go anywhere, I want to know just what happened last night. Why did Ali say his daughter had been executed? Because that particular word brings up a very particular picture in my head."

"He used that word because it was right word." Flat as the

middle of Manhattan Island, that voice. "It was an execution. The Princess Paksima was shot."

We were all quiet, all still, just waiting. It was so obvious Patrick was picking his words, being careful, that I had another one of those flashes, about what he was going to say.

"She took a single bullet to the brain, from close enough range to leave powder burns. I gather they think the muzzle of the gun was held against her temple." He cleared his throat, an odd little noise, very unlike Patrick. "There was an additional act of mutilation performed, that points to this being an execution, Manaari style. I assume all of you remember what happened after the Super Bowl?"

Oh, fuck me, yeah, we remembered, all right. Hard to forget a Styrofoam cooler covered with dip corps *do not open* stickers and with four severed hands in it, being left at our hotel. Ali had refused to turn his daughters' murdering bodyguards over to the New York police. He'd stood in our San Francisco living room and told us there would be punishment, or justice, or some damned thing. That was his definition, apparently. He'd sent his nasty little prezzie direct to Luke.

"Are you saying someone shot that girl in the head?" Bree was dirty-white, and I got one arm round her in a hurry. "And then cut her hands off? Oh god, *god*...Patrick?"

His voice was gentle. "I'm sorry, Bree. I only had about five minutes with Bengt last night—he's in charge of the investigation and he was pretty shaken up—but that's what he tells me happened. Of course he's worried, on several levels."

"No shit, yo. He's the guy in charge of keeping the family safe. One of them gets their head blown off and their fingers in a jar, that goes on the permanent record. And we already knew Mac's old school friend goes for the biblical shit, big time. Sucks for Bengt, but he cashes the cheque. Comes with the gig." Domitra was in the doorway, looking ready for trouble. When the girl thinks things ought to be happening, she doesn't stand about and

202

natter. "Cool, so now we know what happened to Twin Number Two. I'm down with checking out whether JP's right. Anyone want to come with? Mac, stay behind me, and don't even think about arguing with me—yo, Carla, Ian, glad you could join the party. We're heading down the hall. JP thinks maybe we got some squatters at the back of the shack. You want to hang out and drink Bree's coffee, or you want to come along?"

"You trying to be funny?" Ian was even gruffer than usual, probably as much out of sheer exhaustion as anything else. I noticed that Carla had taken time to get dressed, right down to sensible shoes. So, yeah, she'd already sussed that some kind of action was going to need to be taken, and she'd dressed for it. No one's fool, is our Carla. "You're damned right we're coming along. Patrick give you the details? Right. Let's go."

So, right, there we were, band and management, together again. One big happy family, or at least back on the same page; whatever Mac had planned by way of schooling our braintrust on why leaving the band out of band business was a crap idea would probably end up getting shelved for a while, or at least watered down a bit.

Domitra and Patrick were heading up the expedition, side by side with Mac half an arm's length off Domitra's right shoulder. We went down the corridor in a single line, Bree behind me; behind her, Luke was filling Carla and Ian in on why we were traipsing down the hall like we were about to break out into a damned conga, or maybe more like something out of a Pink Panther flick.

We weren't bothering about how much noise we were making by then. No point to it; if someone had really been able to share the palace with us for over a week without us catching on, they probably knew every exit, hiding place and bolthole between the Queen's Palace and downtown Cairo. Still, it was a surprise to hear Cal, ahead of me, humming under his breath. It took me minute to track the tune down in my head, but I found myself grinning when I realised what it was: Robert Palmer's song, "Sneakin' Sally Through the Alley."

To be fair to all of us—as a group, I mean—we hadn't actually had any reason to go wandering down past the Wilsons' suite, or to push aside the gaudy hanging tapestry curtains and rattle the fancy brass hardware on the door at the end of the corridor. We hadn't had much time, either; we'd got there and gone straight into rehearsal and tech specs and build mode. Even Bree, who's got as much curiosity about her surroundings as anyone, hadn't had much time to go exploring; she'd spent a lot of what time she did have available before Nordine was killed learning how to drive the Veyron without killing herself in it.

And even though it felt as if we'd been there about a hundred years, it was actually less than two weeks. I'm not making excuses, but all that was just basic fact. Besides, Ali had gone out of his way to assure us we had the digs all to ourselves, for our exclusive use. That had actually been part of the contract rider for the gig. If we hadn't had the curiosity or the time to go poking about, we hadn't been given any reason to assume our host was wrong or lying to us, either.

What we hadn't known, any of us, was that the corridor we were all sleeping in was one of four arms. Turned out the Queen's Palace had been designed as a cross inside a square building, with only two of the arms having access to the outside world. That was probably part of the original design, back when you wanted to be able to keep an eye on where your naked dancing girls and your pet eunuchs were. The other two had windows, which was another reason we'd assumed Nordine and the rest had come from outside. After all, if whoever it was had walked right past our doors, chances are we'd have heard them.

So we basically had a quadrangle inside a big square block of a building. Dom, who got to the door at the end of the corridor perfectly ready to kick it down if that's what was needed, pulled the curtains aside, got a hand on the ornate brass bird's head that passed for a doorknob, twisted, and pushed with her full shoulder. She nearly fell on her nose as the door swung open in front of her. It hadn't even been locked.

"Oi! Steady on, brat." Mac knew better than to offer an arm or any physical support, but he was close behind, peering over her shoulder. "I don't remember Ali showing us this when he gave us that first Grand Tour. I don't even remember him mentioning it—of course, there was quite a lot of construction going on. What have we got here? The rest of the palace?"

"Looks like it." Patrick went through right behind Dom, straightening up and looking around. "I think this part of the place is clear. Ian? Carla...?"

So, yeah, a cross within a square. And there were doors the length of the two sides of the corridor than continued straight on past ours. The other two arms were solid wall, no way in or out to anywhere except to the other corridors.

"I wonder why they built it this way?" Katia was staring around, obviously fascinated. "Why waste the space on a hallway that doesn't go anywhere? That's just weird."

"Maybe so that whoever was on one side of the wall couldn't hear the screams. I wouldn't put it past them." Tony got hold of his wife's hand. He didn't look happy. "Let's check out the other end, the one with the door to the great outdoors. That one looks like it goes somewhere. I just wish it went to a fucking plane out of here."

Six doors, three to a side, leading to three suites a side, just like the six at our end. A mirror image, that hallway was, at least on the corridor side. I also got a question answered, something I'd been wondering about: those windows in the corridors, the ones high up that provided even the little bit of light? Those were slightly higher than the level of the roof over our suites. Ingenious bit of engineering that was, especially since it had to have been done centuries ago...

"Well, now. This is interesting."

Patrick's voice—pure cop—pulled me out of wondering about the architecture of the windows. Good job, too, because I'd nearly walked straight into Tony.

We all moved up, crowding together, peering through the door. It was the last room on the same side as mine and Bree's, the one closest to the gate that led out to the courtyard and the mineral pools. The door, unlocked like the rest of them, was standing wide open. I don't know whether it had been like that when we'd got there, or whether Patrick or Dom had opened it. Like I said, I hadn't been paying attention.

Ali had told us that, by the time we'd got back for the show, the suites would be completed and with every possible luxury, nothing left out. This wasn't one of our suites, but it was still luxurious, in a rather different way. It had the same basics as ours: a big bed, raw silk coverlet, wide-screen TV, minibar, the lot. The silk coverlet was rumpled, as if someone had got up and got out of the room in a hurry. But there were some personal touches as well, signs of someone who definitely wasn't one of ours: fancy antique scent bottles on every table. A pair of pricey-looking high heels for what looked to be a pair of small feet; one shoe was upright and the other one on its side, half-hidden under the bed.

There was also a rocking throne, just like the one in our suite. Over the back of it was a familiar-looking spangled silk headscarf.

"Bull's-eye." Domitra was inside, picking up the scarf, running it between her fingers. I got a whiff of something, not much, just a bit: perfume. "Or eureka, or whatever you want to call it. JP, dude, I'd say you called it. Looks like the twins were hanging out right here the whole time."

I've spent more than my share of odd mornings. It comes with the territory; when your working life starts after dark and involves the stuff a touring musician's job involves, you're going to run into weirdness eventually. That's just the way it works. You add the last decade or so, all the effects of the MS on how I react to the rest of what the world throws at me, and weirdness takes on a few new definitions.

Still, end to end, that morning was in a class by itself. It went beyond basic weirdness, even by rock and roll standards.

No one seemed to know what to do about what we'd found out. Yeah, it was gratifying to find out I'd got it right, but there didn't seem to be any place to take the information, or any way to actually put it to use. Trotting round to Ali and waving his daughter's scarf at him wasn't on, not under the circs.

"Dom, do me a favour, please?" Carla was holding her fancy phone up close to her face. Whatever I'd thought about it, she obviously had a few ideas of her own. "Can you put that scarf back where it was, pretty much just the way you found it? Great, thanks. And can everyone move back and let me get some clear shots of this, and of those shoes? Because after that whole deal with whoever it was cleaning out that hut, I think we should avoid another 'proof, what proof' incident, if we can do it."

Right. Typical: while the rest of us were standing about like garden gnomes, Carla was getting to the core of whatever needed doing, and getting it done. It's why we pay her so much. We got out of her way, and let her get on with it.

She took at least a dozen photos, not just of the scarf, but of the scent bottles and the high heels, as well. There was something unsettling about those shoes, something pathetic and evocative.

Still, about half the pictures she took were of the headscarf, close up from different angles. I wondered about that, but only for a moment. It made sense, really: the shoes might have been anyone's, but that headscarf couldn't be explained away. We'd all seen it on at least one of the twins.

That done, she got the lot downloaded, sorted, and sent to

every one of our emails, as well as to David Walters' email back in London, all in less than five minutes. It hadn't quite gone seven in the morning yet, and we had hard evidence of the al-Wahid girls squatting in our personal digs scattered all the way through the Blacklight global network. There was no way Bengt or Ali or anyone else was going to be able to do the whole outraged innocence thing and claim we were all full of shit. Raised eyebrows and acting as if we were mental wasn't going to cut it.

"There." She slid the phone back into her pocket. "I don't know if anyone's planning on confronting Ali's people with this or not. We might want to keep this up our sleeves until we need the firepower, assuming we do need it. In fact, that's my official suggestion. But this way, we're covered. If anyone at the Manaari end calls us liars, or drops any delicate little hints that we're all having acid flashbacks and hallucinating, send them over to me."

There was a definite snap in her tone, and I saw Mac shoot her an appreciative look. I had the feeling that quite a lot of his shirtiness at management's recent high-handedness had just been dissipated. I also got the feeling that if anyone at Ali's end gave Carla any aggro over it, they'd be shown a few different ways to regret it, and maybe regretting it in a few positions they hadn't known existed before. At the very least, she'd probably smile sweetly, show them the photos, and mention *Rolling Stone* and what a lovely cover story it would make. The girl earns her pay, every cent of it and more. I was beginning to get just how much she'd resented being jerked around by the Manaari contingent.

With that covered, we backed out of the suite and headed back to our own digs. No one seemed comfortable hanging about in there. Besides, there was no reason to hang about. We'd found out what we wanted to know.

There was something elbow-jogging away at the back of my head, though, and it was getting on my nerves, because I couldn't quite nail it down. It wasn't until we'd got back to our suite, and

Bree was putting up a third pot of coffee, that it suddenly came clear in my head.

"Oi. Dom, what you said back there, about the twins being here all the time. We don't know that, do we?"

"JP's right." Patrick had already worked out the problem in his own head. "Twin, singular, not plural. There was only one pair of shoes, and only one headscarf. At first look, the evidence supports the presence of only one of the girls."

"I wonder which one?" Bree's shoulders were up high and hard again. She saw me watching her, and visibly tried to relax. "Sorry. It just—someone was down there the whole time without us knowing they were there, and it just makes my skin crawl. I know I'm being silly, it's not as if anyone can do anything about it, but it's creeping me the hell out. I can't help it."

"I don't call that silly, Bree. I call it straight sense." Ian had made short work of his first cup of coffee and was already up and pouring a second one. "You want the truth? I'm feeling a right berk. Knowing what we already knew about the al-Wahid twins coming into this mess, I'll be buggered if I can sort out why we didn't suss it out straight away. I never even suspected it, but just look back at what we know about those two. Does anyone here really believe they'd be good little girls and keep off our patch, just because their dad told them to? Christ, JP found them out there skinny-dipping, and none of us thought past that. What, we all get the desert sand between our ears, to stop us thinking straight?"

No one said a word. Ian drained his cup, and sighed.

"Sorry. Truth is, everything about this show has been bad luck or bad news or both, right from the first. And there's no end in sight, not yet." He looked well beyond glum. "Everyone knows we're not likely to be getting out of here today, right? We clear about that? Even if Ali gave us the thumbs up, we've got problems at the other end."

That got a few heads up and some noise, especially from the blokes. Ian held up a hand.

"No, don't flip your shit, any of you. It's nothing to do with what's happening here—just your basic Act of God, that's all. I got an email late last night from David Walter, back in London. We've got a travel logistics nightmare. Turns out half Europe's under massive whiteout conditions, and it's the half we want. That blizzard that was supposed to blow in on Boxing Day blew in good and hard, and it's still there and still dumping snow. Paris and Rome are already under weather emergencies, and there's no trains moving in Southern England, either. Forget Scandinavia— even Scotland's locked down tight until the weather eases up. The North Atlantic's a solid wall of falling snow and high winds to go with it. So unless you fancy a week in Tripoli or Cairo, we're short on choices. The backup on flights is going to mean delays for days, no matter where we wanted to go. And that's assuming we could get a jet booked at this end, and clearance to fly out. I'm not holding my breath on any of it."

No one answered, or looked to have anything to say. Ian wasn't piling on the agony, but he wasn't prettying it up, either.

I took a quick look round at the band family. Mac looked disgusted, Dom wasn't bothering about trying to hide her irritation, and both the Wilsons were looking resigned. Cyn Corrigan made an unhappy noise and dropped her face down on her folded arms, and Stu got busy rubbing her back. I saw Karen close her eyes for a moment, but whether it was hiding her reaction from Luke or just being up so early catching up with her, I couldn't have said.

I spent a moment watching my own wife, or rather, her hands. They'd woven together, hard and tight. I had the feeling that, if I'd turfed everyone out and given her a chance, she'd have hurled the coffee cup, and possibly a few other things, smash into the nearest wall. Not happy, not happy at all.

"All right." Patrick had stayed quiet while Ian did his thing, but it was obvious Ian had said his piece. "So now we all know the situation. Until such time as we get some kind of word from the palace or from Bengt, the most we can do about the situation here is to see what can figure out for ourselves, and decide on the appropriate course of action. Personally, I can't see any point in talking to the British consulate, since about the only place we could actually get to is somewhere else in Arabia, and with the backup Ian mentioned, it would be days anyway."

He stopped, just waiting. Nice clear way of putting things Patrick's got. He always seems to get even clearer when whatever he's talking about is stuff I don't want to hear. He gave it a minute, but it was obvious no one was up for talking.

"My question for all of you is, do you want me to see what information I can pick up about what's happening with the investigation? It probably won't be too much, since I'll have to get what I can without actually asking Bengt about it, and he's going to be pretty busy anyway."

"Fuck yes." Mac sounded nice and definite. If there was any chance Ian or Carla had a different take, they were going to have to get through Mac first. He wasn't alone, either; Luke was nodding. "Do you seriously think you have to ask that, Patrick? Of course we do. It's bad enough being little birds in Almanzor's gilded cage. I'm damned if I want to do it with a blanket over my head."

"What about the American embassy, or whatever we've got here?" Tony had obviously been thinking. Right then, he was beginning to sound like old-school Tony: *I'm Italian-American, yo, don't fuck with me, my uncle was a Navy SEAL and I got friends in Jersey.* "I'm a US citizen. What about talking to them? Hell, we've got to have some clout, having an embassy here. I say we make use of—Carla, why are you shaking your head? Shit, you're an American citizen too."

"Not for this trip, I'm not. None of us are." Nice and crisp and to the point. "We're here specifically on a group work visa issued by the Emirate of Manaar. The work visa was stamped and okayed through the British office in London, and it includes the entire Blacklight party, British citizens or not."

"But we're Americans, goddamnit!"

"Not for purposes of this gig." She sounded stone flat patient. "Under the conditions of the visa, we're legally allowed to be in Manaar for six months, and we're here as visitors from the United Kingdom. It would be nice to call in the Marines, but Uncle Sam isn't going to be useful as a problem-solving device this time. Sorry, Tony."

"Shit." He doesn't do helpless very well. "Isn't that just fucking swell?"

Carla clearly had more on her mind. "I want to be honest here: I don't think that leaning on the Emir to let us leave is the smartest move at this point anyway. In fact, throwing a fit and demanding he get us a plane to anywhere that isn't here would be PR suicide. We've already cashed in to the tune of about forty million dollars at the current exchange rate, for one night's work, and that's what the rest of the world is going to see. Besides, where's our justification? Just wanting to go home isn't an excuse. It's not as if we're being treated as anything other than honoured guests."

"Except for that whole 'soldiers aiming guns at us' thing, true enough. And Ali did made it very clear he hadn't ordered that." Mac had gone from looking cross to looking thoughtful. "Carla, you've got an excellent point, there. We don't want to look a collection of cold-hearted shits, and if we're one breath the wrong side of clumsy, that's going to be how it comes off. Since we can't get home until the weather clears anyway, what's the next step? Public sympathy and offering whatever cooperation they want?"

She nodded. Ian was looking around the suite, taking the roll call of reactions; it was obvious he was getting ready to calm down anyone who disagreed. But there was nothing for him to do. Carla and Mac had both called it: Smile, close our eyes, and think of England.

"All right." Patrick rubbed the stubble on his jaw. "My God, I need a shave. The last time I got this bristly, I was staking out a drug lord in South Beach with DEA. Anyway, so you'll officially let the palace know the band is right here and willing to help in any way possible, and Carla will decide how much of that official stance is unofficially made clear to the world press. In the meantime, I can be a little less official with Bengt. It seems to me I've got two things I can use as starting points."

"That's two more than me." Crikey, Ian really was sounding glum. "Want to share, mate? Believe me, I'll take whatever you've got."

"The first thing might not be possible, at least not without being pretty blunt with Bengt. It might need a lot of pressure, and right now, I'm really not certain what I've got to use as leverage, unless you want to count those pictures Carla took. But I'd like to pursue the question of just why the guards stormed the band's dressing room with guns last night, and who ordered that action. Because as Mac's already pointed out, it clearly wasn't al-Wahid."

"Good call, if you can do it." Ian reached for a clean cup. "Bree, sorry, I think I've got the last of this. Patrick, you said there were two things. What's the second one? And is it likely to be any easier than the first one?"

"No." His voice changed suddenly. "No, it isn't."

I jerked my head round, and I wasn't alone. He didn't sound like Blacklight's head of security just then. That note, that tight quiet tone—that was the hunter, suddenly come front and centre.

"Dish, mate." I'd locked up with him, eye to eye, stare to stare. Just like old times, yeah? "Turn up the volume. What are you on about?"

"We had a dead man: Nordine Benhamou. We saw his body. He was killed on the path outside and bled out in the pool itself. We saw his body removed."

I got hold of one of Bree's hands. "Yeah, we did. What's your point, Patrick?"

"You and Bree both looked through the window of that hut. You both saw what you saw." He was watching me, very steady. "Someone died in that hut. It wasn't Nordine. And it certainly wasn't the Princess Paksima—for one thing, a single shot to the head would not have produced the amount of blood you both observed. The removal of her hands was post-mortem—Bengt told me that much—and could not possibly have produced what you described. For another, had she died that far in advance of the show, we would have known about it."

"Right." Bree's hand was paper-dry and very cold. Once we turfed everyone out, I was going to come the heavy husband and order her back to bed for a nap. Hell, I was going to try for one myself. "So the idea is to find out what happened out there, in that hut? That it?"

"Finding out what happened." He got up, and headed for the door. "And who it happened to."

Chapter Thirteen

The more I thought about Patrick's stagy little exit, the more I realised something: there was a damned good chance we'd get out of Manaar and back home without ever finding out what in hell had actually gone down. It wasn't a comfortable idea, for some reason, and I'd got the sense that the rest of the band was feeling pretty much the same way.

I don't know if Patrick had been trying to plant that in our heads, or not: trying to prepare us in advance for not ever getting the story, yeah? All I know is, we'd listened to the sound of the Range Rover as he pulled away and out of the seraglio, and no one had said a word since he'd left.

Dom finally broke the silence. "So, anyone else think maybe Big Boss over at the palace might have plans? Like maybe keeping the details about whatever the fuck actually happened all in the family? Anyone taking bets?"

"Not tell us, you mean?" The idea plainly hadn't crossed Katia's head, and it obviously didn't appeal to her much, either. "After we got put through all this bullshit? Oh man, Dom, if you're right, I swear my head's going to explode. All this crap, and never knowing what happened? That would suck like a vacuum cleaner on crystal meth."

"We may not get a vote." Ian was turning his empty cup round in his hands, over and over. He sounded grim. "I'm not sure what Patrick can actually do. Maybe nothing at all. But I want to get a consensus on something right now, just in case. Suppose we do get word from the palace? Suppose Ali or one of his talking heads shows up and says greetings mates, your jet's on the tarmac, diplomatic priority landing clearance arranged in Istanbul or Athens or wherever, thanks so much for a lovely visit, visa stamped, now get the hell out of it, effendi, and don't let the door hit your arses on the way out. What do you want me to tell them? That we're not going anywhere until we know what went down? Because if that's the way everyone in the band family wants it, I have to say I think you're all stone fucking bonkers, and I'm prepared to argue until I run out of air."

"Of course you are." Mac was watching Ian with his head tilted. I couldn't read what was going on in there; Mac had his face all the way under control. "Because the band's safety is the issue. That's the reasoning, Ian, is it?"

"You're damned right it is."

Shit.

Yeah, so, Mac had it under control. Ian didn't. The words had been snapped, and it looked as if our manager was just about to snap as well.

The pair of them were locked up tight, and something at the bottom of my stomach had locked up even tighter. Carla's face was a mask, totally unreadable; she was staying quiet, but it seemed to me she inched up closer to Ian's shoulder. That was a shock, for some reason, her being that obvious about where her loyalty was.

"If that's sarcasm, Mac, I'd appreciate you making it nice and clear." The vibe in the room had suddenly gone tense to the point of electricity; the suite was damned near crackling with it. "That way, we'll know where we all stand. I can tell you to fuck off, I quit, and we can be done with it. You think I've got some agenda beyond keeping you people safe, you might want to show a little bottle and say so. I've had more than enough of having my loyalty questioned. You've been doing it since that fucking over by Ali and Bengt, and I'll be buggered if I'm putting up with any more of it."

That might have been the longest three or four seconds I've ever been through during my tenure with Blacklight, and the most uncomfortable. No one was talking. I wasn't sure anyone was actually breathing. It seemed to go on for hours. It wasn't possible, the idea that we were going to have to get between Mac and Ian, choose one or the other, take sides...

Mac grinned. It was a real grin, too.

"Not a chance, mate. You try quitting Blacklight, I solemnly swear I'll personally chase you down and drag you back where you belong, which is right here with the band."

Ian's jaw dropped. Sounds like a cliché, but it's what happened—his whole face went loose and a bit soft, somehow.

"I'm sorry, Ian." Mac wasn't grinning anymore. "I know it's been iffy. Be fair, you did shake us up the wrong way. We had good reason to worry about it. From where I'm sitting, though, we've done with that rubbish, and it's time to move on. The thing is, you had to be the one to put it out there. There really was no opening for me or anyone else to say *oi, stop flipping your shit, you made a bad decision but you did it with Ali's gun to your head, we get that, not to worry, we're over it.* Now that it's out there, I can point out that the situation has been about as unnatural as a nun doing a fan dance in a urinal. We've all been off our heads."

Ian seemed to be having trouble keeping his face under control. Odd, that was, because he doesn't show a lot of feeling, most days. Gruff is his usual thing.

"I'm really sorry, mate." Mac held out his right hand. "That's a genuine apology, by the way—I'm not taking the piss, or being sarcastic. You had to step into the biggest shoes that ever walked, after Chris Fallow died, and you've done it better than anyone alive could have done it. So I'll say it again, and I'm fairly sure I'm speaking for the whole band: we know this mess wasn't any kind of cock-up on your part, and we trust you completely. We good?"

"Yeah, we're good." Ian reached out a hand, and shook Mac's. His voice was gruff, back to normal. "Thanks."

I heard a soft exhale, then another one. For a moment I wasn't sure if it was Carla, or Bree, letting their breath out. Took me a moment to realise at least one of those was me.

"Good, because all this emo stuff is exhausting." Mac yawned suddenly. "Christ, I'm knackered. And by the way, I nearly forgot about that question you asked. I don't know about the rest of you, but if Ali hands us a plane and a landing zone anywhere on the fucking planet that isn't Manaar, I'm out of here so fast, I'll probably leave skid marks. If Patrick wants to ass about playing Sherlock Holmes, good on him. I'm gone."

"Mac, you said it, man." Tony was stretching, letting his joints crack. The air in the suite had suddenly got a lot cleaner and easier to breathe, I'm not sure how. "I'm with you, every fucking word. Guys, look. Is there anything we can do right now? I mean, is there anything we need to take care of? I'm beginning to feel like I'm in the middle of a football huddle, or something. If no one's calling any plays, why are we all hanging out, not doing shit?"

"Tony, dude, lose the passive-aggressive. It doesn't look good on you." Dom shook her head at him. "Spit it out. What you mean is, any reason for us not to go back to sleep for a couple of hours? Me, personally, I can't think of anything. But I do what Mac says."

"Dom, angel, you make me feel so macho sometimes. Very flattering." He blew her a kiss and got up. "Seriously, I've had too much of everything this morning, except sleep. Personally, I vote for going back to bed and clearing the cobwebs out of the circuitry. A hot soak before or after is definitely possible. Besides, I'm betting Johnny and Bree might like a bit of peace and quiet, and they won't get it with us infesting their digs. What time is it, anyway? Oh bloody hell, eight in the morning. Consensus? On the sleep question, that is? Because I'm off. Oh, by the way, a happy new year."

I didn't actually get back to bed straight away, but that was my own doing. Mac's mention of a soak in the tub had got itself lodged in my head and, having decided it sounded brilliant, I ran myself as hot a bath as I could do with.

The MS had settled into a rhythm, a steady miserable physical backbeat with jabs and jerking muscles everywhere. There was no way I was running the jets, not with my skin that hypersensitised, but I did use a double handful of Bree's mineral bath salts. She offered to run the bath for me, and hang out for a conversation, but I shooed her off to bed, after she'd got her morning meds. She might not have been copping to it, but she was wiped out, run off her feet.

She wasn't best pleased with me about that, but she went, after I promised I wouldn't go off and do anything mad without waking her up and giving her a shot at talking me out of it first. That turned out to be a good call all the way round; by the time I'd turned off the taps and eased myself down into the water, I could hear her snoring gently in the other room.

So, yeah, that was one of us conked out, at least. If I was hoping for my own brain to slow down, though, I was out of luck.

The body was happy to oblige, at least as much as the stabby little miseries in my legs and feet allowed for, but the engine running the show wasn't having any of it. A lot of it was probably the body getting the message to the brain that things were dodgy down below, time to sharpen up. It's just one more way this damned disease manages to never give me any peace. And of course the brain decided where it wanted to go, straight off: back to that hut, where someone—who?—had died.

I can't imagine why no one had done the math until Patrick brought it up, but from the reactions in our suite when he did, not one of us had put that together until he did. Whatever had gone down out there had left the place spattered with blood. Christ, the sheets and blankets had looked to be soaked through. I'd seen it, and so had Bree; lying there in the tub, up to my chin in hot water, I closed my eyes and felt my throat tighten up for a second, remembering the smell of stale blood carried out through the slit windows, and Bree on her knees, retching into the dust and sand.

That much blood hadn't just got there by itself. Someone or something had died in there. But Patrick had called it: everyone was present, accounted for, alive and breathing. Whoever had got taken out in that hut wasn't anything to do with Blacklight.

So there it was, a nice simple basic sum: someone had got taken out and we weren't short anyone. One plus nil, and there was no answer, just a huge question: who the hell had died in that hut?

I might have been fed up with Manaar and wanting to go home just as badly as the rest of the band, but I'll tell you what, if I could come up with a way to bring that amazing hot water supply back to London with me, I'd do it. Even our plumbing in San Francisco, the best money could buy, wasn't half as properly hot as what we'd got in the seraglio. What's more, the bathwater stayed hot longer than anywhere I've ever been before. Besides, the tubs were enormous; I was in up to my chin with room to stretch the legs, just letting the salts and the heat do their thing. They were working, too. Usually, when the body decides to back down, my brain's got enough sense to take the offer and follow. But that morning, the more the body relaxed, the faster and clearer my head seemed to be working.

Okay. So we weren't short anyone. That meant it had to have been someone on the Manaari end. And if that was the story, I couldn't see any way we were going to find out the truth unless someone decided to tell us. Patrick was wasting his time.

Bollocks to that, mate. Want to be honest? If that's the story, there's not much reason for any of us to give a toss one way or the other, is there?

Not a pretty thing to have to admit, but true enough: if someone we'd never heard of before had got themselves written off in that filthy little hut, it had fuck-all to do with Blacklight. Sad, okay, maybe even tragic; there was no way to know, because for all any of us knew, whoever it was had been a flaming berk and had got what was coming to them. That was the whole point: it was nothing to do with us.

It took all of about ten seconds to chuck that idea. It wouldn't fly, because if whatever had gone down had nothing to do with us, then nothing made any sense at all.

I settled down deeper into the water. The body was definitely lightening up, but the brain just kept ticking over.

What in hell had Bengt been playing at, lying to us about what we'd seen in that hut? Why would he, or his boss, think we'd have touched one hair under either of the twins' spangled headscarves? Never mind what Ali had said to us—even if they knew we had nothing to do with Nordine dying, they had to have thought we knew something about the princess's death. The Emir's personal thugs showing up in our band room and holding us at gunpoint made that much pretty clear. They hadn't decided to wander over after the gig and scare the shit out of us because they hadn't dug the encore. They'd been sent.

And where did Nordine dying come into it? Because it must have done. There was no way I was swallowing three people who'd got themselves messily dead within ten days and half a mile of each other as some kind of coincidence. Bollocks to that.

The water was finally cooling off, just enough to make me have to decide whether I wanted a longer soak badly enough to risk waking Bree by turning the gushers back on. That's the one downside to pipes hooked straight into the natural hot springs: they're not quiet. There's a good loud gurgle goes on, there.

I had a quick look at the fancy clock over the sink. It was after nine. I'd been marinating in salty water over an hour, everything was going wrinkled and turning me into a prune, and the brain was finally beginning to slow down.

I got out of the tub and dried off, rotating first one ankle, then the other, testing for how bad the jabs were. The bath had been a good call: the pains were still there, mostly in the right thigh and foot, but they'd backed down enough to let me think about drying off and climbing into bed for some kip with my old lady.

Bree was fathoms deep when I climbed in next to her—she didn't even stir. Good. I had the feeling I wasn't going to get quite as far down into REM sleep as she'd managed, not unless I could turn the brain entirely off, but I was damned well going to try.

I did fall asleep easily enough, once my core temperature had come down far enough from the bath heat to stop me sweating. Unfortunately, I'd been right about the REM sleep being difficult; some part of my head just didn't want to let go of the waking world completely. It was probably some sort of survival instinct kicking in, yeah? That's the thing about deep sleep: Once you're out, you're vulnerable.

So I don't know how long it actually took me to get under, or how long I'd been dozing, before I started dreaming that I was back in one of my least favourite experiences in the world: stuck inside a metal tube, with rhythmic pulses being bounced off my skull.

Tap Tap Tap THUMP.

I turned over, trying to wake up, or at least shift it somehow. It had been a couple of years since I'd had an MRI, and thanks to the tickybox, I was likely never going to have to cope with that particular flavour of misery again. The last thing I needed was to be dreaming about it.

Taptaptaptap RATTLE.

Back when I used to get the damned things on an annual basis and sometimes more often than that, my tech had been a kid named Ramon. He'd used to snap at me because of course I'd dealt with it, gone Zen, by making music out of the pulses, and me humming would mess with the test.

This particular rhythm, the one I was dreaming, had just changed on me. It sounded urgent, somehow.

Wake up, Johnny. All the way up. That's not a pulse being banged off your skull. There's someone at the door.

It's a funny thing, really. Looking back at it now, I don't actually remember getting out of bed, or pulling a bathrobe on. I'm not sure I'd really woken up at that point. The only thing I remember clearly was being frantic to get the door before whoever it was woke Bree with their knocking.

I was biting back muttering, because I didn't want that waking Bree, either; she needed her sleep. And I hadn't really wiped the sleep out of my eyes or out of my brain, when I got across the suite and unlatched the door and realised that there wasn't much point in me worrying about waking Bree, not now, because staying asleep had just stopped being an option.

"Please." No headscarf and no high heels, not just then. She was standing there in our doorway, whispering. Her face was a clogged tearstained mess and her eyes were enormous. The Princess Azra was terrified, scared shitless. "Please help me. I am begging you. Please."

Awhile back, in San Francisco, I'd opened our front door to the wrong person.

I'd been expecting someone delivering our dinner from our favourite takeaway, and I'd opened the door without checking to see who it was first. Bad idea on my part: turned out the bloke on the front stair, with his finger on our doorbell, was a fugitive from a murder investigation in Los Angeles. He'd also been an employee of Carla's at the time, and I'd had to make a snap decision: to let him in, or not?

Yeah, well, *snap* was the word, all right. I'd pulled him indoors, shoved him into our front room, and told him to wait. I'd also told him that if he made any noise at all, I'd have the rozzers down to haul him away before he could blink. Not a brilliant choice, but it had been the only thing I could think of doing at the time: Bree and Katia were back in the kitchen, Katia was already a sobbing wreck dealing with Tony's meltdown, and I wasn't having either of them made accessories to a murder, if the kid had turned out to be guilty. Even if I'd been willing to saddle my wife with that, I'd got no right dumping it on Katia. She'd had more than enough on her plate just then. And turning him away wouldn't have been too bright either; one way or another, he'd had information we needed.

So I'd opened the door. That decision, letting him in and not telling my wife about it, had nearly cost me everything I care about; Bree'd found out about it, called me on being a hypocrite, and walked out. It had taken some very fancy dancing on my part to convince her to stay with me. I still break out in a chilly little sweat, bringing that memory up in my head.

Now here I was again, standing there gawking at probably the last person I would have expected to find in my doorway asking for help, facing another one of those *oh bloody fuck now what* moments. Part of my head was wondering why in hell they kept showing up at our place. You'd think we were trouble magnets, or something...

"Get in here. And close that door. *Hurry.*"

I'd been so busy playing over the possibilities in my head, and being unnerved by all of them, that I hadn't heard Bree get out of bed. That whisper from behind me nearly stopped the tickybox in mid-beat. But there she was, awake and with her hair tousled. She was also completely stark.

She had one hand on the princess, pulling her inside, pushing the door closed with one naked hip. She'd got it bolted before either I or the princess could get a word out; I got the feeling that, if there's been anything like a deadbolt or a security chain, she'd have made good use of them.

"Thank you." The surviving twin found her voice first. She was keeping her voice low herself, just above a whisper, and she was watching Bree, not me. The thought went through my head: this was probably the first time in her life she'd ever given the wife her attention, rather than the husband. Still, it was just as well I'd got something on before I'd answered the door. "I am sorry for any trouble I am causing you. But I have no other place where I can go."

"Sit down, please." There was something about Azra that seemed to be keeping my wife formal. "I'm going to put some clothes on, and then I'm going to make some coffee, and maybe some breakfast, too. Have you slept? You look very tired."

"Where would I sleep?" Quiet as a mouse. "There is no place safe left here for me. There is no safe place anywhere."

"When was the last time you ate?" Something was happening to Bree's face; it was sharpening up, getting fierce in way I don't usually see, unless it's me she's getting fierce about. "Are you hungry?"

225

The thought popped into my skull and stayed there: she looked like a mother bear, about to put on a scary defence of an injured cub. Except that, when you came down to it, that was stone fucking nuts, completely insane. Azra al-Wahid wasn't her cub. There wasn't a single thing I could think of that the surviving twin had ever done to make my wife get that fierce look going on. The twins had been trouble from the first time we'd laid eyes on them, and the trouble had just got deeper and worse. So why –

"I ate nothing yesterday." Still quiet, nice and simple, none of the giggles or dimples or fluttering lashes. Maybe she needed her sister with her to pull that stuff off effectively, or maybe whatever had been going down had left her with no place to hide, the way she'd said. Whatever. I don't know. The point is, she was just answering the question, like a good little schoolgirl. "I could eat nothing," she told my wife. "I am not hungry."

"Well, tough shit, because you don't get a vote." Yeah, well, so much for that whole formality thing. "You're eating a decent meal. Sit down."

We were both staring at her now. She caught my eye, just long enough for her to see the *what the fuck is all this*, *then* in there, and turned back to the girl.

"Look." She was still keeping her voice pitched low; not whispering, but still low enough to where no one outside the door to the suite would be likely to hear it. She sounded reasonable, but pretty damned definite, as well. "I don't know why you came to us. For all I know, we were just the nearest door. But whatever made you pick this particular door, you're a guest here, and this is the way it works. This is my house and these are my rules, and you're going to eat some breakfast, so please don't argue with me. Nobody can think straight or get things done when they don't eat. Now sit down and be quiet, please. You can tell us all about it after you get some food down. John? How do you want your eggs, or would you rather I made you some oatmeal?"

"Eggs are fine." Right. If she was losing her mind, might as well go along for the ride. "Scrambled, boiled, doesn't matter. However you're doing yours, that works. Might want to put some clothes on first though, love, all right? You don't need to spatter yourself with hot oil, whipping up an omelette or whatever. Just give me a minute. I want to get dressed."

I headed for the bathroom at a fast trot. I wasn't admitting it to myself, not until I'd actually got my trousers on and zipped, but just the idea of having that girl within sight of my bed was enough to put me off my breakfast. That was one thing, and considering the past history of her and her sister hitting on me, it made sense. Next to the idea of having her anywhere near me, and me with nothing but a bathrobe on, though, that was nothing. That was actually making my skin pucker up with how cold it made me feel.

I'd got all the way to the point of fastening my shoes before I asked myself the obvious question: why should something as simple as putting a layer of street clothes between me and whoever might come looking for the girl make me feel safer? And of course the answer to that was right there, in the question: *Whoever might come looking.*

Shit, shit, *shit.*

It hit me, right between the eyes. Getting dressed in my street clothes wasn't going to appease anyone, or protect me from anything, and I'd been a bloody dimwit to think it might. Because there wasn't any room for doubt about it: if the cherished pampered surviving daughter of the ruling house was so frightened of whoever she'd pissed off that she'd knocked on our door of all doors looking for a hole to crawl into, then someone was coming after her. There was no safety for anyone concerned in this mess, not until it got resolved somehow.

Yeah, you clot, and you left her out there, alone with Bree. Brilliant.

I got my shoes done up, and that took longer than it ought to have done, because my hands were shaking. That was silly, really—I didn't honestly think the girl was getting up to anything, and anyway my wife could have folded her up with one hand and stuffed her through one of those tiny grilled overhead windows with no help from me—but logic wasn't coming into this one, not anywhere. Every reaction I was having just then came straight from the pit of my stomach, or the bottom of my spine, and every damned one of those reactions was telling me right, no slacking, and not good to be out of the action for a second longer than it took to get back to it.

There was also the fact that, the way things had gone in Manaar from the first, whoever showed up was likely to be armed to the teeth. I didn't ever need to hear that particular oily-sounding click again. Once had been more than enough.

Having escalated all that tension in my own head, it was a bit of a letdown to hurry back out into the suite and get hit with the smell of eggs cooking, and fresh coffee. There was another smell, more exotic, one I couldn't put a name to quite so easily: it took me a minute of just letting it percolate through the back of my taste buds to realise it was mint I was smelling. The Princess Azra was perched on one of the kitchen chairs with a plate in front of her. For all that *oh I couldn't possibly eat* nonsense, she was packing down my wife's cooking.

"John, good, ready for some eggs? I've been saving yours for last. And do you want coffee, or would you rather have some tea? There's some left in the pot."

Nice homey domestic scene, right out of some bad daytime telly drama thing, you know? Tasty smells, food cooking, coffee, pretty girl with big eyes scarfing down her breakfast and washing it down with mint tea. *Morning in Manaar*, or something. All we needed was a film crew to get it going. Everything you'd want for a show like that was there: the girl was up to something, her sister had been executed and her hands taken off, my wife's driver had been slashed to death, and who knows who or what had left blood all over a hut out there in the desert.

I couldn't wrap my head round it. The girl had been so flipped out that she'd come to us looking for a place to hide, and here was Bree, acting like a nutter, apparently buying into whatever Azra was up to and playing mother to this dangerous little bit of trouble who probably had men with guns looking for her –

"John?"

I jerked my head up and met Bree's eye. She can't do the "one eyebrow up" thing that I do—it's both or nothing. Both her brows were up, and there it was, that nice marital mind-reading thing, full throttle, and right that moment I decided I was going to let Bree play it any way she wanted.

My wife wasn't buying into anything. It was so clear, I could practically hear her say so.

The kid was in trouble and she'd fetched up here, right, but the big thing was, she was hungry. So she was getting fed and then, if I was reading Bree right, Azra al-Wahid was going to get asked a few big questions. And I was pretty sure that she wasn't leaving without providing a few answers. Fuck, I'd go stand with my back to the door, if that's what was wanted.

"John –?"

"Oh—sorry, love. Coffee, please." I settled in at the end of the table. "And two eggs. Scrambled will do me. Ta."

That had to be the weirdest meal I've ever eaten. Not your basic breakfast: me, the missus, and the potentate's surviving daughter who, for all I knew, might be hiding out from her dad's personal yobbo squadron, or maybe even from her dad. I ate my eggs and toast, I drank my coffee, I accepted a glass of cold orange juice from Bree, and all the time I had one eye on the Princess Azra and one ear tuned out of doors, listening for anyone or anything who might be showing up to break some hell loose. No one said a word the entire meal.

Bree finished first, ahead of me. She did just what I'd seen her do a dozen times before when we had guests for a casual meal: sit back and wait for them to finish before she got up to clear the table. Under normal circs, I'd have done just what I'd usually do as well, which is getting up and offering to help with the washing up.

That morning, I sat and waited. I wasn't about to do a damned thing that might interfere with whatever Bree had in mind for a nice after-breakfast chat, and besides, I wouldn't have known what to ask, or what to say. The truth was, leaving aside Bree's unwillingness to leave anyone in her vicinity feeling hungry, I didn't trust the princess as far as I could throw her dad's million-dollar supercar, with or without her dad in it. All things considered, it was best to leave the driving to Bree.

"Have you had enough breakfast?"

"Yes. Thank you." The girl had put her napkin in her empty plate. She looked less strained, a bit less like she was scared someone was going to use her for a coconut shy. Her looking more comfortable didn't make me trust her any better. "I am very grateful to you. The food was very good."

"Glad you enjoyed it." Bree was talking over her shoulder, putting plates in the sink, running just enough water over them to keep them easy to wash later. She hates dishes piled in her sink, but that morning, she had different priorities happening. "And now that we're all done with that, I sincerely hope you're up for a nice conversation, because we both want to know what in the name of hell is going on."

Azra was quiet. I could almost see the mask drop into place, see her get her head into game-playing mode.

"Azra." I heard my own voice, nice and sharp, a grownup talking to a kid. I didn't remember picking up my cell, but I must have done, because I was holding it. "You showed up here. You came to us, not the other way round. You've been fed. We don't

230

owe you a thing, yeah? So here's the way it's going to be: you either come across with the answers to whatever we ask you, or I ring our chief of security and get him over here. And don't even think about strolling out the door. Get this into your head: You're not going anywhere until we get some gen."

She'd paled out, about as ashy as that deep olive skin was going to get. I couldn't tell if it was fear or temper, but either way, I'd got her attention. She whipped round to look at Bree. If she'd been hoping Bree'd be a softer touch, she dumped that little notion straight off. The girl would have had to be a complete idiot to misread my wife's face.

"You would not touch me." Maybe she was an idiot, after all. Either that, or she was trying a bluff. "You dare not."

"Touch you?" Bree smiled at her, and I jumped in my chair. I've never seen a look like that on her face before, and I don't much want to again. "Oh, honey. I'd rather touch a scorpion, but that wouldn't stop me. Hell, I'd just sit on you while John calls Patrick Ormand. You want to stop wasting time and knock off the bullshit now? You aren't going anywhere until you answer some questions. You might as well just lie back and enjoy it. You know, the way all those boys did, back when you and your sister were enjoying yourselves on the Book of Days tour, before your dad's bodyguards killed them?"

"I tell you nothing." Yeah, it had been rage, all right. Her English was slipping. "You cannot force me to tell."

"Like hell we can't." I was getting pretty pissed off myself. "Who died in that hut?"

Silence, nothing, not a word. She'd clamped her lips down to a single thin dark line.

"Fuck it." I flipped open my phone. "Bree, I'm ringing Patrick. It's his gig, not ours. I've had enough of this bullshit. Let Patrick and Bengt handle it—oi!"

She was on her feet. She'd moved too fast for either of us to anticipate, slapping the phone out of my hand. It hit the floor and skittered under the table. She was halfway across the suite before I'd got my head together enough to suss out that she was streaking for the door.

Bree was faster, though. She was up and across the room, with her back planted against the door, a half breath before the princess got there.

"You've got two choices." Bree was just about a foot taller than Azra was, and a couple of stone heavier as well. She wasn't moving an inch. "You came in here terrified, scared half to death. Either you tell us what we want to know, or you leave here with our head of security."

"Why are you doing this to me?" Her eyes were full of tears and her lips were shaking. She could barely get the words out. "If I tell you, I will be killed. Why would you do this?"

"Believe it or not, it's not all about you." Good. I'd had a bad moment there, wondering if Bree's nurturing thing was strong enough to take that kind of hit. "People are already dead— Nordine, your sister. Who died out there in that hut?"

"No one that matters." She must have seen Bree's face change, or maybe she caught how ugly she sounded, even thick-skinned and privileged as she was, because she hurried to explain. "Someone who was already dead, I mean."

She stopped, because Bree had held up one hand. A moment later, I saw the panic in the girl's face, and heard what they'd both heard.

Noise, coming from out in the courtyard: a truck's engine. It sounded like Patrick's Range Rover.

"Please." She was whispering, clutching Bree's sleeve. She was the colour of dirty chalk. "You must not give me up to them. If you do they will take me and kill me. You could not be so cruel. Please, please –"

A car door slammed. There were footsteps, not hurrying; I

could hear whoever it was walking across the courtyard, into the corridor. For some reason, it didn't sound like Patrick out there. Very light on his feet, Patrick is.

"Please." I don't know if she said it, or mouthed it, or what. I never got the chance to ask.

Behind Bree's back, I heard a click. Not the nasty oily noise I'd heard from the guards' guns; this was something else, the sound of a key in a lock.

A moment later, my wife staggered forward, straight into me. She hit me off-balance, sending us both backwards and into the side of the table. Bree stayed on her feet, but I went down. Whoever had put the key in the lock had shoved the door open as hard as it would go, with no warning and with all their own weight behind it.

I heard the princess scream, short and sharp and pitched to carry. The scream was cut off. And then there was that other kind of click.

"*There* you are." Bengt Ekberg had one hand wrapped good and hard in Azra's hair, at the back of her skull, jerking her head all the way back so that she was looking at the ceiling. The girl wasn't moving, and I didn't blame her. From where I was sitting on the floor, trying to get my wits and my balance back, I could see Bengt's other hand. The gun was pressed hard under her jawline, pointing straight up. "I had the feeling you'd come here. I've been looking all over for you."

Chapter Fourteen

I'm not sure how many people actually do get confronted with the chance to do something clever in a life or death situation. Not genuinely clever—that would be finding a quiet corner and climbing into it until the shit blew over and it was safe to come out. Self-preservation's what you do if you're actually being clever. Maybe the word I want is heroic.

Heroic, clever, whatever. All I know is, sitting on my arse on the floor and looking up at Bengt with his gun jammed into the soft underside of Azra al-Wahid's jaw, I realised that my phone was still on the floor, under the table, just out of reach.

It was a good bet Bengt couldn't see it from where he was standing. Besides, his attention was elsewhere. If I could just reach it, press the number 8, that would ring Patrick's phone. I wouldn't have to say a word—just having the line open, he'd be able to hear what was going on, and suss it out on his own.

I inched one hand under the table. *Right, Johnny, keep your shoulders still. You even let him think you're doing something to upset him, he might just go all Wild West and start shooting the place up.*

The phone seemed to have slid further under the table than I'd thought. I edged one finger forward, a fraction of an inch, slow and careful. I still wasn't finding anything but floor. Where the hell was the phone…?

"Sit down, please." He was talking to Bree. She'd been staring at him, not saying anything. Good call, I'd say; you don't want to piss off the bloke with the hardware. "That chair beside you will do fine. And if you'd help your husband off the floor, he ought to be sitting too. Where I can see both of you. Thank you."

Yeah, well, so much for Hollywood-style heroics. Probably just as well, really.

Bree helped me up and got me into the chair; I was off-balance and shaky. I glanced down at the floor, just for a moment, and she shook her head at me, nice and open. She was probably right—doing the action hero deal, managing to turn the phone on without Bengt's knowing about it and somehow letting Patrick know that something was going down in the Seraglio, wasn't going to happen today.

So we sat there, me and Bree side by side at the breakfast table, and Bengt stood there with the girl's hair in one hand and a gun in the other. We really must have looked a complete bunch of waxworks, because no one was saying anything and no one was moving, either. We just sat.

I had a really bad feeling, even beyond the obvious reason. Bengt hadn't been bothered about staying quiet. He'd driven the Range Rover straight into the courtyard—we'd all heard the motor. He could have left it outside on the road, but he hadn't done that. He hadn't worried about going on tiptoe, either. Our door had given a good loud bang when he'd thrown it open, not to mention that scream of Azra's, that he hadn't bothered telling her to muffle.

For someone who was about to get himself beheaded or worse for manhandling the boss's daughter, he was being pretty front and centre about it. So far as I could see, there was only one reason for that made any sense: he didn't give a shit who knew what he was doing. And that meant he was prepared to go down in a hail of bullets, to get done whatever it was he was planning to do.

"Bengt?" Bree sounded so normal, I had a mad moment of thinking she was going to offer him eggs and coffee. "Do you mind if I ask you something?"

He laughed, and my stomach tightened up even harder. It was a nice cheerful little laugh, but for just a moment there, he hadn't looked or sounded sane; he'd looked and sounded like what he was, a head case on the edge, holding a gun and holding us hostage. If we got out of this alive, I wasn't coming near Arabia again, never mind Manaar.

"Sure," he told her. "But I bet I can guess what you want to know. Want me to guess?"

"If you like." She had her head tilted, watching him steadily. Or was she? It seemed to me she'd glanced past his shoulder, the tiniest flick of her head for just for a second, as if something had caught her attention out there, just beyond the opened door. "I get the feeling you've known all about it all along. Am I wrong or right about that?"

"A little of both." She'd seen something, all right; even keeping my eyes on Bengt, I caught movement out there on the corridor wall, a shadow, something… "It took me too long to understand some of it. Didn't it, Azra?"

The girl was silent and pop-eyed. I watched the knuckles wound in her hair go white as he tightened his grip. "I said, didn't it? *Didn't it, you little bitch!*"

"You said you wanted to guess." How in hell Bree was keeping her voice so calm, I couldn't have guessed; the tickybox was doing a samba and I was having some trouble breathing around it. "But maybe I should just ask. Who died in that hut?"

"Well, now." Bengt moved, suddenly enough to make us both jump. He came all the way into the suite, dragging Azra with him, the gun never wavering. If he was hoping to provoke a noise, any noise, out of the girl, he wasn't making a good job of it. She was stone silent. "That's the big question, isn't it? Funny thing: it's what I came along to find out myself. Well—not exactly. It's the wrong question. I already know who died out there in that hut. What I want to know is who the father was. Once we have the answer to that, we'll be cooking with gas, won't we, Azra dear? There might even be a pop quiz later."

Oh, Christ.

I'd got it now, at least that part of it. Bree's shoulders were still down, still relaxed, but I could see the effort.

"Cleaning up all that blood." He sounded conversational, same Bengt we'd been dealing with the whole time. It suddenly hit me: he really was round the twist, completely off his head. "So messy and nasty. All those stinking sheets. Wasn't that nice of me? Of course, it wasn't as nasty as carrying that little blue corpse out of there and burying it in a pillowcase, out in the dunes. Really, Azra, you owe me. So just between you and me and these nice people here, before I blow your head off your shoulders, clue me in. Who fathered that baby? Was it me, or was it Nordine? I'm okay with not knowing which one of you girls actually killed him, but the rest—no. And don't bother telling me you don't know, that your miserable whore of a sister didn't tell you all about it. If she knew, you know. Whose baby, Azra?"

Silence. You'd have thought the girl was already dead, for all the response he was getting from her. And through the clang of the penny dropping and my own *fuck he's going to have to kill us*,

237

he can't not terror, I was aware of noise: doors opening, coming out, footsteps in the hall…

"*Oi!*" Someone was yelling, and that shocked the shit out of me, because it turns out it was me. I hadn't planned on opening my gob. Next to me, Bree sucked in her breath. "Bengt's in here and he's got a gun! Stay outside!"

He laughed. That laugh made it really clear: the fucker was off his nut. He didn't give a damn who walked in and who didn't.

"Azra." It was Bree, sounding gentle. She was getting her wits back. Mine still seemed to be walkabout, unfortunately. "Was that a miscarriage, or an abortion? Please say something. You have nothing to lose, not now. Bengt, if you want her to answer you, move that gun. She can't talk with it in her face."

He stared at her. "You know, you're right. I get the feeling you're right a lot. I would personally find that very annoying. But you make a good point."

He moved his arm down, until the gun was off the girl's throat and up against her ribs. Not much of an improvement from where I was sitting, but it opened the floodgates; she was talking, suddenly, babbling, and she wasn't stopping.

"The baby was dead. It was already dead. It died inside my sister but it would not let go." There were tears streaming down her face, splashing to the floor. "She could not live with a dead thing inside her, no one could bear such a horror. We could not tell my father. We asked Nordine to help us, my sister and me. And he took the dead thing out of her, but he was not a surgeon, him, and there was blood, too much. She was damaged inside. We did not know what to do."

Next to me, I heard a soft noise from Bree and with no conscious thought, I got an arm around her and pulled her close. Fuck Bengt Ekberg if he had a problem with it—he could sodding well shoot me, and have done with it. My wife had a painful messy miscarriage of her own when she was younger than the al-

238

Wahid girls, and she'd lost the ability to carry a child because of it. She was getting all my attention just then, and the crazy Swede with the gun could fuck off if he didn't like it.

Bengt ignored us. Holding on to Bree, I found myself remembering the day I'd dinged up my knees, taken that fall, and found the twins climbing out of the mineral pools. One of them, presumably Azra, had been completely stark. Her sister had been wrapped in a towel.

"That's fascinating, dear. But it doesn't answer my question." The gun was planted under her rib cage. "So Nordine helped you abort a dead baby. Whose dead baby? Mine or his? And you know, sweet-cheeks, I'm beginning to get annoyed having to repeat myself—oh, look, we seem to have company. Come on in. The more the merrier."

"Mac. Stay behind me." Domitra was in the doorway. I'd have expected her to have dropped into full battle stance, but she hadn't, and that surprised me. Presumably Mac was doing what he was told; I couldn't see him or hear him out there. Anyone with one good eye could have seen just how tricky this was for Dom, because she doesn't do helpless very well. She was jonesing to start something, launch a few good kicks, take Bengt down and rearrange his face for him—you couldn't miss it—but of course, he had the gun and the princess and all the cards, and none of us had a damned thing. Even if Dom hadn't given a rat's arse about whether the princess got shot or not, all Bengt had to do was move the gun a few inches and he could take out Bree, or me, or both of us. The only thing Dom could do just then was her job, and that meant protecting Mac.

Unfortunately, she seemed to realise that. "Out," she said, over one shoulder, and then backed out herself. A moment later, she was gone, probably dragging Mac and off to safety somewhere.

"How did you know she'd come here?"

Bree still sounded completely calm. She wasn't—I had one arm around her and I could feel how cold she was—but you wouldn't have known it from her voice. She sounded curious, period.

"What?" The simple question had thrown Bengt off balance, for some reason. "What do you –"

"You said you guessed she'd probably come here." Calm, rational, almost relaxed. "When you let yourself into our suite. If you suspected she was coming here, you must know something we don't, because this is about the last place I would have thought she'd come. We were the ones who demanded that she and her sister be kept away from us in the first place. So why in the world would you think she'd come here?"

He laughed. That laugh settled it, for me. Bengt Ekberg was mental.

"Are you as naïve as you sound?" He was watching my wife, and the contempt in his voice was staggering. "Why here? Because you're as soft a touch as anyone this pampered little bitch here has ever seen in her life, that's why. Because she's been missing since she saw me kill her sister yesterday—probably hiding behind all those portable toilets. Suitable place for her, hey, Azra? Because she was scared and she was bound to be hungry. And you can't say no, can you?"

"Not to hungry people, no. Why should I? Feeding people is something I do. I'd have fed you too, if you'd wanted a meal. But you didn't ask." Bree'd probably felt me tense up—I'd taken a breath, ready to rip the bloke's head off—and her voice was a shrug, basically. "So was that why you sent the guards to our tent? Because you thought she might be there?"

I don't know why it took me as long as it did to sort out what Bree was doing. I swear, I must have been half off my head myself, for it to take so long to get through. Whoever was still out there in the hallway probably sussed it before I did.

Yeah, she wanted to know the answers. Yeah, she was asking genuine questions, stuff we all wanted to know, questions none of

240

us fancied dying without getting the answers to.

And none of that had a damned thing to do with what she was up to. She was buying time, a half-minute at a pop.

That whole thing, about trying to be heroic, getting my cell out and somehow letting Patrick know what was happening? The entire rest of the band family, everyone out there in the hall, had probably reached for their phones as soon as they'd heard what was happening.

Bengt had to know that. He had to know Patrick would be on the way, probably with Azra's dad and the Forty Thieves and maybe a small army. And Bree had to know that, as well. So why was she stalling him...?

"Why do you care? Just curious?" Bengt let go of Azra's hair suddenly, and slid the arm around her waist, holding her up against him. The gun was still jammed up against her ribs. "Of course that was why. I wanted to find her before her father did. What a stupid question."

"Was that before or after you did that funky shit with the hands? You're a sick motherfucker, you know that?"

Bengt's head jerked towards the door. So did mine. Whatever was moving through Tony's voice, that was something I'd never heard in there before.

"Now there's a funny thing." There was a thin bead of sweat along Bengt's hairline, and I didn't think it had been there a minute before. "That business with the hands wasn't me. I was too busy trying to chase down her sister, when she ran off into the audience. I just put the bullet into Paksima's cheating whoring little skull. Someone else did that stuff with her hands while I was out hunting her sister. I found them on my desk when I got back."

"What?" It was Luke's voice, from out in the hall. I couldn't see him, but he had to be just the other side of the door. Staying out of range; I wondered if Karen was out there with him, refusing to leave him there. "Are you joking? Are you asking us to believe you shot that girl to death but you didn't mutilate her afterwards?"

"I'm sure this will come as a shock, but I really don't give a damn what you believe." He was definitely sweating now, and it wasn't because the room was any warmer. He had one ear cocked, listening to something we couldn't hear, or maybe listening for something he couldn't hear. I was listening too, wondering if that was actually a motor I was hearing in the distance: the hum of a single engine, getting closer by the moment. "But yes, that's what happened. I don't know who it was. I just know it wasn't me."

It was a motor I'd been hearing, all right, but just one. If there was more than one car, I couldn't have told you how many. Only one set of footsteps came down the seraglio corridor and only one person stood in the doorway, looking in at us.

The first time I'd ever seen Almanzor al-Wahid, he'd been toe to toe with Bree on the doorstep of 2828 Clay. At the time, I'd thought he'd looked too damned arrogant for his own good. He'd been perfectly polite, mind you, no bad manners or rudeness, but I'd got the impression that it was only because we were too far beneath him to bother being rude to. He'd looked at us as if he'd thought we were black-beetles, or something.

You'd have thought, under the current circs, that he'd have been a bit less cocky, carried a bit less of the toff about him. He'd lost one daughter already, the bloke who'd done her had the other daughter under the gun, but I'll be damned if he wasn't standing there with that same "right, you're all just the stuff I scrape off my shoes" thing going on. If he was worried about anything at all— including his chief of security blowing his only remaining child's head off—he wasn't showing it. He wasn't saying anything, either.

And he'd come alone. No guard, no backup, nothing. It was just him.

We hadn't moved, me and Bree. I had no clue who was still out in the hall, not beyond Luke and Tony; there was no way to see round the edge of the door, not from where we were inside the suite. Part of me was hoping they'd all gone, that if there were going to be headlines splashed all over the world press about members of the Blacklight family going down in a firefight in Arabia, it would at least be limited to me and Bree. Yeah, that would make it easier for the YouTube mashers to put together a fake video or two, probably with "Remember Me" as the soundtrack, but at least we'd keep the collateral damage down...

"Good morning to you all." He was eye to eye with Bengt, and he sounded bored. "Ah, Bengt. I see you found my daughter, alive and well. Good."

I sat there and gawked. I'd thought it couldn't get any more surreal than it already was, but I'd been wrong about that. Next to me, Bree swallowed a noise at the back of her throat. I thought I was about to do the same, so the sound of my own voice was a bit of a shock.

"Don't suppose you happened to notice the gun? Or the fact that he's got your kid as a hostage? Not to mention me and my wife?"

The dark eyes flickered towards me for a moment, then went back to focussing on Bengt. He was ignoring Azra entirely.

"I did not know, until last night, why Paksima had been killed, or by whom. Once I knew—my surgeon told me that she had recently aborted a child—it was clear to me, of course, both the why and the who. I had long suspected her involvement with Nordine—what was found in the second pool outside these windows confirmed it—but so long as nothing came of it, there was nothing to worry me. My daughters enjoyed their dalliances. It has always been my policy not to interfere." He smiled suddenly. "But something did come of it."

Azra whimpered. No other word for that noise—she'd stayed

dead silent the whole time the crazy bloke with the gun had that grip on her hair, but she whimpered now. She looked so scared, she was pop-eyed with it. Her dad was still smiling, and my heart was seriously thinking about shutting down altogether, it was slamming so hard.

"I confess I knew nothing of your affair, Bengt. It is a pity that you were foolish enough to execute her—you could have left that safely in my hands. Of course you are a dead man, both for the affair and for the execution, but you know that already. Did you get my message? My orders were that it—they—should be delivered to you."

He waved one hand, very casual. He wasn't bothered about making the bloke with the gun jumpy, from the looks of it. "But of course, you must have, or you would not have come here. Would you?"

Next to me, Bree was holding her breath, and I was right with her. There didn't seem to be any air in the suite just then. Bengt had told the straight truth, when he said he hadn't mutilated his girlfriend's corpse.

"Father?" If I hadn't been standing there, seeing Azra trying to get the words out, I wouldn't have recognised the girl's voice. "Please...?"

Ali finally broke the stare with Bengt. He didn't answer his daughter, though, whatever it was she was trying to say. You'd have thought she was invisible to him, or as dead as her sister was. Whatever had happened here, it didn't look to be something Ali was going to forgive.

"I apologise for the intrusions into your privacy." It took me a moment to realise he was talking to us, to me and Bree. "I have learned, too late for any remedy, that my daughters were using the unfinished end of this palace for their trysting place. I offer my regrets. It was my chief of security's duty to prevent such things, but of course there were reasons he was derelict. Still, in the end, the onus is mine. To let them remain at home was poor judgement on my part—I should have had them sent out of the country. To care for one's children too much is a weakness."

He turned back to his daughter. There were tears on her face, as if she knew what he meant, what he was on about, what he was going to say. She seemed to have forgotten about that gun jammed into her ribs, or maybe she'd just stopped caring. I didn't really know what was happening to that family, but one thing was obvious: whatever it was, it mattered to both of them more than Bengt and his weaponry did.

He and Azra had the same eyes, not just the colour, but the shape and the way they were set under those heavy brows. Hard to believe two pairs of eyes could look so much the same and so different at the same time.

The look I'd seen on Ali's face, last night in the tent, was back: smoothed out, as if he'd gone eye to eye with something and blanked himself out over it. If he gave a shit about whatever was behind those tears of hers, he wasn't showing it. He was off somewhere, behind high, high walls.

A phrase popped into my head, I don't know from where or where I'd heard it before: *all passion spent.* I'm not sure what it means, either, but that's what he looked like to me just then, talking about his daughters. You'd have thought Azra was as dead as her sister, that he'd thought about it and decided not to care anymore. "I have overlooked their bad behaviour in the past. It has cost many people. Some things cannot be overlooked. What this one's sister did –"

"*She didn't have an abortion.*" Bree was breathing hard, through her nose. "It was a stillbirth. That baby was dead. What kind of culture punishes women for stillbirths? Are you barbarians, or just insensate?"

I jerked around, to stare at my wife. So did Bengt. Azra kept her eyes on her dad's face. A weird notion popped into my head:

245

she was afraid that if she looked away, she'd stop existing or something, fade out like a ghost...

Ali turned, and met Bree's eye. There was nothing in that face, nothing at all. Emptied out, as smooth as glass.

"You are free to think so, certainly. Our laws are what they are. My daughter—both my daughters—knew they were breaking them. But even if they had not, there is the matter of Nordine's death to be paid for, and it is that of which I speak. It is not only our culture that claims a life as fair exchange for a life taken. Your own does the same, I believe, though I know many disapprove. My daughter Paksima killed her lover. Her sister aided her." He looked at Bengt. "As did you, by your silence. I am betrayed by my family, by those in whom I placed my trust."

"He threatened us!" Azra had found her voice again. "He said that Paksima must marry him or that he would tell you. He said he would lie, that you would believe him. He would not listen—he had no heart. Father –"

"*Be silent.*" Not a glance her way, nothing, but she stopped in mid-sentence. He was back to doing the locked-stare thing with Bengt. "I have no illusions as to Nordine Benhamou's character. He was a useful servant to me, from a family of long service to mine, but he was ambitious and greedy. I am unsurprised to learn him capable of blackmail, of threats, of anything he might have done to better his position. It does surprise me that he was enough of a fool to think he might marry my daughter without my approval. He must have known he would have faced beheading for daring such a thing."

His voice changed. I'm not sure I've heard anything quite like that before or since, and I don't much want to. Whatever it was that made him sound human suddenly blinked out.

"But his foolishness does nothing to change the truth. To have helped in the death of my servant is to forfeit your life." He raised his voice. "And so it will be."

246

He hadn't quite got that last word out when Bree finally moved. And all hell broke loose.

Time's funny, you know? The part of my mind that had got detached and was watching things happen was thinking *right, this flick needs an editor, much too long, they need to cut it back about half an hour.* The reality was just a few seconds start to finish, movie over, house lights up, please drop your empty popcorn buckets in the dustbin on your way out.

I had no idea what was happening, no idea why, no idea what was about to happen next. The only thing I was sure of was that something about what Ali had said, or maybe about the way he'd said it, had brought the situation to flashpoint.

I don't know that Bree'd ever moved as fast as she did just then. One second she was sitting in her chair next to me, and the next she was on her feet, kicking her chair out of her way, grabbing me by the shoulders and pulling me off my own chair. Mine toppled onto its side; hers skittered into Bengt's left leg. He loosened his hold on the princess and I saw her stumble forward, towards her dad.

Bengt turned, and the gun turned with him. It was pointing toward Bree, now, or maybe at both of us.

"Down, get under the table, John please, oh God God, John just *go!*"

Maybe it was just reflex, Bengt being trained to look at the source of whatever was suddenly different in his immediate vicinity. I don't know, now, whether or not he meant to put a bullet into me, or into my wife.

It doesn't matter anyway, not beyond basic curiosity, because he never took the shot. Someone else did.

I heard it, as we hit the floor and rolled under the table. It was nuts, how loud it sounded, the way it echoed—I couldn't tell who'd shot at whom, where it had come from, nothing. I knew Bree hadn't been hit, because we had our arms round each other.

247

But the floor where my chair had been was suddenly covered in a filthy spray of red mist. I could hear Azra screaming, finally, a long drawn-out noise that sounded as if she'd pulled it loose from some place inside that all of us have got, even if we don't want to admit it.

I must have got some of my reaction time back, and thank God for it, because I'd got one hand up at the back of my wife's hair, pulling her face hard into my shoulder and away from any chance at all of her looking at Bengt Ekberg and I hadn't known I was doing it. Bengt was slumping to the floor, knees first. There was something really graceless and lumpy about the way he was moving: horror-movie stuff, just not real, you know?

He slid all the way down, and onto what had been his face. He looked to be missing most of his head.

The floor of the suite just beyond Bree's back looked like a slaughterhouse. There was blood everywhere, droplets and splatters, and a few shards of bone as well. I had no clue what the fuck had just gone down; I just knew Bengt was as dead as dead gets. So far as I could tell, Ali had done a magic trick: he'd said *abracadabra* or something, and instead of a rabbit jumping out of someone's hat, Bengt's head had exploded.

I wasn't worrying about how it had happened—Christ, at that point, I was too confused and disoriented to give a shit. I just lay there, hanging on to my wife. The tickybox was revving like that bloody Bugatti, and I stayed where I was and let it do its thing. Nothing in the world seemed to matter just then beyond making damned sure Bree didn't look behind her. If she'd shown any inclination to turn round for a closer look, I'd have pinned her, but she wasn't going anywhere. It took me a few moments to figure out that she was doing the same thing I was: keeping me from trying to get up and go anywhere until the whole safety thing got itself sorted out. I felt her breath, short warm gusts, tickling the hollow of my throat.

248

Azra's screams had tapered off into sobs, with words lacing through them. I don't speak the local jabber, so I didn't know what she was saying, but the tone was clear. If she was hoping for comfort, though, she was out of luck. Her dad had already made it pretty clear that whatever he'd be offering his daughter, it wasn't going to involve petting and soothing and promising to buy her a pony.

Maybe she already knew that. In any case, she quieted down; the sobs became sniffling and hiccoughing, just quiet enough so that I heard the footsteps, coming down the long corridor. Whoever was heading towards our suite wasn't quite running, but they weren't taking their time about getting here, either: it sounded like a quick, purposeful trot. The footsteps stopped in our doorway.

I opened my eyes. Looking over the top of Bree's head, I found myself focussing on a pair of men's shoes. Halfway up the bloke's trouser leg was a familiar hand. It had a good grip on a really unpleasant-looking gun, much bigger than Bengt's and a lot more dangerous-looking, somehow.

"Is everyone okay?" Patrick might have kept his steps even, but he wasn't bothering about trying to get his voice to behave. That was the nearest I've ever heard him get to flipping his shit. "Ian, excuse me please, I need to get in. JP? Bree? For heaven's sake, talk to me!"

I let go of Bree and pulled myself out from under the table. Not easy, because I had to inch forward instead of taking the easy way and just rolling out the way I'd gone under in the first place. Problem was, that side of the table was where all the mess was, including what was left of Bengt. My stomach was already thinking about doing the fandango, and I was damned if I wanted to add my breakfast to all that gore.

"Yeah, we're fine, I think. Patrick, what the fuck, mate? You fire that shot? Where were you? Look, can someone find a sheet or something? Bree, don't even think about looking at that, all right?"

She sounded pretty calm, all things considered. "Okay. But I really don't want to stay under the table. I promise I won't look, John, but I'm a little too close to it down here." Suddenly, she didn't sound quite so calm. "It—I can smell blood. And yes, can someone please cover him?"

"Go." Ali hadn't touched his daughter, or used her name. He jerked his head at her, as if she was an unsatisfactory servant he was planning on sacking, or maybe having flogged. "Go and fetch a shroud for your sister's lover. Bring a coverlet from the bed she used to seduce my servants."

Azra, her eyes cast all the way down, went. Meanwhile, Bree was pulling herself out, the same way I'd done. She wasn't looking at what was left of Bengt, and she wasn't waiting to hear Patrick answer my question, either; she was too busy moving him out of the way, gun and all. She'd remembered we had family, out there in the hallway.

Everyone was there, and from the general tone of my wife's questions and the answers she got, everyone was in one piece and no one was really flipping their shit, even if some of them were a bit freaked out. Sometime between us diving under the table and Patrick showing up and doing his Dirty Harry act, the whole band family had got themselves back into the corridor: even Carla and Ian had come over from the main palace. Ian was just outside the door, from the sound of it. I wondered how long he'd been there. Me, I was using the time to get my own breath back under some kind of control.

Mac and Domitra had joined the party as well, all the way at the back and well out of range. I heard Bree say something about it being all clear and then Domitra's voice, announcing that Mac was staying where he was until she decided it was all clear, thank you very much. Bree didn't wait for an answer. She was back with me in less than a minute.

250

Personally, I was still waiting for an answer from Patrick. The bare fact seemed obvious enough: someone had shot Bengt and here was our chief of security, on the spot, with a sodding huge gun in his hand. What I couldn't sort out was how it had been possible. I realised suddenly that I'd never seen him with a gun before, not even when he was a homicide lieutenant. If I'd ever wondered about it, I'd have said I thought he didn't much care for the damned things.

"Patrick? You want to tell us how you worked this one, mate? Because we've got all the shutters closed and the only other windows are up on the roof. So how...?"

He jerked his head towards the shutters, and I noticed he was wearing his Bluetooth in one ear. He's never been much for talking to hear himself talk, but he seemed even more terse than usual. "Shutters are closed, but not latched. And you left the window on the left open, about two inches. That's plenty of sightline for a clean kill shot, especially with this gun. I couldn't miss with a Desert Eagle at this range. But it's a good thing the window was open."

I turned my head for a look. Ali was going to have to spring for some repairs; there was wood missing.

"It was a little tricky." Patrick had looked back that way as well. "Standing on the groundskeeper's ladder wasn't much help. I'm just glad Bree figured out what was happening, or at least I assume she did, from how fast she moved. Not having to worry about hitting either of you made it possible for me to take the shot. Something else to be grateful for. Thanks for showing some good sense."

He wasn't smiling, and he wasn't bragging, either. I got the feeling—damned if I know why, but it was very strong—that something about having used that gun to kill Bengt Ekberg had triggered a very different reaction to what I'd assumed would happen.

From the day I first laid eyes on the bloke, I'd backed away from him for just that reason: the whole predator deal, the smell of blood in the water giving him a rush, all that. I don't like people who get their jollies off other people in pain. It's always kept me from actually liking him.

I wasn't getting that off him now; just the opposite, actually. It was obvious that he didn't want to talk about it, that he wasn't going to talk about it unless he had to. And that meant he hadn't wanted to do it. He was keeping those dirty-ice eyes completely away from the dead man on the floor. Not only wasn't he getting turned on from having done the shooting, he wasn't letting himself look at the results.

Someone must have left their own windows open, because there was a cross-breeze in the room. And out of nowhere, the clock rolled back and I was facing off with Patrick, toe to toe in a garden in the South of France, because he was using my wife as bait to catch a killer. Someone had killed a woman called Louise Goff, whom he'd obviously had feelings for, as well as his partner, back when he was DEA in Miami. What had he said? Something about one bullet to the head for each of them, and dumped on Patrick's doorstep like garbage, left for him to trip over...

"JP?"

Patrick was watching me. He'd seen me remember, seen me suss it out. And it was there in his face: I'd been right. This gun, this death, the smell of this particular blood, was going on the dark side of whatever the hell he used as a ledger. I wasn't likely to ever really know why, and that was fine. Fair enough. It wasn't my business anyway.

Bree had come back in, and Azra was at her heels. She wasn't looking at anyone except her father, and she only did that once more that morning. She looked up at him, eye to eye. If I've ever seen pleading in someone's face, it was there in hers.

"Cover him." Distant as the moon. "You aided in his death,

252

and in Nordine's. See what you helped bring about. Look at him."

"I did nothing to him. I did nothing to Nordine." She'd given up even trying to catch his eye. I wondered who she was trying to convince, while she was dropping the gaudy silk cover over what had been her dad's chief of security. "I will do as you tell me, but I am not to blame. I killed no one."

Nothing. Not a look, not a word, no acknowledgement that the girl was still alive or had even ever existed.

"I must thank you, Patrick, for your promptness in arriving and the precision of your shooting. We might have had more deaths, else. And there have been more than enough."

He was looking at the pile on the floor. The small pools of blood were already beginning to brown up, and I caught a faint smell. It reminded me of the morning we'd found that blood-soaked hut.

"My people have already left messages for Mr. Hendry and Ms. Fanucci, that the airports in southern Italy are opening to international traffic. I have arranged for a priority clearance. Your plane will be ready for you within the hour."

Chapter Fifteen

I can't speak for anyone else in the band family, but personally, I've never been happier about getting on a plane in my entire life. About the only person happier about it than me was my wife. If we could have got out of Manaar the day before last week, it wouldn't have been too soon for Bree.

I was saving my questions for the trip to the airport in Sicily; we were going to have a few hours in the air coming up. But yeah, there were going to be questions. There was still a shitload of things I wanted to know. Patrick might not want to talk about it, but he wasn't getting a vote, yeah? I wasn't the only one likely to be hitting him with it.

In the meantime, Bree was itching to get us packed and gone. Normally, if Blacklight's on tour, we travel with staff who handle all that. The Manaar gig had been a one-off, though, and very short notice as well. This gig, we were doing it ourselves; the only crew we'd brought along were band management and tech. All the housekeeping stuff was supposed to be provided by our host, but that didn't seem to extend to packing to get the hell out of the country. Even if it had done, I doubt Bree would have waited.

Under normal circs, my wife's got a nice clean easy way of getting everyone out of our digs when she's decided it's time they all left. Tony, who's been watching her do it for decades, calls it her "thanks for coming everyone please get the hell out and go home now" approach. It's about as subtle as a backhoe, but just then, she was going to have to be even less subtle than usual. She couldn't actually turf the Emir out, what with him owning the place. There was also the matter of the dead body under the silk coverlet.

"If our plane's almost ready, I'd like to start packing now." She'd apparently decided that straight and upfront was definitely the way to go. "Can someone please come and take Bengt off our floor?"

"Of course. I will have this taken care of at once." He turned for the door. "Azra. You will come with me."

"No, she won't. Not without your word that she won't be harmed in any way."

When Bree sounds definite, you can't miss it. The tone of voice means she's ready to go down fighting for whatever it is. I certainly wasn't expecting to hear it just then.

Ali stopped where he was. I could see his shoulders—they were as tense as Bree's own get. He turned slowly back, and stared at her. So did I, and my stomach went into lockdown mode. The green eyes were as fierce as they get. She wasn't going to back down an inch, not on this one.

"I beg your pardon?" Something was moving in that smoothed-out face of his. I had a bad feeling it was rage. "By what right do you demand such assurances?"

"Why did you offer to let me drive your Bugatti?"

It occurred to me that this was probably the last time they'd ever be in the same place again, and that Bree had sussed that out on her own. Even if he came out to the airport to see the plane off the ground, they weren't likely to be talking. This was the last shot at getting that one question answered. Ali had singled her out from the moment we'd got here, and no one had known why.

Still, the timing of her asking it was pretty dammed odd. She doesn't usually answer questions with questions anyway; she's too blunt and definite for that sort of game-playing. But I'm damned if Ali didn't answer her.

"You permitted me to cross your threshold, back in San Francisco. I was uninvited and unwelcome, but you allowed me into your home. You treated me with the courtesy you would have shown an invited guest. That is no small thing for a Manaari, in however low esteem you hold our culture. When I was told you would accompany your husband, I took the trouble to learn what might please you, and was told that you drive a powerful automobile. That suggested a love of speed. I offered the Veyron as a gesture in kind."

Yeah, well, score two points for the Emir. That answer had taken everyone by surprise, except for my wife.

"You just answered your own question," she told him. "Your daughter ate at my table. She was my guest, and she wasn't invited either. That's where I get the right. And if you have a problem with that, it's just too damned bad. Deal with it."

I'm not quite sure how it was possible, but my wife, the Irresistible Force, was managing to be the Immovable Object as well. And her voice wasn't taking any prisoners—that *deal with it* had been too close to being spat for comfort. If Ali hadn't known how little she liked him, he knew now. She might have been talking to a spider. Christ, even I hadn't realised how much she loathed him. She wasn't done with him, either.

"Don't you stand there looking down your nose at me. And you can lose that pushy arrogant tone, while you're at it. Considering that you mutilated your own child's corpse for the crime of not having a child of her own, you don't have a lot of credibility. So how about you stop wasting both our time? You either swear on the Koran or whatever you claim you believe in that your daughter won't be harmed in any way, or she doesn't leave this room with you. Got it? Clear now? Do you want me to write it down for you?"

I wonder, now, how long and how hot the desire to give the bloke a damned good hiding had been bubbling away. If things hadn't been so tense, it would have been almost funny: he was gawking at her, literally slackjawed with disbelief. Patrick was watching, ready to step in if things got out of hand, and he was still holding the gun. Azra wasn't staring at the floor anymore; her head was snapping back and forth between her dad and my wife. I remember thinking she was in for a bad case of whiplash, she kept that up.

"Oh, for fuck's sake, Ali, just get on with it, will you?"

Apparently Domitra had decided it really was clear, because Mac had got himself up to our end of the action. He was leaning against the door, and he sounded sardonic.

"She's right, you're wrong, and that's an end to it. Besides, I know Bree and you don't—such a fierce girl. If you argue with her, we'll miss our plane and that will make everyone cross. You'll lose the argument anyway, so why bother? I can safely promise you we'll all help her make sure your daughter's safe. That business with the hands? Not exactly delicious. All things considered, I doubt any of us are willing to cut you much slack right now. Just do it, Ali. Swear. Then we can all get the fuck out of here."

Ali's mouth was clamped so hard shut, he might as well have had no lips. He was breathing through his nostrils like some kind of pissed-off racehorse.

Bree shrugged. She walked right in front of him, dropped an arm around Azra, and planted herself. The girl's eyes were about the size of the cat dishes we use back at 2828 Clay. My wife's message was definitive: *This is how it is. Swear or she doesn't go with you.*

I had an odd passing thought: this was a new definition of that whole home court advantage thing my wife values so much. Ali might own the physical ground we were standing on, but Bree had just redefined the moral ground. And Ali knew it.

"Do it."

Ian had jumped the queue outside our suite. He slipped inside, in front of Mac and Dom. He was holding his phone.

"I should probably clue you in: Carla and I both recorded every word that just got said in here on our phones, and sent both recordings back to our own offices. I was out there in the hall with my phone getting everything from the moment you showed up. You walked around me to get in, remember? I've got the whole damned thing, including the bit where you said you cut your kid's hands off. We've got some pictures of Bengt, as well. I'm not squeamish and neither is Carla. You want that all over the English language edition of Al-Jazeera, you've got it."

Ian was keeping things icy, but Bree was smiling. It was clamped down, but I know every muscle in my wife's face, and there was a smile there, trying to get out. I'm guessing it was a sort of "finding a kindred spirit" deal, you know? Finding that Ian was just as pissed off at Ali as she was. And crikey, he was pissed off.

"You try any rubbish, anything at all, you'll have the whole story as a viral YouTube video. And don't bother wondering if I'd really do it, either. You jerked me around, you put a wedge between me and the band, and you nearly cost me my job. You tried to screw us and you put us and our crew in jeopardy. We don't owe you a fucking thing. What Bree said is dead right: you've got no cred."

Ali was grey with rage. Ian held up his phone, barely a foot away from Ali's face.

"Get on with it." There was a good hard snap in his voice. "Tell the world you've got no plans to damage your daughter. Say it nice and clear, no mistake possible, and crank up the fucking volume. Soon as you've done, we're off to pack and get the hell out of here. I want that plane on the tarmac and ready to go, and no arguments or excuses, either."

"As you wish." I don't know how Ali got the words out without choking on them, but there they were, and we'd all heard him say it. "She will not be harmed. I give my word."

"Accepted. For the moment, anyway." Bree wasn't smiling anymore. "If you go back on it, I'll call you a liar from San Francisco to Medin-Manaar and back. I'll shout it from the rooftops. But I don't think you will. And now, if you don't mind, I want to pack. If everyone will please excuse us? Mac, you're blocking the doorway. Patrick, be careful not to slip. There's blood on the floor."

Considering how many years Bree's packed for me going out on tour, I probably shouldn't have been surprised at how fast she had every last sock, pair of knickers and three-ounce travel sized bottle of hair product stowed away in our bags. She's packed for so long, she's got an eye for it, and getting all the gear and food she needs for the occasional catering gig back in San Francisco to fit into a rented SUV probably doesn't hurt either. But this was quick even by her standards.

You'd think the entire morning had been surreal enough, but it turned out Manaar wasn't quite done with us yet. Bree'd got nicely into her rhythm and was folding the last bits of my stage gear when we heard footsteps, more than one set of them, coming down the corridor. A moment later, someone knocked, a nice clean sharp rapping. Not the Princess Azra tapping away like a scared rabbit, not this time.

"John?" Bree had one of my jackets half folded. She wasn't slowing down. I suddenly realised, she was keeping her eyes away from the mess on the floor. "Can you get that?"

There were three blokes out in the corridor, waiting politely for me to stand back and let them in. These were definitely Ali's uniforms, probably members of the household guard, but there were no guns in sight. Instead, there was a stretcher, a mop, and a huge bucket full of what looked like cleaning supplies. I saw what looked like a dustpan, and the handle of a small whisk broom, poking out the top.

I'll give Ali this much: he wasn't a slacker. The Emir might have been having fantasies about having Bree strung up and flogged in the middle of Amina Plaza for insubordination or whatever, but he'd got right on his promise to deal with what was left of Bengt. He'd even remembered the pine-scented cleaner and the industrial strength rubber gloves.

There wasn't one word spoken the entire time, not by them and not by us, either. Bree kept folding, and two of them carefully loaded Bengt up onto the stretcher, silk coverlet and all. They got him off the floor and onto the stretcher in total silence. No communicating with each other, not a word to us, nothing. They might as well have been mutes. I just stood back and let everyone get on with it.

It was also really damned disturbing to realise just how good they were at what they were doing. I mean, we've got roadies who've been with Blacklight twenty years who aren't that smooth, yeah? And what the hell, how many chances did these blokes get to practice? I had a mad moment of picturing Ali training his people to load the headless corpses of his enemies onto stretchers without bothering the tourists, and wondering just what he used for the corpses.

They got Bengt off the floor, squared up on the stretcher and out the door without letting anything slip out from under the coverlet. There was none of that 'one limp hand dangling' thriller nonsense. I was quite thankful for that—we were already taking enough bad memories of Manaar with us as it was. Of course, by that time, he'd probably stiffened up anyway.

Before the first two uniforms had got the stretcher halfway through the suite door, the third one got down on both knees and got busy with the cleaning supplies. He used the small whisk-broom and got the shards of bone up and into the dustpan, and then went to work on cleaning up the blood. He was done in under three minutes, bob's your uncle, everything back in the bucket and out the door, with one small nod towards us. So far as I could tell, Bree hadn't let herself look anywhere near the proceedings the entire time they'd been here.

After I locked the door behind him, I found myself staring at the floor. There were already stains, and from the look of them, they were probably there for good. Ali was going to have to spring for a small pile of dosh redoing this particular suite, unless he fancied keeping it as it was and maybe renting it out to rich thrill-seekers as a haunted chamber or something. Maybe next time, he'd get the stones sealed before someone else bled all over them.

"Damn, my back hurts." Bree'd snapped the locks on the last suitcase into place, and was straightening up, slow and careful. "I wish I had some time to do a little yoga before we left. I'm too old to go without sleep."

"Rubbish. If you're old, what does that make me?"

I knew, we both knew, what she'd really meant: it wasn't a question of enough time, it was about a place to do it. Even with her yoga gear and mat already rolled up and packed, she could have pulled the coverlet off the bed and done a nice little yoga workout; if we got the call that the car was outside and ready, they'd wait for us. Hell, in the headspace Bree was in, she'd probably have enjoyed making them wait.

But she wasn't getting down on that floor. The stones were still dark and wet where they'd been scrubbed, still stained a really nasty blackish red underneath those damp patches. Like it or not, our suite had been the site of an execution...

"John?" She'd caught at my thought; the marital mind-reading was running hot and strong. "Would it be okay if we waited outside for the car? I'm sorry—this room is creeping me out."

We left the luggage just inside and headed out into the courtyard. Getting from one end of the corridor to the other, I could hear murmurs behind doors; everyone still seemed to be busy getting their own gear packed up. Out of doors, it was your basic day in Manaar: nice soft breeze, nice clean sunlight, the mineral pools sparkling in the sun.

"How soon do you think the car will get here?" Bree was staring towards the gates in from the main road, craning her neck. Her entire body looked to be straining to get the hell out of here.

"Not to worry—Ian'll text us first. We don't need to sit indoors. Anyway, it's quite pleasant out here."

I wasn't watching the road, or even listening for a car. I was busy reminding myself to ask Patrick about something Ali had said to Bengt, just before the shooting started. What had that been? He'd been saying something about how he'd already known or suspected that one of the twins had been involved with Nordine, and then something about what they'd found in the pool...

"I wonder what they found in that other pool? And when they found it?"

I did a double-take, and Bree hurried into speech. "He said something like that, didn't he? About suspecting that Paksima was having a thing with Nordine, and about how what they found in the second pool confirmed it? I thought –"

"Yeah, he did. You made me jump, that's all. I was just thinking that exact thing myself, but I couldn't remember what he'd said." I glanced out at the mineral pools, clear and shining in the sun. "No idea what they found, but I'm betting I know when they found it. Remember the day after Nordine got slashed, when Ali dragged you all over to the palace to have lunch, and he wouldn't take anyone's no? When we got back here from the band practice he tricked Ian into calling us out for, we found those two tankers. My money's on it being then. Must have been, yeah? They were emptying out both pools, not just the one, and bottom line is, Nordine only died in one of those pools. I'd lay a few bob on whatever it was being something Paksima's dad recognised as hers, straight off."

She was looking pinched, suddenly, and I got an arm round her shoulders. My arm was shaking a bit, just a tiny tremor, and I hoped to hell she'd put it down to nerves, or the warm weather, or not enough sleep.

"It's okay, baby." I had my lips up against her hair. "No point in letting it get to you, is there? We're out of here as soon as the car shows up to get us to the airport, and after that, fuck it, not coming back here again. But there's a few things I want to know, and what you asked, about the second pool, is right up there on my list. I hope Patrick doesn't think he's using the flight for a nice long kip. He's got questions to answer. As soon as we –"

I stopped, because the phone in my trousers pocket had suddenly vibrated. I pulled it out—Ian had texted, right on schedule. *Cars on the way, eta five minutes, plane ready, be packed.*

The limos showed up a few minutes later, along with Ian and Carla and a pair of SUVs for the luggage and guitars. The rest of the crew, Ronan and Nial included, were probably still working their arses off, back at the site: tearing down, checking shipping manifests, packing the gear. As loadouts go, Blacklight had certainly done bigger ones; the stage sets for Book of Days had been monsters compared to this. Still, everything had to be accounted for and crated up. I was just glad our staff wasn't responsible for all those portable toilets. They'd have been stuck in Manaar until midsummer.

Everyone had got Ian's text, and no one was dawdling or hanging about. By the time the cars showed, the suites were empty of people. Everyone had come out of doors to wait.

"Ian, what about our people?" Mac was watching Ali's boys get suitcases stowed in the Range Rovers; they were almost as fast doing that as our impromptu cleaning staff had been. "Are we sure there won't be any problems with them getting out of Manaar? I'm not exactly thrilled with the idea of leaving them behind, all things considered."

"Not an issue, Mac. We're not leaving anyone behind." Nice and gruff; our tour manager was sounding almost normal again. He had one eye watching Ali's people loading our stuff into the SUVs. "All of our people are on the same plane. Ronan and Nial have been onsite most of the night, working with the PA guys. The Clare Brothers staff's handling whatever's left to do. They couldn't head out yet even if they fancied a side trip to Sicily— the contract says they're ultimately responsible for the PA gear, so they've got to make sure everything's done. They're getting on with it. But Blacklight family, all of us, we're going out together. The crew's heading to the airport straight from Amina. They'll meet us at the plane. Everyone ready? Let's go."

Funny thing about that ride out to the airport. I'd got used to basically empty highways on our side of Medin-Manaar—after all, there was really nothing that side of the capital beyond the seraglio and Ali's own digs. That morning, the roads weren't empty. There wasn't much traffic, very few cars, but there were people, what looked to be an endless stream of them, walking along the main road.

"Holy shit, check out all the fans!" Tony was peering out the window on his side of the limo. He sounded a bit freaked, and I got why: the fans had obviously sussed out who was in the limos, and there was some commotion out there. "I never even stopped to think about how they were getting out of here. Are we even going to be able to get on a plane?"

It was a good question. There were a quarter of a million people looking to get to somewhere that wasn't Manaar. On top of that, today was an international holiday, and any flights would be dealing with the aftermath of really bad weather at the arrivals end of most of the destinations they'd likely be headed to. We were looking at a scheduling nightmare.

Even if our plane was the only flight off the ground today, the airport was likely to be buried under people waiting for a way home. I had no clue how we were going to get through the mob. I was about to ask Ian when, out of nowhere, we had company: a half dozen motorcycles on either side of the convoy, the Manaari flag fluttering off the back of each one, keeping a safety zone between the pedestrians and the limos. Next to Bree, Luke grunted.

"Efficient sod, isn't he? Nice little police escort—he thinks of everything. Tony, don't worry about the crowds. They'll drive us straight to the plane, the same way we handled it during Book of Days. I'm betting the yobs out there on the bikes get between us and the rest of the world. Does anyone want to take bets on whether al-Wahid comes out to officially wave us off? Or at least makes sure that we get out of his emirate?"

Next to him, Karen moved in her seat, sliding up a little closer to Luke. "Oh god. I don't want to sound rude, but I really hope he doesn't. I just want to go home to Draycote. I want to forget about this place."

We did the rest of the ride in total silence, not a word said by anyone. Karen sounded so stressed, so completely miserable and played out, no one seemed to want to say anything. Luke got hold of her hands and just held them. The bullet-proof windows made a good job of keeping noise out, as well. It was so quiet, we could have been in the middle of outer space.

Luke had nailed it. We were driven straight onto the airfield, two motorbikes leading the way and the rest forming a cordon behind us to make sure we weren't bothered. And yeah, it was needed. The fans were going nuts, yelling and pointing and cheering. It's something I thought I'd got used to over the years, but every time it happens, it feels new and odd. And the older I get, the more I find myself taken short by the whole thing, more surprised when I hear my own name come out of one of those mobs.

We climbed out of the limos just as the steps were being wheeled up to the plane. The cargo bay doors were open, and they were already loading luggage and gear. Patrick was waiting, and right behind him I saw Ronan and Nial and Jas. Ian, first out of the limo he was sharing with Carla, the Corrigans and the Wilsons, stood peering around. His lips were moving, doing a headcount.

"All present and accounted for." He jerked his head towards the plane. "Don't know about you lot, but I'm ready to get the fuck out of here. I see the Emir didn't bother to come out to kiss us goodbye. Everyone ready? The weather forecast has clear skies. We should be in Sicily in time for dinner."

266

Chapter Sixteen

As it turned out, Patrick did manage an hour's worth of kip on the way home, after all. We'd barely got ourselves strapped in for takeoff when he lifted his voice above the noise of the engines warming up.

"Hey, guys? Ian's suggested that I give my full report as soon as we're in the air. Is everyone okay with that?"

So, yeah, Ian had already sussed we wanted to know what in hell had just gone down, and that none of us wanted to wait to hear it. That was reassuring, in a way; after all, thinking ahead to make sure things get taken care of as smoothly as possible is what we pay Ian for. Comes with the job, yeah? Manaar had cocked things up badly, but it looked as if our tour manager was back to normal, and thank God for it.

I'd been expecting a bumpy flight, but there was no sign of

turbulence. Either we were behind whatever weather fronts were still messing up commercial air travel, or else we were out of the trouble zones. I didn't really give a toss, either way; I was too glad for a nice calm ride to southern Europe.

We'd only been up for about ten minutes before the little lights telling us it was safe to undo the belts went on. The flight attendant serving drinks and nosh did her thing, but no one seemed interested. We were all waiting on Patrick, and he knew it.

This wasn't the first time we'd heard him come across with an actual official report—he's had to do a few of them since we'd hired him on as Blacklight's security chief. But this was the first time he'd had the entire immediate band family there to listen: last time, it had just been the band and Carla getting the gen. This time, he had all the wives, and the full crew as well. Just as well he's not a shy bloke, you know? All those eyes might have put him off. As it was, he didn't look to have made up his mind about where to start.

"I'm not sure what the best way to handle this is." He was talking to all of us, but he was looking at Carla. "As much as I'd like to able to wrap this up cleanly, there are things I can only guess at."

"Really?" Funny thing—Barb Wilson had seemed just as wiped out as the rest of us, but now that we were safe off Manaari soil and headed for Europe, she'd perked right up. Hell, everyone was looking happier. "Such as?"

He took the question seriously. "Well, I don't have anything beyond guesswork for any of the emotional issues. I do have certain hard facts I can share, and of course I will. But all I have to offer, about what was motivating any of these people to do what they did, would be pure guesswork. I don't even know why Ali al-Wahid was willing to pay the kind of money he was willing to pay out to get Blacklight to play his show."

"Guilt. That would be my guess, anyway."

We all looked at Mac. He wasn't smiling. "It's not rocket science, Patrick. I was at school with him, remember. I've probably got a better look at how his mind works than you do. And I can tell you this much: he was writhing over the trouble his twin terrors' bodyguards caused during Book of Days—that whole 'shame of my family' thing is huge in his culture. I suspect this was his way of evening things out: reparation, or whatever he needed to make himself feel that debt was paid off in full. He was smart enough to know he couldn't simply offer us money and quiet down his guilty conscience that way, especially not after I hung up on him twice. The gig, and that ridiculous paycheque, were his way of coping. He did what he always does. He reached for his chequebook."

Stu grunted. "What, executing the bastards wasn't good enough for him? You're probably right about him writhing, but I don't think it was guilt. If he was writhing over anything, it was you and Luke taking him apart back in San Francisco, when he showed up at JP and Bree's place that day. I don't believe he'd have given a fuck one way or the other, if it hadn't been for that. It was the slap to his pride did it."

"He had it coming." Luke was stony-faced enough to give Patrick a run for his money. "And I'll cash his cheque. We earned it. We played the hell of a show."

"That sounds about right." Patrick was tapping on the table in front of him, that rhythmic thing he does with his fingers when he's eager for everyone to stop interrupting and let him get on with things. "Meanwhile, for the facts I do know, it all goes back to Paksima al-Wahid getting sexually involved with both Nordine Benhamou and Bengt Ekberg."

"At the same time?" Carla shook her head. "Wow. Just from the brief dealings I had with those two guys, I can't imagine how that girl thought she could handle both of them. Not a chance. Was she an idiot, or just too spoiled to care?"

"I don't know." Patrick sounded patient. "I could speculate about the emotional reasons, but if you don't mind, I'll stick with the facts. And the fact is that, a few months back, the princess discovered she was pregnant."

"She didn't know whose it was, did she?" Bree's voice was almost too quiet. I reached for her hand, but she had both of them clasped in her lap, out of reach. "I got that much from what her sister said this morning—at least, I think that's what she meant. And then the baby died. I wonder if Paksima thought that solved the problem of whose it was? Because Azra told us this morning that they didn't know what to do, that Paksima asked Nordine for help getting rid of that stillbirth. I can't believe she would have done that, if she thought even for one minute that he'd raise hell over it. She must have read him all the way wrong, if she did that. I only got to know him over learning to drive the Veyron, and even I could tell he wasn't the kind of man anyone could jerk around, not safely anyway."

"Yes, that's apparently what happened." I couldn't get a read on Patrick just then, what he was really thinking or feeling. He had the old homicide rozzer's poker face on. "I got confirmation of a few things from the Emir this morning, on the way over from the royal palace."

"What?" I was staring at him. "You mean Ali just let it bleed? Sorry, mate. Not meaning to be rude, but I don't think I'm buying that. Why would he share a damned thing with you or anyone else, especially if it made his family look bad?"

Patrick turned to answer me, and I got a shock. I'd seen that look on his face once before, back in the South of France. He doesn't show his personal weak spots very often, so when he does, I remember it.

"He shared because he had no choice." Flat as a rock, that voice was. "The information he had was my price for picking up that gun. I made it clear that unless I was aware of as many of the facts he had in his possession, I wouldn't take the shot. Excuse me a minute, I'm a little scratchy-throated."

We stayed quiet while he got a mouthful of cold water. It's like I said, sipping a drink's a great way of stalling for time while you get your shit together. After a minute, he went on.

"So Paksima was pregnant. I gathered from my conversation with Ali this morning that she'd visited her usual doctor, and that the doctor had come directly to him and told him the princess had aborted a foetus. I don't know how Ali convinced the guy to break his patient's confidence, and I don't think the knowledge is pertinent. I don't know when that happened, either. He wasn't forthcoming about it, and I didn't press it. There were things I was more interested in."

"He found out last night. Ali said that to Bengt, just before the shooting started. He said the doctor had told him all about the abortion. I'm betting that's what led to that sick bullshit with the hands. But hang on a minute, all right?"

I'd managed to get hold of one of my wife's hands. The way this conversation was headed was likely to bring up some bad memories. Something had just occurred to me, though, and it wanted out. I took a breath and turned back to Patrick.

"I don't know if you could hear Azra this morning, when she dished. She said they'd gone to Nordine to abort the baby, since it was dead anyway, and that he'd seen it as leverage, a way to marry into the royal family. She said he'd threatened to tell her dad all about it. And I'll tell you what, I think maybe everyone's on the wrong track here. I think we're doing that girl an injustice."

Patrick blinked at me. I went on, sorting it out as I talked.

"Where's the proof that Paksima was actually involved with Nordine? Because that's not what it sounded like, you know? Her sister said something this morning, about how they'd gone to Nordine for help, that he'd messed her up inside and then

271

threatened to go to their dad with it if Paksima didn't marry him. Remember, Bree? She said Nordine threatened to lie to Ali, and that Ali would believe him, yeah? But why in hell would he have to lie, if there was any shot the kid actually was his? Doesn't make any sense, does it? And another thing—the way Azra said it this morning, the way she put it out to her dad, it sounded like they went to him because they'd known him forever. Someone they knew, someone they thought they could trust."

"Oh man." Bree's breathing had gone choppy. "Oh shit. John, yes. And Ali said that Nordine's family had served the royal family for generations, or something."

I nodded. "I think that kid was Bengt's. I'm betting she was never involved with Nordine at all."

Dom had stayed quiet so long, her voice made me jump. "So, what? You think all that shooting and the stuff with the hands, everything that went down, all those people getting killed, it was just a mistake? Man, that's some sad shit right there."

"If JP's right, then yes. And I think maybe he is." Patrick was watching me. The cop face had softened into something else; I had the feeling he might actually be feeling sorry for everyone involved. Bit of a departure, that would be. "But in any case, there appears to be no doubt about the fact that Paksima killed Nordine. And yes, I'm sure of that."

"Why?" Katia sounded as if she really wanted to know. "I mean, why are you so sure?"

"Because her clothes, everything she was wearing when she killed him, were found by Bengt in the second pool the morning after the murder." Nice and impersonal. "Even after it had been in the water overnight, there was apparently still enough blood spatter to be obvious. The forensic evidence, in this instance, was very clear. There was also Azra's reaction. The evidence here would be enough to satisfy a jury. She killed him."

This time, it was Bree's hand tightening around mine. I won-

272

dered if she was seeing the same picture in her head as I was: the girl, all done up in her usual gear from the Paris runways, confronting Nordine, him issuing his threat, her doing—what, exactly? She must have had something in her hand, something sharp enough to do what she'd done to Nordine's throat. And that meant she'd come to that meeting knowing she might be wanting a weapon...

"We're never going to have all the details." Patrick was watching my wife, and he wasn't making any bones about it, either. This time, I didn't mind; she was pale as Manaari desert sand just then. "But clearly Paksima went into that rendezvous suspicious about what Nordine was going to do, because she went armed. And whatever he threatened her with, it was enough to get her to react by killing him."

"She went a little crazy." Bree sounded sad, but she was getting her colour back. Good. "Her hormones were probably off the charts. You're right, we'll never know all of it. But John and I may know a few things you don't."

Patrick lifted an eyebrow at her. "Bengt was—talking," Bree told him. "This morning. I was asking him questions, a little because I wanted to know the answers, but mostly because I thought he was going to have to shoot us and I wanted to be alive a few more minutes. So I kept asking him stuff."

She stopped, just to take a breath. No drama, she was just stating what she'd been up to, but right then, the plane's engines sounded louder than ever, because no one seemed to be breathing. I don't think she knew the effect she'd had, because she just picked up where she'd paused.

"He seemed to want to talk. He was totally whacked out—he must have been having a huge adrenalin rush, or maybe just the whole situation, knowing he wasn't getting out alive. I guess he knew he had nothing to lose, so he just answered things. He said he'd taken the baby's corpse, and buried it out in the desert. And

273

he said he could live without knowing for certain whether Paksima had killed Nordine, but he wanted to know whose baby it had been. He was convinced Azra knew. I think that's why he killed Paksima—the idea that she'd have asked him to bury that baby, when it might not have been his. I don't know why I think that. I just know I do."

"I heard that bit, out in the hall." Ian sounded even gruffer than usual, but he leaned over and patted my wife's arm. Coming from Ian, that was mindblowing. He's the only human being I know who's got less time for stray pats than Bree does. "So he thought they'd been having it off. From all that shite the Emir said to his daughter, he seemed to think so too. But you and JP think he was wrong?"

Bree nodded. She seemed to have run out of words.

"I'm with JP and Bree on this one." Mac waved at the flight attendant. "I don't see that girl asking Nordine to do what she asked him to do if there was any way in hell that child could physically have been his. Oh, yes, I'd like some hot tea, please. Does anyone else fancy a nice cuppa? Because I want something comforting right now. What a hideous pointless mess this whole thing has been."

"Agreed. No, no tea for me, but I'd love a beer." Patrick stifled a yawn. "Where was I? More facts? Ali told me that Bengt was sent to make sure all traces of Nordine in the mineral pool were cleaned out, while Ian and I were told to find some way of getting everyone out of the seraglio. Bengt must have caught sight of Paksima's stuff in the second pool, and got the tankers to suction everything away. Of course he would have recognised the clothes—they'd been having an affair. He would have seen the significance immediately, since they'd been using the back end of the seraglio as their private little pleasure dome."

"He went off his head, didn't he?" I was thinking out loud. "Just lost it. He had a day or two to let it build up. He must have

274

been right off his head. And in the middle of all that, me and Bree spotted the three of them outside our window and went out looking the next morning. That was when we found the hut where the mess with Paksima's baby went down. Wonder who the third person was?"

"Probably Azra." Bree leaned against my shoulder. It's always nice to know that, times like these, I'm who she reaches for. And when it comes to comfort, only Bree'll do for me. "Why did Bengt send the guard to our tent after the show? Or is that speculation and not fact?"

Patrick smiled at her. It was a genuine smile, gone a second later. It suddenly hit me, how tired he was.

"My guess would be to keep everyone's attention diverted while he went out after Azra. You realise, she must have seen her sister executed? There's no other reason for her to have been frightened, or to have run off into that crowd. He would have been desperate to find her and silence her before she could tell her father or anyone else what he'd done. Of course, Bengt couldn't have known that while he was trying to chase down the surviving twin, their father –"

One of the women, I'm not sure who, made a noise, and Patrick broke off. "Well. In any case, that's basically all I've got in the way of actual facts. Unless anyone has questions I might be able to answer, I'd like to try for a quick nap before we land. I'm a little short on sleep."

When it comes to weather, London in January isn't any less miserable than it is in December. Of course, that goes for most of Europe, really; it's probably just as well Bree and I'd honeymooned in southern Europe in warm weather, or she might have thought the entire continent was like this all the time.

We spent three chilly days decompressing in Italy and got back to about as cold a London night as I can remember: the entire city looked to be made of frost. It probably felt even colder than it was, coming from the desert. Letting ourselves into the mews house, I was psyching myself up to huddling with Bree, having a cuddle under a duvet on the sofa until the furnace kicked in. So it was a nice surprise to walk in and find the house a comfy seventy degrees.

"Oh thank heavens!" Bree headed straight for the kitchen, and I followed on. "I bet Carla asked someone at the office to come by and turn the heat on. Man, she's good."

"Yeah, she really is." I'd pulled up one of the kitchen chairs. "Is there anything edible in the house, or do you want to send out for something? Probably too much to hope for, expecting Carla to ask the staff to stock the fridge, as well."

Bree had filled the electric kettle, and plugged it in. "No, it's pretty bare in there. I cleaned the fridge out before we left, so we're basically down to crackers and some frozen stuff, but I can always—is that your phone?"

It was, and I'd left the damned thing in my coat pocket, out in the hall. By the time I got to it, it had clicked over to voicemail. I headed back to the kitchen, where the kettle was on the boil. Bree was dropping a mesh strainer full of decaf Earl Grey into one of the small teapots that came with the rental. She looked up at me, waiting.

"Ian," I told her. "No clue what he wants. Hang on, let me get this. Have we got any honey?"

"*(beep) JP? Ian. Look, I know everyone's only just got home, but Mac wants a dinner meeting at Fallow tomorrow night, full band. This is about early planning for the 'thank the fans' gigs—no worries, there aren't any problems. But since you and Bree are heading back to the States soon, it makes sense to get it done early. Ring me back, will you?*"

"John?" She sounded anxious. "Is everything okay?"

That startled me. She must have seen from my face that nothing much was happening, but that hadn't stopped her from tensing up, you know? I found myself wondering just how much damage the stuff that had gone down in Manaar had really done. Not just to Bree, either; I hadn't been sleeping well, not since the shooting in our suite. The whole time in Italy I'd kept waking up, never really getting too deep into real sleep, and I didn't think it had much to do with the MS, for a change. What was it soldiers got, after they've had too much shit going on around them, gunfire and being afraid all the time and too much death? Post traumatic something or other...?

"Yeah, everything's fine. Just Ian letting me know that Mac wants a get-together at Fallow House for dinner tomorrow night. He says it's about getting a jump on the planning for the festival gigs this summer. They know we're heading home in a few days, and they want to do it while we're still here. Probably going to be a lot of tossing ideas about, unless someone comes up with something straight off." I watched her shoulders loosen up, and patted her hand. "No worries, love. You can hang out here if you'd rather pass on it. I should go, though—at least they'll have a hot supper waiting. Speaking of supper, what are we doing about tonight...?"

In the end, we both went to the Fallow House meeting. That was just as well, because it turned out that between me ringing Ian back to say *yeah, we'll be there* and the hire car dropping us off at the front stairs the next night, someone actually had come up with something, and it was a corker.

Before we'd headed out, though, Bree'd gone off to get enough groceries to get us through the rest of our time in London. We had tickets booked to get us home to San Francisco at the end of the week. The minute she was out the door, I rang Carla's office in Los Angeles and left her a message.

There was something I wanted to book myself, that I didn't want Bree in on. It had nothing at all to do with Blacklight, and I was going to need Carla's help on this one; I knew what I wanted, but I hadn't got the first clue where to start getting it done, or who to talk to. I left her a nice detailed message, right down to remembering to tell her to not let Bree get wind of it. It was six in the morning in California, so she'd find it when she got there. No need to wake her up, you know? She'd only got home from Italy two days ago herself.

Time's a funny old thing, the way it telescopes itself. We'd been at Fallow House maybe six weeks before, but so much had gone down since then, it felt more like six months or maybe six years. At the same time, there was this weird sense of *deja vu*: big gas fireplace warming the place up, sideboard covered with hot chafing dishes, hired wait staff hanging about until they were wanted to do the clearing up, cars pulling up in front of Fallow House to drop people off and disappearing down the Kings Road to park somewhere until it was time to bring everyone home again. Just like the last big supper do we'd had here.

And this time, everyone was there. Ian had even got David Walter and Maureen Bennett, the London office's two honchos, out for this one, and everyone in the band had brought his missus, as well. Patrick had stayed in London, and he'd come along. It wasn't until the hired crew had bundled the last of the dirty dishes out of the way that Ian finally got down to business, and he wasn't wasting any time.

"Everyone have enough to eat? Good, because I told Carla I'd ring her as soon as we were done here. She says she's got a few things she wants to share with the band, and that it's got a direct bearing on the festival dates, and no, I haven't got a clue what it is. She said she wants to run it past everyone at the same time."

Of course she was ready and waiting for us. Marjorie, her assistant, picked up on the first ring and put us straight through.

"Ian?" If she was jetlagged, it wasn't showing. "Is everyone there? Can we get started? Oh, hi guys."

278

"All here, the lot of us. Half a mo, all right?" Ian said it over one shoulder—he was waving the hired help out through the main doors. "Yeah, thanks, good night. Carla? We're ready to rock. What have you got?"

"Three locations, with dates." Nice and crisp, and the truth is, having Carla and Ian sounding completely themselves again somehow put Manaar that much farther behind us. "Let's get Europe out of the way first. What would you say to two European shows? One in mid-June, one in late August?"

"I'd say brilliant, depending on where they were." Mac was sounding normal again, as well. "I wouldn't much fancy playing a goat pasture in Turkey somewhere. Want to share, please?"

Funny thing: Carla performs miracles on a regular enough basis to not even notice what she's pulling off. Just then, though, I'd have sworn I heard a touch of the smug in her voice.

"First thing is the June date. I just finished up with the organisers of Rock am Ring—that's June third through fifth, this year. They've agreed to Blacklight having an entire weekend at the Nürburgring two weeks after the official festival, acts of our choosing, the whole nine yards."

"Bloody hell!" Stu was blinking at the speaker. "Carla, how the fuck do you pull this stuff off? Have you got photos of all these people in bed with donkeys, or something?"

That got a laugh out of her. "Nice idea, Stu, but no, I don't. Does that work for everyone? JP, anything planned in California with the Geezers that might conflict?"

"No, nothing at all. Sounds brilliant." Inside, I was grinning ear to ear. Early or middle June, Germany, nice and close to Bree's birthday: yeah, Carla had got that phone message I'd left, all right. From the sound of it, she'd run with it. "I'm on. What was that about a second Euro show, though? Did you say something about August? What'd you pull out of your hat this time, Hyde Park or something?"

"Well—yes." Gordon *Bennett*. "The last Saturday in August, the twenty-seventh, is ours if we want it. I know it's a short lead time for getting two festivals together, but they're two months apart. Is that enough for planning and booking the other acts we want? And do the venue capacities work for everyone, or do we need two-day events for the kind of traffic you're thinking about?"

Silence. The entire room was just sitting there gawking, at the phone or at each other. Even Mac was slackjawed.

"Guys? Hello? Is everyone still there?"

"Um—yeah, still here." Ian got himself back together. "So you've got us the Nürburgring and Hyde Park, if we want either or both. People? Consensus, please, show of hands. Nürburgring show in June? Any reason to not go for it? I'm not talking tech stuff and prep, I'm asking about personal commitments. Is everyone open for the booking? Right. Carla, every hand in the room's in the air, so I'd say we're good to go for that one. Send me the contact stuff and I'll get it rolling from here. What about a Hyde Park gig? That one seems like a no-brainer—yeah, right, everyone's in? Carla, it's unanimous for both. We'll hammer out the details, no worries. Brilliant job. Was there anything else?"

"Actually, yes, one more thing. I got a call out of the blue about an hour ago, from a guy named Ryder DeWitt. Do any of you know who he is?"

"What, you mean the Las Vegas hotel guy?" Cal had both his eyebrows up. "Yeah, of course. We lent him two of my basses for an exhibition of classic instruments at one of his places, a few years back. What about him, Carla?"

"Apparently he's decided that one of his resort hotels, the Ravenna, is too old to compete with the newer ones, and he's going to build a new state of the art replacement. The site's being razed flat. We're talking about sixty acres of prime land in the middle of Vegas, a nice level lot with nothing on it, as of mid-July." She took a breath. "He says that if Blacklight Corporate is willing to cover the costs of running the required City services into the site—water, gas, that kind of thing—we can have it for the North American festival dates. The only drawback is that he'd need to have the services in and done before the middle of October; something about his permits. So what would you say to a North American festival date in Sin City? Maybe the weekend before Halloween, when the weather in the desert has cooled off? There are no major events scheduled that weekend—I already checked with the Convention and Visitors Bureau. We can get it locked in early and get the Chamber of Commerce resources guaranteed."

Of course, that brought down the house. Everyone was talking, everyone trying to cut through each other's babble, while Carla and Ian just sat back and waited. I turned to Tony, who was sitting just to my left and looking about as happy as I'd seen him look since Book of Days. I was about to say something when Luke's voice came across the table at us.

"...Traitors Gate for the Hyde Park show? Because they haven't toured in a while, and they all live within half an hour of London. Remember the Hall of Fame show? Tony, you and Winston locked up that night. I'd love to play with those guys again. Maybe give Greg Carver or Winston Dupres a ring...?"

Tony went rigid.

There was no other word for it; Bree at her stiffest doesn't come close to how hard Tony closed up. Katia was next to him on the far side, and I watched her react to it, pulling back, staring at him. Whatever had triggered him, she didn't look to be clued in. I watched him gather himself, visibly try to control it, get a handle on it.

"Uh—" Tony's not usually stuck for what to say, but he was now. He was being careful, not just hunting for words but making damned sure every one he used was the right one. He'd got everyone's attention, too. The entire conference room listening. "I'm not too sure that's a good idea, Luke. They might not be— available."

I don't know what twigged it for me. Maybe it was the tone of voice, or maybe how uncomfortable he sounded. All I know is, I was suddenly back at the mews house, the night before Tony checked himself into rehab. My head brought the memory back, nice and clear: Tony and Katia, eating Bree's roast. They'd gone over to the Recovery Centre earlier that day, been shown around the place by the director, Robert Mourdain. Bad weather, sleety cold, the sort of weather in which no one in their right mind would want to be sitting out in a garden...Bits of the conversation, things Tony had said, came back to me, along with the taste of that roast, and everything else.

(*There was someone out in the garden...Mourdain got me back inside in a hurry...they weren't expecting anyone to be out in that weather...we'd seen each other...we recognised each other...you'd have recognised him too...*)

Winston? Greg? Was it blow, or crack, or booze, or maybe something worse? What in hell had happened, and who had it happened to?

My stomach was doing a slow crawl. I couldn't ask Tony, even though Winston, in particular, had become a damned good friend, even though we lived half a world away from each other. Anonymity's got to be respected—that's at the core of the whole recovery deal. Tony hadn't told us back before he checked into the Centre himself, and I couldn't ask him now.

I was staring at Tony, and he was busy making damned sure he wasn't meeting my eye. I jerked myself back to the here and now, but the talk had moved on. I'd missed some of the chatter, but in the end it was simple enough: Ian took an official vote, and confirmed we were unanimous on all three events. Patrick was asked to supply what he thought he'd need for full security for all three gigs, and said he would. Carla thanked everyone and rang off. For a meeting with that much important stuff going on, it was over in record time.

Afterwards, waiting just inside for our driver to pull up with the car, Luke pulled me aside.

"JP, look." His voice was all the way down. "I wasn't about to push Tony, but I got the feeling something was going on. You're good friends with Winston. Is something wrong with him, or Greg?"

"Don't know, mate." I met his eye. "And truth is, if I did, I wouldn't be sharing. That's not how rehab works. But there's nothing to share. I don't know. I'll ring Winston tomorrow—I was planning on asking him over for a meal before we headed home. But I don't know. Oi, Bree, that our car?"

Saying goodbyes, knowing we weren't likely to see most of them again until we got together for early planning and then first rehearsals for the Nürburgring show. Bree offering Karen a solid hug, heading down the hall to the small office where we'd stashed our coats. My phone pinged, letting me know someone had sent me a text. I pulled it out and flipped it open. It was from Carla.

"*Bree confirmed for Ehra-Lessien June 12 happy rocking early birthday mum's the word CF.*"

"John?" She'd come back, the green cashmere coat already buttoned. She was holding mine out to me. "Was someone on the phone? Is everything okay? What are you smiling about?"

"Everything's fine," I told her, and we headed out into the cold and frost, towards the mews house and another three days to get ready for the long ride home.

Epilogue

June 2011

"Mr. and Mrs. Kinkaid? I am Lothar Eichel, track director. Welcome to Ehra-Lessien. I hope your trip was comfortable. It is a great pleasure to meet you both. Please call me Lothar."

I've always thought of myself as a piss-poor actor. This time, though, unless Bree'd suddenly developed some serious acting chops of her own, I'd managed to get my wife out of bed at half past six in the morning and get her from the Grandhotel Schloss Bensberg in Koln to Volkswagen's test track just outside Wolfsburg without her sussing out what I was up to.

And mind you, that was with me giving her fashion advice on what not to wear for the two hundred mile plane ride, something I never do. You'd have thought me telling her *no, comfy clothes and leave the high heels at home today love, they really aren't suitable,* would have either clued her in or left her considering having me committed to the local corn bin; she knows how much I love her in high heels. But either she didn't connect the dots or she honestly didn't know why I'd have stashed her birthday present halfway across Germany.

Still, we'd got here, and the surprise looked to still be intact. I'd been ready to grit my teeth and put up with a helicopter ride for transport. Truth be told, I don't fancy choppers much—I mean, yeah, my head knows that they aren't actually sardine tins with pinwheels on top instead of proper wings, ready to fall out of the sky if the pilot sneezes, but that's got fuck-all to do with what happens to the pit of my stomach and the small of my back whenever I've had to ride in one. Besides, they're bloody uncomfortable.

But a last-minute back and forth texting session with Carla, after the band had checked into the Bensberg until the Nürburgring fan festival was done with, had got that particular worry taken care of. It turned out that Volkswagen not only owns the track at Ehra-Lessien, they operate their own air service in and out of the Wolfsburg airport for their guests. So instead of a couple of hours having my MS tweaked and my tailbone bruised rattling about in a chopper, we were driven from the hotel to Koln airport and settled in on a nice comfy plane. I spent the next hour checking the weather out the window. For what I'd paid for, the weather conditions had to be just right.

Once we'd landed, we'd climbed into another chauffeur-driven car and headed for Ehra-Lessien. Getting in had been scary; the guards at the checkpoints were carrying firepower and not trying to hide it. I found myself wondering if what had gone down in Manaar had left me with some deeper emotional ditches than I'd realised; even though the guards glanced at our driver's papers and waved us straight through, I clenched up so hard and tense, I was sweating. And Bree looked just as tense. There might be some trauma counselling in our future, if that didn't ease up. That could get tricky, because Bree really doesn't like shrinks.

But here we were, finally, climbing out of the car deep inside Volkswagen's no-fly zone, shaking hands with the bloke who'd put everything to do with Bree's birthday prezzie together. Carla had actually introduced us in email, just me and Lothar Eichel. I shook hands with him and grinned, watching the driver help Bree out of the car. Any moment now, the penny was going to drop, and I wanted to be watching her face when it did.

And right on cue, from the opposite direction we'd come in from, I heard the sound of an engine. Lothar, who was shaking Bree's hand, lifted his head and looked over her shoulder. "Ah, right on time. Lanzo has arrived with your car."

First time I'd heard that engine, I'd thought of a lot of coked-up bassists hitting the same low note at the same time. It still sounded like that. Bree'd heard the engine as well, and turned fast, and I caught the look on her face. I was grinning like an idiot.

"Lanzo! Come and meet Mr. and Mrs. Kinkaid. Mrs. Kinkaid, allow me to introduce you to Lanzo Caruselli of Bugatti. Lanzo is our Veyron specialist. Even if you were new to the car, he could show you how to drive it—it's designed to be driven easily, very intuitive. But we were given to understand that you are not completely unfamiliar with it, and that is even better. It will take less time for him to acquaint you with the track, so that you can take the car to its maximum—"

He got out of the way just in time. Bree's never really been the sort of woman who shrieks and clutches, but she was right there, both arms around me, so fast he barely had time to move his arse. If he hadn't, she'd have gone straight through him, and I'm pretty sure I heard something that might have been a stifled shriek, as well. I got a good hold on her; she was whispering under her breath, something that sounded like *omigod omigod omigod*, over and over again. I pulled back and planted a nice noisy kiss.

"Happy birthday, baby." The two techs were watching us, both looking approving. We must have appealed to their sense of sentiment, or something. "Yeah, I bought you a track day. Take the car up as fast as it'll go. I know you want to."

"John..." She bit her lip. "Are you sure? Because I got the impression you really didn't want me doing that. Are you really okay with it? This is the fastest car in the world."

"Yeah, I'm okay with it. Why wouldn't I be? You've been driving me around for thirty years." I patted her bottom. "Go drive the fancy car."

Of course, it wasn't that simple. There were liability releases that had to be signed first, and one that seemed to be Bree signing on the dotted line to admit that her training on the car had been in private one-on-one and not at some place in France where Bugatti usually wants their one-offs to train. There was a very thorough briefing that I basically understood about ten words of, and yeah, it was in English, supposedly. There was Lanzo telling us that, normally, she'd be taking the car out for the final run on her own, but that, what with what he called the slightly unusual nature of her training, they felt that having the ace driver with her for the last lap was best. If she was disappointed or insulted, she didn't show it.

It also turned out that she could have worn the highest heels in her collection and it wouldn't have mattered, because they weren't letting her drive in street clothes anyway. They'd got a fire-proof suit thing ready for her, and a crash helmet. If I hadn't been nervous before, the suit would have done it—it made her look like she was about to drop some comment about this being one giant step for mankind. Carla'd asked for Bree's measurements early on, and I'd sent them along and forgotten about it, and never actually asked what they were needed for. Turns out they even make you wear fireproof long johns, if you take one of these drives.

Ali's Veyron had been black and orange. Not this one; this was white and silver, end to end. I stood with Lothar, listening to the Italian explain things to Bree in nice clear English sentences, watching her visibly remember where things were in the beast, telling myself that it was okay, she wasn't going to crash the thing and get herself killed, it was going to be fine. She hadn't been wrong about how I felt about it. Bree risking her neck pretty much heads my 'oh fuck no' list.

The bottom line, though, is that I trust her. She's never given me any reason to not trust her, you know? She's the most capable human being I've ever known, and what's more, she hasn't got much of a secret death wish. If she doesn't think she can do something, she doesn't bother with it, even if it looks to be fun. And she obviously thought she could do this particular thing, because she put the helmet on, headed back over and climbed straight into the driver's seat.

Not being a driver or knowing anything about cars except where the doors and tires are, I couldn't make sense of the explanations Lanzo Caruselli kept offering up. I do remember one point, when he said something about dropping the car into race mode and how it needed a second key. I wasn't sure if Bree'd got that far with Nordine's lessons, but this part was new to me. I don't know that she was expecting the entire car to hunker down round her. I know I wasn't. I jumped a mile.

They went round four times all told, Bree at the wheel every time. Each time was faster than the last, and they'd gone round three times when they both climbed out and sent the car in for a once-over, and a look at the tires. That made me blink—I already knew that each set of tires cost over forty thousand dollars. I was hoping an extra set of new feet wasn't going to be needed when I realised that my wife wanted to say something, and wasn't sure how to say it. Unusual for her, you know? I jerked my head at her and we stepped away.

"John—listen." She'd left me keeping an eye on her purse while she drove; for some reason, she'd refused to check it with the rest of her gear. Now she'd picked it up and was unzipping one of the inner pockets. "I actually have something I want to give you, too. I just—I want to do it now."

Both of my eyebrows were up. My own birthday, back in early March, had been one of those milestone things: I'd turned sixty. I'd told Bree, flat out, that I was damned if I wanted to make a big deal over it, and I hadn't been joking, either. She'd thrown me a dinner party, close friends and music, all my favourite things that she cooks, with the real prezzie coming after we'd said goodnight to the last guests and gone upstairs. So this wasn't a birthday thing, because I'd had that...

"I was going to wait until we got to London in August to give you this, but I think I'll give it to you now. Just because." She paused, just for a moment, not long enough for me to ask her what that *because* was in aid of. "Just in case."

She pulled out what looked to be a simple cream-coloured envelope, European size rather than American, and yeah, they're different. She wasn't smiling, but her face was soft.

"I've been carrying this around for the last two weeks, when I got everything signed off on. I couldn't give it to you on your birthday because you said you didn't want a fuss made, and anyway I didn't have it yet. I do now, though. Happy birthday, John."

For one wild moment, I wondered if she was handing me divorce papers or something: the envelope had a London solicitor's imprint in the upper left corner. It also had something heavy inside. I loosened the flap, and tilted what was inside into my palm.

Keys, wrapped inside a sheet of paper. The keys were familiar, but it wasn't until I unfolded the sheet of paper, and read my name on the freehold to the London mews house we'd been renting, that I realised which locks they belonged to.

"Right." There was some noise going on under my ribcage. I

got one arm round her, and pulled her close. She doesn't like London much—the balance of crap memories to good ones is tilted pretty badly in the wrong direction. I was born there, and in some sense it was always going to be part of what I think of as home. To Bree, a house is a home. "We'll have to get you a proper oven, and a couple of rocking chairs. Nice to put in some gear of our own, even if we aren't in London all that often. Oh hell, here's Lanzo and Lothar back again. Off you go, lady. I'll be watching from wherever Lothar puts us—probably the pit. That's where he had us for the practice runs. Do a good drive, baby."

Showtime.

I don't how many autos out there go by so fast that the wind pushes people watching from fifteen feet back on their heels, but the Veyron did. Lothar had given me a detailed explanation of what speed points Bree would have to hit and where she'd have to hit them, but truth to tell, he might as well have been speaking Early Martian, for all the sense it made to me. I remember that he said something about tapping some paddles and putting the car in cruise control. I did get that there wasn't any question of setting records; she wasn't experienced enough to try for that. Besides, they were quite happy with the record they'd already got.

"She will likely hit two hundred and forty at the midpoint of the straightaway. Perhaps slightly above."

We were standing together in the pit, behind the protective rail. We couldn't see the car; it was taking the big circuit and heading for the straightaway Lothar had talked about. Nice and flat, apparently, and that was where she'd be taking it as high as she could.

He'd sounded pretty damned certain. Of course, he'd watched the first three practice runs, and he must have seen enough drivers in his day to be able to guess straight off what their skills were.

I must have been looking worried, though, because he caught

my eye. "I doubt she will attempt to take the car up to its limit," he told me kindly. "She is not that style of driver."

"Yeah, well, that's my wife you're talking about, and two hundred forty miles an hour sounds quite fast enough for me, ta." I was craning my neck, watching the road. Nothing. But I thought I could hear something, the deep familiar hum of that coked-up bass-player engine. No, not possible. She'd pulled the Veyron out of the starting house and onto the track about three minutes ago, no more than that.

Time really is funny. Three minutes or three hours or thirty seconds, there was no difference in my head until the engine suddenly got even and clear and loud as hell. And there was the white and silver car going past us, and I staggered backwards in that wind from the speed. The damned thing had gone by too fast to even let me see Bree at the wheel. It wasn't a car, it was a blur.

But right after she'd gone past, the car began to slow down. It must have done, because the wing at the back came up. I'd done some reading up on the car before I'd decided to set this up, and one of the things I remembered was how well it actually stops, something about a special wing to help it brake. I'd got no clue what they'd meant—it's a car, not a plane, and cars haven't got wings, you know? But there it was, a big wing right at the back of the car, where I hadn't seen it up before.

And it did stop, finally, well down the road and out of sight of the pit. I heard the engine, and watched it come back towards us, at a normal speed this time.

Both doors opened and my wife climbed out. She was already pulling the helmet off. It would never have occurred to me that a woman shaking her hair loose from a racing helmet could be that big a turn-on, but it really was. I wondered if I could buy the thing as a souvenir. She'd look brilliant in just the helmet and a pair of her best heels…

291

We met halfway, at the side of the track. She'd actually turned pink, and she was trembling. She looked as if she'd just had some of the best sex of her life.

"Wow." There was heat coming off her in waves. "Sorry. Adrenalin. Wow."

"Gordon *Bennett!*" We were hanging on to each other. I honestly hadn't known how hard I'd been hoping nothing would go wrong out there, how worried I'd been. "How fast did you go?"

"I don't know." She'd started sweating, and her whole body was twitching. That damned thing wasn't a car, it was a sex toy on wheels. "Lanzo had a telemetry box on the dashboard, but it doesn't use miles, it uses kilometres. So I don't know." She shuddered, suddenly, a long ripple, head to heel. "*Wow.*"

It turned out she'd actually got the thing up to two hundred and forty nine miles an hour on the long straightaway, so that was one in the eye for Lothar, who'd doubted she'd get it above two forty. That qualified her for something they called the 400 Drive Club; it sounded rather like having sex in a 747's loo, but Lothar explained that the four hundred in question was kilometres, that she'd hit 400 kilometres an hour. They told us they had a plaque for Bree. I'd rather have had the helmet—it really was having the same effect on me that driving the thing seemed to have had on Bree— but no go, and I made a mental note to just buy one, once we'd got home. Lanzo made some nice comments, complimented her on how good her driving instincts were, and kissed her hand. Of course, he was Italian, and Italians and Frenchmen always kiss the pretty lady's hand, but I got the feeling he meant it.

"Your flight will be ready for you at half past seven. You will only need a short time to get from here to the Braunschweig airport. If I may offer you a cup of tea, or perhaps some of our local beer...? Ah, you would prefer to get back to Koln? If Mrs. Kinkaid would like to shower before she changes back to her street clothes, I will have your driver bring your car."

292

"Yeah, we've got the big show next weekend—the whole band took the day off so that we could come do this." I offered a hand. "Thanks, mate. I don't know I'll ever be able to top this as a prezzie, you know?"

Lanzo was getting into the driver's seat of the Veyron, moving it back indoors for its next tire change. Bree turned for one last look; her eyes were about as deep and bright a green as I'd seen them in years, but I wasn't sure whether that was meant for me or the car. Lanzo waved out the window, and the car was gone from our view. Bree headed indoors for a fast shower. She got to keep the fire-proof suit and the special undies.

The day had been hot, but it was coming on towards evening and the air felt fresh and cool. Off to the west, the outlines of the sun had softened up. Our driver, the same chauffeur who'd picked us up at the airport on the way in, headed towards us with the same car.

"I am curious about something, if you will indulge me." Lothar had his cocked off to one side, looking at Bree. "I was told that you had already had some instruction on driving a Veyron, but I was not given any details—your people in Los Angeles communicated those facts directly with Lanzo. Surely you live in California? I am unaware of any place where taking the car up to true speed is possible there."

"Oh, it wasn't at home." She was waiting for the driver to open the door for her. "It was last year, in Manaar. I was learning to drive the Emir's car, but the driver –"

The words stopped halfway. Something was happening to Lothar Eichel's face. It might have been grief, or pain, or maybe regret. Whatever it was, it silenced both of us.

"Ah, the al-Wahid car. It is always a sad day for us, when we lose one of them. That will perhaps sound odd to you, but you must remember, there are only a few hundred of these in the world, and each is hand-built. To lose one is to lose a member of our family."

293

"What?" I had hold of Bree's hand, and she was holding hard. She seemed to be having trouble breathing. "Lose it? What do you mean, lose it?"

"I am speaking of the accident that took the life of the Emir's daughter earlier this spring."

Bree's mouth opened. She shut it again. I shot her a look, and watched that nice pink glow the Veyron had left her with drain out of her face.

Lothar saw it, as well. "You had heard nothing of this? The girl was alone in the car, apparently, and tried to take it to full speed on a stretch of road along the coast. I gather the Princess was untutored in driving such a car, because she lost control. The Veyron struck the side of a docking office, and then went into the sea."

I was breathing hard. Bree barely seemed to be breathing at all. Lothar shook his head.

"A great tragedy, even more so that I doubt she was given permission to use the car. It is not a vehicle to be driven carelessly, or taken lightly. I understand the Emir is now childless. We were told very little, beyond the bare facts. I believe the Emir has been in complete seclusion, seeing no one since the accident. Thank you both for coming today. I wish you a safe and comfortable flight back to Koln, and all success with your show next weekend."

I've never spent that long travelling with my wife at my side in complete silence. Between Lothar waving at us through the back windows and letting ourselves into our suite at the Bensberg a few hours later, neither of us said a word. We were offered food, but Bree shook her head at the flight attendant and so did I. I did open my mouth to say something, only once, but a quick look at Bree's profile kept me quiet. I know that look, and I hate seeing it there.

Back in the hotel with our door safely locked, Bree turned to me and finally broke the silence. I couldn't have told you what she was feeling just then. I'm not sure she knew, either. I watched her take the deep breath, watched her decide to say it. I knew what she was going to say, too.

"John—did he kill her?"

There was no point pretending I didn't know who she was talking about; there was only one person that "he" could have been. I'd been running it through my head the entire way back from Wolfsburg and I was seeing it now, too clearly: the father and daughter, how things must have been with them. I had my answer ready and I gave it to her straight.

"No. I don't think so, Bree. For one thing, if he was going to use that car as a murder weapon, there'd have been two of them in the car, you know? Main thing, though, is that I can't see him going back on his promise. He didn't want to make it, but he did, and that's a huge deal where he comes from. You want to know what I think, I'll tell you. It's not pretty, but it's not murder, either. I don't believe he lied to us. I think he cut her out of his life and his heart and she couldn't take it. And her sister was already gone."

"Suicide?" She reached out a hand, finding one of the upholstered chairs and easing herself into it. She looked tired suddenly, the kind of bone-weary she gets after she's done a full eight-hour catering event and forgotten to take the proper rest breaks she needs. "You think she couldn't bear to stay alive anymore, so she helped herself to her father's car? You think she got to the coast road and put her foot down and floored it and kept it floored until she lost control of it?"

I nodded. Bree sighed.

"So do I. Because there's no way she lost control of that thing, not unless she took both hands off the wheel and closed her eyes. It had to have been deliberate." Bree closed her own eyes for a moment. Her voice was bleak. "God. That poor kid. I wonder what Ali al-Wahid feels like?"

"If he's lucky, it hurts like hell. Better to feel anything than to feel nothing at all. But I'm betting he's not letting himself feel a bloody thing. He's good at that, numbing himself. And you know what, Bree, there's not a damned thing anyone can do about any of it."

For a moment, we were both quiet. A while back, she'd finally got fed up with thirty years of me telling her not to feel things because feeling them made her unhappy. She'd called me on it, and she'd been right. So I wasn't about to tell her how to feel, or whether to feel. She's quite capable of a lot of things, including knowing how she needs to react.

"True." She reached for the hotel phone. She was still pale, still looked tired, but the look I hated was fading out of her face, like the distant echo of a car engine. "God, I'm hungry. When did we eat last, breakfast? What would you like for dinner...?"

JP Kinkaid

Photo by Nic Grabien

Deborah Grabien can claim a long personal acquaintance with the fleshpots—and quiet little towns—of Europe. She has lived and worked and hung out, from London to Geneva to Paris to Florence, with a few stops in between.

But home is where the heart is. Since her first look at the Bay Area, as a teenager during the peak of the City's Haight-Ashbury years, she's always come home to San Francisco, and in 1981, after spending some years in Europe, she came back to Northern California to stay.

Deborah was involved in the Bay Area music scene from the end of the Haight-Ashbury heyday until the mid-1970s. Her friends have been trying to get her to write about those years—fictionalised, of course!—and, now that she's comfortable with it, she's doing just that. After publishing four novels between 1989 and 1993, she took a decade away from writing, to really learn how to cook. That done, she picked up where she'd left off, seeing the publication of eleven novels between 2003 and 2010.

Deborah and her husband, San Francisco bassist Nicholas Grabien, share a passion for rescuing cats and finding them homes, and are both active members of local feral cat rescue organisations. Deborah has a grown daughter, Joanna, who lives in LA.

These days, in between cat rescues and cookery, Deborah can generally be found listening to music, playing music on one of eleven guitars, hanging out with her musician friends, or writing fiction that deals with music, insofar as multiple sclerosis—she was diagnosed in 2002—will allow.

Visit her website at www.deborahgrabien.com

THE

DEVELOPMENT

Nine Stories

JOHN BARTH

Houghton Mifflin Company

BOSTON ◆ NEW YORK

2008

For information about permission to reproduce selections
from this book, write to Permissions, Houghton Mifflin Company,
215 Park Avenue South, New York, New York 10003.

www.houghtonmifflinbooks.com

Library of Congress Cataloging-in-Publication Data
Barth, John, date.
The development : nine stories / John Barth.
p. cm.
ISBN 978-0-547-07248-7
I. Title.
PS3552.A75D48 2008
813'.54 — dc22   2008011092

Book design by Melissa Lotfy

Printed in the United States of America

DOC 10 9 8 7 6 5 4 3 2 1

Earlier versions of stories in this book first appeared in the following pe-
riodicals: "Peeping Tom" and "Assisted Living" in *Subtropics,* Winter/
Spring 2006 and Fall 2007; "The Bard Award" in *Zoetrope* 10:1, Spring
2006; "Toga Party" in *Fiction* 20:1, 2006 (reprinted in *The Best American Short Stories 2007*); "Teardown" in *Conjunctions* 47, 2006; "Progressive Dinner" in *New Letters* 73:2, 2007; "The End" in *Mississippi Review* 35:31, 2007; "Us/Them" in *The Hopkins Review* 1.2, Spring 2008.
My thanks to Jin Auh and her knowledgeable associates at The Wylie
Agency for arranging these initial publications as well as their collection in the present volume; also to Jane Rosenman and Larry Cooper of
Houghton Mifflin for seeing this volume through the press. And thanks
most of all to my wife, the book's dedicatee, for (among much else) her
unerringly on-the-mark editorial suggestions.

For Shelly

Contents

Peeping Tom

DON'T ASK ME (as my wife half teasingly did earlier this morning) who I think is reading or hearing this. My projected history of our Oyster Cove community, and specifically the season of its Peeping Tom, is barely past the note-gathering stage, and there's nobody here in my study at 1010 Oyster Cove Court except me and my PC, who spend an hour or three together after breakfast and morning stretchies before Margie and I move on to the routine chores and diversions of a comfortably retired American couple in the dawn of the new millennium and the evening of their lives. Maybe our CIA/FBI types have found ways to eavesdrop on any citizen's scribbling? Or maybe some super-shrewd hacker has turned himself into a Listening Tom, the electronic equivalent of Oyster Cove's peeper, even when I'm talking to myself?

Don't ask me (but in that case you wouldn't need to, right?); I just work here. For all I know, "You" — like the subject of this history, in some folks' opinion — may not actually, physically exist. Unlike him, however (and we all assume our P.T., whether real or imagined, to have been a Him, not a Her), you're an invited guest, who- and whatever You are, not an eavesdropper. Welcome aboard, mate, and listen up!

As I was saying, I just work here, more or less between nine and noon most mornings, while Margaret the Indispensable does her ex-businesswoman business in her own workspace upstairs: reviews and adjusts our stock-and-bond accounts and other assets; pays the family bills and balances our checkbook; works the phone to line up service people; schedules our errands and appointments; plans our meals, vacation trips, grandkid visits . . . and Next Big Moves.

Which last-mentioned item prompts this whatever-it-is-I'm-doing. Margie and I have pretty much decided (and she'll soon e-mail the news to our middle-aged offspring, who'll be Sad But Relieved to hear it) that what with my ominously increasing memory problems and her near-laming arthritis, the time has come for us to list this pleasant "villa" of ours with a realtor and get ready to get ready to shift across and down the river from good old Heron Bay Estates (of which more presently) to TCI's assisted-living establishment, Bayview Manor.

Even Margie — a professional real-estate agent herself back in our city-house/country-house days, when she worked the suburban D.C. residential market while I taught history to fifth- and sixth-formers at Calvert Heights Country Day School — even Margie rolls her Chesapeake-green, macularly degenerating eyes at all that developers' lingo. Heron Bay Estates, now approaching the quarter-century mark, was the first large gated-community project of Tidewater Communities, Inc.: a couple thousand acres of former corn and soybean fields, creeper-clogged pine woods, and tidewater wetlands on Maryland's river-veined Eastern Shore. By no means "estates" in any conventional sense of that term, our well-planned and "ecologically sensitive" residential development is subdivided into neighborhoods — some additionally gated, most not — with names like Shad Run and Egret's Crest (low-rise condominiums), Blue Crab Bight (waterfront "coach homes," the developer's euphemism for over-and-under duplexes, with small-boat dockage on the adjacent tidal creek), Rockfish Reach (more of a stretch than a reach, as the only water in sight of that pleasant clutch of mid- to upper-midrange detached houses is a winding tidal creeklet and a water-hazard pond, ringed with cattails, between the tenth and eleventh holes of HBE's golf course, whose Ecological Sensitivity consists of using recycled "gray water" on its greens and fairways instead of pumping down the water table even further), Spartina Pointe (a couple dozen upscale McMansions, not unhandsome, whose obvious newness so belies the fake-vintage spelling of their reeded land-spit that we mockingly sound its terminal *e:* "Spartina Pointey," or "Ye Oldey Spartina Pointey") — and our own Oyster Cove, whose twenty-odd "villas" (on a circular "court" around a landscaped central green with a fountain that spritzes recycled water three seasons of the year) have nothing of the Mediterranean or Floridian that that term implies: In the glossary of HBE and of TCI generally, "villas" are side-by-side two-story duplexes (as distinct from those afore-mentioned "coach homes" on the one hand and detached houses on the other) of first-floor brick and second-floor vinyl clapboard siding, attractively though nonfunctionally window-shuttered, two-car-garaged, and modestly porched fore and aft, their exterior maintenance and small-lot landscaping managed mainly by our Neighborhood Association rather than by the individual owners. Halfway houses, one might say, between the condos and the detached-house communities.

Indeed, that term applies in several respects. Although a few of us are younger and quite a few of us older but still able, your typical Oyster Cove couple are about halfway between their busy professional peak and their approaching retirement. Most would describe themselves as upper-middle-incomers — an O.C. villa is decidedly *not* low-budget housing — but a few find their mortgage and insurance payments, property taxes, and the Association's stiff maintenance assessments just barely manageable, while a few others have merely camped here until their Spartina Pointe(y) (Mc)Mansions were landscaped, interior-decorated, and ready for them and their Lexuses, Mercedeses, and golf carts (3.5-car garages are standard in SpPte). An Oyster Cove villa is typically the first second home of a couple like Margie and me fifteen or so years back: empty nesters experimenting with either retirement or a transportable home office while getting the feel of the Heron Bay scene, trying out the golf course and Club, and scouting alternative neighborhoods. The average residency is about ten years, although some folks bounce elsewhere after one or two — up to Spartina Pointe or Rockfish Reach, down to an Egret's Crest condo, more or less sidewise to a Blue Crab Bight coach home, or out to some other development in some other location, if not to Bayview Manor or the grave — and a dwindling handful of us old-timers have been here almost since the place was built.

To wind up this little sociogram: The majority of Heron Bay Estaters are White Anglo-Saxon Protestants of one or another denomination, but there are maybe three or four Jewish families, a few more Roman Catholics, and probably a fair number of seculars. (Who knows? Who cares? Firm believers in the separation of church and estate, we don't pry into such matters.) Politically, we're split about evenly between the two major parties. No Asians or African Americans among us yet — not because they're officially excluded (as they would have been fifty years ago, and popular though the adjective "exclusive" remains with outfits like TCI); perhaps because any in those categories with both the means and the inclination to buy into a gated community prefer not to be ethnic-diversity pioneers on the mostly rural and not-all-that-cosmopolitan Eastern Shore.

"Gated": That too is a bit of a stretch in Oyster Cove, and (in Margie's and my opinion, anyhow) an expensive bit of ornamentation for Heron Bay. In a low-crime area whose weekly newspaper's police blotter runs more to underage tobacco and liquor purchases and loud-noise complaints in the nearby county seat than to break-ins and crimes of violence, there's little need for round-the-clock gatekeepers, HBE Resident windshield stickers, phone-ahead clearance for visitors, and routine neighborhood drive-throughs by the white-painted Security car — though it's admittedly a (minor) pleasure not to bother latching doors and windows every time we bicycle over to the Club for tennis or drive into town for medical/dental appointments, a bit of shopping, or dinner. As for the secondary gates at Spartina Pointe, Blue Crab Bight, and Oyster Cove — unmanned (even though some have gatehouses), their swing-gates operated by push-button code and usually closed only at night — pure snobbery, many of us think, or mild paranoia, and a low-grade nuisance, especially on rainycold nights when you don't *want* to roll down your car window and reach out to the lighted control box, or oblige arriving guests (whom you've had to supply in advance with the four-digit entry code) to do likewise. And both gates — Reader/Listener take note — screen motor vehicles only: Bicycles and pedestrians come and go freely on the sidewalks, whether the gates are open or shut. Our own Oyster Cove gates, by near-unanimous vote of the Neighborhood Association, have remained open and inoperative for the past dozen years. We use the attractively landscaped little brick gatehouse for storing lawn fertilizer, grass seed, and pavement de-icer for the winter months: a less expensive alternative to removing the whole structure, which anyhow some residents like for its ornamental (or prestige-suggesting) value. Since, as aforementioned, the average O.C. residency is a decade or less, it's only we old-timers who remember actually having used those secondary gates.

But then, it's only we who remember, for better or worse and as best some of us can, when the neighborhood was in its prime: "built out," as they say, after its raw early years of construction and new planting, its trees and shrubbery and flower beds mature, the villas comfortably settled into their sites but not yet showing signs of "deferred maintenance" despite the Association's best efforts to keep things shipshape. Same goes for HBE generally, its several neighborhoods at first scalped building lots with model homes at comparatively bargain prices, then handsomely full-bloomed and more expensive, then declining a bit here and there (while still final-building on a few acres of former "preserve") as Tidewater Communities, Inc., moved on to newer projects all around the estuary. And likewise, to be sure, for the great Bay itself: inarguably downhill since residential development and agribusiness boomed in the past half-century, with their runoff of nutrients and pollutants and the consequent ecological damage. Ditto our Republic, some would say, and for that matter the world: downhill, at least on balance, despite there having been no world wars lately.

Nor are we-all what we used to be, either.

But this is not about that, exactly. M. and I have quite enjoyed our tenure here at 1010 Oyster Cove Court, our next-to-last home address. Of the half-dozen we've shared in our nearly fifty years of marriage, none has been more agreeable than our "villa" of the past fifteen and sole residence of the past ten, since we gave up straddling the Bay. We've liked our serial neighbors, too: next door in 1008, for example, at the time I'll tell of, Jim and Reba Smythe, right-wingers both, but generous, hospitable, and civic-spirited; he a semiretired, still smoothly handsome investment broker, ardent wildfowl hunter, and all-round gun lover; she an elegant pillar of the Episcopal church and the county hospital board. On our other side back then, in 1012, lively Matt and Mary ("M&M") Grauer, he a portly and ruddy-faced ex–Methodist minister turned all-purpose private-practice "counselor"; she a chubbily cheerful flower-gardener and baker of irresistible cheesecakes; both of them avid golfers, tireless volunteers, and supporters of worthy, mildly liberal causes. And across the Court in 1011, then as now, our resident philosopher Sam Bailey, recently widowered, alas: a lean and bald and bearded, acerbic but dourly amusing retired professor of something or other at an Eastern Shore branch of the state university, as left of center as the Smythes were right, whose business card reads *Dr. Samuel Bailey, Ph.D., Educational Consultant*—whatever *that* is. Different as we twenty-odd Oyster Cove householders were and are—and never particularly close friends, mind, just amiable neighbors—we've always quite gotten along, pitched in together on community projects (most of us, anyhow: What community doesn't include a couple of standoffish free riders?), and taken active part in OCNA, our neighborhood association. Indeed, for the past twelve years I've served as that outfit's president; it's a post I'll vacate with some regret when the For Sale sign goes up out front. And despite my having been, please remember, a mere history *teacher*, not a historian, I find myself inclined to set down for whomever, before my memory goes kaput altogether, some account of our little community, in particular of what Margie and I consider to have been its most interesting hour: the summer of the Peeping Tom.

And when was that? Suffice it to say, not many years since. Odd as this may sound from an ex–history teach, the exact dates aren't important. Truth is, I'd rather not be specific, lest some busybody go through the records and think: "Mm-*hm:* Just after the [So-and-Sos] bought [Twelve-Sixteen, say], which they sold a year later and skipped out to Florida. I *thought* there was something fishy about that pair, him especially. Didn't even play golf!" When in fact the poor guy had advanced emphysema and shifted south to escape our chilly-damp tidewater winters. So let's just say that the time I'll tell of, if I manage to, was well after "Vietnam," but before "Iraq"; more specifically, after desktop and even laptop computers had become commonplace, but before handheld ones came on line; after cordless phones, but before everybody had cellulars; after VCRs, but before DVDs.

Okay? The name's Tim Manning, by the way — and if You've got the kind of eye and ear for such things that Matt Grauer used to have, You'll have noted that in all four of the families thus far introduced, the men are called by one-syllable first names and their wives by two-, with the accent on the first (Sam Bailey's late mate, a rail-thin black-haired beauty until cancer chemotherapy wrecked her, was named Ethel). So? So nothing, I suppose, except maybe bear in mind Dr. Sam's wise caution that a Pattern — of last names, happenings, whatever — doth not in itself a Meaning make, much as we may be programmed by evolution to see patterns in things, and significance in patterns.

Okay?

Okay. "It all began," as stories so often start (and if I were a storyteller instead of a history-teller, I'd have started this tale right here, like that, instead of where and how I did), late one mid-May evening in 19-whatever: already warm enough here in Chesapeake country to leave windows open until bedtime, but no AC or even ceiling fans needed yet. After cleaning up the dinner dishes, Margie and I had enjoyed a postprandial stroll around Oyster Cove Court, as was and remains our habit, followed by an hour's reading in 1010's living room; then we'd changed into nightclothes and settled down in the villa's family room as usual to spend our waking day's last hour with the telly before our half-past-ten bedtime. At a commercial break in whatever program we were watching, I stepped into the kitchen to pour my regular pale-ale nightcap while Margie went into the adjacent lavatory to pee — and a few moments later I heard her shriek my name. I set down bottle and glass and hurried herward; all but collided with her as she fled the pissoir, tugging up the underpants that she wears under her shortie nightgown on warm end-of-evenings.

"Somebody's *out* there!" In all our years of marriage I'd seldom seen my self-possessed helpmeet so alarmed. "*Looking* at me!"

I flicked off the light and hurried past her to the open lavatory window, near the toilet. Nothing in sight through its screen except the Leyland cypresses, dimly visible in the streetlight-glow from O.C. Court, between us and the Smythes, which give both houses privacy enough to make closing our first-floor window blinds unnecessary. "Call Security," I said (Heron Bay's main gatehouse); "I'll go have a look outside." Hurried back into the kitchen, grabbed the big flashlight from atop the fridge, and headed for the back door.

"Do you think it's safe to go out there?" Margie worried after me. "In your PJs?"

"Not safe for that snooping bastard," I told her, "if I get my hands on him." Though what exactly I would have done in that unlikely event, I'm not sure: haven't been in a physical scuffle since third grade; never served in the military or had any other form of hand-to-hand-combat training; hope I'm not a coward, but know I'm not the macho sort either. Was maybe a bit surprised myself, not unpleasantly, at my impulsive readiness to go unarmed out into the night for a possible-though-unlikely confrontation with a prowler. Went anyhow, adrenaline-pumped, through laundry room and garage to night-lighted rear driveway and around to side yard — shining the flashlight prudently ahead to warn of my approach.

No sign of anyone. The night was sweet; the air moist, mild, breezeless, and bug-free. The grassy aisle between those cypresses and our foundation planting of dwarf junipers wasn't the sort to show footprints; nor was the shredded-hardwood mulch around those junipers obviously disturbed under the lavatory window, as far as I could tell. Standing among them, I verified that a six-footer like myself could just see over the shoulder-high sill into the lavatory and (with a bit of neck-craning) over to the toilet area. I shrugged a "Who knows?" or "Nobody in sight" sign to Margie, standing inside there with cordless phone in hand, then stepped back onto the grass and checked with the flashlight to see whether *my* footprints were visible. Couldn't say for certain, but guessed not.

"Well, I damned sure didn't imagine it," Margie said a bit defensively when — having inspected the length of our side of the duplex and as much of the front and rear yards as I could without attracting the neighbors' attention — I was safely back indoors.

"Nobody said you did, hon." I gave her a hug, and to lighten things up added, "Great night for prowling, by the way: no moon or mosquitoes. You called Security?"

"They're sending the patrol car around for an extra check and keeping an eye out for pedestrians leaving the grounds this late in the evening. But they're not armed, and they don't go into people's yards except in emergencies. They offered to call 911 or the sheriff's office for us, but I said we'd call them ourselves if you saw anything suspicious out there. What do we think?"

We considered. What *she'd* seen was certainly suspicious — alarming, even — but was it worth involving the county sheriff and the state police? On the one hand, the prowler might for all we knew have been armed and dangerous, scouting the premises with an eye to Breaking and Entering, as it's called in the crime reports, and been spooked when Margie caught sight of him. On the other hand, he might have been some Oyster Cover out looking for a strayed house pet and mortified to find himself glimpsing Margaret Manning in mid-urination . . .

In either case, "A white guy," she affirmed, her pulse and respiration returning to normal as we brushed our teeth and made ready for bed. "No eyeglasses or mustache or beard as far as I could tell, though I couldn't see his face clearly out there through the screen. High forehead but not bald, unless he maybe had some kind of cap on. It was just a glimpse, you know? Kind of a pale moon-face that popped up and looked in and then ducked and disappeared when he saw I'd seen him and heard me holler for you."

So what did we think? In the end — maybe partly because by then it was past eleven and neither I nor the main-gate security guys (who phoned us after their pass through the neighborhood) had seen anything amiss — we decided not to notify the sheriff's office, much less call the 911 emergency number, until or unless something further turned up. I would take another look around in the morning, and we would definitely alert our neighbors, ask them to pass the word along and keep an eye out.

"Sonofabitch peeps in on *my* wife," Jim Smythe growled, "I'll blow his damn head off." He had a way, did swarthy Jim, of making those less belligerent than himself seem reprehensible, wimpy: a habit at which Reba, to her credit, rolled her fine brown eyes. Ethel Bailey, on the other hand, was impressed that I'd gone out there alone and unarmed in the dark. She would *never* have let Sam do that, Margie said she'd said — characteristically admiring husbands other than her own while implying that their wives were less appreciative of them than was she. Sam himself good-naturedly questioned my "risk-benefit analysis" while freely admitting that he'd be too chicken to do what I'd done even if he judged it the best course of action, which he didn't. Matt Grauer, too, as fond of proverbs as of patterns, reminded me that discretion is the better part of valor, but jokingly declared himself envious of the Peeping Tom. "Margie on the can!" he teased the two of us. "What an eyeful!" To which his plump Mary added, "If it'd been me, he'd've gotten a different kind of eyeful: I'd've wet my pants." "Not likely," Margie reminded her, "when you've already dropped them to do your business. Anyhow, guys, they don't say 'scared shitless' for nothing: I here report that it applies to Number One as well as Number Two." Whereupon Sam and Matt, our neighborhood eggheads (though only Sam was bald), bemusedly wondered whether the colloquialisms "It scared me shitless" and "It scared the shit out of me" are two ways of describing the same reaction or (understanding the former to mean "It scared me out of shitting" and the latter to mean "It scared me into shitting my pants") descriptions of two opposite, though equally visceral and involuntary, manifestations of fear.

Thus did we banter the disconcerting event toward assimilation, agreeing that the prowler/peeper was in all likelihood a one-time interloper from "outside": some bored, beered-up young redneck, we imagined, of the sort who nightly cruised the shopping-plaza parking lots in their megabass-whumping, NASCAR-stickered jalopies and smashed their empty Coors bottles on the asphalt. Until, less than two weeks later, Becky Gibson (with her husband, Henry, the new owners of 220 Bivalve Bend, one of several saltily named side streets off Oyster Cove Court) glimpsed a pale face pressed to the glass of their back-porch door as she passed by it en route through their darkened house to turn off a kitchen light inadvertently left on when the couple retired for the night. Like my Margie, she called for her husband; unlike me (but this was, after all, the second such incident), he unhesitatingly dialed 911. Although the responding officer considerately didn't sound his siren at one in the morning, a number of us noticed the patrol car's flashers even through our closed eyelids and bedroom-window curtains. As OCNA's president, I felt it my responsibility to slip as quietly as I could out of bed and into my pajama bottoms (which Margie and I have always slept without, originally for romantic reasons, latterly out of long habit and urinary convenience in our three-pees-a-night old age) and to step outside and see what was what.

Another fine May night, still and moonless. I could see the distant flashers pulsing from somewhere around the corner on Bivalve Bend, but couldn't tell whether they were from one of the county's multipurpose emergency vehicles or a sheriff's patrol car. Not a fire truck, I guessed, or there'd have been sirens. Lest I be mistaken for a prowler myself, I ventured no farther along the curb than the edge of our property, tempting as it was to continue past the next two duplexes to the corner. Other folks were quite possibly looking out their front windows, and anyhow one had to draw some line between being a concerned neighbor and a prying one. As I turned back, I saw the Heron Bay security patrol car — an "environmentally sensitive" hybrid bearing the Blue Heron logo of HBE — turn into Oyster Cove Court through our ever-open gate and head for Bivalve Bend. Rather than hailing or waving it down in my pajamas to ask what was happening, I stepped behind a nearby large boxwood (standard walkway-flanking shrub around our circle) and crouched a bit for better cover until the vehicle hummed past.

"Looks like we have ourselves a problem," all hands agreed next day, after details of the past night's alarm had circulated through the community. Like Margie, silver-curled Becky Gibson could say only that the figure at her back-door window had been a beardless adult white male, either dark-haired or wearing a black bill cap backwards; whether it was the same intruder or another, two Peeping Tom incidents in successive weeks in the same small neighborhood obviously spelled trouble. As had been the case with us, neither the Gibsons nor in this instance the sheriff's deputies had found any trace of the prowler, who'd presumably vanished as soon as he knew himself to have been seen. Mary Grauer, wakened like me by the reflected flashes, was almost certain she'd seen from their living room window somebody skulking in our joint front-walk shrubbery: probably the Gibsons' peeper beating a retreat from Oyster Cove. I was tempted to explain and laugh it off, but held my tongue lest anyone get the wrong idea. Even to Margie I said only that I'd stepped outside to have a look, not that I'd walked to the curb in my PJs and ducked for cover when Security came by.

The third incident, just two nights later, was less unequivocal than its forerunners: Reba Smythe, looking from a window just after dark as we all seemed to be doing now with some frequency, *thought* she might have glimpsed a furtive figure in the Baileys' front yard, and phoned to alert them. Her husband hurried over, nine-millimeter pistol in hand, just in time to quite frighten Sam Bailey, who deplored handgun ownership anyhow, as he stepped out to see whether anyone was there. The two men then did a perimeter check together, and found nothing. Reba acknowledged that she might have been mistaken: She'd recently suffered what ophthalmologists term a vitreous separation in her left eye, in consequence of which her vision was pestered by black "floaters" that she sometimes mistook for flying insects or other UFOs, as she liked to call them. But she was equally insistent that she might *not* have been mistaken; she just couldn't say for sure, although whatever she'd seen was certainly larger than her usual dark specks.

At a sort-of-emergency meeting of the Neighborhood Association the following afternoon (at our place, with jug wines and simple hors d'oeuvres), we decided to reactivate the Oyster Cove secondary entrance and exit gates as a warning and possible deterrent, even though our P.T., as we'd begun to call him for short, was pretty clearly a pedestrian. And we would press HBECA, the overall community association, for additional nighttime security patrols, even if that entailed an increase in everyone's annual assessment; for it needed no Matt Grauer to point out that three such incidents constituted an alarming pattern, and while they'd been confined thus far to Oyster Cove, it was to be expected that the peeper might try other Heron Bay venues, particularly now that ours was on a geared-up lookout for him.

As we most certainly were: unpleasantly on edge, but reassuringly drawn together by a common nuisance that, while not yet quite an overt threat, was definitely scary.

"Not a threat?" Mary Grauer protested when I described our problem in those terms. "You don't think we feel threatened when some creep might be peeking at us in the shower?"

Posing like a Jazz Age flapper with her glass of chablis in one hand and a brie-smeared cracker in the other, "Speak for yourself, dear," Ethel Bailey teased. "*Some* of us might find it a turn-on."

Less publicly, Matt Grauer and Jim Smythe shared with me the disturbing possibility — just theoretical, mind, not a genuine suspicion yet — that our P.T. might actually be *one of us:* if not an Oyster Cover, maybe some unfortunately perverted resident of an adjacent neighborhood. Or somebody's kinky visiting son, perhaps, or adolescent grandson, out on the prowl unbeknownst to his hosts?

No way to check on that last, really: Nearly all of us being empty-nesters and most of us retirees, there was a constant stream of visiting progeny and out-of-town friends in Heron Bay. But the One of Us hypothesis was reinforced, amusingly though ambiguously, a week or so later, when by early-June full moonlight both Bob and Frieda Olsen (in 1014, on the Grauers' other side from us) spotted a stocky, hatless somebody in dark shorts and shirt crossing stealthily, as it seemed to them, from their backyard into "M&M's." The alarm was quickly passed by telephone from the Olsens to the Grauers to us. We all clicked our backyard lights on, and while Margie rang up the Smythes, we three husbands stepped out back to investigate — and interrupted Jim Smythe, pistol in one hand again and flashlight in the other, completing what he unabashedly declared to us (even as Reba was confirming it by phone to Margie) was the first of the one-man armed patrols of Oyster Cove that he intended to make nightly until either HBECA increased the frequency of its security rounds or he caught and apprehended our P.T. in the act — or, better yet, gunned the sick bastard down as he fled. Not a ready acknowledger of his mistakes, Jim was dissuaded from this self-appointed mission only by our unanimous protest that it was at best more likely to trigger false alarms than to prevent real ones, and at worst might lead to his shooting some innocent neighbor out stargazing or merely enjoying the spring air. "Yeah, well, all right then," he grudgingly conceded (while Reba, who'd joined us along with our wives, did her signature eye-roll). "But they'd better stay in their own backyard, 'cause anybody I catch mooning around in mine, I intend to plug."

"Gun nuts, I swear," Sam Bailey sighed to me next day, when we shook our heads together over the fellow's presumption and shortsightedness. "Doesn't he realize that if one of *us* happened to be a guy like him, he'd have gotten himself shot last night?"

"Maybe *he's* been the P.T. all along," I ventured — not seriously, really, and none of us cared to tease Jim with that proposition.

Less alarming, if we count the foregoing as Peeper Incident #4, was the one that followed it the very next evening, as reported by its perpetrator and sole witness, Sam himself, when I happened to walk out to fetch our morning newspaper off the front walk at the same time as he, the pair of us still in robe and slippers before breakfast and Sam wearing the French beret that he'd affected ever since teaching a Fulbright year in Nanterre three decades past. "So at nine last night Ethel turns on one of those TV sitcoms that I can't stand, okay?" he tells me. "So I step into the library," as the Baileys like to call their book-lined living room, "to read for an hour till bedtime, and I catch sight of some movement just outside the picture window," which, flanked by smaller double-hung windows, overlooks the front yard, the street, and the commons beyond in all Oyster Cove Court villas. "So I cross the room to check it out — in my robe and PJs, same as now? — and the guy comes at me from out there on the porch as I come at him from inside, and I'm thinking, Isn't *he* a brazen bastard, and traipsing around there in his nightclothes too! Until I realize it's my own reflection I'm looking at. So I stand there contemplating myself in the picture window and feeling foolish while my pulse calms down, and then I experiment a bit with different lights on and off — table lamps, reading lamps, the track lights over the bookshelves — to see how a person inside might be fooled by his own reflection in different amounts of light from different angles. Because it's occurring to me that our Peeping Tom might be not only *one* of us, but *each* one of us who's seen him. In short" — he touched his beret — "*Monsieur Voyeur, c'est moi.*"

Nonsense, all hands agreed when Sam's report and theory made the rounds: What had so alarmed Margie at our bathroom window and Becky Gibson at her back door had been a youngish, medium-built man, not the reflection of a gracefully aging though less-thin-than-she-used-to-be woman. And it was Jim Smythe on his reckless neighborhood patrol that the Olsens had spotted behind 1014, not Bob and Frieda's joint reflection.

"On the other hand," Ethel Bailey pretended to consider seriously, squinting over-shoulder at her husband, "that beret of Sam's *could* be mistaken in the dark for a backwards bill cap, *n'est-ce pas?* Do you suppose our Oyster Cove pervert might turn out to be the guy I've been sharing a bed with for forty-three years?" Come to think of it, though, she added, the ladies' P.T. had been *sans* eyeglasses, and Doc Sam couldn't find his own weenie without his bifocals. No fun being a voyeur if you can't see what you're peeping at!

"Seriously though, people," Sam bade us consider while all this was being reviewed, with edgy jocularity, at our next OCNA meeting. "Granted that what the Olsens saw was our pistol-packing Jim-boy, and that whatever Margie and Becky saw, it wasn't *literally* their own reflection. Same with these new reports from Blue Crab Bight and Rockfish Reach . . ." in both of which neighborhoods by then, one resident had reported a peeper/prowler sighting to the HBE Community Association.

"They're just jealous of us Oyster Cove women getting all the attention," Reba Smythe joked, to her husband's nonamusement.

"Better pickings over there, d'you suppose?" Matt Grauer pretended to wonder — and added, despite Mary's punching his shoulder, "Guess I'll have to give it a try some night."

"What *I* worry," Jim Smythe here growled, "is we might have a copycat thing going: other guys taking their cue from our guy."

Ethel Bailey tried to make light of this disturbing suggestion: "Another Heron Bay amenity, maybe? One peeper for each neighborhood, on a rotating basis, so we don't have to undress for the same creep week after week?" But a palpable *frisson* of alarm, among the women especially, went through the room.

With a gratified smile, "You're all making my point for me," Doc Sam declared.

"Your *pointey*," I couldn't resist correcting, and felt Margie's elbow in my ribs. "P-O-I-N-T-E, as they spell it up the road."

But there was a nervousness in our joking. He was not maintaining, Sam went on in his mildly lectorial fashion, that every one of these half-dozen or so sightings had literally been the sighter's own reflection, although his own experience demonstrated that at least one of them had been and raised the possibility that some others might have been too, it being a well-established principle of perceptual psychology that people tend to see what they expect to see. No: All he meant was that to some extent, at least, the P.T. might be — might *embody, represent*, whatever — a projection of our own fears, needs, desires. "Like God," he concluded, turning up his palms and looking ceilingward, "in the opinion of some of us, anyhow."

"Objection," objected Matt Grauer, and Sam said, "Sorry there, Reverend."

"Are you suggesting," Becky Gibson protested, "that we *want* to be peeped at on the potty? Speak for yourself, neighbor!"

More edgy chuckles. Sam grinned and shrugged; his wife declared, "I don't know about you-all, but I've taken to checking my hair and makeup before I undress, just in case."

But scoff though we might at Sam's "projection" theory, at least some of us (myself included) had to acknowledge that for Jim Smythe, say, the P.T. could be said to have addressed a macho inclination to which Jim welcomely responded — as perhaps, changes changed, had been the case with Ethel Bailey's touch of exhibitionism. And we were, as a neighborhood, agreeably more bonded by our common concern than we had been before (or would be after), the way a community might become during an extended power outage, say, or by sharing cleanup chores after a damaging storm. Thanks to our Peeping Tom, we were coming to know one another better, our sundry strengths and shortcomings, and to appreciate the former while accepting the latter. Matt Grauer might tend to pontificate and Sam Bailey to lecture, but their minds were sharp, their opinions not to be taken lightly. Jim Smythe was a bit of a bully, and narrow-minded, but a man to be counted on when push came to shove. Ethel Bailey was a flirt and a tease, but she had put her finger on an undeniably heightened self-consciousness in all of us — perhaps especially, though not merely, in the Oyster Cove wives — as we went about our after-dark domestic routines. And when some days later, for example, it was reported that a fellow from over in Egret's Crest, upon spotting or believing he'd spotted a face at the bathroom window of his first-floor condo as he zipped his fly after urination, had unzipped it again, fished out his penis, marched to the by-then-dark window saying "*Eat* me, cocksucker!" and afterward boasted openly of having done so, his account told us little about the interloper (assuming that there had in fact been one) and rather much about the interlopee, if that's the right word.

For all our shared concern and heightened community spirit, however, by July of that summer we Heron Bay Estaters could be said to be divided into a sizable majority of "Peeping Tommers" on the one hand (those who believed that one or more prowlers, probably from Outside but not impossibly one of our own residents, was sneak-peeking into our domiciles) and a minority of Doubting Thomases, convinced that at least a significant percentage of the reported incidents were false alarms; that, as Sam Bailey memorably put it, we had come collectively to resemble an oversensitive smoke alarm, triggered as readily by a kitchen stove burner or a dinner-table candle as by a bona fide blaze. My wife was among the true believers — not surprisingly, inasmuch as her initial "sighting experience" (Sam's term, assigning our P.T. to the same ontological category as UFOs) had started the whole sequence. I myself was sympathetic both to her conviction and to Sam's "projection" theory in its modified and expanded version set forth above — in support of which I here recount for the very first time, to whoever You are, the next Oyster Cove Peeper Incident, known heretofore not even to Margie, only to Yours Truly.

Hesitation. Deep breath. Resolve to Tell All, trusting You to accept that Tim Manning is not, was never, the P.T. per se. But . . . :

On a muggy tidewater night toward that month's end, while Margie watched the ten o'clock TV news headlines from Baltimore, I stepped out front to admire a planetarium sky with a thin slice of new moon setting over by the gatehouse, off to westward, from where also flickered occasional sheet lightning from an isolated thunderstorm across the Chesapeake. Although our windows were closed and our AC on against the subtropical temperatures, the night air had begun to cool a bit and dew to form on everything, sparkly in the streetlamp light. In short, an inviting night, its southwest breeze pleasant on my bare arms and legs (not this time in my usual after-nine pajamas, I happened to be still wearing the shorts and T-shirt that I'd donned for dinner after my end-of-afternoon shower). No problem with mosquitoes: The Association sprays all of Heron Bay Estates regularly, to the tut-tuts of the ecologically sensitive but the relief of us who enjoy gardening, backyard barbecues, and the out-of-doors generally. Time was, as I may have mentioned, when the two of us and others would take an after-dark stroll around Oyster Cove Court, to stretch our legs a bit before turning in for the night. Since the advent of the Peeping Tom, however, that pleasant practice had all but ceased, despite Jim Smythe's reasonable urging of it as a deterrent; one didn't want to be mistaken for the P.T., and most would prefer not to encounter him in mid-peep, lest he turn out to be not only real but armed and dangerous.

So I had the Court to myself, as it were — or believed I did, until I thought I saw some movement in the corridor between Sam and Ethel's 1011 and the villa to its right. A little flash of light it was, actually, I realized when I turned my head that way, which to my peripheral vision had looked like someone maybe ducking for cover over there, but which I saw now to be either the shadow of movement from inside one of the Baileys' lighted windows or else light from that window on some breeze-stirred foliage outside. More and more of us, as the P.T. incidents persisted, had taken to keeping all blinds and draperies closed after sunset; it was unusual to see light streaming from an uncurtained window of what was evidently an occupied room — the Baileys' main bathroom, in fact, by my reckoning, our Oyster Cove floor plans being pretty much identical. It occurred to me then to check our own bathroom window, to make certain that with its venetian blinds fully lowered and closed nothing could be seen — through some remaining slit at the sill, for example, or at the edges of the slats. Creepy as it felt to be spying on oneself, so to speak, I was able to verify that nothing could be seen in there except that the light was on; no doubt Margie making ready for bed.

What must it be like, I couldn't help wondering, to be that sicko bastard snooping on unsuspecting people as they washed their crotches and wiped their asses? I found myself — I'm tempted to say *watched* myself — returning to the street and strolling as if casually across the Court toward that light from 1011, assuring myself that in good-neighborly fashion I was making certain that nothing was amiss over there, but at the same time realizing, with a thrill of dismay, that what I might really be about to do was . . .

Wearing only her underpants, slim Ethel Bailey stood at her bathroom window, facing its curtained and unlighted counterpart across the shrubberied aisle in 1013 (its floor plan the mirror image of 1011's). Eyes closed, thin lips mischievously smiling, head turned aside like an ancient-Egyptian profile and chin outthrust in amused, faux-modest challenge, she cupped her small breasts in her hands as if in presentation and swiveled her upper torso slightly from side to side, the better to display them. As I watched from behind a small cypress, she then slid one hand down across her flat belly and into the front of her jay-blue undies, moved it around inside there, and twitched her pelvis as if to the beat of some silent music. Turned herself hind-to; flexed and unflexed her skinny buttocks practically on the windowsill as she worked her panties down! Hot-faced with appall at both of us, I beat as hasty a retreat as prudence allowed. Was relieved indeed to see no one else out enjoying the night air. Hoped to Christ Jim Smythe wasn't checking for prowlers from his front window.

Already in bed, sitting propped against its king-size headboard and working her Sunday *Times* crossword puzzle while she waited for me to join her, "Where've *you* been?" Margie asked, in a tone of mock-petulant amusement, when I came in. "Out peeping on the neighbors?"

"Nobody out there worth peeping at," I declared as lightly as I could manage, and moved past her to the bathroom to hide my flushed face. "All the hot stuff's right here in Ten-Ten."

"Yes, well," she called back — playfully, to my immeasurable relief. "It *is* a bit sticky in here. Maybe turn the ceiling fan on when you come back in?"

I did, having undressed, washed up, brushed teeth, peed (uncomfortably conscious of the window virtually at my elbow), and donned a short-sleeved pajama top — and found that Margie had already shed hers and set aside her puzzle, expectantly. At that period of our lives, we Mannings still made love at least a couple of times a week (the so-clinical phrase "had sex" was not in as general use back then as nowadays, and never between ourselves), most often in the mornings, but also and usually more ardently at bedtime or even on a foul-weather weekend afternoon. That night, as the low-speed overhead fan moved light air over our skin and I was simultaneously stirred and shamed by the unexpungeable image of Sam Bailey's naked wife, we came together more passionately than we had done for some while. Entwined with her then in spent contentment, guilty-conscienced but enormously grateful for our happy and after-all-faithful marriage, I wondered briefly — and unjealously — whom my wife might have been fantasizing as *her* lover while we two went at it.

But "Wow," she murmured in drowsy languor. "That night sky of yours must've been some turn-on. You'll have to try it more often."

"*You're* my turn-on," I assured her — dutifully, guiltily, but nonetheless sincerely as we disconnected our satisfied bodies and turned to sleep.

And there You pretty much have it, make of it what You will. Relieved both as self-appointed chronicler and as a prevailingly moral man to put that discreditable aberration behind me, I wish I could follow it now with a proper dramatic climax and denouement to this account of the Oyster Cove Peeping Tom: Some rascally local teenager, say, or migrant worker, is caught red-handed (red-eyed?) in the disgusting act and turned over to the Authorities, unless gunned down *in flagrante delicto* by Jim Smythe or some other Oyster Cover, several of whom had seen fit to arm themselves as the sightings multiplied. Or better yet, for dramatic effect if not for neighborhood comity, the P.T. turns out indeed to have been one of us, who then swears he was only keeping an eye out for prowlers, but fails to convince a fair number of us despite his mortified wife's indignant and increasingly desperate defense of him. More or less ostracized, the couple list their villa for sale, move somewhere down south or out west, and divorce soon after.

Et cetera. But what You're winding up here, if You happen to exist, is a history, not a Story, and its "ending" is no duly gratifying Resolution nor even a capital-E Ending, really, just a sort of petering out, like most folks' lives. No further Oyster Cove P.T. sightings reported after July, and only one more from elsewhere in Heron Bay Estates — from an *arriviste* couple just settling into their brand-new Spartina Pointey mansion and, who knows, maybe wanting in on the action? The late-summer Atlantic hurricane season preempted our attention as usual; perhaps one of its serial dock-swamping, tree-limb-cracking near misses blew or washed the creep away? Life in the community reverted to normal: New neighbors moved in, replacing others moving up, down, sideways, or out. Kitchens and bathrooms were remodeled, whole villas renovated, older cars traded in for new. Grandchildren were born (never on grandparental location, and often thousands of American miles away); their parents — our grown-up children — divorced or didn't, remarried or didn't, succeeded or failed in their careers or just muddled through. Old Oyster Covers got older, faltered, died — Ethel Bailey among them, rendered leaner yet in her terminal season by metastasized cervical cancer and its vain attendant therapies; Jim Smythe too, felled by a stroke when Democrats won the White House in '92. We reactivated our secondary security gates, and some of us resumed our evening *paseos* around the Court. Already by Halloween of the year I tell of, the P.T. had become little more than a slightly nervous neighborhood joke: "Peekaboo! I see you!" By Thanksgiving, the OCNA membership bowed heads in near unison (the outspokenly atheist Sam Bailey scowling straight ahead as always) while ex-Reverend Matt Grauer gave our collective thanks that that minor menace, or peace-disturbing figment, had evidently passed.

"I can't help wondering," Mary Grauer declared just a month or so ago, when something or other reminded her and Margie of the Good Old Days, "whether that's because there's nothing in Oyster Cove these days for a self-respecting pervert to get off on. Who wants an eyeful of *us?*"

Her husband loyally raised his hand, but then with a wink acknowledged that the likeliest candidates for voyeuring the current femmes of Oyster Cove Court were the geezers of TCI's Bayview Manor, were it not too long a round-trip haul for their motorized wheelchairs. Margie and I exchanged a glance: We had just about decided to make our "B.M. Move," as we'd come to call it between ourselves, but hadn't announced our decision yet.

"You know what?" my wife said then to the four of us (Sam Bailey having joined our Friday evening Old Farts Happy Hour in 1010's family room, with cheesecake provided by Mary Grauer). "Sometimes I almost *miss* having that sicko around. What does that say about Margaret Manning?"

"That she enjoyed being sixty," Sam volunteered, "more than

she enjoys being seventy-plus? Or that for a while there we were more of a neighborhood than before or since? Life in Oyster Cove got to be almost *interesting*, Ethel liked to say."

"I *do* sort of miss those days," Margie said again to me at that evening's end, as we clicked off the TV and room lights and made our way bedward. "Remember how we'd go at it some nights after you came in from checking outside?"

Replied I (if I remember correctly), "I do indeed," and gave her backside a friendly pat.

Indeed I do.

Toga Party

I F "DOC SAM" BAILEY — Dick Felton's longtime tennis buddy from over in Oyster Cove — were telling this toga party story, the old ex-professor would most likely have kicked it off with one of those lefty-liberal rants that he used to lay on his Heron Bay friends and neighbors at the drop of any hat. We can hear Sam now, going "Know what I think, guys? I think that if *you* think that the twentieth century was a goddamn horror show — two catastrophic world wars plus Korea and Vietnam plus assorted multimillion-victim genocides, purges, and pandemics plus the Cold War's three-decade threat of nuclear apocalypse plus whatever other goodies I'm forgetting to mention — then you ain't seen nothing yet, pals, 'cause the twenty-first is gonna be worse: no 'infidel' city safe from jihadist nuking, 'resource wars' for oil and water as China and India get ever more prosperous and supplies run out, the ruin of the planet by overpopulation, the collapse of America's economy when the dollar-bubble bursts, and right here in Heron Bay Estates the sea level's rising from global warming even as I speak, while the peninsula sinks under our feet and the hurricane season gets worse every year. So really, I mean: What the fuck? Just as well for us Golden Agers that we're on our last legs anyhow, worrying how our kids and grandkids will manage when the shit really hits the fan, but also relieved that we won't be around to see it happen. Am I right?"

Yes, well, Sam: If you say so, as you so often did. And Dick and Susan Felton would agree further (what they could imagine their friend adding at this point) that for the fragile present, despite all the foregoing, we Heron Bay Estaters and others like us from sea to ever-less-shining sea are extraordinarily fortune-favored folks (although the situation could change radically for the worse before the close of this parenthesis): respectable careers behind us; most of us in stable marriages and reasonably good health for our age (a few widows and widowers, Doc Sam included at the time we tell of; a few disabled, more or less, and/or ailing from cancer, Parkinson's, MS, stroke, late-onset diabetes, early-stage Alzheimer's, what have you); our children mostly middle-aged and married, with children of their own, pursuing their own careers all over the Republic; ourselves comfortably pensioned, enjoying what pleasures we can while we're still able — golf and tennis and travel, bridge games and gardening and other hobbies, visits to and from those kids and grandkids, entertaining friends and neighbors and being by them entertained with drinks and hors d'oeuvres and sometimes dinner at one another's houses or some restaurant up in nearby Stratford — and hosting or attending the occasional party.

There now: We've arrived at our subject, and since Sam Bailey's *not* the one in charge of this story, we can start it where it started for the Feltons: the late-summer Saturday when Dick stepped out before breakfast as usual in his PJs, robe, and slippers to fetch the morning newspaper from the end of their driveway and found rubber-banded to their mailbox flag (as would sundry other residents of Rockfish Reach to theirs, so he could see by looking up and down their bend of Shoreside Drive) an elaborate computer-graphic invitation to attend Tom and Patsy Hardison's *TOGA PARTY!!!* two weeks hence, on "Saturnsday, XXIV Septembris," to inaugurate their just-built house at 12 Loblolly Court, one of several "keyholes" making off the Drive.

"Toga party?" Dick asked his wife over breakfast. The house

computer geek among her other talents, between coffee sips and spoonfuls of blueberry-topped granola Susan was admiring the artwork on the Hardisons' invitation: ancient-Roman-looking wild-party frescoes scanned from somewhere and color-printed as background to the text. "What's a toga party, please?"

"Frat-house stuff, I'd guess," she supposed. "Like in that crazy *Animal House* movie from whenever? Everybody dressing up like for a whatchacallum . . ." Pointing to the fresco shot: "Saturnalia?"

"Good try," Doc Sam would grant her two weeks later, at the party. "Especially since today is quote 'Saturnsday.' But those anything-goes Saturnalia in ancient Rome were celebrated in December, so I guess Bacchanalia's the word we want — after the wine god Bacchus? And the singular would be bacchanal." Since Sam wasn't breakfasting with the Feltons, however, Dick replied that he didn't know beans about Saturnalia and animal houses, and went back to leafing through the *Baltimore Sun*.

"So are we going?" Sue wanted to know. "We're supposed to RSVP by this weekend."

"Your call," her husband said or requested, adding that as far as he knew, their calendar was clear for "Saturnsday, XXIV Septembris." But the Feltons of 1020 Shoreside Drive, he needn't remind her, while not recluses, weren't particularly social animals, either, compared to most of their Rockfish Reach neighborhood and, for that matter, the Heron Bay Estates development generally, to which they'd moved year-round half a dozen years back, after Dick's retirement from his upper-midlevel-management post in Baltimore and Susan's from her office-administration job at her alma mater, Goucher College. To the best of his recollection, moreover, their wardrobes were toga-free.

His wife's guess was that any wraparound bed sheet kind of thing would do the trick. She would computer-search "toga party" after breakfast, she declared; her bet was that there'd be a clutch of websites on the subject. "It's all just *fun*, for pity's sake! And when was the last time we went to a neighborhood party? Plus I'd really like to see the inside of that house of theirs. Wouldn't you?"

Yeah, well, her husband supposed so. Sure.

That less-than-eager agreement earned him one of Sue's see-me-being-patient? looks: eyes raised ceilingward, tongue checked between right-side molars. Susan Felton was a half-dozen years younger than Richard — not enough to matter much in her late sixties and his mid-seventies, after forty-some years of marriage — but except for work he inclined to be the more passive partner, content to follow his wife's lead in most matters. Over the past year or two, though, as he'd approached and then attained the three-quarter-century mark, he had by his own acknowledgment become rather stick-in-the-muddish, not so much *depressed* by the prospect of their imminent old age as *subdued* by it, de-zested, his get up and go all but gotten up and gone, as he had observed to be the case with others at his age and stage (though by no means all) among their limited social acquaintance.

In sum (he readily granted whenever he and Sue spoke of this subject, as lately they'd found themselves doing more often than formerly), the chap had yet to come to terms with his fast-running mortal span: the inevitable downsizing from the house and grounds and motorboat and cars that they'd taken years of pleasure in; the physical and mental deterioration that lay ahead for them; the burden of caregiving through their decline; the unimaginable loss of life-partner ... The prospect of his merely ceasing to exist, he would want it understood, did not in itself much trouble him. He and Sue had enjoyed a good life indeed, all in all. If their family was less close than some that they knew and envied, neither was it dysfunctional: Cordially Affectionate is how they would describe the prevailing tone of their relations with their grown-up kids and growing-up grandkids; they could wish it better, but were gratified that it wasn't worse, like some others they knew. No catastrophes in their life story thus far: Dick had required bypass surgery in his mid-sixties, and Sue an ovariectomy and left-breast lumpectomy in her mid-menopause. Both had had cataracts removed, and Dick had some macular degeneration — luckily of the less aggressive, "dry" variety — and mild hearing loss in his left ear, as well as being constitutionally overweight despite periodic attempts at dieting. Other than those, no serious problems in any life department, and a quite satisfying *curriculum vita* for each of them. More and more often recently, Richard Felton found himself wishing that somewhere down the road they could just push a button and make themselves and their abundant possessions simply disappear — *poof!* — the latter transformed into equitably distributed checks in the mail to their heirs, with love ...

These cheerless reflections had been center-staged lately by the business that he readdressed at his desk after breakfast: the periodic review of his and Susan's Last Will and Testament. Following his routine midyear update of their computer-spreadsheet Estate Statement, and another, linked to it, that Susan had designed for estimating the distribution of those assets under the current provisions of their wills, it was Dick's biennial autumn custom, in even-numbered years, to review these benefactions, then to call to Sue's attention any that struck him as having become perhaps larger or smaller than they ought to be and to suggest appropriate percentage adjustments, as well as the addition or deletion of beneficiaries in the light of changed circumstances or priorities since the previous go-round: Susan's dear old all-girls prep school, e.g., had lately closed its doors for keeps, so there went Article D of Item Fifth in her will, which bequeathed to it three percent of her Net Residual Estate after funeral costs, executors' fees, estate taxes, and other expenses. Should she perhaps reassign that bequest to the Avon County Public Library, of which she and Dick made frequent use? Estate lawyers' fees being what they were, they tried to limit such emendations to codicil size, if possible, instead of will-redrafting size. But whatever the satisfaction of keeping their affairs in order, it was not a cheery chore (in odd-numbered-year autumns, to spread out the morbidity, they reviewed and updated their separate Letters to Their Executors). The deaths in the year just past of Sam Bailey's so-lively wife, Ethel (cervical cancer), and of their own daughter Katie's father-in-law out in Colorado (aneurysm) — a fellow not even Dick's age, the administration of whose comparatively simple estate had nevertheless been an extended headache for Katie's husband — contributed to the poignancy of the current year's review. Apart from the dreadful prospect of personal bereavement (poor old Sam!), he had looked in vain for ways to minimize further the postmortem burden on their grown-up daughter and son, whom they most certainly loved, but to whom alas in recent years they'd grown less than ideally close both personally and geographically. Dick couldn't imagine, frankly, how he would survive without his beloved and indispensable Susan: less well than Sam Bailey without Ethel, for sure, whose lawyer son and CPA daughter-in-law lived and worked in Stratford, attentively monitored the old fellow's situation and condition, and frequently included him in family activities.

For her part, Susan often declared that the day Dick died would be the last of her own life as well, although by what means she'd end it, she hadn't yet worked out. Dick Junior and Katie and their spouses would just have to put their own lives on hold, fly in from Chicago and Seattle, and pick up the pieces. Let them hate her for it if they chose to; she wouldn't be around to know it, and they'd be getting a tidy sum for their trouble. "So," she proposed perkily when the couple reconvened at morning's end to make lunch and plan their afternoon. "Let's eat, drink, and be merry at the Hardisons' on X-X-I-V Septembris, since tomorrow et cetera?"

"Easy enough to say," her grave-spirited spouse replied. "But whenever I hear it said, I wonder how anybody could have an appetite for their Last Supper." On the other hand, he acknowledged, here they were, as yet not dead, disabled, or devastated, like the city of New Orleans by Hurricane Katrina just a week or so since: No reason why they *shouldn't* go to the party, he supposed — if they could figure out what to wear.

Over sandwiches and diet iced tea on their waterside screened porch, facing the narrow tidal creek of Rockfish Reach agleam in end-of-summer sunshine, "No problem," Sue reported. She'd been on the Web, where a Google search of "toga party" turned up no fewer than 266,000 entries; the first three or four were enough to convince her that anything they improvised would suffice. It was, as she'd suspected, an old fraternity-house thing, made popular among now-middle-aged baby boomers by John Belushi's 1978 film *Animal House*. One could make or buy online "Roman" costumes as elaborate as any in such movies as *Ben-Hur* and *Gladiator*, or simply go the bed-sheet-and-sandals route that she mentioned before. Leave it to her; she'd come up with something. Meanwhile, could they be a little less gloom-and-doomy, for pity's sake, and count their blessings?

Her husband thanked her wholeheartedly for taking charge of the matter, and promised her and himself to try to brighten up a bit and make the most of whatever quality time remained to them.

Which amounted (he then honored his promise by *not* going on to say), with luck, to maybe a dozen years. No computer-adept like his wife, Dick nonetheless had his own desktop machine in his study, on which, between his more serious morning desk chores, it had occurred to him to do a little Web search himself. "Life expectancy," entered and clicked, had turned up nearly fourteen *million* entries (more than a lifetime's worth of reading, he'd bet), among the first half-dozen of which was a questionnaire-calculator — age, ethnicity, personal and family medical histories, etc. — that, once he'd completed it, predicted his "median quartile" age at death to be 89.02 years. In (very!) short, fourteen to go, barring accident, although of course it could turn out to be more or fewer.

Only a dozen or so Septembers left. How assimilate it? On the one hand, the period between birth and age fourteen had seemed to him of epochal extent, and that between fourteen and twenty-eight scarcely less so: nonexistence to adolescence! Adolescence to maturity, marriage, and parenthood! But his thirties, forties, and fifties had passed more swiftly decade by decade, no doubt because his adult life-changes were fewer and more gradual than those of his youth. And his early sixties — when he'd begun the gradual reduction of his office workload and the leisurely search for a weekend retreat somewhere on Maryland's Eastern Shore that could be upgraded to a year-round residence at his and Sue's retirement — seemed the day before yesterday instead of twelve-plus years ago.

So: Maybe fourteen years left — and who knew how many of those would be healthy and active? Eat, drink, and be merry, indeed! About what?

Well, for starters, about not being a wiped-out refugee from the storm-blasted Gulf Coast, obviously, or a starving, gang-raped young African mother in Darfur. "God's only excuse is that He doesn't exist," Sam Bailey liked to quote some famous person as having said (Oscar Wilde? Bertrand Russell? Don't ask Dick Felton, who anyhow regarded it as a pretty lame excuse). But here they were, he and his long-beloved, on a warm and gorgeous mid-September afternoon in an attractive and well-maintained neighborhood on a branch of a creek off a river off a bay luckily untouched (so far) by that year's busier-than-ever Atlantic hurricane season; their lawn and garden and crape myrtles flourishing; their outboard runabout, like themselves, good for a few more spins before haul-out time; their immediately pending decisions nothing more mattersome than whether to run a few errands in Stratford or do some outdoor chores on the property before Sue's golf and Dick's tennis dates scheduled for later in the day.

So they would go to the goddamn party, as Dick scolded himself for terming it out of Susan's hearing. Some hours later, at a break in whacking the yellow Wilson tennis balls back to Sam Bailey on the Heron Bay Club's courts (since Ethel's death, Sam had lost interest in playing for points, but he still enjoyed a vigorous hour's worth of back-and-forthing a couple of times a week, which had come to suit Dick just fine), he mentioned the upcoming event: that it would be his and Sue's first toga party, and that they'd be going more to have a look at their new neighbors' Loblolly Court mansion and get to know its owners than out of any interest in funny-costume parties. To his mild surprise, he learned that Sam — although an Oyster Cover rather than a

Rockfish Reacher — would be there too, and was in fact looking forward to "XXIV Septembris." As a longtime board member of the Club, Sam had met Tom and Patsy Hardison when they'd applied for membership, even before commencing their house construction. And while he himself at age eighty could do without the faux-Roman high jinks, his Ethel had relished such foolery and would have loved nothing more than another toga party, if the goddamn nonexistent Almighty hadn't gifted her with goddamn cancer.

They resumed their volleying, until Sam's right arm and shoulder had had enough and the area behind Dick's breastbone began to feel the mild soreness-after-exertion that he hadn't yet mentioned either to Susan or to their doctor, although he'd been noticing it for some months. He *had* shared with both his life partner and his tennis partner his opinion that an ideal way to "go" would be by a sudden massive coronary on the tennis court upon his returning one of Sam's tricky backhand slices with a wham-o forehand topspin. "Don't you *dare* die first!" his wife had warned him. All Sam had said was "Make sure we get a half-hour's tennis in before you kick."

"So tell me about toga parties," Dick asked him as they packed up their racquets and balls, latched the chain-link entrance gate behind themselves, and swigged water from the drinking fountain beside the tennis court restrooms. "What kind of high jinks should we expect?"

The usual, Sam supposed: like calling out something in Latin when you first step into the room . . .

"Latin? I don't know any damn Latin!"

"Sure you do: *Ave Maria? Tempus fugit?* After that, and some joking around about all the crazy getups, it's just a friendly cocktail-dinner party for the next couple hours, till they wind it up with some kinky contest-games with fun prizes. Susan will enjoy it; maybe even *you* will. *Veni, vidi, vici!*"

"Excuse me?"

"You're excused. But *go*, for Christ's sake. Or Jove's sake, whoever's." Thumbing his shrunken chest, "*I'm* going, goddamn it, even though the twenty-fourth is the first anniversary of Ethel's death. I promised her and the kids that I'd try to maintain the status quo as best I could for at least a year — no major changes, one foot in front of the other, et cetera — and then we'd see what we'd see. So I'm going for her sake as much as mine. There're two more passwords for you, by the way: *status quo* and *et cetera.*"

Remarkable guy, the Feltons agreed at that afternoon's end, over gin and tonics on the little barbecue patio beside their screened porch. In Dick's opinion, at least, that no-major-changes-for-at-least-the-first-year policy made good sense: Keep everything as familiar and routine as possible while the shock of bereavement was so raw and overwhelming.

But "Count me out," said Sue. "Twenty-four hours tops, and then it's So long, Susie-Q. But what I *really* want is the Common Disaster scenario, thanks" — a term they'd picked up from their estate lawyer over in the city, who in the course of this latest revision of their wills had urged them to include a new estate-tax-saving gimmick that neither of them quite understood, although they quite trusted the woman's professional advice. Their wills had formerly stipulated that in the event of their dying together (as in a plane crash or other "common disaster"), in circumstances such that it could not be determined which of them predeceased the other, it would be presumed that Dick died before Susan, and their wills would be executed in that order, he leaving the bulk of his estate to her, and she passing it on to their children and other assorted beneficiaries. But inasmuch as virtually all their assets — cars, house, bank accounts, securities portfolio — were jointly owned (contrary to the advice of their lawyer, who had recommended such tax-saving devices as bypass trusts and separate bank and stock accounts, not to the Feltons' taste), the Common Disaster provision had been amended in both wills to read that "each will be presumed to have survived the other." It would save their heirs a bundle, they'd been assured, but to Dick and Sue it sounded like Alice in Wonderland logic. How could each of them be presumed to have survived the other?

"Remind me to ask Sam that at the party, okay? And if he doesn't know, he can ask his lawyer son for us."

And so to the party they-all went, come "XXIV Septembris," despite the unending, anti-festive news reports from the Louisiana coast: the old city of New Orleans, after escaping much of the expected wind damage from Hurricane Katrina, all but destroyed by its levee-busting storm surge and consequent flooding; and now Hurricane Rita tearing up the coastal towns of Mississippi even as the Feltons made their way, along with other invitees, to the Hardisons'. The evening being overcast, breezy, and cool compared to that week's earlier Indian-summer weather, they opted reluctantly to drive instead of walk the little way from 1020 Shoreside Drive to 12 Loblolly Court — no more than three city blocks, although Heron Bay Estates wasn't laid out in blocks — rather than wear cumbersome outer wraps over their costumes. The decision to go once made, Dick had done his best to get into the spirit of the thing, and was not displeased with what they'd improvised together: for him, leather sandals, a brown-and-white-striped Moroccan caftan picked up as a souvenir ten years earlier on a Mediterranean cruise that had made a stop in Tangier, and on his balding gray head a plastic laurel wreath that Susan had found in the party-stuff aisle of their Stratford supermarket. Plus a silk-rope belt (meant to be a drapery tieback) on which he'd hung a Jamaican machete in its decoratively tooled leather sheath, the implement acquired on a Caribbean vacation longer ago than the caftan. Okay, not exactly ancient Roman, but sufficiently oddball exotic — and the caesars' empire, as they recalled, had in fact extended to North Africa: Antony and Cleopatra, *et cetera*. As for Sue, in their joint opinion she looked Cleopatralike in her artfully folded and tucked bed sheet (a suggestion from the Web, with detailed instructions on how to fold and wrap), belted like her husband's caftan with a drapery tieback to match his, her feet similarly sandaled, and on her head a sleek black costume-wig from that same supermarket aisle, with a tiara halo of silver-foil stars.

Carefully, so as not to muss their outfits, they climbed into her Toyota Solara convertible, its top raised against the evening chill (his car was a VW Passat wagon, although both vehicles were titled jointly) — and got no farther than halfway to Loblolly Court before they had to park it and walk the remaining distance anyhow, such was the crowd of earlier-arrived sedans, vans, and SUVs lining the road, their owners either already at the party or, like the Feltons, strolling their costumed way toward #12.

"Would you look at that?" Dick said when they turned into the tree-lined keyhole drive at the head whereof shone the Hardisons' mega-McMansion: not a neo-Georgian or plantation-style manor like its similarly new and upscale neighbors, but a great rambling beige stucco affair — terra-cotta-tiled roof, great arched windows flanked by spiraled pilasters — resplendent with lights inside and out, including floodlit trees and shrubbery, its *palazzo* design more suited in the Feltons' opinion to Venice or booming south Florida than to Maryland's Eastern Shore. "How'd it get past Heron Bay's house-plan police?" Meaning the Community Association's Design Review Board, whose okay was required on all building and landscaping proposals. Susan's guess was that Tidewater Communities, Inc., the developer of Heron Bay Estates and other projects on both shores of the Chesapeake, might have jiggered it through in hopes of attracting more million-dollar-house builders to HBE's several high-end detached-home neighborhoods, like Spartina Pointe. She too thought the thing conspicuously out of place in Rockfish Reach, but "You know what they say," she declared: *"De gustibus non est disputandum"* — her chosen party password, which she was pleased to have remembered from prep school days. "Is that the Gibsons ahead of us?"

It was, Dick could affirm when the couple — she bed-sheet-toga'd like Susan, but less appealingly, given her considerable heft; he wearing what looked like a white hospital gown set off by some sort of gladiator thing around his waist and hips — passed under a pair of tall floodlit pines flanking the entrance walkway: Hank and Becky Gibson, Oyster Covers like Sam Bailey, whom the Feltons knew only casually from the Club, Hank being the golfer and Becky the tennis player in their household.

"*Et tu, Brute!*" Sue called out (she really had been doing her homework; that "Bru-tay" phrase sounded familiar, but Dick couldn't place it). The Gibsons turned, laughed, waved, and waited; the foursome then joked and teased their way up the stone walk beside the "Eurocobble" driveway to #12's massive, porte-cochèred main entrance: a two-tiered platform with three wide, curved concrete steps up to the first marble-tiled landing, and another three to the second, where one of the tall, glass-paned, dark-wood-paneled double doors stood open and a slender, trim-toga'd woman, presumably their hostess, was greeting and admitting several other arrivals.

"A miniskirted toga?" Hank Gibson wondered aloud, for while the costume's thin white top had a fold-and-wrap toga look to it, below the elaborately figured multipaneled belt were a short white pleated skirt and sandal lacings entwined fetchingly almost to her knees. "*Amo amas amat!*" he then called ahead. The couple just entering turned and laughed, as did the hostess. Then Sam Bailey—whom the Feltons now saw stationed just inside the door, in a white terry-cloth robe of the sort provided in better-grade hotel rooms, belted with what appeared to be an army-surplus cartridge belt and topped with a defoliated wreath that looked a bit like Jesus' crown of thorns—called back, "*Amamus amatis amant!*" and gestured them to enter.

Their sleek-featured hostess—more Cleopatran even than Sue, with her short, straight, glossy dark hair encircled by a black metal serpent-band, its asplike head rising from her brow as if to strike—turned her gleaming smile to them and extended her hand, first to Susan. "Hi! I'm Patsy Hardison. And you are?"

"Sue and Dick Felton," Sue responded, "from around the bend at Ten-Twenty Shoreside? What a beautiful approach to your house!"

"And a house to match it," Dick added, taking her hand in turn.

"I *love* your costumes!" their hostess exclaimed politely. "So *imaginative!* I know we've seen each other at the Club, but Tom and I are still sorting out names and faces and addresses, so please bear with us." As other arrivals were gathering behind them, she explained to all hands that after calling out their passwords to Sam Bailey, whom she and Tom had appointed to be their Centurion at the Gate, they would find nametags on a table in the foyer, just beyond which her husband would show them the way to the refreshments. "Passwords, please? Loud and clear for all to hear!"

"*De gustibus non est disputandum!*" Sue duly proclaimed, hoping her hosts wouldn't take that proverb as any sort of criticism. Dick followed with "*Ad infinitum!*" — adding, in a lower voice to Sam, who waved them in, "or *ad nauseam*, whatever. Cool outfit there, Sam."

"The Decline and Fall of the You Know What," their friend explained, and kissed Sue's cheeks. "Aren't *you* the femme fatale tonight, excuse my French. Ethel would've loved that getup."

"I can't *believe* she's not in the next room!" Sue said, hugging him. "Sipping champagne and nibbling hors d'oeuvres!"

"Same here," the old fellow admitted, his voice weakening, until he turned his head aside, stroked his thin white beard, and cleared his throat. "But she couldn't make it tonight, alas. So *carpe diem*, guys."

Although they weren't certain of the Latin, its general sense was clear enough. They patted his shoulder, moved on to the nametag table on one side of the marble-floored, high-ceilinged entry hall, found and applied their elegantly lettered and alphabetically ordered stick-on labels, and were greeted at the main living room step-down by their host, a buff and hearty-looking chap in his late fifties or early sixties wearing a red-maned silver helmet, a Caesars Palace T-shirt from Las Vegas, a metallic gladiator skirt over knee-length white Bermuda shorts, and leather sandals even higher-laced than his wife's on his dark-haired, well-muscled legs. With an exaggeratedly elaborate kiss of Susan's hand and a vise-hard squeeze of Dick's, "*Dick and Susan*

Felton!" he announced to the room beyond and below, having scanned their name stickers. "Welcome to our humble abode!"

"Some humble," Dick said, his tone clearly Impressed, and Sue added, "It's *magnificent!*"

As indeed it was: the enormous, lofty-ceilinged living room (What must it cost to heat that space in the winter months? Dick wondered), its great sliding glass doors open to a large, roofed and screened terrace ("Lanai," Susan would later correct him), beyond which a yet larger pool/patio area extended, tastefully landscaped and floodlit, toward the tidal covelet where the Hardisons' trawler yacht was docked. A suitably toga'd pianist tinkled away at the grand piano in one corner of the multi-couched and -cocktail-tabled room; out on the lanai a laureled bartender filled glasses while a minitoga'd, similarly wreathed young woman moved among the guests with platters of hors d'oeuvres.

"Great neighborhood, too," Dick added, drawing Sue down the step so that their host could greet the next arrivals. "We know you'll like living here."

With a measured affability, "Oh, well," Tom Hardison responded. "Pat and I don't actually *live* here, but we do enjoy cruising over from Annapolis on weekends and holidays. Y'all go grab yourselves a drink now, and we'll chat some more later, before the fun starts, okay?"

"Aye-aye, *sir*," Dick murmured to Susan as they dutifully moved on. "Quite a little weekend hideaway!"

She too was more or less rolling her eyes. "But they seem like a friendly enough couple. I wonder where the money comes from."

From their husband-and-wife law firm over in the state capital, one of their costumed neighbors informed them as they waited together at the bar: Hardison & Hardison, very in with the governor and other influential Annapolitans. What was more, they had just taken on their son, Tom Junior, as a full partner, and his younger sister, just out of law school, as a junior partner: sort of a family 4-H Club. And had the Feltons seen the name of that boat of theirs?

"Not yet."

"Stroll out and take a look." To the bartender: "Scotch on the rocks for me, please."

Susan: "White wine spritzer?" And Dick: "I'll have a glass of red."

The barman smiled apologetically. "No reds, I'm afraid. On account of the carpets?" And shrugged: not *his* house rule.

"Mm-*hm*." The living room wall-to-wall, they now noted, was a gray so light as to be almost white. Poor choice for a carpet color, in Sue's opinion — and for that matter, what color *wouldn't* be stained by a spilled merlot or cabernet? But *de gustibus, de gustibus*. "So make it gin and tonic, then," Dick supposed.

"*Ars longa!*" a late-arriving guest called from the hallway.

Sam Bailey, behind them, asked the bartender for the same, predicted that that new arrival was George Newett, from the College, and called back "*Vita brevis est!*" His own *vita* without Ethel, however, he added to the Feltons, had gotten *longa* than he wanted it to be. Raising his glass in salute, "Fuck life. But here we are, I guess. *E pluribus unum.* Shall we join Trimalchio's Feast?"

The allusion escaped them, but to make room for other thirsters they moved away from the bar, drinks in hand, toward the groups of guests chatting at the hors d'oeuvres tables at the lanai's other end, and out on the pool deck, and in what Susan now dubbed the Great Room. As Sam had foretold, once the admission ritual was done, the affair settled into an agreeable Heron Bay neighborhood cocktail party, lavish by the standards of Rockfish Reach and Oyster Cove if perhaps not by those of Spartina Pointe, and enlivened by the guests' comments on one another's costumes, which ranged from the more or less aggressively noncompliant (the bearded fellow identified by Doc Sam as "George Newett from the College" wore a camouflage hunting jacket over blue jeans, polo shirt, and Adidas walking shoes; his wife an African dashiki), to the meant-to-be-humorous, like Tom Hardison's casino T-shirt and Dick Felton's caftan-cum-machete, to the formally elaborate, like Patricia Hardison's and some others' store-bought togas or gladiator outfits. Although not, by their own acknowledgment, particularly "people" people, husband and wife found it a pleasant change from their customary routines to chat in that handsome setting with their neighbors and other acquaintances and to meet acquaintances of those acquaintances; to refresh their drinks and nibble at canapés as they asked and were asked about one another's health, their former or current careers, their grown children's whereabouts and professions, their impression of "houses like this" in "neighborhoods like ours," their opinion of the Bush administration's war in Iraq (careful stepping here, unless one didn't mind treading on toes), and their guesses on whether Chesapeake Bay, in places still recovering from the surge floods of Tropical Storm Isabel two years past, might yet be hurricaned in the current hyperactive season.

"Just heard that Rita's blowing the bejesus out of Gulfport and Biloxi. I swear."

"Anybody want to bet they'll use up the alphabet this year and have to start over? Hurricane Aaron? Tropical Storm Bibi?"

"As in B. B. King?"

"C. C. Ryder? Dee Dee Myers?"

"Who's that?"

"E. E. Cummings?"

"Who's *that?*"

"I can't get over those poor bastards in New Orleans: Why didn't they get the hell out instead of hanging around and looting stores?"

"Did you hear the one about Bush's reply when a reporter asked his opinion of *Roe versus Wade*? 'I don't care how they get out of New Orleans,' says W, 'as long as it doesn't cost the government money.'"

"*George Newett*, is it? At my age, I wish *everybody* wore nametags."

"On their foreheads. Even our grandkids."

"*Love* that headband, by the way, Pat. Right out of *Antony and Cleopatra!*"

"Why, thanks, Susan. Tom's orders are that if some joker says I've got my head up my *asp*, I should tell them to kiss it. Now is that nice?"

"Some cool djellaba you've got there, Dick."

"Caftan, actually. Some cool yacht you've got out there! Is that your RV too, the big shiny guy parked down by your dock?"

It was, Tom Hardison readily acknowledged. In simple truth, he and Pat enjoyed *owning* things. Owning and doing! "What the hell, you only get one go-round."

George Newett's wife (also from the College, and with a last name different from her husband's) explained to Susan, who had asked about Sam Bailey's earlier reference, that Trimalchio's Feast is a famous scene in the first-century *Satyricon* of Petronius Arbiter: an over-the-top gluttonous orgy that became a sort of emblem of the Roman Empire's decadence. "The mother of all toga parties, I guess. But talk about over the top . . ." She eye-rolled the sumptuous setting in which they stood. The two women agreed, however, that Patricia Hardison really did seem to be, in the best sense, *patrician:* upscale but good-humored, friendly, and without affectation; competent and self-assured but nowise overbearing; as Amanda Todd (i.e., Mrs. George Newett, poet and professor, from Blue Crab Bight) put it, superior, but not capital-S Superior.

"I like her," Susan reported to her husband when they next crossed paths in their separate conversational courses. "First poet I ever met. Is her husband nice?"

Dick shrugged. "Retired from the College. Describes himself as a failed-old-fart writer. But at least he's not intimidating."

"Unlike . . . ?"

Her husband nodded toward their host, who was just then proclaiming to the assembled "friends, Romans, countrymen" that the dinner buffet (under a large tent out beside the pool deck) was now open for business, and that Jove helps those who help themselves. "After dinner, game and prize time!"

En route past them toward the bar, "Me," Sam Bailey said, "I'm going to have me another G and T. D'ja see their boat's name? Bit of a mouthful, huh?"

Sue hadn't. She worried aloud that Doc Sam was overdoing

the booze, maybe on account of his wife's death-day anniversary; hoped he wouldn't be driving home after the party. "I doubt if he cares," Dick said. "*I* sure wouldn't, in his position." The name of the boat, by the way, he added, was *Plaintiff's Complaint.* Which reminded him: Since both Hardisons were lawyers, maybe he'd ask Emperor Tom about that "each survives the other" business in their wills, and Sue could ask her new pal Cleopatra. Or was it Sheba?

"Come on," his wife chided. "They're friendly people who just happen to be rich as shit. Let's do the buffet."

They did it, Sue chatting in her lively/friendly way with the people before and after them in the help-yourself line and with the caterers who sliced and served the roast beef au jus and breast of turkey; Dick less forthcoming, as had lately more and more become his manner, but not uncordial, and appreciative of his mate's carrying the conversational ball. Time was when they'd both been more outgoing: In their forties and fifties they'd had fairly close *friends,* of the sort one enjoys going out with to a restaurant or movie. By age sixty, after a couple of career moves, they had only office lunch-colleagues, and since their retirement not even those; just cordial over-the-fence-chat neighbors, golf/tennis partners, and their seldom more than annually visited or visiting offspring. A somewhat empty life, he'd grant, but one which, as afore-established, they enjoyed more than not, on balance — or *had* enjoyed, until his late brooding upon its inevitably approaching decline, even collapse, had leached the pleasure out of it.

So "I'll fetch us another glass of wine," he said when they'd claimed two vacant places at one of the several long tables set up under the tent. And added in a mutter, "Wish they had some *red* to go with this beef."

"Shh. Mostly club soda in mine, please." Then "Hi," she greeted the younger couple now seating themselves in the folding chairs across from theirs: "Dick and Sue Felton, from down the road."

"Judy and Joe Barnes," the man of them replied as they scanned one another's nametags: "Blue Crab Bight." He extended his hand first to seated Susan and then to Dick, who briefly clasped it before saying "Going for a refill; back in a minute."

Speaking for him, "Can he bring you-all anything?" Sue offered. "While he's at it?"

They were okay, thanks. He ought to have thought of that himself, Dick supposed, although he'd've needed a tray or something to carry four glasses. Anyhow, screw it. Screw it, screw it, screw it.

Some while later, after they'd fed themselves while exchanging get-acquainted pleasantries with the Barneses — Sue and Judy about the various neighborhoods of Heron Bay Estates, Dick and Joe about the effects of global warming on the Atlantic hurricane season and the ballooning national deficit's impact on the stock market (Joe worked in the Stratford office of a Baltimore investment-counseling firm) — "Aren't *you* the life of the party," Susan half teased, half chided her husband, who on both of those weighty questions had opposed Joe Barnes's guardedly optimistic view with his own much darker one. The two couples were now on their feet again, as were most of the other guests, and circulating from tent to pool deck and lanai.

"Really sorry about that, hon." As in fact he was, and promised her and himself to try to be more "up." For in truth he had enjoyed meeting and talking with the Barneses, and had had a good postdinner conversation with young Joe out by the pool while Susan and Judy visited the WC — "on the jolly subject of that Common Disaster provision in our wills."

"You didn't."

"Sure did — because *he* happened to mention that his clients often review their estate statements with him so he can help coordinate their investment strategies with their estate lawyer's advice, to reduce inheritance taxes and such."

"O joy."

"So naturally I asked him whether he'd heard of that 'each survives the other' business, and he not only knew right off what

I was talking about but explained it simply and clearly, which Betsy Furman" — their estate lawyer — "never managed to do." What it came down to, he explained in turn to not-awfully-interested Susan, was that should they die "simultaneously," their jointly owned assets would be divided fifty-fifty, one half passing by the terms of his will, as if he had outlived her, and the other half by hers, as if she'd outlived him. "So you make us up another computer spreadsheet along those lines, and we can estimate each beneficiary's take."

"O very joy." But she would do that, she agreed, ASAP — and she appreciated his finally clarifying that little mystery. Nor had she herself, she would have him know, been talking only girlie stuff: When Pat Hardison had happened to speak of "her house" and "Tom's boat," upon Sue's questioning their hostess had explained that like most people she knew, the Hardisons titled their assets separately, for "death tax" reasons: Their Annapolis place was in Tom's name, this Stratford one in hers; same with the boat and the RV, the Lexus and the Cadillac Escalade, their various bank accounts and securities holdings. *So* much more practical, taxwise: Why give your hard-earned assets to the government instead of to your children? Weren't Sue and her husband set up that way?

"I had to tell her I wasn't sure, that that was your department. But my impression is that everything we own is in both our names, right? Are we being stupid?"

Any estate lawyer would likely think so, Dick acknowledged. Betsy Furman had certainly encouraged bypass trusts, and had inserted that "each survives the other" business into their wills as the next best thing after he'd told her that they were uncomfortable with any arrangement other than joint ownership, which was how they'd done things since Day One of their marriage. He was no canny CPA or estate lawyer or investment geek, one of those types who tell you it's foolish to pay off your mortgage instead of claiming the interest payments as a tax deduction. Probably they knew what they were talking about, but it was over his head and not his and Susan's style. "If the kids and grandkids and the rest get less of the loot that way than they'd get otherwise, they're still getting plenty. Who gives a shit?" What he really cared about, he reminded her, was not their death, much less its payoff to their heirs, but their Last Age and their dying. It required the pair of them in good health to maintain their Heron Bay house and grounds and the modest Baltimore condo that they'd bought as a city retreat when they'd retired, sold their dear old townhouse, and made Stratford their principal address. The day either of them joined the ranks of the more than temporarily incapacitated would be the end of life as they knew and enjoyed it; neither of them was cut out for long-term caregiving or caregetting. A Common Disaster, preferably out of the blue while they were still functioning, was the best imaginable scenario for The End: Let them "each survive the other" technically, but neither survive the other in fact — even if that meant making the necessary arrangements themselves.

"My big bundle of joy," Susan said, sighing, and hugged him to put a stop to this lately-so-familiar disquisition.

"Sorry sorry sorry, doll. Let's go refill."

"Hey, look at the lovebirds!" Sam Bailey hollered, too loudly, across the deck from the lanai bar. The old fellow was pretty obviously overindulging. A few people paused in their conversation to glance his way, a few others to smile at the Feltons or raise eyebrows at the old fellow's rowdiness. By way of covering it, perhaps, Tom Hardison, who happened to be standing not far from Sam, gave him a comradely pat on the shoulder and then strode behind the bar, fetched out a beribboned brass bugle, of all things, that he'd evidently stashed there, blew a single loud blast like an amplified, extended fart, and called "Game and prize time, everybody!" The "Great Room" pianist underscored the announcement with a fortissimo fanfare. When all hands were silent and listening, perky Pat Hardison, holding a brown beer bottle as if it were a portable microphone, repeated her husband's earlier "Friends, Romans, countrymen," politically correcting that last term to country*folk*, "lend me your ears!"

"You want to borrow our *rears?*" Sam Bailey asked loudly.

"We've got those covered, Sam," the host smoothly replied; he too now sported a beer-bottle mike in one hand, while with the other placing the bugle bell-down on his interrupter's head, to the guests' approving chuckles. "Or maybe I should say *un*covered, since tonight's Special Olympics consist of Thong-Undie Quoits for the ladies, out on the pool deck, and for the gents, Bobbing for Grapes wherever you see them, as you very soon will. I'll be refereeing the quoits"—he held up a handful of bikini briefs for all to see—"and Pat'll oversee the grapes, which every lady is invited to grab a bunch of and invite the bobber of her choice to bob for."

"Here's how it's done, girls," Pat explained. Out of the large bowl of dark grapes the bartender had produced from behind his station, she plucked a bunch and nestled it neatly into her cleavage. "You tuck 'em in like so, and then your significant other, or whoever, sees how many he can nibble off their stems—without using his hands, mind. The couple with the fewest grapes left wins the prize." Turning to her husband: "Want a no-grope grape, sweetie-pie?"

"Yummy! Deal me in!" Doffing his helmet, he shmushed his face into his wife's fruited bosom and made loud chomping sounds while she, with a mock what-are-you-going-to-do-with-men? look at the laughing bystanders, uplifted her breasts with both hands to facilitate his gorging, and one of the hors d'oeuvre servers began circulating with the bowl among the female guests. A number of them joined in; as many others declined, whether because (like Susan's) their costumes were non-décolletaged, or they preferred watching the fun to joining it, or chose the quoits contest instead. More disposed to spectate than to participate, the Feltons moved with others out to the far side of the pool deck to see how Thong-Undie Quoits was played. Tom Hardison, his grape-bobbing done for the present ("But save me a few for later!" he called back to Patricia), led the way, carrying a white plastic bin full of varicolored thong panties in his left hand while twirling one with his right. On the lawn just past the deck, a shrubbery light illumined a slightly tipped-back sheet of plywood, on the white-painted face of which were mounted five distinctly phallic-looking posts, one at each corner and one in the center: six-inch tan shafts culminating in pink knobs and mounted at a suggestively upward angle to the backboard.

"Here's how it's done, ladies," Tom explained; "not that you didn't learn the facts of life back in junior high . . ." Holding up a robin's-egg-blue underpant by its thong, from behind a white-taped line on the deck he frisbeed it the eight feet or so toward the target board, where it landed between pegs and slid to the ground. With a shrug he said, "Not everybody scores on the first date," and then explained to the waiting contestants, "Three pairs for each gladiatrix, okay? If you miss all three, you're still a virgin, no matter how many kids and grandkids you claim to have. Score one and you get to keep it to excite your hubby. Two out of three and you're in the semifinals; *three* out of three and you're a finalist. All three on the same post and you win the Heron Bay Marital Fidelity Award! Who wants to go first?" Examining the nametag on one middle-aged matron's ample, grapeless bosom, "*Helen McCall*," he announced, "*Spartina Pointe*. How about it, Helen?"

The lady gamely handed her wineglass to her neighbor, pulled three panties from the bin, called out "We who are about to *try* salute you!" and spun the first item boardward, where it fell two feet short. "Out of practice," she admitted. Amid the bystanders' chuckles and calls of encouragement she tossed her second, which reached the board but then slid down, as had the host's demonstration throw.

Somebody called, "Not everybody who drops her drawers gets what she's after," to which someone else retorted, "Is that the Voice of Experience speaking?" But Ms. McCall's vigorous third toss looped a red thong undie on the board's upper left peg, to general cheers. Tom Hardison retrieved and presented it with a courtly bow to the contestant's applauding husband, who promptly knelt before her, spread the waistband wide, and insisted that she step into her trophy then and there.

"What fun." Susan sighed and took Dick's hand in hers. "I wish *we* were more like that."

"Yeah, well, me too." With a squeeze, "In our next life, maybe?" He glanced at his watch: almost nine already. "Want to hang around a while longer, or split now?"

Incredulously, "Are you *kidding?* They haven't awarded the prizes yet!"

"Sorry sorry sorry." And he was, for having become such a party-pooping partner to the wife he so loved and respected. And it wasn't that he was having an unenjoyable evening; only that —as was typically the case on the infrequent occasions when they dined out with another couple—he reached his sufficiency of good food and company sooner than Susan and the others did, and was ready to move on to the next thing, to call it an evening, while the rest were leisurely reviewing the dessert menu and considering an after-dinner nightcap at one or the other's house. To his own surprise, he felt his throat thicken and his eyes brim. Their good life together had gone by so fast! How many more so-agreeably-routine days and evenings remained to them before . . . what?

Trying as usual to accommodate him, "D'you want to watch the game," Sue asked him, "or circulate a bit?"

"Your call." His characteristic reply. In an effort to do better, "Why not have a go at the game yourself?" he proposed to her. "You'd look cute in a thong."

She gave him one of her looks. "Because I'm *me,* remember?" Another fifteen minutes or so, she predicted, ought to wind things up, gamewise; after the prizes were handed out they could probably leave without seeming discourteous. Meanwhile, shouldn't he maybe go check on Doc Sam?

Her husband welcomed the errand: something to occupy him while Susan made conversation with their hostess, a couple of her golf partners, and other party guests. He worked his way barward through the merry grape-bobbers, their equally merry encouragers and referees ("How many left down there? Let me

check." "No, me!" "Hey hey, no hands allowed . . ."), and the occasional two or three talking politics, sports, business. Couldn't immediately locate his tennis pal, in whose present position he himself would . . . well, what, exactly? Not hang around to *be* in that
position, he hoped and more or less re-vowed to himself. Then he
heard the old fellow (but who was Dick Felton, at age five-and-
seventy, to call eighty "old"?) sing out raucously from the living
room, to the tune of "Oh Holy Night":

"O-O-Oh ho-ly shit! . . ."

Sam stumbled out onto the lanai, doing the beer-bottle-mi-
crophone thing as the Hardisons had done earlier, but swigging
from it between shouted lines:

"The sky, the sky is fall-ing! . . ."

Smiling or frowning people turned his way, some commenting behind their hands.

"It is the end . . . of our dear . . . U-S-A! . . ."

Dick approached him, calling out as if in jest, "Yo, Sam! You're
distracting the thong-throwers, man!"

"And the grape-gropers, too!" someone merrily added. Thinking to lead him back inside and quiet him down, Dick put an arm
around the old fellow's bony shoulders. He caught sight of Pat
Hardison, clearly much concerned, heading toward them from
the food tent. But as he made to turn his friend houseward, Sam
startled him by snatching the machete from its sheath, pushing
free of its owner, raising it high, and declaring, "If there's no red
wine, I guess I'll have a bloody mary."

"Sam Sam Sam . . ."

Returning to his carol parody, *"Fall . . . on your swords!"* Sam
sang. *"Oh hear . . . the angels laugh-ing! . . ."*

Too late, Dick sprang to snatch back the blade, or at least to
grab hold of its wielder's arm. To all hands' horror, having mock-
threatened his would-be restrainer with it, Sam thrust its point
into his own chest, just under the breastbone. Dropped the beer
bottle; gripped the machete's carved handle with both hands and
pushed its blade into himself yet farther; grunted with the pain
of it and dropped first to his knees, then sideways to the floor,

his blood already soaking through his robe front onto the lanai deck. Pat Hardison and other women screamed; men shouted and rushed up, her husband among them. An elderly ex-doctor from Stratford — whose "toga" was a fancied-up set of blue hospital scrubs and who earlier had complained to the Feltons that the ever-higher cost of medical malpractice insurance had pressured him into retirement — pushed through the others and took charge: ordered Tom Hardison to dial 911 and Pat to find a bunch of clean rags, towels, anything that he could use to stanch the blood flow; swatted Sam's hands off the machete handle (all but unconscious now, eyes squint shut, the old fellow moaned, coughed, vomited a bit onto the deck, and went entirely limp); withdrew and laid aside the bloody blade and pressed a double handful of the patient's robe against the gushing wound.

"Bailey, you idiot!" he scolded. "What'd you do *that* for?"

Without opening his eyes, Sam weakly finished his song: "*It was the night . . . that my dear . . . Ethel died . . .*"

"We should call his son in Stratford," Sue said, clutching her husband tearfully.

"Right you are." Dick fished under his caftan for the cell phone that he almost never used but had gotten into the habit of carrying with him. "Where's a goddamn phone book?"

Pat hurried inside to fetch one. "Tell him to go straight to the Avon Health Center!" the doctor called after her.

Men led their sobbing mates away. A couple of hardy volunteers applied clean rags to the blood and vomit puddled on the deck; one considerately wiped clean the machete and restored it to its owner when Dick returned outside from making the grim call to Sam Junior.

"Jesus," Dick said, but gingerly resheathed the thing. The EMS ambulance presently wailed up, lights flashing; its crew transferred the barely breathing victim from floor to stretcher to entranceway gurney to vehicle without (Susan managed to notice) spilling a drop of his plentifully flowing blood onto the carpeting. The ex-doctor — *Mike Dowling*, his nametag read, *Spartina Pte* — on familiar terms with the emergency crew from his years of medical practice, rode with them, instructing his wife to pick him up at AHC in half an hour or so. The Feltons then hurried to their car to follow the ambulance to the hospital, promising the Hardisons (who of course had their hands full with the party's sudden, unexpected finale and the postparty cleanup) that they would phone them a report on Sam's condition as soon as they had one.

"I can't believe he'll live," Sue worried aloud en route the several miles into Stratford, the pair of them feeling ridiculous indeed to be approaching the hospital's emergency wing in their outlandish costumes. "So much blood lost!"

"Better for him if he doesn't," in Dick's opinion. The sheathed machete, at least, he left in the convertible, cursing himself for having included it in his getup but agreeing with Susan that in Sam's desperate and drunken grief he'd have found some other implement to attack himself with, if not at the party, then back at his house in Oyster Cove. Their headdresses, too, and any other removable "Roman" accessories, they divested before crossing the parking lot and making their way into the brightly lit ER lobby. The few staff people they saw did a creditable job of keeping straight faces; the visitor check-in lady even said sympathetically, "Y'all must've been at that party with Doctor Dowling . . ." The patient's son, she informed them, had arrived already and was in a special standby room. They should make themselves comfortable over yonder (she indicated a couch-and-chair area across the fluorescent-lighted room, which they were relieved to see was unoccupied); she would keep them posted, she promised.

And so they sat, side by side on one of the dark gray plastic-cushioned couches, Sue's left hand clasped in Dick's right; they were too shocked to do more than murmur how sad it all was. On end tables beside them were back issues of *Time, Fortune, People, Chesapeake Living, Sports Illustrated, Field & Stream*. The sight of their covers, attention-grabbing reminders of the busy world, made Dick Felton wince: Never had he felt more keenly that All That was behind them. If Dr. Dowling's wife, per instructions, came to retrieve her husband half an hour or so after he left the toga party, Sue presently speculated, then there must be a special entrance as well as a special standby room, as more time than that had passed since their own arrival at Avon Health Center without their seeing any sign of her or him. Eventually, however, the receptionist's telephone warbled; she attended the message, made some reply, and then called "Mister and Miz Felton?" There being no one else to hear, without waiting for them to come to her station she announced Dr. Dowling's opinion that there was no reason for them to stay longer: Mr. Bailey, his condition stabilized, had been moved to intensive care, in serious but no longer critical condition. He had lost a great deal of blood, injured some internal organs, and would need further surgery down the line, but was expected to survive. His son was with him.

"Poor bastard," Dick said — meaning either or both of the pair, he supposed: the father doomed to an even more radically reduced existence than the one he had tried unsuccessfully to exit; the dutifully attentive but already busy son now saddled with the extra burdens of arranging the care of an invalid parent and the management of that parent's house until he could unload it and install the old fellow in Bayview Manor, across and downriver from Heron Bay Estates, or some other assisted-living facility.

"Loving children *do* those things," Sue reminded him. "Sure, it's a major headache, but close families accept it."

Lucky them, they both were thinking as they drove back to HBE, through the main entrance gate (opened by the night-shift gatekeeper at sight of the Resident sticker on their Toyota's lower left windshield-corner), and on to their Rockfish Reach neighborhood, Sue having cell-phoned her promised report to the Hardisons as they left the AHC parking lot. How would either of themselves manage, alone, in some similar situation, with their far-flung and not all that filially bonded son and daughter?

"We wouldn't," in Dick's opinion, and his wife couldn't disagree.

All the partygoers' cars were gone from Loblolly Court, they observed as they passed it, but lights were still on in #12, where cleanup no doubt continued. By the time they reached their own house's pleasantly night-lighted drive and entranceway, the car's dashboard clock read the same as their Shoreside Drive house number: 1020. Noting the coincidence, "Now *that* means something," Susan said — a Felton family joke, echoing Dick's late mother (who'd fortunately had a devoted or anyhow dutiful unmarried middle-aged daughter to attend her senile last years in western Maryland). But her effort at humor was made through suddenly welling tears: tears for herself, she explained when her husband remarked them as he turned into their driveway; tears for them both, as much as for poor Sam Bailey.

Dick pressed the garage door opener button over the rearview mirror, turned their convertible expertly into the slot beside their station wagon, shifted into Park, clicked off the headlights, and pressed the remote button again to roll the door back down. Instead of then shutting off the engine and unlatching his seat belt, however, after a moment he pushed the buttons to lower all of the car's windows, closed his eyes, and leaned his head back wearily against the driver's headrest.

"What are you doing?" There was some alarm in Susan's voice, but she too left her seat belt fastened, and made no move to open her door. "Why'd you do that?"

Without turning his head or opening his eyes, her husband took her hand in his as he'd done back in the hospital waiting room, squeezing it now even more tightly. "Shit, hon, why not? We've had a good life together, but it's done with except for the crappy last lap, and neither of us wants that."

"*I* sure don't," his wife acknowledged, and with a sigh backrested her head, too. Already they could smell exhaust fumes. "I love you, Dick."

"I love *you*. And okay, so we're dumping on the kids, leaving them to take the hit and clean up the mess. So what?"

"They'll never forgive us. But you're right. So what?"

"We'll each be presumed to have survived the other, as the saying goes, and neither of us'll be around to know it."

The car engine quietly idled on.

"Shouldn't we at least leave them a note, send them an e-mail, something?"

"So go do that if you want to. Me, I'm staying put."

He heard her exhale. "Me too, I guess." Then inhale, deeply.

If Doc Sam Bailey were this story's teller, he'd probably end it right here with a bit of toga-party Latin: *Consummatum est; requiescat in pacem* — something in that vein. But he's not.

The overhead garage light timed out.

Teardown

I N L A R G E gated communities like our Heron Bay Estates development, obsolescence sets in early. The developers knew
their business: a great flat stretch of former pine woods and
agribusiness feed-corn fields along the handsome Matahannock
River, ten minutes from the attractive little colonial-era town of
Stratford and two hours from Baltimore/Washington in one direction, Wilmington/Philadelphia in another, and Atlantic beach
resorts in a third, converted in the go-go American 1980s into
appealingly laid-out subdevelopments of condos, villas, coach
homes, and detached-house neighborhoods, the whole well
landscaped and amenitied. The first such large-scale project on
the Eastern Shore end of Maryland's Chesapeake Bay Bridge, it
proved so successful that twenty years later it was not only all but
"built out" (except for a still controversial proposal for midrise
condominiums in what was supposed to remain wood-and-wet-
land preserve), but in its "older" subcommunities, like Spartina
Pointe, already showing its age. In Stratford's historic district, an
"old house" may date from the early eighteenth century; in Heron
Bay Estates it dates from Ronald Reagan's second presidential
term. More and more, as the American wealthy have grown ever
wealthier and the original builder-owners of upscale Spartina

Pointe (mostly retirees from one of those above-mentioned cities, for many of whom Heron Bay Estates was a weekend-and-summer retreat, a second or even third residence) aged and died or shifted to some assisted-living facility, the new owners of their twenty-year-old "colonial" mini-mansions commence their tenure with radical renovation: new kitchen and baths, a swimming pool and larger patio/deck area, faux-cobblestone driveway and complete relandscaping — all subject, of course, to approval by the HBE Design Review Board.

Which august three-member body, a branch of our Heron Bay Estates Community Association, had reluctantly approved, back in the 1980s, the original design for 211 Spartina Court, a rambling brick-and-clapboard rancher on a prime two-acre lot at the very point of Spartina Point(e), with narrow but navigable Spartina Creek on three sides. It was a two-to-one decision: None of the three board members was happy to let a ranch house, however roomy, set the architectural tone for what was intended as HBE's highest-end neighborhood; two- and three-story plantation-style manses were what they had in mind. But while one of the board folk was steadfastly opposed, another judged it more important to get a first house built (its owners were prepared to begin construction immediately upon their plan's approval) in order to help sell the remaining lots and encourage the building of residences more appropriate to the developer's intentions. The third member was sympathetic to both opinions; she ultimately voted approval on the grounds that preliminary designs for two neighboring houses were exactly what was wanted for Spartina Pointe — neo-Georgian manors of whitewashed brick, with two-story front columns and the rest — and together should adequately establish the neighborhood's style. The ranch house was allowed, minus the rustic split-rail fence intended to mark the lot's perimeter, and with the provision that a few Leyland cypresses be planted instead, to partially screen the residence from street-side view.

The strategy succeeded. Within a few years the several "drives" and "courts" of Spartina Pointe were lined with more or less imposing, more or less Georgian-style homes: no Cape Cods, Dutch colonials, or half-timbered Tudors (all popular styles in easier-going Rockfish Reach), certainly nothing contemporary, and no more ranchers. The out-of-synch design of 211 Spartina Court raised a few eyebrows, but the house's owners, Ed and Myra Gunston, were hospitable, community-spirited ex-Philadelphians whom none could dislike: organizers of neighborhood parties and progressive dinners, spirited fund-raisers for the Avon County United Way and other worthy causes. A sad day for Spartina Pointe when Myra was crippled by a stroke; another, some months later, when a For Sale sign appeared in front of those Leyland cypresses.

All the above established, we may begin this teardown story, which is not about the good-neighbor Gunstons, and for which the next chapter in the history of their Spartina Point(e) house, heavily foreshadowed by the tale's title, is merely the occasion. We shift now across Heron Bay Estates to 414 Doubler Drive, in Blue Crab Bight, the second-floor coach home of early-forty-ish Joseph and Judith Barnes — first explaining to non-tidewater types that "doubler" is the local watermen's term for the mating stage of *Callinectes sapidus,* the Chesapeake Bay blue crab. The male of that species mounts and clasps fast the female who he senses is about to molt, so that when eventually she sheds her carapace and becomes for some hours a helpless "softcrab," he can both shield her from predators and have his way with her himself, to the end of continuing the species: a two-for-one catch for lucky crabbers, and an apt street name for a community of over-and-under duplexes, whose owners (and some of the rest of us) do not tire of explaining to out-of-staters.

Some months have passed since the space break above: It is now the late afternoon of a chilly-wet April Friday in an early year of the twenty-first century. Ruddy-plump Judy Barnes has just arrived home from her English-teaching job at Fenton, a small private coed junior-senior high school near Stratford, where she's also an assistant girls' soccer coach. This afternoon's intramural game having been rained out, she's home earlier than usual and is starting dinner for the family: her husband, a portfolio manager in the Stratford office of Lucas & Jones, LLC; their elder daughter, Ashleigh, a Stratford College sophomore who lives in the campus dorms but often comes home on weekends; and Ashleigh's two-years-younger sister, Tiffany, a (tuition-waived) sixth-form student at Fenton, who's helping Mom with dinner prep.

Osso buco, it's going to be. While Judy shakes the veal shanks in a bag of salt-and-peppered flour and Tiffany dices carrots, celery, onions, and garlic cloves for preliminary sautéing, Joe Barnes is closing his office for the weekend with the help of Jeannine Weston, his secretary, and trying in vain to stop imagining that lean, sexy-sharp young woman at least half naked in various positions to receive in sundry of her orifices his already wet-tipped penis. *Quit that already!* he reprimands himself, to no avail. *Bear in mind that not only do you honor your marriage and love your family, you also say amen to the Gospel According to Mark, which stipulates that Thou Shalt Not Hump the Help.* "Mark" being Mark Matthews, his boss and mentor, first in Baltimore and then, since Lucas & Jones opened their Eastern Shore office five years ago, in Stratford. That's when the Barneses bought 414 Doubler Drive: a bit snug for a family of four with two teenagers, but a sound investment, bound to appreciate rapidly in value as the population of Avon and its neighboring counties steadily grows. The girls had shared a bedroom since their babyhood and enjoyed doing so right through their adolescence; the elderly couple in 412, the coach home's first-floor unit, were both retired and retiring, so quiet that one could almost forget that their place was occupied. In the four years until their recent, reluctant move to Bayview Manor, they never once complained about Ashleigh's and Tiffany's sometimes noisy get-togethers with school friends.

Perhaps Reader is wincing at the heavy New Testament sound of "Mark Matthews Lucas and Jones"? "Thou shalt not wince," Mark himself enjoys commanding new or prospective clients in their first interview. "Why do you think Jim Lucas and Harvey

Jones [the firm's cofounders] hired me in the first place, if not to spread the Good Word about asset management?" Which the fellow did in sooth, churning their portfolios to the firm's benefit as well as theirs and coaching his protégé to do likewise. That earlier gospel-tenet of his, however, he formulated after breaking it himself: In his mid-fifties, coincident with the move from Baltimore to Stratford, he ended his twenty-five-year first marriage to wed the striking young woman who'd been his administrative assistant for three years and his mistress for two. "Don't hump the help," he then enjoyed advising their dinner guests, Joe and Judy included, in his new bride's presence. "You should see my alimony bills!" "Plus he had to find himself a new secretary," trim young Mrs. Matthews liked to add, "once his office squeeze became his trophy wife" — and his unofficial deputy account manager, handling routine portfolio transactions from her own office in their Stratford house, "where unfortunately I can't keep an eye on him."

But "*Eew*, Mom!" Tiffany Barnes is exclaiming in the kitchen of 414 Doubler Drive, where she's ladling excess fat off the osso buco broth. "Even without this glop, the stuff's so *greasy!*"

"Delicious, though," her mother insists. "And we only have it a couple times a year."

"We have it *only* a couple times a year," her just-arrived other daughter corrects her. An English major herself, Ashleigh likes to catch her family's slips in grammar and usage, especially her English-teacher mother's. Patient Judy rolls her eyes. "Dad says I should open a cabernet to breathe before dinner," the girl then adds. "He'll be up in a minute. He's doing stuff in the garage."

"Just take a taste of this marrow," Judy invites both girls, indicating a particularly large cross-section of shank bone in the casserole, its core of brown marrow fully an inch in diameter, "and tell me it's not the most delicious thing you ever ate."

"*Ee-e-ew!*" her daughters chorus in unison. Then Tiffany (who's taking an elective course at Fenton called The Bible As Literature that her secular mother frowns at as a left-handed way of sneaking religion into the curriculum, although she quite respects the colleague who's teaching it) adds, "Think not of the marrow?" Judy chuckles proudly; Ashleigh groans at the pun, musses her sister's hair, and goes to the wine rack to look for cabernet sauvignon, singing a retaliatory pun of her own that she'd seen on a bumper sticker earlier in the week: "*Life is a ca-ber-net, old chum . . .*"

Sipping same half an hour later with a store-bought duck pâté in the living room, where a fake log crackles convincingly in the glass-shuttered fireplace, "So guess who just bought that house at the far end of Spartina Court?" Joe Barnes asks his wife. "Mark and Mindy Matthews!"

"*Mindy*," Ashleigh scorns, not for the first time: "What a lame name!" Though only nineteen, she's allowed these days to take half a glass of wine with her parents at cocktail time and another half at dinner, since they know very well that she drinks with her college friends and believe that she's less likely to binge out like too many of them on beer and hard liquor if, as in most European households, the moderate consumption of wine with dinner is a family custom. Tiffany, having helped with the osso buco, has withdrawn to the sisters' bedroom and her laptop computer until the meal is served.

"That ranch house?" Judy asks. "Why would the Matthewses swap their nice place in Stratford for a run-of-the-mill ranch house?"

Her husband swirls his wine, the better to aerate it. "Because, one, Mark's buying himself a cabin cruiser and wants a waterfront place to go with it. And, two, by the time they move in it'll be no run-of-the-mill ranch house, believe me. Far from it!"

Judy sighs. "Another Heron Bay remodeling job. And we can't even get around to replacing that old Formica in our kitchen! But a renovated rancher's still a rancher."

Uninterested Ashleigh, pencil in hand, is back to her new passion, the sudoku puzzle from that day's *Baltimore Sun*. She has the same shoulder-length straight dark hair and trim tight body that her mother had when Joe and Judy first met as University of Maryland undergraduates two dozen years ago, and that Jean-

nine Weston (of whose tantalizing figure Joe is disturbingly reminded lately whenever, as now, he remarks this about his eldest
daughter) has not yet outgrown. He and Judy both, on the other
hand, have put on the pounds — and his hair is thinning toward
baldness, and hers showing its first traces of gray, before they
even reach fifty . . .

"Never mind remodeling and renovation," he says. "That's not
Mark's style." He raises his glass as if in toast: "Heron Bay Estates
is about to see its very first teardown!"

. . . plus her generous, once so fine, firm breasts are these days
anything but, and "love handles" would be the kindest term for
those side rolls of his that, like his belly, have begun to lap over
his belted trouser top. Men, of course, enjoy the famously unfair advantage that professional success may confer upon their
dealings with the opposite sex: Unsaintly Mark, e.g., is hardly the
tall/dark/handsome type, but his being double-chinned, pudgy,
and doorknob bald didn't stand in the way of his scoring with
pert blond Mindy — and what in God's name is Joe Barnes up
to, thinking such thoughts at Happy Hour in the bosom of his
family?

Thus self-rebuked, he takes it upon himself to clean up the
hors d'oeuvres and call Tiffany to set the table while Judy assem-
bles a salad and Ashleigh pops four dinner rolls into the toaster
oven. As is their weekend custom when all hands are present,
they then clink glasses (three wines, one diet Coke) and say their
mock table-grace — "Bless this grub and us that eats it" — before
settling into the osso buco. *I love you all, goddamn it!* lump-
throated Joe reminds himself.

"So what do the Matthewses intend to put up in place of their
teardown?" Judy asks. "One of those big colonial-style jobs, I
guess?"

"Oh, no." Her husband grins, shakes his head. "Wait'll you
see. You know that fancy new spread on Loblolly Court, over in
Rockfish Reach?" Referring to an imposing Mediterranean-style
stucco-and-tiled-roof house built recently in that adjacent neighborhood despite the tsk-tsks of numerous homeowners there.

"Ee-e-ew," comments Tiffany.

"Well, this morning Mark showed me their architect's drawings for what he and Mindy have in mind — Mindy especially, but Mark's all for it — and it makes that Loblolly Court place look as humble as ours."

"Ee-e-*ew!*" Ashleigh agrees with her sister: a putdown not of their coach home, which she's always happy to return to from her dorm even though their bedroom has become mainly Tiffany's space these days, but the pretentiousness, extravagance, and inconsiderate arrogance, in her liberal opinion, of even the Loblolly Court McMansion, which at least was built on an unoccupied lot.

A month or so later, on a fair-weather A.M. bicycle ride through the pleasantly winding bike and jogging paths of Heron Bay Estates, Judy and the girls and a couple of Tiffany's Fenton classmates pedal up Spartina Court to see what's what (Joe's in Baltimore with his boss and secretary at some sort of quarterly meeting in the Lucas & Jones home office). Sure enough, the Gunstons' rambling rancher and its screen of trees have been cleared away completely and replaced by a building-permit board and a vast shallow excavation, the foundation footprint of the Matthewses' palatial residence-in-the-works.

"A perfectly okay house," indignant Ashleigh informs her sister's friends, "no older than ours and twice as big, and *wham!* They just knock it down, haul it to the dump, and put up Buckingham Palace instead!"

"More like the Alhambra," in her younger sister's opinion (Tiff's art history course at Fenton includes some architecture as well).

"Or Michael Jackson's Neverland?" offers one of her companions.

"Dad showed us the latest computer projections of it last week?" Ash explains with the rising inflection so popular among her generation. "Ee-e-*ew!* And he thinks it's just fine!"

"Different people go for different things," her mother reminds them all. "*De gustibus non est disputandum?*"

"See what I mean?" Tiffany asks her friends, and they seem to, though what it is they see, Judy prefers not to wonder.

"Anyhow," Ashleigh adds, "whatever's right by our dad's boss is fine with our dad."

"Ashleigh! Really!"

Tiffany's exaggerated frown suggests that on this one she sides with her mother, at least in the presence of nonfamily. To Judy's relief, Ashleigh drops the subject, and they finish their bike ride.

Over their early Sunday dinner, however—which Joe, as promised, has returned from Baltimore in time for, before Ashleigh goes back to her dorm—the girl takes up her cudgel again. It's one thing, she declares, to build a big pretentious new house like that eyesore in Rockfish Reach, if that's what a person wants? But to tear down a perfectly okay quote-unquote *older* one to do it is, in her opinion, downright obscene—like those people who order a full-course restaurant meal and then just nibble at each course, leaving the rest to be tossed out. Gross!

"Weak analogy," her teacher mother can't help pointing out. "Let's think up a better one."

"Like those people who buy a new car every two years?" Tiffany offers. "When their quote *old* one's in perfectly good condition with maybe ten thousand miles on it?"

"No good," in her sister's opinion, "because at least the old car gets traded in and resold and used. This is more like if every time they buy a new one they *junk* their perfectly okay old one."

"Good point," Judy approves.

"Or like Saint Mark Matthews," bold Ashleigh presses on, "dumping the mother of his kids for a trophy blond airhead half his age."

Alarmed, Tiffany glances from sister to mother to dad. But Joe, who until now has seemed to Judy still to have city business on his mind, here joins the conversation like the partner she's loved for two dozen years. "Beg to disagree, guys? Not with your analogies, but with your judgment, okay? Because what the heck, Ash: The ranch-house people weren't evicted or dumped; they put their place up for sale and got close to their asking price for it. Seems to me the whole business calls for nothing more than a raised eyebrow — more for the new house's design, if you don't happen to like it, than for the replacement idea itself."

"I think I second that," his wife decides.

"And Mindy Matthews, by the way, is no *airhead*," Joe informs his daughters. "She's sharp as a tack."

"Hot in bed, too, I bet," Tiffany makes bold to add. Her father frowns disapproval. Judy declares, "That's none of our business, girls."

"But what still gets me, Dad," Ashleigh persists, less belliger-ently, "is the *extravagance* of it! We learned in poly sci this week that if Earth's whole human population could be shrunk to a vil-lage of exactly one hundred people — with all the same ratios as now? — only thirty of us would be white people, only twenty would live in better than substandard housing, only eight would have some savings in the bank as well as clothes on our back and food in the pantry, and only *one* of the hundred would have all that plus a college education! And you're telling us that this tear-down thing isn't disgraceful?"

"That's exactly what I'm telling you," her father amiably agrees. "We live in a prosperous free-enterprise country, thank God. Mark Matthews — whom I happen to very much admire — earned his money by brains and hard work, and he and Mindy are entitled to spend it as they damn well please. And their architect, builder, and landscaper are all local outfits, so they'll be putting a cou-ple million bucks into Avon County's economy right there, along with their whopping property taxes down the line." He turns up his palms. "Everybody benefits; nobody gets hurt. So what's your problem, Lefty?"

This last is a family tease of a couple years' standing. Ashleigh Barnes was in fact born left-handed, as was Judy's mother, but the nickname dates from her ever more emphatic liberalism since her fifth- and sixth-form years at Fenton. It's a tendency that her younger sister has lately been manifesting as well, although apart from their mother and a few of Judy's colleagues, the school, its faculty, and its students' families are predominantly center-right Republicans.

Her problem, Ashleigh guesses with a sigh, is that she just doesn't like fat cats.

"Mindy Matthews *fat?*" Tiffany pretends to protest. "She's downright anorexic! Speaking of which," she adds to her father, "at least one person sure got hurt when Saint Mark changed horses: Sharon Matthews." Mindy's predecessor.

Judy looks to her husband with a smile and raised eyebrows, as if to ask, How d'you answer *that* one? But Joe merely shrugs and says, "With the alimony payments she's getting for the rest of her life, that woman can cry all the way to the bank. So let's enjoy our dinner now, okay?"

His wife sees their daughters give each other their we-give-up look. She does likewise, for the present, and the family returns to enjoying, or at least making the best of, one another's company.

Later that evening, Ashleigh drives back to campus in her hand-me-down Honda Civic, Tiffany busies herself in her room with homework and computer, Judy takes a preliminary whack at the Sunday *New York Times* crossword puzzle before prepping her Monday lesson plans, Joe scans that newspaper's business section while pondering what Mark Matthews told him that morning en route back from Baltimore in Mark's new Lexus (Mark and his secretary in the front seat, Joe and Jeannine Weston in the rear) and that he hasn't gotten around yet to sharing with Judy—and the new downstairs neighbors' little Yorkshire terrier starts the infernal yip-yipping again that's been driving them batty ever since the Creightons moved into 412 a month ago. They're a pleasant enough younger couple, he an assistant manager at the Stratford GM dealership, she a part-time dietitian at Avon Health Center and busy mother of their four-year-old son. But the kid is noisy and the dog noisier — a far cry from the unit's previous owners! — and although the Creightons respond good-naturedly to the Barneses' tactful complaints, promising to see what if anything they can do about the problem ("You know how it is with kids and pets!"), it gets no better.

He slaps the newspaper down in his lap. "We've got to get out of this fucking place, hon."

"I'm ready." For rich as it is with five years' worth of family memories — the girls' adolescence, their parents' new jobs — the coach home has never really been big enough. No home-office space; no TV/family room separate from the living room; a dining area scarcely large enough to seat six. No guest room even with Ashleigh in the dorm; no real backyard of their own for gardening and barbecuing and such. But the place has, as they'd predicted, substantially appreciated in value, and although any alternative housing will have done likewise, by Joe's reckoning they're "positioned," as he puts it, to move on and up. What Judy would go for is one of the better Oyster Cove villas, a side-by-side duplex instead of over-and-under: three bedrooms, of which one could be her study/workroom and another a combination guest room/den once Tiffany's off to college; a separate family room with adjacent workshop and utility room; and their own small backyard for cookouts, deck lounging, and as much or little gardening as they care to bother with. But what Joe has in mind lately is more ambitious: to buy and renovate one of those older detached houses in Rockfish Reach. A dining room big enough for entertaining friends and colleagues in style, as well as Ash and Tiff and *their* friends; a *real* yard and patio; maybe a pool and some kind of outboard runabout to keep at their own private dock. And they should finally cough up the money to join the Heron Bay Club on a golf membership and take up the game, without which one is definitely *out* of the social scene (so Mark told him, among other things, in the car that morning).

Judy's flabbergasted. "Are you *kidding?* A twelve-thousand-buck initiation fee plus, what, two-hundred-a-month dues? Plus a house to renovate and two college tuitions coming up, dot dot dot question mark?" It's a thing she does now and then.

"Leave that to me, hon," her husband suggests, in a tone she's been hearing him use lately. "I've learned a thing or two from

Master Mark about estate building." *Among other things,* he silently adds and she silently worries — not without cause, although "Tennis, maybe, but count me out on the golf" is all she says aloud. "Not this schoolmarm's style."

Amiably, not to alarm her, "Folks can change their style, you know," he says — and then shares with her part of what's been distracting him all day, since Mark announced it on the drive home. Jim Lucas, one of the firm's founding partners, intends to retire as of the fiscal year's end. Mark Matthews will be replacing him as senior partner and codirector of the company's home office (he and Mindy are buying a condo on the city's Inner Harbor to supplement their Spartina Pointe weekend-and-vacation spread). "And Saint Mark's successor as chief of our Stratford office will be . . . guess who? Whoops, sorry there, Teach: Guess *whom.*"

"Oh, *sweetie!*" She flings aside her crossword and lays on the congratulatory cries and kisses; calls for Tiffany to come hear Daddy's big news; asks him why in the world he didn't announce it while Ashleigh was there to hear it too; but laughingly agrees with him that the girl will scornfully assign them to the *crème de la crème* of her hypothetical hundred-person village — and refrains from pointing out to him that the nominative-case "guess who" is in fact correct, the pronoun being the transposed subject of the verb "will be" rather than the object of "guess." No champagne in the house to toast his promotion with; they'll get some and raise a glass to him when Ashleigh's next with them. And in their *new* house, maybe he can have the wine cellar he's always yearned for! Meanwhile . . .

"Congratulations, Dad!" cheers Tiffany, piling onto his lap to kiss him. And when Mom and Dad retire not long afterward to their bedroom for the night, Judy gives her crotch a good washcloth-wipe after peeing, to freshen it in case he goes down there in the course of celebratory sex. Since the commencement of her early menopause, she's been bothered by occasional yeast infections, with accompanying vaginal discharge and sometimes downright painful intercourse — not that they go at it as often or as athletically as in years past.

But this night they do, *sans soixante-neuf* and such but vigorously *a tergo* and, to her mild surprise, in the dark. Normally they leave Joe's nightstand light dimmed during lovemaking, to facilitate his finding, opening, and applying their personal lubricant and to enjoy the sight of each other's so familiar naked bodies. Tonight, however, it's only after he clicks off the light and snuggles up to say goodnight (also to her surprise) that Joe seems to change his mind. He places his right hand on his partial erection and raises himself on one elbow to lift her short nightie, kiss her navel and nipples, and begin fingering her vulva — all the while scolding himself for imagining a certain younger, leaner body responding to his caresses. In the car that afternoon, when Mark broke the big news of his own and Joe's promotions, Jeannine Weston had squealed with excitement, flung her arms around her boss (those fine breasts of hers pressing into his right upper arm), and planted a loud wet kiss on his cheek. Alice Benning, Mark's secretary since Mindy's promotion to wifehood, had then declared to all hands that she'd asked Jeannine earlier whether she'd be interested in shifting to Baltimore to become the hot-stuff new front-desk receptionist for Lucas & Jones, LLC, and that the girl had replied, "As long as Joe Barnes wants me, I'm his." "Tattletale!" Jeannine had mock-scolded the older woman, and squeezed her chief's right hand in both of hers and leaned her head fondly on his shoulder. Mark, winking broadly at the couple in his rearview mirror, had teased, "Don't forget Rule Number One, Joe," and when Jeannine asked what *that* might be, Alice turned in her seat to whisper loudly, "It's *Hands off the help* — a good rule to live by, says I." So "Shoo, girl!" Joe had duly then bade his young assistant with a broad wink of his own — and to his startlement, in the spirit of their sport, she had slid laughing over to her side of the seat, crossed one arm over those breasts, and with her other hand cupped her crotch as if protectively. It is those body parts that Joe Barnes helplessly finds himself picturing now, and that tight little butt of hers, bare and upraised for him to clutch in both hands while he thrusts and thrusts and thrusts and *ahhh!* . . . collapses atop his accommodating spouse in contrite exhilaration.

Now: This teardown story could proceed from here in any of several pretty obvious directions, e.g.: (1) Joe Barnes "comes to his senses," his love for Judy and the family reaffirmed by that short-lived guilty temptation. While his office relationship with Jeannine Weston retains an element of jocular flirtation, no adultery follows. A year later the young woman is reoffered that receptionist post in the Baltimore office, and this time she takes it. Her replacement in Stratford is a married woman slightly older than Joe: amiable and competent, but not the stuff of lecherous fantasies. Alternatively, (2) somewhat to his own appall, Joe does indeed succumb to temptation and "humps the help," either in what used to be Mark Matthews's office but is now his or in some motel far enough from town for anonymity. The imaginable consequences range from (*a*) Next to None (adultery goes undiscovered; both parties, ashamed, decide not to repeat it; Jeannine meets and soon after marries a young professor at Stratford College who eventually moves to a better-paying academic post in Indiana), to (*b*) Considerable (Joe confesses to Judy and asks for divorce with generous settlement. She brokenheartedly agrees to what she condemns as a "marital teardown." Joe and Jeannine then wed and do a modified Mark-and-Mindy, renovating a large house in Rockfish Reach. The girls, both in college by that time, are shocked, embarrassed, and angry, but in time come more or less to terms with the family's disruption. Judy remarries — an estate lawyer from her southern Maryland hometown — and all parties get on with their lives' next chapter, neither unscarred nor, on balance, unhappy), to (*c*) Disastrous (Judy discovers the affair, goes ballistic, sues for divorce, and bars Joe from the house. Their daughters turn against him for life. The small-town scandal obliges Jeannine to quit her job and Joe to shift, under a cloud, to Lucas & Jones's far-western-Maryland office. "What'd I tell you?"

Mark scolds triumphantly. Judy stays on at her Fenton post and in the Blue Crab Bight coach house, where the downstairs dog yips maddeningly on to the tale's last page and beyond).

My personal inclination (George Newett here, Reader, who's been dreaming up this whole story: Tale Teller Emeritus [but no tale bearer] in Stratford College's Department of English and Creative Writing and, like "Joe and Judy Barnes," resident with my Mrs. in Blue Crab Bight) is to go with (3) None of the Above. This being, after all, a teardown story, I'm deciding to tear the sumbitch down right about here, the way people like "Mark and Mindy Matthews" might decide to tear down not only the Gunstons' "old" ranch house on Spartina Court but also the barely started *hacienda grande* that they're in the costly process of replacing it with. Mindy, let's say, has been belatedly persuaded by her longtime friend and fellow Stratford alumna Faye Robertson (now on the Fenton Day School faculty, Judy Barnes's colleague and Tiffany's art history teacher) that a mission-style *palacio* in Spartina Pointe will be as in-your-face and out of place as that neo-Neapolitan *palazzo* of Tom and Patricia Hardison's in Rockfish Reach, and that for the sake of Heron Bay Estates' "aesthetic ecology," the Matthewses really ought to have considered a Williamsburg-style manse instead. "Never too late to reconsider," I imagine bold Mindy declaring to her astonished friend with a Just You Watch sort of laugh and then announcing her mindchange to "Saint Mark," who wonders whether *he'd* better reconsider what he's gotten himself into with this woman. Maybe time for a midstream change of horses on *that* front too? But he then decides it'd be a better demonstration of upscale panache just to shrug, chuckle, and say, "Whatever milady desireth . . ."

You see how it is with us storytellers — with some of us, anyhow, perhaps especially the Old Fart variety, whereof Yours Truly is a member of some standing. Our problem, see, is that we invent people like the Barneses, do our best to make them reasonably believable and even simpatico, follow the rules of Story by putting them in a high-stakes situation — and then get to feeling more responsibility to *them* than to you, the reader. "Never too late to reconsider," we end up saying to ourselves like Mindy Matthews, and instead of ending their teardown tale for better or worse (sorry about that, guys), we pull its narrative plug before somebody gets hurt.

Here's how:

The Bard Award

O F THE MANY TIDAL rivers on Maryland's Eastern
Shore of Chesapeake Bay, most bear Indian names, as
does the great Bay itself; names antedating the fateful
arrival of white colonists four centuries ago, but filtered through
those English ears into their present form and spelling: Poco-
moke, Wicomico, Nanticoke, Choptank—and the handsome
Matahannock, near whose ever-less-wooded shores I write these
lines. A mile wide where it ebbs and flows past our Heron Bay
Estates, the Matahannock (like these opening sentences of this
would-be story) then winds on and on: another dozen-plus miles
upstream, ever narrower and shallower, northeastward through
the agribusiness corn and soybean fields and industrial-scale
chicken farms of our table-flat Delmarva Peninsula to its petering out (or in) at its marshy headwaters somewhere near the Delaware state line, and about the same distance downstream from
here, ever wider and somewhat deeper, southwestward past ma-
rinas, goose-hunting blinds, crab- and oyster-boat wharves, former steamboat landings, eighteenth-century estates, twenty-
first-century mega-mansions, and more and more waterfront
developments, until it joins our planet's largest estuarine system,
which itself flows from and ebbs into the Atlantic and thence all

the other oceans. Although no Heron Bay Estater has yet done so or likely ever will (we being mostly Golden Agers), one could theoretically set out from HBE's Blue Crab Marina Club, sail down the Matahannock, under the Bay Bridge and on south into Virginia waters, then hang a left at Cape Charles and cruise on to the Azores, Cape Town, Tahiti — right round the world!

The region's counties, on the other hand, like the state they subdivide, have Anglo names — not surprisingly, since they didn't exist as geographical entities until the natives' dispossessors claimed, mapped, and laid them out: Dorchester, Talbot, Avon, Kent — most of them boundaried by the above-mentioned rivers. Ditto those counties' seats and other towns, their American characters quite out of synch with their historic English names. Cambridge and Oxford, for example, on opposite shores of the broad Choptank, are pleasant small towns both, but absent anything remotely like their Brit counterparts' venerable universities.

Likewise "our" Avon County's Stratford (the gated community of Heron Bay Estates is five miles downriver, but Avon's county seat is our P.O.). A colonial-era customs port on the slightly wider river-stretch where Stratford Creek joins the Matahannock, it's now a comfortable town of six or seven thousand that nowise resembles its famed English antecedent: not a thatched roof or half-timbered gable-end to be found in our Stratford's red-brick-Georgian historic district. Unlike those Choptank towns aforenoted, however, it does in fact boast a modest institution of higher learning. Stratford College is no Oxford or Cambridge University, but it's a good small liberal-arts college, old by American standards like the town itself. We currently enroll some fifteen hundred students, mainly from our tri-state peninsula, with a double handful from across the Bay and nearby Pennsylvania and half a handful from remoter venues. As might be expected of a Stratford in, if not quite on, an Avon, the college gives particular emphasis and budgetary support to its Department of English and Creative Writing. *Who'll be our Shakespeare?*, our student-recruitment ads ask prospective applicants: *Maybe you!* — adding that many a potential bard not *born* in Stratford has been *reborn* in the College's Shakespeare House, headquarters of the writing program, "under the benignly masterful tutelage of experienced author-professors on the faculty and distinguished visitors to the campus." What's more (those ads bait their hook by declaring further), every budding playwright, poet, and prose writer in the program has a shot at winning the College's Shakespeare Prize, awarded annually to the graduating senior with "the most impressive body of literary work composed in his or her courses."

And this is where Yours Truly comes in, eventually. Stratford's "Bard Award," as everybody on campus calls it, is a hefty prize indeed, endowed some decades ago by a wealthy alumnus who had aspired unsuccessfully to playwriting but later flourished as the CEO of Tidewater Communities, Inc., his family's real-estate development firm. His munificent Shakespeare Fund pays the honoraria and travel expenses of an impressive series of visiting lecturers, maintains Shakespeare House and its associated quarterly lit mag, *The Stratford Review,* and annually showers one lucky apprentice writer with a cash award currently twice the size of—get this—the Pulitzer Prize, the National Book Award, and PEN's Faulkner Prize combined: the equivalent of at least two years' tuition at the College or the annual salary of one of its midrange professors! Little wonder that competition is intense among the ten to fifteen seniors who submit portfolios (StratColl .edu is a small operation, remember), and the pressure considerable on the half-dozen of us faculty folk who review and, to the best of our ability, judge them.

That "us" and "our" . . . After thirty-some years of teaching at Stratford, I'm newly retired from academe these days, but I still enjoy hanging out at Shakespeare House with new students and old colleagues (my wife among them, who has a couple of years yet to go before joining me in geezerdom) and serving on the Prize Committee. Mandy and I are a pair of those "experienced author-professors" mentioned in the school's ads, who out of teacherly habit here remind you that Experienced doesn't necessarily mean Good, much less Successful. Not likely you'll have heard of the "fictionist" George Newett or his versifying spouse Amanda Todd, even if you're one of those ever scarcer Americans who still read literature for pleasure (as you must be if you're reading this, if it ever gets published, if it ever gets written). Oh, I scored the occasional short story once upon a time, and Mandy the occasional lyric poem, mainly in serious quarterlies not much more widely read than our *Stratford Review:* little magazines that we ourselves rarely glance at unless something of ours or our colleagues is in them, which was never often and, in my case anyhow, is now nearly never. *The New Yorker? Harper's? Atlantic Monthly?* Neither of us ever made it into those prestigious (and better-paying) glossies. I did manage to place a novel forty years ago — not with one of the New York trade houses, alas, but with my midwestern alma mater's university press. On the strength of that modest publication plus three or four lit-mag stories, an M.F.A. from the Iowa Writers' Workshop, and two years of assistant-professoring at one of our state university's branch campuses, I was hired at Stratford, where then-young Mandy was already an instructor with an M.A. from Johns Hopkins and a comparably promising track record in poetry. A fine place to raise kids, she and I were soon happily agreeing in and out of bed — and so the town and its surroundings proved to be. Over our wedded decades, however, our separate and never loquacious muses more or less clammed up here in Oyster and Blue Crab Land, as they doubtless would have in any other venue, and we learned to content ourselves with trying to help others do better than their coaches were doing. The circumstance that as of this writing no Stratford alum has managed that not-so-difficult achievement does not prove our pedagogical labors fruitless, at least in our and most of our colleagues' opinion. Our program's graduates are better writers by baccalaureate time than they were at matriculation: more knowledgeable about language, literary forms and genres, and the achievements of three thousand years' worth of their predecessors. If they then become law clerks, businesspeople, schoolteachers, or whatever else, rather than capital-W Writers — well, so did their profs, and we don't consider *our* careers wasted.

Do we?

We don't, really, most of us more-or-less-Failed Old Farts, at least not most of the time. For one thing, showing all those apprentice scribblers what wasn't working in *their* works (that worked so well in the works of the great ones they were reading) showed us FOFs, on another level, the same thing vis-à-vis our own, if you follow me, and our consequent self-silencing spared posterity a lot of second- and third-rate writing, no? Though, come to think of it, most of our never-finished-if-ever-even-started stuff wouldn't have found a publisher anyhow, and most of what managed to find one would've mostly gone unread. So what the hell.

That being the case, why in the world am I writing *this,* and where, and to whom? The *where,* at least, I can answer: I'm in my office-cum-guest-room in our empty-nest coach home in Blue Crab Bight, a neighborhood of over-and-under duplexes in the sizable community of Heron Bay Estates, itself one of several extensive developments — residential and commercial, urban/ suburban/exurban — built by the virtual patron of Stratford's Shakespeare Prize Fund, the afore-mentioned Tidewater Communities, Inc. Indeed, inasmuch as our house purchase made its tiny contribution to TCI's profitability and thus to the wealth of its philanthropical CEO, we Newett-Todds feel triply linked to that problematical award: as coaches of its candidates, as judges of their efforts, and as (minuscule, indirect) contributors to the winner's outsized jackpot.

It's a jackpot that Stratford's apprentice writing community regards, only half humorously, as jinxed: Shakespeare's Revenge, they call it, or, if they know their *Hamlet,* the Bard's Petard ("For 'tis the sport to have the enginer / Hoist with his own petard," the Prince observes grimly in act 3) — as if, having hit the literal jackpot on some gargantuan slot machine, the unlucky winner then gets crushed under an avalanche of coins. Much as our Public Information Office welcomes the publicity attendant on every spring's graduation exercises, when the Shakespeare Prize routinely gets more press than the commencement speaker, its ever more embarrassing side is that of the nearly two-score winners over the decades since the award's establishment, nearly none so far has managed to become "a writer" — i.e., a more or less established and regularly publishing poet, fictionist, essayist, screenwriter, journalist, or scholar — even to the limited extent that their coaches did. Worse yet, some who aspired simply to additional practice in one of our Republic's numerous master of fine arts programs have had their applications rejected by the more prestigious ones despite their not needing a teaching assistantship or other financial aid. And the few of our B.A.s who *have* gained admission to those top-drawer graduate programs happen not to have been among our Shakespeare laureates: a circumstance in itself no more surprising than that a number of the world's finest writers — Joyce, Proust, Nabokov, Borges, Calvino — never won the Nobel Prize, while not a few of its winners remain scarcely known even to us lovers of literature. *C'est la vie, n'est-ce pas?* But awkward, all the same, for the Bard awardees and awarders alike.

In vain our efforts to reduce the pot to some more reasonable though still impressive size — four or five thousand dollars, say, or even ten — and divert the surplus to other of our program's amenities: more munificent honoraria to attract eminent visitors, better payment for contributors to *The Stratford Review,* upgrades of Shakespeare House's facilities, larger salaries for the writing faculty ... Our benefactor's team of canny lawyers saw to it that the terms of the endowment are un-fiddle-withable. In vain too what I thought to be Mandy's and my inspired suggestion to a certain noted novelist on whom the College conferred an honorary Litt.D. ten years ago: that once the doctoral hood was hung on her, just before the awarding of the Prize, she announce, "By the authority invested in me by the Muse of Story and the Trustees of Stratford College, I declare that what I've been told is called Shakespeare's Curse is hereby lifted, both henceforward and retroactively. My warm congratulations to whoever may be this year's winner: May your efforts bear rich fruit! And my strong encouragement to all previous winners: May the Muse reward with future success your persistence in the face of past disappointment! Amen."

The audience chuckled and applauded; the media were duly amused; that year's prizewinner (a high-spirited and, we judges thought, quite promising young African-American poet from Baltimore) hip-hopped from the podium over to the seated dignitaries, check in hand, to bestow a loud kiss on his would-be savior — and returned triumphantly after the ceremony to his ghetto 'hood across the Bay, only to be killed later that summer in a "drug-related" drive-by shooting. Nor did his forerunners' and successors' fortunes appreciably improve, although several of my thus-far-luckless novel-writing protégés from commencements past have kept on scribbling vainly with their left hands, so to speak, while pursuing nonliterary careers with their right, their old coach having warned them that unlike violinists, mathematicians, theoretical physicists, and even lyric poets, for example — all of whom tend to blossom early or never — many novelists don't hit their stride until middle age.

Or later.

"So am I there yet?" one such perennially hopeful thirty-five-year-old asked me not long ago in a cover note to the typescript of her opus-still-in-progress, which she'd shipped to Blue Crab Bight for my perusal and comments despite my standing request to our graduates that they pass along all their future *publications*, to warm their old coach's heart and encourage his current coachees, but show me *no more unpublished writings ever*, please. A few pages plucked grudgingly from the thick pile's opening, middle, and closing chapters attested that their author wasn't, alas, "there yet." To spare her that blunt assessment, I e-mailed my praise for her persistence, reminded her of my No More Manuscripts policy ("We'd be shortchanging our present students if we kept on critiquing our alumnae"), and reminded her further always to enclose a self-addressed stamped envelope with any manuscript that she wanted returned to her. No reply, and so after a fair-enough interval I recycled her eternally gestating opus through my word processor, using its pages' bare white backside for next-draft printouts of my own work-in-regress at the time.

Namely? Well, since you asked: a "story" provisionally titled "The Bard Award," not by Yours Truly, George Newett, but by "Yours Falsely, George Knewit" — a.k.a. a certain Ms. "Cassandra Klause" (quotes hers), beyond question the most troublesome, gifted, and all-round problematical coachee that "Yours Falsely" and his colleagues (my wife included) ever had the much-mixed privilege of coaching, and of being coached by.

Those quotation marks; that saucy sobriquet and *nom de plume,* as openly provocative as the "bare white backside" of a few lines back (all typical Klause touches) ... Who knows how a youngster born to and raised by stolid Methodist parents on an Eastern Shore poultry farm and educated in marshy lower Delmarva's public school system came by age eighteen to be the unpredictably knowledgeable, aesthetically sophisticated, shyly brash and unintimidatable "literary performance artist" (her own designation) who, even as a Stratford freshman, was signing her term papers and exam bluebooks (always in quotes) "Sassy Cassie," "Sandy Claws," or "[in]Subordinate Klause," and contrived on her driver's license and other official documents to have her true name set between quotes? ("It's like that on my birth certificate," "C.K." once declared in class with her puckish smile. "My folks thought it looked more *official* that way.")

"And anyhow," she added this time last year in my old Shakespeare House office, "what's in a name?, as Uncle Will has that poor twat Juliet ask her hot-pants boyfriend. Best way to find out is to try on different ones for size, right? Like pants or penises. Now then, Boss: my final exam. *Ta-da!*" Whereupon she turned her back to me, bent forward, and yanked down her low-cut jeans to display, on her unpantied bare white et cetera, the marker-penned title and opening lines of her latest composition: *A Body of Words, by Nom D. Plume.* I didn't seriously believe, by the way, did I (she nattered calmly on as I hurried to reopen the office door, which she herself had closed before displaying her lettered derrière, and call for my across-the-hall colleague, the FOF poet Amanda Todd, to please come verify that if anyone in the House was Behaving Inappropriately, it was our student, not her teacher), that that bumpkin of a glover's son from the Stratford boondocks actually wrote those plays himself? About as likely as a down-county chicken farmer's hatchling's winning next year's Bard Award!

Which in fact, however, she added as my wife came to my rescue, she was dead set on doing, this time next year. "C'mon, Doc, *examine* me!"

"Ms. Klause is up to her old tricks," said I with a sigh to Professor Todd, and gestured toward our saucy pupil's "final exam."

"*New* tricks, guys." She turned her (plumpish) "text" to the pair of us — and to the open door, which my wife quickly reclosed behind herself. "Just call me Randy Sandy, Mandy."

A calmer hand than her spouse in situations involving bareassed coeds bent over one's office desk, my Mrs. granted briskly, "Very amusing, Cass. And we get your point, I think: all that feminist/deconstructionist blather about Writing the Body? Up with your pants now, please, or you get an Incomplete for the semester."

Undaunted, "Cass my ass, Teach," the girl came back, and maintained her position: "If y'all don't read Cassie's Ass, her semester's incomplete anyhow."

Said I, "Excuse me now, everybody?" and consulted my wife's eyes for her leave to leave: "Professor Todd will review and evaluate your final submission, Ms. Klause —"

To my desktop she retorted, "*Semi*final submission. You ain't seen nothing yet."

I'd seen more than enough, I declared. I would wait in Professor Todd's office while its regular tenant examined and evaluated the rest of the text for me. "Your title and pen name pretty well establish the general idea."

To my departing back, as with a headshake I thanked Mandy and got out of there, "No fair, Chief. You read 'em out of cunt-text!"

Some while later, over lunch at a pizzeria just off campus, my wife and I shook heads over this latest, most outrageously provocative bit of *Klauserie*. What she had seen further of *A BODY OF WORDS*, she reported (feet, arms, belly, back, and neck had been enough for her), confirmed her opinion of its being a not-unclever assemblage of quotes from all over the literary corpus, having to do literally or figuratively with the various anatomical items upon which they were inscribed: Virgil's "I sing of arms" on her forearms, the Song of Solomon's "Thy belly is like a heap of wheat set about with lilies" encircling her navel, etc. "She said she'd intended to 'perform the whole text,' quote-unquote, in class, but then decided to hear your editorial suggestions first."

"Very considerate of her. What a handful that wacko kid is!"

"A *figurative* handful, we presume you mean?" Because though no beauty by fashion-mag standards, the ample-bodied Ms. Klause, we agreed, was a not unclever, not unattractive young woman, not unpopular with her classmates both male and female.

"Listen to us," I said to my spinach-mozzarella stromboli: "'Not unclever, not unattractive, not unpopular' . . . The girl's extraordinary! One tour de force after another, while everybody else in the room is still doing 'It was a dark and stormy night.' She *deserves* a fucking prize!"

"Better one of those than the Bard Award, we bet."

A certain small voltage had built across the table during this dialogue; it dispersed, if that's what voltages do, when I here declared, "The PITA Prize is what she deserves: Pain In The Ass." Back to being the dedicated, indeed impassioned teacher/colleague/wife I loved, "The girl's amazing," my wife enthused (a verb that she hates, but that her husband sometimes finds convenient). And "While we're talking about writing," she went on, although we hadn't been, exactly, "Ms. PITA Prize suggested to me that you should, and I quote, 'get some *description* done in that lame Bard Award story that he and I are supposedly collaborating on,' close quote. By which she meant you and her. Question mark?"

"*What?*"

That afore-noted small voltage resurged. "Her very words, George." Raising two fingers to make a quote mark, "'Like give the Gentle-Ass Reader some idea of how things feel, smell, sound, and *look*, for pity's sake, beyond Cassie's Bare White Et Cetera and Ms. Mandy's Jealous-Green Eyes, don't you think?' End of quote — and *what the fuck story is she talking about,* please? What's this *collaboration?*"

I was damned if I knew, and energetically swore so, adding that of course Ms. Klause and I had spoken in conference about the much coveted but problematical Shakespeare Prize, I being after all her faculty adviser, and that (partly as a result of that discussion) it had in fact occurred to me that there might be a George Newett short story in there somewhere: about an eccentrically gifted student "writer," say, whose "texts" are collages, rearrangements, pastiches of the words of others. But despite a few notebook notes and a false-start draft page or two, I had yet to work out what that story might be — and most certainly, to my knowledge, hadn't discussed it with "Cassandra Klause." When a potential story of mine is still that nebulous, she might remember, I don't speak of it even to my beloved fellow-writer spouse, much less to my students. And "Could we please change the subject now, hon? Enough voltage already!"

We duly did: spoke of our distant pair of adult children and of our grandchild, already high school age, up in Vermont; of our plans for the weekend; of some of our other, less troublesome Stratford students. But my mind remained at least half on "Cass Klause"'s editorial suggestion, with which I found myself so in accord that I itched to get back to my desk at home and experiment with a bit of sensory detail (never my strongest writerly suit) in that story-not-quite-yet-in-embryo: to "flesh out," for example, such lame lines as *"The girl's amazing," my wife enthused* with enhancements like *My wife closed her* [Matahannock-greenbrown?] *eyes, shook her* [uh, very attractive? ruddy-cheeked? short-walnut-hair-framed?] *head, and* [um, enthused?] *"The girl's amazing!"*

Better yet, maybe go back and cut out all that river-name and gated-community stuff at the tale's front end and get right to the action: the day when a certain budding prankster/performance *artiste* proposed to her writing coach that instead of submitting to the class a manuscript of his own for *them* to criticize (as she'd heard I'd done once or twice in the past, half in jest, at semester's end), I should let her submit one of mine under *her* name — as if for a change she was making up her own sentences and paragraphs, characters and scenes, instead of rearranging and "performing" other people's, when in fact she wouldn't be! That way I'd get some *really* objective feedback, right? As could scarcely be expected otherwise, except from her outspoken self ("Too many parentheses and dashes, in this reader's opinion; not enough *texture*," etc.). Plus maybe submit as mine a story of hers: She'd try to hack out something conventional, maybe about life in a tacky gated community like Heron Bay Estates, or about a professor whose maverick student puts an additional small strain on his prevailingly quite happy marriage by teasing him with her "corpus" . . . that sort of thing. Which is pretty much what Ms. "Cassandra Klause" did, Reader, at the time here told of — and here we go, almost.

Additional small strain, somebody just said, on a *prevailingly* happy marriage. Mandy's and mine has been that, for sure; keenly aware of each other's strengths and shortcomings, we feel much blessed in each other, on balance. But of course there've been trials, strains, bumps in our road: the undeniably disappointing atrophy of our separate literary talents, to which however we feel we have, on the whole, commendably accommodated; one serious temptation apiece, somewhere back there, to adultery — which however we each take credit for candidly acknowledging and, we swear, resisting; never mind the details. And our inevitably mixed feelings, as we've approached or reached the close of our academic careers, not to mention of our lives, about what each and the other have accomplished, professionally and personally: about what we've done and not done, who we've been and not been, separately and together, during our joint single ride on life's not-always-merry-go-round. Hence those occasional small voltage surges above-noted: nothing that our coupled domestic wiring can't handle, as I'm confident we'd agree if we spoke of it, which we seldom do. Why bother? It's an electrical field potentiated over the past year by "Cassandra Klause" at one pole and at the other by my Shakespeare House "replacement," Professor Franklin Lee — who would've been introduced earlier into this "story" if its "author" didn't have a chip on his shoulder with respect to that smug sonofabitch. That tight-assed, self-important asshole. That . . .

Oh, that not untalented, not unhandsome, undeniably dedicated, generally quite capable and personable forty-five-year-old who joined the Stratford faculty half a dozen years ago upon the publication, two years before *that*, of his first (and eight years later still his only) novel — as utterly conservative, conventional, and unremarkable an item as its corduroy-jacketed author, but (to give the devil his due) not a bad job, really: issued by a bona fide New York trade house, not an academic press, and politely enough received by its handful of reviewers. Long since out of print, of course, but who among us isn't? A second novel allegedly still "going the rounds" up in Manhattan, and its author altogether mum about what, if anything, he and his strait-laced muse have been up to since.

In short and for better or worse, the guy's one of us, toward whom Mandy feels less animus and more colleagueship than does her spouse. "Frank Lee?" she'll tease when I get going like this on the subject. "Frank-*ly*, my dear, I don't give a damn, and neither should you." She's right, as usual, and I probably wouldn't, so much, except that it's been "Miz Klause's mizfortune," as that young woman herself puts it, to have Professor Lee as her official senior-year adviser, coach, and critic — and there, in her workshop mates' no doubt relieved opinion, go any hopes she might have entertained of so much as a long shot at this year's Shakespeare Prize.

But not in her own irrepressible estimation, nor in that of her FOF former coach. Shit, Reader (as Franklin Lee would never say): I'm no avant-gardist; would anytime rather read (or have written) the works of Ernest Hemingway, John Steinbeck, or Scott Fitzgerald, e.g., than those of Gertrude Stein or the later James Joyce. About contemporary "experimental" fiction — inter-active electronic hypertext and the like? — I have only the most dutiful, professorial curiosity. Or used to, anyhow, back in my professoring days: used to urge my Stratford charges to keep an open mind and interested eye on the edges of their medium's en-velope, reminding them that like the highest and lowest octaves on the classical eighty-eight-key piano — which, though rarely used, may be said to give a sort of resonant *optionality* to the middle octaves, making their use the composer's or performer's choice rather than a constraint — so likewise et cetera, you get the point. I therefore welcomed into my last year's workshop, after my initial startlement, the flagrantly unconventional "submissions" (misleading term!) of the apparently unscrupulous but actually strong-principled *faux-naïve provocateuse* "Cassandra Klause." The academic year that culminated last spring in *A BODY OF WORDS, by Nom D. Plume* had kicked off in the previous autumn with such unconventionalities as the opening pages of *Don Qui-xote* over the name "Pierre Menard" ("Borges's story, you know?" she had to explain to her baffled classmates. "About the guy who recomposes Cervantes's novel word for word?" They didn't get it); cribbed pages of a Joyce Carol Oates story signed "Toni Mor-rison," and vice versa (the "point" being that those two eminent Princeton colleagues must surely feel some rivalry, and might mischievously [etc.]); followed by other pointed or pointless but always transparent "plagiarisms" signed "The Grace of God," "The Way," "A Long Shot," "Extension," or "Bye Baby," leaving the reader to supply the missing "by." Never a sentence of her own compos-ing, but invariably a presentation more original than anything else in the room, even when flagrantly cribbed, chopped, and re-assembled from the previous week's workshopped efforts of her classmates and re-presented as [by] "D. Construction" or "Tryst-'em Sandy." And then that *BODY OF WORDS*, which she openly declared to be her trial run for the Bard Award ("Hey, it's for the quote 'most impressive *body* of work' unquote, right?") and "performed" for a handful of fellow workshoppers in her dorm room after its preview by me and Mandy. And the "author" of these brazen stunts, mind, was an invariably unassuming, perky but shy-mannered young woman who also happened to be the most astute and candid yet diplomatic critic in the room (except perhaps for her coach) of her colleagues' literary efforts, so earnest but clunkily unimaginative by comparison.

One can readily imagine how less than edifying, instructive, or even entertaining Professor Franklin Lee found this sort of thing. In conference before the opening classes of her senior fall semester (my ex-student reported to me by e-mail), he pleasantly but firmly let her know that *his* Advanced Fiction Writing seminar, "unlike some," was no theater for avant-garde gimmickry, but a serious workshop in "the millennia-old art of rendering into language the human experience of life": more specifically, in the less ancient art of "inventing and constructing short dramatic prose narratives for print, involving Characters, Setting, Plot, and Theme, in the noble tradition of Poe and Maupassant through Hemingway and Faulkner, Eudora Welty and Flannery O'Connor, to such contemporary masters of the form as Jorge Luis Borges and John Updike." If she found too constraining for her unconventional tastes a genre so splendidly various and accommodating (though rigorous), he advised, she should drop his course and sign up for something in the way of Experimental Theater, perhaps.

And when I pointed out to him that the Stratford catalogue doesn't offer any such courses [her e-message went on], *he smirked that tweedy little smirk of his and said, "Maybe Professor Emeritus Newett will be willing to do some sort of Independent Study project with you in his retirement, unless his wife objects. If he isn't willing, or if she says no, it might just be that Stratford isn't really the right venue for you." In his class, however, while we were free to write in the comic or non-comic mode, the realistic or*

the fantastic, the traditional or the innovative, what we were go-
ing to make up and set down was STORIES, not "marginally in-
teresting aesthetic points presented by non-narrative means."

So HELP!!!!! (me, God) (And why wd yr wife object to a few
extracurricular sessions, just you&me&my rambunctious muse,
either somewhere on campus or maybe @ yr place, while Ms.
Todd's meeting her classes?) (Just kidding, Ma'am ;-)

Adieu[10]/0 (= Much Ado Over Nothing),

Yrs (truly), "CK"

"I personally think Frank has a point," opined Mandy when I showed her this message (she and I have no secrets from each other, that I know of). "And damn straight I object! She's so obviously coming on to you, whether she means it seriously or not." If I chose to celebrate my academic retirement by humping a coed forty-five years my junior, she added, thereby dishonoring our longtime solemn vow to keep hands off our students, I should go right the hell ahead, and there'd be "much adieu" indeed: adieu to our marriage and to my academic reputation, for starters. My call.

This-all said no more than half seriously, she crediting me with no such intentions. And of course I abandoned the notion of any such tête-à-tête tutorials, if I'd ever really half entertained it. But I maintained Cassie's and my e-mail connection, offering to show my wife any and all such communications if she wished to monitor them — which she hoped I was kidding even to suggest. Because, truth to tell, my previous year's exposure to "Nom D. Plume"'s "rambunctious muse" showed signs of stirring my own muse from her extended hibernation. During Klause's second junior-year semester with me, and over the following summer, I had found myself reviewing two decades' worth of George Newett story-scripts (most of them rejected after serial submissions), including a half-dozen comparatively recent ones that I hadn't bothered to show Mandy. After my experience of "CK"'s freewheeling, no-holds-barred imagination, they all struck me as, well, earnest but clunky; "not untalented" but nowise exceptional; the sort of stuff that a Franklin Lee might produce, with none of the sparkle that marked Cassie's more imaginative perpetrations. Pallid rehashes, they were, of "the 3 Johns" (her dismissive label for Messrs. Cheever, O'Hara, and Updike): the muted epiphanies and petty nuances of upper-middle-class life in a not-all-that-upscale gated community on Maryland's endearingly funky Eastern Shore. Not impossibly, I had come to feel, some infusion of "CK"ish radicality might goose that muse of mine into rejuvenated action in my Golden Years, and George Newett would be remembered as a once-conventional and scarcely noticed writer who, in his Late Period, produced the refreshingly original works that belatedly made his name.

Meanwhile, however (not having lost my marbles altogether), I respected Frank Lee's ultimatum, sort of, or at least his right to declare it, as Amanda most certainly did as well. But I was determined to come to my former student's aid somehow or other. With some misgivings, therefore, I confided all the above to her by e-mail as her senior-year registration date approached, and we came up with a plan, mostly but by no means entirely hers, to kill several birds with one stone. So to speak? I would supply her with drafts of those unpublished and abandoned later stories of mine: the ones that not even Mandy had seen. She would then edit, revise, and/or rewrite them as much or as little as she chose and submit them to Professor Lee's workshop as her own, perhaps over such Klausean pen names as "John Uptight," "(Over A-)Cheever," "Scareless O'Hara" — surely Professor Lee wouldn't object to *that!* The payoff for me would be fresh input (including his) on those old efforts, for whatever that might be worth, which I could perhaps then re-revise and present to some book publisher as a story collection. For "Sandy," the reward would be her baccalaureate and a shot after all at the Shakespeare Prize (one of whose judges I still was, along with Mandy, Frank Lee, another literature professor, and the head of the English Department). In competition for which she would submit . . . what? Perhaps a "body of work" comprising specimens of her provocative junior-year stunts, her senior-year experiments with conventional forms and straightforward realism, and some sort of capstone piece embodying both, to demonstrate her "Hegelian evolution" as a writer (her term for it), from Thesis versus Antithesis to a Synthesis triumphantly combining and transcending both.

Yes, well, reader of these strung-out pages: We did that, my star ex-coachee and I — unbeknownst to my wife, to Franklin Lee, and to my other Stratford ex-colleagues — and all parties were impressed. Ms. Klause had been, remember, the ablest critic in my workshop; now she showed herself to be by far the best editor/rewriter as well. Those ho-hum scribblings of mine took on a resonance, texture, and sparkle that they'd formerly manifested only here and there, if at all — on the strength of which example I dared hope to return to my long-abandoned second novel and CPR it back to new life. "Best damned writing student I ever had," Frank Lee marveled to Amanda and me over a colleaguely lunch one April day in the Stratford Club, "by a factor of several!" He would never have guessed, he went on, that those jim-dandy stories that she had come up with for his workshop were Crazy Cassie's, if not for their jokey pen names — "which of course we will get rid of before she sends them off to *Harper's* and *The New Yorker.*"

That winking, almost conspiratorial "we": So surprised and delighted was Fussy Frank by "our problem child's metamorphosis" that he generously included among its causes my earlier patient encouragement of her, along with his own "less permissive" standards. "Like Thesis and Antithesis, right?" he actually remarked to Mandy. "And she's our Synthesis." Hence the lunch-in-progress (his suggestion), to which he'd also invited my wife on the strength of her having rescued me a year ago from that *BODY OF WORDS*, by now a campus legend.

"I'll drink to that," she allowed, and raised her glass of faculty-club merlot to mine and to our colleague's de-alcoholized chardonnay (he had a class to teach that afternoon, he explained — but then, so did Mandy). As we nibbled our smoked-turkey-and-bean-sprout wraps, he even hinted, shyly, that if our joint protégée needed some extra cash this summer, he might actually hire her to review the typescript of his second novel and make editorial suggestions, so impressed was he by her acumen in that line. "Not that she'll likely be short on funds," he added with a chuckle — inasmuch as he would soon be presenting to the Prize Committee her assembled portfolio, which in his candid, considered, and confidential opinion need consist of nothing more than those half-dozen first-rate contributions to his senior seminar to make her a shoo-in for the Bard Award. "Who'd've thought, last September, that I'd hear myself saying that?"

I could have raised my hand, but of course did not. Among the things of which my lunchmates were unaware was that our Triumphantly Synthesizing student's senior-year output included two items that would not appear in her portfolio: a story of mine that she had submitted under her name to three good quarterlies simultaneously, without editing or revising it, as what she termed a "control" (all three had rejected it, as then had she), and one of her own under *my* name, programmatically imitative of my style, subject matter, and thematic preoccupations, but evidently superior to her model, as it was promptly accepted for publication by a lesser but still worthy periodical.

Consider it a thank-you for all you've done for me, the girl explained by e-mail when I (1) received the lit mag's baffling acceptance letter (she'd supplied my Heron Bay Estates address on the obligatory self-addressed stamped envelope), (2) made a puzzled inquiry of the editor, (3) quickly surmised what was afoot, (4) canceled the publication (at least under my name), (5) provided the actual author's name and address in case the magazine was still interested (it was, but would need to Inquire Further), and (6) demanded from that author an explanation of this latest jaw-dropper. *XOXO Mwah!,* her message signed off, *cklause2@stratcoll.edu.*

Mwah my fat ass! I messaged back, demanding now both apology and cross-her-heart promise of no further such embarrassments — and at once regretted that angry imperative, to which she responded, *Just name the time and place, Coach.*

(And yours isn't all that *fat, by the way: You shd see* mine *these days! ;-)*

Aiyiyiyiyi: How to get out of this me-made mess, and this mess of a nonstory about it by Who Knows Whom: a "story" that opened so George Newett–like, with a serene little disquisition on Eastern Shore river and place names; that proceeded smoothly through a half-dozen pages on Stratford College and its problematical Bard Award, establishing en route its newly retired narrator/ protagonist and his not-yet-retired wife/colleague — and that then derailed just when it ought really to have got going, with the introduction of Conflict in the form of Troublesomely Brilliant Student "Cassandra Klause"? Should FOF Newett now commit his maiden adultery, so to speak, by humping one of his not-quite-ex students — at her initiative, to be sure, but still . . . — thereby blighting both his long happy marriage and his academic retirement, disgusting his colleagues and grown-up children, but perhaps reactivating (for what they're worth) his so-long-quiescent creative energies? And if so, so what? Or ought we to have the guy come to his moral senses (if necessary, since we've seen thus far no incontestable sign of his being *seriously* tempted by "CK"'s flagrances) and not only decline her seductive overtures but terminate altogether their somewhat sicko connection, make a clean breast of it to his faithful, so-patient Amanda before that breast gets irrevocably soiled, and content himself with his writerly Failed-Old-Farthood and his inarguably good works as teacher and coach of future FOFs? But again: If so, so what?

Or could/should it turn out to be at least possibly the case that *nothing thus far here narrated has been the* (actual, nonfictive) *case?* And if so . . . ?

"Well of *course* it hasn't been, dumdum!" he imagines his frisky new sex mate teasing as he mounts her latest cleverly lettered performance piece, BARTLETT'S DEFAMILIARIZED QUO-TATIONS, [by] *"Gosh & Golly,"* the two of them on all fours on the faux-oriental living room rug in her new apartment, rented with a bit of her Shakespeare Prize money and her earnings as editorial assistant to Professor Franklin Lee. "Do I need to remind *you*, of all people, that this whole she-bang is a made-up story? There *is* no 'Cassie-Ass Klause' or Georgie-Boy Newett! No you, no me, no Frankie-Pank Lee! No StratColl dot e-d-u, nor any Bard Award! All just freaking fictions! So sock it to me, Coach! *Unh! Unh!*"

Yes, well: No thanks, *chérie;* not even in an Effing Fiction. And as for the question with which you're now about to pull the rug from under your narrator — How to wrap up a longish story that has no proper plot development anyhow? A story that for all one knows (or cares) may be being written by Not-Yet-Failed Fictionist Franklin Lee, say: beneath his corduroy camouflage a less straitjacketed writer than some mistake him to be, ha-ha, and longtime secret lover of a certain poet-colleague of his, ha-ha-ha, as well as of her pathetic husband's ex-protégée "CK," ha-ha-ha-ha! . . . ?

No problem, mate (ha-ha-ha-ha-ha & *UNH!*) . . . :

THE END

Respectfully submitted to the Shakespeare Prize Committee [by]
"Hook R. Crook"
(Copywrong ☺ *Twenty-Something* [G. I. Newett])

Progressive Dinner

1.

HORS D'OEUVRES AND APPETIZERS

"Hey, Rob! Hey, Shirley! Come on in, guys!"

"And the Beckers are right behind us. Hi-ho, Debbie! Hi-ho, Peter!"

"Come in, come in. Nametags on the table there, everybody. Drinks in the kitchen, goodies in the dining room and out on the deck. Yo there, Jeff and Marsha!"

"You made your taco dip, Sandy! Hooray! And Shirley brought those jalapeño thingies that Pete can't keep hands off of. Come on in, Tom and Patsy!"

TIME: The late afternoon/early evening of a blossom-rich late-May North Temperate Zone Saturday, half-a-dozen-plus springtimes into the new millennium. Warm enough for open doors and windows and for use of decks and patios, but not yet sultry enough to require air conditioning, and still too early for serious mosquitoes.

"So, did you folks see the Sold sign on the Feltons' place?"

"No! Since when?"

"Since this morning, Tom Hardison tells us. We'll ask Jeff Pitt when he and Marsha get here; he'll know what's what."

"The poor Feltons! We still can't get over it!"

"Lots of questions still unanswered there, for sure. Where d'you want this smoked bluefish spread, Deb?"

"In my mouth, just as soon as possible! Here, I'll take it; you guys go get yourself a drink. Hey there, Ashtons!"

PLACE: 908 Cattail Court, Rockfish Reach, Heron Bay Estates, Stratford, Avon County, upper Eastern Shore of Maryland, 21600: an ample and solidly constructed two-story hip-roofed dormer-windowed Dutch-colonial-style dwelling of white brick with black shutters and doors, slate roof, flagstone front walk and porch and patio, on "Rockfish Reach," off Heron Creek, off the Matahannock River, off Chesapeake Bay, off the North Atlantic Ocean, etc.

"So, Doctor Pete, what's your take on the latest bad news from Baghdad?"

"You know what I think, Tom. What all of us ivory-tower-liberal academics think: that we had no business grabbing that tar baby in the first place, but our president lied us into there and now we're stuck with it. Here's to you, friend."

"Yeah, well. Cheers? Hey, Peg, we all love our great new mailboxes! You guys did a terrific job!"

"Didn't they, though? Those old wooden ones were just rotting away."

"And these new cast-metal jobs are even handsomer than the ones in Spartina Pointe. Good work, guys."

"You're quite welcome. Thanks for *this,* Deb and Pete and everybody. *Mmm!*"

"So where're the Pitts, I wonder?"

"Speak of the devil! Hi there, Marsha; hi-ho, Jeff! And you-all are . . . ?"

OCCASION: The now-traditional season-opening progressive dinner in Heron Bay's Rockfish Reach subdivision, a

pleasantly laid out and landscaped two-decade-old neigh-
borhood of some four dozen houses in various architectural
styles, typically three-bedroom, two-and-a-half-bath affairs
with attached two-car garage, screened or open porches, decks
and/or patios, perhaps a basement, perhaps a boat dock,
all on low-lying, marsh-fringed acre-and-a-half lots. Of the
nearly fifty families who call the place home, most are empty-
or all-but-empty-nesters, their children grown and flown.
About half are more or less retired, although some still work
out of home offices. Perhaps a third have second homes else-
where, in the Baltimore/Washington or Wilmington/Phil-
adelphia areas where they once worked, or in the Florida
coastal developments whereto they migrate with other East
Coast snowbirds for the winter. Half a dozen of the most com-
munity-spirited from the Reach's Shoreside Drive and its
adjacent Cattail and Loblolly Courts function as a neigh-
borhood association, planning such community events and
improvements as those above-mentioned dark green cast-
metal mailboxes (paid for by a special assessment), the
midsummer Rockfish Reach BYOB sunset cruise down the
Matahannock from the Heron Bay Marina, and the fall pic-
nic (in one of HBE's two pavilioned waterside parks) that
unofficially closes the season unofficially opened by the pro-
gressive dinner, here in early progress.

As usual, invitation notices were distributed to all four
dozen households a month before the occasion, rubber-banded
to the decorative knobs atop those new mailboxes. Also as
usual, between fifteen and twenty couples signed on and paid
the $40-per-person fee. Of the participating households (all
of whom have been asked to provide, in addition to their fee,
either an hors d'oeuvre/appetizer or a dessert, please indicate
which), six or seven will have volunteered to be hosts: one for
the buffet-and-bar opening course presently being enjoyed by
all hands, perhaps four for the sit-down entrée (supplied by
a Stratford caterer; check your nametag to see which entrée
house you've been assigned to), and one for the all-together-

*again dessert buffet that winds up the festive occasion. The
jollity of which, this spring, has been somewhat beclouded
— as was that of last December's Rockfish Reach "Winter
Holiday" party — by the apparent double suicide, still unex-
plained, of Richard and Susan Felton (themselves once active
participants in these neighborhood events) by exhaust-fume
inhalation in their closed garage at 1020 Shoreside Drive,
just after Tom and Patsy Hardison's elaborate toga party last
September to inaugurate their new house on Loblolly Court.
Recommended dress for the progressive dinner is "country
club casual": slacks and sport shirts for the gentlemen
(jackets optional); pants or skirts and simple blouses for
the ladies.*

"Hi there. Jeff insists that we leave it to him to do the honors."

"*And* to apologize for this late addition to the guest list, *and* to
cover the two extra plate charges, *and* to fill in the nametags —
all courtesy of Avon Realty, guys, where we agents do our best
to earn our commissions. *May I have your attention, everybody?*
This handsome young stud and his blushing bride are your new
about-to-be neighbors Joe and Judy Barnes, formerly and still
temporarily from over in Blue Crab Bight but soon to move into
Number Ten-Twenty Shoreside Drive! Joe and Judy, this is Dean
Peter Simpson, from the College, and his soulmate Deborah, also
from the College."

"Welcome to Rockfish Reach, Joe and Judy. What a pleasant
surprise!"

"Happy to be here . . . Dean and Mrs. Simpson."

"Please, guys. We're Debbie and Pete."

"*Lovely* house, Debbie! And do forgive us for showing up
empty-handed. Everything happened so *fast!*"

"No problem, no problem. If I know Marsha Pitt, she's probably brought an hors d'oeuvre *and* a dessert."

"Guilty as charged, Your Honor. Cheesecake's in the cooler out
in our car for later at the Greens'; I'll put these doodads out with
the rest of the finger food."

"And *your* new house is a lovely one too, Judy and Joe. Pete and I have always admired that place."

"Thanks for saying so. Our daughters are convinced it'll be haunted! One of them's up at the College, by the way, and her kid sister will be joining her there next year, but they'll still be coming home most weekends and such."

"We hope!"

"Oh my, how *wonderful* . . . Excuse me . . ."

"So! Go on in, people. Jeff and Marsha will introduce you around, and we'll follow shortly."

"Aye-aye, Cap'n. The Barneses will be doing their entrée with us, by the way. We've got plenty of extra seating, and they've promised not to say that our house is the Pitts'."

"*Ai*, sweetheart, you promised not to resurrect that tired old joke! Come on, Joe and Judy, let's get some wine."

("You okay, hon?"

"I'll make it. But that daughters thing really hit home."

"Yup. Here's a Kleenex. On with the party?")

HOSTS: The "associates": Deborah Clive Simpson, fifty-seven, associate librarian at Stratford College's Dexter Library, and Peter Alan Simpson, also fifty-seven, longtime professor of humanities and presently associate dean at that same quite good small institution, traditionally a liberal-arts college but currently expanding its programs in the sciences, thanks to a munificent bequest from a late alumnus who made a fortune in the pharmaceuticals business. The Simpsons are childless, their only offspring, a much-prized daughter, having been killed two years ago in a multicar crash on the Baltimore Beltway during an ice storm in the winter of her sophomore year as a premedical student at Johns Hopkins. Her loss remains a trauma from which her parents do not expect ever to recover; the very term "closure," so fashionable nowadays, sets their teeth on edge, and the coinciding of Julie's death and Peter's well-earned promotion to associate dean has leached much pleasure from the latter. Neverthe-

*less, in an effort to "get on with their lives," the Simpsons last
year exchanged their very modest house in Stratford — so rich
in now-painful memories of child-rearing and of the couple's
advancement up the academic ladder from relative penury to
financial comfort — for their present Rockfish Reach address,
and they're doing their best to be active members of both their
collegiate and their residential communities as well as generous supporters of such worthy organizations as Doctors Without Borders (Médecins Sans Frontières), to which it had been
Julie's ambition to devote herself once she attained her M.D.*

"So we bet those new folks — what's their name?"

"Barnes. Joe and Judy. He's with Lucas and Jones in Stratford,
and she teaches at the Fenton School. They seem nice."

"We bet they got themselves a bargain on the Feltons' place."

"More power to 'em, *I* say. All's fair in love, war, and real estate."

"Don't miss Peggy Ashton's tuna spread, Rob; I'm going for
another white wine spritzer."

"Make that two, okay? But no spritz in mine, please. So, Lisa:
What were you starting to say about the nametags?"

"Oh, just that looking around at tonight's tags reminded me
that friends of ours over in Oyster Cove told us once that nine out
of ten husbands in Heron Bay Estates are called by one-syllable
first names and their wives by two-syllable ones: You Rob-and-
Shirley, we Dave-and-Lisa, et cetera."

"Hey, that's right. I hadn't noticed!"

"And what exactly does one make of that sociocultural infobit,
s'il vous plaît?"

"I'll let you know, Pete-and-Debbie, soon's I figure it out.
Meanwhile . . ."

"What *I* notice, guys — every time I'm in the supermarket or
Wal-Mart? — is that more and more older and overweight Americans —"

"Like us?"

"Like some of us, anyhow — go prowling down the aisles bent

forward like *this,* with arms and upper body resting on their shopping cart as if it was some kind of a walker . . ."

"And their fat butts waggling, often in pink warmup pants . . ."

"Now is that nice to say?"

"It's what Pete calls the American Consumer Crouch. *I* say 'Whatever floats your boat . . .'"

"*And* keeps the economy perking along. Am I right, Joe Barnes?"

"Right you are, Jeff."

"So, Deb, *you* were saying something earlier about a long letter that Pete got out of the blue from some girl in Uganda?"

"Oh, right, wow: *that* . . ."

"Uganda?"

"I should let Pete tell you about it. Where are you and Paul doing your entrée?"

"Practically next door. At the Beckers'?"

"Us too. So he'll explain it there. Very touching — but who knows whether it's for real or a scam? Oh, hey, Pat: Have you and Tom met the Barneses? Joe and Judy Barnes, Tom and Patsy Hardison from Loblolly Court."

"Jeff Pitt introduced us already, Deb. Hello again, Barneses."

"Hi there. We've been hearing great things about your Toga Party last fall! Sounds cool!"

"All but the ending, huh? We can't *imagine* what happened with Dick and Susan Felton that night . . ."

"Has to've been some kind of freak accident; let's don't spoil this party with that one. Welcome to Rockfish Reach!"

"Joe and I love it already. And your place on Loblolly Court is just incredible!"

"Jeff pointed it out to us when we first toured the neighborhood. Really magnificent!"

"Thanks for saying so. An eyesore, some folks think, but it's what we wanted, so we built it. You're the new boss at Lucas and Jones, in town?"

"I am — and *my* boss, over in Baltimore, is the guy who

stepped on lots of folks' toes with that teardown over in Spartina Pointe. Maybe you know him: Mark Matthews?"

"Oh, we know Mark, all right. A man after my own heart."

"Mine too, Tom. Decide what you want, go for it, and let the chips fall where they may."

"Well, now, people: Excuse me for butting in, but to us lonely left-wing-Democrat dentist types, that sounds a lot like our current president and his gang."

"Whoa-ho, Doctor David! Let's not go there, okay? This is Lisa Bergman's husband Dave, guys. He pulls teeth for a living."

"And steps on toes for fun. Pleased to meet you, folks."

"Entrée time in twenty minutes, everybody! Grab yourselves another sip and nibble, check your tags for your sit-down-dinner address, and we'll all reconvene for dessert with the Greens at nine!"

"So, that Barnes couple: Are they golfers, d'you know?"

2.

ENTRÉE

The assembled now disperse from the Simpsons' to shift their automobiles or stroll on foot to their various main-course addresses, their four host-couples having left a bit earlier to confirm that all is ready and to be in place to greet their guests. Of these latter, four will dine with George and Carol Walsh on Shoreside Drive; six (including the newcomer Barneses) with Jeff and Marsha Pitt, also on Shoreside; eight (the Ashtons, Bergmans, Greens, and Simpsons) with Pete and Debbie's Cattail Court near-neighbors Charles and Sandy Becker; and ten with Tom and Patsy Hardison over on Loblolly Court. Stratford Catering's entrée menu for the evening is simple but well prepared: a caesar salad with optional anchovies, followed by Maryland crabcakes with garlic mashed potatoes and a steamed broccoli-zucchini mix, the vegetables cooked in advance and reheated, the crabcakes prepared in advance but griddled on-site, three minutes on each side, and the whole accompanied by mineral water and one's choice of pinot grigio or iced tea.

The Becker group all go on foot, chatting together as they pass under the streetlights in the mild evening air, their destination being just two houses down from the Simpsons' on the opposite side of the cul-de-sac "court." To no one in particular, Shirley Green remarks, "Somebody was wondering earlier whether the Barneses got a bargain price on the Feltons' house? None of our business, but *I* can't help wondering whether the Beckers' house number affects *their* property value."

"Aiyi," Peggy Ashton exclaims in mock dismay. "*Nine-Eleven* Cattail Court! I hadn't thought of that!"

If *he* were Chuck Becker, Rob Green declares to the group, he'd use that unfortunate coincidence to appeal their property-tax assessment. "I mean, hell, Dick and Susan Felton were just two people, rest their souls. Whereas, what was it, three *thousand* and some died on Nine-Eleven? That ought to count for something."

His wife punches his shoulder. "Rob, I *swear!*"

Walking backward to face the group, he turns up his palms: "Can't help it, folks. We accountants try to take everything into account."

Hisses and groans. Peter Simpson takes his wife's hand as they approach their destination. He's relieved that the Barneses, although certainly pleasant-seeming people, won't be at table with them for the sit-down dinner to distress Debbie further with innocent talk of their college-age daughters.

The Beckers' house, while no *palazzo* like the Hardisons', is an imposing two-story white-brick colonial, its columned central portico flanked by a guest wing on one side and a garage wing on the other, with two large doors for cars and a smaller one for golf cart and bicycles. The eight guests make their way up the softly lighted entrance drive to the brightly lit main entry to be greeted by ruddy-hefty, bald-pated, silver-fringed Charles Becker, a politically conservative septuagenarian with the self-assured forcefulness of the CEO he once was, and his no-longer-sandy-haired

Sandy, less vigorous of aspect after last year's successful surgery for a "growth" on her left lung, but still active in the Neighborhood Association, her Episcopal church in Stratford, and the Heron Bay Club. Once all have been welcomed and seated in the Beckers' high-ceilinged dining room, the drinks poured, and the salad served, their host taps his water glass with a table knife for attention and says, "Let's take hands and bow our heads for the blessing, please."

The Simpsons, seated side by side at his right hand, glance at each other uncomfortably, they being nonbelievers, and at the Bergmans, looking equally discomfited across the table from them. More for their sake than for her own, Debbie asks, as if teasingly, "Whatever happened to the separation of church and dinner party?" To which Charles Becker replies smoothly, "In a Christian household, do as the Christians do," and takes her left hand in his right and Lisa Bergman's right in his left. David shrugs his eyebrows at Pete and goes along with it, joining hands with his wife on one side and with Shirley Green on the other. Peter follows suit, taking Debbie's right hand in his left and Peggy Ashton's left in his right; but the foursome neither close eyes nor lower heads with the others while their host intones: "Be present at our table, Lord. / Be here and everywhere adored. / These mercies bless, and grant that we / May feast in Paradise with Thee. Amen."

"*And*," Paul Ashton adds at once to lighten the little tension at the table, "grant us stomach-room enough for this entrée after all those appetizers!"

"Amen and *bon appétit*," proposes Sandy Becker, raising her wineglass. "Everybody dig in, and then I'll do the crabcakes while Chuck serves up the veggies."

"Such appetizers they were!" Lisa Bergman marvels, and then asks Paul whether he happens, like her, to be a Gemini. He is, in fact, he replies: "Got a birthday coming up next week. Why?"

"Because," Lisa declares, "it's a well-known fact that we Geminis prefer hors d'oeuvres to entrées. No offense intended, Sandy and Chuck!"

Her husband winks broadly. "It's true even in bed, so I've heard — no offense intended, Paul and Lisa."

Sipping their drinks and exchanging further such teases and pleasantries, all hands duly address the caesar salad, the passed-around optional anchovy fillets, and the pre-sliced baguettes. Although tempted to pursue what she regards as presumption on their host's part that everyone in their community is a practicing Christian, or that because the majority happen to be, any others should join in uncomplainingly, Debbie Simpson holds her tongue — as she did not when, for example, the Neighborhood Association proposed Christmas lights last winter on the entrance signs to Rockfish Reach (she won that one, readily granting the right of all residents to decorate their houses, but not community property, with whatever religious symbols they cared to display), and when the Heron Bay Estates Community Association put up its large Christmas tree at the development's main gatehouse (that one she lost, and at Pete's request didn't pursue it, they being new residents whom he would prefer not be branded as troublemakers). She gives his left hand a squeeze by way of assuring him that she's letting the table-grace issue drop.

"So tell us about that strange letter you got, Pete," Peggy Ashton proposes. "From Uganda, was it? That Deb mentioned during appetizers?"

"Uganda?" the hostess marvels, or anyhow asks.

"*Very* strange," Peter obligingly tells the table. "I suppose we've all gotten crank letters now and then — get-rich scams in Liberia and like that? — but this one was really different." To begin with, he explains, it wasn't a photocopied typescript like the usual mass-mailed scam letter, but a neatly handwritten appeal on two sides of a legal-size ruled sheet, with occasional cross-outs and misspellings. Polite, articulate, and addressed to "Dear Friend," it was or purported to be from a seventeen-year-old Ugandan girl, the eldest of five children, whose mother had died in childbirth and whose father had succumbed to AIDS. Since their parents' death, the siblings have been lodged with an uncle, also suffering from AIDS and with five children of his own. Those he dresses properly and sends to school, the letter writer declares, but she and her four brothers and sisters are treated harshly by him and his wife, who "don't recognize [them] as human beings." Dismissed from school for lack of fee money and provided with "only two clothes each" to wear and little or nothing to eat, they are made to graze the family's goats, feed the pigs, and do all the hard and dirty housework from morning till night. In a few months, when she turns eighteen, she'll be obliged to become one of some man's several wives, a fate she fears both because of the AIDS epidemic and because it will leave her siblings unprotected. Having (unlike them) completed her secondary education before their father's death, she appeals to her "dear Friend" to help her raise 1,500 euros to "join university for a degree in education" and 1,200 euros for her siblings to finish high school. Attached to the letter was a printed deposit slip from Barclays Bank of Uganda, complete with the letter writer's name and account number, followed by the stipulation "F/O CHILDREN."

"How she got *my* name and address, I can't imagine," Pete concludes to the hushed and attentive table. "If it was in some big general directory or academic Who's Who, how'd she get hold of it, and how many hundreds of these things did she write out by hand and mail?"

"And where'd she get paper and envelopes and deposit slips and postage stamps," Lisa Bergman wonders, "if they're so dirt poor?"

"And the time to scribble scribble scribble," Paul Ashton adds, "while they're managing the goats and pigs and doing all the scutwork?"

Opines Rob the Accountant, "It doesn't add up."

"It does seem questionable," Sandy Becker agrees.

"But if you could see the letter!" Debbie protests. "So earnest and articulate, but so unslick! Lines like 'We do not hope that our uncle will recover.' And 'I can't leave my siblings alone. We remained five and we should stick five.'"

Taking her hand in his again and using his free hand to make finger quotes, Pete adds, "And, quote, 'Life unbearable, we only pray hard to kind people to help us go back to school, because the most learnt here is more chance of getting good job,' end of quote."

"It's heartbreaking," Shirley Green acknowledges. "No wonder you-all have so much of it memorized!"

"But the bottom line is," Chuck Becker declares, "did you fall for it? Because, believe me, it's a goddamn scam."

"You really think so?" Dave Bergman asks.

"Of course it is! Some sharpster with seven wives and Internet access for tracking down addresses sets his harem to scribbling out ten copies per wife per day, carefully misspelling a few words and scratching out a few more, just to see who'll take the bait. Probably some midlevel manager at Barclays with a PC in his office and a fake account in one of his twelve daughters' names."

"How can you be so *sure?*" Lisa Bergman wants to know.

With the air of one accustomed to having his word taken, "Take my word for it, sweetie," their host replies. Down-table to his wife then, "Better get the crabcakes started, Sandy?" And to the Simpsons, "Please tell me you didn't send 'em a nickel."

"We didn't," Debbie assures him. "Not yet, anyhow. Because of course we're leery of the whole thing too. But just suppose, Chuck and everybody — just *suppose* it happens to be authentic? Imagine the courage and resourcefulness of a seventeen-year-old girl in that wretched situation, with all that traumatic stuff behind her and more of it waiting down the road, but she manages somehow to get hold of a bunch of American addresses and a pen and paper and stamps and deposit slips, and she scratches out this last-chance plea for a *life* . . . Suppose it's for real?"

"And we-all sit here in our gated community," Lisa Bergman joins in, "with our Lexuses and golf carts and our parties and progressive dinners, and we turn up our noses and say, 'It's a scam; don't be suckered.'"

"So what *should* we do?" Paul Ashton mildly challenges her. "Bet a hundred bucks apiece on the *very* long shot that it's not a shyster?"

"I'm almost willing to," Shirley Green admits. Her husband shakes his head no.

"What we *ought* to do," Dave Bergman declares, "is go to some trouble to find out whether the thing's for real. A *lot* of trouble, if necessary. Like write back to her, telling her we'd like to help but we need more bona fides. Find out how she got Pete's name and address. Ask the American consulate in Kampala or wherever to check her story out. Is that in Uganda?"

"You mean," his wife wonders or suggests, "make a community project out of it?"

Asks Debbie, "Why not?"

"Because," Rob Green replies, "I, for one, don't have time for it. Got a full plate already." He checks his watch. "Or soon will have, won't we, Shirl?"

"Same here," Dave Bergman acknowledges. "I know I ought to *make* time for things like this, but I also know I won't. It's like demonstrating against the war in Iraq, the way so many of us did against the war in Vietnam? Or even like working to get out the vote on Election Day. My hat's off to people who act that strongly on their convictions, and I used to be one of them, but I've come to accept that I'm just *not* anymore. Morally lazy these days, I guess, but at least honest about it."

"And in this case," Chuck Becker says with ruddy-faced finality, "you're saving yourself a lot of wasted effort. Probably in those other cases too, but never mind that."

"Oh my goodness," his wife exclaims. "Look what time it is! I'll do the crabcakes, Chuck'll get the veggies, and Paul, would you mind refreshing everybody's drinks? Or we'll never get done before it's time to move on to Rob and Shirley's!"

3.

DESSERT

The Greens' place on Shoreside Drive, toward which all three dozen progressive diners now make their well-fed way from the several entrée houses to reassemble for the dessert course, is no more than a few blocks distant from the Becker and Simpson residences on Cattail Court — although the attractively winding streets of Heron Bay Estates aren't really measurable in blocks. Chuck and Sandy Becker, who had earlier walked from their house to Pete and Debbie Simpson's (practically next door) for the appetizer course, and then back to their own place to host the entrée, decide now to drive to the final course of the evening in their Cadillac Escalade. The Greens themselves, having left the Beckers' a quarter-hour earlier to make ready, drove also, retrieving their Honda van from where they'd parked it in front of the Simpsons'. The Ashtons, Paul and Peggy, walk only far enough to collect their Lexus from the Simpsons' driveway and then motor on. Of the five couples who did their entrée at 911 Cattail Court, only the Simpsons themselves and the Bergmans decide that the night air is too inviting not to stroll through it to Rob and Shirley's; they decline the proffered lifts in favor of savoring the mild westerly breeze, settling their crabcakes and vegetables a bit before tackling the dessert smorgasbord, and chatting among themselves en route.

"That Chuck, I swear," Lisa Bergman says as the Beckers' luxury SUV rolls by. "So *sure* he's right about everything! And Sandy just goes along with it."

"Maybe she agrees with him," Peter suggests. "Anyhow, they're good neighbors, even if Chuck can be borderline insufferable now and then."

"I'll second that," Dave Bergman grants. Not to walk four abreast down a nighttime street with no sidewalks, the two men drop back a bit to carry on their conversation while their wives, a few feet ahead, speak of other things. Charles Becker, David goes on, likes to describe himself as a self-made man, and in considerable measure he is: from humble beginnings as a small-town carpenter's son —

"Sounds sort of familiar," Peter can't help commenting, "except our Chuck's not about to let himself get crucified."

"Anyhow, served in the Navy during World War Two; came

home and went to college on the G.I. Bill to study engineering; worked a few years for a suburban D.C. contractor in the postwar housing boom; then started his own business and did very well indeed, as he does not tire of letting his dentist and others know. No hand-scrawled Send Me Money letters for *him:* 'God helps those who help themselves,' et cetera."

"Right: the way he helped himself to free college tuition and other benefits not readily available to your average Ugandan orphan girl. Hey, look: Sure enough, there's Jeff Pitt's latest score."

Peter means the Sold sticker on the For Sale sign (with *The Jeff Pitt Team* lettered under it) in front of 1020 Shoreside Drive, the former residence of Richard and Susan Felton. The women, too, pause before it — their conversation having moved from the Beckers to the Bergmans' Philadelphia daughter's latest project for her parents: to establish a Jewish community organization in Stratford, in alliance with the College's modest Hillel club for its handful of Jewish students. Lisa is interested; David isn't quite convinced that the old town is ready yet for that sort of thing.

"The Feltons," he says now, shaking his head. "I guess we'll never understand."

"What do you mean?" Debbie challenges him. "I think *I* understand it perfectly well."

"What do *you* mean?" David cordially challenges back. "They were both in good health, comfortably retired, no family problems that anybody knows of, well liked in the neighborhood — and *wham*, they come home from the Hardisons' toga party and off themselves!"

"And," Peter adds, "their son and daughter not only get the news secondhand, with no advance warning and no note of explanation or apology, but then have to put their own lives on hold and fly in from wherever to dispose of their parents' bodies and house and belongings."

"What a thing to lay on your kids!" Lisa agrees. The four resume walking the short remaining distance to the Greens'. "And you think that's just fine, Deb?"

"Not 'just fine,'" Debbie counters: "*understandable.* And I agree that their kids deserved some explanation, if maybe not advance notice, since then they'd've done all they could to prevent its happening." What she means, she explains, is simply that she quite understands how a couple at the Feltons' age and stage — near or in their seventies after a prevailingly happy, successful, and disaster-free life together, their children and grandkids grown and scattered, the family's relations reportedly affectionate but not especially close, the parents' careers behind them along with four decades of good marriage, nothing better to look forward to than the infirmities, losses, and burdensome caretaking of old age, and no religious prohibitions against self-termination — how such a couple might just decide, Hey, it's been a good life; we've been lucky to have had it and each other all these years; let's end it peacefully and painlessly before things go downhill, which is really the only way they can go from here.

"And let our friends and neighbors and children clean up the mess?" David presses her. "Would you and Pete do that to us?"

"Count *me* out," Peter declares. "For another couple decades anyhow, unless the world goes to hell even faster than it's going now."

"In our case," his wife reminds the Bergmans, "it's friends, neighbors, and *colleagues*. Don't think we haven't talked about it more than once since Julie's death. I've even checked it out on the Web, for when the time comes."

"On the *Web?*" Lisa takes her friend's arm.

Surprised, concerned, and a little embarrassed, "The things you learn about your mate at a progressive dinner!" Peter marvels to David, who then jokingly complains that he hasn't learned a single interesting thing so far about *his* mate.

"Don't give up on me," his wife says. "The party's not over."

"Right you are," Debbie agrees, "literally and figuratively. And here we are, and I'll try to shut up."

The Greens' house, brightly lit, with a dozen or more cars now parked before it, is a boxy two-story beige vinyl-clapboard-sided affair, unostentatious but commodious and well maintained, with fake-shuttered windows all around, and on its creek side a large screened porch, open patio, pool, and small-boat dock. Shirley Green being active in the Heron Bay Estates Garden Club, the property is handsomely landscaped: The abundant rhododendrons, azaleas, and flowering trees have already finished blossoming for the season, but begonias, geraniums, daylilies, and roses abound along the front walk and driveway, around the foundation, and in numerous planters. As the foursome approach, the Bergmans tactfully walk a few paces ahead. Peter takes his wife's arm to comfort her.

"Sorry," Debbie apologizes again. "You know I wouldn't be thinking these things if we hadn't lost Julie." Her voice thickens. "She'd be fresh out of college now and headed for med school!" She can say no more.

"I know, I know." As indeed Peter does, having been painfully reminded of that circumstance as he helped preside over Stratford's recent commencement exercises instead of attending their daughter's at Johns Hopkins. Off to medical school she'd be preparing herself to go, for arduous but happy years of general training, then specialization, internship, and residency; no doubt she'd meet and bond with some fellow physician-in-training along the way, and Peter and Debbie would help plan the wedding with her and their prospective son-in-law and look forward to grandchildren down the line to brighten their elder years, instead of Googling "suicide" on the Web . . .

Briefly but appreciatively she presses her forehead against his shoulder. Preceded by the Bergmans and followed now by other dessert-course arrivers, they make their way front-doorward to be greeted by eternally boyish Rob and ever-effervescent Shirley Green.

"Sweets are out on the porch, guys; wine and decaf in the kitchen. Beautiful evening, isn't it?"

"Better enjoy it while we can, I guess, before the hurricanes come."

"Yo there, Barneses! What do you think of your new neighborhood so far?"

"Totally awesome! Nothing like this in Blue Crab Bight."

"We can't wait to move in, ghosts or no ghosts. Our daughter Tiffany's off to France for six weeks, but it's the rest of the family's summer project."

"So enjoy every minute of it. Shall we check out the goodies, Deb?"

"Calories, here we come! Excuse us, people."

But over chocolate cheesecake and decaffeinated coffee on the torch-lit patio, Judy Barnes reapproaches Debbie to report that Marsha Pitt, their entrée hostess, told them the terrible news of the Simpsons' daughter's accident. "Joe and I are *so* sorry for you and Peter! We can't *imagine . . .*"

All appetite gone, "Neither can we," Debbie assures her. "We've quit trying to."

And just a few minutes later, as the Simpsons are conferring on how soon they can leave without seeming rude, Paul and Peggy Ashton come over, each with a glass of pale sherry in one hand and a chocolate fudge brownie in the other, to announce their solution to that Ugandan orphan girl business.

"Can't wait to hear it," Peter says dryly. "Will Chuck Becker approve?"

"Chuck shmuck," says Paul, who has picked up a few Yiddishisms from the Bergmans. "The folks who brought you your dandy new mailboxes now propose a Rockfish Reach Ad Hoc Search and Rescue Committee. Tell 'em, Peg."

She does, emphasizing her points with a half-eaten brownie. The informal committee's initial members would be the three couples at dinner who seemed most sympathetic to Pete's story and to the possibility that the letter was authentic: themselves, the Bergmans, and of course the Simpsons. Peter would provide them with copies of the letter; Paul Ashton, whose legal expertise was at their service, would find out how they could go about verifying the thing's authenticity, as David Bergman had suggested at the Beckers'. If it turned out to be for real, they would then circulate an appeal through Rockfish Reach, maybe through all of Heron Bay Estates, to raise money toward the girl's rescue: not a blank check that her uncle and aunt might oblige her to cash for their benefit, but some sort of tuition fund that the committee could disburse, or at least oversee and authorize payments from.

"Maybe even a scholarship at Stratford?" Paul Ashton suggests to Peter. "I know you have a few foreign students from time to time, but none from equatorial Africa, I'll bet."

"Doesn't sound impossible, actually," Peter grants, warming to the idea while at the same time monitoring his wife's reaction. "*If* she's legit, and qualified. Our African-American student organization could take her in."

"And our Heron Bay Search and Rescue Squad could unofficially adopt her!" Lisa Bergman here joins in, whom the Ashtons have evidently briefed already on their proposal. "Having another teenager to keep out of trouble will make us all feel young again! Whatcha think, Deb?"

To give her time to consider, Peter reminds them that there remains the problem of the girl's younger siblings, whom she's resolved not to abandon: "We remained five and we should stick five," et cetera. Whereas if she "went to university" in Kampala for at least the first couple of years, say, she could see the youngsters into high school and then maybe come to Stratford for her junior or senior year . . .

"Listen to us!" He laughs. "And we don't even know yet whether the girl's for real!"

"But we can find out," David Bergman declares. "And if we can make it happen, or make something *like* it happen, it'll be a credit to Heron Bay Estates. Make us feel a little better about our golf and tennis and progressive dinners. Okay, so it's only one kid out of millions, but at least it's one. I say let's do it."

"And then Pete and I officially adopt her as our daughter," Debbie says at last, in a tone that her husband can't assess at all, "and we stop eating our hearts out about losing Julie, and everybody lives happily ever after."

"Deb?" Lisa puts an arm around her friend's shoulder.

"Alternatively," Debbie suggests to them then, "we could start a Dick and Susan Felton Let's Get It Over With Club, and borrow the Barneses' new garage for our first meeting. Meanwhile, let's enjoy the party, okay?" And she moves off toward where the Pitts, the Hardisons, and a few others are chatting beside the lighted pool. To their friends Peter turns up his palms, as best one can with a cup of decaf in one hand and its saucer in the other, and follows after his wife, wondering and worrying what lies ahead for them — tonight, tomorrow, and in the days and years beyond. They have each other, their work, their colleagues and friends and neighbors, their not-all-that-close extended family (parents dead, no siblings on Debbie's side, one seven-years-older sister of Peter's out in Texas, from whom he's been more or less distanced for decades), their various pastimes and pleasures, their still prevailingly good health — for who knows how much longer? And then. And then. While over in Uganda and Darfur, and down in Haiti, and in Guantánamo and Abu Ghraib and the world's multitudinous other hellholes . . .

"They had *nothing* like this back in Blue Crab Bight, man!" he hears Joe Barnes happily exclaiming to the Greens. "Just a sort of block party once, and that was it."

"Feltons or no Feltons," Judy Barnes adds, "we've made the right move."

Nearby, florid Chuck Becker is actually thrusting a forefinger at David Bergman's chest: "We cut and run from I-raq now, there'll be hell to pay. Got to *stay the course.*"

"Like we did in Nam, right?" unintimidated Dave comes back at him. "And drill the living shit out of Alaska and the Gulf Coast, I guess you think, if that's what it takes to get the last few barrels of oil? Gimme a break, Chuck!"

"Take it from your friendly neighborhood realtor, folks," Jeff Pitt is declaring to the Ashtons: "Whatever you have against a second Bay bridge — say, from south Baltimore straight over to Avon County? — it'll raise your property values a hundred percent in no time at all, the way the state's population is booming. We won't be able to build condos and housing developments fast enough to keep up!"

Peggy Ashton: "So there goes the neighborhood, right? And it's bye-bye Chesapeake Bay . . ."

Paul: "*And* bye-bye national forest lands and glaciers and polar ice caps. Get me outta here!"

Patsy Hardison, to Peter's own dear Deborah: "So, did you and Pete see that episode that Tom mentioned before, that he and all the TV critics thought was so great and I couldn't even watch? I suspect it's a Mars-versus-Venus thing."

"Sorry," Debbie replies. "We must be the only family in Heron Bay Estates that doesn't get HBO." Her eyes meet Peter's, neutrally.

Chuckling and lifting his coffee cup in salute as he joins the pair, "We don't even have *cable*," Peter confesses. "Just an old-style antenna up on the roof. Now is that academic snobbishness or what?" He sets cup and saucer on a nearby table and puts an arm about his wife's waist, a gesture that she seems neither to welcome nor to resist. He has no idea where their lives are headed. Quite possibly, he supposes, she doesn't either.

Up near the house, an old-fashioned post-mounted school bell clangs: The Greens use it to summon grandkids and other family visitors in for meals. Rob Green, standing by it, calls out, "Attention, all hands!" And when the conversation quiets, "Just want to remind you to put the Rockfish Reach sunset cruise on your calendars: Saturday, July fifteenth, Heron Bay Marina, seven to nine P.M.! We'll be sending out reminders as the time approaches, but *save the date*, okay?"

"Got it," Joe Barnes calls back from somewhere nearby: "July fifteenth, seven P.M."

From the porch Chuck Becker adds loudly, "God bless us all! And God bless America!"

Several voices murmur "Amen." Looking up and away with a sigh of mild annoyance, Peter Simpson happens at just that moment to see a meteor streak left to right across the moonless, brightly constellated eastern sky.

So what? he asks himself.

So nothing.

Us/Them

T O HIS WIFE, his old comrades at the *Avon County News,* or his acquaintances from over at the College, Gerry Frank might say, for example, "Flaubert once claimed that what he'd *really* like to write is a novel about Nothing." In his regular feature column, however — in the small-town weekly newspaper of a still largely rural Maryland county — it would have to read something like this:

FRANK OPINIONS, by Gerald Frank
Us/Them

The celebrated 19th-century French novelist Gustave Flaubert, author of *Madame Bovary,* once remarked that what he would *really* like to write is a novel about Nothing.

After which he might acknowledge that the same was looking to be the case with this week's column, although its author still hoped to make it not quite about Nothing, but rather ("as the celebrated Elizabethan poet/playwright William Shakespeare put it in the title of one of his comedies") about Much *Ado* About Nothing.

There: That should work as a lead, a hook, a kick-start from which the next sentences and paragraphs will flow (pardon Gerry's mixed metaphor) — and voilà, another "Frank Opinions" column to be e-mailed after lunch to Editor Tom Chadwick at the *News* and put to bed for the week.

But they *don't* come, those next sentences — *haven't* come, now, for the third work-morning in a row — for the ever-clearer reason that their semiretired would-be author hasn't figured out yet what he wants to write about what he wants to write about, namely: Us(slash)Them. *In Frank's opinion,* he now types experimentally in his column's characteristic third-person viewpoint, *what he needs is a meaningful connection between the "Us/ Them" theme, much on his mind lately for reasons presently to be explained, and either or all of (1) a troubling disconnection, or anyhow an increasing distinction/difference/whatever, between, on this side of that slash, him and his wife — Gerald and Joan Frank, 14 Shad Run Road #212, Heron Bay Estates, Stratford, MD 21600 — and on its other side their pleasant gated community in general and their Shad Run condominium neighborhood in particular; (2) his recently increasing difficulty — after so many productive decades of newspaper work! — in coming up with fresh ideas for the F.O. column; and/or (3) the irresistible parallel to his growing (shrinking?) erectile dysfunction* [but never mind *that* as a column topic!].

Maybe fill in some background, to mark time while waiting for the Muse of Feature Columns to get off her ever-lazier butt and down to business? Gerry Frank here, Reader-if-this-gets-written: erstwhile journalist, not quite seventy but getting there fast. Born and raised in a small town near the banks of the Potomac in southern Maryland in World War Two time, where and when the most ubiquitous Us/Them had been Us White Folks as distinct from Them Coloreds, until supplanted after Pearl Harbor by Us Allies versus Them Japs and Nazis (note the difference between that "versus" and the earlier, more ambivalent "as distinct from," a difference to which we may return). Crossed the Chesapeake after high school to Stratford College, on the Free State's Eastern Shore (B.A. English 1957), then shifted north to New Jersey for the next quarter-century to do reportage and editorial work for the *Trenton Times;* also to marry his back-home sweetheart, make babies and help parent them, learn a few life lessons the hard way while doubtless failing to learn some others, and eventually — at age fifty, when those offspring were off to college themselves and learning their own life lessons — to divorce (irreconcilable differences). Had the immeasurably good fortune the very next year, at a Stratford homecoming, to meet alumna Joan Gibson (B.A. English 1967), herself likewise between life chapters just then (forty, divorced, no children, copyediting for her hometown newspaper, the *Wilmington* [Delaware] *News Journal*). So hit it off together from Day (and Night) One that after just a couple more dates they were spending every weekend together in her town or his, or back in the Stratford to which they shared a fond attachment — and whereto, not long after their marriage in the following year, they moved: Gerry to associate-edit the *Avon County News* and Joan ditto the College's alumni magazine, *The Stratfordian.*

And some fifteen years later here they are, happy with each other and grateful to have been spared not only direct involvement in the nation's several bloody wars during their life-decades, but also such personal catastrophes as loss of children, untimely death of parents or siblings, and devastating accident, disease, or other extraordinary misfortune. Their connection with Gerry's pair of thirty-something children, Joan's elder and younger siblings, and associated spouses and offspring is warm, though geographically attenuated (one couple in Oregon, another in Texas, others in Vermont and Alabama). Husband and wife much enjoy each other's company, their work, their modest TINK prosperity (Two Incomes, No [dependent] Kids), and their leisure activities: hiking, wintertime workouts in the Heron Bay Club's well-equipped fitness center and summertime swimming in its Olympic-size pool, vacation travel to other countries back in more U.S.-friendly times, and here and there in North America since 9/11 and (in Gerald Frank's Frank Opinion) the Bush administration's Iraq War fiasco (U.S./"Them"?). Also their, uh . . . friends?

Well: No F.O. column yet in any of *that*, that Gerry can see. While typing on from pure professional habit, however, he perpends that paragraph-ending word above, flanked by suspension points before and question mark after: something to circle back to, maybe, after avoiding it for a while longer by reviewing some other senses of that slash dividing Us from Them. Peter Simpson, a fellow they know from Rockfish Reach who teaches at the College and (like Joan Frank) serves on the Heron Bay Estates Community Association, did a good job of that at one of HBECA's recent open meetings, the main agenda item whereof was a proposed hefty assessment for upgrading the development's entrance gates. As most readers of "Frank Opinions" know, we are for better or worse the only gated community in Avon County, perhaps the only one on Maryland's Eastern Shore. Just off the state highway a few miles south of Stratford, Heron Bay Estates is bounded on two irregular sides by branching tidal tributaries of the Matahannock River (Heron and Spartina Creeks, Rockfish and Oyster Coves, Blue Crab Bight, Shad Run), on a third side by a wooded preserve of pines, hemlocks, and sweet gums screening a sturdy chain-link fence, and on its highway side by a seven-foot-high masonry wall atop an attractively landscaped berm, effectively screening the development from both highway noise and casual view. Midway along this side is our entrance road, Heron Bay Boulevard, accessed via a round-the-clock manned gatehouse with two exit lanes on one side, their gates raised and lowered automatically by electric eye, and two gated entry lanes on the other: one on the left for service vehicles and visitors, who must register with the gatekeeper and display temporary entrance passes on their dashboards, and one on the right for residents and nonresident Club members, whose cars have HBE decals annually affixed to their windshields. So successful has the development been that in the twenty-odd years since its initial layout it has grown to be the county's second-largest residential entity after the small town of Stratford itself—with the consequence that homeward-bound residents these days not infrequently find themselves backed up four or five cars deep while the busy gatekeepers simultaneously check in visitors in one lane and look for resident decals in the other before pushing the lift-gate button. Taking their cue from the various E-Z Pass devices commonly employed nowadays at bridge and highway toll booths, the developers, Tidewater Communities, Inc., suggested to the Association that an economical alternative to a second gatehouse farther down the highway side (which would require expensive construction, an additional entrance road, and more 24/7 staffing) would be a third entry lane at the present gatehouse, its gate to be triggered automatically by electronic scansion of a bar-code decal on each resident vehicle's left rear window.

Most of the Association members and other attendees, Joan and Gerry Frank included, thought this a practical and economical fix to the entrance-backup problem, and when put to the seven members for a vote (one representative from each of HBE's neighborhoods plus one at-large tie-breaker), the motion passed by a margin of six to one. In the pre-vote open discussion, however, objections to it were raised from diametrically opposed viewpoints. On the one hand, Mark Matthews from Spartina Pointe — the recentest member of the Association, whose new weekend-and-vacation home in that high-end neighborhood was probably the grandest residence in all of Heron Bay Estates — declared that in view of HBE's ongoing development (controversial luxury condominiums proposed for the far end of the preserve), what we need is not only that automatic bar-code lane at the Heron Bay Boulevard entrance, but the afore-mentioned second gated entrance at the south end of the highway wall as well, and perhaps a third for service and employee vehicles only, to be routed discreetly through the wooded preserve itself.

In the bluff, down-home manner to which he inclined, even as CEO of a Baltimore investment-counseling firm, "Way it is now," that bald and portly, flush-faced fellow complained, "we get waked up at six A.M. by the groundskeepers and golf course maintenance guys reporting for work with the radios booming in their rusty old Chevys and pickups, *woomf woomf woomf,* y'know? Half of 'em undocumented aliens, quote unquote, but never mind *that* if it keeps the costs down. And then when we-all that live here come back from wherever, the sign inside the entrance says Welcome Home, but our welcome is a six-car backup at the gate, like crossing the Bay Bridge without an E-Z Pass. I say we deserve better'n that."

"Hear hear!" somebody cheered from the back of the Community Association's open-meeting room: Joe Barnes, I think it was, from Rockfish Reach. But my wife, at her end of the members' table up front, objected: "Easy to say if you don't mind a fifty percent assessment hike to build and staff those extra entrances! But I suspect that many of us will feel the pinch to finance just that automatic third entry lane at the gatehouse — which I'm personally all for, but nothing beyond that unless *it* gets backed up."

A number of her fellow members nodded agreement, and one of them added, "As for the racket, we just need to tell the gatekeepers and the maintenance foremen to be stricter about the no-loud-noise rule for service people checking in."

Mark Matthews made a little show of closing his eyes and shaking his head no. The room in general, however, murmured approval. Which perhaps encouraged Amanda Todd — a friend of Joan's and an Association member from Blue Crab Bight — to surprise us all by saying "Gates and more gates! What do we need *any* of them for, including the ones we've got already?"

Mild consternation in the audience and among her fellow members, turning to relieved amusement when Joan teased, "Because we're a gated community?" But "Really," Ms. Todd persisted, "those TCI ads for Heron Bay are downright embarrassing, with their 'exclusive luxury lifestyles' and such. Even to call this place Heron Bay *Estates* is embarrassing, if you ask me. But then to have to pass through customs every time we come and go, and phone the gatehouse whenever we're expecting a visitor! Plus the secondary nighttime gates at some of our neighborhood entrances, like Oyster Cove, and those push-button driveway gates in Spartina Pointe . . . Three gates to pass through, in an area where crime is practically nonexistent!"

"Don't forget the garage door opener," Mark Matthews reminded her sarcastically. "That makes *four* entrances for some of us, even before we unlock the house door. Mindy and I are all for it."

"Hear hear!" his ally called again from the back of the room, where someone else reminded all hands that we weren't *entirely* crime-free: "Remember that Peeping Tom a few years back? Slipped past the main gatehouse and our Oyster Cove night gates too, that we don't use anymore like we did back then, and we never did catch him. But still . . ."

"You're proving my point," Amanda argued. Whereupon her husband — the writer George Newett, also from the College — came to her support by quoting the Psalmist: "Lift up your heads, O ye gates! Even lift them up, ye everlasting doors, and the King of Glory shall come in!"

"Amen," she said appreciatively. "And *leave* 'em lifted, I say, like those ones at Oyster Cove. No other development around here has gates. Why should we?"

"Because we're *us*," somebody offered, "with a community pool and tennis courts and bike paths that aren't for public use. If you like the other kind, maybe you should move to one of *them*."

Mark Matthews seconded that suggestion with a pleased head-nod. But "All I'm saying," Ms. Todd persisted, less assertively, "— as Robert Frost puts it in one of his poems? — is, quote, 'Before I built a wall, I'd ask to know what I was walling in and walling out, and to whom I'm likely to give offense,' end of quote. Somebody just mentioned *us* and *them:* Who exactly is the Them that all these walls and gates are keeping out?"

To lighten things a bit, I volunteered, "That Them is Us, Amanda, waiting at the gate until we get our Heron Bay E-Z Pass gizmo up and running. Shall we put it to a vote?"

"Not quite yet, Gerry," said Peter Simpson — also from the College, as has been mentioned, and chairman of the Association as well as its member from Rockfish Reach. "Let's be sure that everybody's had his/her say on the matter. Including myself for a minute, if I may?"

Nobody objected. A trim and affable fellow in his fifties, Pete is popular as well as respected both in the Association and on campus, where he's some sort of dean as well as a professor. "I'll try not to lecture," he promised with a smile. "I just want to say that while I understand where both Mark and Amanda are coming from, my own inclination, like Joan's, is to proceed incrementally, starting with the bar-code scanner gate and hoping that'll do the trick, for a few years anyhow." He pushed up his rimless specs. "What's really on my mind, though, now that it's come up, is this Us-slash-Them business. We have to accept that some of us, like Amanda, live here because they like the place *despite* its being a gated community, while others of us, like Mark, live here in part precisely *because* it's gated, especially if they're not full-time residents. The great majority of us, I'd bet, either don't *mind* the gate thing (except when it gets backed up!) or sort of like the little extra privacy, the way we appreciate our routine security patrols even though we're lucky enough not to live near a high-crime area. It's another Heron Bay amenity, like our landscaping and our golf course. What we need to watch out for (and here comes the lecture I promised I'd spare you) is when that slash between Us and Them moves from being a simple distinction — like Us Rockfish Reach residents and Them Oyster Cove or Spartina Pointers, or Us Marylanders and Them Pennsylvanians and Delawareans — and becomes Us not merely *distinct* from Them, but more or less *superior* to Them, as has all too often been the case historically with whites and blacks, or rich and poor, or for that matter men and women."

Up with the glasses again. Mark Matthews rolled his eyes, but most present seemed interested in Pete's argument. "At its worst," he went on, "that slash between Us and Them comes to mean Us *versus* Them, as in race riots and revolutions and wars in general. But even here it's worth remembering that *versus* doesn't always necessarily mean inherently superior: It can be like Us versus Them in team sports, or the Yeas versus the Nays in a debating club, or some of the town/gown issues at the College that we try to mediate without claiming that either side is *superior* to the other."

Here he took the glasses off, as if to signal that the sermon was approaching its close. "I'm sure I'm not alone in saying that some of Debbie's and my closest friends live outside these gates of ours."

"Amen," Joan said on his behalf. After which, and apologizing again for nattering on so, Pete called for a vote authorizing the Association to solicit bids and award a contract for construction of an automatically gated HBE Pass third lane at our development's entrance. When the motion passed, six to one, Amanda Todd good-naturedly reminded Mark Matthews, the lone dissenter, that "Us versus You doesn't mean we don't love you, Mark." To which that broad-beamed but narrow-minded fellow retorted, "You College people, I swear."

"Objection!" Amanda's husband called out.

"Sustained," declared Peter Simpson, rising from his chair and gathering the spec sheets and other papers spread out before him. "No need to pursue it, and thank you all for coming and making your opinions known." Offering his hand to Matthews then, with a smile, "Here's to democracy, Mark, and parliamentary procedure. Agreed?"

"Whatever."

And that had been that, for then. But en route back along sycamore-lined Heron Bay Boulevard to our condominium in "Shad Row," as we like to call it (punning on that seasonal Chesapeake delicacy), we Franks had tsked and sighed at Mark Matthews's overbearing small-mindedness versus Pete Simpson's more generous spirit and eminently reasonable review of the several senses of Us/Them. "Like when people born and raised in Stratford talk about 'us locals' and 'them c'meres,'" Joan said, using the former's term for out-of-towners who "come here" to retire or to enjoy a second home. "Sometimes it's a putdown, sometimes it's just a more or less neutral distinction, depending."

"And even when it's a putdown," her husband agreed, "sometimes it's just a good-humored tease between friends or neighbors — unlike Lady Broad-Ass's Us/Thems in our condo sessions," he added, referring to his Shad Run Condominium Association colleague Rachel Broadus, a hefty and opinionated widow-lady who, two years ago, had vehemently opposed the sale of unit 117 to an openly gay late-middle-aged couple from D.C., early retired from careers in the federal government's General Services Administration — even letting the prospective buyers know by anonymous letter that while it was beyond the Association's authority to forbid the sale, homosexuals were not welcome in Heron Bay Estates. A majority of the Association shared her feelings and had been relieved when the offended couple withdrew their purchase offer, although most agreed with Gerry that the unsigned letter was reprehensible; he alone had spoken on the pair's behalf, or at least had opposed the opposition to them. When in the following year Ms. Broadus had similarly inveighed against the sale of unit 218 to a dapper Indian-American pharmacist and his wife ("Next thing you know it'll be Mexicans and blacks, and there goes the neighborhood"), he'd had more company in objecting to her objection, and the Raghavans had come to be well liked by nearly all of their neighbors. "Even so," Gerry now reminded his wife, "Broad-Ass couldn't resist saying 'Mind you, Ger, I don't have anything against a nice Jewish couple like you and Joan. But *Hindus?*'"

Joan groaned at the recollection — who on first hearing from Gerry of this misattribution had said, "You should've showed her your foreskinned shlong already. Oy." Or, they'd agreed, he could have quoted the Irish-American songwriter George M. Cohan's reply to a resort-hotel desk clerk in the 1920s who refused him a room, citing the establishment's ban on Jewish guests: "You thought I was a Jew," said the composer of "The Yankee Doodle Boy," "and I thought you were a gentleman. We were both mistaken." Rachel Broadus, they supposed, had heard of Anne Frank and had readily generalized from that famed Holocaust victim's last name, perhaps pretending even to herself that the Them to which she assigned the Shad Run Franks was not meant pejoratively. It was easy to imagine her declaring that "some of her best friends," et cetera. Gerry himself had used that edged cliché, in quotes — "Some of Our Best Friends . . ." — as the heading of a

"Frank Opinions" column applauding the progress of Stratford's middle-class African Americans from near invisibility to active representation on the Town Council, the Avon County School Board, and the faculties not only of the local public schools but of the College and the private Fenton Day School as well.

All the above, however, is past history: the HBECA lift-gate meeting and us Franks' return to Shad Run Road for a merlot nightcap on our second-story porch overlooking the moonlit creek (where no shad have been known to run during our residency) before the ten o'clock TV news, bedtime, and another flaccid semi-fuck, Gerry's "Jimmy" less than fully erect and Joan's "Susie" less than wetly welcoming. "Never mind that pair of old farts," Joan had sighed, kissing him goodnight before turning away to sleep: "They're Them; we're still Us." Whoever *that's* getting to be, he'd said to himself — for he really has, since virtual retirement, been ever more preoccupied with his approaching old age and his inevitable, already noticeable decline. To her, however, he wondered merely, "D'you suppose they're trying to tell us something?"

"Whatever it is," she answered sleepily, "don't put it in the column, okay?"

The column: Past history too is his nattering on about all the above to his computer for four work-mornings already, and now a fifth, in search of a "Frank Opinions" piece about all this Us/Them stuff. By now he has moved on from Joan's "Us Franks" as distinct from "Them body parts of ours," or the singular "I-Gerry/Thou-'Jimmy,'" to Gerry's-Mind/Gerry's-Body and thence (within the former) to Gerry's-Ego/Gerry's-Id+Superego, and while mulling these several Us/Thems and I/Thous of the concept Mind, he has duly noted that although such distinctions are *made* by our minds, it by no means follows that they're "all in our minds."

Blah blah blah: Won't readers of the *Avon County News* be thrilled to hear it?

Yet another Us/Them now occurs to him (just what he needed!): It's a standing levity in Heron Bay Estates that most of its male inhabitants happen to be called familiarly by one-syllable first names and their wives by two-: Mark and Mindy Matthews, Joe and Judy Barnes, Pete and Debbie Simpson, Dave and Lisa Bergman, Dick and Susan Felton — the list goes on. But while we Franks, perhaps by reflex, are occasionally fitted to this peculiar template ("Ger" and "Joanie"), we're normally called Gerry and Joan, in exception to the rule: an Us distinct from, though not opposed to, its Them.

So? So nothing. Has Gerald "Gerry" Frank mentioned his having noticed, years ago, that his normal pulse rate matches almost exactly the tick of seconds on his watch dial, so closely that he can measure less-than-a-minute intervals by his heartbeat? And that therefore, as of his recent sixty-eighth birthday, he had lived for 24,837 days (including 17 leap days) at an average rate of 1,400 pulses per day, or a total of 34,771,800, give or take a few thousand for periods of physical exertion or unusual quiescence? By which same calculation he reckons himself to have been mulling these who-gives-a-shit Us/Thems for some 7,200 heartbeats' worth of days now, approaching beat by beat not only his ultimate demise but, more immediately, Tom Chadwick's deadline, and feeling no closer to a column than he did five days ago.

Maybe a column about that? Lame idea.

Tick. Tick. Tick. Tick. Tick.

He believes he did mention, a few thousand pulses past, that the Shad Run Franks, while on entirely cordial terms with their workmates and with ninety-nine percent of their fellow Heron Bay Estaters, have no *friends*, really, if by friends one means people whom one enjoys having over for drinks and dinner or going out with to a restaurant, not to mention actually vacation-traveling together, as they see some of their neighbors doing. They used to have friends like that, separately in their pre-Us lives and together in the earliest, pre-Stratford period of their marriage. Over the years since, however, for whatever reasons, their social life has atrophied: annual visits to and from their far-flung family, lunch with a colleague now and then (although they both work mainly at home these days), the occasional office cocktail party or HBE community social — that's about it. They don't particularly *approve* of this state of affairs, mildly wish it were otherwise, but have come to accept, more or less, that outside the workplace that's who they are, or have become: more comfortable with just Us than with Them.

As if his busy fingers have a mind of their own, *To be quite frank, Reader,* he now sees appearing on his computer screen, *old Gerry hasn't been being quite Frank with you about certain things. E.g.:*

— He and his mate share another, very different and entirely secret life, the revelation whereof would scandalize all Stratford and Heron Bay Estates, not to mention their family.

— Or they *don't,* of course, but could sometimes half wish they did, just for the hell of it.

— Or they *don't* so wish or even half wish, for God's sake! Who does this nutcase columnist take us for, that he could even *imagine* either of them so wishing?

— Or he has just learned that the precious, the indispensable Other Half of our Us has been diagnosed with . . . oh, advanced, inoperable pancreatic cancer? While *he* sits scared shitless on his butt counting his heartbeats, her killer cells busily metastasize through that dearest of bodies. Maybe a dozen thousand ever-more-wretched tick-ticks to go, at most, until The End — of her, therefore of Us, therefore of him.

— Or he's just making all this crap up. Trying it out. Thinking the unthinkable, perhaps in vain hope of its exorcism, or at least forestallment. But such tomfoolery fools no one. While his right hand types *no one,* his left rummages in a drawer of the adjacent inkjet-printer stand for the reassuring feel of the loaded nine-millimeter automatic pistol that he keeps in there for "self-defense": i.e., for defending Joan and Gerry Frank yet a while longer from murder/suicide — which they agree they'd resort to in any such scenario as that terminal-cancer one above-invoked — by reminding himself that they have the means and the will to do it, if and when the time comes.

But they don't — have the means, at least; at least not by gunfire. There is no pistol, never has been; we Franks aren't the gun-owning sort. Should push come to shove *chez nous,* in our frank opinion we'd go the route that Dick and Susan Felton went last year: double suicide (nobody knows why) by automobile exhaust fumes in the closed garage of their empty-nest house in Rockfish Reach, with not even a goodbye note to their traumatized, life-disrupted offspring.

Well, we guess we'd leave a note.

Maybe this is it?

Nah. Still . . .

Deadline a-coming: Tick. Tick.

Deathline? Tick.

FRANK OPINIONS: Us/Them
or,
Much Ado About

Assisted Living

L IKE ANY NORMAL PERSON, Tim Manning (speaking) used to think and speak of himself as "I," or "me." *Don't ask me,* the old ex–history teacher would start off one of his "His-Stories" by typing on his computer, *who I think is reading or hearing this* — and then on he'd ramble about his and Margie's Oyster Cove community in Heron Bay Estates, and the interesting season when they and their neighborhood were bedeviled (or at least had reason to believe they were) by a Peeping Tom. Stuff like that. *I grabbed the big flashlight from atop the fridge,* he would write, *told Margie to call Security, and stepped out back to check.* Or *"I do sort of miss those days," Margie said to me one evening a few years later* ...

That sort of thing.

But that was Back Then: from the Depression-era 1930s, when Timothy Manning and Margaret Jacobs were born, a few years and Chesapeake counties apart, through their separate childhoods and adolescences in World War Two time, their trial romances and (separate) sexual initiations in late high school and early college years, their fortuitous meeting and impulsive marriage in the American mid-1950s, their modest contributions to the postwar baby boom, and their not unsuccessful careers (he guesses they'd agree) as high school teacher (him), suburban-D.C. realtor (her), and life partners (them!). Followed, in their sixties and the century's eighties, by their phased retirement to Heron Bay Estates: at first Bay-Bridge-hopping between their city house near Washington and their new weekend/vacation duplex in Heron Bay's Oyster Cove neighborhood, then swapping the former for a more maintenance-free condominium halfway between D.C. and Annapolis (where Margie's real-estate savvy found them a rare bargain in that busy market), and ultimately —when wife joined husband in full retirement—selling that condo at a healthy profit, unloading as best they could whatever of its furnishings the new owners had no interest in buying, and settling contentedly into their modest villa at 1010 Oyster Cove Court for the remainder of their active life together.

Amounting, as it turned out, to a mere dozen-plus years, which feels to Tim Manning as he types these words like about that many months at most. Where did the years go? He can scarcely remember—as has been becoming the case with more and more things every year. Where'd he put the car keys? Or for that matter their old station wagon itself, parked somewhere in the Stratford shopping plaza that he still manages to drive to now and then for miscellaneous provisions? As of this sentence he hasn't yet reached that classic early-Alzheimer's symptom of forgetting which keys are for what, or which car out there is their Good Gray Ghost (excuse him: *his* GGG, damn it, now that Indispensable Margie—his "better two-thirds," he used to call her—is no more), but he sure forgets plenty of other things these days.

E.g., exactly what "Tim Manning" was about to say before this particular His-Story wandered. Something having to do with how—beginning with the couple's reluctant Final Move three years ago from dear "old" Oyster Cove to Bayview Manor and especially since Margie's unassimilable death just one year later —he has found himself standing ever more outside himself: prodding, directing, *assisting* Tim Manning through the increasingly mechanical routines of his daily existence. Talk about Assisted "Living" . . .

And who, exactly, is the Assistant? Not "I" these days, he was saying, but old T.M.: same guy who'll get on with telling this story if he can recollect what the hell it is.

Well, for starters: In a way, he supposes, "T.M." is replacing (as best he can't) irreplaceable Margie as Tim Manning's living-assistant. In the forty-nine and eleven-twelfths years of their married life, she and he constantly assisted each other with everything from changing their babies' diapers to changing jobs, habitations, outworn habits, and ill-considered opinions as their time went by. In more recent years, as her body and his mind faltered, he more and more assisted her with physical matters — her late-onset diabetes, near-crippling arthritis and various other -itises, their attendant medicos and medications — and ever more depended on *her* assistance in the memory and attention departments as his Senior Moments increased in frequency and duration. While at the same time, of course, they continued to assist each other in the making of life decisions.

Such as . . .

Ahem: *Such as?*

Sorry there: got sidetracked, he guesses, from some sidetrack or other. *Such as,* he sees he was saying, their no-longer-avoidable joint recognition — after some years of due denial, so unappealing were the alternatives — that what with Margie now all but wheelchaired and her husband sometimes unable to locate the various lists that he'd come to depend on to remember practically everything, even the housekeeping of their Oyster Cove duplex was becoming more than they could manage. Time to check out Assisted (ugh!) Living.

Not long after the turn of the new millennium, they apprised their two grown children of that reluctant intention, and both the Son in St. Louis and the Daughter in Detroit (that alliteration, their father was fond of saying, helped him remember which lived where) dutifully offered to scout suitable such operations in their respective cities. But while the elder Mannings quite enjoyed their occasional visits to Bachelor-girl Barbara and

Married-but-childless Michael, they felt at home only in tidewater country, where they still had friends and former workmates. Dislocation enough to exchange house and yard, longtime good neighbors, and the amenities of Heron Bay Estates for a small apartment, communal meals, and a less independent life, most probably across the Matahannock Bridge, in another county. Although they went through the motions of collecting brochures up and down the peninsula from several "continuing care retirement communities" whose advertisements they'd noted in the weekly *Avon County News* ("Quality retirement lifestyles! Gourmet dining! On-site medical center! A strong sense of caring and community!"), and even took a couple of Residency-Counselor-Guided Personal Tours, they agreed from the outset that their likeliest choice would be Bayview Manor. Situated no farther from the town of Stratford on the river's east side than was Heron Bay Estates on its west, Bayview was a project of the same busy developer, Tidewater Communities, Inc. It was generally regarded as being at least the peer of any similar institution on the Shore, and among its residents were a number of other ex–HBE dwellers no longer able or inclined to maintain their former "lifestyles" in Shad Run or Oyster Cove, much less in the development's upper-scale detached-house neighborhoods. Depending upon availability — and one's inclinations and financial resources — one could apply for a one- or two-bedroom cottage there (with or without den) or choose from several levels of one- and two-bedroom apartments, all with a variety of meal plans. Standard amenities included an indoor pool, a fitness center, crafts and other activities rooms, a beauty salon, gift shop, and branch bank office, and periodic shuttle service to and from Stratford; also available were such extra-cost options as linen and personal laundry service, weekly or biweekly housekeeping, a "professionally staffed" Medical Center, and chauffeured personal transportation. For a couple like the Mannings who didn't yet require *fully* assisted living, the then-current "base price entry fees" ranged from $100,000 for a small one-bedroom apartment (refundable minus two percent for each month of occupancy) to just under $500,000 for a high-end two-bedroom cottage with den (ninety percent refundable after reoccupancy of unit by new resident when current occupants shift to Med Center residence or to grave). Housekeeping and other service fees ranged from $2,000 to $4,000 monthly, and meal plans from individual dining room meal charges for those who preferred to continue preparing most of their own meals at home to about $800 monthly for a couple's thrice-daily feed in the dining hall.

"Jesus," Tim wondered. "Can we even consider it?"

They could, his wife (the family investment manager) assured him. But what about the fact that Bayview, no less than the other places they'd checked out, got its share of bad reviews as well as good? On the one hand were those happy Golden Agers in the brochure photos, duly apportioned by gender and ethnicity and handsomely decked out in "country club casual" attire while bird-watching or flower-arranging, painting and quilting and pottery-making, or smiling at one another across bridge and dining tables. On the other, such Internet chatroom grumbles both from some residents and from their relatives as *The food sucks, actually, if you've been used to eating* real *food,* and *Be warned: It's college dorm life all over again — at age eighty!,* and *Frankly, it's the effing pits.* The best Margie and Tim could guess was that temperamentally upbeat, outgoing, people-enjoying types were likely to find their continuing-care situation at least as much to their liking as what had immediately preceded it in their *curriculum vitae,* while the more easily dissatisfied were, well, dissatisfied. They themselves, they supposed, fell somewhere between those poles.

"May we not fall on our geriatric asses between them," they more or less prayed; then gave each other a determinedly cheerful high-five over white wine and champignon cheese at Happy Hour on their screened porch overlooking Oyster Cove, and took the plunge: what they'd come to call the Old Farts' B.M. Move. Given the ever-rising value of Heron Bay real estate, Margie figured they could list for $400K the free-and-clear villa for which they'd paid slightly more than half that amount fifteen years ago, take out a $300K mortgage on it to finance either a midrange Bayview cottage or one of those high-end apartments, pay off the mortgage shortly thereafter when good old 1010 Oyster Cove Court sells for, say, $375K, and shift across the river with most of their present furnishings at a tidy profit — the more since ex-realtor Margie would be handling the sale and saving them the seven percent agent's commission.

Thus the plan, and thus it came to pass — even a bit better than their projection, but at their age a wrench and hassle all the same. In a mere five months, the villa found a buyer for $380K, and between its sale and closing dates a high-end Bayview apartment became available, its widowed and emphysemic tenant obliged to move into the Manor's Medical Center. While they'd thought that "transitioning" to one of the cottages might be less of a jolt, they took the apartment, reminding themselves that they had, after all, rather enjoyed that interim condominium over near Annapolis, and that as they grew older and less able than presently, the apartment would be more convenient — to that same Medical Center, among other things. So okay, they would miss gardening, outdoor barbecuing, and the relative privacy of a house. But what the hell, they had adjusted readily enough back in the '80s from detached house to duplex living; they could hack it in a comfortable apartment.

So hack it they did: quite admirably all in all, given Margie's physical limitations. As their nation enmired itself in Afghanistan and Iraq, the Mannings bade goodbye to their Oyster Cove neighbors and other Heron Bay friends (who were, after all, a mere thirty-minute drive from Bayview), scaled down from two cars in a garage to just Old Faithful in a designated parking-lot space, and packed and unpacked their stuff for what must surely be the last time. Over the next year-and-a-bit — from late summer 2003 to mid-autumn '04 — they repositioned their furniture and knick-knacks, rehung their wall art, reshelved as many of their books as they had room for, donated the rest to the Avon County Library, and gamely set about making new acquaintances, sampling the

Manor's sundry activities, and accustoming themselves to their start-out meal plan: breakfasts and lunches together in the apartment, dinners in the dining hall except now and then in a Stratford restaurant. Pretty lucky they were, T.M. supposes in retrospect, to have made their "B.M. Move" when they did, before the nationwide housing-market slump just a few years later, not to mention before the recent, all-but-total destruction of Heron Bay Estates by that spinoff tornado from Tropical Storm Giorgio in an otherwise eventless hurricane season. And most certainly not to mention ... the Unmentionable, which however is this His-Story's defining event and therefore *must* be mentioned, to say the least, not far hence.

And a pretty good job they did, all in all (he believes he was saying), of making the best of their new life. Okay, so they shook their heads occasionally at the relentless professional cheeriness of some of the Bayview staff; and they had no taste for the bridge tournaments, square-dance and bingo nights, and some other items on the Activities menu; and the dining hall fare, while it had its fans, was in their opinion mostly blah. But on the plus side were some of the Manor's sightseeing excursions to places like the du Pont estate's Winterthur Garden, up near Wilmington, and the Chesapeake Bay Maritime Museum down in St. Michaels (the Mannings had got out of the habit of such touring), the Happy Hour and dinnertime socializing in the Blue Heron Lounge and dining hall, which one could do as much or little of as one chose (sipping from one's personal wine supply at the bar), and the comforting-indeed knowledge that, if needed, assistance was as near at hand as the Help Alarm button conveniently located in every residence unit. They were doing all right, they assured their children and their Heron Bay Estates friends; they were doing all right ...

Until, on a certain chill-but-sunny midmorning in November 2004, as suddenly and without warning as that above-mentioned fluke tornado two years later, out of nowhere came the End of Everything. After a late breakfast of orange juice, English muffins, and coffee (they'd been up past their usual bedtime the night before, watching with unsurprised dismay the presidential election returns on TV), Tim had withdrawn to his computer desk in the apartment's guest-bedroom/study to exchange disappointed e-mails with Son and Daughter, who shared their parents' stock-liberal persuasion. Margie, still in her nightclothes, lingered at table over a second coffee to read the *Baltimore Sun's* painful details of John Kerry's unsuccessful bid to thwart George W. Bush's reelection — a disaster for the nation, in the Mannings' opinion — after which she meant to move as usual to *her* computer in their little den/office/library to do likewise and attend to some family business before lunch and whatever. But he had no sooner sat down and booted up than he heard a crash out there and, bolting kitchenward, found his without-whom-nothing life partner, his bride of half a century minus one month, his Margie!Margie!Margie! face-down and motionless on the breakfast-nook floor tiles, coffee from the shattered porcelain mug staining her nightgown and the crumpled pages of the *Sun.* With a half-strangled cry he ran to his fallen mate, her eyes open but not moving, her face frozen with alarm. Some years previously, the Mannings had signed up at the Heron Bay Estates Community Activities Center for a half-day course in Cardiopulmonary Resuscitation and Warning Signs of Stroke and Cardiac Arrest, and had vowed to review the various drills together at least annually thereafter — but never got around to doing so. Now he desperately felt for a pulse, put his face near hers to check for respiration, and detected neither; dashed to locate and press that Help button (on the wall beside the main-bath toilet); dashed back to try whether he could recollect anything whatever of the CPR routine; pressed his mouth to Margie's in what was meant to be some sort of forced inhalation but dissolved into a groaning kiss and then collapsed into a sobbing, helpless last embrace.

Helpless, yes: He still damns Tim Manning for that. Not that anything he or anyone else might have done would likely have saved her, but had their situations been reversed — had the thitherto undetected and now fatally ruptured aneurysm (as the

Cause of Death turned out to be: not, after all, the news of Bush and Cheney's reelection) been his instead of hers — Margie Manning, for all her alarm and grief, would no doubt have taken some charge of things. She'd have dialed 911, he bets, and/or the establishment's Medical Center; would have shouted down the hallway for help and pounded on their neighbors' doors — all the usual desperate things that desperate people in such situations typically do, even if in vain. And would then have somehow collected herself enough to deal as needed with Med Center and other Bayview functionaries; to notify children and friends, comfort and be comforted by them, handle the obligatory farewell visits, and manage the disposition of the Departed's remains and estate and the rearrangement of the Survivor's life. But except back in his high school history-teaching classroom before his retirement and in a few other areas (tending their former lawn and shrubbery, making handyman repairs, presiding over their Oyster Cove cookouts), Margie was ever the more capable Manning — especially in emotionally charged situations, which tended to rattle and de-capacitate her husband. Now (i.e., then, on Election Day + 1, 2004) he lay literally floored, clutching his unbelievably dead mate's body as if he too had been stroke-stricken, which he desperately wished he *had* been. Unable to bring himself even to respond to the Manor's alarm-bell First Responder (from the nurses' station over in Assisted Living) when she presently came knocking, calling, doorbell-ringing, and doorknob-twisting, he lay closed-eyed and mute while the woman fetched out her passkey, turned the deadbolt, and pressed in with first-aid kit and urgent questions.

Don't ask T.M. how things went from there. Death is, after all, a not-unusual event in elder-care establishments, whose staff will likely be more familiar with His visitations than will the visited. As it happens, neither Tim nor for that matter Margie had had any prior Death Management experience: Their respective parents' last days, funeral arrangements, and estate disposition had been handled by older siblings, whose own life closures were then overseen by competent grown offspring who lived nearby and shared their parents' lives. The Bayview responder — an able young black woman named Gloria, as Tim sort of remembers — knelt to examine the pair of them, spoke to him in a raised voice, cell-phoned or walkie-talkied for assistance, spoke to him some more, asking questions that perhaps he answered or at least endeavored to, and maybe did a few nurse-type things on the spot. After a while he was off the floor: in a chair, perhaps mumbling apologies for his helplessness while Margie's body was gurneyed over to the Med Center to await further disposition. Although unable to take action, not to mention taking charge, he eventually became able at least to reply to questions. *To be notified?* Son in St. Louis, Daughter in Detroit. *Funeral arrangements?* None, thankee. *None?* None: Both Mannings preferred surcease *sans* fuss: no funeral, no grave or other marker, no memorial service. *You sure of that?* Sure: Organs to be harvested for recycling if usable and convenient; otherwise forget it. Remaining remains to be cremated — and no urn of ashes or ritual scattering, *s.v.p.;* just ditch the stuff. All her clothes and other personal effects to the nearest charity willing to come get them. Oh: and if Nurse happened to have in her kit a shot of something to take him out too, they could do a two-for-one right then and there and spare all hands more bother down the road.

Because what the fuck (as he explained to S-in-S and D-in-D when both were "B-in-B": Billeted, for the nonce, in Bayview): He and Margie had been fortunate in their connection and had relished their decades together. Unlike their Oyster Cove neighbor Ethel Bailey, for example, with her metastasized cervical cancer, Margie had been spared a lingering, painful death; she'd gone out in one fell swoop, a sort of Democrat parallel to their other O.C. neighbor Jim Smythe's fatal stroke in '92 upon hearing of Bill Clinton's defeat of George Bush *père*. Better yet — so he can see from his present perspective — would've been for the two of them to go out together like George and Carol Walsh over in Rockfish Reach last year, when T.S. Giorgio's freak tornado flattened most of Heron Bay Estates. On second thought, though, that must have been scary as shit: Best of all (if they'd only known that that goddamn aneurysm was about to pop) would've been to take matters into their own hands like those other Rockfish Reachers Dick and Susan Felton, who for no known reason drove home one fine September night from a neighborhood party, closed their automatic garage door, left their car's engine idling and its windows down, and snuffed themselves. Way to go, guys! Yeah: Pour Margie a glass of her pet pinot grigio and himself a good ripe cabernet, crank up the Good Gray Ghost, hold hands, breathe deep, and sip away till the last drop or last breath, whichever.

Whoops, forgot: no garage these days over here in Geezerville. Nor much get-it-done-with gumption either, for that matter, in this lately overspacious apartment, where T.M. pecks away at his word processor *faute de* fucking *mieux* (but No thankee, Barb and Mike: Dad'd rather stay put than change geographies this late in the day). Left to himself, Yours Truly Tim Manning is ... well ... *left to himself,* making this minimal most of his hapless self-helplessness by chewing on language like a cow its cud.

Assisted Living? Been there, done that.

So?

Well. Somewhere on this here QWERTYUIOP keyboard — maybe up among all those *F1–F12, pg up/pg dn, num lock/clear* buttons? — there ought to be one for Assisted Dying ...

Like, hey, one of these, maybe: *<home? end>?*

help

Worth a try:

enter

The End

W E DELMARVANS . . . Delmarva Peninsulars? Anyhow, we dwellers on this flat, sand-crab-shaped projection between the Atlantic Ocean and Chesapeake Bay, comprising the state of Delaware and the Eastern Shores of both Maryland and Virginia, are no strangers to major storms. Even before global warming ratcheted up our Atlantic hurricane season — pounding the Caribbean, the Gulf of Mexico, and the East Coast of the USA from July into November with ever more numerous and destructive tropical tempests — there had been slam-bangers every decade or so for as long as anybody can remember. The nameless Big One of 1933, for example, cut a whole navigable inlet through our peninsula's coastal barrier islands, decisively separating the resort town of Ocean City, on Fenwick Island, from undeveloped Assateague Island, below it. Hurricane Hazel in 1954 roared over the Outer Banks of North Carolina into Chesapeake Bay, sent crab boats through second-story windows in our marshy lower counties, and sank the five-masted tourist schooner *Levin J. Marvel* in mid-Bay, with considerable loss of life. Even in George and Carol Walsh's dozen and a half years in Heron Bay Estates, at least three formidable ones have "impacted" that gated community and environs: Hugo in

'89, which downed trees and power lines hereabouts after ravaging the Carolinas; Floyd in '99, with its humongous basement-flooding downpours; and Isabel in 2003 — a mere tropical storm packing less wind and rain than those hurricanes, but piling a record-breaking eight-foot storm surge into the upper Bay that tore up countless waterfronts and flooded historic riverside houses in nearby Stratford that had been dry, if never high, since the eighteenth century. Nothing so catastrophic hereabouts to date as the great Galveston hurricane of 1900 or Katrina's wipe-out of New Orleans in 2005, but we tidewater Marylanders keep a weather eye out and storm-prep list handy from Independence Day to Halloween.

That earlier holiday, with its traditional patriotic fireworks display upriver in Stratford and Heron Bay's own smaller one off our Blue Crab Marina Club pier (rebuilt after T.S. Isabel), was just a few weeks behind us when Tropical Storm Antonio fan-fared this year's season by fizzling out north of Puerto Rico after sideswiping the Leeward Islands with minimal damage. On Antonio's Latino heels a fortnight later came his *gringuita* sister Becky, who during her transatlantic passage rapidly graduated from Tropical Depression to Named Tropical Storm (sustained winds between 50 and 73 miles per hour on the Saffir-Simpson scale) to Category 1 Hurricane (74–95 mph) before turning north-northwest in midocean, passing harmlessly east of Bermuda as if en route to Nova Scotia, but dissipating long before she got there. To all hands' surprise then — not least the National Hurricane Center's, which had predicted another busier-than-average season — there followed the opposite, an extraordinarily stormless summer: fewer-than-normal ordinary thundershowers, even, along our mid-Atlantic Coast, and a series of tropical depressions only a handful of which achieved named-storm status, much less hurricanehood. In vain through August and September the severe-weather aficionados (of whom the afore-mentioned George Walsh was one) daily checked Weather.com for signs of the promised action. The autumnal equinox passed without a single hurricane's whacking Florida and points north or west — a far cry indeed from '05's record-breaking season, which in addition to wrecking the Gulf Coast had exhausted that year's alphabet of storm names and obliged the weather service to rebegin in October with the Greek alphabet. This year Columbus Day came and went, Halloween approached, and we were no farther down the list than Tropical Storm (T.S.) Elliott, with the inevitable lame jokes about its name's proximity to that of the author of *The Waste Land.*

But then — *ta-da!* — after Elliott fizzled in the Windward Islands and then Frederika, right behind him, petered out off the Leewards, there materialized in midocean the tempest that might have been dubbed George if that name hadn't been used already, but since it had been (1998), was dubbed Giorgio instead, in keeping with the Weather Service's storm-naming policies of ethnic diversity and gender alternation. And now, perhaps, this nonstory called "The End" can begin.

"Giorgio?" I imagine George Walsh wondering aloud to his wife, who's at her computer, as is he his, in the adjoining workrooms of their ample Georgian-style house on Shoreside Drive, in Rockfish Reach. "Is that me in Spanish?"

"In Spanish you'd be J-o-r-g-e," I hear Carol call back through the open door between His and Hers — in which latter she's checking out the websites of various resort accommodations on the Hawaiian island of Kauai, where they hope to vacation next February: "Pronounced *Hor*-hay. Giorgio's Italian. Wherefore ask ye, prithee?"

She talks that way sometimes. Her husband then explains what he's just seen on Weather.com: that a tropical depression near the Cape Verde Islands off West Africa, which he's been monitoring for the past several days, has organized and strengthened into the seventh named storm of the season as it crossed toward the Antilles, and is currently forecast to escalate in the Caribbean from Tropical Storm Giorgio to a Category 1 hurricane.

"O joy," Mrs. W. would likely respond, her tone the auditory equivalent of a patient eye-roll, and go back to her Internet chatroom on the pros and cons of those vacation lodgings, as does Mr. to his storm-tracking.

So meet the Walshes, Reader, as I reconstruct them — who, despite prevailingly robust health in their seventh decade of a successful life and fourth of a good marriage, have only eight remaining days of both until The End. Longtime Stratfordians before they shifted the five miles south to Heron Bay Estates, like the majority of their neighbors they're more or less retired at the time of this "story." Carol, sixty-five, is the ex–vice principal of Avon County High School, where for years she'd been a much-loved teacher of what the curriculum called Literature & Language and she called Reading & Writing. Outgoing and athletic (though less trim and more fatigue-prone nowadays, I'd bet, than she's used to being), she still enjoys tennis, swimming, and bicycling, and "to keep her hand in" coaches a number of college-bound ACHS seniors for their SATs as well as presiding over weekly meetings of the Heron Bay Book Club. Her husband, sixty-eight, was born and raised in Stratford, where his father directed a local bank. After graduation from the county high school at which his future wife would later teach and administrate, he crossed the Bay to take a baccalaureate in business at the University of Maryland, where Carol (from the Alleghenies of western Maryland) happened to be working toward her degree in education. By happy chance among so many thousands of College Park undergraduates, in her freshman and his senior year they met, introduced by a fraternity brother of George's who happened to be an old high school friend of Carol's and who, shortly after her graduation three years later, would be best man at their wedding. The bridegroom being by then busily employed at Stratford Savings & Loan, the newlyweds set up housekeeping in his hometown. While George — on his own merits, be it said — rose rapidly in the ranks of his father's firm, Carol completed at Stratford College the requisite postgrad credits for teacher certification. The two then thrived in their chosen fields, moving through the decades to high, though never top, positions in each (George would no doubt have succeeded his father as president of SS&L had he remained there rather than shifting in the early 1980s to a promising position with the Eastern Shore wing of Tidewater Communities, Inc., just breaking ground for its Heron Bay Estates project). Although less extroverted and community-spirited than Carol, he got along easily with colleagues and business associates, and in his retirement still enjoys attending Rotary Club and TCI board meetings. Husband and wife agree that like their differing genders, their differing temperaments, interests, and even metabolisms enhance rather than detract from their connection (despite his hearty appetite, George's body has shrunk with age, and his posture is becoming bent already, as was his father's). Their one child — a sometimes difficult but much-loved daughter with her mother's smile and her father's frown — went off to college in Ohio and never returned to Tidewaterland except to visit her parents. Now forty, lesbian, childless, and currently companionless as well, Ellen Walsh works in the editorial offices of the *Cleveland Plain Dealer* to support herself while pursuing, thus far without success, what she believes or anyhow hopes is her true vocation, the writing of serious literary fiction. Her parents content themselves with their hobbies and household routines: the pleasures and activities above-mentioned plus some gardening and small-scale renovation projects. Also, of course, household chores, errands, and dealings with maintenance-and-service people — yard crew, housecleaner, roofer and plumber and painter and electrician — all more frequent as their house gets older by HBE standards. To which must be added visits to the sundry doctors, dentists, and pharmacists who tend to their similarly aging bodies.

In all, a comfortable, fortune-favored life, as they well appreciate: ample pensions, annuity income, and a solid, conservative investment portfolio; not-bad health; no family tragedies; few really close friends (and no house pets), but no enemies. To be sure, they fear the prospect of old age and infirmity; can't help envying neighbors with married children and grandkids near at hand to share lives with and eventually "look after" them. Over their seven decades, separately and together, they've done this and that if not *this* or *that;* traveled here and there though not there and there; succeeded at A, B, and C if not at D, E, and F. No extraordinary good luck beyond their finding each other and being thus far spared extraordinary bad luck. Could wish for some things they never had, but feel graced indeed with each other, with their family (siblings and nieces and nephews in addition to their daughter), their neighbors and neighborhood, and the worthy if unremarkable accomplishments of their past and present life. They wish it could go on for a long while more! And have, after all, no reason to expect that it won't, for at least another decade or so.

But it won't.

"Yup," George reports next morning, or maybe the morning after that. "We've got ourselves a Cat. One hurricane. Looks like old Giorgio's going to pass under Puerto Rico and smack southern Haiti."

His wife sighs, shakes her head, adjusts her reading glasses. "Just what that poor miserable country needs."

I see them at breakfast in their nightclothes, George scanning the *Sun*'s weather page while Carol reads with sympathetic indignation an op-ed criticism of the Bush administration's ill-funded public-education program called No Child Left Behind: all show and no substance, in her and the columnist's opinion. The news from Iraq, as usual, is all bad: Husband and wife agree that their government's preemptive invasion of that country was unnecessary, poorly planned, and disastrous, but neither has a firm opinion on what's to be done about the resulting debacle. Things aren't going well in Afghanistan either, and the news from sub-Saharan Africa remains appalling. After breakfast, stretching exercises, and an hour or so at their desks, Carol will change into warmup clothes for her tennis date at the Club while George attends to some errands in town. They'll kiss goodbye as usual, remeet for lunch — perhaps out on their pleasant screened porch, the day being sunny and unseasonably warm for late October — and plan their afternoon: a bit of autumn yard cleanup, maybe, before next month's major leaf-fall from the neighborhood's maples, oaks, and sycamores; some cricket spray around the house foundation before the first frosts bring the critters indoors. Then perhaps a bicycle ride on Heron Bay's bike and jogging paths, if they're not too tired, before cocktails and hors d'oeuvres on the patio, a shower, dinner prep (still good weather for barbecuing), and after dinner their customary hour or so of reading and/or Internet stuff, a nightcap hour of television, and to bed after the ten o'clock news and a check of the Weather Channel.

So?

So nothing, really. In a proper Story, one would by now have some sense of a Situation: some latent or overt conflict, or at least some tension, whether between the Walshes themselves or between them on the one hand and something exterior to them on the other (a neighbor, a relative, a life problem, whatever); then some turn of events to raise the dramatical stakes. In short, a story-in-progress, the action of which is felt to be building strategically to some climax and satisfying denouement. The narrative thus far of this late-middle-aged, upper-middle-class, early-twenty-first-century, contented exurban North American married couple, however, its teller readily acknowledges to be no proper Story, only a chronicle: Its Beginning now ended, its Middle has begun, and its End draws nearer, sentence by sentence, as Hurricane Giorgio, after hitting Haiti with 90-mile-per-hour winds, turns northwest, crosses eastern and central Cuba (diminishing inland to Tropical Storm force and then restrengthening to Category 1 in the warm Florida Straits), veers north-northwest, and at a leisurely forward speed of 8 mph approaches landfall between the Keys and Miami. But an End is not the same as an Ending.

Just wanted to get that clear. Over the several days following, while Carol and George carry on with their drama-free lives, Tropical-Storm-again Giorgio drenches southeast Florida, turns north-northeast into the Atlantic below Cape Canaveral, and re-regains hurricane force before his next landfall, between Capes Fear and Lookout in North Carolina's Outer Banks; he then weakens yet again from Cat. 1 to Borderline T.S. as he makes his way toward Norfolk and the mouth of the Chesapeake, leaving

the usual trail of flash floods and power outages. Closely following his progress, the Walshes and their fellow Delmarvans hope
he'll turn out to sea or at worst pass just offshore; instead, at bicycle speed he moseys straight up our peninsula, his sustained
winds diminishing to 35–40 mph with occasional higher gusts,
before his disorganized remnants pass up into Pennsylvania and
New Jersey. Much (welcome) rain to relieve a droughty autumn,
and overall not a lot of damage: some roads temporarily flooded;
relatively few trees and power lines down, the ground having
been abnormally dry; the routine handful of casualties (macho
teenager drowned in flash flood while trying to cross rushing
stream; elderly couple killed in collision with skidding SUV on
I-95 between Baltimore and Wilmington); some messed-up basements and damaged boats at docks and marina slips, but nothing
like '03's shoreline-wrecking Isabel.

Except that, as happens on rare occasions, the system spun off
a single, short-lived but *very* strong tornado, watches for which
had been posted for much of Maryland's Eastern Shore but generally ignored beyond the typical storm-prep stuff, our Tidewaterland being non-twister-prone. Subsequently rated a high-end
F3 on the Fujita scale (winds just above 200 mph), the thing
touched down here in Avon County a few miles south of Stratford, fortunately sparing that colonial-era college town but bull's-
eyeing instead, not one of those mobile-home parks that such
tempests seem to favor, but handsome Heron Bay Estates.

I.e., us. Established by TCI during the Reagan administration as the area's first gated community. Successfully developed
through the George Bush Senior and Bill Clinton years from
blueprints and promotional advertisements to built-out neighborhoods of detached and semidetached houses and low- and
mid-rise condos, all generously landscaped and tastefully separated from one another by tidal creeks and wetland ponds, winding roads, golf-course fairways, and small parkland areas. Amenitied with grounds- and gatekeepers, security patrols, clubhouses,
tennis courts, marina facilities, pool and fitness center and activities building, community and neighborhood associations, web-

site, and monthly calendar-magazine; also with sightseeing excursions to D.C., Baltimore, Philadelphia, and various Atlantic beach resorts; interest groups ranging from contract bridge, book discussion, gardening, and investment-strategy clubs to political, religious, and community-service organizations; Internet and foreign-language classes; neighborhood picnics, progressive dinners, and holiday parties. Populated by close to a thousand mostly white Protestant, mostly late-middle-aged, mostly middle- and upper-middle-class families, nearly all empty-nesters, many retired or semiretired, a considerable percentage with other homes elsewhere, plus a few quite wealthy individuals and a sprinkling of Catholics, Jews, Asians, and other minorities — even a half-dozen school-age children. Our lack of such urban attractions as museums, concert halls, nightclubs, and extensive restaurant and shopping facilities largely offset both by our reasonable proximity to those afore-mentioned cities and by nearby Stratford College, with its public lecture and concert series, continuing-education programs, and varsity sports events. In sum, a well-conceived and admirably executed project — nay, *community* — developed to completion over two dozen years and then, in half that many minutes, all but obliterated.

Not for the first time in these pages, "So?" one might reasonably inquire: on the scale of natural catastrophes, a trifle compared to Hurricane Katrina or the 2004 Southeast Asian tsunami, with its death toll of some 230,000. Indeed, although Heron Bay Estates was effectively wrecked, the human casualties of that spinoff tornado were remarkably low: only two deaths (one fewer than the earlier-mentioned toll of Giorgio's unhurried movement up the peninsula) plus numerous bone fractures and assorted lacerations, sprains, and contusions from flying debris, several of which injuries required emergency room treatment.

Indeed, that so many dwelling places and other structures could be destroyed with so comparatively few people seriously hurt, not to mention killed, would seem as fluky a circumstance as the twister itself — the more so since, unlike hurricane warnings, tornado watches hereabouts don't prompt evacuation.

Granted, it was the forenoon of a late-October weekday: Those half-dozen youngsters were in school, their working parents and other office-going adults at their jobs in Stratford or elsewhere, and others yet doing various errands beyond our gates. Many of the snowbirds had migrated already to their winter quarters in more southern climes; numerous of those for whom Heron Bay was a weekend/vacation retreat were at their primary residences in the Washington-to-Philadelphia corridor, and some of our year-round resident retirees were off traveling. Even so, not a few HBEers were at home in their Egret's Crest or Shad Run condos, their Oyster Cove villas or Blue Crab Bight coach homes, their detached houses in Rockfish Reach or Spartina Pointe — at work in home offices, fiddling with their computers, or doing routine chores — while some others were enjoying bridge games at the Club, workouts at the fitness center, etc. And our staff, of course, were about their regular employment at the entrance gates, the golf course and grounds maintenance depots, the Community Association office, and the Heron Bay and Blue Crab Marina clubhouses. Bit of a miracle, really, that so many survived such devastation so little scathed — collapsed buildings ablaze from leaking propane lines or flooded by ruptured water pipes (in some cases, both at once) — and that only a couple were killed.

"A couple" in both senses: M/M George and Carol Walsh, of what used to be 1110 Shoreside Drive in what used to be the Rockfish Reach neighborhood of what once was Heron Bay Estates, in what manages to go on being Avon County, upper Eastern Shore of Maryland, USA 21600. Crushed and buried, they were, in the rubble of that not-unhandsome residence: two red-brick-sided, white-trimmed, black-shuttered-and-doored, slate-roofed stories, of which only the far end of one chimneyed exterior wall remained standing after the tornado had roared through the community into Heron Bay proper, where it waterspouted and then quickly dissipated in the adjoining Matahannock River. Their bodies (his more or less atop hers) not excavated therefrom until quite a few days later, when stunned survivors managed to tally the injured, review the roster of those known or thought to have been in residence, note the unaccounted-for, and attempt to contact next of kin while salvaging what they could of their own possessions, assessing their losses, and scrambling to make at-least-temporary new living arrangements for themselves. A traumatic business, especially for the elderly among us and most particularly for those without a second home or nearby relatives to take them in. No makeshift Federal Emergency Management Agency trailers for us Heron Bay Estaters, thanks!

"So?" you not unreasonably persist: Why should you care, other than abstractly, as one tsks at the morning newspaper's daily report of disasters large and small around the globe? And while you're at it, who's this "I," you might ask, the presumptive teller of this so-called tale, who speaks of "we" Delmarvans and "our" HBE? Am I perhaps, for example, Dean Peter Simpson of Stratford College, a Rockfish Reacher like the Walshes and, with my Ms., one of the hosts of that neighborhood's annual progressive-dinner parties, as were George and Carol? Or maybe I'm another George: that self-styled Failed-Old-Fart Fictionist George Newett, also from the College once upon a time and, with *my* Ms., erstwhile resident of what used to be HBE's Blue Crab Bight? George Newett, sure, why not, who . . . let's see . . . let's say . . . once upon a dozen-years-ago time permitted himself, to his own surprise and likely hers as well, a one-shot adulterous liaison with . . . guess who: Carol Walsh! In her early fifties she was back then, his fellow Heron Bay Estates Community Association member and, shall we say, ardent community servicer? Never mind the details. Or wait: Maybe I'm that Miz of his, the poet Amanda Todd, who (you know how it is with us poets) upon her husband's shamefacedly confessing his uncharacteristic lapse, sought poetic justice, shall we say, by bedding George Walsh in turn — or would have so done, except that that astonished and out-of-practice chap couldn't get it up even to the point of consenting to let her try getting it up for him?

Good tries yourself there, Comrade Reader — to which you might add the possibility that I'm *Ellen Walsh*, George and Carol's errant, Sapphic daughter! Ellen Walsh, sure: Early wire-service reports of that freak Delmarva tornado reach my office at the *Plain Dealer*, followed by more specific accounts of a certain gated community's near-total destruction. I repeatedly phone both "home" and the HBE Community Association office, in vain: All phones in the area are out. No point in calling Uncle Cal and Aunt Liz in Virginia or Uncle Ray and Aunt Mattie in Delaware yet, who're no doubt making the same anxious, fruitless inquiries; soon enough they'll be phoning me, to hear what I've learned of Mom and Dad's situation. It occurs to me to try the offices of the *Avon County News* in Stratford, or maybe just hop the next flight to Baltimore/Washington International, rent a car, and get my butt over the Bay Bridge to HBE, since no matter what my parents' fate, I ought surely to be there to aid and comfort them, pick up the pieces, whatever. But — paralyzed, maybe, by some combination of anxiety, denial, anticipatory grief, self-pity, and who knows what else — to my own dismay I find myself staying put for a day, and then another and another. I turn off my phone-answering machine and decline even to answer the caller-ID'd attempts of aunts, uncles, and others to reach me, with whatever tidings, though for all I know some of the *un*identified calls could be from my folks themselves, reassuring me that they're safe somewhere but needing my help. I go through the motions of my work, my "life," steering clear of the few officemates and "friends" who know where I grew up (i.e., in Stratford, back before HBE was built) and who might be wondering . . .

Nay, more, now that I think of it: I find myself staying put in the little apartment that I share with a ten-gallon tropical-fish tank and a past-its-prime computer and *losing* my fucked-up self in what I've long wished, to no avail, had been my true vocation, the writing not of interoffice memos but of serious-type fiction stories. Like maybe one about an only-child daughter who, coming to realize that she's a lez, leaves small-town Maryland after high school, goes to university somewhere Midwest, and returns thereafter only for dutiful visits to her parents — unlike the tale's author, who never left "home" but often wishes she had, instead of winding up as a sexless spinster in an entry-level Egret's Crest condo partly financed by her folks and miraculously spared by Giorgio's tornado. A tornado that never actually occurred, it occurs to her to imagine, except in her heartbroken, wish-granting imagination — wherein, while she's at it, she fancies that she's only *fancying* that she "stayed behind" in Avon County! Or, on the contrary, that she long ago left it and never moved back . . .

Thus do I find myself by losing myself: While the directors of Tidewater Communities, Inc., at their next board meeting, observe a moment's silence in honor of their late colleague and his Mrs., and then debate the pros and cons of rebuilding Heron Bay Estates — weighing the projected (and environmentally ruinous) ongoing population surge in the Chesapeake Bay region against the recent nationwide slump in new and existing home sales and the predicted hyperactive hurricane seasons, with their attendant steep hikes in H.O. and flood-insurance premiums — "I" invent a pleasant, "eco-sensitive" gated community called Heron Bay Estates, replete with a natural preserve, recreational facilities, good neighbors and Peeping Toms, toga parties and progressive dinners, neighborhood- and community-association meetings, house renovations and teardowns, adulteries and suicides — the works. Sometimes I almost get to thinking that the place is real, or used to be; even that *I* am, or once was. Other times, that I dreamed both of us up, or anyhow that *somebody* did.

In whichever case (as happens), B followed A, and C B, et seq., each perhaps the effect, at least in part, of its predecessors, until . . .

THE END • 153

Rebeginning

WHERE IN THE WORLD to begin, and how? Maybe with something like *In the beginning, Something-or-Other created Creation* — including what became our local galaxy and solar system . . .

On whose third-from-the-sun planet, a primordial land mass divided over the eons into a clutch of continents . . .

Along the eastern coast of one of which (named "North America" by a certain subset of an animal genus that evolved together with the geography), the off-and-on glaciations and other geological morphings developed that particular planet's largest estuarine system — called "Chesapeake Bay" by the "English" colonizers who displaced its aboriginal human settlers after appropriating many of their place names along with their place . . .

Which those newcomers then named "Maryland" . . .

In what their descendants would call "the USA" . . .

And lo, on the "Eastern Shore" of this same river-intricated Bay, near the small college town of "Stratford" in ever-less-rural "Avon County," an enterprising outfit trade-named "Tidewater Communities, Inc." developed in the "1980s" a soon-thriving gated community called by its developers "Heron Bay Estates" . . .

Which project prospered just long enough for its thousand-

and-some inhabitants to begin to feel that their variously laid out and well-shrubberied neighborhoods constituted not only a successful residential development but a genuine community . . .

Until, a mere two dozen years after its inception, that development was all but totally flattened in fewer than two dozen minutes by an F3-plus tornado, rare for these parts, spun off from an ever-less-rare tropical storm — the one called "Giorgio," in the "October" of "2006," during that year's annual hurricane season — and here we refugee-survivors of that freak twister freaking *are,* and that's more than enough already of this strung-out, quote-mark and hyphen-laden blather, the signature stylistic affliction of Failed-Old-Fart Fictionist George I. Newett, emeritus professor of more-or-less-creative writing @ the above-alluded-to Stratford College, who here hands the figurative microphone to his former colleague and fellow displaced Heron Bay Estatesman Peter Simpson, just now clearing his throat to address the first postapocalyptic meeting of the Heron Bay Estates Community Association (HBECA, commonly pronounced "H-Becka"), convened *faute de mieux* in a StratColl chemistry lecture hall thanks to Chairperson Simpson's good offices as associate dean of said college and open to all former residents of that former development. Your podium, Pete, and welcome to it: Rebegin, sir, *s.v.p.!*

"Yes, well," Dean Simpson said to the assembled — then paused to reclear his throat and adjust with experienced hand the microphone clamped to the lectern perched between lab sinks and Bunsen burners on the small auditorium's chemistry-demonstration rostrum: "Here we-all are indeed — or *almost* all of us, anyhow, and thanks be for that!" He shook his balding but still handsome late-fiftyish head and sighed, then with one forefinger pushed up his rimless bifocals at the nose piece, smiled a tight-lipped smile, and continued: "And the question before us, obviously, is *Do we start over?* And if so, how?"

"Excuse me there, Pete," interrupted one of the six official neighborhood representatives seated together in the lecture hall's front row — plump Mark Matthews from Spartina Pointe, Heron Bay's once-most-upscale detached-house venue — "*I* say we oughta start over by starting this here *meeting* over, with a prayer of thanksgiving that even though Heron Bay Estates was wrecked, all but a couple of us survived to rebuild it."

"Amen to that," some fellow gruffed from an upper rear row — beefy-bossy old Chuck Becker, Pete saw it was, from Cattail Court, in his and Debbie's own much-missed Rockfish Reach neighborhood — and there were other murmurs of affirmation here and there in the well-filled hall. But "Objection," a woman's voice protested from elsewhere in the room — the Simpsons' friend and (former) neighbor Lisa Bergman: Dr. Dave the Dentist's wife and hygienist-partner, and HBECA's trim and self-possessed rep from their late lamented subdivision. "If we're going to bring Gee-dash-Dee into this meeting," she went on, "— which I'm personally opposed to doing? — then before we thank Him-slash-Her, at least let's ask Her-slash-Him to explain why He/She killed George and Carol Walsh and wrecked all our houses, okay?"

"Hear hear!" agreed her swarthy-handsome husband and several others, including Pete's afore-mentioned Debbie, the Stratford poet-professor Amanda Todd, and *her* spouse, Yours Truly, the off-and-on Narrator of this rebegun Rebeginning. Enough present objected to the objection, however — both among the official representatives from what used to be HBE's Shad Run, Egret's Crest, Oyster Cove, Blue Crab Bight, et al., and among the general attendees of this ad hoc open meeting from those several neighborhoods — that Peter was obliged to restore order by tapping on the microphone before proposing that in the interests of all parties, a few moments' silence be observed forthwith, during which those inclined to thank or supplicate the deity of their choice would be free to do so, and the others to reflect as they saw fit upon the loss of their homes and possessions and the survival of their persons. "All in favor please raise your hands. Opposed? Motion carried: Half a minute's silence here declared, in memory of our late good neighbors the Walshes and our much-missed Heron Bay Estates."

While all hands prayed, reflected, or merely fidgeted, their chairperson could pretty well tell who was doing what by raising his eyes while lowering his head, stroking his short-trimmed beard, and noting the lowered heads with *closed* eyes (Spartina Pointers Mark Matthews and his self-designated trophy wife, Mindy; Mark's investment-counseling protégé Joe Barnes from Rockfish Reach; and his afore-mentioned cheerleaders Chuck and Sandy Becker, among others), the defiantly raised heads and wide-open eyes (notably Pete's own wife, Debbie, of whom more anon; the afore-noted Bergmans; the weekly *Avon County News* columnist Gerald Frank from Shad Run; and us Newett/Todds, late of Blue Crab Bight), and other somewhere-betweeners like Pete himself (e.g., Joe Barnes's wife, Judy; Gerry Frank's Joan; the tirelessly upbeat party hosts Tom and Patsy Hardison from Annapolis and Rockfish Reach; and, somewhat surprisingly, the Oyster Cove ex-pastor Matt Grauer, whose conversion from Methodist minister to educational consultant perhaps reflected some weakening of faith?). As Dean Pete makes his unofficial tally, your *pro tem* Narrator will take the opportunity to stretch this thirty-second Moment of Silence into a more extended patch of what in the trade we call Exposition before getting on with the business at hand and this story's Action, if any — rather like that other windbag, our Giorgio tornado, expanding its few-minute life span into what seemed an eternity to us hapless and terrified HBEers huddled in our basements and walk-in closets while windows and skylights blew out and trees and walls came a-tumbling down.

Okay, okay: weak analogy; scratch it. But whether or not this Moment of Silence helps any present to decide where we go from here, both as individuals and as a community, there's no doubting that those other moments of horrifying wind-roar changed the lives of most of us who survived it (not to mention the Walsh couple who didn't) and of many others lucky enough to have been in Stratford or elsewhere at the time but unlucky enough to have lost their primary or secondary dwelling place.

E.g., in that latter category, those Matthewses, Mark and Mindy, whose weekend-and-vacation establishment — an imposing faux-Georgian McMansion in Spartina Pointe — had scarcely been finished and landscaped when F3 all but wrecked it. The pair were over in Baltimore at the time, Mark in his downtown office at Lucas & Jones, LLC, whereof he is CEO, and his ex-secretary Mindy in their nearby harborfront penthouse condominium. Thanks to its no-expense-spared construction, enough of their Heron Bay house remains standing to make its restoration feasible, but for Mark the question is whether to rebuild at all in a community that may or may not follow suit, or to take what insurance money he can get, claim the rest as a casualty-loss tax deduction, clear the ruins, list the lot for sale, kiss HBE bye-bye, and build their *second* second home on higher ground somewhere less flood- and hurricane-vulnerable, like maybe the Hunt Valley horse country north of the city or the Allegheny hills of western Maryland. With their well-diversified equities portfolio, their Baltimore condo plus a couple of other "investment units" here and there, and a certain offshore account in the Cayman Islands, they're in no great pain. Indeed, for pert and upbeat Mindy the wreck of 211 Spartina Court is as much opportunity as setback: Long and hard as she'd worked with architect, designers, and decorators on that house's planning and construction — including radically changing its original "design concept," at no small cost, from mission-style *hacienda grande* to Williamsburg colonial — they had enjoyed the finished product just long enough for her to wish that she'd done a few things differently: better *feng shui* in the floor plan, especially in the mansion's wings, and maybe one of those "infinite edge" swimming pools instead of the conventional raised coping right around. Something to be said for going back to Square One, maybe, whether with TCI in a redesigned and even better-amenitied Heron Bay or with some other architect/builder elsewhere . . .

No such temptations for the Hardisons, among others: those prosperous, high-energy Annapolis lawyers whose Rockfish Reach *palazzo* was the second most expensive casualty of the storm. They want the *status quo ante* restored as quickly as possible, not only at their Loblolly Court address but in all of Heron Bay Estates, so that they can get back to their weekend golf and tennis, their costume parties, progressive dinners, and Chesapeake cruising on their forty-foot trawler yacht, *Plaintiff's Complaint*. While for the elderly Beckers (who have flown up from their winter retreat on Florida's Gulf Coast to attend this meeting), the question isn't whether to rebuild what had been their primary residence on Rockfish Reach's Cattail Court or to build or buy another elsewhere in the area, but whether instead to give up altogether their annual snowbird migrations between two houses, shift their primary domicile to state-income-tax-free Florida, and escape its sweltering summer season on cruise ships, Elderhostel tours, and such — including, for Sandy Becker especially, frequent Stratford revisits to keep in touch with her many Episcopal church and Heron Bay Club friends.

Nor any such options and luxurious dilemmas for us reasonably well-off but by no means wealthy Simpsons, Bergmans, Greens, Franks, and Newett/Todds, whose wrecked houses and ruined possessions were our *only* such, and who've been reduced to making shift as best we can in generally inadequate temporary lodgings — motel rooms, in some instances — in small-town Stratford while still reporting daily to our company workplaces, our college or other-school classrooms, or our improvised laptop-and-cell-phone "home" offices. For pity's sake, cry we, let's get old HBE up and running, however rudimentary its resurrection! And the same goes in spades for those elderly widows and widowers like Rachel Broadus, Reba Smythe, and Matt Grauer, who had been managing well enough, all things considered, in their Shad Run condos or Oyster Cove villas, but are now renting unhappily like us or squatting with their grown children, and in either case wondering whether the time has come for them to pack it in as homeowners and shift across the Matahannock River to TCI's Bayview Manor Continuing Care Community.

End of overextended Exposition. Back to you, Peter?

"Okay," that ever-reasonable fellow declared to the assembled, glancing at his agenda notes and tapping the microphone again to end their memorial Moment of Silence: "Let's start again —which of course is this meeting's agenda exactly." Comradely grin; stroke of close-cut gray-black beard. "The questions are Where, and How, and To What Extent, and In What Order we do whatever we end up deciding to do." Sympathetic head-shake. "I quite understand that most of you have your hands as full as Debbie and I do, squatting in temporary quarters while we deal with insurance adjusters"—boos and hisses from here and there, not directed at the speaker—"and scrabble around to make do while trying to keep up with our jobs and all. It's overwhelming! I want to emphasize that what each of you does with your damaged or destroyed property is entirely up to you, as long as you bear in mind HBE's covenant and building codes. All rebuilding plans for detached houses need to be cleared with our Design Review Board, obviously, just as they were back when those neighborhoods were first built. The condominium and villa and coach-home communities we presume will be rebuilt pretty much as before—assuming they *are* rebuilt—by a general contractor selected by each of the neighborhood associations, and the plans passed along to H-Becka, whose unenviable job it'll be to coordinate and monitor the several projects. Reconstruction of the Heron Bay Club and the Marina Club and piers will be up to each one's board of governors, subject to the same review protocols. And TCI, I'm happy to report, will be standing by to advise and consult on HBE's infrastructure and on any changes we may want to make in its overall layout—even though it's our baby these days, not its original developer's."

He paused, glanced around the hall, readjusted his eyeglasses, and returned to his notes. "I know that several of you have ideas and proposals for a 'new' [*finger quotes*] Heron Bay Estates, while others of you would be more than content to have things put back as much as possible the way they were before. It's important for you to understand that this meeting is for *preliminary input only,* not for any final decisions. And some kinds of things can be put off till we get our homes rebuilt and reoccupied — may the day come soon! But even in that department there may be some suggestions that we ought to be considering as we plan our repairs and reconstruction. So the floor's open, folks: We'll make note of any and all proposals, talk 'em over in committee, and report back to you at our next open meeting. Let me remind you that you can also make written suggestions and comments on the H-Becka website." Smile of invitation. "Who wants to go first?"

Several hands went up at once, among the neighborhood representatives (my wife's, for one) and in the general audience (among them, mine). Before the chair could call on any, however, Mark Matthews heaved to his feet, turned his ample dark-suited back to Peter Simpson, and loudly addressed the hall: "Friends and neighbors! Mark Matthews here, from Spartina Pointe and the Baltimore office of Lucas and Jones — an outfit that knows a thing or two about turning setbacks into opportunities, as Joe Barnes yonder, from our Stratford office, can testify. Am I right, Joe and Judy?"

In a fake darkie accent, "Yassuh, boss," the male of that couple called back. A few people chuckled; his wife, sitting beside him, did not. Nor did Pete, who raised his eyebrows and stroked his chin but evidently decided not to interrupt, at least for the moment, this interruption of normal meeting procedure.

"Now, then! Mindy and I personally haven't made up our minds yet whether or not to rebuild our Spartina Court place, but I can tell you this, folks: The current downturn in the housing market — all those contractors hungry for work? — is such a golden opportunity for all hands present that if TCI isn't interested, Charlie Becker and I might just get into the construction racket ourselves! You with me there, Chuck?"

That elderly Becker (in fact the retired CEO of a Delaware construction firm) grinned and cocked his white-haired head as if considering the suggestion. And "Hear hear!" duly seconded Joe Barnes.

"But if we do," Matthews went on, "it won't be just to get back to where we were. No sirree! It'll be to build a *bigger and better* Heron Bay Estates! And here's how." Raising his stout right thumb: "First off, we buy us a couple hundred more acres of cornfields and woodlots, either next door or across the highway or both, for an *HBE Phase Two!*" Now his thick forefinger: "Then we build us a couple more mid-rise-or-higher condominium complexes and detached-house neighborhoods — to *raise our base,* know what I mean?" Middle finger: "Plus we build ourselves an Olympic-size *indoor* pool and spa complex at the Club to use in the cooler months, and maybe even a second golf course on some of that useless preserve acreage of ours that just *sits* there. Et cetera et cetera: a whole new ball game!"

Tom Hardison it was, for a change, who said, "Sounds about right to me, Mark." Joe Barnes, of course, echoed assent, and there were approving or at least worth-considering nods from Chuck Becker and Stratford realtor Jeff Pitt as Matthews, clearly much pleased with himself, plumped back into his seat and beamed almost defiantly up at Peter Simpson. But "It sure sounds anything but right to *me*," my Amanda objected, also rising as if to address the gathering at large, but then turning to the podium: "However, instead of just grabbing the floor, I'll ask the chair's permission before I sound off."

Obviously welcoming the return to parliamentary procedure, "Permission granted," Simpson said at once. "Let's hear what you have to say, Amanda."

In her firm but gentle professorial voice, "What I have to say," she declared to the assembly, "is just about a hundred and eighty degrees from what you've just heard." Tucking a lock of gray-brown hair behind her ear, she smiled down at Matthews, who appeared to be studying the spread fingers of his left hand. "I agree with Mark that the catastrophe we-all have suffered can be turned into an opportunity. But in my opinion — and I'm not alone in this — what it's an opportunity *for* is not to *destroy* our precious preserve land and adjacent acreage and grow bigger-bigger-bigger, like too many already-overweight Americans —"

"*Objection*," Mark Matthews complained, and seemed about to rise again from his seat, but didn't.

"Noted but overruled, Mark," Peter declared, and nodded to Amanda to continue.

"Let's imagine instead a very *different* kind of Heron Bay makeover," my wife proposed. "Given what we all know the future has in store for us with global warming and such, and the critical importance of reducing our carbon emissions and foreign-oil dependency, here's our chance to make HBE a model 'green' community!" The adjective in finger quotes. "Solar panels on every building, plus whatever other energy-saving technologies we can deploy — expensive to start with, but they soon pay for themselves in lower utility bills, and what's bad news for Delmarva Power and Light is good news for the environment. *Fewer* grass areas to be fertilized and irrigated, instead of more; *more* preserve instead of less, and natural 'xericulture' landscaping wherever possible, instead of high-maintenance flower beds and shrubbery. Energy-efficient houses and condos, and propane-powered shuttle buses to Stratford and back every hour, like the ones they use in some of our national parks, to cut down on gasoline consumption and car-exhaust emissions every time we need to get into town. What an example we could set for twenty-first-century America!"

"I'll second that," called Debbie Simpson.

"And I'll third it," added Joan Frank. "We might just want to reconsider the whole gated-community concept too, while we're at it, as Mandy suggested last year."

"Whoa-ho-*ho!*" Jeff Pitt protested, rising from his seat in the audience and, like Mark, not waiting for acknowledgment from the chair: "Excuse me, ladies, but you take this tree-hugging stuff far enough and next thing we know you'll be telling us to donate the whole shebang to the Nature Conservancy instead of rebuilding at all!"

Uneasy chuckles here and there. Unfazed, "Don't think I

haven't considered that option, Jeff," Amanda replied: "Collect our insurance payouts and take our casualty-loss deductions and then buy or build in an already-existing population center like Stratford: smart growth instead of suburban sprawl! But I'm trying to be less radical than that: We keep our entry gates and our golf course; we rebuild our beautiful Heron Bay Estates and even keep that pretentious last word of its name, if that's what most of us want; but we rebuild it more green and eco-friendly, for our own good as well as the planet's! Thank you all for hearing me out."

Your Narrator applauded, proud as usual of his spunky mate, though disinclined to go quite so far as she in the extreme-makeover way. What *I'd* settle for, frankly, at my age and stage, is to be back with my dear high-mileage Apple desktop in my snug little study in our snug little coach home in HBE's snug little Blue Crab Bight subdivision exactly as it was before Mister Twister hit the Delete button, pecking away my Old-Fart-Emeritus autumn mornings at yet another rambling prose piece while Amanda, in *her* snug little et cetera, invokes the Muse of Less-Than-Immortal Versifiers but Damned Good Teachers to see her through yet another StratColl.edu semester or three before she joins her gin-and-tonic-slurping mate out in the pasture. Yes indeedy, Cap'n Gawd: Get us back Just Where & As We Were, Sir, *s.V.p.* — rolling our fortune-favored eyes at the word "Estates" and the 24/7 entrance gates and security patrols in our all-but-crime-free neck of the tidewater Maryland woods; tsking our liberal tongues at the U.S. fiasco in Iraq and at sundry other disasters around the world; shaking our snotty-intellectual heads at our community's toga parties and old-fashioned socials while at the same time quite enjoying them.

O bliss!

But no such luck, of course. Fabulator though G. I. Newett by vocation may willy-nilly be, the subject of these present fumbling fabulations is (anyhow *was*) a subdivision of the Real World — wherein, as Reader may have had occasion to note, nothing once truly whacked is ever quite restorable to What It Was Before. Best one can do is bid Mister Chairperson to tap the old microphone/gavel and proceed with our proceedings. Okay, Pete?

"Okay," declared Peter Simpson, and did just that: tapped the mike and thanked Amanda for her input, which he pronounced most certainly worth serious consideration even by those who — like himself and no doubt numerous others present ("Not including my wife," he acknowledged with a small smile: "She's with *you*, Amanda") — inclined to a more conservative conservationism, so to speak: the reconstruction of Heron Bay Estates as expeditiously as possible and as close as possible to what it was before, perhaps with "green" enhancements where convenient and cost-effective. Reduced community-assessment fees, say, for energy-efficient and/or eco-sensitive building and landscape designs?

"Right on," somebody agreed — Gerry Frank, I'd guess, or Dave Bergman — and there was a general rustle of approbation in the hall. No need for motions and seconds, Pete reminded us, since this wasn't a formal meeting, just a sort of solidarity and opinion-gathering session for us lucky-but-hard-hit survivors. "Your neighborhood reps and I will be getting together as often as we can to review and approve rebuilding proposals from individual homeowners, as well as from the condo and villa and coach-home associations and the Club and Marina Club boards, and we'll green-light as many as we possibly can in keeping with HBE's covenant, using what we've heard from you today as our guidelines." Deep exhale; stroke of beard. "So: The floor's open now to any others who want to be heard."

A few more did, mainly to affirm one or another already-voiced position, after which the aspiring teller of this would-be tale took it upon himself to thank our Association chairman for his good offices on our behalf. "No call for that," Dean Pete modestly replied, gathering up his notes. And then, to the house, "On behalf of H-Becka, it's I who thank *you*-all for coming to this get-together and making your opinions known. We're all plenty stressed out, for sure. But one way or another, by George . . ." As if just realizing what he'd said, he grinned meward. "One way or another, we'll *rebegin!*"

Yeah, right. And while we're about it, friends and neighbors, let's rebegin our derailed lives, okay? Taking a more or less alphabetical clutch of us as we've appeared in the Faltering Fables of G. I. Newett, let's have Sam Bailey's wife Ethel *not* die of cervical cancer this time around, so bereaving my old ex-colleague and Oyster Cove neighbor that he skewers himself (unsuccessfully) with a borrowed machete at the Hardisons' toga party in Rockfish Reach. Okay? And let those other RRers Dick and Susan Felton *not* feel so prematurely finished with their lives' prime time that they drive home from that same bloodily disrupted fest and off themselves with auto exhaust fumes in their garage, *sans* even a farewell note to their distant kids! Let good Pete and Debbie Simpson's daughter, Julie — their much-prized only child, on track to graduate from Johns Hopkins, go on to med school, and thence to service in some selfless outfit like Doctors Without Borders — *not* be car-crashed to death in her sophomore year by a drunken driver on the Baltimore Beltway, so traumatizing both parents (but Deb in particular) that they haven't enjoyed a truly happy hour in the several years since! Let George and Carol Walsh *not* be crushed to a bloody mush in the rubble of their house on Shoreside Drive (Rockfish Reach again) by that fucking five-minute F3 funnel-cloud! Et cetera? And while we're about all *that*, let's rebegin us Newett/Todds, making my Mandy this time around *not* merely an okay Poet + Damned Fine Teacher, but the Essential Lyric Voice of Early-Twenty-First-Century America + DFT!

And her husband?

Yes, well. *In the beginning* (that chap believes he was saying once upon a time) there was this place, this "development." There were these people: their actions, inactions, and interactions, their successes and failures, pleasures and pains, excitements and boredoms, in a particular historical time and geographical location.

Nothing very momentous or consequential in the larger scheme of things: one small tree-leaf in the historical forest, its particular spring-summer-and-fall no doubt to be lost in Father Time's vast, ongoing deciduosity. But just as, now and then, one such leaf may happen against all odds to be noticed, picked up, and at least for some while preserved — between the leaves of a book, say — and may with luck outlast its picker-upper as the book may outlast its author and even its serial possessors, so may this verbal approximation of the residential development called Heron Bay Estates and of sundry of its inhabitants survive, by some fluke, that now-gone place and its fast-going former denizens — whether or not it and they in some fashion "rebegin," and even if this feeble re-imagining themof, like the afore-invoked leaf-pressed leaf, itself sits pressed and scarcely noted in Papa T's endless, ever-growing library —

Or, more likely, his recycling bin.

— [Good]By[e] George I. Newett